THE MASTER'S APPRENTICE

A Retelling of the Faust Legend

OTHER TITLES BY OLIVER PÖTZSCH

The Hangman's Daughter Series

The Hangman's Daughter

The Dark Monk

The Beggar King

The Poisoned Pilgrim

The Werewolf of Bamberg

The Play of Death

The Council of Twelve

The Black Musketeers Series

Book of the Night

Sword of Power

Knight Kyle and the Magic Silver Lance

Holy Rage

THE MASTER'S APPRENTICE

Translated *by* Lisa Reinhardt

Oliver Pötzsch

AMAZON **CROSSING**

Text copyright © 2018 by Oliver Pötzsch and Ullstein Buchverlage GmbH

Translation copyright © 2020 by Lisa Reinhardt

Previously published as *Der Spielmann: Die Geschichte des Johann Georg Faustus 1* by Ullstein Buchverlage GmbH in Germany in 2018. Translated from German by Lisa Reinhardt. First published in English by Amazon Crossing in 2020.

Published by Amazon Crossing, Seattle

www.apub.com

Amazon, the Amazon logo, and Amazon Crossing are trademarks of Amazon.com, Inc., or its affiliates.

ISBN-13: 9781542009980

ISBN-10: 1542009987

Cover design by M. S. Corley

Printed in the United States of America

For Aliahmad Alizade:
as clever and ambitious as Faust, and as lovable and
buoyant as Margarethe.
On winding roads to the finish line.

These people never smell the old rat, e'en when he has them by the collar.

—Johann Wolfgang von Goethe,
Faust, Part I (translated by Charles T. Brooks)

HISTORICAL NOTE

AROUND THE YEAR 1500, A MAN WE KNOW VERY LITTLE ABOUT traveled the German empire; the few sources and countless myths surrounding this man have led historians to believe that he really existed. He was the greatest magician of his time, and a con artist, astrologer, and charlatan. He was as clever and learned as a dozen scholars and as cunning as the Borgias. Not long after his violent death, a book was written about him, which many consider the first German bestseller. Playwrights including Christopher Marlowe and Johann Wolfgang von Goethe wrote dramas about him, and he became a popular character in puppet shows. To this day he is the symbol of the ambitious, restless individual who is prepared to make a deal with the devil to gain fame and fortune—but ultimately pays with his soul.

His name was Johann Georg Faustus.

This is his true story.

Prologue

IN THE FALL THAT THE CHILDREN DISAPPEARED, THE JUG-
glers came to town.

From an alcove in the upper city gate, little Johann stood with his mouth open, watching the boisterous, dancing, singing train of colorful people. Like a small army, they crossed the drawbridge spanning the boggy moat, marched through the wide-open gate, and filled Knittlingen with life. At the front of the train, two dark-skinned men were doing cartwheels, followed by a handful of musicians with tabor pipes, bagpipes, and tambourines. Next came masked acrobats, a hunchbacked dwarf in a fool's costume, sword-wielding show fighters, and a real-life shaggy bear, which a giant was leading by a chain. Johann had never seen such splendor! Almost as if the emperor himself had traveled to the small town in the Palatinate. The huddled stone houses suddenly seemed to glow in a strange light, and Johann smelled something new and tantalizing—the scent of the wide world.

One after another the jugglers moved past him, followed by a crowd of laughing children who had been longing for this day as much as Johann had. One of the acrobats winked at him; someone laughed and gave him a nudge that almost tripped him. Johann realized he'd been so busy gaping at the jugglers that he hadn't noticed he was stepping out onto the road. Wagon wheels rolled past him within a hair's breadth, leaving deep furrows in the ground, which was still wet from the last rain. Cold autumn fog crept down from the wooded hills surrounding the town, but Johann didn't feel it. He couldn't take his eyes off the noisy, never-ending caravan of people, carts, horses, and oxen pouring into town.

Where do they all come from? he wondered. *From faraway Nuremberg? From foreign lands beyond the Alps—or even beyond the ocean? Where sea serpents, lions, and dragons live . . .*

Johann's world didn't extend beyond the hills of the Kraichgau. Behind those hills began the world of myths, fairy tales, and legends. Whenever his mother found the strength, she told him stories: stories of the sleeping emperor Barbarossa; of knights, gnomes, and fairy queens; of the boogeyman in the woods; of imperial diets in Augsburg and Regensburg; and of grand feasts. Johann would sit in her lap and listen, entranced by her soft voice.

After the jugglers came the itinerant merchants, some pulling carts while others carried their goods bundled on their backs. Every year, on the day of Saints Simon and Jude, the merchants set up their stalls along Market Street, which led from the upper city gate to Saint Leonhard's Church. The autumn market was Knittlingen's biggest fair—even bigger than the Cantate market in spring. Peddlers came from Bretten, Pforzheim, and even Heidelberg to sell their wares.

Johann had been looking forward to this day for weeks. He was eight years old, and last year's autumn market was nothing but a faint memory. He'd taken up position at the city gate early this morning so he wouldn't miss the arrival of any artists or merchants, but only now, as lunchtime neared, was the town truly starting to get busy. When the last peddler had passed through the gate, Johann followed the caravan into town. Hawkers fought over the best spots near the church; a bearded, already-drunken itinerant preacher announced the imminent end of the world from atop a wine barrel; musicians played dancing tunes; the first cask was tapped with loud hammering outside the Lion Inn. The air smelled of beer mash, cider, horse dung, smoke, and delicious cooking smells from the many street kitchens. And under all that lay the first hint of snow. Peasants said that on Saints Simon and Jude Day, winter knocked at the door.

The whole of Knittlingen had spruced up for this day. The wealthier residents wore their best Sunday frock coats and fustian shirts; the women covered their hair with skillfully tied scarves. Johann struggled to make his way through the crowd of bickering, laughing, and bartering grown-ups. Every now and then he passed other children he knew: the baker's red-haired twins, Josef and Max;

the blacksmith's broad-shouldered son, who was as strong as an ox at twelve years of age; and short, skinny Hans from the Lion Inn. But as usual, they avoided Johann or whispered behind his back as soon as he'd walked past them. Johann was so used to it that he hardly noticed. Only sometimes, when he roamed the woods around Knittlingen alone with his dreams, would he feel sad.

His mother told him not to mind the other children. He was different— smarter, brighter than them. Of noble blood, she'd once told him, though Johann didn't understand what she meant.

Johann had quickly grown bored at the German school he attended over at the hostel. While the rest of the students struggled with math, German, and the few scraps of Latin from the catechism, learning came easily to Johann. Sometimes he even corrected the teacher, a bitter old man who doubled as Knittlingen's sacristan. Johann often wanted to dig deeper, asking about foreign countries, the phases of the moon, the force of water—but no matter what he asked, the old man never had an answer. And when the other boys beat up Johann, the teacher just stood by, trying to suppress a grin.

"Watch where you're going, midget! If you step on my toes again, I'll turn your smart-aleck face to mush."

Ludwig, who was two years older and almost two heads taller than Johann, and the son of the Knittlingen prefect, punched him in the stomach. Johann gasped and held his belly but, thinking of his mother's words, didn't fight back. If he was truly of noble blood, then why had God made him so darn scrawny? He would gladly give some of his brains for more muscles—the only currency that counted for anything among children.

"Piss off!" Ludwig snarled and picked a piece of smoked sausage from between his teeth. Fat was running down his chin. "Go wipe your ass with books instead of standing around in people's way!"

Johann said nothing and took to his heels before Ludwig could punch him again.

At last he'd elbowed his way to the small square in front of the church, where the jugglers had set up their stage using wooden planks and four barrels and had begun performing their tricks. One musician started a drumroll while another struck a cymbal to announce the next act. Jugglers threw colorful wooden balls and burning torches through the air, catching them at the very last moment— much to the pleasant horror of the Knittlingers.

Johann applauded the jugglers eagerly, as well as the following act, a hunch-backed dwarf performing raunchy poems about wine, women, and song until a giant dipped him into a tankard as big as a barrel. The audience hooted with laughter, and Johann didn't hear the soft voice beside him. Then someone pulled on his ear, and he started with fright. He thought it was Ludwig, ready for another round.

"Hey, are you deaf? Did one of the jugglers cast a spell on you and turn you to stone?"

Johann spun around and smiled with relief. Standing in front of him was Margarethe, Ludwig's younger sister. She wore a gray dress with a white apron, its hem already spattered with dung. Her flaxen hair looked wild and windswept, as usual. Margarethe was one of the few children in Knittlingen who liked Johann and spent time with him. Twice already she'd saved him from the other boys by threatening to tell her father. Even Ludwig listened to her. Johann had to pay for her kindness with double beatings afterward, but it didn't hurt as much as it normally did. He'd simply close his eyes and think of Margarethe's hair glowing like wheat in the summer sun. However, there was one problem: whenever Margarethe spoke to him, his mouth appeared to be sealed—it was jinxed! Now, too, he couldn't get out a single word.

"You like the jugglers, don't you?" Margarethe asked and bit into a juicy red apple.

Johann nodded silently, and Margarethe continued as she chewed: "Did you know that jugglers and musicians are children of the devil?" She gave a shudder. "That's what the church says. Whoever dances to their music they lead straight to hell." She lowered her voice and made the sign of the cross. "Perhaps they took the children, too. I wouldn't be surprised."

"Don't talk nonsense," said Johann. "The wolves took them, even the hunts-men say so. And they must know!"

Despite the cheering and laughter, a chill suddenly ran down his spine as though he were standing alone in the forest. Four children had gone missing in recent weeks: seven-year-old Fritz from Knittlingen, his five-year-old brother, and two girls from neighboring Bretten. The two Bretten girls had been playing in the woods; Fritz, the butcher's boy, had disappeared from Marktgasse Lane, and his brother, little Peter, had been herding a pig in nearby Eichenloh Forest. The sow had arrived home alone. Some folks said wild beasts had killed the children. Others said there were hungry and ruthless outlaws living in the woods who preferred the tender flesh of children to that of poached deer. Someone had seen smoke rise up from the edge of the distant forest on the hills; apparently, a whiff of burning meat had been in the air.

Johann clenched his teeth and silently stared at the jugglers on stage. Suddenly the smell from the street kitchens made him feel sick.

Burning meat . . .

A murmur went through the crowd, rousing him from his thoughts. Margarethe squeezed his hand, and he gave another start. He shuddered and couldn't tell whether it was because of Margarethe's touch or because of the missing children.

Or because of *him*.

"Didn't I tell you?" whispered Margarethe. "Just look at him! He must be straight from hell."

The man stepping onto the stage indeed looked like a demon incarnate. He was tall and haggard and wore a black-and-red-striped coat billowing behind him like the wings of a bat. His face was as pale as though there was no blood in him, his nose sharp like the beak of a bird of prey. He wore a wide black felt hat with a red feather, like those of traveling scholars.

Most frightening of all were his eyes, gleaming black and deep like pools in a swamp. To Johann they seemed like the eyes of a man much older than their owner seemed to be. When those eyes moved across the crowd, everyone fell silent. For a brief moment, Johann thought he could feel the man's gaze like fingers reaching out to touch him. Then the strange man slowly and ceremoniously raised his head and looked up at the cloudy sky. A light drizzle set in.

"The stars," he began in a voice that was at once quiet and penetrating, audible across the whole church square. His accent was slightly foreign, soft, like that of travelers from beyond the Rhine.

"The stars don't lie! They're invisible during the day, and yet they are there. They shine above us, guide our path—a path that has been predestined for each one of us." He paused dramatically, his eyes moving across the crowd again. "*Ah oui, c'est vrai!* I can read those paths for you. I am a master of the seven arts and keeper of the seven times seven seals! I'm a doctor of the university of black magic in Krakow."

"A sorcerer," Margarethe whispered. "I knew it!"

Johann said nothing and waited for the mysterious stranger to continue. The man now addressed his audience with his arms outstretched, like a priest.

"Is there anyone who would like to know their future?" he asked loudly. "One kreuzer per question." He gave a thin smile. "If I foretell your imminent death, the answer is free."

A few people laughed, but it sounded hollow and nervous. A tense silence had descended upon the square. Finally a young, sturdy farmer's son raised his arm, and the foreigner asked him up on stage.

"What would you like to know?" asked the magician as the trembling young man handed over a coin.

"I, well . . . ," the peasant said awkwardly. "My Elsbeth and me, we've been together for over a year. But the dear Lord still hasn't granted us a child. I'd like to know if fate will smile upon us."

The foreigner took the man's hand, which was calloused from laboring in the fields, and bent over it. Johann thought it looked as though he sniffed the hand, even licked and tasted it like an animal would a salty rock. A considerable amount of time passed as the magician ran his fingers across the young man's palm, murmuring almost inaudibly. Finally he straightened back up.

"Your wife is going to carry your child before next spring. And it will be a boy! He'll be healthy and strong, born under the constellation of Pisces. The stars have spoken!"

The strange man raised his hands and—seemingly out of nowhere—a black raven flew up into the sky. The crowd gasped with surprise, and somewhere at the back, an elderly maidservant fainted.

Bowing and scraping, the farmer's son left the stage, and another nervous client took his place. Johann watched with excitement as the creepy stranger foretold a good harvest, a successful house build, the best day for sowing, and three more healthy sons and daughters for Knittlingen. Two crows flew up from his previously empty hand, playing cards with mysterious blood-red symbols tumbled to the ground out of nowhere, and he pulled a real black cat out of his hat. Johann was so captivated that he almost forgot to breathe. He'd never seen anything like it. This man was a real magician! He'd cast a spell on all of them.

At last the show was over. The foreigner took a bow and strode gracefully off the stage. The acrobats took his place and started to perform their tricks. But no matter how high they leaped, no matter how many somersaults they tumbled,

Johann now found their show dull. He had seen true magic, had caught a glimpse of another world beyond the earthly world he knew! And now it was already over? Johann trembled with disappointment. Not even Margarethe's presence cheered him up. She was still beside him, holding his hand. The funny harlequins and jugglers seemed to appeal to her much more than the scary magician had.

"How did he do it?" muttered Johann again and again, mostly to himself. "How did he do it? How did he make the raven and crows fly up, and where did the cat come from? What's his secret?"

"Ravens, crows, black cats—I told you he's in league with the devil," groused Margarethe without taking her eyes off the jugglers. "And now hush or I'll have nightmares about that man. Brr! I only hope he leaves town today."

Johann was shocked by the thought. If the mysterious stranger left town today, Johann would never find out what lay behind his tricks! He looked around. Where had the man gone? Johann couldn't see him next to the stage, where the other jugglers waited for their turn. Had he already left?

Johann let go of Margarethe's hand and made his way toward the stage. Margarethe was focused on the acrobats and didn't even notice him leaving. He turned left and walked around the church. It was much quieter away from Market Street. A blind beggar tapped his stick along the dirty cobblestones; a drunken man vomited in a corner. No one else was in sight. Gray autumn fog seeped through the lanes. It almost seemed to Johann it was thicker here than on the other, busier side of the church. Viscous.

Then he saw the wagon.

It stood a little off to the side, next to the empty town hall, and was covered with a dirty canvas embroidered with strange symbols and runes Johann couldn't read. A tired-looking old horse was munching on barley from a bucket tied around its neck. On the wagon's outside wall above the box seat hung a large, rusty cage that held two crows and a raven. The cage creaked and swayed when the birds moved.

How did he do it? How did he make the raven appear?

Entranced, Johann walked toward the birds as they flapped their wings restlessly. What if they were enchanted? He tiptoed quietly toward the cage, reached out his hand—

"If you're hungry, let me warn you: those birds are tough. And they dissolve in your stomach and return to me, their creator. You wouldn't find them very satisfying."

Johann spun around and looked into the face of the pale magician, who was standing right behind him, looking down at him. How could he not have noticed the man approaching? Was that another spell?

The man frowned at first, then his lips twisted into a smile. Johann saw small, sharp teeth, like those of a predator.

"Oh, it's the boy from the front row." The man's eyes twinkled with amusement. "I could have fitted a barn inside your gaping mouth." He leaned down to Johann, who thought he could smell a faint waft of sulfur. "How old are you, boy?"

"I . . . I'm eight," Johann said hoarsely, feeling very uncomfortable. He thought the air suddenly grew much colder; it felt like the middle of winter. The music and noise from the fair seemed to come from far away, as if from the other side of a heavy door.

"Hmm . . ." The man tilted his head to one side, just like the birds in the cage beside him. Then, after what felt like an eternity, he straightened up to his full height.

"And what's your name?" he asked abruptly.

"I . . . My name is Johann Georg, son of Jörg Gerlach, the farmer," replied Johann. "But my mother calls me Faustus."

"Faustus, I see . . . What a beautiful yet strange name." The man gave a quick smile. For a moment Johann thought the stranger's black eyes flashed, like sheet lightning behind storm clouds. "Then I'm sure you know the meaning of this Latin word?"

"It means 'the lucky one,'" Johann replied eagerly. "Or 'the bearer of luck,' 'the blessed one.' My mother always says I was born under a lucky star. She believes fate has great plans for me." He shrugged. "Though I don't really know what she means by that. She says I'm of noble blood."

"Of noble blood? That's a good one! You'd have to wash more often to pass as a nobleman." The man laughed. "In any case, your mother seems to be a wise and ambitious woman. Our names can shape our destinies."

He suddenly grabbed Johann by his arm and pulled him very close. He opened Johann's fist and studied his palm. Something about it seemed to irritate him. He brought his face even closer to Johann's hand. As before onstage, he sniffed it, and for a brief moment Johann thought he felt a rough tongue on his skin, like that of a billy goat.

"Those lines . . . those lines," he whispered, as if muttering an ancient incantation. "Indeed . . ." He stared at Johann. "Do you know when you were born, boy?"

Johann hesitated. He'd always wondered why his mother remembered the exact day of his birth. Most children knew only their saint's day. "April twenty-three in the year of our Lord 1478—on Saint George's Day," he said eventually. "My mother told me to remember the date well."

The man tilted his head to the side once more. "The day of the prophet. Hmm . . ." His fingers dug into Johann's shoulder, stinging like long, sharp talons. "Maybe I should—"

Right then Johann heard a high-pitched wail that frightened him to the core. It sounded like someone was being strangled to death. He spun around in panic. At first he thought it had been the crows or the raven, but then he realized it had come from inside the wagon. Now he heard soft whimpering and whining from the same direction. The stranger heard it, too.

"Cats," he said with a smile. "My old Selena just had a litter of five. I'll have to drown them all if they keep up the noise."

The whining stopped abruptly.

"Forget what you heard! Trust me—it's better for you."

The magician let go of Johann. He took the cage off its hook, turned, and climbed onto the box seat. He set down the cage beside him and picked up the reins. The black birds watched Johann from small, evil-looking eyes.

"I must be off," the magician said impatiently. "I want to be in Bruchsal by sundown. Work to do. So much work, and I'm not getting any younger!" He gave a cackling laugh, then turned serious.

"Those lines," he muttered again. "Born on the day of the prophet . . ." He shook his head in disbelief. "Well, young Faustus, we might meet again one day. The stars don't lie!"

He cracked his reins, and the wagon jerked forward.

As the carriage slowly rolled toward the lower gate and into the late autumn fog, Johann heard the high-pitched wailing sound once more. Just before the wagon disappeared behind one of the last houses, the canopy suddenly trembled, then stretched and bulged as if someone was desperately pushing against it from the inside. Then the fog closed in like a white curtain.

Johann remained standing in the middle of the lane, unable to move. He thought he was in a dream. What was magic, what was real? At last he shook himself and walked back around the church with trembling knees, back to the noisy fair, where the masses soon swallowed him up. The musicians played, jugs were handed around, and as the sun slowly disappeared behind the city wall, the Knittlingers celebrated the day of Saints Simon and Jude, on what might have been the last warm day of the season. One thing Johann knew for certain: no matter how many years went by, he'd never forget the magician.

Act I

The Man from the West

1

THE SUN BLAZED AS IF IT WANTED TO SET FIRE TO THE world.

Johann lay on his back with his eyes closed, feeling the warmth bake into his body. The last winter had been long and was replaced by a wet, cold spring. The first sowing had been washed away during a massive thunderstorm, like so often in recent years here in the Kraichgau region, north of the Black Forest. It wasn't until now, in July, that summer seemed to have fully arrived. The grain on the fields around Knittlingen stood tall and offered the ideal hiding place for snoozing, daydreaming, and avoiding work.

Or for a first stealthy kiss.

Johann squinted, turned his head almost imperceptibly, and saw that Margarethe was lying just as still as he was, soaking up the warmth. They'd been lying next to each other in silence for a while now, listening to the wind and the chirping of the swallows. It was the Lord's day, and most Knittlingen farmers stayed at home or frequented one of the many taverns; hardly anyone worked the fields. An ancient, weathered stone cross in the middle of a rye field formed the center of their hiding place. Johann had flattened the stalks with his feet. As long as they were close to the ground, nobody could see them.

It was the perfect love nest.

It had taken all of Johann's courage to ask Margarethe to meet him here. For days he'd hung around her, unable to open his mouth. In the end he wrote her an encrypted letter. They'd had their secret code for a few years now: with a needle Johann pierced tiny holes in individual letters, and put together, those letters spelled a message.

This time the message had read that he wanted her to meet him here and that he would show her a new trick. He hadn't said what kind of trick.

Johann had often visited Margarethe at the Knittlingen prefecture in recent years. It was only a stone's throw away from his parents' house. For as long as he could remember, he'd made Margarethe laugh with his tricks and entertained her with Aesop's animal stories or one of the funny Greek comedies he'd found at the library of the Maulbronn monastery. When they'd been younger, they used to play in the hay or hide in the prefecture's huge storehouse. But they were no longer children. A fuzz of black hair was sprouting on Johann's face. He'd turned sixteen a few months ago, just like Margarethe. The Knittlingen lads had been making eyes at her for a while now.

The unkempt, sassy, flaxen-haired girl with the dirty dress had grown into a bright young woman. Her skin wasn't tanned from the sun like that of the other girls her age but was almost as white as marble, like the skin of a highborn princess, and covered with freckles. She had also been graced with an ample bosom. Most importantly, Margarethe was the daughter of the Knittlingen prefect and was the best catch in town. And he, Johann Georg Gerlach, second-youngest son of farmer Jörg Gerlach, had managed to meet her in the fields.

Only question was, What next?

Johann stretched awkwardly and gave a loud yawn. Margarethe turned to look at him. Her eyes were as blue as the cornflowers growing in the rye field. She also stretched and sat up.

"Didn't you say you were going to show me a new trick?" she said, giving him a half-curious, half-challenging look. "That's why we came here. Or did you have other plans for a poor, innocent girl like me, Herr Johann Georg Faustus?" Like so many others in town, she used his nickname with a mocking undertone. But he didn't mind.

"No, no." Johann sat up hastily and fished a tattered pack of cards from under his jerkin. "This is . . ." He faltered when he saw the disappointment in Margarethe's face.

"You asked me here because you want to play cards? That's for the boys at the tavern." She wagged one finger. "If they don't arrest you first!" The game with cards was still relatively new and frowned upon by the authorities. The church called playing cards "the devil's prayer book."

"Wait and see!" Johann fanned out the cards in his hand. "Here, pick one card. Any card. And think about your sweetheart."

"How dare you, you cocky devil!" Margarethe giggled and reached for a card. She passed it to Johann, who flipped it over with a dramatic gesture.

It was the jack of hearts with a rose in his hand.

Johann returned the card to the deck with a triumphant smile. "So you did think of your sweetheart after all."

"Pure coincidence. Let me try again." Margarethe picked out another card, and it was the jack of hearts once more. When the trick worked a third time, she clapped her hands excitedly, like she used to as a child. "How did you do it?" she demanded impatiently. "Go on, tell me!"

Johann grinned. It was this innocence and her readiness to be amazed that had always fascinated him about Margarethe. She never seemed sad, never brooded like he did. Her laugh was high and clear, and when he heard it ringing out across the church square, the gloomy thoughts that often buzzed around him like fat moths dispersed.

"It is magic," he declared theatrically.

"Magic? Bah! You're nothing but a charlatan. Just you wait!"

Margarethe jerked the cards from his hand and sent them flying through the air. Shrieking with laughter, she threw herself on him, and soon they tussled like a pair of young dogs. A pleasant shiver ran down Johann's spine. They had scuffled in play many times before, but the sensation he experienced now with Margarethe's thighs pressing against his was new.

New and very, very nice.

"What is this?" asked Margarethe with a chuckle, placing her hand on his crotch. "Another deck of cards?"

Johann had been in love with Margarethe for as long as he could remember. There were a few girls in Knittlingen who gave him suggestive looks, but she was the only one who interested him. Still, he struggled to show it. Usually, he was considered quick-witted and scathingly sarcastic, and many Knittlingers called him insolent or a know-it-all. But with Margarethe he found himself tongue-tied, just like when he was a little boy. He couldn't come up with a reply to her coquettish question.

"It's . . . it's nothing," he replied lamely.

"Nothing? Let me see if there's nothing in the pants of Herr Faustus, Knittlingen's greatest trickster and braggart!"

Margarethe tried to pin him to the ground, but Johann was quicker and rolled on top of her.

"Braggart," she gasped, her eyes blazing with a mix of fear and desire. "You're nothing but a braggart. Admit it!"

Johann had hoped the card trick would impress her. Ever since seeing the eerie magician at the fair eight years ago, he'd been fascinated by conjuring tricks—much to the dismay of his father, who considered such things heretical nonsense. Johann made coins appear from ears; put live mice in his pockets, whereupon they reappeared from beneath Margarethe's skirts, accompanied by her screams; juggled with balls, knives, and torches; and turned sour wine into sweet wine just by blowing across the cup. Every time jugglers and magicians came through town, Johann studied their tricks. Sometimes they'd explain one to him, and he'd practice secretly in the stable behind the house. Rehearsing magic tricks hadn't helped his reputation among the Knittlingers. Folks believed sleight of hand to be the work of the devil—as much as they enjoyed watching the traveling artists in their bright garments.

As he and Margarethe chased each other across the field, Johann felt the small leather satchel he'd put in his trouser pocket that morning. It contained a strange powder he'd bought off a traveling juggler for a slice of ham and two eggs the week before. When lit with a flame, the powder smoked, flashed, and cracked loudly. Johann had hoped to impress Margarethe with the show.

But perhaps he no longer needed the powder.

"Ha! Got you!"

Shrieking, Margarethe hurled herself at him again. She pinned Johann's arms to the ground, which he didn't mind at all. Her face was so close to his that he could smell her warm breath and her hair, which carried a wonderful scent of honey, hay, and sunshine. They pressed their hips against one another, and Johann felt Margarethe's hot, damp skin beneath her thin dress. He'd waited for this moment for so long.

His whole life, really.

"You . . . you charlatan," Margarethe gasped. "Johann Georg Gerlach, you're nothing but a charlatan. But a very likable charlatan, admittedly."

A dreamy look entered her eyes and she brought her face even closer, until their lips almost touched.

"You're special," she whispered and brushed a strand of his raven-black hair from his forehead. "So different from the other boys. What's your secret, Johann Faustus? Tell me, what's your secret?"

Johann was sweating. It was as hot as a baker's oven, and his mouth felt completely dry.

"Margarethe, I—" he whispered.

Fingers dug into his upper arm and yanked him to his feet. Margarethe cried out with surprise when she was also pulled up by a hand. Between them stood Johann's father, a burly, bullnecked man with a sunburned face. He shook the young lovers like a pair of kittens. Then he let go of Margarethe and slapped Johann across the face so hard that he fell backward into the rye.

"What do you think you're doing, God damn it?" shouted Jörg Gerlach. "The prefect's daughter! Are you insane? Pray that her father doesn't hear of this, or he'll thrash you from one end of town to the other."

"But we didn't do anything!" protested Margarethe.

Gerlach raised his finger, trembling with fury. "I ain't stupid, girl! I know what I saw. You're not children anymore. Don't try to fool me!" He shot a look of disgust at his son, who was still lying amid the stalks and wiping a trickle of blood from his chin. Then he turned back to Margarethe. "I've put up with my son making eyes at you for too long. He's put a spell on you with his accursed tricks, and you fall for them like a silly goose!"

"But, Father," Johann said, holding his burning cheek. He tried to curb his anger. If he provoked his father even more, he'd be forbidden from seeing Margarethe again. "Nothing happened—honestly."

"Nothing happened?" Gerlach spun around. "Don't you see what damage you're causing with your wanton behavior? Margarethe is promised to a merchant's son from Bretten! He won't marry a girl who's been touched by another. And then the prefect will raise my interest out of spite. I'm already the town's laughingstock, thanks to you. You won't ruin my reputation any longer. Not you!" He stamped on the playing cards. The jack with the rose in his hand was lying under the farmer's heel, smeared with muck and dirt.

"Stuff of the devil," he snarled.

Johann moved backward. Until now, Margarethe being promised to a merchant's son had been nothing but idle gossip. Margarethe had never mentioned anything. But his father's words had turned rumor to reality—and Johann's dream of a future with Margarethe burst like a bubble. This blow hurt so much more than his father's slap.

"Stuff of the devil!" shouted Jörg Gerlach again and ripped the jack of hearts into small shreds. "Accursed, heretic stuff of the devil! Made for jugglers, scoundrels, and fraudsters!"

Johann had never seen his father this angry before. His face was scarlet with rage. It seemed like he was letting out everything that had long been stewing in him. They had never been close, but lately they'd grown even further apart. Johann's elder brothers, Karl and Lothar, were his father's favorites. He took them out on the horse, asked them along on trips to neighboring markets—and Karl, the eldest, was even allowed to join their father at the tavern and drink wine at the same table. The Gerlachs were a respected family with a large farm. Their house was right by the Knittlingen church. Everyone knew that Karl would inherit the farm, and Lothar, who was apprenticed to the blacksmith, would take over the smithy one day. The two youngest sons, Johann and seven-year-old Martin, would go empty handed.

"I don't want that pimply Bretten boy for a husband," said Margarethe angrily. She had jumped to her feet and stood with her hands on her hips. "I've only seen him twice, but that was enough. Adalbert Schmeltzle is as dumb as an ox, with teeth like a horse. I'd rather enter a nunnery!"

Jörg Gerlach's face twisted into a sneer. "You've got no say in the matter, girl. That's between fathers. Now run along before word gets out that you're rolling in the field with my son. And you . . ." He turned back to Johann. "Go home as fast as you can. Mother is worse, and she's been calling for you." He shook his head. "Aren't you ashamed? While you're out playing silly games in the field, your mother is coughing her lungs out! You promised to look after her—seeing as you're no good for anything else."

Johann, back on his feet, doubled up as if he'd been struck. His father knew he'd hit a sore point, and dealt the next blow.

"The priest said after mass that he'd soon have to administer the last rites. Who knows how many days she's got left." He nodded grimly. "Perhaps it's better for everyone if she leaves us sooner rather than later."

"How can you speak about Mother that way? You . . . you . . ."

Johann raised his arm, caught himself, and lowered it again. He spun around and started to run. He raced through the tall stalks of grain toward town, almost blind and deaf with grief. He didn't hear Margarethe's desperate cries and stumbled toward the city gate, his eyes swimming with tears of anger and despair. While he realized that his father just wanted to hurt him, he also knew in his heart that he was right.

His mother was dying.

With clenched teeth, Johann kept running, through the open gate, past the dozing guard. It was noon, and the lanes of Knittlingen lay deserted. It was unbearably hot, even in the shade, and it hadn't rained more than a few drops for weeks. Regardless of the heat, Johann ran up toward the church, which was situated atop a low, slanting ridge. Laughter could be heard from the taverns and inns, where farmers and tradesmen had gathered for their traditional pint following Sunday mass. Someone called out to Johann but he didn't stop. He could still hear his father's cruel words in his head.

Who knows how many days she's got left . . .

He shouldn't have left his mother's side—not for this long. His father always knew where it hurt the most. His mother had been sickly for years, but for the last few months, she hadn't been able to leave her bed at all. Johann would sit with her for long hours, reading from books he'd borrowed from the Maulbronn monastery or telling her stories he'd picked up from travelers at the taverns. Today had been the first day in a long time he hadn't sat by her bedside.

Instead he'd gone into the fields to meet a girl for a first kiss. A girl who was promised to another.

His mother's cough had been bad this morning, her phlegm streaked with red. Johann couldn't remember a time when his mother hadn't been ill. And his father had always treated his mother's illness with a cold indifference that frightened Johann. Sometimes he thought his father would be glad if she died. If she were an old horse, he'd probably put her down and look for a younger horse. But as it was, he left the task of caring for his sick wife to Johann.

Over the years, Johann had learned much from his frequent visits to the Knittlingen barber-surgeon and to the nearby monastery library, where he'd read countless books about healing—though he'd found many of the books rather strange. A lot of them spoke of the breath of hell, witches' brimstone, and pious invocations, but there weren't many useful recipes. Books were often like that: whenever he reached a point where he wanted to know more, they called upon God or blamed the devil.

Running out of breath, Johann climbed the last few steps to his home. The house of the Gerlach family sat on the hillside between Saint Leonhard's Church and the prefecture, which served as an administrative center and housed the town's wine and fruit presses. Johann's house was large, several stories high and with an attached barn and several stables for cows, horses, and smaller livestock. Jörg Gerlach owned more than sixty acres of land around Knittlingen, making him one of the wealthiest farmers in town. He employed a dozen maids and farmhands.

Johann rushed through the doors and past the hunchbacked old maidservant who was lighting the stove in the hallway. His two older brothers, Karl and Lothar, were there, sitting at the large table in the kitchen, shoveling stew into their mouths. Johann guessed they'd just arrived back from the fields. The strong young men had to work even on a Sunday. Johann was still short and slight and hardly any use in the fields. The two brothers looked up angrily when they heard Johann arrive.

"So Father finally found you, you slug," grumbled Karl, the eldest brother. "If you don't help in the fields, you could at least look after Mother." He gestured at the door to her chamber. "Hurry up and go inside before she soils her bed again."

Johann bit his lip. Neither Karl nor Lothar had ever cared for their mother. They'd lost interest in her the day she could no longer breastfeed them. They had literally sucked her dry. The older brothers considered the weak, sickly woman in the back room a burden.

"Go on!" growled Lothar. "Get a move on, midget! We worked our asses off while you were probably lying in the sunshine."

The smoke of the open fire didn't vent well through the opening in the ceiling, and Johann's eyes stung as he walked down the low hallway braced by sooty beams. He knocked softy at his mother's door but got no reply. He entered.

The chamber smelled of herbs, vomit, and moldy rushes. It was dark because the shutters were closed. The barber-surgeon was of the opinion that sunlight was bad for his mother, that even plain daylight could kill her in the long run. A sliver of fatwood was burning on the table in the middle of the chamber. There were a crude chest, a cross on the wall, and a bed, where his mother lay under a thin woolen blanket, pale and with her eyes closed. For a brief moment Johann thought she had died. But then her eyelids fluttered and she smiled.

"Ah, my Faustus," she said hoarsely. "Are you back from your walk?"

Johann hadn't told her that he was going to meet Margarethe, but she might have guessed something. He merely nodded and brushed her sweat-dampened hair from her forehead.

His mother's face was small and wrinkly, like that of a baby bird fallen from its nest. Her hair was thin and gray. Once upon a time she'd been a stunning beauty with blonde curls, but giving birth to four children, suffering several stillbirths, and being struck by disease had turned her into an old woman before she'd seen forty summers. Only her eyes still burned with a fire that must have bewitched Jörg Gerlach all those years ago. That and the large dowry. Johann's mother came from a wealthy family. Her grandfather used to be a goldsmith in Mainz.

"Please, do me a favor and open the shutters," she asked Johann. "I want to see the sunshine."

"But the barber—" Johann started.

"He is a miserable quack," said his mother with a cough. "Please open them before I wither like a flower in the dark."

Johann pushed open the shutters, and light flooded into the room. Dust shimmered in the rays of sunshine, and the fresh air smelled of summer and hay.

"That's better. Come, sit with me." She patted her mattress. Johann sat down beside her and let his mother stroke his hair. "Your hair is as beautiful and black as the feathers of a young raven," she whispered.

"F . . . Father said you were feeling worse," Johann said softly.

Instead of a reply, his mother started to cough again. Johann handed her a filthy old rag. She spat into it and then dropped it, her hand limp. Johann noticed with a fright that there was blood on the rag again. But he didn't say anything, not least to keep his own fear at bay.

"Tell me what you've heard from travelers in the taverns," his mother asked eventually.

Johann hesitated briefly. Then he began to talk, his voice growing steadier. When he was a child, she used to tell him stories about the big, wide world, and now he was her window to the outside. He had been for years now.

"They broke a robber on the wheel in Speyer—he'd been operating on the imperial road with his gang," he said. "Allegedly, he cut the throats of five merchants. Hans Harschauber from the Lion Inn was at the execution. He said it was a huge spectacle with hundreds of people watching."

"What else?" asked his mother with her eyes closed, breathing calmly now.

"The farmers in Württemberg are unhappy because of the cold spring, the poor harvest, and the high taxes. Many starved to death last winter or went into the woods. Apparently, Count Eberhard is a harsh ruler. Oh, and near Venice, a huge fish washed ashore. It's supposed to be as big as the Cologne Cathedral!"

His mother laughed, triggering another coughing fit. "Sounds like a fairy tale to me," she said, gasping for breath. "Do you believe it?"

"I heard it from a Venetian merchant staying at the Lion."

For a few years now, a new post road that led from the Netherlands to Tirol and from there across the Alps had run right past Knittlingen. Many travelers came to town along with the mounted messengers. Whenever he got a chance, Johann sat in a hiding place at the Lion Inn and listened to their tales. His mother used to do the same before she got too ill. The strangers told stories about a world so much bigger, more colorful and beautiful than Johann ever dared to dream.

"Give me your hand, my boy," his mother suddenly demanded.

Johann moved closer and held out his arm. She squeezed his hand so hard that it almost hurt. Johann hadn't known his mother still possessed such strength.

"My little Johann," she whispered. "My Faustus, my lucky child."

She called him that only when they were alone. One time his older brothers had heard the nickname and teased him with it for weeks. They knew their mother indulged him, and they were jealous.

"Why do you call me your lucky child when I'm not lucky at all?" he asked. "No one likes me, and Father calls me lazybones and a weakling. He says I've nothing but nonsense in my head."

"Oh, your father. Just let him talk. Who cares?" She smiled, and for an instant Johann saw in her eyes the lively girl with blonde curls from long ago. Young and beautiful like Margarethe, and her laughter just as clear and cheerful.

"I know there's more in you," she said, patting his hand. "You ask too many questions, and people don't like that. They only believe what they see, and they don't want anything to change. But you look further and dig deeper. You always have, even as a small boy." She raised her head a bit. "How is school going for you?"

"Good. Very good, even." Johann nodded. The thought of school brightened his mood a little.

A few months ago, his mother had asserted her wish that he be allowed to attend the higher Latin School, even though he'd completed his time at school. His father had been against it, especially because Latin School was expensive and usually reserved for the sons of wealthy patricians. But Jörg Gerlach had soon realized that this was very important to his wife and she'd never leave him in peace until he agreed. Since then, Johann had been learning Latin, grammar, arithmetic, and even a little astronomy. Along with his trips to the nearby Maulbronn monastery, his hours at Latin School were Johann's small escapes from the bleakness of everyday life in town. Sometimes he dreamed of studying at a university, like the one in Heidelberg, or even farther away. But he knew his father would never let him.

"Father Bernhard taught us about the heavenly bodies and star constellations," he continued. "He said there are scholars who claim that the sun, not the Earth, is the center of the universe."

"Heresy!" His mother smiled. "Don't let the priest hear you say that."

"Next Sunday night, the father wants to show us the stars from the steeple. He even has an astrolabe! He'll use it to show us the constellations the seafaring folk use to find their way on their journeys. Cassiopeia, the Great Bear, Pisces, Scorpius . . ." Johann hesitated.

"What is it?" asked his mother.

"You've often said that I was born under a lucky star. That's why I know the date of my birth. But what star was it?"

"Well, which one do you think, silly?" His mother winked at him, and he caught yet another glimpse of the young girl from long ago. "Jupiter, of course, the lucky planet! God has great plans for anyone born under Jupiter. He who is born under the lucky star is possessed by a deep longing for freedom and knowledge. He is never content but forever trying to get to the bottom of things. He is a prospector in the mine of knowledge, always searching for the truth. And he is someone who can lead people."

"How do you know all that?"

She paused. "A . . . a wise man once told me. A very wise and widely traveled man. He was a sage despite his young age. He told me fate would smile especially upon you. That's why I named you Faustus. It was his idea. Born on the day of the prophet, he said."

Johann frowned. His mother had never spoken to him like this before. He vaguely remembered someone else talking about a prophet—the magician he'd met on that memorable day at the fair years ago.

"Who was that man?" he demanded.

His mother hesitated. "He went away long ago. He . . . he came from the west . . ." Another coughing fit gripped her. It got so bad that Johann feared she'd suffocate. When she handed him the dirty cloth with a weak gesture, he saw that it was saturated with blood. Johann sprang to his feet.

"You need medicine," he said. "I'll go to the barber-surgeon right away."

His mother closed her eyes and breathed heavily. "Forget the barber. I've told you many times he's a quack. No better than all those charlatans at the fairs. All I need is rest. Rest and the stories you tell me."

The Knittlingen barber-surgeon was a drunkard who firmly believed he could heal any disease with bloodletting and purging. He thought any new findings in the art of healing were nonsense, just like the ancient knowledge of the monks and Arabic scholars. But there was no doctor in Knittlingen, and the physician in nearby Bretten was much too expensive.

"Then . . . then I'll go to the Maulbronn monastery," Johann said. "Father Antonius will know a remedy. He's helped us before."

But his mother didn't reply; she seemed to have fallen asleep. Her breathing was shallow but calm. Johann squeezed her hand.

"I'm going to see Father Antonius at Maulbronn," he whispered. "I'll be back in a few hours. Promise."

He stroked her cheek one last time. Then, quietly, he left her chamber.

~

His mother gazed after him for a long while. Her eyes rested on the worm-eaten, knotty pinewood door her son had closed behind him. As a child, Elisabeth Gerlach had always dreamed of a prince, a man who would carry her to faraway lands on his white steed. But all she'd gotten was a drunk Knittlingen farmer.

The other girls had said Jörg Gerlach was a good catch, a bear of a man and rich to boot. But his mind was narrow and his soul didn't want to soar; to him happiness was a steaming field, a good harvest, a folk dance on the fiddle, and a mug full of brown ale or wine.

Elisabeth had known soon after their wedding that she'd never be happy with Jörg Gerlach. But who cared? No one ever said joy and happiness played a role in marriage. People married to have children and to share the workload of the house and the fields. So every time Jörg had climbed atop Elisabeth and heaved and groaned, she'd closed her eyes and dreamed of distant lands and her prince on his white horse.

She gave birth to four live sons and became ill and weak. Two were like their thick father and one, the youngest, was a lovable cripple who'd always be dependent on others.

Only Johann was different.

She had sensed it when he lay in her arms as a newborn. Those alert eyes that seemed to take in everything, absorbing the world like a sponge. She had always known that fate had great plans for him.

And the man from the west had said it, too, and smiled strangely. The beautiful young man with raven-black hair as soft as silk.

Her prince.

Elisabeth closed her eyes and dreamed the man would return and take her away on his white horse, far away to a land with no disease and no pain.

Born on the day of the prophet . . .

"My Faustus," she whispered. She coughed again and spat blood into the rushes on the floor. Then she drifted off to sleep, a small, frail body, withered by the little bit of life she had been granted.

~

Outside the house, Johann ran into his little brother, Martin. The younger boy seemed to have been waiting for him and broke into a happy smile when Johann came out the door.

"H . . . h . . . here you are!" he called out. "Margarethe told me I'd find you at home." Johann just kept walking, and Martin struggled to keep up with his older brother. He jogged alongside Johann in his crudely carved clogs. Martin was small and scrawny, with a crooked back, and he stuttered—especially when he was excited. Sometimes, when Johann wasn't around, the other children called him a dimwit or a dwarf.

"Wh . . . wh . . . what's the matter?" asked Martin. "Wh . . . wh . . . where are you going?" He gave him a conspiratorial wink. "Are you going to make m . . . m . . . magic again? I won't tell!"

Johann sighed. Seven-year-old Martin stuck to him like a burr. Karl and Lothar were too old to play with their pitiful little brother, and they were ashamed of him. Martin often followed along when Johann wanted to practice his tricks alone in the woods. The younger boy would jump up and down like an eager puppy, would climb trees by the wayside, would pester Johann with questions, and wouldn't be persuaded to turn back. Nonetheless, Johann loved his little brother very much. Martin was so much more like him than like Karl and Lothar. Despite the stammer and the hunchback, Martin was smart and thirsty for knowledge, and just like Johann, he was closer to their mother than to their father, who didn't have much attention for the small latecomer.

"I don't have time for you right now," Johann said, rushing ahead with long strides. "Mother is very ill. I'm on my way to the monastery to get some medicine."

"B . . . bring me with you!"

"It'll take too long," Johann replied with a shake of his head. "I want to return to Mother as fast as I can." He stopped, leaned down to Martin, and gave him a serious look. "But I have an important task for you, do you hear me? Stay with Mother and look after her. Wipe the sweat from her forehead, fetch hot water for her, and sweep up the old rushes. They smell like death. If she gets worse, run and get the barber, all right?"

Martin nodded. He could tell by his brother's eyes that he was serious.

"And you'll c . . . c . . . come back soon?" asked Martin anxiously.

Johann patted his shoulder. "That's why I want to go on my own, so I can come back as fast as possible. Now go to Mother. She needs you."

Martin obeyed, and Johann went on his way. He hurried along Market Street toward the upper city gate, which he passed a short while later. Knittlingen was a small town of about two thousand souls. Its walls were surrounded by a foul-smelling moat fed by a handful of brooks. The church and the prefecture formed the center of town. For as long as anyone could remember, Knittlingen had been in the tenure of the Maulbronn monastery, which also appointed the prefect. The monastery itself was about an hour's walk from town.

Johann left the city and turned right, where the old imperial road led south. The path was dry and dusty, and hardly anyone was traveling this Sunday. Johann could make out a cart in the distance, and one lone horseman cantered past him; other than that, the road was quiet.

He'd walked this road many times before, knew every step, every tree, every field along the path. The track wound its way through cornfields and past gently sloping vineyards before climbing steeply toward the forest. Johann gazed at the fields and vineyards, spreading like a chessboard to his left and right. Everything around Knittlingen was well ordered, everything had its proper place—farmers, monks, the mighty Kraichgau houses of knights, the count palatine in Heidelberg, and above him, the king and the pope. Sometimes Johann felt he was the only one who didn't fit into the fabric of the world.

He thought about the argument with his father. He'd often wondered why they always clashed. He guessed it was because they were so different. His father was a strong man with a bushy brown beard and a broad back, while Johann was delicate and sinewy, with raven-black hair, and he was much too short for his age. They were also worlds apart in their opinions, their desires, and what made them happy.

Johann wasn't entirely sure yet what he considered happiness.

On the hilltop, he passed the ancient Knittlingen execution site, a square of mortared stones with old gallows. No one hung there today, but on many other occasions Johann had walked past the gently swaying remains of a convict. The German king himself afforded protection on all imperial roads, and to preserve safety, robbers and thieves were always hanged in elevated places by the roadside—a warning to other scoundrels near and far. To Johann, the stinking corpses were a reminder of the transitory nature of life.

He'd slowed down for the last steep part, but now, atop the hill, he ran until his heart raced. His thoughts were a jumble. Worry for his mother, anger about his father, and his feelings for Margarethe whirled through his mind like a storm. He passed an oxcart on its slow and steady way to the monastery. The driver was almost asleep from the heat. Then the forest ended and the road wound its way down into a lovely valley fringed by vineyards. On the left lay the well-known monastery.

It was an imposing complex made of sandstone with a wall, a church, and several other buildings. Eight fortified towers and a round walk showed that the monks were willing to defend their property. But they hadn't needed to in a long time. Maulbronn grew and prospered, like so many monasteries in the German empire.

Johann entered the abbey through a huge gate into a courtyard that was bordered by another wall at the back. Here, in the front part, the worldly facilities were situated, like the bakery with the granary, the smithy, a mill, and accommodation for pilgrims and travelers. The narrow lanes between the sandstone buildings were as busy as ever. Two lay brothers in brown robes rolled an empty wine barrel toward the building housing the wine press; a shaggy dog lifted his leg at the trough outside the inn and got booted by the innkeeper; a group of pilgrims in dusty traveling frocks searched for their quarters. A broad-shouldered, bearded monk in the smithy slammed a piece of iron with his hammer. Pacing through the lanes in silent prayer were choir monks, who, in contrast to the lay brothers, were shaved and wore white robes with black scapulars. Many of them were noblemen who were in search of a simple life—or who, as second- or third-born sons, were excluded as heirs.

Johann loved the monastery's aura of scholarship and eternity. Time seemed to stand still here. The sandstone walls were hundreds of years old, and the knowledge hoarded behind them was legendary. Johann visited the abbey as often as he could and occasionally ran small errands for the brothers. Sometimes he was even allowed to visit the library—always a very special occasion. So many books, so many answers to his questions! Normally, outsiders weren't allowed to set foot in the famous library—let alone a sixteen-year-old boy. But Johann enjoyed the friendship of a powerful benefactor at Maulbronn, someone who even permitted him to take home a book every now and then. And Johann wanted to see this man today.

He approached a lay brother who was driving a squeaking pig toward the butchery. "God be with you, Brother," he said in greeting. "Do you know where I might find Father Antonius?"

"Where do you think, boy?" The monk grinned and pointed at the tall monastery church. "At the infirmary, of course. Both the cellarer and the prior have been struck down by a nasty summer fever, and so have a number of brothers. He's got his hands full."

Johann nodded gratefully and went on his way to the church behind the next wall. This was where the spiritual, quiet part of the monastery began. The porter knew the boy and merely grunted as Johann passed. The Maulbronn librarian was a good friend of Father Bernhard, Johann's teacher at Latin School. But Father Antonius wasn't just the librarian. His medical skills were known far beyond the walls of Maulbronn. Johann felt certain the man would have a remedy that would help his mother.

Johann reverently entered the church, whose sandstone blocks were painted in blue and red. The tall windows allowed slanted sunlight to illuminate the altar and the adjoining choir, with its elaborately carved stalls. In a side chapel, a monk was quietly reading a mass. Johann had heard that the Cistercians used to work their fields themselves once upon a time, but now they were too busy managing a fortune that grew with each generation. The monastery called more than a dozen villages in the surrounding area its own. The farmers paid their duties more or less willingly. That was how it had been since time immemorial: knights fought, monks prayed, and farmers toiled.

And what am I going to do? Johann asked himself as he walked past the tall cross above the altar. *What plans does God have for me?*

He left the church through the silent cloister and followed the corridor that led to the infirmary. Rows of beds stood to his left and right, most of them holding coughing monks under thin blankets. A younger monk was scattering fresh rushes while an old, gray-haired brother poured steaming water into a bowl with herbs. A pleasant fragrance spread through the long, high-ceilinged room. When the old man heard Johann's hurried footsteps, he looked up. A tired smile spread on his face.

"Johann!" he exclaimed. "I should have known you'd come today. It's your day off." His expression turned serious. "But I'm afraid I must disappoint you. I'm too busy to visit the library with you." He gestured toward the full beds. More coughing and sniffling could be heard. "We've got our hands full with a nasty fever. Dear Father Jeremias died of it just yesterday, though he was very old, too. God rest his soul." He sighed deeply and made the sign of the cross. "How is my dear friend Father Bernhard? I hope he's doing well?"

"Father Bernhard is well and sends his greetings," Johann replied. "But my mother is very ill."

The other monk, a clean-shaven young man in a white robe, looked up and frowned at them. The Cistercians followed the rule of silence closely, and often they communicated merely with hand signals. The rule wasn't always enforced in the infirmary, but one was still expected to keep a low voice.

Father Antonius waved Johann to an alcove off to the side and listened to the boy's report. Then he nodded gravely. "She's coughing blood, you say? I don't want to jump to conclusions, but . . ."

"What is it?" Johann said, giving the monk a pleading look. "Please, tell me!"

Father Antonius sighed. "You know your mother hasn't been well for a long time. When a body is weakened thus, diseases find an easy target. Nasty diseases like the white plague."

Johann closed his eyes to hide his fear. He'd heard about the white plague. Travelers often brought it from Venice, Geneva, or Rome. Those who caught it grew increasingly weak, slept more and more, and coughed. The disease seemed to consume them from the inside—which was why it was also known as consumption. It wasn't quite as bad as the black plague, but eventually they both resulted in death.

"And there is no remedy?" said Johann. "You know so much about healing, Father. Please!" He felt a thick lump in his throat. If Father Antonius didn't know of any medicine, only the dear Lord could help his mother.

"Hmm, there might be a remedy." Father Antonius moved his head from side to side, considering. "But I don't keep it here. It's down in the store." He hesitated briefly, then he patted Johann on the shoulder. "I'm sure they can cope without me here for a short while. Come, there's something else I want to show you. It might just cheer you up."

Father Antonius gently pushed the boy ahead of him. They walked to the cloister, where a group of monks stood by a bubbling fountain, talking in hushed voices. They faltered when they saw Johann, but the father paid them no heed. Together they entered a small room. A set of stairs led to a lower chamber illuminated by narrow windows high against the ceiling.

This was the store, and it smelled musty and fragrant at the same time, mixed with a slightly metallic, caustic smell Johann couldn't place. Barrels and crates were stacked against the walls alongside many shelves; salted legs of ham hung from the ceiling together with sausages and bundles of dried herbs. On the far side of the room stood a table with a strange apparatus that reminded Johann vaguely of a fruit press. In front of it stood several open crates, and on the floor, glinting in the light of the afternoon, sticks of iron were scattered about, like the broken teeth of some kind of mythical creature. The metallic smell seemed to come from the apparatus.

"What is that?" asked Johann, puzzled.

"That's just what I was going to show you. Ha, I knew you'd be interested! It is a printing press." Father Antonius winked mischievously and walked to the press. "The prior and I managed to convince the abbot to buy one for the monastery. We got it quite cheaply from a monastery near Worms, along with some boxes of Latin and Greek books for the library. Once we start using the press, things will change around here. And not only here." The father made a sweeping gesture with both arms. "A new age is dawning, I'm sure! So many new insights and discoveries reach us—not only from Italy but also from the Spanish moors and faraway Constantinople. Old Latin, Greek, and even Jewish manuscripts are being rediscovered, and now we can print and duplicate them all! Just imagine, everything humanity has ever thought up can be put down with letters—and will still be legible centuries down the line. Knowledge will become immortal! I'm so grateful for the privilege of witnessing such exciting times at my old age."

Johann's eyes grew big. He'd heard about printing presses but never seen one before. Every now and then, a printed leaflet found its way to Knittlingen, usually bearing religious content. The playing cards Johann had bought from his savings and that his father trampled into the dirt had also been printed.

The pages of printed books were made with paper instead of the blotchy parchment used in most old books at the Maulbronn library. In the past, monks had copied each book by hand using iron gall ink to duplicate it, but now presses increasingly took over this task. The letters were cast from lead and tin. A job that used to take months or even years could now be done within days. Johann struggled to imagine how many books could be produced thus in a short space of time. Hundreds? Thousands? Already there were more books than he could ever read!

As he slowly walked around the printing press and touched the metallic, ink-stained shafts with the back-to-front letters, Father Antonius lifted a small clay bottle from one of the shelves.

"I made this medicine last week with a recipe from an old monastic book," he explained. "The book was in one of the boxes from Worms." The father smiled. "It's mainly made of . . . well, cheese mold."

Johann looked at him with surprise. "Cheese mold?"

"And a little sheep dung and honey." Father Antonius raised his hand. "I know, it sounds a bit strange. But it's an old recipe and supposed to help with the white plague. You don't have to tell your mother exactly what it contains." He handed Johann the corked bottle. "Give her one sip today and then one sip morning and night every day for the next week. Praying won't hurt, either."

"Thank you, Father." Johann was about to leave when one of the books in the crates by the printing press caught his eye. A few months at Latin School had improved Johann's Latin greatly, and so he stared with surprise at the title and author of the book on top of the pile.

Speculum Astronomiae.

"Mirror of Astronomy," he muttered. "By Albertus Magnus, venerable brother of the Dominicans and bishop of Regensburg."

Astronomy, Johann knew from Father Bernhard's class, was the knowledge of the stars, just like astrology. He recalled his mother mentioning the stars and the day of his birth yet again earlier this day. But he hadn't realized men of the church also took an interest in the stars.

"Does the church believe in the power of the stars?" he asked Father Antonius.

"Well, it's a thin line between what the church believes and what it condemns as heresy," the monk replied. "The stars are an expression of God's will, says the pope, and so does the great Albertus Magnus, who wrote this book more than two hundred years ago. Even bishops occasionally have their horoscopes cast." Father Antonius gave a small grin. "Although personally, I don't really believe in it. Albertus Magnus also wrote about alchemy and magic. Some say he was a sorcerer himself. But where does black magic begin? And what is God's will?" He smiled. "Why do you ask?"

"It's . . . it's just . . ." Johann was about to tell the father about his conversation with his mother when he realized how long he'd already been at the monastery. He had to return to Knittlingen! His mother needed the medicine as soon as possible.

"I'm afraid I don't have any money on me," Johann said hesitantly. "But I'm sure my father will reimburse you." Deep down, he doubted it. His father was a miser who considered the monks a bunch of quacks.

"No need to trouble your father." Father Antonius waved his hand dismissively. "It's a gift of the church. If you ask me, the farmers of Knittlingen have paid us more than enough. May God protect your mother and may the medicine bring her relief."

"Thank you so much, Father!" Johann briefly squeezed the father's hand before rushing outside and stuffing the precious bottle under his shirt. During his conversation with Father Antonius he'd almost forgotten how ill his mother was, and now he'd have to hurry if he wanted to make it home before nightfall.

Johann left the church and ran past the smithy and the inn, through the monastery gate, and toward the hill that separated Maulbronn from Knittlingen. The sun was low on the horizon, and the trees cast long shadows. The small bottle pressing against his chest, Johann ran up the steep path until he reached the dense beech forest. There was a spring in his step now that his worries weren't weighing him down as much. He felt certain the medicine would help his mother—Father Antonius had always been right. All would be well! And next time he visited Maulbronn, the father might tell him more about this Albertus Magnus who might have been a sorcerer.

Soon Johann had reached Gallows Hill. The place appeared much gloomier now that it was getting dark. The branches of an elm tree near the gallows groaned in the wind like a hanged man drawing his last breath.

And someone was awaiting Johann there.

Three figures were sitting on the stone platform. When Johann came closer, they jumped off the wall and walked toward him.

Johann started with fright. At first he thought they were highway robbers out to get him, but then he recognized them as three boys from town. They were a little older than him, and he knew them well. Two of them used to beat him up occasionally at his old school when he asked too many questions in class. But the third one was the most dangerous: Ludwig, Margarethe's older brother.

Ludwig was nearly eighteen now, a whole head taller than Johann, with a pockmarked face and shifty eyes. He often knocked about with Johann's elder brothers, drinking and fighting with the boys from neighboring villages. Ludwig had bullied Johann for as long as the younger boy could remember. The prefect's son had never liked the fact that his sister was meeting up with the village misfit and know-it-all. Ludwig had no time for Johann's magic tricks. Sometimes he even seemed envious when Johann enchanted Margarethe and her friends with chicken eggs and scarves.

Now Ludwig's vigorous and triumphant demeanor told Johann that this time he wouldn't get away with a joke and a few smart lines.

"Look at that, your tiny cripple of a brother was right," Ludwig scoffed. "We only had to give the dwarf a little shake and he spilled. You were over at Maulbronn with those Bible thumpers again. I bet you wiped their asses with parchment." Ludwig had always hated books at school; evidently his attitude hadn't changed.

"I went to get medicine for my mother," Johann replied firmly and felt for the small bottle under his shirt. "She is very ill."

"When is your mother ever not ill?" Ludwig jeered and looked around at his younger friends for approval. "Do you know what folks are saying? The say Elisabeth the harlot caught the French disease. She went to bed with some foreign mercenary, and God is punishing her for it."

"What did you call my mother? Say it again and I'll . . . I'll . . ." Johann took one step toward Ludwig. His anger was greater than his fear now, his voice trembling. It wasn't the first time boys from town had teased him with the fact that his mother had been seen with other men in the past. They were careful never to do so while Johann's father was around, though, as he'd respond with brutal violence. Still, Johann's mother had a certain reputation in Knittlingen.

"You'll what?" asked Ludwig. When Johann didn't reply, the older boy continued. "Your mother is a whore. Do you hear me? A dirty whore! And I won't stand by and watch my sister become one, too."

It was too much for Johann. Shaking with anger, he raised his fist—when it suddenly dawned on him why Ludwig and the two others had ambushed him here: someone must have seen him and Margarethe in the field! And now Ludwig felt compelled to defend his little sister's honor. Even if he fought with Ludwig now, the rumor was out, and it was more damaging to Margarethe than to him, especially since her father wanted to marry her off to a merchant's son from Bretten. He had to pull himself together, for Margarethe's sake.

"Listen," Johann said in a conciliatory tone. "I don't know what you've heard, but there's nothing going on between Margarethe and me—"

"It's too late for excuses," Ludwig shouted angrily. "You need a good tanning. Grab him!"

The two other boys stepped toward Johann at Ludwig's command. Instinctively, Johann reached into his pocket where he'd put the powder earlier that day. It had a strong, pungent smell and was supposed to explode amid loud hissing and popping—but even unlit, Johann thought, it might serve him well. With one swift movement he hurled the powder into the face of one of the boys, who dropped to his knees almost instantly, rubbing his eyes and crying.

"He blinded me!" he whimpered. "The bastard blinded me! Help!"

"You'll pay for this!" screamed Ludwig, lunging at Johann, who tried to escape. But Ludwig, strong as an ox, grabbed him. Johann didn't stand the faintest chance.

While the boy with the powder in his eyes still rolled on the ground crying, Ludwig and the third boy started in on Johann. He thrashed as much as he could, but it was no use. They had brought a strong length of rope, and they tied his hands and feet until he lay before them as a twitching bundle.

Ludwig looked down at him and grinned. "Well, how do you like it now, smart-ass? Your tricks can't help you now." He turned to his friend. "Let's carry him behind the gallows, like the mangy crook he is."

The two of them grabbed Johann and lugged him over to the crumbling platform where the gallows rose into the night sky like a warning finger. When they came to the other side of the platform, Johann realized what they had planned for him.

Behind the execution site lay a huge anthill. It was almost up to Ludwig's hips.

Johann screamed and squirmed, but the boys paid him no heed. The hill was a bustling scurry of tiny red insects busy carting pine needles and small twigs. Not far from it, half covered by dirt, lay a human skull and bones, presumably belonging to a hanged man. The wood ants had carefully cleaned the bones of any remaining sinews and flesh.

The lads pulled down Johann's pants and whipped his naked buttocks with pine branches until blood ran down his legs. He raged and screamed with pain and anger at this humiliation—but no one heard him way up here, far from

Knittlingen. The bottle of medicine he'd been clutching in his fingers fell to the ground, and Ludwig kicked it away like trash.

Then, still using a branch, he pummeled Johann like a madman. "You think you're better than the rest of us, do you?" shouted Ludwig, panting. "Ha, how's your learning helping you now, and all your smart comments? What's the use of your heretic tricks now?"

Breathing heavily, Ludwig finally let go of the blood-smeared branch. Beads of sweat stood on his forehead.

"Now, in he goes!" he shouted. "This'll be a lesson to the filthy bastard—he won't roll around in the fields with my sister again."

The third boy staggered toward them with half-closed eyes, his swollen face twisted into a grimace of hate. "One, two, three!" shouted Ludwig. "Enjoy your meal, you little beasts."

The three boys hurled Johann right into the anthill.

The insects started to attack him instantly. They crawled over Johann's naked, bleeding haunches, biting by the hundreds and spraying their acid, which burned like fire in his open sores. Johann screamed. The pain almost took his breath away. He tossed his body back and forth, yanked on his fetters, but the ants were everywhere—in his hair, his ears, his eyes, his mouth, on his skin. A murderous army of tiny soldiers, out to destroy him. There was no escape.

Laughing, the three boys turned to leave.

"Oh, and your medicine," Ludwig said and turned one last time to Johann, who tossed and squirmed like a hare in a trap. Margarethe's brother picked up the small corked bottle from the ground beside the anthill.

"If those white monks gave it to you, it'll only be water and vinegar or whatever else they sell people," Ludwig said. "Your father agrees. He won't mind if we use it to feed the ants. I'm sure the little beasts will love it."

He pulled the cork out of the bottle and slowly poured out its contents, creating a small puddle among the pine needles that soon seeped into the ground. Ludwig wrinkled his nose in disgust.

"Yuck! I told you, nothing but expensive hocus-pocus. Your mother should consider herself lucky she doesn't have to drink this." He signaled for his friends to follow him. "Come on, let's go. If he really knows how to do magic, he can free himself."

With one last smirk in Johann's direction, the three went on their way, leaving the groaning and whimpering boy in the anthill. The insects' bites felt like needles. Johann thought of the pale bones nearby and screamed loudly again as he tossed back and forth. After a while he managed to crawl a little way away from the hill and into a muddy, damp wallow, which had probably been used by wild boars the night before. The cool mud eased the worst of his pain. The ants gradually dispersed until there were just a few left on his scalp and in his pubic hair, searching for an invisible adversary.

Johann didn't manage to undo his ties until it was fully dark. With his last remaining strength he limped through the night toward Knittlingen, bleeding and filthy.

When he reached home, his mother was dead.

2

THE FOLLOWING DAYS AND WEEKS SEEMED LIKE A NEVER-
ending nightmare to Johann.

He'd only seen his mother one last time before she'd been carried to her grave, looking almost unreal—like a small, dried-up doll. In the middle of summer, dead bodies decayed very fast, so the funeral took place the day after her death, at the cemetery of Saint Leonhard's Church. Almost all the burghers of Knittlingen had come, as well as the day laborers, maidservants, and other workers. They shook the quiet widower's hand and patted Johann's and Martin's heads, while Lothar and Karl stood around listlessly, showing little emotion—as if it had been some distant relative who'd passed away. Margarethe and her father had also attended but remained at the back. Johann was relieved that Ludwig hadn't come. He thought he might have struck down Margarethe's brother with a stone right there at the cemetery.

The priest said a brief prayer as the casket was lowered into the grave. Then Johann's mother was nothing but a memory.

The end had come fast. Apparently his mother had called for Johann in her last few hours and coughed up much blood. She'd wanted to tell him something important, it seemed. When little Martin had left to fetch the barber, she'd died, all alone. In the grief-stricken commotion, no one had asked why Johann had returned from the monastery with torn, bloody trousers, his body covered in welts. His father had merely given him an angry look.

He gave him the same look now at the funeral. "Why weren't you by her side?" he whispered at Johann. "*You* were supposed to look after her, not that stupid cripple brother of yours. Instead you're God knows where, getting into fights. This is your fault alone!"

Johann said nothing. His face was puffy and red from all the tears he'd cried the night before. He knew his father was being unfair, but he felt guilty nonetheless. If he'd only returned sooner from the monastery! Father Antonius's medicine might have saved his mother's life. He didn't tell his father what happened at Gallows Hill; the farmer probably wouldn't have believed Johann, anyhow. Instead, when he wasn't at Latin School with Father Bernhard, which brought him some distraction, he spent the following days roaming the woods, vineyards, and hills around Knittlingen on his own. He barely saw Margarethe during that time, and if he did, Ludwig was always nearby, casting dark glances at him and quickly pulling his sister along. Johann wrote letters to her in their secret code, but she didn't reply.

As days became weeks his wounds healed, but the pain inside remained. The pain and a quiet longing for revenge. He would never forget what happened at Gallows Hill. His mother was gone, forever! He felt terribly alone in the world. Little Martin clung to him more than ever, as if afraid his beloved brother would leave him just like their mother had.

Every night Johann stood by the small, crooked cross in the graveyard. He prayed to and railed against God at the same time, asking countless questions without ever receiving an answer.

Summer came to an end and fall arrived with fog, wind, and rain. The grain harvest was in, and next up was the grape harvest. People began to look forward to the next Saints Simon and Jude Fair—the highlight of their year. The wheel of life kept turning.

Every hand was needed for the grape harvest, so there was no school. Day after day, rain or shine, Johann stood side by side with the other Knittlingen boys and girls on the slopes of the vineyards, picking grapes, throwing them into the basket strapped to his back, and carrying his load to one of the three *Keltern*—the buildings housing the wine presses—at the prefecture. It was hard work, and Johann's back ached as if he'd been whipped, but he still went to his mother's grave every evening with a fresh bundle of flowers.

When he arrived home one particularly foggy evening, his father was sitting at the kitchen table, a half-empty mug of wine in front of him. Jörg Gerlach's red face told Johann that his father had had a fair bit to drink, like so often in recent weeks. People were saying it was because he grieved for his beloved (if somewhat strange) wife, but Johann knew better. His father was a drunkard, always had been. And now that his mother was no more, there was no one left to restrain him.

"I told the father that you won't return to Latin School after the grape harvest," Gerlach said to his son. His eyes looked glassy and red; his face was doughy like a dumpling.

Johann staggered backward as if he'd walked into a wall. "But—why?"

"What they teach you there is useless. And the school's far too expensive. Why d'you need to learn all that nonsense when all you're going to do in life is muck out stables?"

"So that's what you've got planned for me, is it?" Johann glowered at his father, his voice shaking. It was the first time his father had spoken to him in a long while—and now this. No sympathy, no kind words, just the end of his dreams. "You want me to be a stable boy?"

Jörg Gerlach shrugged his shoulders. "I need neither a priest nor a scholar. What did you expect? I've got four sons, but only Karl can inherit the farm. And you're no good for anything other than picking grapes or mucking out— or can you conjure up roast pigeons and make milk and honey flow in the Knittlingen moat? Do your oh-so-clever books teach you anything useful like that?" He laughed and took a long sip of his wine. His tongue sounded heavier when he continued to speak. "What did your mother use to call you? Faustus the lucky one? She spoiled you for far too long! Better get used to the fact that this is the start of different, less lucky years for you. It's time you got to know real life, Johann, and stopped reading and dreaming all day long. You'll thank me one day! Oh yes, you'll thank me. Did you hear me, you . . . you juggler! Good-for-nothing!"

But Johann didn't hear the last words. He'd turned away and stormed out of the house. What did he ever do to his father that the man had to torture him at every turn? Latin School had been the last ray of light in his life, now that Mother was dead and Margarethe couldn't or wouldn't see him anymore. Secretly he'd hoped that he might enter the monastery as a lay brother following Latin School, as a kind of assistant to Father Antonius. But that wouldn't happen if he didn't learn Latin!

He hadn't seen Father Antonius in a long time. The old monk had been made prior a few weeks earlier, after the previous prior died of that accursed summer fever. Since then, the father had been too busy with administrative tasks to have time for Johann's worries and dreams.

Johann walked aimlessly through the lanes and alleyways of Knittlingen in the dim light of dusk, until he suddenly found himself on Market Street outside the Lion Inn. It seemed to him like a stroke of fate. This was where his mother used to sit as a girl, secretly listening to the stories of travelers. And Johann used to love being here, too. But since his mother's death he'd avoided the place; the memories were just too painful.

At that moment he saw the wagon.

It stood next to the inn, tied to the hitching rail where usually the post riders' horses received their hay. Even though it had been eight years, Johann recognized the wagon instantly: it belonged to the magician Johann had met during the Knittlingen fair. The dirty canvas showed the same strange runes, and even the old horse munching on his feed seemed to be the same. Johann felt oddly restless, and his depressing thoughts drifted into the background. His curiosity aroused, he opened the door to the inn and looked inside.

Since the post road led past Knittlingen, the Lion was always busy. All sorts of strangers chose to spend the night. Now, too, several travelers sat beside numerous locals at the scratched tables, sharing jugs of wine. Something was going on toward the back of the room. A whole throng of Knittlingers—Margarethe's father, the prefect, among them—were standing together, so that Johann couldn't see the table behind them. Some of them whispered to each other, while others led loud discussions. Hans Harschauber, the innkeeper, walked toward Johann with a mug of beer. He smiled and patted Johann's shoulder.

"Well, Johann," he said in greeting. Harschauber was one of the few people in Knittlingen who always treated him kindly. "Are you fetching a keg for your father? It's good to see you here. Too much moping about the house isn't healthy."

Johann didn't reply. He scanned the room but didn't see the one he was looking for. Harschauber followed his gaze. He winked and nodded toward the group of men in front of the table.

"A traveling astrologer is lodging here," he explained quietly. "Apparently he's staying for the fair. But he's already relieving our Herr Prefect of his money!" Harschauber laughed. "He's having his horoscope cast as we speak. He's probably just been told that he'll make it to emperor one day."

"A . . . an astrologer?" Johann's heart beat faster. He walked toward the noisy crowd until he finally caught a glimpse of the man at the table.

It was the magician.

Just like his wagon, he was unchanged. He wore the same felt hat with the red feather he had worn eight years ago, and the same black-and-red-striped coat, which made his lean body look even more gaunt than it already was. His eyes gleamed like old copper buttons in his extremely pale face, his nose protruding sharply. Johann guessed the magician was somewhere between forty and fifty years old. But on second look, he wasn't so sure. The man might just as well have been much younger or much older. On the table in front of him lay blotchy scrolls of parchment with confusing charts and drawings, similar to those depicted on the wagon canvas. The prefect stood beside him and listened intently.

"Fourteen hundred ninety-four is a good year for you," the magician was saying, running his long, skinny fingers across the parchment. His voice still had the soft, exotic sound of the west. Johann thought the man probably came from the Alsace or even France. "*Oui*, 1494 is good. But 1495 is going to be better yet, for you and for your town! The sun will be in Leo and the moon in Saturn, and a hot summer and a good harvest await. Hmm, however . . ." He paused dramatically.

"What is it?" asked the prefect, and the men around him fell silent with anticipation.

"*Mon Dieu!* I see bad weather in April, with lots of storms and hail. Hold back some of your seed, because you're going to need it."

A murmur went through the crowd, and the prefect kneaded his hat, which he'd been clutching tightly the whole time. "Thank you, Magister," he said quietly, placing a few coins on the table.

The foreigner wrinkled his nose in distaste. "Who do you think I am?" he growled, and his voice was suddenly as rough as the bark of an angry dog. "A charlatan or a swindler? That is not enough! A few kreuzers might buy you a line from some little old herb woman, but not a decent horoscope. I've studied at Avignon, Krakow, and even Paris!"

"And if I refuse to pay more?" asked the prefect briskly. "What are you going to do? The horoscope's already cast."

The foreigner flashed a smile, and then his lips turned into two thin lines. He glared at the prefect with eyes that were no longer gleaming but dark and cold like the blackness behind the moon.

"Pay me. Only the stars and I know what happens if you don't."

The foreigner had spoken quietly, yet everyone in the room seemed to have heard him. For a few moments, the barroom grew strangely silent. Then the prefect placed two silver coins on the table, put his hat on, and walked out. The others followed him, glancing back at the stranger with fear in their eyes. In the end, only Johann was left.

"Dumb peasants," the magician muttered, and Johann wasn't sure if he'd spoken to him or just to himself. The sinister man rolled up his parchment scrolls and pocketed the coins. At some point he looked up and saw Johann standing there.

"What do you want?" he asked. "Question time is over, boy. Go home like the rest of the numbskulls."

"I . . . I . . . ," Johann stammered. He wasn't sure what he was doing here. But, just like last time, he felt a strange fascination radiating from the foreigner—and also something frightening.

Suddenly the man's expression changed and he frowned. "Hang on—I know you! You're the boy I met before in this town, aren't you? Let me see your hand." His arm darted forward like a snake, grabbing Johann's hand, and he began to read his palm. Then he smiled. "Indeed, it's you! Johann Georg Faustus, right? The lucky one."

Johann straightened up with surprise. "You . . . you still know my name? After all these years?"

The foreigner laughed and let go of Johann's hand. "Name is but sound and smoke, but those lines don't lie. I can recognize anyone by their palm. How is your mother?"

"She . . . she died a few weeks ago," Johann replied softly. "The white plague, most likely."

"I'm sorry." The stranger nodded. "I would have liked to speak with her again. Well . . ." He gathered his scrolls and stood up. "I must go look after the horse and birds. Come back tomorrow if you like—I'll be offering my services here at the Lion again, and I'll be in the area until the fair."

"What services do you offer?"

"Oh, the usual." The foreigner shrugged. "I cast horoscopes, read palms, and sometimes dabble in a bit of hydromancy or pyromancy—whatever people desire."

"Pyro . . . what?" Johann was puzzled. "Is that magic? Are you a magician?"

The man laughed again. "Ha, don't call me a magician! I don't want to end up at the stake. The church doesn't particularly like wizards and magicians." He raised a finger. "No, I'm not a magician but an astrologer. A traveling magister, versed in the arts of alchemy and"—he winked at Johann—"yes, admittedly, also a little in the art of magic, such as it is taught at the University of Krakow. White magic, that is, not black. And now, if you'll excuse me."

He left Johann where he was, crossed the barroom, and climbed the stairs. Johann's head was full of words. White and black magic, alchemy, astrology, hydromancy . . . clearly, this man was far more than just a traveling juggler.

Johann was about to turn away when he noticed something glinting under the table. He leaned down and saw a small knife, about as long as his hand. The handle appeared to be worked from some kind of bone and was adorned with black patterns and lines. The surprisingly heavy blade was wide with a narrow point and sharp as a razor. There was a small hole in the end of the handle.

Johann ran his thumb along the blade thoughtfully. The knife must have belonged to the foreigner. He'd have to give it back—he was no thief, after all. And Johann had a feeling it wasn't a good idea to steal the blade of a magician. Surely that would bring bad luck. But it was such a nice knife! Why couldn't he just keep it overnight, or for a few days? The magician would be in town until the fair. Johann could always return the knife to him then and say he found it in the streets.

He weighed the knife in his hand, glanced around furtively, then slid it into the pocket of his jerkin. The weapon felt cool and hot at the same time against his skin, like a burning stone.

Still deep in thought, Johann walked out onto the dark street, and immediately his gloomy thoughts returned. Inside the warm, brightly lit inn, he'd forgotten all about his father and Latin School. Maybe Johann could talk to him again, promise to work harder? School was all he had left!

Johann was about to head for home when he heard a low whistle from a small alleyway. He spun around and his heart leaped with joy. Margarethe! He realized now just how much he had missed her.

"Margarethe!" he called out and ran toward her. "I thought you didn't want to see me anymore. Didn't you read the letters I wrote you?"

She held a finger to her lips. "My brother can't catch us," she whispered. "Or he'll tell Father. And he already knows too much about us! They're trying to keep me away from you because they're worried about the wedding. Ludwig says if he catches me with you one more time, Father will send me to a nunnery."

"Your brother can go to hell!" replied Johann grimly.

"Johann, don't you understand?" Margarethe gave him a pleading look. "I'm supposed to marry! It's a done deal between my father and the Schmeltzle family. They shook hands on it just a few days ago—as if I were a horse at market." She paused. "We'll celebrate my engagement next spring, when I'm seventeen. Old enough, my father says."

"Then let's go away from here," Johann said. "There's nothing to keep me in Knittlingen."

"Go away?" Margarethe gave a sad laugh. "And live off what? Your tricks, perhaps?"

"I'll think of something!"

"Oh Johann, my Faustus," sighed Margarethe. "I'd love to. Believe me. But there's no way out."

He took her hand and felt her shudder. He thought about their time together in the field, only a few weeks ago, how they had almost kissed, and the salty sweat on her skin. "You'll never find happiness with that man!"

"Happiness?" Margarethe laughed again, but this time tears twinkled in the corners of her eyes. "Who said I'm supposed to find happiness? I must bear his children and be a good wife. His family will elevate ours. The dear Lord never said happiness was part of married life."

"Margarethe, you don't believe that. Let's go away from here. We could—"

Johann noticed Margarethe's frozen expression and spun around. Ludwig was standing behind him with a whole gang, all of them eyeing him with loathing. In his excitement at seeing Margarethe again, Johann hadn't even heard them approach.

"Ludwig, don't!" pleaded Margarethe.

But her brother ignored her. He shoved Johann deeper into the alleyway. "Didn't I tell you to stay away from my sister?" he snarled. "Haven't you had enough? You just wait. When I'm finished with you this time, you won't be able to sit down until Christmas. You'll wish you'd never been born!" He leaned down and grabbed a nail-studded length of timber from a pile of rotten boards.

Johann clenched his fists. There were too many of them to fight back. Should he run? Call for help? But who would help *him*—the village smart aleck and good-for-nothing? People would say he had it coming.

Then Johann remembered the knife.

His fingers went to his pocket. The handle felt cool and pleasant. But he hesitated. If he stabbed Ludwig now, he'd be a murderer and branded forever. He couldn't do it! The price was too high. So he merely stood as still as a rabbit that smells the hunter but doesn't flee.

"Leave him!" shouted Margarethe, trying to run up to him. "Johann!" But two of the young men held her.

"Pull down his pants!" snarled Ludwig. "I'm going to teach him a lesson he won't forget for the rest of his life."

Johann thought of the knife again. It throbbed in his pocket like a small, breathing animal. How he'd enjoy cutting Ludwig's plump cheek open!

Ludwig raised the plank and was about to strike when a voice rang out from the street.

"There you are, you lazy layabout! Have you forgotten? You were supposed to take care of my horse! What did I give you a kreuzer for?"

Johann started. The foreigner stood in the alley and waved at him as if they'd known each other for a long time. In the dim light of night, only his outline with the wide coat was visible, resembling a scarecrow in the fields.

"Is that your new friend?" jeered Ludwig. "A skinny, dishonorable juggler? Ha! He can't help you now."

He raised his length of timber once more when the stranger spoke again.

"If you don't come right now, boy, I see great misfortune. Very great misfortune, for everyone here. The stars don't lie, and they shine wanly upon you boys. *Do you understand me?*"

It was the same voice the stranger had used earlier to threaten Ludwig's father inside the Lion. Low and cold, like a wind from the far north sweeping through the lanes. His last words had been clipped and as sharp as the blade of a butcher's knife. Ludwig lowered his arm slowly, as though someone were forcing it down.

"Damn it . . . All right, I'll let you get away this time," he said uncertainly to Johann. "But next time, you're done. I will get you—if not today, then tomorrow or next week. You mangy bastard! That's what you are. A bastard!"

He turned around and signaled for his friends to follow. Margarethe managed to break away and rushed over to Johann. "Tomorrow morning by the Trottenkelter press at the prefecture!" she whispered. "When the bells chime six o'clock, before morning mass. I—"

Ludwig dragged her away before she could finish.

"Your mother is a dead whore!" he shouted at Johann as he walked away. "D'you hear me? A dead whore!" Then the gang disappeared around a corner, Margarethe in tow.

Torn between fear, anger, and the hope of seeing Margarethe again the next day, Johann staggered into the street, where the magician waited for him with a smile.

"I believe you owe me a favor," he said when Johann stood in front of him. "It looks like I just saved you from a good beating. The least you can do is tell me what those boys wanted from you." He grinned a wolfish grin. "Let me guess: something to do with that freckled girl."

"One . . . one of them is her brother," Johann replied haltingly. He was still shaking. "He doesn't want us to see each other. He beat me up before and threw me into an anthill with my hands and feet tied."

"Into an anthill? Wow, that's nasty."

For a few moments neither of them spoke, and Johann's breathing gradually slowed. They could hear music and the laughter of men coming from the inn. Then Johann remembered the knife in his pocket. The cold metal he'd admired earlier suddenly repulsed him. He pulled the weapon from his jerkin and held it out to the stranger.

"You must have lost this under the table earlier. I picked it up for you."

"Yes, that's my knife." The foreigner raised an eyebrow in surprise. "Well, thank you." He took the knife and weighed it in his hand, thinking. Then he gave Johann an appraising look.

"Hmm, did I just hear that boy call your mother a dead whore?"

Johann nodded.

"And you just put up with it? If someone threw *me* into an anthill and called my mother a dead whore, do you know what I would do to him?"

Johann looked at the magician expectantly.

"I would wait until he sleeps, then I would bash his skull in with a cudgel. And once the blood ran from his nose and eyes, I would use this knife to cut off his lips. His lips and his goddamned tongue. So he would never say such filth about my mother again."

Johann waited for the man to laugh at his joke. But he didn't laugh; his pale face remained completely unmoved.

"Why do you put up with it, boy?" the man asked eventually, running his finger along the blade. "Are you always going to put up with it? Have you never thought of revenge?"

Revenge . . .

Johann closed his eyes for a moment. Oh yes, he had! In his many sleepless nights over the last few weeks he'd seen the same image over and over in his head: himself, lying bound and naked in an anthill, while Ludwig poured out the medicine with an evil smile on his lips. The same medicine that might have saved his mother's life. Oh yes, Johann had thought about revenge. He'd fantasized about wringing Ludwig's neck as if he were a chicken, and about slitting open his fat guts with a knife. The thought had entered his mind and burrowed its way into his brain like a tick he couldn't shake.

"Ahhh, you feel it, don't you?" The stranger's lips twisted into a triumphant smile. "Don't be afraid to admit it. I can see it in your eyes. Hatred burns inside you, and that is nothing to be ashamed of. Hatred can be very healing, purging the soul like fire. But it needs a direction, and it needs closure. You do want that boy to be dead, don't you? Dead like your mother?"

Johann said nothing, but then he nodded slowly.

"Then say it," the man urged. "It'll make you feel better! Just like sweet medicine."

"I . . . I want Ludwig to be dead," Johann said hoarsely before he knew what he was doing.

The man nodded and gave him a pat on the back. "There you go. You'll see, you'll feel much better." He gave a wide grin and bared his teeth, which gleamed unnaturally white in the light of the moon. Then he held the knife out to Johann.

"I'm giving this to you. You found it, so it shall be yours. I get the impression you could use a knife. It's a throwing knife and very old. I just sharpened it. It cuts skin and sinews like butter."

Johann hesitated, but the foreigner placed the weapon in his hand. "Take it, you silly boy. If you don't know what else to do with it, use it to peel turnips."

"Thank you," Johann said and put the knife back in his pocket. It felt much heavier than before.

"Oh, how terribly rude of me—I haven't even introduced myself." The stranger held out his hand to Johann. "My name is Tonio. Tonio del Moravia. Krakow magister of the seven arts and keeper of the seven times seven seals. Tonio to my friends. Shake hands."

Johann took Tonio's hand; it felt cold and damp, like the scaly skin of a fish.

"It was a pleasure to meet you," Tonio said and patted Johann's shoulder. "Now keep your eyes open on your way home. I can't bail you out every time."

Whistling, he untied his horse and walked away. A cool breeze suddenly swept the fallen leaves through the dark lanes, and a chill ran down Johann's spine.

Summer in Knittlingen was truly over.

~

The man who called himself Tonio led his horse into the stable and tied it to the wagon, which the lads working for the innkeeper had pushed in there. Above the box seat dangled the cage holding the raven and two crows. The birds screeched and flapped their wings when they recognized their master.

"So, what do you think?" asked the man with a wink. He stood below the cage, speaking to his birds as though they could understand him. "The boy strikes me as promising. Reminds me of you, Baphomet." The man laughed and gave the cage a nudge, making it swing from side to side with a squeaking sound. The raven fluttered wildly with his wings, struggling to stay on his perch, and stared at his master from mean yellow eyes.

"*Kraa,*" the bird called and it sounded almost like a human word. "*Kraa!*"

"Shh!" said the man. "Don't worry, Baphomet, you're still my favorite. At least until we find the right one and all this searching can come to an end." He uttered a sudden curse and gave the cage another push, causing the raven to scream like an angry child.

"Damn it, Baphomet, and I was so certain about you! I truly thought the day had come. Well, perhaps I'm mistaken yet again. It's been a while . . ." The stranger looked pensive, then he shook his head. "I must be mistaken. It can't be. Not yet—it's too soon. But it's worth a try, I think. Don't you?"

The birds fluttered and screeched.

"Easy, easy, you little beasts," the man said. "You had your time. Don't complain. Here, take this and be quiet."

He fished a few chunks of dried meat from a pouch and threw them into the cage. The birds pounced and devoured the chunks.

"And remember," the man said with a smile. "If he isn't the one, you get his liver. Promise."

He turned around and walked out of the stable, humming softly.

∼

The next morning, Johann rose before sunrise.

He and Martin shared the attic room, where rats and martens scurried among the shingles. He dressed as quietly as he could, hoping his brother wouldn't wake. He'd hidden the knife Tonio had given him in his straw-filled pillow. If his father found it, he'd almost certainly accuse him of stealing it. He took out the knife and studied it in the sparse light. It looked valuable. The black inlay on the bone handle gleamed like gemstones. He noticed only now that three letters had been carved into the handle:

G d R.

What was their meaning? Could they be the initials of a name? The magician was Tonio del Moravia, so they couldn't be his. Perhaps he had stolen the knife from someone or bought it off its previous owner? But maybe the letters stood for something entirely different.

Johann weighed the knife in his hand, feeling its heaviness. He guessed he could always sell it if he found he had no use for it. Quietly he lifted the end of one of the floorboards and hid the knife underneath. It was better if Martin didn't see the knife; the young boy wasn't good at keeping secrets.

After hesitating for another moment, Johann replaced the floorboard and sneaked downstairs. Outside the house, he scooped a few handfuls of water from a bucket, washed his face, and combed his hair with his fingers. Then he hurried toward the prefecture, which lay behind the church.

The prefecture was surrounded by a high wall, like a town inside the town. Behind the walls were the wine presses, the tithe barn, the prefect's quarters, stables, more barns, and the jail, as well as a torture chamber. The inner part was protected by an additional moat and drawbridge. During times of war, the prefecture acted almost as a castle. But now, during grape-harvest season, the bridge was down and the gates wide open. The sun hadn't fully risen; a rooster crowed somewhere, but other than that, all was quiet. Not even the servants were out yet.

Johann entered the first courtyard and turned left toward the Trottenkelter, the building housing the oldest type of press at the prefecture. For decades people here had been pressing grapes to extract the juice with their feet. Three huge tubs that were almost as tall as a man stood inside the cool stone building, and barrels were stacked along the walls. The smell of mashed grapes was so overwhelming that Johann grew dizzy for a moment.

He and Margarethe had met up secretly here before. From the ground, no one could see a person hiding inside the tubs. And at the moment, most of the work took place at the large screw presses in the buildings on the opposite side of the courtyard. Therefore, this high-ceilinged, drafty building served as an ideal hiding place.

Johann climbed the ladder leaning against the left-hand tub. Soon he saw Margarethe's flaxen hair gleaming below. He jumped down into the tub and almost slipped and fell on a bit of old mash. Margarethe giggled.

"Don't fall," she said. "Or everyone will smell where you've been hiding."

"Where *we've* been hiding, you mean." Johann smiled. He'd missed Margarethe's chuckle so much. Her chuckle and her full red lips, which he'd almost kissed once.

Margarethe grew serious. "I'm sorry about what happened yesterday," she said. "I should have known my brother would follow me. At least I know for certain that he isn't after me now—Father is making him clean the big presses over at the Grosse Kelter before breakfast, as punishment for loitering about town last night instead of helping at work."

Johann nodded grimly. "Your father is a fair man. My father lets Karl and Lothar get away with murder while I have to do the dirty work. And he doesn't give a damn about Martin." His expression darkened even more. "Especially now that Mother is no longer with us. He even wants to take me out of Latin School."

"Oh God, Johann, I'm so sorry!" Margarethe gave him a hug.

It felt good to be so close to her. He'd never told her what had happened at Gallows Hill that night. There hadn't been an opportunity, but he was also too ashamed. He felt safe now in Margarethe's arms, almost as if he were in the arms of his mother. But then he remembered that he'd soon lose Margarethe, too.

"You can't go to Bretten," he whispered.

Margarethe stiffened and pushed him away. "I . . . I don't want to talk about it. Not today. Let's not think about next year for now." She closed her eyes. "I often think about that day in the field. You and me together by the old stone cross. Your kiss . . ."

"I . . . I wasn't going to kiss you!"

"Really? I remember it differently. See, our lips were this close." She pulled him close to her again. "This close . . ."

Johann stroked her hair. It smelled sweet and alluring, of grapes, milk, and cider . . .

Margarethe suddenly loosened her embrace. "What was that?" she asked quietly. "Do you hear that?"

Johann listened, and after a few moments he heard it, too.

It sounded like a soft whining. Desolate and cold, like wind pushing through cracks in a wall, but definitely human. For a second, Johann even thought he could hear words, but before he could make anything out, the sound stopped.

"It's nothing," he said with a shrug. "A crying child, perhaps."

"I don't know." Margarethe shivered. "What if it's something else?"

"What do you mean?" asked Johann.

"You haven't heard?" Margarethe lowered her voice. "Three children disappeared from the Schillingswald Forest in the last few days. The first one was a four-year-old boy who must have gotten lost. His siblings went out looking for him and didn't come back. People are whispering that the kobolds snatched the children and took them to their underground realm."

Johann realized he'd been too preoccupied with his own worries recently to listen to any news. He shuddered when he thought about how many times he'd roamed through Schillingswald Forest by himself since the death of his mother. The forest stretched from the city's southern boundary for many miles toward Pforzheim. It would be easy for someone who didn't know the forest well to get lost.

"And do you believe it was the kobolds, too?" asked Johann mockingly. He didn't want her to see that he was also a little frightened.

"Of course not!" Margarethe shook her head vehemently. "They could have been taken by robbers or wild animals—wolves or bears, perhaps. Maybe they simply got lost. Remember? Two years ago, little Liesl Müller went missing for more than a week, and then a hunter found her, almost starved to death."

Johann nodded, thinking back on the incident. He remembered the mother's wailing and then the cries of joy all over town when Liesl was found. Since that time, the girl had been strangely quiet and withdrawn.

And then Johann remembered the other missing children.

They had disappeared eight years ago, around the time Johann had first seen Tonio the magician. Johann had always remembered the magician's face as clearly as if he'd seen him just the day before, but he'd forgotten about the missing children. Suddenly he recalled something else, like from a dream.

The magician's wagon driving away behind the church, the canvas bulging briefly as if from a gust of wind, and a soft wailing sound. Of baby chickens or kittens.

Or of children . . .

But the image disappeared as fast as it had arrived. Johann couldn't tell if the memory had been real or if it had been the imaginative mind of an eight-year-old.

"What is it?" asked Margarethe, concerned. "Is it because of your mother?"

Johann shook himself. "It's nothing." He attempted a smile. "Nothing to do with us, anyhow."

"Well, in any case, Father doesn't want me to go beyond the city walls until they know why the children have disappeared." Margarethe rolled her eyes. "As if I was a little child who couldn't look after herself. I'm sixteen! It's ridiculous. He's probably just using the excuse to prevent us from meeting in the fields again."

"Then we just meet here," Johann replied.

"And why should I do that again?" Margarethe winked at him. "You were rather naughty last time, throwing an innocent girl to the ground and—"

She broke off when they heard the whining once more. But this time it was louder, much louder, and it turned into wailing and crying. Then someone screamed as though they were terrified. The screams came from somewhere across the courtyard. Doors and shutters were thrown open; hurried footsteps crossed the yard.

"Something must have happened!" said Johann, unwilling to let go of Margarethe. "Fire, maybe?"

"Let's go see." Margarethe climbed to the top of the tub. Johann followed her and, in his haste, splattered red grape mash on his pants. They jumped off the edge of the tub and ran out into the courtyard. Several workers and maids were running toward the open gate of the Grosse Kelter, the building housing the biggest presses, where the screams were coming from.

And also a piercing wail that sounded like a large dying bird.

"That's Mother!" shouted Margarethe. "Oh God, something terrible must have happened!"

Together they ran to the Grosse Kelter. Inside stood four presses far larger than those in the Trottenkelter. Heavy beams made of entire trees provided the necessary weight to squash the grapes. A crowd of people had gathered around the second press, staring at something in horror.

Underneath the press lay Ludwig.

Johann almost didn't recognize him. The pressing plate must have come down on him while he was cleaning the basket underneath. Blood and mash were mixed in a red mass and covered Ludwig's face and hands. His rib cage was pushed in like a large rotten apple, and his arms were dangling lifelessly over the rim of the basket. When one of the workers poured a bucket of water over the dead body, they could see Ludwig's face. Bulging, empty eyes stared up at the ceiling. His lips were twisted into a grimace of pain and terror, and a thin stream of blood ran from the corner of his mouth and into the vat.

"Oh God, my son, my son!" Ludwig's mother cried over and over, like a madwoman. "My poor son!"

She knelt beside Ludwig and held his limp, lifeless hand. Her cries gradually grew quieter and eventually turned into a mournful lament. Johann watched her dress become soaked with blood and grape mash. The prefect stood stone still among his workers, seeming unable to grasp what had happened.

"The beam must've come loose when he was cleaning the basket," whispered a broad-shouldered day laborer next to Johann. "I bet the mounting was rotten. I told the old man a long time ago he needs to replace the press—but he didn't want to hear! And now he's lost his only son."

Margarethe stared at the horrific scene in silence. Johann knew she'd never liked her older brother very much—but he still was her brother. He thought of the sounds they'd heard from their hiding place earlier. Had it been Ludwig's soft whimpering as he lay dying under the wine press, drowning in his own blood? Johann thought he wouldn't wish this kind of death upon his worst enemy.

Then he flinched.

My worst enemy . . .

Hadn't he wished Ludwig dead the night before? Tonio the magician had encouraged him to say it out loud. And now Ludwig was dead! How was this possible? It must have been a terrible coincidence, because anything else would be too awful to even think about. He looked at Ludwig's twisted face, contorted in horror. What was it Tonio had said?

Hatred can be very healing . . . But it needs a direction . . . and closure . . .

This here was the closure.

Johann suddenly felt sick to his stomach. He started to gag and turned away so he wouldn't have to see Ludwig anymore. When he looked down, he saw his own slimy red trouser legs. He hadn't eaten anything yet, and his mouth filled with sour bile.

This is the taste of revenge, he thought. *Not sweet, but sour.*

Johann sank to his knees and spat out thick green mucus while the lamenting of Ludwig's mother rose and fell like a never-ending chorale. When he had no more left to vomit, Johann looked down at himself, his lips trembling.

His fingers, pants, and shirt were red with grape mash, but it could also have been blood.

Ludwig's blood.

3

Johann hardly saw Margarethe in the following days. The prefect's family was busy with the funeral preparations. It pained Johann to see how much effort was put into Ludwig's last journey. Johann's mother had deserved as much.

They washed Ludwig and dressed him in his best shirt. His casket wasn't a rough-and-ready box but crafted from heavy beechwood, and the funeral feast took place at the house of the prefect, with ham, sausages, and fragrant loaves of wheat bread. Ludwig had been the family's only son; all the other children except Margarethe had died in infancy. He was supposed to be the heir, and now there was only Margarethe. Johann's father told him and his brothers about the large crowd of mourners and rambled on about Ludwig—what a great fellow he'd been, strong as an ox, hardworking, and loyal to his father, just like his own eldest sons.

"Oh Lord, protect us from misfortune!" he prayed and threw his arms around Karl and Lothar. "I don't know how I'd carry on without you two."

Johann knew: if he should die before his father, the man wouldn't shed a tear for him.

Johann gave the Lion Inn a wide berth during those days. He couldn't stop thinking about how Tonio had encouraged him to say the death wish out loud. At night he tossed and turned for hours while rats scurried across the floorboards. He thought about how he'd shaken Tonio's hand after he'd voiced his desire for revenge, almost as if they'd sealed a pact. Johann had longed for Ludwig's death and then it had arrived. If this was indeed a pact, then what would he have to pay? Or had he unwittingly given something already? He hadn't gone near the knife under the floorboard again since, as if it were cursed.

But then Johann called himself a fool. Tonio might be an astrologer, a juggler, and a creepy magician, but surely he couldn't kill anyone just by wishing them dead. It was nothing but an unfortunate coincidence. A sad coincidence, nothing more.

Johann had heard from workers at the prefecture that the mounting holding the tree trunk above the press basket had indeed been rotten. Still, an uneasy feeling remained, along with a fear that Johann didn't understand. During one of his sleepless nights, he remembered some of the protective signs his mother had once taught him. He wrote them on a scrap of parchment, put the parchment inside a small leather satchel, and pushed it into a knothole in the threshold to his and Martin's room. People had shielded themselves from evil for centuries this way, and Johann immediately felt a little better—although he had an inkling that those words and symbols were just make-believe.

To take his mind off his fears and gloomy thoughts, he worked even harder in the vineyards, where the harvest was slowly drawing to a close. He carried almost two dozen loads each day, filled to the brim with the best grapes. But his father wouldn't change his mind. His decision stood firm: Johann wasn't allowed to return to Latin School.

His father hadn't visited his mother's grave in days. In fact, he seemed to be looking for a new, younger wife already. Only Johann and little Martin walked to the cemetery every day, bringing a fresh bunch of flowers. Summer blooms had turned to autumn flowers, and now that it was almost November, some days the only blossoms they could find came from the monk's pepper in the Maulbronn monastery garden. Johann knew his mother had particularly liked this inconspicuous plant.

All of Knittlingen was excited about the Saints Simon and Jude Fair. When the day finally arrived, Johann stood by the upper city gate like he'd done so many times over the years, watching the merchants and jugglers parade into town. But unlike in the past, he wasn't feeling excited. He and little Martin drifted with the crowd, snacking on something here and watching the jugglers for a while there, but the magic of the past had gone. And Johann heard people talk about the missing children. The number had gone up to seven, and all of them came from in and around Knittlingen.

But the children weren't the only topic of conversation at the fair. In the summer of 1493, the wise old emperor Friedrich, who had ruled the country for half a century, had died after a prolonged battle with a gangrenous leg. His son Maximilian, an adventurous knight who loved jousting, was now the sole German king. Word from faraway Granada was that the heathen Moors had finally been banished from Spain for good. And a Genoese man supposedly had found a new sea route to India and China via the Atlantic, although most people doubted it. Why should this nobody of a man succeed where the Portuguese had been trying and failing for many years? Although they had been following the coastline of Africa to the south—a lost cause. News from the Alsace was more reliable: another peasant uprising had been crushed swiftly; the leaders, as usual, had been drawn and quartered as a warning to others.

These days, messengers on horseback spread such stories faster than wildfire. The old folks shook their heads, reminiscing over a cup of mulled wine about the good old days when politics ended behind the next hill and God alone steered history.

Johann looked around and noticed some whispering girls glancing in his direction. He guessed they were gossiping about him and Margarethe. He'd spoken with her only a handful of times since her brother's accident. Every time he asked her about the impending marriage, she avoided his question. It was as if she had closed her eyes to what awaited her. Johann hoped to run into her at the fair soon. He might even snatch a few moments alone with her, like in the old days.

There was no sign of the magician on the square or in the lanes around Saint Leonhard's Church. Had he left town already? Surely the fair meant lucrative business for him. But deep down, Johann was glad he didn't have to see the eerie foreigner again. The man reminded him too much of Ludwig's cruel death. Still, he couldn't get the magician out of his head, like a melody that had etched itself into his memory.

"Will th . . . the devil get me, too, if I'm n . . . naughty?" said a familiar voice beside him.

Johann looked down and sighed. He thought he'd shaken his little brother, but now Martin had found him again. The boy clung to the tail of his shirt, afraid of losing his big brother in the crowd once more. Spellbound, Martin watched the puppets in a theater show moving back and forth in the window of a shabby box with filthy curtains and a painted background. Just then the devil himself appeared, dragging a poor sinner in the shape of a monk into the abyss. Johann couldn't help but smile.

"No, Martin, he won't," he said. "The devil only takes bad children."

"Did he also take the seven children that have gone missing?"

"You're talking nonsense. Satan has better things to do than take a bunch of brats to hell. But if you keep clinging to me like a burr, he just might."

He tried to walk away, but Martin followed him like a puppy. Annoyed, Johann spun around.

"I'm looking for Margarethe, and you're slowing me down."

"I know wh . . . where she is," Martin said proudly. "I saw her not long ago. If . . . if you take me with you, I can show you."

Johann rolled his eyes and took Martin by the hand. "You win. Take me to her."

Margarethe was sitting on the edge of a fountain a little way off the market square. She seemed deep in thought. Her brother's death had hit her quite hard, considering she'd feared Ludwig more than she'd loved him. Unlike her mother, though, she no longer wore black. It had been a terrible accident, but now life went on.

"May I?" Johann sat down beside her, and she smiled.

"I've got a stomachache from all the sweets," she said. "I think that's one thing about the fair that never changes. Not as far as I can think back, anyhow."

Johann laughed. "Do you remember the time we ate so much candy that I spewed on your lovely white dress? Your father gave me a good belting. And Ludwig—" He broke off. "I'm sorry," he said softly. "I wasn't thinking."

Margarethe shrugged. "It's all right. He was a monster, even though he was my brother. We both know it. Maybe he had some good inside him, but if he did, he never showed us. To him, I was a possession, not a sister."

They sat in silence as little Martin balanced along the edge of the fountain like the tightrope walkers performing in the square. It was afternoon by now, and the first drunken figures staggered through the lanes. Soon the musicians would play dancing tunes—much to the dislike of the church, which considered dancing to be the devil's wanton temptation. The air smelled of wine and rotten pomace, reminding Johann of Ludwig lying in the press basket like a squashed grape.

"Do you feel like going down to the Weissach River with me?" suggested Margarethe abruptly. "We can go back to the fair later."

Johann frowned. It was typical of Margarethe to come out with such a spontaneous idea; she was like a leaf in the wind, moved by her whims. Maybe she just wanted to get away for a while because Knittlingen and the fair reminded her of her brother and his horrible death.

"Didn't your father forbid you to leave the city?" he asked cautiously.

Margarethe waved her hand dismissively. "I'm nothing but thin air to him since Ludwig's death. He spends his days staring at the ceiling, just like Mother. Ludwig was the apple of their eyes. I'm just a girl who'll be married soon and out of the house."

"B . . . but what about the m . . . missing children?" stammered Martin, squeezing Johann's hand. "Our father also said not to l . . . leave town."

Indeed, just before the fair, Jörg Gerlach had told Johann explicitly not to go out into the fields with Martin. It had almost sounded as if the old farmer remembered his fatherly duties for once, but Johann suspected he was just trying to prevent him from meeting up with Margarethe.

"Do you know what I think?" said Margarethe. "I think those children have just gotten lost. Schillingswald Forest is huge—they could be in Pforzheim by now for all anyone knows."

"And what if it was the k . . . kobolds or the b . . . boogeyman?" asked Martin anxiously.

"Oh, Martin, you're such a scaredy-cat!" Margarethe laughed. "They only exist in your imagination!" She stood up. "I tell you what. We're going to Schillingswald Forest to look for the children. Imagine if we find them! They'd celebrate us in the whole of the Kraichgau!"

"You're not serious, are you?" asked Johann.

But Margarethe crossed her arms on her chest defiantly. "You're just shitting your pants like everyone else here! If you don't come, I'll go by myself."

Johann gave a sigh. He knew that when Margarethe made up her mind to do something, nothing would stop her. And of course he wouldn't let her go into the woods by herself. At least it was a way to be alone with her.

"All right," he said with a shrug. "But only until it starts to get dark. We must be back before the city gates close." He turned to Martin. "You better go home now. This isn't for little children."

"B . . . but I want to come!" said Martin in protest. "If you d . . . don't take me, I'll tell F . . . Father where you've gone and w . . . with whom," he added angrily.

Johann was about to make a harsh reply, but Margarethe cut him off: "Let him come. At least this way people can't gossip if anyone sees us."

Johann nodded reluctantly. "All right, then." He turned to Martin again. "But don't wet your pants if we do see a kobold after all."

Cursing under his breath, Johann walked ahead. He'd been thrilled at the thought of being alone with Margarethe, and now he'd have to put up with Martin! Would it never end?

Together they left the church and the fair behind and hurried toward the lower city gate. The shouts of the drunks and the noise of the fair faded away. All of Knittlingen seemed to be on Market Street and in the square, and the lanes on the far side of the church lay deserted. Finally they arrived at the gate, which was still open at this time of day. The only remaining guard had dozed off over a jug of wine presumably brought to him by a sympathetic colleague. The three explorers sneaked past him without problems.

Beyond the moat lay a few fields with a meandering stream, and behind the fields the forest began.

Even though the sun was still high in the sky, Johann thought the trees looked sinister and menacing, like an impregnable black wall rising up in front of them. He'd been here many times before, but today the edge of the forest seemed like the boundary to a foreign, evil land. They ran across a stubble field and soon reached the blackberry and hawthorn bushes at the forest edge. A jay screeched somewhere, and something big, probably a deer, disappeared rustling into the bushes.

"And now?" asked Johann, who was considering Margarethe's idea increasingly stupid. "What do we do now?"

Margarethe pointed at the stream entering the woods. "A path begins there. I know it from when I used to go into the forest with my father. If we follow the stream, we can't lose the path. It leads to a clearing with some large rocks and a cave. Maybe the children are hiding there."

"And you think no one else has thought to look there?" asked Johann mockingly.

"I don't know." Margarethe walked ahead. "But I do know one thing: if we stand around here for much longer, we might as well turn back around and let the others search."

Johann gave a shrug and followed her into the forest. Underneath the trees, it looked like dusk had already fallen. Many of the beech and oak trees hadn't lost all their foliage yet. Patches of thick undergrowth made it hard to see the path. The stream gurgled along peacefully, and it was as though a large bell hung over the woods, muffling every sound within.

They followed the stream in silence, as if they feared waking sleeping beasts. Johann knew the area. He used to bring the pigs here to fill their bellies on acorns, although he never went deeper than a few hundred steps into the woods. Beyond lay the unknown, inaccessible territory of hunters, forest workers, and outlaws.

The deeper they walked into the forest, the darker it got. Fir trees took the place of beeches and oaks, barely allowing any light to reach the forest floor. Thickets of thorny bushes slowed their progress even more, as well as fallen trees overgrown with moss and fungi. Several times they had to take a detour around obstacles and struggled to find the stream again. They reluctantly called out for the children, but it seemed to Johann their voices were instantly swallowed up by the trees.

"I . . . I'm scared!" whined Martin. His small, hunched body was trembling, and his stammer had grown worse, which always happened when he was afraid. "Wh . . . what if the b . . . b . . . boogeyman finds us a . . . and eats us?"

"I told you not to come, damn it!" swore Johann.

"Don't be afraid, Martin," Margarethe said soothingly. "The boogeyman would spit someone like you right back out." Her face was smeared with dirt and sweat, making her look like an angry forest sprite.

Johann knew the tales of the boogeyman and the kobolds. The stories were as old as time. But while he thought kobolds were just a myth, he wasn't so sure about the boogeyman. Every now and then, travelers told stories about dirty, ragged figures hanging about the woods; outcasts, the insane, wanted criminals—the forest was their home, and Johann, Martin, and Margarethe shouldn't have been there.

"I think we should turn back. It's late," he said to Margarethe. "We can come again tomorrow."

"Just to the clearing," Margarethe replied. "I'm sure we're nearly there. I came here with Father once."

Indeed, a short while after, they arrived at a small clearing drenched in afternoon sun. A handful of ducks fluttered into the air, quacking loudly, from a pond the stream flowed into; a pile of large, moss-covered boulders stood in the center of the clearing, forming a small cave at their base.

"Ha, I told you!" exclaimed Margarethe triumphantly.

Johann looked around the clearing. He'd never been here before. It was a quiet, peaceful spot, and he could indeed imagine that lost children might seek shelter here. They fanned out and searched the cracks in the boulders and the cave. But they found nothing, apart from old bear droppings and animal bones. Johann found a symbol scratched into one of the boulders: a bearded head with horns.

"What is that?" he asked, running his fingers along the moss-covered lines. "It looks very old."

"I bet the boogeyman drew this," Margarethe said with a wink. "That's just what he looks like—same as you if you don't wash your face."

Laughing, she ran down to the pond and washed her own face, arms, and legs, lifting up her dress high enough for Johann to see her marble-white thighs. He followed and washed himself, too, casting furtive glances at her. The water was surprisingly warm for the end of October. The sun shone onto the surface, and the two of them looked at their reflections in the water: Margarethe's freckled face with her flaxen curls, and Johann's narrow, pale face with the dreamy expression in his eyes and the raven-black hair his mother had loved so much.

Meanwhile, Martin had climbed atop one of the biggest boulders and waved from up high. His fears seemed forgotten.

"I can see the city from up here!" He laughed, clearly feeling at ease; even his stammer had vanished for the moment. "Let's stay a little longer, please?" he begged. "It's so nice here!"

Margarethe looked at Johann, and eventually he nodded. He also enjoyed the tranquil atmosphere of this place. "All right!" he called up to Martin. "But you stay in the clearing, understood?"

Martin threw his arms in the air and whooped—this hunchbacked little person reminding Johann of one of those mythical kobolds. He loved his brother more than anything in that moment. After his mother's death, Martin was the only one in the family he felt he belonged to. How could he ever have considered leaving Knittlingen? He had to stay for Martin. Martin needed him, and he needed Martin.

"He looks so happy up there," Margarethe said with a smile, watching Martin's little dance of joy.

"I think he likes being with us," Johann replied. "We're his family."

Margarethe laughed. "You mean like father, mother, child?" She started pulling him toward the cave. "Then quick, let's go into our house and cook a sorrel soup, like we used to when we were children, my dear husband." She sounded playful, yet there was an undertone of desire.

Johann was glad to let Margarethe lead him away.

~

Martin stood atop the boulders as if he were the king of the world.

He'd never been so happy in his life! He had been shunned and despised for as long as he could remember. People called him a cripple and a fool. But he didn't care, because all that mattered to him was his brother Johann. Especially now that Mother was dead. Johann protected him, played with him, and, most important, explained the world to him. Martin had so many questions. Why did the sun rise and set again? Where did lightning and thunder come from? Who made plants grow in the fields and calves in the stables? Why had the dear Lord given him, little Martin, a hunched back and a stammering tongue?

Johann didn't always know the answer, but he always went searching for an explanation. And now his big brother had taken him into the woods with beautiful Margarethe. They had brought him, the little cripple, along with them. Johann, Margarethe, and Martin. They'd always be together, for certain! His brother would never forsake him.

Martin climbed down from the boulder and walked toward the pond. He knew Johann and Margarethe were doing naughty things inside the cave. Earlier, Johann had made him promise to leave him and Margarethe alone for a little while. So he played among the reeds and made small boats from tree bark, letting them float on the pond. Then he tried to hit them with pebbles and watched them go under. One of the little rafts sank right in front of him. He leaned forward and thought he saw a black shadow in the depths, like a monstrous, slimy fish. Frightened, he shot up and stepped back.

There was a gurgling sound, and a bubble rose to the pond's surface. A slight smell of sulfur wafted across the clearing.

Martin thought of all the scary stories people told about the Schillingswald Forest. He thought about the kobolds and the boogeyman, who snatched little children. Suddenly the old rhyme the other children sang when they played no longer sounded funny, out here in the woods.

Who's afraid of the boogeyman? No one! And if he comes? Then we run!

But then he heard Margarethe giggle in the cave, the afternoon sun shone brightly, and the shadow in the water had disappeared as quickly as it had come. The smell of sulfur also faded. Martin breathed a sigh of relief.

Still, the pond now seemed unappealing. He stood up and went looking for a nice stick he could practice using his little knife on. Maybe he'd carve a heart on it and give it to Johann or Margarethe.

Martin knew the best sticks wouldn't be in the middle of the clearing but near the edge, where the forest began. He was walking toward a gnarly old oak when he heard an unusual sound. He paused and listened.

It was the sound of a willow whistle.

Martin knew willow whistles because he'd once made one with Johann. But he'd never extracted such heavenly tunes from it. The whistle he was hearing now played a soft melody, cheerful and sad at the same time.

It came from somewhere in the forest, not far from him.

Martin hesitated for a moment, then he entered the woods and immediately noticed how much darker it was than in the clearing. Again he heard the melody, but this time it seemed to come from another direction.

Martin was afraid, but at the same time he wanted to find out where the melody came from and who played it. With grim determination he clutched his little knife tightly and walked deeper into the forest. He didn't dare to call out. A strange magic lay in the air; the trees seemed to bend down to him like friendly, curious giants.

The whistle sounded very near now.

Martin closed his eyes for a moment. What a wonderful melody! It almost sounded as if his mother were singing by his bed. He hoped the song would never end.

Susie, dear Susie, what's rustling in the straw?

'Tis the little goslings, they don't have any shoes.
Susie, dear Susie, what's rustling—

There was a cracking sound and the melody broke off.

"What—?" he just managed to say.

Then Martin knew that the boogeyman was real.

And it was much worse than in his nightmares.

~

Johann and Margarethe were lying in the cave, where it was dark and cozy. The moss-covered ground made for a soft bed. They lay close together and Johann trembled all over, although he hoped Margarethe wouldn't notice.

"Now I can tell you," Margarethe whispered and leaned over him. Her hair tickled his nose. There was so little space in the cave that her breasts were pressed against his chest. "I didn't want to come here because of the missing children, but because of you."

"B . . . because of me?"

Margarethe chuckled. "You stammer like your little brother. Don't act more foolish than you really are! Didn't you notice the girls' looks at the fair? I think it's time we gave them something to gossip about." She brought her lips close to his. "You've tried to kiss me twice before. It's now or never."

Johann turned crimson with embarrassment and didn't know what to say. But he didn't need to say anything. Margarethe kissed his lips. She tasted so sweet, sweeter than honey or apples. They embraced tightly while she continued to kiss and caress him. Margarethe took his hand and placed it on her bosom, which had grown considerably in the last year.

"Touch me here," she breathed.

Johann didn't need to be told twice. At first he stroked her very gently, but then he pushed his hand under her bodice. He touched her nipples, which were hard with excitement. A shiver went through Margarethe's body.

"That's good," she whispered. "You're the first to touch me like that, you know. I've always loved you, Johann. From the moment I first saw you. You're so . . . so different. There's something great inside you—I can feel it." Then she chuckled again and her hand traveled to his codpiece. "I wasn't talking about *that*."

Johann tried to turn away in embarrassment, but she held him. "It's all right, Johann. It's all right."

They stroked and kissed each other, and Margarethe proved to be the more adventurous one. "If I must be engaged soon, at least I want to know what to do," she said softly. "It's my gift to you. But I must remain a virgin—we have to be careful."

Johann closed his eyes and let it happen. His fingers moved instinctively, sliding under her skirt and between her legs. She opened her thighs with a soft moan.

"My Johann," she whispered. "My Faustus . . ."

All his dreams seemed to come true at once. He loved Margarethe and she loved him back! What could keep them apart now? Perhaps they'd convince her father to break off the engagement, or perhaps he'd simply run away with Margarethe and Martin. Anything was possible!

They kissed, licked, and tasted each other in the most intimate, forbidden places. While Margarethe stroked him, he let his fingers circle, playfully at first, then more and more urging, until Margarethe's excitement erupted with a cry she struggled to suppress. They were so engrossed in their lovemaking that they didn't notice how fast the sun went down outside.

When Johann finally stumbled back into the darkening clearing, Martin had gone.

"Martin, where are you? Martin! Martin!"

Johann had climbed atop the highest boulder, where his little brother had stood and waved to them not long ago. With growing despair he scanned the clearing below, which was steadily being swallowed up by long shadows. At first he'd thought Martin was playing tricks on them. He and Margarethe had searched every crack in the boulders, hoping Martin would jump out of one at any moment. But his brother wasn't by the rocks or anywhere else in the clearing. How was this possible? Why would Martin go into the woods by himself? Unless . . . Ice-cold fear shot through Johann.

The pond!

He jumped off the boulder and ran toward the water.

"Wait!" called Margarethe after him. Her hair was full of bits of bark and moss from the cave, her face filled with anguish. All the feelings of happiness they'd shared a few moments before had vanished. "Where are you going? Don't leave me alone!"

But Johann didn't listen. He ran to the pond and jumped into the murky water, which didn't feel nearly as warm as an hour or two ago. Martin couldn't swim. The water wasn't more than waist deep, but Johann knew that was enough for someone to drown in. Just the year before, the smith's three-year-old son had drowned like a rat in the shallow city moat. His older sister had taken her eyes off him for only an instant.

"Martin! Martin!"

Panicked, Johann trudged through the pond, waving his arms back and forth in the water and hitting countless sticks with his feet on the slimy bottom. But he couldn't see Martin anywhere. Margarethe arrived at the pond, panting.

"Do you think he might have gone home without us?" she asked.

"Never! He was much too frightened. You heard what he said about the boogeyman!"

Suddenly Johann remembered the drawing on the rock—a bearded man with horns like a billy goat.

Horns of the devil.

Fear gnawed at Johann's stomach like a small animal.

"We have to search for him!" he shouted. "He . . . he must be somewhere in the woods!"

Again he rushed off without waiting for Margarethe. The entire clearing lay in the shade now; only the tip of the highest boulder still bore a patch of sunlight. The place Johann had found so peaceful earlier now seemed gloomy and menacing.

When Johann entered the forest, he realized how late it had become. Here, among the fir trees, night had already fallen. The trunks were black lines and the space in between was foggy gray twilight, and Johann could barely make out the ground. He stumbled and fell over roots and shrubs several times but got back to his feet and pressed on every time. He had promised to look after his little brother, and now Martin had disappeared. Swallowed up by this forest!

Or by something unspeakably evil.

"Johann! Johann! Wait for me!"

Margarethe's voice rang out behind him, sounding scared and quite far away now. Johann stopped, gasping for breath. It was completely pointless! The forest was huge. He'd never find his brother this way.

"Martin!" he shouted into the twilight. "Martin, can you hear me? Where are you?"

But he received no reply.

Instead, he heard something else.

It was a soft whimpering, a plaintive moaning that seemed to come from the trees themselves, or the fog surrounding them. Johann froze.

"Martin?" he croaked. His voice almost failed him. "Martin, is . . . is that you?"

It was impossible to tell where the sound was coming from; it seemed to come from all directions at the same time. Johann knew it could be difficult to rely on one's hearing for orientation in the forest. The Knittlingen prefect sometimes held hunts in Schillingswald Forest, and Johann had helped as a beater before. The beaters flushed small game out of their hiding places by swinging sticks and shouting, but they always stayed within sight of each other. They knew how quickly the woods could play tricks on you.

Johann held his breath and listened intently. He felt certain now. What he was hearing was the whimpering of a child.

"Martin!" he shouted into the darkness. "I can hear you! Where are you?"

Suddenly there was a piercing scream somewhere behind him. Johann thought it was Martin. But then he heard Margarethe's voice. She sounded frightened.

"Oh my God, go away, *go away!*" Her voice became more and more shrill, and she sounded scared to death. Johann had never heard Margarethe scream like this before.

"Margarethe!" he called out. "What is it?"

"Away, away, away!" she screamed again, high pitched, almost like an animal. And the forest echoed Margarethe's screams tenfold.

Away . . . away . . . away . . .

Johann spun around in panic. What was going on? Who or what else was in the forest with them?

"Margarethe?" he shouted again, and the trees seemed to swallow his calls. "Margarethe! Where are you?"

The screams had come from the clearing, he thought. Johann decided to look for her there. She was in danger! He picked up a solid branch and headed back. It seemed to be getting darker by the moment. Trees and background blended to a blackish gray. Johann kept running. Where was the damned clearing? There! He could see a spot that seemed a little lighter than the rest. Holding the cudgel tightly, Johann sped up and soon found the clearing.

But there was no sign of Margarethe or the mysterious attacker.

The screams and the whimpering had stopped. It was utterly still; even the birds had stopped singing, as if they waited for a signal.

"Margarethe!" shouted Johann. "Martin!" And he kept shouting, more and more desperate: "Margarethe, Martin! Margarethe, Martin!"

Ducks quacked by the pond and flapped their wings. Apart from that, Johann heard only his own voice as a jarring echo, as if an insane doppelgänger mocked him.

Margarethe . . . Martin . . . Margarethe . . . Martin . . . Margarethe . . . Martin . . .

The boulders were completely black now, like ink or blood seeping into the clearing.

Johann was gripped by an unspeakable fear.

He turned around and ran like never before in his life, racing along the stream. He stumbled and fell, got back to his feet, fell again, and kept running, out of breath, unable to form a single clear thought. All he heard were the thuds of his feet on the forest floor, the wind in the treetops above him, and the echo of his own voice inside him.

Margarethe . . . Martin . . . Margarethe . . . Martin . . . Margarethe . . . Martin . . .

Then suddenly there was more light and he staggered out into the fields. The lights of Knittlingen glowed warmly on the far side of the fields, and he could hear cheerful music coming from the fair.

Johann broke down crying.

He had made it out of the woods. But the only two people in the world he loved and whom he'd sworn to protect hadn't. Something evil lurking in the depths of the forest had taken them.

4

JOHANN SAT AT THE TABLE IN THE PREFECT'S HOUSE AND felt the eyes of the people in the room on him like daggers. They all glowered at him in silence, except Margarethe's mother, who was crying softly in the background.

"So you ran away," said Jörg Gerlach angrily, repeating what Johann had just told them in a trembling voice outside at the fair. "You left your little brother and Margarethe alone in the forest and ran away like a frightened rabbit. Not only did you disregard my order to stay inside the city walls, but you also acted cowardly! You . . . you . . ." Trembling with rage, he raised his hand to strike Johann, but the prefect stopped him.

"Leave it, Jörg," he said. "It's important that we find out what exactly happened."

Unlike Johann's father, the prefect was a level-headed man. Grief for his son had painted dark rings around his eyes. The news that now his daughter—his only remaining child—had gone missing had turned his face even more gray and wrinkled. He looked more dead than alive. Johann had found him and his own father at the fair and told them in brief, broken words what had happened. Jörg Gerlach had grabbed his son by the arm, and together with a handful of other men, including the priest and the bailiff, they'd gone to the prefect's house to question Johann.

"You're saying there was someone else in the forest with you?" asked the prefect.

Johann nodded uncertainly. "At least, I . . . I think so."

"What do you mean, you *think* so?" snarled his father. "Speak plainly!"

"Margarethe kept shouting 'Go away!' and I heard a whimpering."

"A whimpering? The boy's out of his mind!" said the bailiff.

As the head of the city watch, the serious old man was in charge of the questioning. They were sitting around the table in the living room. No one touched the full jugs of wine in front of them.

"It could be robbers living in the woods," the blacksmith suggested. "I heard them talking about a band of highwaymen in Tiefenbach waylaying carriages. Not even the imperial road is safe any longer!"

"Let us send out men with torches immediately!" said the prefect. "We have to find our children—now, before it's too late!"

"And what about the boy?" asked the priest, studying Johann, who was shivering all over. "He still seems to be out of his senses."

"Put him in the hole!" ordered Gerlach. "Maybe it'll help him remember what really happened—it has worked for others. And it's still a mild punishment for what he's done."

The bailiff hesitated at first but then nodded. "You're right, Jörg. Perhaps he'll come to his senses and then he can tell us the truth."

They took Johann, who was unsteady on his feet, by the arms and walked him to the prefecture's tower, which stood at the far end of the courtyard. The prison room was a dark, musty chamber with one tiny, barred window and a heavy, iron-studded door, which crashed shut behind him. Johann was alone. Soon he could hear the shouts of men outside and dogs barking—the search had begun. They would comb the forest the same way they did during a hunt, including the clearing Johann had described to them. He hoped and prayed they would find Margarethe and Martin. But deep down inside he felt that the two had gone forever, like the other children before them.

Johann's knees buckled.

Racked by silent fits of crying, he sank onto the dirt floor. Until then, a shell of fear and shock had enclosed him. He'd replied to the men's questions like a puppet, but now an icy wave of reality came crashing over him. He had sinned gravely, and prison really did seem like a mild punishment for his crimes. How could he have run away and left Margarethe and Martin behind? What had possessed him to do such a thing? No one had attacked him or pursued him. Everything that had seemed like the most wonderful thing in the world before— Margarethe's kiss, touching her body all over, their whispers and moans—all that seemed dirty and bad to him now. Perhaps the church was right to condemn lust as the tool of the devil, because the two of them seemed to have called upon the devil, upon pure evil, with their doings.

He had been punished by God.

Johann desperately tried to figure out what had happened in the forest. Had there been outlaws about, like the blacksmith suspected? The whimpering could have come from Martin with someone holding a hand over his mouth. Margarethe fought back and shouted, "Go away," so it would seem there was only one assailant, not several. He would have stood a chance against one man! He should have at least tried, instead of running like a chicken. The devil's face etched into the rock, Margarethe's screams, the twilight, the whimpering—everything had frightened him so much that he'd panicked.

The whimpering . . .

An old memory rose to the surface.

The wagon . . . The cage with the raven and the crows . . . The canvas billowing in the wind . . .

He'd heard a similar kind of whimpering before, eight years ago, when the magician was leaving town with his wagon. Could Tonio be behind all this? One misfortune after the other had occurred since the man had returned to Knittlingen. First he had made Johann wish for Ludwig's death, where-upon it became reality. And now Martin and Margarethe had gone missing in Schillingswald Forest. Johann realized he hadn't seen Tonio at the fair.

Because he was in the forest?

Of course Johann knew that children and youths were abducted from time to time. There were horror stories of hungry outcasts, of lunatics and wild men who caught little children and ate them. But Johann didn't really believe that part. The poor souls were probably sold to the highest bidder and spent the rest of their days as mine workers below ground, as slaves in faraway countries, or as child harlots. But the suspects were always gangs of robbers—a single man with a child would be too conspicuous. Tonio's presence in town and the terrible events could only be a stupid coincidence.

Johann huddled down in a corner of the prison chamber and thought about his life. Faustus, his mother had called him, the lucky one. The name had never seemed more wrong to him as in this dark hour. All his cleverness, his wit, his thirst for knowledge had led him not to the top, but into this abyss with no way out.

Time passed very slowly. Every now and then he could hear shouts and the barking of dogs in the distance. Half of Knittlingen was probably out in the forest, while he, the coward, the loser, was sitting in the hole.

When the first twilight broke through the dark of night, the shouts and barking suddenly became louder. The men were coming back. Soon afterward, heavy footsteps approached the door to his cell, then the bolt was pushed back and the door opened. The gray rectangle was filled by the bailiff, his coat ripped and muddy at the hem, his face damp with sweat and dew. But the man smiled as he lifted a lantern to illuminate Johann's face.

"Good news, boy," he said. "At least the prefect won't bite off your head now. They found Margarethe."

It would be a whole week before Johann was allowed to see Margarethe.

During that time, the people of Knittlingen—adults as well as children—acted as though he weren't there. When he returned to the grape harvest in the vineyards, they avoided him. He worked by himself among the almost-bare vines, and when he carried his full basket to the carts, the farmers stared at him in silence and spat on the ground. As soon as he walked away, they whispered behind his back. Johann was too ashamed to go to Maulbronn. Surely Father Antonius would shake his head at a boy who first lost the medicine for his deathly ill mother and then failed to help his little brother and his friend.

Martin remained missing, and the hope of finding him alive dwindled with every passing day.

The fair came to an end, and the jugglers and merchants left Knittlingen. Tonio the magician must have departed earlier—his wagon hadn't been parked outside the Lion for a while now. Hans Harschauber, the innkeeper and one of the few people who still talked to Johann, told him that the itinerant astrologer had indeed left town the morning of the first day of the fair.

Meanwhile, a group of men led by Jörg Gerlach and the prefect continued to search for Martin. They combed the forest with dogs almost as far as the Black Forest and past Bruchsal. They sent messengers to villages and towns near and far, but it was as if the earth had swallowed the boy. All that was found of Martin was a small, crudely carved wooden shoe lying near the clearing.

The worst were the evenings and nights at home. Neither his father nor his brothers, not even the maids, spoke with Johann. His bowl with soup or barley porridge was put in front of him in silence, and he wasn't included in the meal-time prayers. For many hours Johann would lie in his chamber upstairs, staring at Martin's empty bed beside him. What had happened to his little brother? Was he still alive? And if so, how was he doing? Was he sitting locked up in some stable or cage, crying, cursing his older brother who hadn't protected him? Was he lying in chains in the belly of a ship traveling down the Rhine, in the hands of slave traders who treated him like livestock?

Johann also worried about Margarethe. He'd gathered from a few whispered remarks made by the servants that she hadn't spoken since the incident in the woods. She merely lay in her bed in silence, getting spoon-fed, staring at the ceiling with wide eyes. She seemed to have been frightened out of her wits. Johann's heart ached with concern for Margarethe. If only he could see her! But the house of the prefect—the entire prefecture, in fact—remained barred to him. Whenever he approached the entrance, two or three servants appeared and made it clear that he wasn't welcome.

On the eighth day, the prefect visited the Gerlachs' house and spoke with Johann's father behind closed doors. Afterward, Gerlach addressed his son for the first time in a week.

"The prefect wants you to talk to Margarethe," he said frostily. "He reckons you might get through to her, help her get better. And maybe she knows something about Martin. Although I doubt she'll talk to the boy who abandoned her."

Johann was filled with renewed hope. If he could bring Margarethe to speak again, all would end well! She'd describe the men who abducted Martin. They'd search for them across the whole Kraichgau, find them, and break them on the wheel or draw and quarter them. Martin would be brought home safely and Margarethe would love him again, just like she'd told him inside the cave.

He ran over to the prefecture, where the prefect awaited him in the court-yard. In the last few weeks, the once strong, tall man seemed to have aged by years. His hair had turned gray, and deep furrows lined his face.

"She's in the back chamber," he said to Johann, gesturing toward his house. "Try your best, boy. I'm just not sure what else to do. The devil knows what she saw in the forest. It seems to me the dear Lord has turned his back on our family."

Johann walked past Margarethe's father like a whipped dog, crossed the courtyard, and entered the house.

In the chamber, Margarethe lay still on her bed, her eyes wide open. Johann came closer, his heart thumping loudly. But she didn't stir, even when he touched her cautiously. Her skin was as white as chalk, with blue veins showing underneath, and even now, in this sad moment, her beauty mesmerized Johann. He thought about their time together in the cave. That seemed like a lifetime ago. He had fantasized about becoming her husband then, and now she lay in front of him like a corpse.

"Margarethe," he whispered and took her hand. "Can you hear me?"

Her gaze remained blank, her lips unmoving. Only her calm breathing showed that she was still alive.

"Margarethe," Johann continued and knelt beside her. "I . . . I'm so sorry! I should have been there for you, for both of you. Please, talk to me! Just one word, so I know you can hear me. I . . . I love you!"

He squeezed her hand, which was cold and limp, like wet bread. Just when he thought she'd never speak again, her lips began to tremble. The words she breathed were so low that Johann couldn't understand them at first. He had to lean down close to Margarethe's face before he finally understood what she was whispering to him.

It was just two words, and they hit him like a blow to the stomach.

"Go . . . away."

It was the same words she had screamed in the forest when he'd abandoned her—and now they were addressed to him. And then her lips formed a phrase that would forever be etched into Johann's memory.

"Go . . . away . . . You . . . are . . . the . . . devil!"

Johann began to tremble, and everything around him suddenly seemed black and gray. The world was drained of all color. With tears in his eyes, he stood up.

"Goodbye, Margarethe," he whispered. "I will never forget you."

He ran his hand over Margarethe's flaxen hair one last time, then he turned around and walked to the door. Who did she think she saw in him? Or what?

You are the devil . . .

Johann stumbled through the lanes like a ghost, without direction, without aim. His true love—his only love—had cursed him.

~

The following morning, his father called him before breakfast. Like so often in the last few months, Jörg Gerlach was sitting at the kitchen table with a jug of wine, his face red from the alcohol. But unlike other times when he called upon his son, he asked Johann to sit. He stared at his son in silence for a long while before addressing him.

"Your brother Martin still hasn't been found," he said slowly. "And I don't think he will be found. The ravens are probably pecking away at his crooked bones by now."

His father's coldness sent shivers down Johann's spine.

"I want to be honest with you, boy. You're not welcome here any longer. Folks have never thought very highly of you—your tricks, your nosy questions, your fancy ways, acting like you're better than them—but now you've gone too far. Because of you, your brother died in the wilderness and the prefect's daughter is bedridden, more dead than alive." His father looked at him with contempt. "You've brought shame to my family, and I don't want you under my roof any longer."

Johann was dumbstruck. Margarethe had cursed him, and now his father was doing the same. Strangely, his father's words didn't affect him very much; it was as if they couldn't touch him deep down inside. The shock of Margarethe's rejection was too fresh.

"Of course, I can't force you to leave," Gerlach said with a shrug. "A father casting out his son doesn't look proper, even with a mongrel of a son like you. But if you stay, your life will be hell on earth—I promise. No one is going to speak with you, not even your brothers. You'll perform the most menial tasks and take your meals with the dogs outside." He took a sip of wine and stroked his beard. "But I'm not a monster. Upstairs in your room, you'll find a purse with a few coins, a warm coat, and a pair of solid leather shoes. Take it and go with God, or with the devil for all I care. I don't want to see you here tomorrow morning. The people will say you ran away, and everyone will understand." Gerlach made to get up, but when Johann started talking, he sat back down.

"Where does all this hatred come from, Father?" asked Johann calmly.

"Where?" Gerlach gave a laugh. "I think you can answer that yourself."

"I'm not talking about the woods or the fact that I wasn't with Mother when she died. You've always hated me. Am I not right? I've never had a gentle word from you. I was never allowed to sit on your lap. You've never given me as much as a piece of apple for a treat or a spinning top to play with. You even treated little Martin better than me. Why?"

His father said nothing for a while and stared at him from small, bloodshot eyes. Then he cleared his throat. "What the hell. You're leaving anyway, so why shouldn't you know?" He leaned forward and Johann smelled his alcoholic breath.

"Yes, it's true," Jörg Gerlach said quietly. "I never loved you like a son— because you aren't my son."

Johann winced as if he'd been slapped.

"Your mother was the most beautiful woman in town, but by God, people were right, she was a goddamn whore!" spat Gerlach, his eyes flashing with hatred. "I would have given her everything, but I was never enough for her. The whole of Knittlingen wasn't enough for her! She thought she was better than the rest of us, just like you. At home she acted all meek and quiet, but at the inn with the travelers, she laughed and danced and did as she pleased. I could never prove anything, but folks were talking, and I always knew that something was going on. Especially when that young fellow came to town, that . . . that sorcerer!"

"Sorcerer?" Johann felt as if he were in a dream. "What . . . what sorcerer?"

"A pale, black-haired fellow carrying a pack full of magic knickknacks. He was from the west, from beyond the Rhine. Some kind of scholar, traveling student, and juggler." Jörg Gerlach snorted derisively. "Claimed he could read the stars and speak with the dead. He put a spell on your mother, that's what he did! He only looked about twenty years old with his silky black hair, same as yours. But his eyes—I swear it—his eyes were those of an old man. Like the devil's eyes! They met up secretly in the forest, she and he. I'm sure of it. Because afterward she was a different woman, and cold as a fish in bed. Nine months later, you were born, you . . . you bastard!"

Gerlach spat out the last words, spraying saliva all over Johann's face.

"The man had the nerve to come back to town after you were born," Gerlach continued scornfully. "If only he'd taken you with him. But I made sure he left for good. By God, if he hadn't taken to the hills at the last moment, we'd have set that sorcerer alight like a straw puppet." He gave a brief laugh but then turned serious again.

"Since then, people call me a cuckold behind my back. They think I don't notice, but I feel it, every day. Every time I see you I'm reminded of my shame."

Jörg Gerlach rose to his feet. "Now get out of my house! You're not one of us and you never have been! Go and never come back to Knittlingen, so this curse can finally come to an end."

The last Johann saw of his father was his broad back and his bull neck as he stomped out of the kitchen, leaving Johann alone at the table.

Johann remained sitting there for a while. He looked at the devotional corner with the cross and the dried roses; the chicken cages under the bench, where he used to hide as a child; the chest with his mother's dowry; the faded, crooked picture of Saint Christopher that had brought him so much consolation over the years. Then he cast everything off like an old skin. He stood and went upstairs.

His father hadn't lied. On Johann's bed lay a small purse, a coat, and a sturdy-looking pair of shoes. Johann put on the shoes and coat, tied the purse to his belt, and reached for the staff he'd once made for little Martin.

He was about to leave when he remembered the knife under the floorboard. Traveling all by himself—it probably wasn't a bad idea to carry a weapon. And perhaps he could sell the knife. It looked valuable enough. So he bent down, lifted the floorboard, pulled out the knife, and slipped it in his pocket. On his way out, he helped himself to a piece of cheese and half a loaf of bread, placing both in an inside pocket of his coat.

Then he left his home for the last time and went on his way. Johann didn't yet know that this way would lead him to the highest of highs and lowest of lows.

Into the whole world and beyond.

It was still early in the morning, and the lanes and alleyways were empty. A light, cold drizzle set in, blowing against Johann's face. Many Knittlingers would still be working in the vineyards today, bringing in the last few sweet grapes. It was the final day of the harvest, and tonight, everyone would be celebrating. Without Johann, though—from now on, he was an outcast.

Strangely enough, Johann didn't feel sad. On the contrary: with every step he took toward the upper city gate, his spirits rose. He had a small purse full of coins, and he was clever and deft—surely some farmer would employ him as a laborer. And then he'd see. But first he needed to put as many miles as possible between himself and Knittlingen, not least to help him get over Martin, Margarethe, and everything else that had happened there.

He walked through the open city gate without seeing a guard. The old, wide imperial road stretched out before him, leading out into the world. The road led northwest on one side and to the southeast on the other. To the north lay Bretten, then the Rhine, Speyer, and Cologne; the southern route led via Maulbronn to the Württemberg lands, then Ulm, Mindelheim, and eventually Innsbruck, where the king resided occasionally. Johann had heard there were mountains there covered in snow all year round, and beyond them lay prosperous Venice, and somewhere beyond Venice came Rome, the eternal city.

He stopped in the middle of the road, unsure of which way to turn. He had a vague feeling that his future depended on the decision he made now. After standing around indecisively for a few moments, he pulled a stained coin out of his purse. Heads for south, tails for north. He tossed the coin high up in the air, caught it, and placed it carefully on the back of his hand.

It showed heads.

South.

Johann sighed. That meant he'd have to walk past the Maulbronn monastery and Gallows Hill. Evidently, fate wanted to remind him of his shame one last time. He grasped his staff tightly and started out without turning around to look at his hometown again. He walked along the bare fields and the vineyards, heading into the rain with grim determination. When he came past the execution site, he spat over his shoulder to ward off bad luck. This was where all his misery had started; from now on, he thought, his future would be brighter.

Soon the Maulbronn monastery appeared behind the fog to his left. Johann felt a pang of regret. How he had longed to find employment as the librarian's assistant here and delve deeper into the world of books and knowledge! For a brief moment he considered paying Father Antonius one last visit, but his shame was too great. If he returned at all, he'd do it as a celebrated scholar!

Johann imagined what it would be like to visit Father Antonius—old and gray by then—many years from now, bringing a whole wagon full of books and medicines as a gift. All of Knittlingen would regret the way they had treated their most famous son. His horrible stepfather would be dead and Margarethe well again. They would marry, and even little Martin would return from his captivity, laden with riches.

Johann was so wrapped up in his thoughts that he didn't even notice the monastery disappearing behind the trees. He had walked past it without realizing—which meant he'd walked farther than ever before in his life. Until then, Maulbronn had been the end of his small world. Now he'd taken the first step into the unknown.

A new, much bigger world lay ahead of him.

The first few nights of his journey Johann spent in barns, freezing. His happy daydreams had burst with the first hailstorm. He'd also learned that no farmer needed a sixteen-year-old laborer this time of year. The harvest was in and the vines empty. The people of the Kraichgau were sitting at home in their warm kitchens, mending their baskets, fixing leaking tubs and broken crates, or looking after their wine in the cellar. If he was lucky, Johann received a stale chunk of bread when he knocked on doors; if he wasn't, the farmer set his dogs on him.

The road seemed to wind endlessly through flat valleys filled with meadows and fields. Gentle slopes rose on both sides, covered with beech trees and oaks. Since ancient times the track connecting the eastern and the western ends of the German empire had run along here, between the Rhine flats and the lands east of the Neckar River. It was a lovely area during the summer, but now, in early November, autumn storms howled down from the mountains, and the rain whipped the last remaining leaves off the trees, leaving them bare and bending in the wind, like skeletons writhing in a dance of death.

Johann's spirits dwindled by the day, and grief filled his whole heart. The silence that often surrounded him reminded him that he was alone in the world. He had no one. His mother was dead, and his father wasn't his father but a nasty man who'd cast him out. He didn't know his real father—probably some traveling juggler who had courted his mother. All he had left as the stranger's son were the raven-black hair and the curse of being a bastard.

During his lonely nights, Johann sometimes pulled out the knife the magician had given him. He whittled small figures from rotten wood by the wayside and pretended they were his mother, Martin, or Margarethe. Often they'd turn out ugly or they broke, and he threw them away.

The handful of travelers going the other way, on horseback or with carts, were wrapped in heavy coats and wore their hoods pulled down low. They barely gave him as much as a nod in greeting, and soon the next rain shower swallowed them up. Johann's clothes were saturated and no longer dried out. He shivered with cold, his shoes were wet, and the drenched coat pulled on him like chains.

At night he was tortured by dreams of Margarethe and Martin standing above him with accusatory faces.

You frighten us, Johann! They called out and pointed their fingers at him. *You are the devil! The devil!*

Johann still didn't know what had happened that evening in Schillingswald Forest and whom Margarethe had seen. It must have been bad enough for her to lose her mind. Had she seen who or what had taken Martin? Johann guessed he would never find out. All of that was behind him now, and before him unfurled the never-ending road.

Though he'd hoped to save his money for harder times, Johann was soon forced to spend some on food. Every night he counted his coins carefully. There were mainly stained kreuzers and tinged copper pennies, with only three silver pennies among them. His stepfather had remained a miser to the last. Johann rubbed the coins as if they were made of pure gold, stacked them up in little towers, and calculated. If he kept spending at this rate, he'd be out of money within a few weeks. He thought about selling the engraved knife, but he didn't do it. Even though it had come from the magician, it seemed to be part of the world he had lost. Selling it seemed like selling a piece of himself. So he kept it and suffered from hunger.

Johann knew that if he carried on this way, sooner or later, he'd die on the side of the road like a stray dog. Unless he started earning money. If not by working as a laborer, then perhaps by doing something else.

And he had an idea just what he might do.

A wide river appeared in front of him—the Neckar, he gathered. This river also passed through Heidelberg, the city where he would have loved to study one day. Now, in late fall, the river shimmered metallic gray. It looked very cold and very deep, and there was no bridge he could see. Johann had to give away another one of his precious coins to an old ferryman, who eyed Johann the whole way across the river as though he was considering robbing him and toss-ing him into the water. Johann's tiny fortune seemed to run through his fingers like melting wax.

In the next village, a few miles on, he gathered all his courage and decided to try his luck.

He was still traveling on the imperial road, and so there was a post station here—an inn with a stable for the horses of messengers and travelers. Johann took a deep breath and entered the small, dark inn. It was late afternoon and raining outside, so the taproom was full. All kinds of travelers had sought shelter at the inn. In the flickering light of the open fire, Johann saw a burly merchant wearing a fur coat and a beret, two itinerant Franciscan monks, and several peddlers, whose tall packs were leaning against the wall behind them. Someone else seemed to sit farther back, but Johann couldn't quite make him out in the dim light. A handful of farmers were also sitting at the tables, enjoying the quiet period following the harvest with a few mugs of wine. They laughed and drank and paused only briefly when Johann came in and headed for one of the empty tables at the rear. But instead of taking a seat, he suddenly jumped onto the table and clapped his hands.

Now there was no going back.

"My esteemed audience!" he declared loudly, just like he'd seen jugglers in Knittlingen do. "Watch and be amazed, because I can multiply your money! Forget your worries and fears, because from today, you'll be swimming in coins!"

The people murmured, some of them laughing, some of them jeering. But Johann had achieved what he wanted. He had their full attention.

With a theatrical gesture, he reached into his pants pocket and pulled out one coin. He held it up, transferred it to his other hand, and placed it in his purse. He did the same with a second and a third coin. The first spectators began to mutter.

"He's moving the coins from his pocket to his purse," one of them grumbled. "What's so special about that?"

Johann raised an eyebrow and pretended to be shocked. "Oh, you're saying I should take the coins from somewhere else? Not from my pocket but . . . from the air, perhaps?" He took another kreuzer and dropped it in his purse. But this time, a new coin appeared in his hand as if by magic, then another and another. Each time, Johann took the coin and placed it in his leather purse, which he held up triumphantly once it was full.

"You see!" he shouted. "The pouch is full! A friendly spirit of the air handed me the coins."

The people laughed and clapped their hands. It was a cheap trick Johann had learned from an itinerant juggler in Knittlingen, but here, in a small village, it worked well.

"Now let's see if I find coins on you, too." Grinning, Johann jumped off the table and walked over to the fat merchant. Johann puffed his cheeks and gestured toward the burly man, who eyed him suspiciously. "This moneybags strikes me as a good place to start. May I?"

He leaned over the merchant and pulled a coin from his nose, and then another one out of his mouth. When he leaned down to the man's broad backside and coins jingled in his hand shortly thereafter, the people hooted with laughter.

"Dear Lord!" exclaimed Johann. "The man shits coins! I want a donkey like him in my stable."

The inn guests held their bellies with laughter while the merchant just sat there with a sour face.

But then the man broke out in a grin and extended his hand demandingly. "What a pretty little trick," he said. "And now give me back my money, boy."

Johann stopped short. "What money?"

"The money you pulled out of my backside. It's mine—you stole it from me, didn't you?" He turned to the people sitting at the tables around him and gestured at a leather pouch by his side. "The lad cleaned me out! This bag was full of coins before, and now it's empty."

Johann's smile froze. He couldn't believe what was happening here. The bag had been empty from the start. The merchant was trying to cheat him out of his money.

"So give me back my money!" demanded the fat man. "It was funny at first, but I swear to you, if you don't hand over my coins right now, you're a thief. And thieves get hanged."

"Give him the money!" shouted some of the other people. "Thief! Thief! Or we'll hang you from the linden tree!"

"But . . ." Johann tried to explain. "I promise you . . ."

"Hang him now!" cried one of the peddlers, a bearded knife-sharpener in rags, his belt heavy with grindstones and knives. "Before he steals our money, too. The boy is nothing but a common thief!"

Some of the farmers had sprung to their feet and held up their fists angrily, and the peddler reached for one of his knives. The angry shouts grew louder and louder.

"Hang him, hang him!"

Johann's hand went to the small knife in his pocket. But what would he achieve with that? He looked around in panic. The way to the door was blocked by the crowd, but there was a narrow window covered with parchment to his right. He ran toward the window and jumped through it headfirst. The parchment ripped and he landed hard in a pile of foul-smelling dung. He could hear angry shouts behind him. He briefly considered running out onto the road, but then he thought the merchant would most likely have a horse in the stable. If he ran, they would catch him faster than he could say the Lord's Prayer—and soon after he'd be dangling from the nearest tree. So he changed his plan. Hunched over, he ran around the building and toward the stable. While the people from the inn poured onto the road, he slipped through the stable door and hid in the straw.

It was warm and dark in the stable. A horse snorted somewhere, but other than that, all remained calm. The shouting outside grew quieter; a door was shut. It seemed the people had abandoned the search and returned to the taproom.

Johann waited a while longer, then he got up cautiously. He was about to open the stable door to go outside when he felt a knife against his throat.

"I had a feeling you might be hiding out here," hissed a voice right behind him. Johann saw from the corner of his eye that it was one of the itinerant Franciscans from the inn. A man of God threatening him with a knife—would this nightmare never end?

"Lovely trick you performed in there," said the monk in a growling voice. Johann could smell brandy and stale sweat. "I'm guessing your purse was full to begin with. And now I'd like to have that purse. Hand it over or I'll slit your throat like a lamb!"

"Please," begged Johann. "It's all the money I have!"

The monk laughed behind him. "Then you should take better care of it, boy. Now give it here!"

Johann thought about the knife in the pocket of his jerkin. He could feel it through the fabric. But if he reached for it, the fellow would most likely cut him open without batting an eyelid. Trembling, Johann reached for the pouch on his belt—when he realized it was still lying on the table in the taproom. He'd forgotten to take the purse in his haste!

"I don't have the money anymore," he said anxiously.

"What tricks are you playing now, damn it! Just you wait, kid, I told you I'd—"

Suddenly the man gave a loud groan. The knife fell from his hand and he sagged to the ground, gurgling. Johann spun around; standing behind the monk was a figure like a huge raven silently spreading its wings. Johann couldn't believe his eyes.

It was Tonio.

"Look at that, the oh-so-lucky boy from Knittlingen," said Tonio with a grin, calmly wiping his bloodied dagger on a bundle of straw. To his horror, Johann saw that his rescuer had slit the monk's throat. The wound gaped like a second, grinning mouth with blood spurting from it. The monk wheezed and jerked while the life drained from his body. One last tremble went through his body, and then he lay still.

"Quite a peculiar juice is blood," Tonio continued as he polished his knife, in a tone as if he were talking about the weather. "As much as you wipe and clean, something always remains. If you have five men with clean daggers and you want to find the murderer, just wait and see which blade the flies choose. They smell the blood even if we can't see it anymore. Interesting, don't you think?"

The magician looked just like Johann remembered him. Tall and haggard, with a narrow face and eyes as black as charcoal. Only he didn't look as pale today—his cheeks had a rosy glow, and his lips were red and full. Tonio placed the dagger back in his belt. Then he adjusted his felt hat and studied Johann. "So we meet again. Shouldn't you be at home with your family?"

Johann remembered the dark figure at the back of the inn. Tonio must have sat there earlier and watched him. Evidently he, too, was traveling along the imperial road.

"I . . . I no longer have a family," Johann replied and, still in shock, continued to stare at the dead monk and the growing puddle of blood on the ground. Tonio raised an eyebrow.

"If you're worried because he's an honorable man of the church," he said, "he isn't. Or rather, he wasn't. He was a scoundrel, a tramp, and a thief, like most people here." He shook his head in disapproval. "Didn't I give you a knife? Why don't you use it? You really ought to be more careful—the imperial road is full of scum. You can consider yourself lucky that I was here."

"Th . . . thanks," Johann whispered. He felt terribly faint all of a sudden. Everything went black before his eyes, and he braced himself against a beam.

"It looks like I helped you out once again," the magician said. He grabbed Johann by the arm and pulled him farther into the stable. Now Johann saw the familiar wagon and horse.

"Climb in the back," Tonio commanded with a low, sharp voice. "Before they come to check the stable."

Trembling, Johann climbed into the wagon. It was dark inside and he couldn't make out much, but it seemed to be lined with chests, and bunches of dried herbs hung from the canvas ceiling. The smell was sweet and sickly. The magician flicked the reins, and the wagon went rumbling out the open gate into the pouring rain.

"This time, you owe me more than a small favor," Tonio said over his shoulder as they drove out of the village in the dim light of dusk. "And I think I know just how you can repay your debt."

They rode in silence for the next few minutes. Johann expected the angry mob to pursue them at any moment, or the fat merchant on his horse. But nothing happened. Johann was shivering with cold; his already damp clothes had become soaked again when he'd escaped through the rain. He still couldn't believe what had just happened. He'd almost been killed and he'd lost all his money! Even the staff he'd carved for Martin once upon a time—his last reminder of his brother—was left behind at the inn.

But the worst part was the memory of the casual ease with which Tonio had slit the monk's throat, like a butcher killing a calf. Then he remembered with horror that the false Franciscan had been about to stab him to death for a pouch of rusty coins. How stupid he had been to think he could travel all alone, without a companion, a writ of protection, or a horse! He'd almost paid with his life for his stupidity.

The wagon squeaked and bumped along. Through a slit in the canvas, Johann could make out Tonio as a dark outline. Evening had turned to night, and the rain gradually eased off.

Once Johann's eyes had adjusted to the dark, he could make out more details inside the wagon. There was a lowered section in the middle that was covered with brushwood; he guessed that was where Tonio slept. What Johann had thought were chests turned out to be bench seats with storage space underneath.

The cage holding the two crows and the raven dangled from the ceiling among the herbs. The large, rusty cage swayed back and forth to the rhythm of the wheels, the raven watching Johann out of almost human eyes. The crows shuffled nervously from side to side on their perches, as if they sensed danger. For the first time Johann could study the birds more closely. The raven frightened him the most. It seemed to be quite old, with some feathers missing and a beak that was scuffed and jagged at the edges. There was something sly in its gaze.

Suddenly, the cart stopped. The canvas at the front was pushed aside like a curtain, and Tonio's head appeared in the opening. He gave Johann a sharp look.

"You're cold," he noted. "If you're not careful, you'll get a fever and die on me. Then I can forget about my payment." The magician tossed an old, musty-smelling horse blanket to Johann. "Wrap yourself up in that and then come out and help me with the fire. Go on!"

They were parked a little way off to the side of the road in a grove of dripping fir trees. Shivering all over, Johann searched for any firewood that wasn't quite as wet as the rest. When he returned to Tonio, the magician had already started a small fire with some twigs. Next to him stood a basket with eggs, a fat lump of bacon, and bread. The magician hung a pot above the fire and added water and various herbs from a pouch. Soon a fragrant, almost biting smell rose from the pot. Tonio took it down, poured its contents into a cup, and handed that to Johann.

"Drink," he ordered.

Johann obeyed. The brew tasted bitter, but it helped to dispel the cold. Tonio watched him in silence. When Johann had drained the cup, the magician spoke.

"Are you feeling better now?"

Johann nodded.

"Then listen to what I have to say." Tonio leaned forward, his angular, rosy face below the black felt hat glowing in the light of the fire. "I don't want to know what happened in that shitty little hometown of yours, or why you're traveling all by yourself. I don't care. The devil knows why fate has brought us together! I only know one thing: I've helped you out for the second time, and so you should be at my service. Quid pro quo! I saw the trick you performed at the inn. It wasn't bad, but it wasn't special. Any old juggler can do that. Do you know any other tricks?"

"Well, I . . . I know a few card tricks," Johann replied reluctantly. "And there's the shell game, the coin trick, juggling, the traveling sticks, the cursed die, the egg in the blanket—"

"The egg in the blanket?" The magician's bored expression changed, and he straightened up with interest. He reached into the basket behind him and picked up an egg. "Show me what you mean. I don't know that trick, and believe me, I know most."

Johann looked at Tonio with surprise. He'd once watched a drunken Venetian juggler perform the trick at the fair in Knittlingen and asked him to explain it for a skin of wine. Could it be true that Tonio didn't know the trick?

Carefully, Johann placed the egg on the ground and spread the horse blanket over it. Then he stood up and paced around the fire, making conjuring movements with his hands and muttering the spell the Venetian juggler had taught him. Apparently, it was derived from twisting the words of a Latin mass: "Hocus, locus, pocus!"

"Hit the blanket as hard as you can," he said to Tonio. The magician shrugged. Then he raised his hand and struck the blanket.

"Shame about the egg," Tonio muttered. "Now we're down to four. Scant supper for you."

Johann pulled away the blanket triumphantly. The egg was gone.

"Now lift your hat," he instructed Tonio.

The magician did as he was asked. The egg was lying in his graying black hair like in a nest. Tonio grinned and took down the egg. For the first time he seemed genuinely surprised.

"The trick is not bad," he said. "We can use that. But we need to work on the story around it. Always remember, the show is everything. It must be big and colorful. The mass can only be impressed by masses."

"I could have done the same with a chicken if we had one," Johann bragged, trying not to let his relief show. The trick with the egg and the blanket was one of the most difficult he'd learned. He'd practiced it for weeks in a small wooded area near Knittlingen. He hadn't been entirely certain it would work this time. Something told him it was very important that he'd performed the trick without mistake—crucially important.

"Well done." The magician placed the egg on the ground in front of him. "Now listen carefully. I am a traveling astrologer and chiromancer—am called magister, doctor, indeed, but it is getting harder and harder to attract an audience, especially in the cities. There are just too many jugglers and acrobats. That's why I need a trickster."

"A trickster?" Johann gave him a puzzled look.

"*Sacre bleu!* Don't you know anything? I thought you were a juggler." Tonio sighed. "There are different occupations among jugglers." He counted on his fingers. "Musicians, jugglers who actually juggle, goliards, false alchemists, bear tamers, tightrope walkers, and tricksters. They are young, cocky jesters who know the small tricks. Coin tricks, cups and balls—all those things. It will be your task to gain the people's attention. You're short and scrawny, but your voice is strong enough, as I heard at the tavern. Can you play the bagpipe?"

Johann shook his head. He'd never learned an instrument. He thought he wasn't very musical at all.

"You'll learn," said Tonio. "The bagpipe is the loudest instrument and easy to master. Whoever plays it draws the people in like with a magic flute." He grinned. "Even if it doesn't sound quite as beautiful. We'll start tomorrow."

"I . . . I'm supposed to travel with you?" asked Johann slowly.

"You finally got it?" The magician laughed. "By the devil, yes! I saved your life, and now you shall serve me for one year, as a test and without pay. After that time, we'll see. The pact is valid until I dismiss you." Tonio tilted his head to one side and eyed Johann. "You can't go back home, I can see it in your face. And traveling by yourself means certain death. Either you starve or you'll get butchered. So, what do you say? You'll fare well with me. You'll be amazed to learn what life holds in store for you. Shake on it."

The magician held out his hand. Johann thought of the last time he'd shaken Tonio's hand. The tall, haggard man with the felt hat still frightened him immensely. But did he have a choice? He had no money, and Tonio was right: he was doomed on his own. Besides, he felt almost magically drawn to Tonio, and the feeling was old and familiar.

It stemmed from his childhood, when he'd seen the magician for the first time.

He clasped Tonio's hand. The man's grip was viselike, and he held Johann's hand for so long that Johann gave a little cry of pain. It felt like the magician was squeezing the blood from his hand. Tonio smiled, and once again he reminded Johann of a wolf.

"Welcome to life on the road," Tonio said. "Our pact is sealed."

Johann pulled back his throbbing hand. "You said earlier that the year was a test," he said. "What if I don't prove worthy, if I don't live up to your expectations? If I don't pass your test?"

"Well, it's just like with eggs," Tonio replied and reached for the brown speckled egg in front of him. He held it in his fist. "Some withstand the pressure, while others . . ." He clenched his fist. There was a crack, and yellow yolk ran through his fingers and dripped into the flames. "Others crumble under it."

He wiped his hand on the ground as easily as he'd wiped the blood off his dagger earlier. Then he reached into the basket and started to cut the bacon.

"But now let's eat and drink. Oh, and one more thing." The magician held up his knife like a teacher's pointer. "From now on, you call me master. Understood?" He smiled. "And believe me—you will learn much from me."

Act II

Tonio the Sorcerer

5

THE FOLLOWING WEEKS WERE THE MOST EXHAUSTING OF Johann's life. Instead of returning to the road, the two men stayed in the forest. The weather was too awful for travel anyhow. The road had turned into a mud pit with wheel ruts deep as ponds. While the rain and sometimes hailstones as large as pigeon eggs beat against the canvas, Tonio made Johann show him every trick he knew. Usually the magician merely gave a bored wave or corrected Johann with a growl. Tonio was a tough master, not tolerating any sloppiness or the tiniest mistake.

"You call that a trick, damn it?" he snarled and struck Johann with a cane. "I saw the coin in your hand! One more time—and roll up your sleeves, for God's sake. Or do you want them to call you a swindler in the next village and string you up? I won't help you again!"

Johann got beaten on his second and third attempts, too. The same happened when he performed his card tricks—even those he'd thought he could do with his eyes closed. Tired, hungry, and sick from days of being cold and wet, he soon struggled to manage even the simplest tricks.

"Are you trying to insult me?" snarled Tonio. "Watch. This is how you do it."

The magician produced a deck of cards in one hand, let them slide into his other hand with a sound like a drumroll, fanned them, and suddenly held only kings. Then he closed the fan and opened it again, and now they were all queens. "And now you," he ordered.

Johann clumsily dropped the entire deck, and the cane came whistling through the air.

Soon Johann's hands hurt so badly that he couldn't hold cards any longer, and the master demanded he juggle balls out in the rain. Tonio's balls were red, blue, and gold and made of hard ash wood. When Johann dropped one of the balls, Tonio hurled it at him. After countless failed attempts, Johann had a huge bump on his head and felt every single muscle in his body.

"Three balls are nothing!" shouted Tonio. "Every peasant can do three. You must master four at least, if not five!"

In the evening they practiced the shell game. This trick was especially important to Tonio, and they spent the largest amount of time on it. Three walnut shells and a pea were lying on a small box in the wagon. The pea went underneath one of the shells, the three shells were shuffled about, and the intended victim had to guess which shell the pea was hidden underneath. Tonio didn't take his eyes off Johann as he pushed the walnut shells back and forth on the box.

"It's important you let them win at first," the magician said. "They must feel sure of themselves before you milk them. You only strike when there's enough money on the table. Understood?"

Johann was quite good at the shell game, and Tonio soon left him alone about it—though not before reminding him several times to never become complacent. To Johann's surprise, the magician didn't ask to be shown the trick with the egg and the blanket again. It seemed to Johann the master begrudged him a trick he didn't know himself.

Beaten and humiliated, Johann fell asleep beside the fire soon after dark every night, while Tonio read his books, murmuring silent verses as if he was learning entire pages by heart. Johann's sleep was dreamless and deep. For the first time in a long while he didn't even dream of Margarethe and Martin. But early in the morning, the torture continued.

They stayed in the forest for nearly two weeks, until Johann had mastered the most important tricks. When the weather improved, they set off again, following the post road to the southeast.

The following days went roughly the same and were almost always accompanied by rain, from drizzle to torrential downpours and everything in between. They always practiced in the late afternoon until long into the night. During the day they rolled along the imperial road toward Ulm, making camp away from the road and getting up at the crack of dawn. The master slept inside the wagon while Johann had to lie by the fire with a threadbare blanket. Throughout each chilly, wet night he'd frequently wake up shivering. He suffered from a terrible cold, his nose running and his head thumping. But the master showed no mercy.

Johann was allowed to rest only during the brief hours they traveled along the bumpy road.

Every morning, after a bite of bread and a sip of watered-down wine, Johann had to feed the horse and hitch it to the wagon. Then they set off and drove until they arrived at a village or a larger township. If there was a market square, that's where they went; if not, they simply parked on the muddy road near the village church, where they'd soon be surrounded first by children, then by the rest of the villagers.

For the next few hours, Tonio would hold court in his wagon while Johann made a lot of noise. He performed his tricks, juggled the balls, and declared loudly that the world-famous astrologer and chiromancer Tonio del Moravia had come to town, a master of the seven arts and keeper of the seven times seven seals, to read the future of anyone who'd like to know. It was never long before there'd be a line outside the wagon. For a few kreuzers, Tonio would read their palms or cast hasty horoscopes for them. In the meantime, Johann would clean out people's pockets with the shell game. At some point during the afternoon, when the crowd dispersed or someone arrived from the local authority—the bailiff or some of his henchmen—they'd move on, find a new place to camp for the night, and practice. And so they moved along the imperial road.

It was a hard life, but not the worst, and Johann might have grown to like it. He might even have learned to put up with Tonio's beatings and constant criticism without complaint—if it hadn't been for that accursed bagpipe.

Johann loathed the instrument, which reminded him of a stubborn animal. It consisted of a leather pouch crafted from a stinking goatskin and several protruding tubes. Two so-called drone pipes produced different but equally howling notes, while the melody pipe or chanter was like a flute and was played with the fingers. Another small pipe served to blow air into the sack.

No matter how hard Johann tried, whenever he blew into the pipe, all that came out was a pitiful squealing or an awful squawking, causing the master to throw up his hands in despair every time.

"*Mon Dieu*, are you trying to frighten off every soul between here and Cologne?" he'd exclaim. "The only creatures you'll attract with this music are the wolves. Try harder, God damn it! The bagpipe isn't hard to play—anyone can do it."

But try as he might, Johann wasn't getting any better at it. The master made him practice every afternoon, sending him deep into the forest in rain, hail, or sun. Johann knew the master could still hear him from over half a mile away. If he paused for too long, he didn't get any supper. If Tonio decided he'd produced only caterwauling again, he didn't get any supper, either. Whenever the master told him off, the birds in the cage joined in, bickering and cawing as if they were jeering at Johann. Johann wished he could wring the raven's neck, but he was afraid Tonio would then do the same to him.

One evening, when the master told him once more what a pathetic juggler and embarrassment he was, Johann finally lost his temper.

"If my playing is that horrible, why don't you play the bagpipe yourself!" he shouted. "Or better still, get yourself on stage and perform your tricks like you used to. You're bound to impress the audience more than I do!"

"How . . . how dare you, boy." Tonio's face turned red and he looked like he was about to explode, his hand raised to strike. But then he paused and gave a grin. "All in good time," he said. "There are masters and apprentices. If the master performs the tasks of the apprentice, he makes a fool of himself. And if the apprentice tries to imitate the master, bad things happen."

"But I want to learn how to cast horoscopes and read palms!" exclaimed Johann with indignation. "I'm never allowed to watch when you read people's futures."

"Like I said, all in good time." Tonio tossed the bagpipe at him. "What does it say in the book of Ecclesiastes? There's a time to be silent and a time to speak. Now go back into the forest and practice, boy. If I hear the wolves howl, no supper for you."

December brought snow to the land. They'd left the Kraichgau region behind long ago, and Württemberg, too. From time to time, stone markers indicated when they crossed into another county, bishopric, duchy, or knight's estate. On many bridges they had to pay a toll; sometimes a quick horoscope or a cup of wine would suffice. Tonio explained to Johann that the German empire consisted of hundreds of small states.

"Everyone here cares only about themselves," he muttered. "Praise be to my France, where Paris is the hub of everything. But that's what the Germans are like—they don't look farther than the next tavern."

The area they passed through next was called Albigoi or Allgäu, and it was mountainous and inhospitable. The people here spoke with an accent Johann could hardly understand, though it must have been German. They drank a sour brown ale, completely different from the beer at home—although home was nothing more than a fading memory now. Only at night, when the blackness of a starless sky covered him like a musty shroud, would he suddenly feel homesick, and then he'd think of his mother, of Martin, and of Margarethe.

As a distraction, Johann often took the small knife into the forest along with the bagpipe. He still hadn't figured out what the engraving on the handle might stand for.

G d R.

He didn't want to ask Tonio. He was afraid the master would once again ask him why he hadn't used the knife to stab the false monk. In Tonio's eyes, Johann was a coward and a weakling.

It was a throwing knife, and Johann practiced by hurling it at dead tree trunks. At the beginning he was just as clumsy as with the bagpipe, but after a while his throws became stronger and more accurate. Sometimes he imagined faces of people on the tree trunks—Ludwig, his older brothers, or his stepfather. But he found that he grew increasingly angry that way, more aggressive with every throw until sweat ran down his forehead. Panting, he'd put the knife back in his pocket, where it felt cold and heavy.

Icy winds swept across the fallow fields; icicles like daggers hung from the bare trees. To the south, they could make out the steep, snow-covered peaks of the Alps. Johann remembered that Rome and Venice lay somewhere beyond that mountain range. But how did pilgrims manage to get across that wall of rock and ice? So far, the master hadn't given him any clues about their destination, but Johann couldn't imagine they'd cross the mountains during winter.

At least they no longer slept outdoors but at inns and taverns along the imperial road—mostly at one of the many new post stations, which offered a decent amount of comfort. There was a station every twenty miles, where post riders changed horses or handed over their mailbags to the next rider. That way, the riders could travel up to a hundred miles each day—a speed, compared to their lumbering cart, that seemed to Johann like the flight of a bird.

At every inn, the master, acting like a noble lord, always took one of the best rooms, while Johann, as his apprentice, slept with the horse in the stable. But at least it was warm there and he was left in peace. Only the suspicious looks of the raven and the two crows disturbed him. It almost seemed like they were spying on him so they could report to the master later.

Tonio often held court in the taproom, just like he had done in Knittlingen. It never took long for a crowd to gather when the great Tonio del Moravia spread his books and scrolls full of mysterious symbols on the table. The tomes bound in crumbling leather were part of the show, demonstrating what a learned man the master was. Now Johann could finally watch Tonio at work.

There appeared to be different ways of predicting the future. Most of the time the master studied the client's palm, running his finger along the various lines and murmuring mysterious phrases. If it was a young woman, he'd say, "Look at that, your Fate line and Heart line cross right here—a good sign! Next spring you'll be standing at the altar with your dapper bridegroom." If he was reading the hand of an old man, he'd say, "The Life line has many small branches, but it runs deep. You've been blessed with a long, interesting life, thank the Lord!"

This was what the master called the art of chiromancy. Tonio never foretold harsh blows or death. Mostly it was rich harvests, an imminent wedding, or unexpected wealth that would befall his clients.

For those willing to pay a little extra, Tonio would read their destiny from a glass of water or the flickering flames of the open fire. Those mysterious arts were called hydromancy and pyromancy. The master could also read from the clouds, crystals, and playing cards.

Very rarely someone requested a nativity chart. Such customers would invariably be wealthy citizens, like the village bailiff or burgomaster, and one time even an abbot. A pile of money would change hands, and Tonio would ask for the client's day and place of birth and then retreat to his chamber, where he'd work all night. The next morning, he'd emerge from his room looking pale and tired, carrying a length of parchment covered with small writing and symbols. Johann could make out circles and drawings of animals, though he didn't understand them. But the clients always seemed very pleased.

Johann was dying to know what the master was doing in his room, but as much as he begged and pleaded, the horoscopes remained Tonio's secret. Neither did he allow Johann to look at his books. When they were on the road, he kept them locked up in one of the chests under the benches. At the inns, he took them to his room. Johann suspected the books were very old and very valuable.

Tonio steered clear of larger towns and cities, which sometimes meant long detours. When Johann asked the master about it, he shook his head.

"People around here aren't always favorably inclined toward chiromancers and astrologers," he said. "They're a rough, superstitious people. Some think we're sorcerers or necromancers. I don't want to end up burning at the stake— even though it'd be warmer than this goddamned Allgäu in this weather. Damn the cold!"

Toward the middle of December, they were hit by the worst snowstorm Johann had ever seen. Icy grains stung them like needles, the wind tore at their coats, and visibility was so poor that Johann sometimes feared he'd gone blind. Drifts of snow piled up on the road, and several times Johann had to climb off the wagon with a shovel to clear their path. They barely made any progress, and behind every bend was another drift. The storm howled as if it were laughing at the little mortals below.

In the afternoon, the wagon became stuck in a deep rut. It took them over an hour and many failed attempts to pull it back out. The horse whinnied and shook the snow from its mane. The old nag didn't look as though it would last five more miles.

"Damn, if I didn't have you slowing me down, I'd long be across the Alps and in the warm countries of the south," groused Tonio, his voice carried off by the howling wind. "We are traveling much too late in the year. But no, I must explain to you even the simplest coin trick again and again! Thank God I know an inn not far from here where we can spend the winter. Come on, now! Or do you want to freeze your ass off here?"

He jumped back on the box seat and cracked his whip. The horse moved forward reluctantly. The thought of spending the next few weeks beside a cozy fireplace made Johann feel a little warmer already. Finally this journey through snow and ice would come to an end. They would celebrate the birth of Christ with a steaming mug of spiced wine at a tavern. Perhaps he'd even get to sleep in a bed and be granted a look at Tonio's books.

It was long after darkness had fallen before they finally saw the lights of a village through the driving snow. Mountains like black giants rose behind the lights, silent and insurmountable. Tonio urged the horse on, and half an hour later they'd reached the first houses. A large inn with stables and several out-buildings was situated in the village center. The buildings were arranged around a courtyard, forming a small fortress with only one gate for an entrance.

"The Black Eagle," Tonio said with a grin and climbed down from the wagon. His mood had improved drastically during the past hour. "The best inn between Kempten and Innsbruck. I spent a winter here once before. Their rooms are tidy and the straw beds fresh, with hardly any fleas or lice. And the wine and food aren't bad, either. Even a real-life emperor once stopped here on his pilgrimage to Rome."

Johann caught a glance inside through the crown-glass window. He heard music and laughter, and the warm glow of the lamps looked inviting. Shivering, he rubbed his almost-frozen fingers and couldn't wait to warm himself with a cup of hot wine. Tonio knocked at the gate, and soon a voice answered.

"Who wants to enter the Eagle at this late hour? You can't be a post rider, because you didn't blow the horn."

"The honorable master Tonio del Moravia, astrologer and chiromancer, scholar of the seven arts, requests admittance," replied Tonio loudly. "He is on the search for winter quarters and willing to pay good money and offer up his legendary skills!"

They heard a few shouts inside, then hurried footsteps. A bolt was pushed back and an obese, bald man wearing an apron appeared in the gate. He eyed Tonio and Johann from small, piggy eyes, shifting his weight from one foot to the other nervously.

"I'm the innkeeper," he said haltingly. "And I'm afraid I must tell you that you can't stay here—not for the winter, anyhow. You may consider yourselves our guests until the morning."

Tonio's smile froze. "And why is that?"

"Well, how can I put this . . ." The innkeeper kneaded his apron. "I'm afraid you've come too late, honorable master. We're already putting up another astrologer, and two of your kind, um . . . Do you understand? I'm afraid people will start talking."

"Another astrologer?" Tonio's voice had grown as cold as the winter storm still raging outside the gate. "And who is that supposed to be?"

"He calls himself Freudenreich von Hohenlohe, a minstrel and itinerant doctor. He says he's the only true white wizard."

"Freudenreich von Hohenlohe?" Tonio laughed derisively. "I've heard of the fellow. He's a cunning swindler. Robs people of their money and sells them salves made of bear shit."

The innkeeper made a wry face. "My wife bought one of his salves. She had terrible pain in her arms and legs, and now it's gone. And the horoscope he wrote up for me was very positive."

"Nothing but lies!" shouted Tonio at the innkeeper. "Throw him out and take us in!"

"I can't," the man replied desperately. "He paid in advance. Please understand. All I can offer you is a room for one night. You have to move on tomorrow, or I'll be in trouble."

Tonio said nothing for a long while. Johann started to think he'd turn around without another word. But then he finally replied.

"Very well," he said quietly. "We won't encroach on your hospitality for more than one night. But I promise you, no matter what that Freudenreich foretold, it won't come true."

He handed the reins to the trembling innkeeper and walked into the courtyard. Johann followed him dejectedly. He'd been so excited at the prospect of spending the winter here. And now they'd have to leave again the following morning. Where would they go?

Together they entered the inn on the left-hand side of the yard. The warmth hit Johann and almost instantly made him sweat. The room was quite full. Most of the patrons were farmers, listening to a young minstrel playing the fiddle. He looked like he wasn't yet thirty years old, and wore a garish tunic, one side colored differently than the other. Lined up on the table beside him were rows of jars and bottles, several sheets of parchment, and a crystal ball sparkling in the glow of the fire. When Tonio looked over to him, their eyes met. A mocking smile played on the minstrel's lips as he performed a satirical song about the winter in a delicate, high-pitched voice.

"Winter, O winter, you frighten me not. I sit by the stove and my fire burns hot. O winter, keep howling, I show thee no mercy. I'm drinking my beer where it's warm and it's cozy . . ."

The people danced and clapped their hands. No one paid any attention to the tall, haggard man with the felt hat and the snow-covered black-and-red coat, standing in the doorway with his apprentice.

"Well, well, the famous Freudenreich von Hohenlohe," hissed Tonio. "He never was any good at singing—nor at telling the future, for that matter."

"You know him?" asked Johann.

"We've met a few times on the road. The whippersnapper calls himself a wizard, but in reality he's nothing but a quack and a balladmonger, robbing people of their money. And someone like that steals my winter quarters." Tonio's lips were as thin as knife blades when he glared at the minstrel once more. "Freudenreich, what an incredibly stupid and unfitting name! He won't find happiness in these harsh climes, oh no, he won't."

Johann found himself shivering at Tonio's words.

The innkeeper assigned them the last available room—a drafty hole in the attic that looked like it hadn't been cleaned in a long time. The straw in the cushions was old and smelled musty, and Johann saw lice and bedbugs crawling in the light of the tallow candle. Strangely, the master allowed Johann to stay with him this time. He'd brought the birdcage upstairs, too, and the crows and the raven flapped about restlessly in the corner. They seemed to sense their master's anger and tension.

For a long while, Tonio just sat on his bed and stared straight ahead. When Johann cleared his throat, the master raised his hand imperiously. "Be quiet. I need to think," he growled. "Or do you want us to freeze to death? We need winter quarters, and I can't think of any other inn this close to the Alps that'll take in an astrologer and his good-for-nothing apprentice."

Finally, Tonio seemed to reach a decision. He nodded with grim determination.

"I might know a place. It's about thirty miles from here—two to three days' travel in this atrocious weather. If we lower our expectations a little, it'll do just fine." Then he grinned. "Who knows—perhaps it's a stroke of fate. It can't be worse than this stinking hole."

Tonio's mood improved dramatically. He reached for the bottle of wine and the ham and moldy cheese the innkeeper had brought upstairs for them. The magician hadn't wanted to eat in the taproom. He filled two cups and pushed one toward Johann. "Go on, drink, so you'll get warm."

Johann accepted the cup gratefully and took a few sips. Never before had the master offered him wine. The alcohol warmed him up almost instantly, and he felt a lot less miserable. His spirits rose. Cautiously, he glanced at the leather bag holding the books Tonio had brought upstairs with him as usual. The magician noticed the direction of his look and laughed.

"The books won't leave you alone, will they? You're a clever lad, even though you'll never get far with the bagpipe. Who cares! I hate musicians these days. So why don't we study a little?" He winked at Johann. "Let's see how you do."

Tonio reached into the bag and pulled out one of the books. It was a stained, heavy volume, its yellowed pages covered in drawings. The magician opened the book at a page depicting a hand with lines, bumps, and symbols.

"Let us begin with chiromancy," said Tonio. "It belongs to the arts of divination, the third path of white magic. Of all the different ways of foretelling, it is the easiest to learn." He gestured at the various lines in the drawing. "See for yourself. No two hands are the same, just as every man has his own fate. The left hand shows your dispositions, and the right hand your future. Look at the Life line, which separates the ball of your thumb from the remaining fingers. It tells you how strong someone is, whether he can expect illness, and how he gets on in life. Each disruption has a particular meaning—sometimes even death. This is the Head line. It stands for your mind, and the Heart line for emotions. They mostly run parallel, and interruptions here can mean a broken heart, but also an impending marriage."

Johann studied his own hand, for the first time paying attention to the many lines. All together they really did look like a map, like roads in a yet-unknown land.

"And what is this line?" Johann pointed at a fourth line on his right hand, which ran straight down from his middle finger and was broken in many places. Johann had also found it in the drawing, where it was marked with a strange letter.

"Ah, that is a very special line! The Saturn line, or line of Fate. It tells us about our destiny. If you know how to read it, you can see right inside a person!"

Johann cleared his throat. "When I was still a child, you read my hand. You told me I was born on the day of the prophet, and my mother also spoke of that. She said I was chosen by God. What does that mean? Can I read my own hand?"

"You're taking the second step before the first one, boy." The master smiled. "I told you before: all in good time. Let us study the art of chiromancy first. It's important that you find your own way to yourself."

Without elaborating further, Tonio pointed at several circles and lines underneath the fingers. "Look here. This is the Mount of Venus. And that one is the Mount of Luna, which tells us about a person's transcendental talents . . ."

The master explained long and patiently. But he didn't mention the day of the prophet, and Johann soon forgot his question. Too mysterious, too intriguing were the many different aspects of chiromancy. He'd waited so long for the master to show him more than a few cheap tricks—and now he was finally learning one of Tonio's arcane secrets. How many more of those secrets were written in his books? How much more was there to learn?

"I'd like to try it," Johann said timidly when the master finished his explanations. "May I read your hand?"

Tonio seemed to hesitate briefly, then he gave Johann a mocking smile. "My hand can't be read. See for yourself." He held out his right hand, and to his surprise Johann saw that there were hardly any lines on it. There were calluses and a few scars, but no Head line, Heart line, or Life line.

As if someone had wiped the map clean.

Johann frowned. How was this possible? The master's hand was like a blank page. Didn't he say that every person was readable, that everyone had those lines?

Tonio quickly withdrew his hand and grinned. "Don't worry. You'll soon get an opportunity to practice your skills. You shall read someone's hand in the next village—a simple peasant, perhaps." He pushed the book toward Johann. "Now memorize the lines and mounts well. You have until the candle burns out. Then we'll sleep and get out of this filthy hole first thing."

Johann leaned over the book and studied the lines and their names while the master watched him thoughtfully. Sometimes Johann asked a question and Tonio answered curtly. Hours passed. Eventually, the flame started to flicker, gave one last jerk, and died. Darkness descended over the chamber, and Johann closed the book and lay down. It had felt so good to read and learn something new, like he used to do at the monastery. His hunger for knowledge was insatiable, and there was so much the master could teach him. Johann thanked God for sending him to the southeast when he hadn't known which way to turn, so that he ended up meeting Tonio del Moravia.

He woke up once during the night to find the master sitting by his bed, stroking his hand and watching him with piercing black eyes as if looking deep inside him. Johann wanted to sit up, but Tonio held him back.

"Sleep, young Faustus, sleep," he whispered. "We'll know more about each other soon. All in good time."

Johann wanted to get up, wanted to ask the master a hundred questions, so many things he'd just thought of in his dreams. But he was overcome by exhaustion so strong that he sank back onto his cushion and was instantly asleep.

∼

Later in the night, the master stood up and walked over to the cage with the crows and the raven. As usual, when their master approached, they beat their wings and squawked—it was hard to tell whether out of fear or excitement. Johann tossed and turned on his bed at the other end of the room, but he didn't wake. Deep in thought, the master pulled a few bits of dried meat from his pouch and tossed them to the birds.

"The boy is truly astounding," he murmured. "Smart and thirsty for knowledge. And those lines . . ." He shook his head. "Maybe our search really is coming to an end. It's possible. The stars can't lie. Or can they? Baphomet, Azazel, Belial—"

The raven pecked at him, and the master quickly pulled his fingers out of the cage.

"Ouch! How dare you, you bastard?"

A few drops of blood fell to the ground and disappeared in the straw. The bird stared at his master expectantly with his small yellow eyes.

"Lousy beast!" hissed Tonio and licked the blood off his finger. "You can't bear the fact that you failed, Baphomet. That he might be the right one. But you had your chance, and it wasn't you. Now shoo!"

Tonio hit the cage. The raven flapped about wildly, attacking the iron bars with his beak.

"*Kraa!*" called the raven, and it sounded almost human. "*Kraa! Kraa!*"

But the master wasn't perturbed. He looked over to Johann, who was twitching in his sleep.

"I think it's a good idea to go to the tower with him," he said pensively. "What do you think? We'll have all the time we need there. And we've got to stock up on our provisions, and I'll be able to hunt there. The meat is rather tough and stale by now."

He put one of the brown lumps between his teeth and started to chew.

"Oh yes, we need fresh provisions."

~

It would be two more days before Johann was allowed to read his first palm.

The next morning, the storm had passed and they left the Black Eagle. They didn't see Freudenreich again, but when they stepped through the gate, the master turned back one more time. His lips formed silent words, and then he leaned down and placed three black pieces of coal in the snow outside the threshold.

"What are you doing?" asked Johann.

"I'm leaving a message for other jugglers and magicians," Tonio replied. He stood up and wiped the soot off his hands. "No winter quarters to be had here. Saves everyone the argument and disappointment."

He climbed onto the box seat and cracked his whip. Johann turned back to look at the inn one last time. Dark clouds were gathering above it, like the fists of an angry god. In front of them, however, the morning sun made the fresh snow sparkle. The storm had turned the trees along the road into sculptures made of ice. The sky was bright blue, and the countryside was covered in a glittering white blanket. The air was clear and fresh, and Johann felt wide awake.

He would have liked to know what place the master had chosen for their winter quarters. But Tonio said nothing. When Johann asked, he only waved his hand. "I think you'll like it. At least it'll be nice and quiet there." He laughed. "As quiet as a grave. None of those superstitious peasant folk will set foot anywhere near the place."

Even though the weather was fine now, it was freezing cold, and they made slow progress. The road led south toward the mountains, and soon they'd reached the first foothills of the Alps. Their way led through rugged hills and past boulders so big that Johann thought giants must have thrown them from the mountains. The handful of cottages at the side of the road all looked battened down, their shutters closed. Smoke rose from the chimneys, but the inhabitants of this inhospitable area didn't seem to have any interest in passing travelers. When they came through the small villages they hardly saw a soul—only occasionally a shadow behind a shutter, a fearful pair of eyes following them.

"Didn't I tell you?" said Tonio. "They think the devil himself rides in this wagon. Now that Saint Thomas Night is near and darkness wins over the day, people are even more superstitious. I hope they'll at least sell us provisions for the winter."

When Johann became too cold, he went into the back of the wagon and wrapped himself up in a woolen blanket. But the cage with the birds hung there, and Johann felt watched. The raven especially seemed to stare at him with loathing.

"*Kraa!*" called the black bird again and again, almost desperately, as if it was trying to tell him something. "*Kraa!*" The monotonous sound rattled Johann's nerves.

And so he never stayed in the wagon for long, despite the cold.

Late in the afternoon of the second day, they came to a large farmstead standing alone in a clearing in the woods. Dogs growled and barked when the wagon came closer to the solid stone house. But the farmer gave them a warm welcome. He was impressed by Tonio's pompous demeanor and his offer of casting a horoscope for the whole next year for a very small sum. The farmer's sheds and pantries were full, and he agreed to sell them flour, bacon, dried meat, onions, and a small keg of wine.

In the evening, they all sat together in the cozy farmhouse kitchen. Children, workers, and maids all sat on the bench seats looking frightened, their eyes glued to the magician. Tonio was telling the farmer about his travels and the latest news. Those stories were often part of the service.

"After I finished my studies at the celebrated University of Krakow, I moved to the warm south, to Castile, where the sun burns so hot that the people are as black as ebony and as hard as kilned clay," he told them while sipping his wine. "Down there is a huge rock called Gibraltar, populated with herds of small, hairy creatures with sharp teeth."

The farmer's family listened with their mouths open as Tonio continued, waving his arms in dramatic gestures. "Then I continued by ship to Crete, the isle of the happy, and on to Constantinople, which was conquered by the accursed heathens a few years thereafter. My travels led me to countries inhabited by animals whose tails grow from their mouths, and horses with necks as tall as trees."

"But weren't you afraid of falling off the edge of the world?" asked the farmer fearfully.

Tonio laughed. "Haven't you heard? The Earth isn't flat—it's a ball! Just this year, in Nuremberg, I saw a map in the shape of a ball that showed all the countries in the world."

"But if the Earth is a ball, then the people at the bottom are upside down," said one of the workers. He scratched his louse-ridden beard. "How's that supposed to work?"

"Well, how do you think, you dimwit?" Tonio shrugged. "They wear shoes with nails at the bottom so that they always stick to the ground." The family nodded and muttered in agreement.

It was quite late by the time the master rose from his seat and stretched. He gave the farmer a nod. "I'm going to retreat now and work on your horoscope," he said and then gestured at Johann. "My apprentice will keep you company. He is skilled in the art of palm reading. Perhaps one or two of you would like to know what life has in store for you." Tonio winked at Johann before climbing the stairs that led up to the quarters the farmer had prepared for his two widely traveled guests.

The family stared at Johann anxiously. For the first time, he could understand what it felt like to be a traveling magician—respected and feared at the same time, an outcast and yet admired. He possessed a knowledge that was inaccessible to simple people. His words—a single look, even—decided the fates of entire villages and towns.

After a few moments, the corpulent farmer's wife shuffled closer to him and held out her trembling hand. "The last harvest was good," she began haltingly, speaking with a throaty accent Johann struggled to understand. "But a lightning strike destroyed our bakehouse just as I was carrying the bucket to the well. Is lightning going to strike me down next time I leave the house in foul weather?"

Johann took her right hand and tried to remember everything the master had told him and what was written in the old book. First he felt the woman's hand to see if it was clammy or dry, and whether there were many calluses and cracks from hard work. He could already draw some conclusions from that. Then he studied the various lines and mounts.

"The lightning that struck your bakehouse was a warning," he said in a low, mysterious voice. "But if you continue to fulfill your duties as good Christians and give shelter to pilgrims and travelers, no harm or storms will come to you. I can't see any serious misfortunes in the coming years."

Indeed, the woman's Life line ran deeply and evenly, and she looked well fed and healthy. Johann told her a few more things about her godly marriage and future blessings. Then a pretty maidservant came and held out her hand shyly.

"Should I stay with this farmer after Candlemas, or should I find somewhere else?" she whispered.

Johann could tell by her frightened eyes and the sour look on the face of the farmer's wife that there was bad blood between the two women. He studied her lines, especially the Heart line, which was broken and splintered. "You better find a new place to work," he replied quietly so the others wouldn't hear. "You'll find happiness somewhere else."

He proceeded similarly with the next two candidates, a worker and another young maid. He looked at their lines, but what he mostly tried to do was find out what their fears and worries were and what they were hoping to hear from him. Johann realized the art of chiromancy was both easier and more complicated than merely applying knowledge from books. It was about really listening to people, and the hand was just an aide.

Finally, the corpulent wife pushed one of her sons toward him. He was a handsome lad of about eight years, whose curious, alert eyes reminded Johann of himself as a boy. As was customary for a son of a well-to-do farmer, his hair was cut above the ears, which made him look more slow witted than he probably was.

"This is Rafael," said the farmer's wife, stroking the boy's hair adoringly. "My youngest and most beloved. The priest reckons he's smart and ought to attend a higher school eventually—perhaps at Innsbruck, even! What do you think, Master?"

Johann smiled. Evidently, the wife thought he was a gentleman or at least a scholar. Sometimes professors and students traveled from town to town, earning money as scribes. Those students were usually university dropouts who thought they were superior, but they actually were the most educated people many of the rural villagers would ever meet.

Johann picked up the boy's hand and studied it closely. His Head line was very strong indeed, but the bright eyes had already told Johann that Rafael wasn't silly. He was about to speak when an odd feeling startled him. It was like a gentle, warm throbbing coming from the boy's hand, as if the lines lit up underneath the skin for a brief moment.

And then he knew. The realization hit him like a blow.

The boy didn't have long to live.

It was nothing more than a dark premonition; the glow beneath the skin had long gone, but Johann sensed it very strongly.

The mother seemed to notice that something was wrong and eyed him suspiciously. "What is it? Is he going to become a farmer after all? No higher school? Speak up!"

"No, no." Johann shook his head. "It's . . . it's nothing." He tried to smile. "The priest is right. Your Rafael is going to become a learned cleric, perhaps even an abbot. The Lord is smiling upon you."

The wife clapped her hands excitedly, then she hugged her youngest son tightly. "You see, I told you, darling. God has great plans for you!"

Johann felt sweat running down his forehead, and his throat was bone dry. He didn't understand what had just happened. This had nothing to do with anything he'd read in the books or heard from the master. He thought of Tonio's words from two days ago.

It's important that you find your own way to yourself.

Was this what the master had meant? Johann hoped fervently that he was simply tired and had imagined the throbbing. He stood up, said a hasty good night, and climbed upstairs. In the chamber, Tonio was sitting at a table, writing on a piece of parchment in the light of a candle. Jerking shadows danced across the walls. The master looked up and eyed Johann expectantly.

"So? Did you read their futures?" he asked.

Johann nodded.

"It's not always pretty, is it? Now you know what it means to walk on the third, dark path." Tonio turned back to his parchment and drew strange-looking figures with his scraping quill. After a while he spoke again, but without looking up.

"When we reach our winter quarters, I will teach you more. More than you like, perhaps. Be patient, my little Faustus."

Johann dropped into his bed and fell asleep almost instantly. His dreams were gloomy and as sticky as spiderwebs enclosing his mind.

6

THEY LEFT EARLY THE FOLLOWING MORNING. THE FARMER had been very pleased with his horoscope—not least because it was written on real, expensive parchment. In return for his services, the famous and honorable Tonio del Moravia had received a smoked leg of ham, a keg of wine, and two small sacks of flour. In addition, they'd purchased nuts, dried fruit, salt, honey, cheese, and salted meat.

As they slowly rolled through the snow-covered alpine foothills at dawn, Johann's thoughts kept returning to the uncanny feeling that had overcome him when he'd read Rafael's palm. Could it be possible that he had foreseen the boy's death? The master hadn't said anything more about his protégé's first experience as a chiromancer, but Johann thought he could feel Tonio's eyes on him. When Johann had turned around to look at the farmstead one last time, Rafael had stood in the window, smiling and waving. Johann had turned away with a shudder, unable to return the wave.

They had left the imperial road the previous day and were traveling west along a narrow path. It became increasingly difficult for the horse to pull the wagon. The track was steep and in some places ran along a sheer drop into the valley below. Once, Johann caught a glimpse of a city by a wide river behind the crests of several hills, with a castle sitting on a peak above the town. But it soon disappeared from view. Snowdrifts blocked their way again and again, and each time Johann had to climb down and clear the track with the shovel. Each drift delayed them for over half an hour. Meanwhile, Tonio sat on the box seat, cursing and cracking his whip impatiently.

"We'll never get there at this pace," he groused. "Do you want to freeze to death so close to the end? Come on, move it—it's snow, not cement!"

But to Johann, every shovelful of snow felt like a shovelful of lead.

In the early afternoon, they left the track near a small village and turned onto an even-narrower path, which was bumpy, covered in tree roots, and only just wide enough for the wagon. It wound through a patch of forest with dark firs and sharp boulders, some of them as tall as trees. The snow was knee deep in places, and while Johann labored with the shovel, clumps of snow and ice rained down on him from the trees, soaking his clothes. Finally, when the wagon was stuck once more and a fallen tree blocked the road ahead, Johann threw the shovel aside angrily.

"Damn it, where is this journey supposed to lead?" he railed. "To hell? There's nothing but rock and ice here!"

The master grinned. "Well, it's a little too cold for hell. The devil doesn't like to freeze. But let me assure you, we're nearly there." Instead of grousing and cracking his whip, the master jumped down from the wagon and helped Johann shovel the snow. Together they were much faster. After another hour, they'd even managed to drag the tree aside. Tonio grabbed the horse by the reins and pulled mercilessly. The old black nag whinnied and shook the ice from its mane, exhausted nearly to death.

When Johann had almost stopped believing they'd ever arrive, the trees suddenly opened up and revealed a hilltop sticking out of the forest, with the tall peaks of the Alps in the background. Atop the hill stood a single stone tower, defiant as a castle, with a derelict stable beside it. The tower looked ancient, its stones polished by countless storms. Several of the battlements had broken off like rotten teeth. Black windows stared at Johann like the eyes of a huge beast. From up here they could see far down into the valley, where gathering clouds warned of the next storm.

To Johann, the tower on the hill seemed like it marked the end of the world.

"We're here." Tonio gestured at the building and wiped the cold sweat from his forehead. "I can tell you now—I wasn't even sure I'd still find the tower. It's been a long time since I was here last." He trudged up the hill while Johann stayed where he was, gaping at the building in front of them. His breath formed little clouds in the icy air. This pile of rocks was supposed to be their winter quarters? He'd expected a hut, or an old mill, perhaps—but this was nothing more than a ruin! Probably an old watchtower that hadn't been used for centuries. How were they supposed to live here until the spring?

Dejected, he followed Tonio up the hill, which was sparsely overgrown with shrubs at the top. The tower, roughly square in shape, was built from solid granite. Johann could tell by the windows that it contained three stories with a platform on top, which might have been roofed in once upon a time. Now the battlements were crumbled and the walls cracked. When Johann came closer he noticed that some of the windows had shutters that didn't look as old as the rest of the tower. And there was a solid wooden door, almost completely buried in snow. Tonio scooped the snow aside with his arms.

"Apparently, the Romans lived in this area a long time ago," he explained as he cleared the entrance. "The Via Claudia Augusta, an old Roman road, leads across the Alps not far from here. Soldiers and their families built this tower as a fortification against hostile tribes on this side of the Alps. There used to be lodges and a small town as well, but at some point the Romans abandoned it all. I'm guessing they were simply overrun—there was great bloodshed. Men, women, and children were crucified, burned alive in huge wicker baskets, or flayed for some forgotten deity." Tonio winked at his pupil. "They say you can still hear their screams in this tower today."

"What a pleasant place to spend the winter." Johann shuddered and helped Tonio clear the snow in front of the door.

"At least it's a place where we'll be left alone," Tonio replied. "Folks believe the tower is cursed. They avoid it, and if we're lucky, not much has changed since my last visit."

Johann noticed only now that a hastily scribbled black pentagram had been drawn on the door. "What's that?" he asked.

"A protection against travelers and other nosy folk," the master said. "Most people turn around and run when they see that symbol. Now all we need is the key." He walked back and forth near the door until his foot hit a stone slab hidden by the snow. "There we go!"

Once he'd kicked the snow off the slab, he pulled out a large, rusty key from underneath, stuck it into the lock, and turned it. The lock creaked loudly, and then Tonio kicked the door until it swung open. He nodded after his first glance inside. "I think we're in luck."

Johann blinked a few times to get his eyes used to the dim light. He could make out some furniture along the walls: a chest, a table, several stools.

Everything was covered in a thick layer of dust, but apart from that, it all seemed to be in good order. A steep set of wooden steps led upstairs.

Old ashes still lay in the fireplace built into the deep wall. It was bitterly cold. Inside, too, pentagrams had been drawn on the walls, in a color that reminded Johann of dried blood. A cup stood on the table, beside a tinged pewter plate holding something tiny and mummified.

"How long ago were you last here?" asked Johann with disgust. "A hundred years ago?"

"Possibly." The master grinned. "Like I said, it's been a while. Let's take a look at the second floor." He climbed up the creaking stairs, and Johann followed. The second floor was also furnished and adorned with pentagrams. It even contained a bed, but the straw inside was rotten.

Once Tonio had looked about for a few moments, he said to Johann, "We're leaving the wagon at the edge of the woods, and the horse goes in the stable. You bring everything into the tower." He pointed down the stairs. "We cook, eat, and study on the first floor. The second floor is yours."

"And the third floor?" asked Johann, noticing the master hadn't checked above them yet.

"That's mine alone, and you've got no business up there." Tonio gave him a stern look. "If I catch you in my room, I'll skin you like a rabbit—just like the barbarians used to do with the Romans. Understood?"

Johann nodded. He walked outside and started to lug the many crates, chests, and sacks up the hill. The master immediately carried the sack of books upstairs.

As Johann cleaned and swept the worst of the dirt and rotten straw from his room and the first floor, he wondered what was hidden in the uppermost chamber.

For the next few days they were busy fixing up the dilapidated tower. They found lengths of timber in the stable to close off the open windows. They found, hidden under the straw from Tonio's last stay, a stash of tools, including a hammer, a saw, and nails. The master turned out to be quite handy as a carpenter, and they made good progress. They reroofed the stable, and Johann cleared out the worst of the trash.

The chimney finally drew properly once Johann had removed several dead birds and mummified rats, and they were able to cook and get some warmth into the old walls. Johann stuffed his bed with fresh straw and covered it with furs. He filled the small chest in his room with his few possessions. He also had a table, where the master permitted him to study selected books. But the third floor remained closed to Johann.

At the end of the day, they'd sit by the open fire—the warmest place in the tower. The cage with the raven and the two crows dangled from the ceiling, the birds eyeing their new home curiously and flapping their wings. Bear and wolf skins served as cushions, and the large table was covered with books, parchment scrolls, bits of cheese rind, and half-empty cups of wine. Tonio had even built a shelf, which was now filled with neat rows of books, like soldiers of knowledge.

Johann soon had to admit that the tower wasn't as inhospitable as he'd first thought. But when the wind whistled through the cracks, howling and moaning, he thought of the tortured Roman souls Tonio had told him about. And sometimes, at night, he heard a soft murmuring and chanting from the master's chamber, together with heavy footsteps pacing the room. It sounded almost as if the master was speaking with another person, as if someone else was in the room with him, someone very large.

Several times Johann thought Tonio was by his bedside, holding his hand like at the Black Eagle Inn.

There is a time for everything, he heard the master's voice say. *A time to be born and a time to die. A time to heal and a time to kill . . .*

But when Johann awoke the next morning, nothing remained but a vague memory, and he told himself that it had been only a dream.

When they sat together by the fire in late afternoon, Johann finally received the long-awaited lessons. At first he learned more about palm reading, and then they turned to the subjects of pyromancy, hydromancy, and aeromancy, which were all elements of the art of divination. Johann took a particular liking to pyromancy. The master threw a handful of salt into the fire and gestured at the dancing flames.

"Learn to read them," he said. "Watch how the flames crackle and lick. You can learn much from the color, too: Are the flames bright red, or blue, or perhaps purple? Do they climb high or are they dying down? Does the smoke rise in a column or is it a cloud of stinging fumes?"

Sometimes, when the sky was clear to the north and the air icy cold, they went outside and studied the clouds, which were getting caught in the mountaintops like sheep wool in a comb. There was much to be learned from them. The master explained to Johann the various shapes of clouds and what kind of weather each one indicated. They watched the flight of a hawk, studying his wide, lofty circles above the forest. At dusk, when the sun disappeared behind the glistening snow and turned it as red as blood, Johann watched the play of colors, mesmerized, while the master explained the different hues of a rainbow.

"Everything has a deeper reason," Tonio said in conclusion, gesturing at the trees, the mountains, and the horizon to the north. "Nothing is without a plan. And when you recognize that plan, the world lies before you like a naked whore."

To Johann's infinite relief, the master no longer asked him to practice the bagpipe. Johann suspected Tonio wanted to spare his own ears. And perhaps he was afraid the noise might attract prying eyes from the nearby village. The accursed instrument stayed in its chest; Johann hoped it would remain there until it rotted. He didn't find much time to practice throwing his knife, either. He was too busy with other things now.

Saint Thomas Night—the longest night of the year—came and went, and soon it was Christmas. In Knittlingen, there was always a Christmas mass followed by a long, cozy evening together, singing and celebrating the birth of Jesus. Johann used to enjoy this day as a child. His mother had been a good singer, and his father—in a generous mood thanks to several cups of mulled wine—used to be a little nicer to him. Johann wondered how Tonio would mark the feast day. But the master didn't look like he was going to celebrate at all on Christmas Eve—he neither prayed nor sang. Instead, he sat in his chair by the fire with a grim look on his face, leafing through an old tome full of tables and drawings. Johann could hear the bells of the village church from over a mile away. He guessed the people were on their way to mass.

Johann cleared his throat and addressed his master. "It's Christmas," he began awkwardly. "You . . . you aren't particularly religious, are you?"

The master frowned and closed his book. "Just because everyone else sings and cries and turns all sentimental about a Jewish urchin doesn't mean I have to join in with such nonsense."

"So you don't believe in anything?" asked Johann, incredulous. He'd never met anybody who spoke like the master. Such talk was a certain road to hell—and to a crackling fire beneath a stake, if anyone heard it.

"Oh yes, I believe." The master grinned. "I believe in higher powers, much more strongly than you can imagine. Most of all, however, I believe in the power of stars. They never lie."

"Then explain them to me," begged Johann. "I've been waiting for so long."

Palm reading and the other manticisms had been interesting, and Johann still didn't fully understand what had happened when he'd sensed Rafael's death. But he'd been eagerly anticipating the day the master would introduce him to the art of astrology. He had a thousand questions, and until now, the master had always evaded them.

Tonio sighed; outside, the bells continued to toll like a cry for help from afar. Eventually, he gave a chuckle. "The hell with it. Maybe today is just the right day to begin the study of astrology. After all, those three old fools also followed a star."

He opened the book he'd been reading and pointed at strange circles covered with drawings and runes.

"The spheres of Ptolemy," Tonio began and traced the individual circles with his long finger. "More than a thousand years ago, this Egyptian divided the heavens into hollow spheres carrying the celestial bodies, which circle around the Earth, producing some kind of lovely music. A load of nonsense, if you ask me—I've never heard any music coming from the stars. But Ptolemy gives us a good basis to work with. In actual fact, astrology is much older still, dating back to the Babylonians, who also used to practice many dark and desirable rites."

"What do all these symbols mean?" asked Johann, leaning closer to the drawing.

"Earth and man are surrounded by celestial bodies." Tonio counted on his fingers. "The sun, the moon, Mercury, Venus, Mars, Jupiter, and Saturn—and each one is attached to a sphere. Those stars and planets are also known as the holy seven. Then follows the sphere of zodiacs, which is divided into twelve signs. Seven and twelve are magical numbers. Do you follow me?"

Johann nodded, and Tonio continued. "Each planet and each sign of the zodiac has an influence on man, on his destiny and his future. There are two kinds of horoscope: the nativity, which is about a person's character, and the progressive horoscope, which tells us something about the outcome of a future event, like a battle or a business decision. This kind of horoscope is much more difficult and therefore more expensive."

Fascinated, Johann studied the drawing and several tables below it. He'd been waiting for this for weeks. How many times had his mother spoken of the stars on the day of his birth and how because of them, he was a lucky child, a Faustus. Now he'd finally learn what all that meant!

"My mother said I was born under the influence of Jupiter," he said quietly. "On April twenty-three in the year of 1478. She always told me to remember the date well, but she never explained why. Can you tell me?"

"It's a strange date indeed. On that day, at your place of birth, the sun and Jupiter stood in the same degree of the same sign. And some of the other celestial bodies formed a, well . . . a very interesting relationship. It's a constellation that occurs only a handful of times in a century."

"When I first met you, you spoke of a day of the prophet," said Johann. "Do you remember?"

"Oh yes, I remember."

Suddenly, the master's eyes became as empty as glass marbles and he gazed into the distance. When he spoke again, his voice was hollow and so quiet that Johann struggled to understand.

"And I stood upon the sand of the sea, and saw a beast rise up out of the sea, having seven heads and ten horns, and upon his horns ten crowns, and upon his heads the name of blasphemy. *Homo Deus est!*"

Johann frowned with confusion. He'd never seen the master like this before. "What did you say?" he asked.

Tonio shook his head and smiled, his eyes normal again. "An old Bible quote, nothing more." He turned the page, and there were more tables with numbers. "Listen, I have a task for you. A Palatinate abbot asked me to write up a simple nativity for him. I haven't gotten around to it yet, and I'd like you to do it. You've got all winter."

"All winter?" Johann looked at him with surprise. "It can't possibly take that long!"

Tonio laughed. "My dear Faustus, you'll soon learn that astrology, along with alchemy, makes up the crown of the arcane arts. The road to mastery is long, stony, and paved with mistakes. And now listen carefully to what I'm telling you about the time of birth and sidereal time. I'll only explain everything once. Understood?"

Johann gradually came to realize that astrology was an extremely complicated field indeed, more difficult than anything he'd studied so far—yes, even more difficult than playing that accursed bagpipe.

In the following days, he studied the signs of the zodiac and their meanings. Each sign in the outermost sphere occupied a space of thirty degrees, of which ten formed a so-called decade. From a person's time of birth and the sidereal time—time reckoned by the movement of the stars rather than the sun—the so-called twelve houses could be calculated. There were ascendants and descendants, and everything had to be determined with the help of complicated formulas. Many nights Johann sat up late working on the chart just to watch the master tear his work to pieces the next morning.

"You're nothing but a jackass," scolded Tonio. "You can't even manage the simplest calculations. From the beginning! If you're not finished by noon, you're not getting any lunch."

Johann thus studied day after day. He thought about his stepfather telling him that his real father, the juggler and traveling scholar, also used to read the stars. Most likely, it had been nothing but hocus-pocus, not true knowledge, although Johann couldn't be certain. He didn't know who his father was. And he'd never find out, since the only person who could tell him was his mother—and she lay dead and buried in the Knittlingen cemetery. Johann's heart ached at the thought, and he decided to stop fretting about his parents. He might no longer have a father or a mother, but he had Tonio.

Sometimes, when the master was satisfied with Johann and the night was crisp and clear, Tonio would take him outside and show him the constellations. Ursa Minor and Major, Aquila, Andromeda with its milky fog. The great Ptolemy had gazed upon them. The stars were eternal. And yet they changed. Constellations traveled, coming and going like ancient companions of Mother Earth.

"Look there: Orion," Tonio said, pointing to a particularly striking constellation. "Canis Minor and Canis Major rise with him in winter. Together with Taurus, Gemini, and Auriga, they form the winter hexagon. In February, the summer constellations begin to return."

"There are so many stars," replied Johann. "And you can't seem to see the end. Is the universe infinite?"

"Remember the heavenly spheres," Tonio said. "There are eight of them."

"And what comes after the eighth sphere?"

Tonio laughed. "If I were a priest, I'd say, 'God only knows.' But I think we don't know because we can't see that far. Most stars can't be seen with the naked eye. But there are . . ." Tonio hesitated. "Possibilities. Your birth constellation, too, is difficult to discern, especially because our narrow-minded way of thinking ends behind the eighth sphere."

"Do you know when it appears next?" asked Johann.

The master smiled mysteriously. "You'll find out soon enough, young Faustus."

Johann was struck by the thought that the very same stars he was gazing at were also sparkling above Knittlingen, and homesickness flared up in him. He remembered how Father Bernhard also used to explain the constellations to him, and how Father Antonius showed him the printing press at Maulbronn and the book of the great Albertus Magnus—the *Speculum Astronomiae*, the mirror of astronomy.

But most of all, he thought of his little brother, Martin, and of Margarethe.

Some nights, when he couldn't go to sleep, his thoughts of Margarethe became so strong that he had to seek relief with his hand. Afterward, he felt ashamed and prayed for Margarethe's health. Perhaps she'd forgotten him by now. For him, too, it would be best to forget her.

But he couldn't.

During the cold days of January, he was often alone in the tower. The master didn't tell him where he was going, but more than once Tonio stayed out overnight. He always locked the trapdoor leading to the upstairs chamber carefully before leaving and reminded Johann what he'd do to his pupil should the young man ever ignore his order.

When the master would return the next morning, he always looked very pleased. A few times he came back with new books—mostly about astronomy and alchemy—and Johann wondered where he got them. Other times, the master carried sealed clay jugs or leather sacks filled with something bulky. The sacks were damp at the bottom, as if whatever was inside was wet. Johann didn't dare ask about it, though, and focused on his books. He got the impression that

Tonio always looked healthier after his nightly expeditions—less pale, somewhat rosier and fleshier in the face. He guessed the master went to the village tavern for a good meal and a few drinks while Johann was stuck in the tower with a grumbling stomach, working on the accursed horoscope of some priest. Sometimes, when he looked up from his work, he felt as though the birds in the cage were watching him so they could tell the master all about his doings.

"Goddamned beasts!" shouted Johann once, throwing a piece of firewood at the cage, causing it to swing back and forth wildly. The birds cawed as if they were mocking him, and the raven glared at him with evil eyes.

"*Kraa!*" croaked the raven. "*Kraa, kraa!*"

Johann held his hands over his ears to shut out the bird's almost-human voice.

When Johann needed a break from the tables and numbers, he went into the forest to chop firewood. He baked delicious-smelling loaves of flatbread over the fire, practiced his magic tricks and throwing his knife, or leafed through books the master had lent him. Johann had always enjoyed reading, and his Latin was getting better all the time. He was a fast reader and remembered most of what he read. When Tonio quizzed him on a book, Johann was nearly always able to give detailed replies. Then the master would lower the book and gaze at Johann pensively.

"It seems to me you're a better scholar than a juggler and musician," he'd say eventually. "Johann Georg Faustus, you're full of surprises."

Indeed, Johann didn't find much time to practice his tricks over the winter; the horoscope the master had entrusted him with kept him busy. After four more weeks, the birth chart of the Palatinate abbot was finally completed. Making one final stroke with his quill, Johann carried it downstairs. As usual, Tonio was sitting at the table with his books.

"Here you go," Johann said defiantly and handed Tonio the scroll. He fully expected the master to tear it up again, but to his enormous surprise, Tonio didn't seem to find a single mistake.

"What a boring fellow he is, this abbot. His stars are gray and insignificant." Tonio laughed. "But the birth chart is all right. Tiny oversights here and there, but generally well done. I didn't expect anything else of you. You've proven in the last few weeks that you're talented—more talented than many other students I've had."

The birds in the cage started to squawk wildly, shuffling back and forth on their shared perch.

"Hush, you beasts," Tonio shouted, turning to them.

Johann breathed a sigh of relief, but the master wagged his finger in warning.

"This was just a simple task, boy. Nothing more than the horoscope of a pale abbot. Don't let it go to your head. There'll be much harder tests for you yet—especially once we turn to alchemy, the jewel in the crown of the arcane arts. But you've done enough for today." He clapped his hands. "We should celebrate your first horoscope. Go down to the village and get us a small keg of wine, bread, and some juicy smoked sausages. What do you say?"

Johann nodded enthusiastically. Until then, the master had always forbidden him to go near the village so they wouldn't arouse suspicion. This would be his first excursion since they'd moved into the tower almost three months ago.

"Wash your face before you go." Tonio winked at him. "And don't mess about with the village girls. You've grown a fair bit in the last few weeks, and you're a handsome chap. Taller and a little stronger. If anyone asks, you're just a traveling tinker's journeyman, understood? We don't want any trouble. And now off with you—I can tell you're itching to go." He handed Johann a few coins. "I don't want the cheapest wine. Woe to you if you come back with swill!"

Johann took the coins with a grin and reached for the coat he had brought from home, which looked rather worse for wear by now and was becoming too short in the sleeves. Then he hurried outside.

The sun was shining and the first birds were singing, welcoming the nearing spring. As Johann ran through the snow, he could feel the stress of the last few weeks fall away from him like a lead weight.

~

The master waited until he could no longer hear Johann before going upstairs to prepare the ritual. The blood he kept in a small barrel was a little congealed, but it would do. Slowly, he stirred the sticky liquid, dipped his finger into it, and sucked it with relish. There was no taste like blood—warm and salty and full of life.

Especially when it was as young as this blood.

He dipped his hand into the barrel, and the liquid dripped onto the floor like paint. Using his fingers, he drew the ancient pattern that had served as a means of communication for thousands of years. He renewed the faded symbol on the floor, and a faint smell of decay spread through the chamber.

He was almost certain.

He hadn't thought it possible at first; he'd studied the ancient maps and watched the skies with the apparatus he'd invented. But the stars didn't lie. The day was close, very close, and it seemed he'd finally found the right one. The chosen one. They had to act now! Or the moment would pass, and no one knew when it would return.

He paced the circle with measured steps like he'd done countless times before, murmuring the ancient words.

"Remember then! Of one make ten, the two let be, make even three, there's wealth for thee . . ."

When the master had finished, he sat down in the middle of the circle, closed his eyes, and waited for a reply.

~

The trees dripped with melting ice, and the path that had been covered with a thick layer of snow just a few days earlier was now sodden with puddles. Johann nimbly jumped across mud and puddles as he headed down the valley, breathing in the fresh air that smelled faintly of the first buds of spring. He felt as though he'd escaped from a prison.

Indeed, spring didn't seem far off. Johann guessed they'd continue their travels soon. Until then, he hadn't thought about where they might be heading. The master had never mentioned anything. Did they even have a destination? Distant Venice, perhaps—the city he'd heard so much about? Or Paris? Rome? During the first few weeks of their travels, Johann had simply been grateful for the roof over his head. Tonio had given him a home, shelter from the hardships of winter. He had promised to stay with the master for one year, and sometimes, when Tonio had worked him too hard, he'd thought about running away sooner. But now he was happy to be the student of a man like him. Tonio could teach him far more than Father Antonius and Father Bernhard together—the whole world stood open to Johann!

But today, he simply wanted to enjoy life. After weeks of loneliness and studying in the tower, Johann looked forward to seeing other people, even if they were just the slow-witted inhabitants of some mountain village.

After about an hour's walk, he reached the road at the bottom of the valley, which ran along a fir-covered foothill of the Alps. In the distance, Johann could make out the snowcapped peaks surrounded by haze. The village lay about half a mile to the east. It was a small backwater with a tiny, decrepit church surrounded by a handful of houses. Next door to the church was the tavern, a low building made from black tree trunks, with dense gray smoke rising from the chimney. A larger trading route led past it.

It was late Sunday morning, and many farmers from the surrounding area had gone to the tavern for a drink or two following mass. Several oxcarts stood by the side of the road, and a group of young maids sat on the edge of a well outside the church. When they caught sight of Johann, they huddled together and whispered. He straightened up and took a playful bow as he walked past them. The girls giggled and squealed and scattered like a flock of hens. Only now did Johann realize how tattered and dirty he looked—with his torn trousers, too-small coat, and matted black hair that had grown long in the last few weeks. He walked over to the well to wash himself. He was surprised when he saw his reflection in the water. His face had become leaner and more angular since fall. Black fuzz had grown around his lips, and his eyes were almost as black and gleaming as those of the master. The weeks in the tower had turned Johann into a serious-looking young man—and, if he interpreted the girls' giggles correctly, a not entirely unattractive young man.

Once he'd removed the worst of the dirt from his clothes and combed his hair with his fingers, he entered the tavern. It was busy, and the air was heavy with stale sweat and spilled beer. Instantly, several pairs of eyes turned to him, and he thought he heard some snide comments. With his head held high, he walked to one of the few empty tables in the corner and sat down while the villagers eyed him suspiciously. Soon the tavern keeper came over.

"What do you want?" asked the man, briskly wiping the dirty, scratched table with a cloth. "If you're here to beg, sit in front of the church."

"A mug of beer, if you please," Johann replied with a smile. "And some provisions for the road. A keg of wine, a handful of sausages, and some bread, please. I'm an itinerant tinker on my way to Innsbruck." He held up one of the coins the master had given him. "And I can pay—in case you're worried."

The tavern keeper tilted his head and stared greedily at the coin, which was made of pure silver. "You'll get your supplies," he said eventually, reaching for the coin. "But you can't sit here. We don't want strangers in the village."

Johann's smile froze. "But why . . . ," he began.

The tavern keeper had already turned away without offering him as much as a beer. Frowning, Johann stayed put. What sort of a place was this? The Knittlingers weren't particularly fond of strangers, either, but they didn't chase them out of town. His good mood vanished.

"Dirty traveling scum," muttered someone nearby. "They're all in league with Beelzebub."

"They should all be hanged before more terrible things happen round here," someone else exclaimed. "There's a foul wind blowing from the mountains."

Intrigued, Johann turned toward the speakers. They were two elderly farmers, one of whom now spat noisily on the ground. "I'm telling you, the devil is on the loose," he grumbled. "He takes our loved ones and burns down the roofs over the heads of those who give him shelter. Have you heard? A magician stayed at the Black Eagle near Kempten over the winter, and now the inn's burned to the ground—and the heretic is over the hills and far away!"

"I don't think the scoundrel lives far from here," the other man whispered, making the sign of the cross. "I heard someone's staying at the old Roman tower—a sorcerer, so help me God! The charcoal burner saw him dance in the forest the other night with his assistant."

Johann winced. Had he heard right? Those farmers were talking about him and the master. Someone must have seen them near the tower and was spreading rumors. Worse, people seemed to have them mixed up with Freudenreich. Johann suddenly noticed that many of the guests were staring at him with hatred. Some even clutched the hilts of their knives; conversations gradually died down.

"Dirty traveling scum," the old farmer hissed once more. "Spawn of the devil!"

Johann was relieved when the tavern keeper returned to his table. The man handed him a heavy burlap sack. "Here's everything you asked for," he growled. "Now get out of here before they cut your throat. I don't want any blood spilled in my tavern!"

Johann took the sack without comment, stood up, and walked to the door. He had barely made it outside when he sensed that he was being followed. Slowly, he turned around. There were three young men, two of them holding gnarly sticks. The third one grasped a knife and approached Johann menacingly.

"What have you done with my little sister?" shouted the young man suddenly, his face contorted with anger. "Did you eat her like a wolf? Are you a werewolf?"

Johann was stiff with fright. "I . . . I'm just a plain tinker," he stammered. "I'm traveling with my master . . . We'd never—"

"You steal our children!" shouted the second man, cutting him off. He swung his cudgel. "Admit it! Our little Elsbeth and all the others. You steal them at night and you eat them!"

"But . . . that's nonsense!" Johann started walking backward. He raised his hands defensively. "We are no—"

A rock struck his head. A boy standing by the well had thrown it. The giggling maids were long gone. Instead, Johann was facing a growing number of angry young men.

"Grab him!" shouted one of them. "We'll beat the truth out of him. And then let's burn him like a Judas puppet so his black soul can't harm us any longer!"

Another stone hit Johann on the head. He turned around and a cudgel came down hard on his back. The pain made him gag.

"Club him to death like a dog!" screamed someone. "Just look at him! With his black hair and evil eyes. He's Satan's henchman! He killed our children!"

"Satan, Satan!" shouted the others.

Johann stumbled and fell, then got back on his feet before more blows struck him. Another rock whirred past his head. He started running down the road as fast as he could, the mob screaming and yelling behind him. The sack over his shoulder felt like it was filled with rocks. He dropped it into the ditch and ran, stones and clumps of ice raining down on him. For a while he still heard steps behind him, but they faded until he couldn't hear them at all. None of the villagers seemed to pursue him any longer, but he kept running as if the devil were after him. Finally, he reached the part of the woods that led up the hill to the tower. He turned off the road, followed the muddy path, and, panting heavily, arrived at the tower.

"Master!" he called out and rapped at the door. "Something . . . something happened! We must leave, now!"

But there was no answer. When Johann opened the door, the room on the other side was empty. The fire had gone out.

There was no sign of the master.

For a while, Johann stood in the middle of the chamber, breathing heavily and listening for any sound. But everything was silent. The books were still lying on the table, next to the abbot's birth chart. Red embers still glowed in the ashes, and the room smelled of smoke and faintly of sulfur. There was also another smell, but Johann couldn't place it.

His heart still racing, Johann thought about how narrowly he'd escaped death. There was no doubt in his mind that the villagers would have stoned or beaten him to death if he hadn't managed to run away.

He particularly remembered one thing they'd said.

You steal our children . . . You steal them at night and you eat them . . .

It would seem that here, too, children had been going missing, just like in Knittlingen all those months ago. In both cases, the master had been staying nearby. Johann thought about how satisfied and fleshy Tonio looked every time he returned from his nightly excursions. He thought about the clay jugs and the wet sacks—especially the wet sacks.

You eat them . . .

Johann shook himself as though waking from an evil nightmare. What a load of nonsense. Tonio del Moravia may have been a gloomy-looking fellow, a conjurer, an astrologer, and a chiromancer, but he was no man-eating monster. He was a wise and stern mentor, a man who could teach him a lot.

You eat them . . .

Johann's eyes turned to the stairs. What in God's name was his master up to in his chamber? Tonio had strictly forbidden him to enter the third floor. But now doubts gnawed at Johann like a thousand tiny rats. He needed to find out what went on upstairs. He'd never stop worrying about it otherwise. He wondered about his chances of getting caught. Tonio had probably gone out for a while, not expecting Johann home before afternoon. He still had time.

Provided the villagers didn't get here first to smoke out the alleged sorcerers.

Quietly, Johann sneaked up to his chamber and farther up the stairs to the trapdoor, which was usually bolted shut. Whenever the master left the house, he locked the bolt with a heavy padlock, and the key was always on his belt. But to Johann's surprise the bolt wasn't even pushed shut. Had the master forgotten to lock it? Or was he asleep upstairs?

Johann listened. On many occasions he had heard Tonio muttering until late at night, heavy footsteps thumping back and forth, and a dragging noise, as if something heavy was being pulled across the chamber floor. But now everything was silent: no footsteps, no muttering, no snoring, not even breathing.

For some reason Johann couldn't explain, he made the sign of the cross. Then he pushed against the trapdoor. It opened with a soft creak. Johann paused, waiting for an angry scream, but nothing happened. So he opened the door completely and climbed the remaining stairs until he stood inside the master's room.

Like in his own chamber, there was a bed and a table covered in books. A pile of clothes sat next to a chest in one corner, the windows were covered in cobwebs moving in the wind, and nothing seemed particularly out of the ordinary.

Except for the floor.

A huge pentagram had been painted on the floor, taking up almost the entire room. At each tip of the five-pointed star stood a burned-out candle, each candle surrounded by a pool of half-cooled wax. Johann knelt down and studied the rust-colored pentagram more closely. The paint was dry and exuded a faintly sweet smell—the same smell Johann had noticed downstairs. Johann sniffed again. It was just how it used to smell at home in Knittlingen when his stepfather butchered a pig to make sausage and ham.

It was the smell of blood.

You eat them . . .

A ladder led up to a square opening in the ceiling. In a daze, Johann climbed the few rungs until his head was outside, overlooking the platform that formed the tower's roof. A cold wind blew into his face. He spotted a strange construction set up on the roof: a large tube about as long as his arm resting on a stand. Johann guessed it must have been in one of the heavy crates he'd had to lift off the wagon and carry up the tower. He couldn't figure out what the apparatus might be. Was that the master's secret? But why wasn't Johann allowed to know about it? And what was the pentagram about?

Johann couldn't resist the temptation. He walked over to the tube; it was made of copper and shaped like a narrow funnel. Each end was covered with a pane of glass, reminding Johann of the eye glasses Father Antonius used to wear occasionally. The monk had told him they helped him to better decipher the tiny writing in books. Could this mysterious construction also be for reading books? Then he'd probably have to look through it.

He reached for the tube with trembling hands and brought his eye down to the skinny end. At first he saw nothing, just blurred blackness. Then he noticed that he could move the tube up and down and left and right. He played around for a bit—and started with fright.

The mountains that had been so far away a moment ago suddenly stood right before him, as if he could touch them with his hand. He clearly saw the snow glistening in the sun, the rugged rocks, and an eagle circling the mountain-tops, just as though they were right there in front of him. When he stepped back, everything was far away again. What a wondrous toy this was! Johann thought of the printing press in the Maulbronn monastery. This tube, too, seemed like an invention capable of changing the world. Was it powerful enough to let him see the stars up close? Would it be possible to see beyond the eighth sphere?

More confident now, Johann spun the tube in the other direction, toward the forest. Again, everything was blurry at first, but after a while he could make out details. The village church looked as if it were directly in front of him, then the road, and the path winding its way up through the woods to the tower.

And the master.

Johann screamed and let go of the tube as if he'd burned his fingers. He had seen the master's sinister-looking face and his thin black hair blowing in the wind. Tonio had appeared so close—and he seemed to have looked right into Johann's eyes. Without the tube, Johann saw only a black dot, but it steadily grew larger as the master rushed up the path.

Johann prayed that Tonio hadn't seen him on the platform. He climbed down the ladder as fast as he could, raced through the master's chamber past the pentagram and the pile of clothes, down the stairs into his own room, and finally down to the first floor, where he quickly sat in front of the cold fireplace with a book in his hands, pretending he'd been reading it all along.

Soon enough he heard the master's footsteps outside. The door was pushed open and Tonio entered. He had apparently been walking fast; sweat gleamed on his forehead, and he breathed heavily. He gave Johann a long, hard look with his piercing pitch-black eyes, and the young man suddenly felt certain Tonio had seen him on the platform. Then the master spoke with a sense of urgency.

"We must leave. I spoke with a merchant on the road. He said the village folk believe sorcerers are staying at the tower. Apparently, there was an incident in the village. Pack your things if you don't want to get burned alive! If we're lucky, they won't come until the morning. They're probably too drunk on a Sunday."

He didn't ask what Johann had been up to and why he was already back from the village. Instead, he went upstairs to his chamber, and Johann heard him packing in a hurry.

While Johann gathered his own belongings, he thought about the clothes he'd seen in the master's chamber. He hadn't paid them much attention earlier, but now, thinking about it, he remembered that there had been a lot of clothes. Many more than the master owned. And he could have sworn that they'd looked small.

Like children's clothes.

Upstairs, he could hear Tonio's footsteps, heavy and ominous, like those of a dark sea captain pacing the deck while their ship slowly sank to the bottom of the ocean.

7

THEY DROVE DOWN TO THE ROAD IN SILENCE. AT THE MASter's command, Johann had hitched the horse to the wagon and loaded their bags, sacks, and crates. The cage with the birds was back in its old place, dangling from the ceiling of the wagon.

One last time Johann turned to look at the tower that had been his home for the last few months, where he had learned so much. Then Tonio cracked his whip, and the tower was soon out of sight. It wasn't long before they had to climb down from the wagon and lead the horse. The snow had gone, but the track was riddled with deep ruts. Tree roots reached out of the ground like fingers of subterranean ghosts and forced them to take many small detours. Twice they had to cross a small stream swollen with meltwater rushing down the valley. The master was silent, pulling on the old nag's bridle when it didn't want to walk through muddy puddles.

Before driving off, they had nailed the windows and door shut and buried a large crate behind the tower. Johann had managed to see that the crate was mostly filled with books, but he'd also seen the copper tube. Apparently, Tonio had disassembled the strange apparatus and hidden it in the crate. After they'd filled the hole, the master made some strange gestures with his hands and laid out five white stones in a circle. "In case we ever come back," he growled. "No one will dare to dig for treasure here. Not if they value their immortal soul." With soot, he painted a black pentagram on the door and secured it with a heavy beam.

Finally, after two hours of pushing and pulling, they reached the bottom of the valley. They turned west, away from the village. After another half hour, the church bells started chiming wildly, as if there was a fire somewhere or an impending storm.

As if the villagers are gathering for a hunt, Johann thought. *A witch hunt.*

The bells grew fainter until Johann could no longer hear them at all, and the journey passed quietly for a while. Johann sat beside the master on the box seat, like he'd done so many times before the winter. Tonio still hadn't spoken. He ground his teeth grimly, as if imagining eating every one of those slow-witted, superstitious peasants alive.

You eat our children . . .

Johann now had time to reflect on what he'd discovered at the tower. Had he actually seen children's garments in Tonio's chamber? Suddenly he wasn't so sure. It had just been a pile of clothes, after all, and there was probably a rational explanation for the pentagram, too. Johann knew that alchemy worked with symbols and a wide variety of substances, including blood. Most likely, what he'd seen on the floor was pigs' blood—disgusting, yes, but nothing to be afraid of. What if his imagination was running away with him? What if he was being just as narrow minded and hysterical as the villagers? Children had gone missing—it happened all the time, everywhere. And there'd be an explanation for Tonio's nightly excursions, too.

Suddenly, Johann felt bad. Hadn't the master been very kind to him in the last few weeks? Hadn't he taught him much? Johann had been blind for so long, and finally someone showed him the light. And there was so much left to learn. About the strange tube he'd found on the roof of the tower, for example, or the legendary field of alchemy the master had just begun to teach him about. Tonio might not have owned a library as large as the one at Maulbronn Monastery, but he seemed to be something of a walking library himself. Sometimes Johann thought the master's knowledge was ancient and infinite, reaching back to the very first knowledge of man. How much Johann could still learn from him! Johann cleared his throat. Perhaps the time had come to ask where their journey was headed.

"Now that the snow is melting, the road across the Alps should be clear, right?" he asked.

The master nodded but didn't reply, holding on tightly to the reins.

"Are we going to travel across the Alps?" asked Johann in another attempt. "Perhaps to . . . to Venice?"

"Our plans have changed," Tonio replied curtly. "We're heading east, to the Kingdom of Poland."

"But why?" Johann couldn't hide his disappointment. He'd been very much looking forward to Venice and Rome, to the warm lands beyond the Alps. He'd wanted to see the ocean, and now they were headed to a country he'd never even heard of before. "Why Poland?"

Now the master turned his haggard, falcon-like face to look at him, eyeing Johann intently, making him feel like Tonio was reading his every thought.

"Have you never wondered where I gained all my knowledge?" asked Tonio. "Do you think it all fell from the sky like a dead star?"

"You . . . you studied," Johann replied. "In Paris, Heidelberg—"

"Yes, yes," Tonio said impatiently. "I visited many universities, a traveling scholar, always on the search for new knowledge. But you can only learn the dark arts at one particular university—Krakow."

Johann remembered the master mentioning Krakow—in Knittlingen he had introduced himself with those words.

Tonio del Moravia. Krakow magister of the seven arts and keeper of the seven times seven seals.

"Once upon a time there were other universities that taught the arcane arts," Tonio continued while the old horse pulled them along the bumpy road. "But the accursed church banned them, even though those arts are much older than the church. Now there's only Krakow left. There's no other place if you want to learn about the seven times seven seals!"

"What are the seven times seven seals?" asked Johann.

"Be patient, young Faustus." The master grinned. "You'll learn about them soon enough. I've sent out a messenger to announce your arrival at Krakow."

"My arrival?" Johann stared at his teacher with disbelief. "But why—"

"Did you never wonder what I was doing when I stayed out all night?" asked Tonio, cutting him off. "I was waiting for news, week after week! When none arrived, I went out myself this morning and gave a letter to a merchant. Our friends need to know that you're coming. The stars are extremely favorable."

"That *I'm* coming?" Johann's astonishment grew. "But . . . but why should they know about me?"

The master opened his mouth to reply, but then shook his head. "It's too soon. We've been disappointed many times, even though I'm quite certain this time." He smiled. "Wait a little longer, young Faustus. I'm sure we'll run into some friends on the way to Krakow. There are many of us, and our numbers are growing. It can't be long now. Giddyup, you lazy old nag, pull!"

He cracked the whip, and the old horse lifted its head and whinnied, almost as if it were laughing. Then it pulled them steadily eastward toward this legendary Krakow. Johann sat on the box seat, brooding. Now he had some sort of explanation for why the master had been out so many nights, but one mystery had been replaced with another, much bigger one. Johann had thought he was nothing but an apprentice, a plain assistant who helped Tonio del Moravia, the great magician, during his performances in the German empire.

But it seemed the master had bigger plans for him.

The following morning, they reached a larger road busy with merchants and pilgrims. It led south toward the mountains, but Tonio turned the wagon north.

"The old Roman road," he explained. "Once upon a time these roads covered the empire like a finely woven net spanning many hundreds of miles. They were paved so the Roman soldiers could travel fast. Each road was wide enough for two carts to pass each other. Watchtowers and forts guaranteed safety for travelers." He pointed out some overgrown cobblestones, remains of a footpath on the side of the road, and a crooked milestone with withered Roman numerals that stuck out of the mud. "Hundreds of years have gone by since, and not much is left. But the little that remains is still better than anything the German kings and emperors have managed since."

"And this road leads to Krakow?" asked Johann.

Tonio laughed. "Not quite. But it'll get us close. It's a long way to Krakow. We'll be traveling for many weeks—weeks I can use to teach you many things." He looked up at the sky and squinted. "I only hope we'll make it in time."

Indeed, the master used their time on the road and the evenings to teach Johann more about astrology and the basics of alchemy.

"Many believe alchemy is just about finding a way to make gold," he explained. "I, too, was once obsessed by this desire. But alchemy is much more than that. Alchemy, as it was taught by the great Hermes Trismegistus in Egypt and later by the Greeks and Arabs, grants us an insight into that which the world contains in its innermost heart and finer veins. Do you understand what I mean?"

Johann nodded, though he felt like he'd only tasted the tiniest drop of a vast ocean of knowledge.

The master was much nicer to him now than before their time at the tower. They had all but stopped practicing their juggling tricks, and Tonio rarely read palms and no longer compiled horoscopes at taverns. He seemed in a hurry to reach Krakow. On clear nights, the master spent a lot of time gazing at the stars. Something seemed to excite him very much.

"It's happening much faster than I thought," he'd say again and again, almost to himself. "Much faster. Who would have thought, this early in the year. The day is near . . ."

When Johann asked what he meant, Tonio merely shook his head and told him he'd find out in Krakow.

"You can't keep walking around looking like that," Tonio said one day, eyeing Johann critically. "You look like a scarecrow, not like the promising apprentice of an itinerant chiromancer and astrologer."

Johann looked down at himself. It was true: his clothes were dirty and torn and much too small.

"We'll need a new outfit for you," the master continued. "Nothing in the garish patterns of jugglers' clothing, nor the colorful garb of a dandy. It wouldn't suit you—you're a student of the arcane arts now, so we'll need something serious, something plain."

They visited a tailor in the next town, and Johann was fitted with a long black tunic, a warm black coat, and shiny leather boots. On his head, instead of a hat he wore a gugel—a type of fashionable hood that covered head and shoulders and was ideal in bad weather. His new trousers were made of the finest wool and felt nice against his skin. The master grinned.

"You look like an honorable scholar. Folks are going to doff their hats and ask you to write up documents for them."

The countryside they were passing through now looked much like the Kraichgau. Johann learned that this region was called Swabia. Small villages were dotted among the patches of forests and the fields. The snow was melting, and it was nearly time for the first sowing. The wheel of life kept turning. Hungry faces marked by hardship stared at them from the fields. It looked as though Swabian farmers, too, had suffered much in recent years.

Once they passed a group of Dominican monks clad in black, chanting loudly and calling on people to repent their sins. The monks were accompanied by heavily armed mercenaries pulling a cart containing a chest with several padlocks. The chest bore metal fittings and, on the front, a painting of the devil with his fork, torturing souls in purgatory.

"Damned shavelings!" groused Tonio before spitting on the ground. "Don't the farmers pay enough in tithes? Now they have to pay for a place in heaven, and one for the long-dead great-grandfather on top!"

Johann had heard of priests selling indulgences as a means of gaining forgiveness for sins. In the past, the only way to atone for one's sins was through prayer or pilgrimage, but now people could shorten the amount of punishment they'd have to undergo with money. It was even possible to reduce the time long-deceased ancestors had to spend in purgatory—provided one had enough coins for the chest.

"People are as stupid as pigs," Tonio continued as they drove past the chanting train. "And why? Because the church and the high and mighty deny them knowledge. But all that is going to change soon. Oh yes, soon! *Homo Deus est!*"

Johann had heard the last phrase from Tonio before. By now he could not only read Latin, but also speak it reasonably well. Despite understanding those three words, however, he still didn't understand what they were supposed to mean together. The phrase didn't make any sense to him.

Man is God . . .

There were more and more crossings in the road now, and increasing numbers of villages and towns. Trading routes led off in all directions, and every road seemed to be busy. Knights cantered past on their mighty steeds; expensively dressed merchants drove their heavily loaded carts along at a snail's pace. Johann and Tonio heard some travelers talking about King Maximilian holding an imperial diet in Worms. The French had invaded Italy, and the accursed Ottomans threatened the borders of the German empire. Merchants were conducting business with faraway lands that had hitherto existed only in legends. The whole country seemed to be in a state of excitement, as if spring was liberating the entire empire from a long frost.

Five days later, the walls of a city appeared in front of them. Countless towers jutted into the sky, a large cathedral in their center. The greenish-gray ribbon of a large river gleamed in the spring sunshine. Hordes of pilgrims and merchants flocked toward the gates. Johann had never seen such a huge city before.

"Augsburg," said Tonio grimly.

Johann had heard of Augsburg. He'd heard travelers in Knittlingen talk about this city; it was one of the largest in the German empire. They said it was ruled by patricians—powerful families of merchants and councilors who were unbelievably wealthy, owning properties all over the world and lending money to bishops, dukes, and even the emperor himself. It seemed like those men were the new masters of the world—not knights, counts, and barons, like in his mother's days.

After spending the last few nights in the wagon by the roadside, Johann was glad they'd soon be staying at an inn again—and in such an interesting place. But, much to his disappointment, Tonio gave Augsburg a wide berth, and soon Johann lost sight of the city's battlements, towers, and cathedral.

"Augsburg is far too dangerous a place for the likes of us," Tonio said. "The bishop gives short shrift to sorcerers. Not too long ago they boiled an alchemist alive because he claimed he could turn iron into gold."

"Could he?" asked Johann.

"Only very few are privy to that secret. The quack in question definitely wasn't one of them. I'm guessing he couldn't even tell the difference between copper and bronze." The master gave a laugh. "Do you know what boiled human flesh smells like? Just like pork! At the end of the day, we all wallow in the same mudhole."

Johann said nothing. Once again he realized that magic was a dangerous business. Something that counted as a harmless weather spell in one place could mean heresy and death in the next town. White magic like astrology, chiromancy, and some alchemy was allowed, but black magic like necromancy and sorcery wasn't.

Soon enough, he'd experience the difference between the two worlds firsthand.

Their journey took them to the north, toward Franconia. The snow had all melted now, and the hawthorn and fruit trees were full of buds, birds chirping among their branches. The master whistled a tune and seemed to grow more cheerful with every mile. At night, he barely glanced up at the sky anymore. It seemed he had reached a decision.

"I am hopeful we'll soon be meeting our friends," he said. "In the town of Nördlingen, we're going to meet a man who can help us on our journey. I've known him for a very long time. If the message I sent off in the mountains has been delivered, he should already be there."

Johann had long since given up asking Tonio about his mysterious friends. The master didn't volunteer any more information, but Johann hoped he'd learn more in Nördlingen. He was itching to know why his arrival was eagerly anticipated in Krakow. The only explanation he could come up with was that he'd shown, during their time at the tower, that he was a gifted student. He was a fast learner, interested in everything the master told him—be it the power of steam as taught by Hero of Alexandria, which Johann observed each night above their cauldron, or the technical secrets of mechanical clocks like the ones they sometimes saw on town halls or church spires. The master also taught him about the herbs growing by the roadside. Their lessons often started with Tonio spotting something and jumping off the wagon.

"Black hellebore," he said one time, pointing at a pretty white flower by the wayside. "You can extract a poison from this plant strong enough to kill emperors and kings. In very small doses, it can ease insanity. If you ever pick black hellebore, make sure you wash your hands thoroughly—or you won't live long enough to regret your mistake."

Another time, he pointed at the black smoke rising from a charcoal pile in the woods. "Grind the coal from an alder buckthorn and mix it with sulfur and saltpeter. The resulting powder is powerful enough to burst the walls of Constantinople—I saw it with my own eyes!"

Johann, sitting on the box seat, listening to Tonio, realized he was learning much faster than back at school in Knittlingen. Thoughts and ideas flew into his mind as if Tonio had tapped some sort of spring inside him that couldn't be stopped.

After two more days, they reached a curious area. A ridge of hills forming a gigantic ring spread before them. It looked to Johann like a giant had thrown a rock into an ancient ocean. Once again he was struck by the perfection of nature, the symmetry of the natural world, as though it had been built by a clock maker. He thought of the beautiful crystals of snowflakes melting in his hand; the wings of butterflies; and flower petals following the sun all day. When he told Tonio his thoughts, the master laughed.

"God as a clock maker—don't let the church hear you talk like that. They suspect heresy behind every rock these days. But I like the image. It makes God kind of human, doesn't it? *Homo Deus est!*"

Finally, they reached another large town surrounded by a high wall. The master explained that this was Nördlingen, where he hoped to meet his friend. The lanes and squares in the town were busy; a cattle market was in full swing. Pigs squealed and geese with tied wings cackled in their baskets. A calf on its way to the butcher's block stared at Johann with big eyes. A huge newly completed church stood in the town's center, still partially enclosed by scaffolding. The tall tower showed all travelers that Nördlingen considered itself on par with Augsburg.

"You should see this place at Whitsuntide," Tonio said, carefully steering the wagon through the narrow lanes. "The fair is so spectacular that you even forget the stink."

The air did smell strongly of blood and urine. Johann guessed the stench came from the many tanneries along the city stream. Old and young tanners washed skins in the water and hung them in their airy attics to dry.

They headed toward a tavern near the church. The tavern was several stories high, with a large gate in the center that led into a courtyard. To the gate's left and right were pub rooms, and a wide set of stairs led up to guest rooms. Heavy oaken floorboards and gilded decorations made the tavern look almost palatial.

"The Golden Sun Inn," Tonio explained. "Emperors have stayed here, and His Majesty King Maximilian just visited a few years ago. I thought we'd treat ourselves to some nice accommodation."

Following their long, arduous journey and the many nights spent by the roadside, Johann went to bed early. The down quilt and fresh reeds on the floor seemed like heaven on earth. He slept like a log and only woke late in the morning to drumrolls and flourishes.

When he rushed to the window, he saw crowds of people heading toward the western gate. The master awaited him downstairs in the taproom.

"Quick, have some thinned beer and honeyed barley porridge," he commanded, gesturing toward a jug and a bowl on the table. "We don't want to miss the show. We've arrived at just the right time," Tonio said, rubbing his hands. "A stroke of luck! My old friend hasn't arrived yet, but there's another acquaintance I wouldn't mind seeing one last time."

"Who is it?" asked Johann, curious.

"Oh, you'll know him," Tonio said with a smile.

Johann still didn't understand. After a hasty breakfast, he followed Tonio out into the street. They joined the crowd heading out of town. Not far from the city walls, Johann saw a hill that had been cleared of trees and was crowned by a large rock.

The people seemed merry, buying nuts and pastries from itinerant merchants who carried their wares through the crowd on large back frames. Children squealed and ran after the drummers, and everyone seemed bound for the rock on the hill. It looked like an enormous table or altar and was more than five heads high. A pile of wood as tall as a man had been stacked on top, and a ladder led to a stake in the center of the pile. Dark-clad monks were swinging incense burners, and the smoke seemed to Johann like the harbinger of a much larger fire.

He understood now what kind of a show the crowd had come for.

"Everything's ready," the master said with a smile, his eyes appraising the hill in front of them. "All that's missing is our friend."

Johann was waiting with Tonio and all the people of Nördlingen, who were shouting and cheering, when a tumbrel pulled by a mangy donkey came jolting up the road. The hangman stood atop the cart, wearing a red shirt and a mask, and next to him, a man bound with ropes swayed back and forth as if he was drunk. Despite his torn shirt, blood-encrusted face, and arms twisted like those of a broken doll, Johann recognized him immediately: Freudenreich von Hohenlohe, the young minstrel from the Black Eagle Inn.

"They arrested him two months ago," Tonio explained as he joined in the rhythmic clapping of the crowd. A kettledrum provided the beat. "The poor bugger conjured up a calf with two heads and a hailstorm that devastated the fields around Nördlingen. If you ask me, he probably didn't pay his bill at the tavern or screw the landlady hard enough. Folks around here are easily angered. Apparently, good old Freudenreich was stubborn during torture, and that's why it took so long to get him sentenced."

The hangman dragged the trembling minstrel down from the cart. He barely resisted. The hangman's assistants had to carry him for the last few yards because he could no longer walk. It looked as though his legs were broken, along with his arms, which were bent at unusual angles.

Tonio began to sing quietly. It was the same song Freudenreich had performed when they'd seen him at the Black Eagle at the start of winter.

"Winter, O winter, you frighten me not. I sit by the stove and my fire burns hot. O winter, keep howling, I show thee no mercy . . ."

Rough-hewn steps led up the rock to the pyre. The assistants tied Freudenreich to the stake and held a burning torch to the wood. The sticks were dry, and the flames devoured them hungrily. Soon the stake was enshrouded in thick white smoke.

Like a giant incense burner, Johann thought.

The crowd fell silent, tense with expectation, even the children. Then a scream rose out from the smoke, animalistic and shrill. Johann thought about how beautifully the minstrel had once sung. And he thought about the master's words back at the Black Eagle.

He won't find happiness in these harsh climes, oh no, he won't.

Johann shuddered despite the heat of the fire. They had denied the great Tonio del Moravia his winter quarters, and he had taken terrible revenge. First the inn had burned down, and now the minstrel burned, too.

Freudenreich's screams turned into inhuman screeching and finally a wailing that stopped abruptly. Then the smoke turned black. Johann smelled burned flesh, and it smelled like pork. He felt sick.

"Keep howling, I show thee no mercy," Tonio sang once more, clapping his hands.

The execution was over, and after staring at the glowing embers for a while, the crowd began to make its way back to town. Johann was still in a daze, snapping out of it only when Tonio tapped him on the shoulder.

"I like fires," he declared cheerfully. "Even though they remind me of darker times. Once I watched a young maiden I was very fond of burn in France. We were like siblings—that's when it all began." He turned around and didn't look at the smoking pyre again. "And now let's go. If we're lucky, my friend has finally arrived."

~

The master's friend arrived in the evening. Tonio had been awaiting him impatiently at a corner table of the Golden Sun. Johann sat next to him, reading a book. The master had been drinking expensive Rhenish wine for hours but didn't seem to be getting drunk—not even tipsy, although Johann noticed that he looked paler than he had back at the tower.

A broad-shouldered man entered the inn, dressed entirely in black, wearing a long coat and a floppy hat like Tonio. He was so tall that he was forced to stoop as he walked through the door. He carried a long staff, like that of a shepherd, except it looked like a little twig in his huge fingers. He smiled as he walked toward their table, but his smile seemed false, as if someone had painted it onto his pockmarked, bearded face.

"*Mon baron*, it is an honor to see you again after such a long time," greeted the man with a rough voice, bowing low. Like Tonio, he spoke with a French accent, but his was much stronger.

"Don't, Poitou," said Tonio. "Not in front of the boy."

The man scrutinized Johann, who suddenly felt naked.

"That's him, yes? Looks rather unremarkable. Pale as a bookworm."

"I'm a bookworm, too, if that's what you want to call it. When will you learn that appearance doesn't matter, Poitou? On the contrary. You may be big and strong, but your mind doesn't allow you to think further than the next meal."

"Oh yes, I like thinking about the next meal." The giant gave a grin. "You're right, milord. I can eat as much as my horse munching on his barley outside the door. I rode for two days and one night straight to proclaim your arrival and meet you here. There is much to talk about."

"*Parle français,*" said Tonio, waving to the innkeeper to bring them more wine.

The men conversed quietly in French, and Johann pretended to be focused on his book while casting furtive glances at the master and the foreigner. Why had the man named Poitou addressed Tonio as a baron? Was the master a descendant of French nobility? The other man's submissive behavior seemed to suggest as much. Johann didn't like the way they'd spoken about him—like a precious object. What were their plans for him?

He listened intently to the strange-sounding conversation, trying to understand anything at all. The words *diable* and *réunion* were mentioned several times and sounded familiar, but other words sounded harsh and throaty to him, like *garache*, *béliche*, and *bête bigourne*. Johann couldn't make any sense of it, and he sank deep into thought.

Following the gruesome execution in the morning, he and the master had returned to the inn, where Johann told the master he wanted to study. But in truth he'd needed some time to think. He owed the master a lot. Tonio had taught him so much already, and he'd teach him more still.

On the other hand, Johann grew more afraid of Tonio every day. He was repulsed by the glee with which the master had watched the execution—he'd enjoyed it, even. But worse still was the suspicion Johann harbored deep down—that Tonio was somehow responsible for both the execution and the fire at the Black Eagle Inn. Could it be possible? Johann remembered the three pieces of coal Tonio had placed at the Black Eagle's threshold, muttering incantations, and also the bloody pentagram at the tower. Were there symbols and formulas that could conjure up lightning and flames, and even kill someone? Or had everything just been a series of unfortunate coincidences? But the coincidences were piling up, and Johann struggled to believe in them any longer.

As if the master had read his thoughts, he paused in his conversation and looked over at Johann. Like an alert wolf or lynx, he seemed to detect something, but then he smiled.

"Look, the boy studies even now," he said to Poitou in French. "He's truly insatiable."

"Then I'm sure he'll like what we have planned for him," replied Poitou with a laugh.

Johann gave a grin, even though he hadn't understood a word, and then returned to his book. He was scared of the big Frenchman—but not as scared as he was of Tonio.

On top of everything else, earlier he'd discovered that someone had rummaged through Johann's few possessions in their room upstairs while he'd been out. For a brief moment, Johann had suspected the two crows and the raven, who always watched his every movement from their cage. Then he realized how ridiculous the thought was. Nothing was stolen, but nonetheless he decided to wear his little knife on a leather string around his neck from now on, underneath his shirt and jerkin, where Tonio couldn't see it.

But supposing the master actually was a sorcerer—why should he care? Tonio was his teacher, and he'd find none better in this world. What were Father

Antonius's superficial knowledge and Father Bernhard's awkward attempts to study the stars compared to the arcane arts, the ancient knowledge about "that which the world contains in its innermost heart and finer veins," as Tonio had put it not long ago. Johann guessed black magic was a part of it. He felt certain the master would teach him about it someday. Johann's nightmares and twinges of conscience were simply the price he had to pay. Perhaps that was exactly what that strange Latin phrase Tonio always recited was supposed to mean.

Homo Deus est . . .

Perhaps God didn't lead man's way, but everyone was responsible for their own path.

Meanwhile, the innkeeper had brought them platters of roast piglet with slices of deliciously fragrant white bread, and a serving of wild onions and carrots in a steaming herb sauce. The men ate ravenously, pausing the conversation. After eating in silence for a long while, Tonio burped loudly, wiped the juices from his lips with the last bit of bread, and leaned back contentedly.

"I haven't eaten like this since the Battle of Patay, and that was a long time ago," he said. "Just what we needed to strengthen us for what comes next." He turned to Poitou. "Is everything prepared?"

The man nodded. "All is ready, milord. You are expected. Although some of them said we should wait till Krakow."

"We don't have time," snarled Tonio. "The stars are favorable right now. Who knows how long it would take us to get to Krakow. I don't want to risk it. We're doing it here—that's my final word!"

Poitou looked at Johann, who had hardly eaten anything and seemed to be focused on his book again. But he was listening to every word. So were they not going to Krakow at all now? What were those two men going to do with him?

"And you really believe he's the right one?" asked Poitou. "I have an uneasy feeling about this. We could pay the midwife here a visit. A different child, born around the same—"

"It's him," Tonio said so quietly that Johann struggled to understand. "If we go about this the right way, he will change the world. But we must act *now*! If we miss the moment, it won't return anytime soon. You know how long we'd have to wait."

He stood up and signaled to Johann to follow. "Let us go." The master gave him a cheerful wink. "All this might seem strange to you now, young Faustus.

But trust me. You'll soon know more. I arranged for your ordination to take place here, so we don't have to wait until Krakow. We have enough friends around here—by now, we have friends everywhere."

"Ordination?" Johann was confused. "What ordination?"

"You'll find out soon enough. And now come, before the moon disappears behind the hills again."

A short while later, they set off. Tonio had sent Johann up to his room to pack his few belongings. The master's crates and the birdcage had already been taken to the wagon. Night had fallen outside, but a full moon bathed the lanes of Nördlingen in a pale light. Tonio and Poitou sat on the box seat while Johann found a place among the chests and sacks under the canvas. They tied Poitou's exhausted horse to the back of the wagon, where it plodded along leisurely.

They drove toward the closed city gate. The road beyond led back to Augsburg; it was the road they'd come from the day before. Poitou whistled, and the gate opened with a soft squeak. Johann guessed the man had bribed the guards earlier. Outside the gate, they turned right. When they passed where Freudenreich the minstrel had been burned to death that morning, Tonio whispered something to Poitou in French and the man laughed out loud. The air still smelled faintly of smoke and roast meat.

The moon was high in the sky as the wagon rolled past fields and small patches of forest. No one else was on the road at this time of night. It was as quiet as if the whole world were asleep—except for once, when Johann heard wolves howling in the distance.

They turned onto an unmarked, narrow track. Their surroundings became increasingly rough and overgrown. Moss-covered boulders were scattered among the trees, looking as if they'd fallen from the sky in ancient times. Johann thought about the giant throwing the huge rock into an ancient sea. Were these boulders remnants of that rock? Had God been the giant?

The master repeatedly looked up at the sky and the pale stars. Each time, he nodded with satisfaction, as if confirming an observation. After about two hours, Poitou asked Tonio to stop. He gave a whistle that imitated the call of a nightingale. Then he waited, and after a short while, an owl hooted three times. "We have arrived," said Poitou, looking around searchingly. "It's not far from

here. I suggest we leave the wagon hidden among the trees over there. And then
we walk."

The three birds in the cage flapped their wings excitedly and cawed, as if they
sensed that someone was nearby. Tonio gave the cage a shove.

"Be quiet, God damn it!" he barked. "I know you're hungry. Not long now."
He turned back to Poitou. "Did you bring what I asked you for?"

Poitou grinned. "It wasn't easy at such short notice." He opened his wide
coat and pulled out a clear vial with a cork, containing a liquid the color of
swamp. "The black potion. La Meffraye herself brewed it."

"Well done." Tonio climbed down from the wagon and led the horses a little
deeper into the forest. Then he waved for Johann to follow him. The three of
them sat down on a rock that gleamed pale in the moonlight, as if it had been
covered with a white sheet. Poitou handed the vial to Tonio, who raised it toward
the moon with both hands.

"The black potion," he announced solemnly. "He who drinks it is close to
Pan."

"So be it," Poitou murmured as if praying. "Now and forever."

The master removed the cork from the vial and handed it to Johann. "You
must empty it in one go," he commanded. "It doesn't taste particularly good,
but it acts fast."

"What . . . what is it?" asked Johann. He still didn't have the faintest idea
what the purpose of their excursion might be. "Why should I drink it?"

"My little Faustus," Tonio sighed and placed one hand on his shoulder in a
fatherly gesture. "I've always encouraged you to ask questions. Only those who
ask will receive an answer. But for once I'm telling you not to. You must cross the
threshold naked and unknowing. It's the rule." He smiled and stroked Johann's
cheek. "But you can trust me. Once you swallow that drink, your knowledge is
going to be infinite. And that is what you want, isn't it, my Faustus? Knowledge
at any cost, just like me. This world is waiting for people like you and me—
people who will finally lift the veil."

Johann hesitated. He sensed that he was once more standing at a fork in
the road, like when he'd set out from Knittlingen. If he took the potion, there
was no way back. But did he really have a choice? He'd left everything behind.
His mother was dead; he didn't know who his father was. His only brother had

vanished, probably eaten by wild animals. And the only girl he'd ever loved had cursed him with words he'd never forget.

Go away. You are the devil.

Tonio gave him a nod. His black eyes seemed to pierce Johann.

"It's time," the master said. "The stars don't wait. Drink."

The liquid felt thick on Johann's tongue; it slowly ran down his throat and into his stomach. It burned like fire and tasted slightly rotten, of sulfur and vomit. Johann coughed and spluttered, and the master grabbed him by the collar.

"It's crucial that you keep the drink down, my boy," he said urgently. "It'll soon be over."

Johann closed his eyes, and the nausea indeed eased. But the feeling of fire in his stomach remained, as if something was eating into his guts. Poitou laughed.

"The first time is the worst. You'll get used to it after a few years. The path to hell is lined with fire—but the ripest fruit awaits you on the other side."

"Shut up, Poitou," hissed Tonio. "Help me get him to the clearing."

He dragged Johann to his feet like a puppet, but the young man shook his head.

"Leave . . . me. I . . . I can walk by myself." With great difficulty, he took a few steps. For some reason he didn't want the master to lead him. No matter what came next, he wanted to walk this path alone.

"As you wish," said Tonio, letting go of him.

The two men walked on either side of Johann as they went deeper into the dense forest of fir trees and gnarled, scattered yews. It was much darker now, but Johann thought he could see better than before, as if the potion had sharpened his senses. A wolf howled somewhere very close to them, and Poitou gave a laugh.

"*Loup-garou,*" he said. "*Tout est prêt.*"

The men started talking in French again, while Johann staggered along like a drunkard. His throat was still on fire, but his legs felt strangely light. He seemed to walk faster and faster, almost flying. He listened to the sounds of the forest and made out dozens of different creatures: the howl of the wolf Poitou had called *loup-garou,* the hooves of a deer on a distant game path, the flapping of a small owl's wings—yes, even the whispering of mice in their little underground caves. The trees seemed to glow with a strange light, their outlines sharp against the black sky. Every branch, every twig seemed unnaturally clear.

"*C'est une bonne nuit pour le diable,*" Poitou was saying. "*La réunion va être une réussite.*"

"*Tais-toi,*" growled Tonio. "*Ne parle pas du diable.*"

Suddenly, something strange happened to Johann. The men were speaking French, and yet he thought he could understand them! Some words, at least, because they were very similar to Latin. Was this the knowledge the master had promised him? Did the potion allow him to understand any tongue in the world, even the oldest? Words flashed through his brain like lightning bolts. *Loup-garou, garache, bête bigourne, Belial, Beelzebub, Satan, Baphomet, béliche, le diable . . .* Johann winced.

Le diable . . .

The beast had many names.

His heart skipped a beat when the realization sank in. The men were speaking of the devil. They were talking about a meeting with the devil, here in the forest. In an instant he saw everything very clearly. The potion allowed him to think faster, and now various memories came together like the pieces of a mosaic. The handshake with Tonio outside the Lion Inn, followed by the death of Margarethe's brother, Ludwig; the missing children in Knittlingen as well as near the old tower; the drawing of the horned creature on the rock; Martin, and Margarethe's screams in Schillingswald Forest that day. It must have been Tonio she'd seen! And it had also been the master she had spoken about in her fever. She hadn't cursed Johann, but Tonio.

Tonio del Moravia. Keeper of the seven times seven seals.

Go away. You are the devil.

Johann's legs, so nimble just a moment ago, suddenly gave way. He tripped on a root and fell, but Tonio caught him as easily as if he were nothing but a leaf in the wind.

"The potion is working," said Tonio. "That's good, very good. Soon the pact will be sealed."

Johann tried to speak, but it felt as if a fat frog were sitting in his mouth. His eyes seemed sticky with a gooey black mass, and his whole body suddenly went numb. His soul tried to flee, but there was no escape, no way out. A wolf howled once more, someone screamed, and a low, dull groan like from a large animal came from somewhere nearby.

"We're nearly there," whispered Tonio.

As Johann's soul frantically searched for a way out—for some kind of escape—Johann heard a familiar sound in the distance, like from another world. He heard beautiful, sparkling laughter ringing out as clear as a bell. For a brief moment, it drowned out all the howling, screaming, and groaning.

It was Margarethe's laughter.

Johann's mouth twitched and saliva ran down his chin while Tonio held him by the collar. Her laughter had always been what he loved most about her. He used to think it wonderfully naive and simple—completely innocent. But in retrospect he felt Margarethe had always laughed at his longing for knowledge, his serious determination, and his need to be someone, to mean something. She had laughed at him like a child who doesn't care about yesterday or tomorrow but only lives in the here and now.

Margarethe was laughing at the devil.

Johann straightened up and shook off Tonio's hand. His tongue still felt heavy.

"Can . . . walk . . . myself . . . ," he managed eventually.

"*Chapeau!*" Poitou gave a cackling laugh. "The boy is tougher than I thought."

Johann walked straight ahead for a few steps, then he veered sharply to the right and ran into the forest. His legs were as soft as molten wax, and he staggered and stumbled, but he didn't fall.

"Stop, little Faustus!" shouted Tonio. "Where are you going? There's only the one road now. The pact is almost sealed."

Johann knew he'd never get away from the master and Poitou. They'd catch him and finish whatever it was they were doing with him. Still he ran on, until he saw the outline of a large boulder in front of him. Johann's eyesight was still blurred, and the rock seemed to grow and shrink at the same time. He staggered around the boulder and dropped to his knees.

Then he stuck a finger down his throat and vomited.

Stinking black bile dripped onto the ground and disappeared among the pebbles and rotting leaves. He scrambled to his feet and stepped out from behind the boulder, where Poitou spotted him immediately.

"I've got him, milord!" he called out, breathing heavily. "He's here. He didn't get far."

"Then bring him to me, God damn it!" shouted Tonio. "Let's get it over and done with."

Now that the potion was no longer in his body, Johann felt a little better. But the drug had already begun to take effect. Everything seemed like a dream. Poitou lifted him up like a bundle of kindling and carried him through the forest. The screaming and moaning grew louder, and Johann made out a faint glow beneath the trees ahead. Soon they reached a clearing with a large bonfire in its center. Ancient, dead oak trees stood in a ring around the opening, their naked branches reaching for him like the fingers of a witch. Johann squinted. There was something hanging in the branches, something that squirmed and whimpered. A thick black liquid dripped to the ground like blood. But every time Johann tried to take a closer look, his eyes watered.

Someone leaned over Johann, and he could smell soil and sweat.

"He is yours, Meffraye," Tonio said, his voice sounding far away.

Hands pulled and tugged at Johann, undressing him. He didn't resist. He felt a mighty erection grow, and then everything felt moist and warm. A chorale of female voices began to sing around him as a voluminous creature he couldn't make out properly with his watery eyes lowered herself upon him.

"O Ostara, hear us," chanted the chorale. "O Belial, hear us!"

There was a smacking sound. The odor of soil was overwhelming now; Johann could smell fresh humus, grown and perished in the everlasting circle of life. Large, heavy breasts appeared in front of his face, and he reached for them, still feeling like he was in a dream. Someone groaned with pleasure, and he gave himself up to the rhythm, to the up and down, like waves in a sea of blood. The groans grew louder, eventually turning into cries, and Johann realized it was his own voice. He was crying out with pleasure and lust. He thought he could also hear Poitou and Tonio cry out and laugh in the distance. The cawing of the raven and the two crows sounded like the laughter of the insane.

The crimson waves grew higher and higher, and Johann sailed on their crests. More hands tugged at him, and suddenly everything around him was naked skin tasting of soil and blood. He grasped a handful of long, matted hair like that of an animal—black curls, and blonde, brown, and red. Countless naked arms, legs, full breasts, and soft buttocks rubbed against him. Tongues licked him everywhere, and he licked, too, tasting salt and also something fishy, like from the depths of the ocean. As the chorale rose and ebbed around him, Johann let himself flow in the wild whirlpool of bodies. Voices whispered in his ear, urged him on, cried and exulted and moaned, together pushing toward the imminent climax.

Then his semen spilled and the moaning stopped abruptly.

Johann fell into a deep black hole.

When he came to, he could see clearly again: the huge, dying fire, and surrounding it, wrapped in blankets, sleeping men and women, exhausted from their shared ritual. Above them, small, lifeless bodies hanging in the branches like burned-out lanterns. Everywhere around him was silence and death. The potion's effect had let up, and reality hit Johann like a bucket of cold water. He scrambled to his feet and ran—stark naked—into the woods. Twigs and thorns tore at his skin, and a cold wind whistled through the trees, but he felt none of it. He ran away like prey running for its life.

Suddenly, an angry scream rang out behind him, followed by the familiar, demanding voice.

The voice of the master.

"Come back, Faustus!" he yelled. "Come back! I command you!"

Ignoring the voice, Johann ran on.

"Stop! Don't do this to me! Don't do this to *you!*"

Something in his voice made Johann slow down. It sounded like he was begging him, pleading with him.

"Come back, Faustus! I can teach you so much more. The world could lie at your feet—at our feet. You have the power to set the world on fire! *Homo Deus est!* Faustus, I'm begging you."

Johann paused for a moment, but then he ran on. He leaped over bushes and fallen tree trunks, crossed streams and ditches, stumbling and falling but getting back up every time, pressing on without looking back. The voice behind him grew more and more plaintive and eventually began to scream furiously.

Johann was still running when the voice fell silent.

Tonio del Moravia, the magician, keeper of the seven times seven seals, had vanished from Johann's life.

Act III

The Train of Jugglers

8

THE EFFECT OF THE POTION DIDN'T FULLY WEAR OFF UNTIL daylight broke. Until then, Johann ran through the forest like a restless wolf, naked and filthy. Whenever his strength failed him and he needed to rest, he'd find a dip in the ground or a rotten, fungi-covered tree trunk to hide behind. But his fear of Tonio and the horror he was running away from was greater than his exhaustion.

Johann kept running as if the devil was after him.

Every now and then he thought he was being pursued by a flock of black shadows attacking him like bats. He screamed and lashed out at them even though he knew they weren't real. He could hear whispering voices; the roar of a great, angry animal; and the soft crying of children. The crying was the worst, because then he again saw the small, lifeless bodies hanging in the trees, and the blood dripping down from them.

Finally Johann's steps slowed. He staggered and then fell flat on his face. He managed to cover himself with twigs and rotting leaves before sleep overpowered him.

When he woke, the sun was high in the sky.

Johann blinked a few times, then shot up as if waking from a long bad dream. He was cold—colder than he'd ever been. His toes and fingers were blue, and his limbs ached, shivering so badly that he struggled to gain control of his movements. Only now did he notice that he still wore the knife around his neck. It was all he had left.

While he slowly rose from his bed among the leaves, images of the previous night returned. He had a pounding headache and struggled to tell the difference between real and imagined memories. He hadn't been able to think straight since Tonio and Poitou had given him the black potion. Father Antonius had told Johann about such drinks. They contained henbane, devil's trumpet, deadly nightshade, and other intoxicants that gave the user the impression of soaring high in the air or brought on hallucinations like lewd, buxom women.

Drink too much of it, though, and you'd go straight to hell.

Father Antonius once told Johann that older boys and girls from remote villages sometimes used those plants to cook up a brew that helped them escape the prisons of their drab lives for a short while. And witches concocted similar potions to mate with the devil. They smeared their broomsticks with the potions for the so-called witches' sabbath and soared up into the thunderclouds. Back then, those stories had seemed like old wives' tales to Johann.

But now he wasn't so sure.

If he wasn't mistaken, Tonio and Poitou had invoked some kind of evil creature in the clearing—perhaps even the devil himself. Evidently they were Satanists, followers of Lucifer who practiced horrific rituals. Had all the women who had kissed, licked, and mounted him really existed? And the large, soft creature that had lowered herself on him?

Had it been a witch? Or something much worse?

Johann looked down at himself. His private parts were sticky, and there were leaves all through his pubic hair. Then he thought of the bloody, whimpering bundles in the trees, and a wave of nausea overcame him.

He broke down and vomited, gasping. He had nothing left but green bile. Nonetheless, he felt a little better afterward. He looked around, his teeth chattering. If he didn't want to freeze to death, he needed to find clothes. Tall fir trees stood all around him, blocking out the sunlight almost completely. He had no idea where he was or what direction he ought to take. He decided to follow a narrow game path, so at least he didn't have to battle the thorny undergrowth.

Trembling and keeping low like a frightened deer, Johann made his way through the forest. He was still terrified of Tonio finding him. The master wasn't someone who gave up in a hurry. Johann started to notice dozens of small wounds on his body. At first he thought they were scratches from running through the trees, but when he looked more closely, he saw that the marks seemed to have been made by long fingernails. Some of the cuts formed symbols he couldn't read.

What in God's name happened last night?

A terrible suspicion sprouted in his mind. What if Tonio hadn't invoked the devil, but if instead . . . The thought was so awful that Johann didn't even want to think it through.

What if Tonio is the devil himself?

Johann remembered that he'd heard Margarethe's laughter through his delirium. Margarethe had saved him—she had opened his eyes. If he hadn't thrown up the potion in the last moment, he'd never have been able to run away from Tonio. Perhaps he'd be hanging in the branches of a dead oak by now, gutted like those poor little creatures; Johann still didn't know whether they had been real or a figment of his imagination.

Johann hoped—prayed—that he'd only imagined them. But then he remembered all the missing children. He thought of Martin, his little brother.

Small, whimpering bundles . . .

He forced the thought aside and banished it to a deep, dark place.

After another hour of aimless wandering, he spotted a column of smoke rising up above the firs about an arrow's shot away. Cautiously, he headed toward it and soon reached the edge of a clearing with a solid two-story log cabin. The clearing was covered in charred tree stumps, and the ground in between them had also been burned. A little way off, a charcoal pile smoldered steadily, filling the air with biting smoke.

Ducking behind a dew-covered blackberry bush, Johann watched the clearing for a while for any signs of life. He could hear the blows of an axe in the distance and guessed that the charcoal burner was out chopping wood somewhere in the forest. The relatively large house suggested he had a family.

Johann sneaked over to the house as quietly as he could. It was built of hefty logs, and the windows were as small as arrow slits. The door stood ajar. Johann nudged it open carefully and found a tidy room within. It was warm inside, and a large bowl of barley porridge stood in the middle of the table—probably breakfast leftovers. Johann devoured it like a famished wolf. Using both hands, he shoveled the sticky mass out of the bowl and into his mouth. When he had cleaned out the bowl, he licked his fingers. He stopped short when he heard creaking footsteps on the boards above him.

There was someone upstairs. He didn't have much time.

He frantically looked around and spotted a chest next to the stove. His heart leaped with joy when he opened the lid. Inside the chest were clay bowls, wooden spoons, a tarnished copper candlestick holder, and—most importantly—clean linen shirts and leggings, like farmers wore in the fields. There was even a pair of wooden clogs. Johann quickly gathered up an armful of the clothes. He was about to run outside when he spotted a bowl of milk in the corner that someone must have left for the cat. He was still so hungry that he knelt down, held the bowl to his lips, and slurped up the milk like an animal.

In that very moment, the door to the next room opened and an older woman wearing an apron and a bonnet gaped at him. There were more people in the house than he'd thought. The woman turned pale and then pointed at the kneeling, naked Johann with a trembling finger, screaming loudly.

"A wolf-man!" she screamed. "God help us! There's a wolf-man in our house!"

Johann dropped the bowl and it shattered on the floor. Holding on tightly to the clothes and the shoes, he ran out of the house while behind him the woman continued to shriek, calling upon all fourteen holy helpers to save them. Much to Johann's horror, the charcoal burner emerged from the forest. His bearded face was black with soot, making his eyes gleam very white. He was holding his axe like a weapon and came running toward Johann between the charred stumps.

"Stop, whatever you are! Stop, beast!" shouted the man.

Swinging his axe, the man cut across the clearing and blocked Johann's way. Johann managed to dodge the axe at the last moment, hearing it whooshing past his ear. He staggered and almost fell but caught himself and rushed toward the forest edge. He could hear the charcoal burner closing in on him.

"Martha, get the workers!" the man shouted. "We must catch the beast. I won't let it get away! Hans, this way!"

From the corner of his eye, Johann saw a younger man with an axe run toward him from the right. The strong-looking lad was about to cut off his escape route. Johann desperately hurled himself shoulder-first at the worker. There was a loud crack, and a sharp pain shot down Johann's arm. The young man cried out and fell to the ground. Johann still clung to the bundle of clothes as if it were a treasure. He got back on his feet and ran into the forest. Soon the fir trees swallowed him up.

"Go back to the hell you came from, you demon!" yelled the charcoal burner. "May God strike you down with a bolt of lightning!"

The shouting gradually eased and eventually stopped altogether, but Johann kept running until he came to a narrow track. After a little while, the trees opened up and Johann saw a larger road that led out of the forest and through fallow black fields.

Johann washed himself as well as he could in a ditch by the wayside before putting on the shirt, leggings, and wooden shoes. Then he stepped out into the road. The sun was high in the sky—Johann guessed it was around noon. He was gasping with exhaustion, and he was shivering—not just with a chill that seemed reluctant to leave his body, but also because he was terrified that the charcoal burner and his workers might appear from behind the next bend. His shoulder hurt like hell. He was too weak to run now, let alone defend himself. But at least he looked like a human again.

Which way should he turn? He had nothing left but the clothes he was wearing, and even those were stolen.

Quo vadis, Faustus?

The choice was made easier when a squeaking horse-drawn cart appeared from the right. At first Johann thought it was the master's wagon, and he was about to jump into the ditch, but then he saw it was just a cart driven by a portly old man—a wealthy farmer or a merchant, he guessed. The man was wearing a fur vest and a warm, woolen coat that was clasped together at the front with a silver pin. Upon seeing the shivering boy in the thin shirt that was much too big for him, and whose face was covered with nasty scratches, the man gave him a look of pity.

"Where are you headed, lad?" he asked, pulling a stalk of straw from between his few remaining teeth. "You don't look like you'll get very far."

Johann hesitated. Then he named the first city that came to his mind. It was the city he would have liked to visit a few days ago, but Tonio had steered clear of it—another reason that it seemed like a good choice. Hopefully, he'd be safe from Tonio and Poitou there. There was a good chance they were still searching for him.

"Augsburg," he said.

The old man grinned. "You're in luck, boy. That's just where I'm taking my wine." He gestured at the load of barrels behind himself. "Jump on up. But don't you dare sample my wine—or I'll drown you in it like a rat!"

And so Johann went to Augsburg—the biggest, loudest, and wealthiest city he'd ever seen.

They had reached the imperial city in two days, arriving around noon.

Like the last time, Johann couldn't get enough of gazing at the countless rooftops and towers rising up behind the battlements of the city wall. Tallest of all was the grand cathedral tower. By comparison, Knittlingen's Saint Leonhard's Church looked like a dirty stable.

"Close your mouth before the flies crawl in, sleepyhead," said the old man with a laugh. "This is golden Augsburg—the wealthiest city in the world. That's what the late, great Pope Pius II called it, and, as God is my witness, it has only grown wealthier since."

The corpulent old man turned out to be a stroke of luck for Johann. He was a wine merchant from Würzburg whose only grandson had been taken by fever a few months prior. Apparently, Johann reminded the man of his beloved boy, who'd died far too young. Therefore, the merchant had bought Johann a bowlful of steaming stew on both nights of their journey, helping to dispel the cold from Johann's limbs. The rest of the time, Johann had slept between the barrels on the wagon like a log. His shoulder still hurt, and the many scratches on his skin were still healing, but he felt strong enough to continue his journey on his own now.

Only where this journey was supposed to lead, Johann didn't know.

He had decided not to think about that terrible night near Nördlingen. God only knew what sort of heathen ritual Tonio and Poitou had been trying to achieve there. Ancient ceremonies that used to serve some nameless god and that the church hadn't entirely managed to exterminate. Tonio called himself a magician, so what did Johann expect? The whole thing had been nothing but cheap hocus-pocus, just like the pentagrams, the black potion, and all the rest. Something unspeakably evil had happened that night. No magic tricks, nothing that had actually invoked the devil—and yet it had been something devilish for which Tonio would someday burn in the deepest depths of hell.

There was a great hustle and bustle outside the gates of Augsburg. Johann and the merchant circled around the city and eventually entered it through the Red Gate, a massive fortification on the Via Claudia Augusta, which led south toward the Alps. The wine merchant had told Johann that Augsburg had been founded by a Roman emperor—and not just any emperor, but the famous

Emperor Augustus, who had lived at the time of the savior. Johann reverently gazed at the worn cobblestones in the streets, imagining Roman soldiers marching across them long ago.

From the Red Gate they came to a busy avenue that was so wide that there were even houses in its center. The street, which led all the way to the cathedral, was lined with huge patrician palaces several stories high and adorned with colorful frescoes. The two men passed wealthy patricians wearing velvet tunics and fur-lined coats, women clad in colorful scarves and the finest fustian, and one man who wore a cap laced with gold thread instead of a hat.

The wine merchant winked at Johann. "Did you see that vain peacock? That was young Jakob Fugger. They say his family will soon be the most powerful family of Augsburg. Since Maximilian is the new king, Fugger has been doing business with him and lending him money. Ha, to think that Jakob's grandfather started life as a simple weaver from the country! That's what it's like nowadays—nothing is certain anymore, and anyone can become someone." He gestured toward an ostentatious building in the middle of the street. "All the high-class ladies and gentlemen—the Fuggers, the Welsers, the Gossembrots, and the Rehlingers—are meeting for the *Geschlechtertanz* here tonight—a fancy dance. Apparently, the youngest Rehlinger girl is getting hitched. It'll be a big night of politics. And that always goes best when the throat is well oiled." He gave a merry laugh. "And that's where I come in. Five barrels of the finest Franconian wine! There's none better far and wide, believe me."

They drove a little farther and reached a long square surrounded by barns and more patrician houses. A huge crowd of people pushed past market stalls and makeshift tables. Behind the stalls and tables, dozens of barrels of every size stood stacked in piles, chalk marks designating each barrel's origin and owner. Merchants walked up and down in front of their stalls, hawking their wares and handing out small jugs for sampling. The cobblestones were red and slippery with spilled wine.

The stench reminded Johann of the Trottenkelter press at Knittlingen, and the image of Ludwig's brutally disfigured body appeared in his mind's eye. He chased away the thought as quickly as he could. Knittlingen, Margarethe, Ludwig, Martin, Tonio—all of that was in the past. The future lay in front of him, even if he didn't yet know where it led.

"Looks like the wine market opened earlier than usual today," the old man growled, looking around anxiously. "Fingers crossed that we aren't too late. Hey, Albertus, old friend! Here I am!"

He jumped down from the box seat and was soon deep in conversation with a grumpy-looking bald-headed man. It wasn't long before a heavy purse changed owners. The wine merchant returned to Johann with a wide grin.

"Albertus has been awaiting me desperately. He supplies the dance hall. Apparently, the Rhenish wine is so sour this year that they have to sweeten it with honey. Two of the barrels he was sold can only be used as vinegar. Albertus thanked God and all the saints when I told him I had five barrels of good wine left—at a price, of course." He opened the purse and tossed Johann a coin. "Here, for you. You brought me luck. And now off with you before I get too softhearted." He frowned. "The devil knows what you've been through. You screamed in your sleep last night as if all seven hounds of hell were after you. I wish you good luck for wherever you're going next."

He gave Johann one last pat on the shoulder, and then he turned away to help the other man unload the barrels.

"Thank you," Johann called after him. "And God bless you!" But the old man seemed not to hear him.

Clutching the coin tightly in his hand, Johann drifted with the crowd until he'd left the wine market behind. Another square with stalls followed—the fish market, judging by the smell, and some of the wares didn't seem to be the freshest. A tall tower rose up behind the fish market, and Johann headed toward it. He walked around the tower and found a mangy bear locked up behind an iron grate. The beast was lying in a corner, looking tired, its dull fur matted with scabs and dried blood. Every now and then children would prod it with a stick until the bear growled and swiped at them angrily before lying back down. The once-proud animal reminded Johann of himself. Tired, hurt, no way out . . .

Thoughtfully, he studied the coin in his hand. It was an old Augsburg penny, so smooth from handling that the image of Emperor Friedrich was barely recognizable. Well, the coin would buy him a warm supper and one night at a flea-infested inn—and then what?

Dejected, he moved on. He felt even more pathetic amid all the splendor of this wealthy place. Perhaps it hadn't been such a good idea to come to Augsburg, the golden city, after all. What was he doing here, surrounded by rich, confidence-oozing burghers? He reached another square and thought the huge building at its far end must be the city hall; it wasn't far from the cathedral. A crowd had formed outside the building. At first Johann thought it was another type of market, but then he heard a loud, cheerful voice and stopped.

"Not three, not four, no, *five* balls are going to be juggled by our very own Emilio! Only the most talented jugglers can accomplish this feat. Watch and be amazed!"

Johann smiled. He thought about the time he and Tonio traveled from village to village as jugglers. It seemed like an eternity ago, though only a few months had passed since then. He made his way through the spectators and soon caught sight of two wagons with colorful canvases. Between them, blue and red ribbons roped off an area where a juggler was throwing leather balls into the air, accompanied by a man on the fiddle. Both wore the typical colorful garb of a juggler: yellow and red for one, the other one clad in green and blue.

The juggler—Emilio, evidently—didn't look much older than Johann, while the fiddle player was probably past thirty. He had fiery red hair and a raw face with a huge beak of a nose. He played faster and faster while the boy threw the balls higher and higher. Small bells attached to the juggler's clothes jingled to the beat of the music. His curly brown hair and his handsome, dark face suggested he came from southern lands.

"And now, it is my pleasure to introduce to you the beautiful Princess Salome from the Orient! Once upon a time she turned the head of John the Baptist," announced the fiddler loudly. "Watch and be amazed! But beware, dear husbands—it's going to be hard to remain faithful to your wives at the sight of the princess."

A young woman emerged from behind one of the wagons, and a murmur went through the crowd. Her jet-black hair reached down to her hips. Her skin was dark—almost as dark as a Moor's. A fire burned in her eyes, and her mouth was hidden behind a veil. She was dressed in colorful silk scarves that she twirled all around herself as the fiddler played an exotic-sounding tune. She moved her hips suggestively as she danced, causing some of the spectators to sigh out loud.

A hulk of a man who was just as dark skinned appeared behind her. He wore tight leggings, and nothing but a leather vest covered his chest, revealing his bulging muscles. He stared straight ahead with dark eyes, his strong arms crossed in front of him. The giant's head was as bald as an egg.

"Mustafa the Strong, an Ottoman eunuch, is always at Salome's side, watching over her," the fiddler declared. "Beware of him! He can rip out entire trees with his arms and bend iron rods. He will demonstrate his skills shortly. But now, behold the Princess Salome!"

On cue, the foreign-looking girl pulled from under her dress several wooden skittles painted gold. She began throwing them to Emilio, one after the other. For each skittle, Emilio threw one ball to her. The woman continued to dance while she managed to keep the balls and skittles in the air like pearls on a string. The crowd exploded in raucous applause. The male spectators couldn't stop gaping. With her low-cut outfit and wide hips, Salome did indeed look like a princess from the Far East. Her flowing black hair was stunning. Women never wore their hair down in public—only dancers and other dishonorable folk went out without a bonnet. Salome, however, wore her hair as proudly as precious jewelry.

The fiddler played one last quick run that ended on a high-pitched, mournful note—and suddenly the balls disappeared, swallowed up by Salome's flowing garments. The juggler caught the skittles, and together they bowed to the fierce applause of the people of Augsburg.

Johann grinned. The show wasn't bad, even if he'd seen better in Knittlingen. Some jugglers performed their tricks with closed eyes or while balancing on a rope; others ate fire or swallowed entire swords. But this girl was as beautiful as the dawn, and the red-haired fiddler played like the devil. Together with the rest of the audience, Johann felt transported to a different, faraway country.

The fiddle player, who appeared to be the leader of the troupe, raised his hands and asked for silence. "We've arrived at our next highlight!" he shouted. "From the hot plains of Jerusalem, we've been joined by a man whose reputation precedes him like the roar of a lion. He once lived as a hermit in the desert and is so wise that sultans and emperors sought his advice. Bow your heads to the widely traveled Magister Archibaldus!"

The cloth covering the door to one of the wagons was pushed aside, and out came a skinny old man with wild gray hair. His almost-white beard reached to his navel. He was wearing a slightly threadbare red frock and held a plain wooden staff, which he used to help him climb down the few steps from the wagon. He tried his best to appear dignified, but he clearly struggled to stay on his feet, swaying from side to side. Countless tiny veins crisscrossed his beefy nose.

"Magister Archibaldus has been fasting for nearly fifty years and consumes nothing but water," the fiddler explained.

"And wine!" shouted one of the spectators, and the people around him laughed.

The red-haired man put on a stern look. "Don't mock him. The venerable master is privy to the secret of the philosopher's stone—do you want to see it or continue to crack jokes?"

The crowd cheered and clapped. Meanwhile, Archibaldus had walked to the middle of the arena, where the strong Mustafa had prepared a copper bowl that looked like a large mortar. The beautiful Salome and Emilio the juggler appeared with flasks and jars.

"Hear, worthy people of Augsburg! I succeeded where Albertus Magnus and Avicenna failed," said Archibaldus with a rasping voice, raising his staff into the air like a monstrance. "I studied the forbidden art of alchemy for many years, and now finally I have found the philosopher's stone. A tincture that has the power to turn any kind of material into gold. Even"—he paused for effect—"even this plain wooden staff from a yew tree."

The audience murmured appreciatively, and Archibaldus turned to Salome.

"Well, then, my beautiful assistant, prepare the magical tincture." He struggled to suppress a hiccup. Then he pointed at the various flasks, one after another, as Salome poured a few drops of each into the bowl.

"The blood of a unicorn," Archibaldus counted. "The tears of a person in love, three ounces of liquid lead, the juice of a whole orange picked in the garden of Eden—"

"No wine—because he drank it all up!" shouted the same joker as before, but the audience ignored him this time. Spellbound, they stared at the bowl while Archibaldus continued with a heavy tongue.

"Dragon saliva from distant India, as well as ground pepper, nutmeg, and cloves—but only a pinch of each!"

With the tips of her fingers, Salome sprinkled a little powder into the bowl before stepping aside with a bow. Then Archibaldus dipped his staff into the bowl, and blue smoke began rising out of it, enshrouding the alchemist like a saint. For a few moments, he was barely visible.

"By the seven times seven magical formulas of Hermes," the old man muttered while moving his stick around in the smoke. "Dust to dust, ashes to ashes, and . . . wood to gold!"

He stepped out of the smoke and held up his staff. A murmur of amazement went through the crowd.

The tip of the staff gleamed golden.

"It is done!" declared Archibaldus, bowing low and staggering a little. The crowd cheered, and a few people tried to grab the stick, but Mustafa the Strong took one step forward and they stopped.

"Magister Archibaldus must rest now," the redhead said loudly, casting a stern look at the old man. "Following the show, you are invited to his wagon to gaze upon some relics the wise man has brought with him from the East. Among others, hay from the crib at Bethlehem and a feather from the wings of Gabriel the archangel. Only one kreuzer per visit." He gave a wide grin. "And for those of you who think they can't afford it, come and win yourself some money. It's child's play!" He snapped his fingers and Mustafa brought a table, which looked like a wooden toy in his big hands. When the fiddler produced three nutshells from his pocket and placed them on the table, Johann knew immediately what was happening.

"Believe me, it has never been easier to make a quick buck," the red-haired man said. "All you need is a fast pair of eyes and your wits." He held up a pea. "I'm going to hide this pea under one of the shells now, and then I'll move the shells around. If you can point to the shell that the pea is hiding under, you get back double the money you put in. Who wants to give it a shot?"

A few curious onlookers came and tried their luck. The first two put in one kreuzer each and guessed correctly. The fiddler handed them their winnings, seeming disgruntled. The participants became braver and put in more money, but increasingly, the fiddler won.

Johann grinned. He'd practiced this trick so many times that he could do it with his eyes closed. The knack was in managing to make the pea disappear in one's hand while lifting one nutshell and transferring it to another without anyone noticing. Every second or third customer needed to win so the audience wouldn't grow suspicious. Occasionally jugglers even paid people to pretend they'd happened to pass by and wanted to play.

Suddenly Johann knew how he could make a little money.

He waited until it grew quieter around the table. Then he approached the fiddler, holding up his coin shyly. The man smiled.

"Ah, someone wants to try his luck. Well, then, my boy." Slowly, he moved the shells from side to side. "Place your coin where you think the pea is hiding."

Johann guessed right, which didn't surprise him. The man wanted him to feel safe.

"Now you have two pennies," said the fiddler with a sigh. "And I have none. Do you want to try again?"

Johann nodded eagerly and the musician started moving the shells around again. This time Johann saw how the man hid the pea in the palm of his hand and then placed it beneath another shell. He was good at it, but not good enough. Without hesitating, Johann placed his coins in front of the right shell, and the fiddler's smile froze.

"Right again. Well done." The redhead waved to Salome. "Be so kind and fetch two more pennies from our savings. A promise is a promise." He gave Johann a challenging look. "Another round?"

"Why not? What do I have to lose?" Johann grinned and placed four coins on the table. "I only started with one penny."

This time the man moved the shells so fast that Johann's eyes could barely follow. But Johann picked the right shell again. The small crowd of onlookers laughed as the fiddler pushed eight pennies across the table with a doleful expression.

"You're good," he hissed from between clenched teeth, watching Johann closely. "You know the game, don't you?"

"I want to play again," Johann said, ignoring the man's comment and dropping his coins onto the table with a jingle. "For all or nothing."

"I think we've had enough for one day," the fiddler said. "Folks still want to see the relics, after all, and Magister Archibaldus—"

"If the boy wants to play, he should play," said a broad-shouldered laborer standing next to Johann. "A promise is a promise. You said so yourself."

Others in the crowd joined in, and the fiddler waved dismissively. "All right, why not? Every winning streak must come to an end."

The shells flew across the table at a speed that made the spectators gasp with amazement. Johann saw that the fiddler kept the pea in his hand.

"Which shell?" asked the man harshly.

Johann shook his head. "I can't say."

The fiddler grinned and reached for the coins. "Ha, you can't say, which means—"

"I can't say because the pea isn't under any of the shells."

"What are you saying?" The man pretended to be outraged. "Just look for yourself, numbskull."

Before the man could touch one of the shells, Johann quickly turned over all three.

The pea wasn't under any of them. A cry of outrage went through the crowd.

"Um, the pea must have rolled off the table," the fiddler said vaguely and leaned down. "It must be here somewhere . . ."

"Cheat!" shouted the man next to Johann. Other spectators joined in. "Cheat! Dishonorable fraudsters! Hang them!"

The table with the nutshells was pushed over, and the first few stones were thrown. The fiddler, Salome, and Emilio the juggler took cover behind a wagon while Mustafa struck one of the assailants. From the corner of his eye, Johann saw several Augsburg city guards run over from the city hall. He bent down and quickly gathered up any coins he could find, and then he strolled off at a leisurely pace. The guards rushed past him with raised halberds. No one cared about the boy in simple peasant clothes.

As Johann walked past the city hall, he could hear cries of pain and the sound of splintering wood behind him. Someone blew a horn. He left the main street and turned onto a smaller lane, and the noise ebbed off.

He counted his winnings with trembling fingers. He'd managed to pick up nine Augsburg pennies—not a bad day's work, even though he felt sorry for the jugglers. The red-haired fiddler had done nothing Johann himself hadn't been doing a few months ago. Johann hoped the outraged people of Augsburg wouldn't hurt the jugglers too badly and the guards wouldn't lock them up.

With the coins in his hand, he prowled through the narrow lanes, wondering how much wine and roast chicken one could buy for a fistful of pennies in the wealthiest city on earth.

A few hours later, Johann came staggering out of a tavern in the hope of sobering up a little in the fresh air. He soon realized that wasn't going to happen quickly.

To celebrate his winnings, he had decided on one of the better taverns near the cathedral. He struggled to remember what had happened after. At first the tavern keeper didn't want to serve the gaunt young boy who clearly came from the country. But when Johann showed him his silver pennies, the man suddenly turned friendly and brought him roast venison with cranberry sauce, white bread baked from the finest flour, and a heavy deep-red wine that, according to the keeper, came from France. Wherever it came from, it was damned strong and just as expensive.

After the third jug of wine and a dessert made from egg yolk and honey, Johann was five pennies poorer. He gave two more to a busty, almost-toothless prostitute who disappeared quickly. In a generous mood fueled by alcohol, he gave the eighth penny to a homeless musician who was hanging around outside the tavern. Johann vaguely remembered that he'd performed card tricks at the tavern—hadn't that tattered beggar played some music to his tricks on his old lute? Whatever the case, now his money was almost all gone, and all he had left was the one coin the wine merchant had given him.

Only just won, already gone, Johann thought in his drunken stupor.

He weaved along the dark lane without knowing where he was headed. He needed a cheap place to stay for the night, but one penny wouldn't get him far in a city like Augsburg. Or should he just sleep out of doors? Chances were some scoundrel would slit his throat while he was asleep. Strangely, Johann wasn't frightened by the thought. What reason was there for him to still be in this world? Everyone he'd ever loved was gone. Mother, Margarethe, his little brother. And his teacher, who had shown him the workings of the world, had turned out to be a profoundly evil man and a heretic. He thought about what Tonio had said to Poitou about him at the Golden Sun Inn.

If we go about this the right way, he will change the world . . .

What a joke! He must have heard wrong. He was a nothing, a nobody.

Grief and self-pity overwhelmed Johann. Tears streamed down his face, and he wanted to die. He felt awfully sick from all the wine and the sweet dessert. He braced himself against the wall of a house and took a deep breath, when suddenly someone slipped a sack over his head from behind.

"Hrmh—" was all he managed before everything turned black.

The attack had come as a complete surprise—he hadn't heard anyone approach. Johann thrashed about widely, but the sack only grew tighter. A rope closed in around his neck, and Johann thought he was being throttled, but then someone lifted him up like a piece of furniture and tossed him over their shoulder. Johann cussed and screamed, and his abductor knocked Johann's head against the wall so hard he thought his skull was going to burst.

Someone growled angrily, like a bear. Johann gathered it was a warning and kept quiet. He tried to figure out what the fellow wanted from him. Was he going to throw him into one of the canals running through the city and leave him to drown? But if he wanted to kill Johann, that would be unnecessary. The man carrying him was strong enough to squash him like a bug.

Johann was bounced through Augsburg like a sack of flour on the man's shoulder. He smelled dust and musty grain but couldn't see a thing. Finally the man's steps slowed. His mysterious abductor lifted him up and threw him onto the hard ground. Johann gasped with pain when he landed on his sore shoulder.

"Open the sack, Mustafa," said a voice he'd heard before.

Johann heard a ripping sound, and then he was blinded by the light of the moon. He blinked repeatedly and waited for his eyes to adjust. It seemed he was lying in a dirty back alley amid piles of foul-smelling garbage. Two wagons he'd seen before stood nearby. Their canvases were torn, the front wheel of one of the wagons was broken, the box seats were damaged, and one of the shafts was shattered.

And standing in front of Johann was the redheaded fiddler.

He wore a dirty bandage around his head, and his right eye was swollen shut. He studied Johann with pinched lips, as Johann, trembling with fear and cold, looked about himself. The muscular body of Mustafa towered behind him, and Salome and Emilio emerged from the shadows of the yard.

"So we meet again," snarled the fiddler, still wearing his yellow-and-red costume. He spoke with a slight lisp, and Johann saw in the pale light that he was missing a tooth. "Soon you'll realize that it was a mistake to mess with Peter Nachtigall. No one makes a fool out of me—no one! Understood?"

"*Madonna*, calm down, Peter," said Emilio in a foreign-sounding southern accent. The little bells on his costume gave a jingle. "No one is helped if you skin the boy alive, eat him up, and spit out his bones. We need him to give us back our money and pay his debts."

"Debts?" said Johann hoarsely, feeling stone-cold sober now. He rubbed his throbbing forehead and slowly got to his feet. "What . . . what debts?"

"Are you kidding me?" shouted Peter. "You . . . you . . ." He lowered his voice. "Our wagons have been trashed—not to mention my face. We can consider ourselves lucky that the guards didn't lock us up and we're allowed to stay in this stinking yard for the night. We must leave Augsburg in the morning because we've been banned from performing here. And all that just because one little good-for-nothing thought he'd pull one over on us!"

"That's not quite right," Johann said quietly. "You were trying to pull one over on me."

"You dirty little smart-ass . . ." Peter Nachtigall raised one hand, ready to strike, but stopped short when Salome laughed out loud behind him. Her voice sounded husky and quite low for her delicate stature.

"He's right, Peter. I told you in Würzburg that the shell game is too dangerous. People see through it—though usually not as quickly as this clever boy." She eyed Johann closely and not without sympathy. He guessed she was about ten years older than him, although it was hard to tell. "I wouldn't be surprised if you turned out to be a juggler yourself. Are you?"

Johann hesitated briefly, then nodded.

"Ha! So you were sent to have us chased out of town," Peter growled. "Who do you work for? Steffen Lautenschläger? Or Karl Froschmaul and his gang? Speak up before I cut out your tongue!"

"For . . . for no one," Johann replied. "I'm on my own. I traveled with an astrologer for a while, but we . . . we went our separate ways."

"With an astrologer?" Salome gave him a wink. "I hope he wasn't an old drunkard like our venerable Magister Archibaldus. I swear, if *you* hadn't blown up our show today, he would have ruined the next. He drinks like a fish and then passes out." She gestured behind herself. "Hear him snore?"

Indeed, Johann heard a wheezy rattling from one of the wagons, followed by a loud fart and more snoring.

"We should cut the old boozer loose, damn it," grumbled Emilio. "His gold trick is ridiculous, and if we're not careful, he'll fall into his own bowl sooner or later."

"You know very well why he's with us," Peter said. "So shut up." He turned to Johann with a challenging look. "Now back to you, boy. Give me back my coins!"

"I . . . I don't have them anymore," Johann replied sheepishly. "I spent all but one at a tavern."

"At the White Lamb, we know." Salome nodded. "You acted like a little lord and splurged on a night out. But your card tricks weren't too bad, apparently."

Johann's jaw dropped. "How do you . . . ?"

"*Maledetto*, we've been looking for you since this afternoon," Emilio exclaimed. "When one of the Augsburg harlots told us there was a young man in peasant's clothes with too much money at the White Lamb, we sent Mustafa."

The giant nodded and cracked his knuckles.

"Search him!" commanded Peter.

Mustafa grabbed Johann, shook him like a wet coat, and patted down his pockets. He pulled out the last coin and handed it to Peter Nachtigall.

"Damn, he wasn't lying," Peter said and tossed the penny onto the dirty ground. "And how are we supposed to fix the wagon now?"

"One of the wagons still goes," said Salome soothingly and picked up the coin. "We can sell the broken one and the old horse and still have enough room for all our gear. The old nag would never have made it across the Alps anyway."

Johann's heart started beating faster. "Across the Alps, did you say? Where are you going?"

"Where do you think?" Emilio gave a shrug. "To the warm lands beyond the mountains. That's where I come from, and I speak the language. Jugglers are always welcome in the cities of Lombardy. Everything is much brighter and friendlier over there, and the people are so wealthy that there's always enough for the likes of us. And we'll have winter quarters in Venice that Archibaldus—"

"That's enough!" barked Peter. "I'm still not convinced that this guy isn't a spy for another troupe. So you better shut it." He pointed at Johann. "And you better run along now, before I tell Mustafa to beat you to a pulp."

"I . . . I could come with you," Johann blurted suddenly. The words had simply slipped out. Ever since he could remember, he'd dreamed of seeing Venice. He had almost traveled across the Alps with Tonio; perhaps this was his last chance.

"Come with us?" Peter raised his eyebrows, then he gave a laugh. "And why should we take a weed like you to Italy with us?"

"I . . . I could pay back what I owe you."

"And how are you going to do that?"

"Jesus, Peter, don't act more stupid than you are," said Salome. "He's a juggler, remember? Clearly, he's one of those little tricksters like Lukas used to be." She gave Johann an encouraging smile. "What can you do, boy?"

Johann swallowed hard. His head felt like thick honey, and his right shoulder ached. Whenever he looked up, he felt dizzy. And yet he knew this was his only chance.

"Does anyone have an egg and a hat?" he asked.

He performed his trick with the egg and the blanket, a few coin and card tricks, the seven Dalmatian knots, the broken stick, and the snake of Giza, whereby a length of rope was brought to life. He briefly considered juggling but decided against it. The troupe already had a juggler; what they needed was a magician, and a good one—who could do more than card tricks.

When Johann was finished, he bowed and awaited their judgment. Cold sweat was running down his forehead, and he thought he might faint.

The jugglers were sitting in a half circle in front of him, eyeing him thoughtfully.

"Not bad," said Peter Nachtigall grumpily. "Almost as good as Lukas—but only almost."

"I think he's better," said Salome, gazing at Johann with a look he couldn't read. "He's charming, and, well . . . not too bad looking. And he can talk. People will like him—the girls, especially."

"The trick with the egg is good," said Emilio. "I've never seen it before. And we can work with the coin tricks. I think he might be a good addition."

"You're not serious about taking him along, are you?" groused Peter. He pointed at his missing tooth. "I've got him to thank for this! And one of our wagons is wrecked!"

"Come on, we've had blowups before," said Salome. "If he hadn't called you out on the shell game, someone else would have." She ran her fingers through her long black hair. "He'll pay back his debt. Coin for coin. Isn't that right?"

Johann nodded, and Salome turned to Mustafa, who hadn't said a word the whole time. "What do you think?"

Mustafa gave Johann a long look. Then he made a few strange signs with his hands.

"What's he saying?" asked Peter.

"He's saying there's some dark secret surrounding the boy," Salome replied. "But he doesn't think he's a spy for another troupe." She gave a grin. "And Mustafa likes the trick with the egg, too."

Peter Nachtigall sighed and raised both hands as if surrendering. "All right. We'll give him a chance." He looked sharply at Johann. "But I promise you one thing, boy: I'm keeping an eye on you. And I'll find out about your dark secret."

9

THEY LEFT AUGSBURG THE FOLLOWING MORNING, USING
the same gate through which Johann had entered the city the day before. He
turned to cast one last glance at the famous golden city with its towers, patrician
palaces, and mighty cathedral. But he no longer felt awe. After just one night,
Johann's enthusiasm had given way to the conviction that there was as much
poverty and misery in the empire's wealthiest city as anywhere else. Only very
few were benefiting from the new times the wine merchant had spoken of, while
the rest went hungry and struggled to get their children through the next winter
or the next drought.

Feeling much better than the night before, Johann walked beside the only
slightly damaged wagon drawn by a skinny gray horse. Emilio had managed to
sell the second, broken wagon and the old nag to the Augsburg knacker. They
hadn't gotten much, but it would be enough to have the other wagon fixed up
in the next town. And they'd bought some food for their journey.

The road followed the Lech River, which was already busy this time of year.
The troupe passed rafts laden with wine, oil, and bales of fabric, which were
wrapped in a waxed layer to protect them from water. Watching all the action
coming downstream, Johann tried to imagine how difficult it must have been to
cart all those wares across the mountains. Now he'd be making the same journey,
only in the opposite direction.

Peter Nachtigall sat on the box seat with the reins in his hand and stared
straight ahead. His eye looked even worse than the day before, and he still wore
the bandage around his skull. Johann guessed it would take some time before
the troupe's leader would say more than a few words to him. Peter still didn't
seem fully convinced that this serious-looking smart aleck was a good addition

to his troupe. But at least Emilio and Salome were on Johann's side. He wasn't so sure about Mustafa—the hulking man hadn't uttered a single word so far. Johann suspected he was mute.

Salome, Emilio, and Mustafa also walked alongside the wagon. The group headed south at a leisurely pace, straight toward the Alps. When Johann discerned the mountains as a white ribbon on the horizon, he walked a little faster. Finally he had a destination. He would see Venice, the best-known city in the world! All he knew about Venice so far were the stories his mother had told him. Apparently, the city was built on islands in the sea and crossed by countless canals. The roofs of the houses gleamed like pure gold, and every day, ships arrived carrying spices and the strangest goods from Africa and India. Hundreds of Christian pilgrims started their journeys to Jerusalem in Venice. For the first time in days, Johann managed to forget Tonio and the gruesome experience in the woods.

Salome was walking a few steps ahead of him. Suddenly she climbed a small tree by the wayside, as nimble as a cat, sat on a branch, and winked at him. Johann looked away with embarrassment. He wasn't sure what the exotic beauty, with her long black hair and voluptuous curves, thought of him. He guessed Salome to be in her late twenties, and if he interpreted Emilio's looks and gestures correctly, the two of them were an item. But he wasn't certain. He decided to be careful, in any case. The last thing he needed right now was more trouble.

Johann could hear soft, flat singing from inside the wagon. It was Magister Archibaldus, who had slept late and now seemed to liven up. So far, Johann had only seen him drunk or asleep.

"Hey, boy!" Peter Nachtigall whistled and nodded at Johann. "Do me a favor and check on the old drunkard in the back, will you? I've got a feeling he's on the wine again. I want to give a show at Landsberg tonight and need him sober."

Johann nodded, glad that Peter had given him a task. He jumped on the back of the wagon, pushed aside the canvas, and climbed in. He was immediately enveloped by a cloud of alcohol fumes and the smell of old man. The wagon was loaded heavily with chests and sacks. In one corner, Archibaldus was leaning over an open chest and seemed to be searching for something, humming softly to himself. Johann awkwardly cleared his throat, and Archibaldus slammed shut the lid with a start.

"Um, I was just making sure the straw of Bethlehem was still there," the old man gabbled. "I was afraid we'd left it behind in the rush." His hair looked as wild as the day before, but his beard was noticeably shorter. Johann realized the straggly, Methuselah-like growth had been a fake.

"If I'm not mistaken, that's the chest with the supplies," Johann said, gesturing at the chest. "The one with the relics is over there."

"Of course, you're right, boy!" Archibaldus slapped one hand against his forehead. "I'm getting old and forgetful." He squinted and looked more closely at Johann. "You're the new fellow, aren't you? Well, at least you're older than Lukas." He winked at him. "And smarter, from what I hear."

"Who is Lukas?" asked Johann. He'd heard the name the day before but hadn't asked about him.

"The question should be, Who *was* Lukas?" replied Archibaldus dryly. "One of the wagon wheels got the poor lad as we were rolling down a hill near Leipzig. His leg broke like a twig. I put a splint on it and treated it with a salve, but fever took him in less than a fortnight. He was only fifteen years young." The old man suppressed a burp. "Shame about the boy. He was a good juggler. Knew a lot of tricks."

"I'm sorry," said Johann.

Archibaldus waved his hand dismissively. "That's just life. We come and we go, and no one knows when his time will be up. I never thought the dear Lord would grant me this many years. Almost seventy now." He gave a grin. "I was a dapper lad when I was your age. And I had a smart mouth on me. A traveling scholar who never turned away a girl, no matter how ugly." He laughed loudly.

"Did you study?" asked Johann. He knew students often traveled from university to university, sometimes succumbing to drink and idleness and ending up as jugglers. Itinerant clergymen known as goliards also frequently joined the performing troupes.

"Oh yes, I come from a good family. Although you wouldn't think so, looking at me now."

Archibaldus had taken a seat on a bench along the side of the wagon, and now Johann joined him. The man's clothing smelled of rancid fat, and his hair was full of nits.

Archibaldus shook his head as he continued. "My father was a wealthy merchant from Hamburg. The Stovenbrannts were once among the most powerful families there. I was the third-born son and supposed to study philosophy and medicine, and law, and ah! Theology, too." He sighed deeply. "Let us speak of other things. I hear you're a good trickster. Who taught you?"

"A . . . widely traveled man. Tonio del Moravia."

Archibaldus frowned. "Tonio del Moravia? I feel like I've heard the name before. Hmm . . ." He paused. "A juggler, you say?"

"A chiromancer and astrologer," said Johann, disliking the intent look Archibaldus was giving him.

"And did he teach you any of the arcane arts?" asked the old man.

"Just bits and pieces." Johann suddenly felt very uncomfortable. Maybe it had been a mistake to mention Tonio's name. Quickly, he changed the subject. "Are you a real alchemist?"

Archibaldus looked surprised. "What makes you think that?"

"Well, the golden tip on your staff . . ."

"Oh, that." The old man laughed. "It's just a little gold leaf. If you smear a little mud on it, you can't see it. The rest is hocus-pocus."

Johann grinned. *"Hoc est enim corpus meum . . ."*

"So you speak Latin. A learned trickster. Wonders never cease!" Archibaldus gave Johann a mischievous wink. "Or is that the only phrase you know?"

"Lingua latina sermo patrius meus est," replied Johann in fluent Latin. *"Deorum antiquorum modo colloqui amo. Homo Deus est."* The last sentence had just slipped out—and Tonio's favorite phrase had a strange effect on Archibaldus: the man flinched as if Johann had struck him.

He gave Johann a long, hard look. "How do you know these words?"

Johann shrugged, rattled by Archibaldus's gaze. "I guess I heard them somewhere." He quickly changed the topic. "Emilio mentioned yesterday that it was thanks to you that the troupe has winter quarters in Venice. Is that true?"

"Hmm," said the old man hesitantly. "It's true. And it's the only damn reason they're letting me come. I know I'm a lousy alchemist and relic peddler these days. The straw from the crib of Bethlehem is moldy, and Archangel Gabriel's wing feather is as tousled as if the cat had got him."

Johann smiled, glad for the change of subject. Relic peddlers traveled the country with more-or-less-genuine relics, displaying them for money. He'd once heard that there were enough pieces of "the true cross" to build an entire city.

Partly to blame was the fact that items were sometimes declared relics when they'd merely touched a relic.

Archibaldus gave an almost-toothless grin. "But I still have a few connections in trading circles because of my family name. Among others, in the German trading post in Venice. That's where we stay for the winter, in exchange for a bit of juggling and music." He snickered. "I've got a letter of recommendation from Hamburg, from very high places. It's my retirement security, so to speak. And—"

"Hey, you two!" shouted Peter from up front. "Are you draining our wine together now? Come here, Johann, I need you to push. There's a hill up ahead, and this horse won't manage on its own."

Johann was about to get up when Archibaldus clutched him by the sleeve.

"Those Latin words you said before," he said quietly. "You know: *homo Deus est*. I don't care where you got them from, but keep them to yourself from now on. You don't want the wrong ears to hear them. Do you understand?"

Johann nodded, even though he wasn't sure he understood. Was the old man trying to frighten him? He turned away and climbed out of the wagon. Long after Johann had left, Archibaldus's eyes remained on the slit in the canvas. Then the old scholar sighed deeply and continued his search for the keg of wine.

With the slightly damaged wagon, their progress went slower than expected, and they ended up spending the night beside the river. Cold fog rose up from the water at sunset. Johann shivered but tried not to let it show. As the new one in the troupe, he sat a little apart from the rest while eating his stew. Salome gave him a few strange smiles.

Following their sparse supper, Peter played his fiddle for a while, and Johann thought once more that he was an excellent musician. Most musicians he knew from Knittlingen were drunken drifters who could barely keep a rhythm. But Peter was bowing his instrument like an angel, closing his eyes and losing himself in the music. Johann envied his apparent ability to shut out all his worries and fears for a while. He himself couldn't do it, and so he slept poorly once more, dreaming of Tonio and small, squirming bodies in a clearing somewhere in the woods near Nördlingen. Several times he was woken by sighs and moans, but it was only Emilio and Salome, enjoying themselves not far from him under a thin fur blanket.

They finally reached Landsberg in the late morning of the following day. Johann was supposed to perform his first show there.

Like Augsburg, this town also lay by the gentle River Lech. A castle sat upon a steep hill in the east, tall defensive walls telling of the city's power and wealth. Peter had been here many times before, and it wasn't long before they were granted permission to perform on the market square.

Along with dozens of other travelers, they crossed the river on a wide wooden bridge with a weir on one side. The salt road led through Landsberg—it was an important trading route on which precious salt was carted from Reichenhall via Munich to Lake Constance. A salt store and road tolls ensured that the people of Landsberg got their share of the daily salt transport.

As soon as their wagon rolled into the market square, the first curious onlookers began to gather. Children flocked around the troupe; old men and women muttered prayers and made the sign of the cross but couldn't help gawking at the jugglers' colorful costumes. Johann knew from his time with Tonio that people were grateful for any distraction. There wasn't much entertainment outside of church fairs and the occasional execution, particularly in smaller towns and villages. One or two convivial hours, a bit of laughter and amazement—jugglers took people on a journey to a land far away from the misery and monotony of their daily lives.

There was a fountain in the center of the square unlike any Johann had seen before. Water spouted into the air several yards high, resembling lances glinting in the light of the sun. Behind the fountain lay the three-story city hall with its tall, crenellated facade and stair turret and many windows. Johann thought about the old well outside the Knittlingen town hall and the moat with its murky waters. The closer they got to the Alps, the wealthier the towns and cities seemed to be.

"Nervous?" asked Peter mockingly. Johann was still gaping at the fountain. "Don't soil your pants—Salome won't want to wash them for you." He laughed and handed Johann some items of clothing. "Put these on. They were a little too big for Lukas, so they should be just right for you."

Johann pulled on a pair of bright-green leggings and a red jerkin with a hood as long as his arm. Colorful pieces of fabric had been sewn onto the jerkin, and it had several slits with yellow cloth showing underneath. It was warm and elaborately made, even if he looked like a fool in it. To his horror, Johann noticed that the right trouser leg had been poorly patched up and was speckled with dried blood.

"It's a good jerkin," said Peter, noticing Johann's look. "Poor Lukas was given it as a gift from a Saxon nobleman who liked his tricks. Just before his death. We cleaned it as well as we could." He gave a grin. "You're not fussy, are you?"

Johann said nothing as he fastened the jerkin.

Their show on the market square was a great success. Emilio juggled, Salome danced with her veils, and Mustafa bent iron rods like willow branches. Even Magister Archibaldus appeared to be relatively sober, and the crowd bought his alchemist story and clapped wildly at the sight of his gilded staff.

Peter's playing was so heartrendingly beautiful that people's eyes welled up with tears. Johann thought he understood now where Peter's name came from— *Nachtigall* meant "nightingale." He wasn't just a gifted musician but also an astounding singer. His voice was loud and clear both when he sang and when he spoke, and his announcements between acts made people laugh and gasp with amazement. Peter was without a doubt a born leader, even if his speech suffered slightly from the new gap in his teeth.

Johann thought his own performance hadn't been too bad, either. The audience loved the trick with the egg; this time, he'd asked a slow-witted butcher's apprentice on stage to pose for him. When Johann lifted the boy's hat and people saw the egg, they roared with laughter. His card and coin tricks worked well, too, especially with Salome acting as his assistant. She handed him the cards and patted him down to prove that he didn't have any additional cards hidden on his body, touching him in places that weren't strictly necessary for the act.

Johann noticed that the young female spectators eyed him differently than had the girls he'd seen a few months ago. He had grown taller and had filled out a little. His hair was black and luscious, and his teeth gleamed white, thanks to a cleansing recipe from his mother using mint and mallow root. Still, he felt rather ridiculous in the slit jerkin and the long gugel hood.

Added to the proceeds from the sale of the broken wagon, the money they made was enough for accommodation at a decent inn near the church and a bowl of hot meat stew for each of them. And the innkeeper promised to have their battered wagon fixed the following day.

They stayed in Landsberg for two more days, giving three shows a day. At first Johann's performance had been a bit rusty, but with each show the tricks came a little more easily. Still, Peter remained cold toward him. Johann feared the man would never forgive him the gap in his teeth.

In the hours before and between shows, Johann practiced juggling with Emilio and learned that the young juggler was deft with a throwing knife. Johann pulled out his own knife and hurled it at a wagon wheel, where the blade came to a trembling halt in the hub of the wheel. He'd had plenty of practice during his time with Tonio, especially when his hatred of all those narrow-minded Knittlingers had become unbearable. Emilio nodded appreciatively.

"If you get a little better, we might be able to turn it into an act," he said with a grin. "With Salome, perhaps. But we better practice without live targets first—I don't want you to make a hole in my pretty girl's dress."

On the second night, Johann needed to empty his bladder long before sunrise. He got up as quietly as he could. He shared a chamber with Archibaldus, who was snoring beside him. As usual, the magister had stayed up drinking until late and reeked like an old barrel of wine. Johann thought even the fleas in the beds must find him disgusting. He sneaked downstairs on tiptoes and walked into the yard behind the inn to the wooden outhouse. When he was finished, he lingered in the yard for a while, gazing at the waning moon. It had been only a week since he'd fled from Tonio beneath the same moon. It seemed to him like a different, long-gone life.

Then he felt a hand on his shoulder.

Johann spun around and saw the fine features of Salome's face. She looked even more exotic in the dark, with her oval face the color of burned clay, high cheekbones, and bushy eyebrows. Her hair was tousled, and she wrapped herself up in a blanket that didn't hide her curves. Her full lips twisted into a mocking smile.

"Are you howling at the moon, my little wolf?"

Johann shook his head. "I'm thinking of something I'd rather forget."

"Aren't we all?" She gave a hoarse laugh, sounding almost like a man. "Archibaldus would like to forget that he's just an old drunk and not an itinerant scholar from a wealthy house. Emilio wants to forget what the mercenaries did to his parents in Lombardy. Peter wants to forget that his time as a great showman is over."

"He really plays like the—"

"Like the devil, I know." Salome grinned. "How appropriate! The church considers jugglers as lures of the devil and dancing as their mass." She swayed her hips suggestively. "And especially dishonorable jugglers' wenches like me. Well, can you feel the lure of the wench? Can you feel it?"

"Peter could play his music at the courts of noblemen," Johann said without responding to Salome. "But instead he travels from town to town with your troupe—why?"

Salome gave him a wink. "Once again it was an accursed wench dragging the man to his demise. As far as I know, Peter is the youngest son of a Franconian knight. He loved a girl—a simple barber's daughter, apparently—and left his family for her. But the lass died young, and not even his music could save her. He's been roaming the empire with a broken heart ever since." She shrugged. "At least that's what he says when he's drunk. And then he's pretty hard to understand. Sometimes, when he's in a really bad state, he talks about some pact that stole the girl from him."

"I understand Peter too well," said Johann glumly.

"Because you, too, loved a girl?" She came closer. "Did you?"

"And what about you?" asked Johann quickly. "Are you also trying to forget something?"

"Every day I forget what happened the night before."

She opened the tattered blanket, revealing her immaculate naked body, with her fuzzy black triangle and full breasts bathed in pale moonlight. He couldn't move. She brusquely pulled him against her and kissed him hard and passionately, her tongue burrowing into his mouth like an angry viper. Johann felt her hand on his crotch, and there was nothing he could do to stop his penis from growing.

"I like your eyes, my little wolf," she breathed. "They're as dark and deep as ponds in the forest. There's something gleaming under the surface I don't understand. Can you explain?"

"What . . . what about Emilio?" he asked, breathing heavily.

"Who is Emilio?" She gave a giggle. "I'm free, little wolf. I belong to no one—not even to a god."

She had pushed him against the rim of a barrel. Johann feverishly grabbed her buttocks and lifted her onto him. Her hips moved slowly and rhythmically, her eyes closed and her delirious face turned toward the crescent moon. They made love in silence except for their gasping breath, wrapped tightly around each other as if they were wrestling. Then Salome gave a soft cry, and her whole body tensed before growing limp. Johann inhaled the scent of her salty sweat. Even though it was cold, he felt as hot as he had that day in the field with Margarethe.

After a few moments she let go of him and wrapped the blanket back around her. She was smiling.

"We should go back before the others wake up. Peter wants to leave early." She ran her thumb over the black fluff growing on Johann's chin. "My cute little wolf," she whispered. "We'll taste each other again." Then she turned around and quickly walked back inside the inn.

Johann stayed in the yard for a long time, spellbound, as in a dream.

Johann could not sleep. He tossed and turned in his bed, thinking about Salome. It had been the first time he'd truly had sex with a woman. Back in the cave in Schillingswald Forest, he and Margarethe hadn't gone the whole way, and whatever happened that night near Nördlingen—he didn't want to think about. When Johann closed his eyes, he thought he could still smell Salome's sweat and the scent of her sex. So that was the great magic everyone talked about. And he had to admit: he was bewitched. Still, how could he ever look Emilio in the eye again without blushing? Would Salome tell him what had happened?

But when they finally sat together in the gray twilight of the taproom downstairs, eating their barley porridge and drinking their thinned beer, Salome didn't even look at Johann. She seemed cool and distant. She never even gave him a smile but bantered with Emilio all the more. Johann was deeply confused at first, but then he thought he understood. If she and Emilio were a couple, the other man couldn't know about his mistress's excursion. Johann thought about Emilio's knife and how quickly men started brawls about women.

Worried and tired, Johann leaned over his bowl and tried to forget about Salome. But he couldn't. What had happened between them had been amazing. Something stirred inside him every time he thought about it. He tried to eat his porridge quickly and hurried outside to brush the horse.

They left Landsberg in the light of the rising sun, following the Lech River until they came to a crossroad near a town called Schongau. Two years before, a fire had devastated the entire town, and not all the houses had been rebuilt yet.

A performance among the ruins didn't seem practical, so they decided to rest outside the town walls.

Johann filled a bucket with water for the horse from a cold, clear stream that was lined with ice crystals. The mountains were much closer now, and he thought he could smell the snow even though it was already the beginning of April. When he returned, Peter and Archibaldus were in the middle of a loud argument, but for once it didn't seem to be about the old man's drinking.

"I'll say it one more time: it's nonsense taking the upper route," Archibaldus was saying, still reasonably sober at lunchtime. "It's longer and more dangerous. I know what I'm talking about—I've traveled through the Finstermünz Gorge before. It's still deepest winter there in April! There'll be avalanches, and storms can break out at any moment. The Eisacktal Valley, by Bozen, on the other hand—"

"Is just as dangerous, if not more so," Peter retorted. "Even though the toll keepers are trying to tell us otherwise—I don't fall for their tricks." His eyes narrowed and he crossed his arms on his chest. "Believe me, old man, I spoke with several merchants about this, just last night in Landsberg, when you were already under the table. The lower route is flooded with meltwater in many places and blocked by landslides. And the locals demand horrendous tolls for the detours. We can't afford those. The upper route may be longer, but it's safer and—most importantly—cheaper. I've traveled it twice myself."

"But the gorge—" tried Archibaldus again.

"That's my final word," snarled Peter, cutting him off. "I'm the leader of this troupe, and I don't let anyone tell me what to do, especially not an old drunkard who last traveled that road in the time of Methuselah."

Grumbling, Archibaldus retreated back inside the wagon.

Johann put the bucket down in front of the horse and gazed at the Alps. They suddenly seemed a lot more menacing. Evidently, there were several different routes across this tall, impregnable-looking wall of mountains, and none of them was absolutely safe. As the sun drifted toward the western horizon, it painted the mountains in a red light, making them look like they were on fire.

That night, as they were sleeping around the wagon, Johann heard Salome's soft cries. Emilio giggled, then groaned loudly. Johann thought of how Salome had cried out for him just the night before, and the thought drove him wild.

He pulled his hood over his ears and held them shut, but he could still hear the moans and lustful sighs of the lovers.

The next evening, the travelers finally reached the foot of the mountains. A newly built castle rose up beside a monastery right where the Lech River came roaring down from the mountains. Below the castle lay the town of Füssen, which Johann had heard of. It was the starting point of the Lech's navigable section; beyond lay nothing but mountainous wilderness. The king himself had visited Füssen on his way from Innsbruck to Augsburg. The tall townhouses were surrounded by a thick wall. Many merchants and pilgrims chose to stay here at the start of their journeys to Italy.

Peter thoughtfully studied the fluffy clouds above, which covered the evening sky like spilled milk.

"The weather's turning," Peter muttered. "Damn it. Pray to God it'll last for a while longer."

After a lengthy search they found an affordable tavern near the town's granary. Over wine, bacon, and eggs, Peter blathered about Füssen's excellent lute makers and a number of new songs he intended to perform in Venice. He said nothing more about the upper route they were going to take the following day, or about the changing weather. Archibaldus sulked in the corner, emptying cup after cup until he finally passed out at the table.

"He's going to drink himself to his grave," said Emilio.

"Let's hope that won't happen before Venice," Peter replied grumpily. "He's the key to our winter quarters. Now let's get to bed—tomorrow is going to be a long day. And don't forget to pray to Saint Peter to chase away the clouds."

Peter didn't play his fiddle that night, and the others also went to bed early. In the middle of the night, Johann got up and sneaked over to the chamber where Salome and Emilio slept. He paused for a while outside their door, listening to the calm breathing of the sleeping people inside. Then he called himself a fool and went back to bed.

But he still couldn't sleep.

The next morning, the sky was overcast and there was a light drizzle as cold as snow. Johann thought about how beautiful the last few days had been—and now it seemed winter wanted to wield its power one more time. Peter scrutinized the mountains, which were enveloped in a gray haze. Clouds stuck to their peaks like poisonous mushrooms. The leader of their troupe spoke with other travelers, and they decided to wait until the weather improved.

They stayed at Füssen for three more days. The mood and the wine worsened, but the weather remained unchanged. It seemed like the snow and hail were lurking in the mountains—waiting for the travelers to start their journey. On the morning of the fourth day, Peter woke the others with loud knocking and ordered them to pack up.

"No one said it was going to be easy," he growled. "Now let's go before we all freeze to death in this place." Archibaldus was about to respond, but Peter silenced him with one stern look.

They joined a group of merchants from Augsburg who also had decided to attempt the crossing. They carried linen, wool, and furs, and they were accompanied by several pilgrims, whose brown woolen coats, wide-brimmed hats, and staffs were a familiar sight on the roads. The pilgrims' number had grown steadily since Augsburg. They were headed for Rome or Venice and the Holy Land, sang and prayed continuously, and weren't intimidated by wind and rain. Johann envied the pilgrims' trust in God, their perpetual smiles and camaraderie. He wondered if he couldn't be a pilgrim, too. But search as he might, he couldn't find the voice of God inside him. He felt perhaps Tonio's black potion had tainted and sealed him from the inside.

The jugglers didn't have to pay for the protection the train of merchants afforded them—but they promised to brighten the cold mountain evenings with music and dance. Peter was glad they didn't have to travel alone, because the French under King Charles VIII had been fighting the Italian cities since the year before. Florence, Rome, and Naples had already fallen, and no one could tell how far north the fighting was going to reach. People were telling tales of horrific slaughters, even in the Vinschgau and Tyrol areas.

"At the imperial diet in Worms, the upper classes demanded an everlasting public peace from the emperor so that the knights can't keep thieving and murdering as they please," said Archibaldus, sitting in the wagon with Peter. "They even want to found an imperial court of judgment and a council that controls the king." He gave a laugh. "And all the while the noble lords can't even keep the lousy French out of Italy. This empire is a joke!"

"The situation is much too serious for a joke," grumbled Peter. "Now shut your trap, old man. I'm getting sick of your grousing."

Slowly, like a fat centipede, the caravan of about thirty people and a dozen wagons moved toward the mountain ranges, which formed a natural gateway near Füssen. The narrow, rocky gorge through which the Lech River rushed right behind the city made Johann shudder. It felt like they were crossing an invisible boundary. Behind him lay the lovely fields and rolling hills of the Allgäu region, and in front of him was the inhospitable world of mountains, with its raging rivers, avalanches, and landslides—and, somewhere to the south, far beyond the horizon, the legendary Venice.

The river was their steady companion for the next two days, growing ever narrower and wilder. Wide valleys stretched between the mountains, which seemed to get taller with every mile. The path climbed gently uphill, but so far they'd had no trouble with the wagons and pack animals.

The area they now traveled through belonged to the county of Tyrol; it was heavily wooded and sparsely populated. Johann thought about his winter with Tonio, spent not far from here. He even thought he recognized some peaks. A shiver ran down his spine.

Is he still looking for me? he wondered.

Sometimes he thought he could still feel Tonio's hand squeezing his as they'd sealed their pact. Peter had also spoken to Salome of an unholy pact. Johann wondered with whom the fiddle player might have made a deal. Another powerful man who'd promised him the world and brought him nothing but misfortune? Johann wiped his hand on his trousers as if it was dirty, but the memory of Tonio stuck to him like a greasy coating. He remembered Tonio's words to him as his apprentice.

The pact is valid until I dismiss you.

In conversation with the merchants and pilgrims, Johann learned that not many travelers chose the upper route these days. Most took the shorter lower route, which led to Venice via Innsbruck and a pass called Brenner. Apparently, it took a horseman only ten days from Augsburg on that road, although by wagon it took much longer, of course. The Romans had established both routes a long time ago, and they were still the main passageways across the Alps. But the lower route currently suffered from severe flooding. Looking up at the cloudy sky, however, Johann feared the upper route wasn't much safer.

The path led them higher and higher. They eventually left the Lech behind near a castle called Ehrenberg, which sat enthroned above them like the nest of an eagle. The road became muddy and rough. Potholes as large and deep as ponds slowed their progress. Archibaldus was forced to climb down from the wagon and walk. Sometimes they had to push, but they still fared better than the merchants, who regularly became stuck in the mud with their heavily laden wagons. On some days, they made only a few miles. Mustafa pulled and pushed like an ox, his muscles moving under his skin like fat snakes. Despite the cold, he still wore only his leather vest, and he still hadn't uttered a word.

"Not long now and we'll need additional draft animals," said Emilio, panting as they heaved the wagon across the next pothole. The rain poured down relentlessly, turning the road into a field of mud. "That'll be expensive. Let's pray we won't get caught in a landslide."

Archibaldus nodded underneath the brim of his hat. "Yes, yes, like I said," he replied, grumbling. "And this is only the first pass. But no one wants to listen to an experienced old traveler."

At one point the road had been washed away for over a quarter of a mile. The detour cost them two extra days. Everything around them was gray and shrouded in fog; only rarely did they catch glimpses of jagged peaks stretching to the horizon.

Salome didn't visit Johann during any of the following nights, either. The weather worsened. Thick snowflakes began to fall from the sky, and a few times it hailed. They still hadn't reached the highest point of their journey. Green lakes sparkled between the rocks; chamois and ibex leaped along narrow tracks impassable to humans. Eagles circled high above them like messengers from another world.

"They look as if they're just waiting for one of us to freeze so they can peck out the liver," said Emilio, shivering in his thin juggler's garb. Now Johann was grateful for his brightly colored jerkin with the ridiculous hood—at least it kept him warm.

They couldn't afford the expensive mountain taverns, tempting as they were with their warm rooms and hot mulled wine. Just like the pilgrims, they slept in flea-infested, drafty hostels where monks served watery gruel. When there was no hostel, they slept underneath the wagon, tortured by wind, hail, and Archibaldus's snoring and farting, which drove Johann to the brink of insanity.

But worse still was the fact that Salome ignored him completely.

Had she only been toying with him? Sometimes, while Johann trudged through the snow and fog, she walked ahead of him like an apparition from another world. He could make out her curves even under her warm coat; her swaying walk, the way she tossed back her hair, and how she shook the snow off her shoulders caused him to think of nothing but her naked body. He became quiet and withdrawn. He felt Peter's hard looks on him from time to time—the troupe's leader had noticed his changed mood. Johann held back in the evenings when the other jugglers entertained the travelers, contributing to the shows only when Peter asked him explicitly. He practiced with the knife in silence, throwing it at tree trunks again and again. Sometimes he imagined Tonio's grinning face in the bark, and other times it was Emilio, his mouth open in a lustful moan.

By now they were following the Inn River, wider than the Lech. They'd been crossing the Alps for nearly two weeks, and the mountains weren't coming to an end—on the contrary, they seemed to rise up higher than ever. The river roared and twisted in its bed between cliffs as high as cathedral towers. At the narrowest point, when Johann thought the path must have ended, a fortification jutted out from the rock face on the opposite bank like a wart on the nose of a giant. A wooden bridge led across the raging river, and in its middle stood a fortified tower with a bretèche, the water foaming up at the tower's base. A wall with a walkway ran along the rock face, although Johann struggled to make out details of the river's far bank through the rain and the sleet.

"Fort Finstermünz," said Archibaldus glumly. "From here, the path winds its way up to the Reschen Pass. Last year a bunch of wagons fell into the river not far from here." He gave a dry laugh. "Of course, our dear Peter Nachtigall didn't tell you that part of the story—nor about the massacres at the hands of Swiss mercenaries nearby."

In the bridge tower they were received by a group of surly Tyrolean soldiers dressed in tattered clothes and rusty armor, whose job it was to collect the toll. Some wagon hands were also stationed there, ready to offer services like additional draft animals for the pass. They spoke in a language that sounded strangely old, like an ancient precursor to Latin.

"See how low the gate is?" Archibaldus asked Johann, gesturing toward the dark passage in the tower. "Those bastards built it that way on purpose. If a wagon can't fit through it, smaller wheels must be fitted. The guards charge three kreuzers for the service—per wheel, that is. And on the other side, when the wheels get changed back, they charge as much again. Damn Tyrolean thieves! They'll never change."

The water below them gurgled, and the bridge quivered and swayed slightly as the wagons drove across it one by one. A few of them indeed had to change their wheels, and oxen and strong draft horses were hitched in front of the merchants' own animals on the other bank to help pull their wagons up the pass. The jugglers waited for their turn to cross. Emilio made to wave over one of the wagon hands, but Peter stopped him.

"We don't need those cutthroats," he said with a growl.

"But our wagon—" began Emilio.

"Isn't nearly as heavy as those of the merchants. We'll get up the pass just fine." Peter grinned. "And we've got Mustafa, remember?"

"If you say so." Emilio didn't seem convinced. He looked over to Archibaldus, who was watching the clouds.

"It looks rather dark in the west," said the old man. "If we don't take extra draft animals, we should at least wait until tomorrow for the weather to settle."

"And pay a fortune for accommodation at the fort?" Peter waved dismissively. "That's precisely what those thieves want us to do. We're leaving now. Everything going well, we'll be up the pass in just a few hours."

"Everything going well," muttered Archibaldus. But he had given up trying to oppose Peter.

It wouldn't be the last time his warnings were ignored.

Disaster struck about halfway up the pass.

It had started to rain heavily again, and swollen brown streams flooded across the path in regular intervals, rushing down into the gorge and making progress difficult. Peter and Salome were up in front with the horse, while Emilio, Johann, and Mustafa pushed from behind; Archibaldus followed with his staff. By the time Peter's cry of warning rang out, it was too late.

There was a low rumble, and then an avalanche of snow and debris came sliding down the mountain and into the caravan. The noise was tremendous, as if the entire mountain were exploding. All around them people screamed, horses neighed, and wood splintered as the avalanche poured across the narrow track. Johann watched in horror as the wagon in front of them, heavily laden with bales and crates, was pushed toward the edge by an enormous force. The driver tried to jump off his seat, but then the wagon plunged into the depths. The man's piercing scream was cut off abruptly when he hit the raging brown floodwaters of the Inn.

A smaller arm of the landslide struck the troupe's wagon at the rear. Emilio, Johann, and Mustafa managed to jump aside at the last moment. The wagon's back axle hovered dangerously above the abyss, the wheels spinning in the air.

"Over here!" shouted Peter. "Help me!"

The horse, trapped in its harness, whinnied in fear and reared up while Peter desperately hung on to the reins. But as much as he pulled on the leather straps, he couldn't manage to soothe the panicked horse. Inch by inch the wagon slid over the edge while Johann just stood there, unable to move. He watched as Mustafa rushed to the horse, grabbed the reins, and yanked them down hard. The horse regained its footing, and Mustafa and Peter dragged it away from the cliff step by step.

At that moment, a second landslide hit the travelers.

Like the first one, it consisted of mud, rocks, and brown lumps of snow and ice, and it came rushing down the mountainside like a huge tongue, swallowing everything in its way with a hungry and awe-inspiring force. Another wagon not far from the jugglers plunged into the gorge, but this time, the avalanche came to a halt just before the troupe's wagon.

Johann was standing with his back against the rock wall when he heard a high-pitched scream. Through the veil of rain he spotted Salome clinging desperately to a splintered tree trunk. She had sought shelter a little farther up the path and had been sucked off her feet by the second avalanche. Her legs were already over the edge, and the trunk steadily pushed her down, moved by a mound of mud and debris. Archibaldus and Emilio were closest to her. The young juggler was about to rush to Salome's aid when another shower of small stones came down the mountainside. Emilio stopped dead in his tracks, his face twisted in a grimace of fear. Then he turned around and sought shelter underneath a ledge.

Johann woke from his daze. He stormed across the mud and debris, fell to his knees, and reached down to Salome, who was struggling to cling to the tree trunk.

"Take my hand!" he shouted, his voice almost completely drowned out by the rain. "Quickly! Take it!"

For a brief moment she looked at him almost defiantly, her lips pinched, her eyes fearless—then she grasped his hand.

Johann immediately felt her weight. He pulled as hard as he could while his feet slipped on the muddy ground. He could feel himself sliding closer to the abyss. Desperately, he dug his toes into the ground and kept pulling, his hands clasped around Salome's as if they were one. With an angry cry he reared up, fell backward, and caught her body in his arms. Her clothes were soaked with water and mud, and she was panting heavily. He could smell her sweat. For a while they remained there, lying on the ground without moving, while all around them people were screaming, praying, and crying for help.

Eventually, Salome sat up and then tried to stand on her shaking legs.

"Thank you," she said softly. "Not everyone would have done that for me."

Visibly shaken, but with her head held high, she walked over to the others. They were standing around the wagon, exhausted but happy to be alive. Archibaldus looked deathly pale leaning against one of the wagon wheels, but none of the jugglers seemed injured.

When Johann stood up from the dirt, he noticed Emilio staring at him with a strange expression.

He couldn't tell whether it was hatred or relief.

It took more than three hours before the path was cleared sufficiently for the caravan to continue its journey. The Augsburg merchants had lost two wagons and three wagon hands. Two pilgrims had been killed by falling debris. Most of the travelers had suffered scrapes and bruises, and one young pilgrim bore a nasty head wound. Johann thought to himself that not even their boundless love of God had saved the pious men. Today the Almighty had been angry, not merciful.

Three more wagons were too damaged to continue on and needed to be pulled back to Fort Finstermünz for repairs. Many of the costly bales of cloth were torn and filthy—a harsh blow for the merchants.

"I knew this journey wouldn't end well," muttered Archibaldus again and again as they made their way up the steep mountain pass in the fading daylight. "I knew it."

He avoided looking Peter in the eye. The troupe's leader had checked and fastened their gear in silence, making sure his new fiddle was unharmed. No one dared to address him—not even Salome, who was fine apart from a few minor scratches.

Finally, long after sunset, they reached the village of Nauders, which lay close to the top of the pass. Utterly exhausted, they sought out the local hostel, where a handful of gout-ridden monks took care of the injured. The rain had finally stopped, and the survivors lay down to rest. Some of the pilgrims sang a hymn, which sounded hollow and desolate among these frigid walls. The dead would be buried in the morning.

Shivering with cold and exhaustion, Johann was lying wrapped in a damp woolen blanket. He'd never felt more tired in his life, and yet he struggled to fall asleep. He closed his eyes and was listening to the prayers of the pilgrims when he felt a hand on his cheek.

It was Salome.

"Come," she whispered.

He got up and quietly followed her past the sleeping travelers, through the gate, out into the fields, until the hostel lay far behind them. A dark castle watched over the plateau, and snow stretched before them like a sea of black pitch.

"Our bed," whispered Salome.

She pulled him down into the snow, and they loved each other passionately, as if it would be the last time. The wind pushed the clouds aside and the snow sparkled in the moonlight. Johann didn't feel the cold, and his exhaustion had vanished as if by magic. Salome was showing him a world he'd never known before. Her hands clawed his back and he cried out, because some of his wounds from that unfortunate night near Nördlingen hadn't fully healed yet.

"What's that?" she asked and ran her fingers over the bumpy scabs. She gave him a wink. "Another woman? Should I be worried, little wolf?"

"Sometimes I ask myself the same thing," Johann murmured. He stroked a long scar that ran right across Salome's back. "And what about this one? What secret are you carrying around with you?"

Salome smiled, but her eyes looked sad. "We all have our little secrets, don't we?"

He grabbed her again and made love to her in silence with an aggression that was new and a little frightening to him. Salome groaned and cried out—he couldn't tell whether with pleasure or pain.

When they sneaked back to the hostel a while later, she gave him one last kiss. "Thank you," she breathed and disappeared inside the wagon.

Johann wasn't sure whether she was thanking him for saving her life in the gorge or for their lovemaking in the snow.

He slipped through the gate and entered the dark, foul-smelling hall. He was about to wrap himself back up in his blanket when he noticed Emilio watching him.

"I guess you think that just because you saved her life she'll be forever at your feet," said the young juggler. "Forget it. That woman can't be owned— you'll learn soon enough."

"I don't want to own her," Johann replied.

"I first met her more than three years ago, when she arrived at the port in Genoa with Mustafa," Emilio continued as if Johann hadn't spoken. "Did you know the two of them are brother and sister? She said they came from Alexandria, where they used to be slaves of a wealthy Syrian merchant. She was his plaything and he raped her several times a day, torturing her with whips, chains, and other instruments. One time, Mustafa tried to defend her, and the merchant had his tongue cut out. The devil knows how those two managed to escape." Emilio gave a sad smile. "Believe me, Salome's had many pets like you. I was her companion for a while, now it's you, and soon enough it'll be someone else. She needs us men to help her forget. We're just her toys."

"I'm tired," said Johann. "I want to sleep now."

"Don't worry, I'm not trying to fight for her. I'm merely warning you. She can eat a man up—that's what she did to me." Emilio hesitated. "Earlier, in the gorge—I was trying to save myself," he said pensively. "Of course I was scared of falling to my death, but more than that, I was afraid of her dragging me down further into her abyss. Good night, Johann."

Emilio turned away and said no more. After a few moments, Johann pulled the damp blanket up to his chin and closed his eyes, aching from the long, hard day. He was filled by a quiet happiness, despite Emilio's words of warning.

His last thought before he fell asleep was that today was April 23—his seventeenth birthday. He'd heard some of the pilgrims mentioning Saint George's Day that morning. In all the excitement in the gorge, he'd almost forgotten the day that used to be so important to his mother. He smiled wistfully.

He was seventeen years old and a man.

10

THE WEATHER IMPROVED THE FOLLOWING MORNING.
Clouds and fog dispersed as they buried the dead at the small hostel cemetery.
They set off when the bells rang the noon hour, and soon after, they reached the
top of the pass. Johann looked down at valleys and lush meadows grazed by fat
cows. The grass was knee high and glinted with the rain of the previous evening.
Colorful meadow flowers and herbs were speckled among the green. But the
mountains weren't finished yet—snowcapped ranges stretched in every direction.

"The Vinschgau," said Peter with a sweeping gesture. "It's a fertile valley with
lots of cattle and grassland. Beyond it is the Etschtal Valley, which leads us to
Meran and eventually Bozen."

"Will these mountains never end?" asked Johann.

Peter laughed. "Not until we reach the Val Padana, and that's still a fair way
off. The great Po River runs through its plains and makes it Italy's granary. The
people there are wealthy and grateful for any diversion. That's where we want to
try our luck before spending the winter in Venice."

Despite the harrowing events of the previous day, Peter seemed rested and
almost cheerful. "Thank you for saving Salome yesterday," he said to Johann,
patting his shoulder. "I didn't think you had it in you. Looks like there's more
to you than I thought."

Johann shook his hand, pleased the troupe's leader finally seemed to have
accepted him. Peter's snarly remarks in the last few weeks had begun to bother
him.

The road was no longer extremely steep; it led gently downhill, past lakes,
meadows, and farmers with scythes doffing their hats. Johann noticed that the
houses and churches looked different here than on the other side of the pass. The

language of the people living here was barely understandable. Peter explained that the inhabitants of this area belonged to an old people who'd mixed with the Romans a long time ago. Here, in the remote mountain valley, its ancient culture had been preserved.

As predicted by Emilio, Salome was much nicer to Johann now. She gave him furtive smiles, squeezed his hand, or brushed against his codpiece when she thought no one was looking. They made love every night of their journey through the Vinschgau and Etschtal Valleys, finding outlying barns and other secluded places. Salome proved to be a good teacher. She knew countless games and positions, and Johann tried not to think about what Emilio had said about her past. He didn't want to be reminded of the source of Salome's knowledge. Much to his relief, Emilio kept his word and didn't try to compete for her. The young juggler seemed relieved.

Every night, they put on a show for their fellow travelers and for the villages they passed through. Each time Johann made an egg appear beneath the hat of a farmer or wagon driver, or made coins disappear and reappear, the spectators laughed and cheered. The warm receptions encouraged Johann to put great effort into each performance.

One evening, after yet another successful show, Peter asked Johann to join him by the fire.

"Magister Archibaldus told me you used to travel with an astrologer and chiromancer. Is that true?"

Johann nodded reluctantly. He wasn't sure what Peter was getting at.

"Does that mean you know how to cast horoscopes?" asked Peter. "Mine, for example?"

"Horoscopes are time consuming," Johann replied. "I'd have to make calculations and check tables I don't have. And I'd need to know the exact date and place of your birth."

"I know the place." Peter's expression turned dark. "Even though I don't like thinking about it. Too many unhappy memories. I don't know the date of my birth, but it must have been the summer the Ottomans conquered Constantinople, in the year of our Lord 1453."

Johann counted back and realized that Peter was over forty years old. He'd always thought the man with the lively eyes and fiery red hair was younger than that. But then Johann realized something else: Tonio del Moravia had also spoken of Constantinople once—of a Constantinople he'd visited *before* the Ottomans had conquered the city. That would have been almost fifty years ago. Could that be right? After all, Tonio hadn't seemed like an old man, but more like someone in his late forties or early fifties. Johann shuddered.

How old was the magician?

"If you can't cast a horoscope for me, at least read my palm," said Peter, tearing Johann from his thoughts. He held out his hand with a laugh. "There's no way every twist and turn of my life can fit on one hand—you'll probably have to continue up my arm."

Johann started to reach for Peter's hand but then paused. He hadn't read a palm since his experience at the Allgäu farmstead. He still didn't understand how and why he'd foreseen the boy's death.

"Go on," Peter said and gave an encouraging wink. "Or I'll have to assume that you're nothing but a fraud."

Johann was glad Peter had finally accepted him, and he didn't want to offend the troupe leader. So he took the hand and bent over it. Peter's fingers were long and slender—not surprising, since he was a talented fiddle player. The Mount of Luna was very pronounced on the outside edge of his palm, which also suggested musicality. The Life line running right across the ball of the hand was furrowed and showed lots of small branches.

Johann was about to start talking when he flinched. He was overcome by the same strange feeling he'd sensed at the farmstead that time: a soft, warm pulsating, as if the lines lit up for the briefest instant. Fear shot through him, and he dropped Peter's hand as if it were on fire. He knew immediately what the pulsating meant.

He had foreseen Peter's imminent death.

"What is it?" asked Peter, who noticed that Johann had turned white as chalk. "Something bad? You're trembling."

"No, it's nothing." Johann shook his head. "Just a fever I must have caught in the last few cold nights."

"Yes, and I know just what kind of fever." Peter grinned. "Salome is one hell of a woman. Don't think I don't see what's going on. I can't blame you!" He laughed and gave Johann a pat on the shoulder. "But be careful Emilio doesn't slit your throat at night. Those southerners can be rather jealous."

Johann gave a strained smile. "We already worked it out like men."

"Like men? Hear, hear! That's good." Peter nodded. "So, then, what do you see in my hand, great chiromancer?"

Johann cleared his throat. Then he told Peter about complex Life lines, interestingly curved Head lines, and a promising future as the leader of his troupe. He hinted at something dark in the man's past, according to the pieces of gossip he'd heard from the other members of the troupe. He tried his best, and Peter was impressed. When Johann had finished, the fiddler frowned.

"I think you understand me better than my dear mother used to, God rest her soul," he said. "I applaud you. We really ought to make this part of our show—for money, of course. What do you say?"

"Let me think about it," Johann replied weakly. He quickly got up and walked away, feeling sick to his stomach.

"I must have a word with Salome," Peter shouted after him. "I'll lose my best juggler if she continues to wear you out like this!"

Johann felt like he was in a bad dream as he staggered past the pilgrims and other travelers who sat around the fire, laughing and drinking. He still had a vivid image of Peter's glowing hand in his mind.

And he prayed that it truly was a fever playing tricks on him, and nothing else.

The farther down the wide valley they went, the warmer it got. Johann noticed that the air smelled different on this side of the Alps. The mild breeze carried the scent of flowers, grass, and, very faintly, something salty. They were still traveling between mountain ranges, but the peaks weren't as high and rugged. Johann also discovered plants and trees he'd never seen before. The sky was blue, and apart from the occasional shower, the weather remained fair.

For the first time since his escape from Tonio, Johann felt lighthearted. He tried to forget what he'd seen in Peter's palm. The man seemed healthy and happy, and Johann came to the conclusion that he'd only imagined the throbbing in Peter's hand. After all, he didn't even know whether the boy from the farmstead had died in the end.

Only rarely and late at night did he think of Margarethe, his young brother Martin, and the eerie gathering in the forest near Nördlingen. His nightly rendezvous with Salome helped him forget his gloomy thoughts. She always came up with new games; occasionally they involved binding her wrists with ropes or blindfolding him. Johann always went along without resisting, and he didn't ask why Salome allowed him to orgasm inside her. He assumed she was unable to bear children or took certain remedies to prevent a pregnancy.

Each night, it was as if he were in a state of intoxication that only ended just before dawn. Accordingly, he was exhausted during the day, but he tried not to let it affect his performances. The applause of the crowd gave him the strength he needed. However, he grew more sullen and moody by the day. The arrogance he'd shown even as a child increasingly came out as violent fits of temper. If something went wrong during a show, he would vent his anger on Emilio and the others. And when he lay with Salome, their play was often like a battle where he was the conqueror.

In the evenings and between performances he continued to practice with his knife, throwing the blade with a force and accuracy that caused Emilio to shake his head. Since their nighttime conversation up on the pass, the two young men had become something like friends, even though Salome still stood between them like an invisible shadow.

"It's amazing how skilled you've grown with the knife in just a few weeks," said Emilio. "You're gifted. But try not to throw with so much force—it's scary to watch." He gave a laugh. "It looks like you're trying to kill someone with every throw."

Maybe I am, Johann thought and hurled the blade at a tree, where it lodged dead in the center of a knothole, the blade quivering.

The following day, they included knife throwing in their show. The audience groaned with fear as Johann threw knife after knife at Salome, who was tied to a board. Every time, the blade landed only a finger's breadth away from her face or her chest. It seemed to Johann that Salome was enjoying the mortal danger. She never so much as blinked and always gazed at him with an encouraging smile. He, too, enjoyed the thrill of the game, the gauging of the boundaries—life and death separated only by a thin, invisible line. He felt almost delirious when he threw the knives, one after the other, driven by an inexplicable fury. But he never performed with the knife Tonio had given him, although he couldn't say why. Maybe it was the absurd thought that it would somehow, magically, find its way to Salome's heart. Johann still didn't know what the strange initials on it stood for.

Another week later they came to a lake that seemed to Johann as large as an ocean. They traveled along its eastern shore until they reached the city of Verona. Johann had never seen anyplace like it. Roman palaces and ruins stood among the tall, imposing patrician villas like witnesses from a long-gone era. There was a huge, crumbling arena that people were using as a quarry. Once upon a time, heretics had been burned in its center; now the old arena was sometimes used for plays. The Italians, Johann realized, loved pomp and all things bright and cheerful much more than the dolorous Germans did. The country reminded him of an elderly, drunken harlot who had applied a little too much makeup but still radiated plenty of charisma.

Peter asked him repeatedly whether he was ready to read people's palms, and each time, Johann made up excuses. Here at Verona, Peter tried again.

"The Veronese are wealthy and superstitious. We could make a pile of money with palm reading." Peter gave Johann a pleading look. "Come on! It's just a bit of hocus-pocus. What's so hard about it?"

But Johann remained stubborn. Archibaldus gave him a thoughtful look. Following their evening performance on the Piazza delle Erbe, which had been used as a market and meeting square since Roman times, the old man sought him out. Together they sat on the bank of the River Etsch, which flowed underneath a huge stone bridge. On the opposite bank, the arena rose up among houses. A small fire at their feet dispelled the chill of the night. Archibaldus took a long sip from a wineskin and burped.

"Did you know that they used to set lions on Christians in arenas like this in Roman times?" he said. "How strange the course of this world is. First the Christians are persecuted and burned as heretics, and then they go and burn heretics themselves. Cathars, Waldensians, sorcerers . . ." He gave Johann a sideways look. "Was your mentor one of those sorcerers?"

"He is an astrologer and chiromancer," replied Johann hesitantly, unsure of Archibaldus's question. "He only dabbles in the kind of white magic that's permitted by the church." Johann had no intention of discussing Tonio's other side with the old magister—the dark, evil side Johann had only really seen at the end.

The old man cleared his throat and scratched his louse-ridden head. "Seems to me you're no friend of chiromancy," he said. "How come? Don't you trust the skills of your former master?"

Johann gave a shrug. "Peter's right. There's a lot of hocus-pocus to it."

"Is that so?" Archibaldus raised an eyebrow. His voice sounded steady and serious now, not at all like that of a drunkard. "Perhaps that's true for some chiromancers. But I've also heard there are a few who can actually foresee a person's fate—even his death." He looked intently at Johann, who gave an embarrassed laugh.

"Oh, I don't know—"

"I've watched you the last few days and weeks, Johann," said Archibaldus, cutting him off. "I've been in this world for a while now, and I think I know a fair bit about people. You're not just a juggler. You're damned clever—the cleverest lad I've ever met. You could become a great scholar—or a fool who mocks the world. There's something dark inside you that I can't read, and the darkness is growing. Something inside you is searching, looking for answers, foraging in depths we mortals aren't supposed to explore. You're changing, Johann, and I'm afraid for you. Those words . . ."

"I . . . I don't know what you're talking about."

"That Latin phrase you used a few weeks ago," Archibaldus said. "I can't stop thinking about it. Remember? *Homo Deus est.* How do you know those words?"

"My . . . my mentor mentioned them once. Why do you ask?"

"Tonio del Moravia. That was his name, wasn't it?" Archibaldus nodded pensively. "An interesting name for an itinerant white magician. I'll find out where I've heard that name before. Man is God . . . Hmm. They like to use those words to identify themselves."

"Who? What do you mean?" asked Johann. But Archibaldus said nothing. The logs crackled in the fire, and Johann thought of the burning minstrel in Nördlingen. He could almost hear his screams—just like the screams of all those Christians chased to death by beasts of prey in the arena of Verona once upon a time.

Archibaldus looked up to the cloudless night sky and the sparkling stars. He gestured upward. "The honorable Bertold of Regensburg, a learned Franciscan and assistant of Albertus Magnus, once said that heaven consisted of ten heavenly choirs, but one of them rebelled against God and became the flock of the devil. According to Bertold, the Earth is also divided into ten groups, one of which is devoted to the devil."

"And who is that group supposed to be?" asked Johann.

Archibaldus smiled. "Haven't you figured it out? It's the jugglers, traveling magicians, and charlatans. Bertold even gave them names of devils. Azazel, Baphomet, Beelzebub, Mephistopheles . . ." He took another sip of wine and burped loudly.

"Damn good wine they make, those Italians. But they should leave the brewing of beer to the Germans." Archibaldus rose to his feet, and Johann saw how exhausted the old man looked. His face was gray and gaunt, covered with a web of red veins and wrinkles. "Those daily shows take it out of me," he said. "I'm very tired. Too tired to drink, even. I must be getting old. Good night, Johann. And stay away from sorcerers."

He nodded at Johann and walked over to the troupe's camp.

That night, Johann made love to Salome so hard that she screamed out loud with pleasure and pain.

With May, summer came to this bright country, which was so different from the cold German lands that had been Johann's home. He thought the light seemed more intense here, making the villages and towns they passed through appear much friendlier than the gloomy backwaters in the Allgäu or in Franconia. It was much warmer, too, and finally he understood why German jugglers preferred to spend winter here.

They arrived at the Val Padana, the valley of the Po River, where endless fields of grain stretched along the banks of the wide, lazy waterway. On their journey through the cities of Lombardy, Johann saw ancient Roman ruins, but also magnificent palaces and stone churches financed by citizens who were conscious of their power and wealth. Northern Italy was ruled by patricians—members of influential dynasties who accumulated their riches through trade, interest, and a good deal of artfulness. The old nobility and faith in the church had been gradually replaced by an all-powerful, unstoppable force: money. Money didn't care about rank or title.

Occasionally, Johann could feel Archibaldus's eyes on him, but they never again spoke about Johann's former master or that which the old man had called the darkness inside him. Johann learned to better control his temper, although anger continued to fester within him. At night, when everyone was asleep and he lay beside Salome, he wondered if it had been Tonio who'd awakened the darkness in him. Or had it always been there and was only becoming more pronounced now that he was growing into a man?

Emilio told him that northern Italy actually still belonged to the German empire, but it had been many years since a German emperor had managed to assert his claim in the region. Decades had gone by since a German ruler last marched an army across the Alps. Over the years, many city-states had evolved; some of the most powerful included Venice, Milan, Florence, and Geneva. In between, countless small fiefdoms remained that were still loosely connected to the empire—and that always welcomed German jugglers and paid well for their performances.

Together the troupe had decided to travel through Lombardy and farther south over the summer. In fall, they'd head for Venice and the trading post where Archibaldus held sway. They knew their journey wasn't without danger. The land they were moving through had been at war since the year before, although at this stage, the fighting took place elsewhere. The French king, Charles VIII, had conquered Naples and Rome in an attempt to gain a foothold in wealthy Italy. Rising up against him was the so-called Holy League, led by the pope and the Venetians. The battle lines were shifting back and forth, and the jugglers heard rumors about groups of marauding mercenaries who terrorized remote parts of the country, even up here in the north. Apparently, Charles VIII was on his way to Lombardy with more than five thousand men to defeat the Holy League for good.

"Damn those Frenchmen!" groused Peter, cracking his whip. "King Charles is an ugly gnome who sends his soldiers anywhere he suspects there's money. The devil take the lot of them!"

Little did he know that his curse would soon come true for many French soldiers—but also for himself.

On a hot, dry day in July, the two opposing armies met in combat near the city of Parma. The battle was short and devastating. Thousands of French soldiers bled to death in the dusty fields of Fornovo, and Charles VIII was forced to retreat from Italy.

Many of his mercenaries stayed behind, however, leaving a bloody trail of torched villages, murdered farmers, and raped women in their wake.

The troupe had given several successful shows at Mantua—a city favorably inclined toward Germans and ruled by the powerful Gonzaga dynasty. Now they wanted to continue on their way, crossing the Apennine Mountains toward Florence and Siena.

The Apennines were a karstic, densely wooded mountain range, and the troupe rarely passed other travelers. The road wound its way across hills that were covered with thick, nearly impregnable brush. The sun beat down mercilessly from a cloudless sky, and the only sound came from the cicadas, singing their monotonous lullaby. Salome had retreated into the wagon, and Mustafa brought her some water. Johann longed to be alone in the wagon with her. But she'd been cold toward him for days now. Things between them usually went like this: at night she loved him and dug her fingernails into his sweat-covered back, and during the day she completely ignored him. Johann had no idea why. *She'll drive me insane,* he thought. Each climax seemed to drain him a little more, as if she sucked the blood from his veins—and yet he couldn't keep his hands off her.

While they passed through a shady ravine one afternoon, Johann heard a conspicuous whirring noise. In the next moment, a crossbow bolt struck the side of the wagon, quickly followed by a second. Johann and Peter dived headfirst off the box seat and, together with Archibaldus and Emilio, sought shelter behind the wagon. They could hear shouts in a foreign language—French, Johann thought. Moments later, half a dozen mercenaries in colorful slashed trousers and rusty cuirasses emerged from the bushes. Two of them were armed with crossbows, while the rest slowly walked toward the troupe with drawn swords. Johann could tell by the look in the soldiers' eyes that they'd show no mercy.

"La fille," growled the front-most mercenary, a tall, bearded man with a poorly healed scar on his face. *"Donne-moi la fille!"* He gestured toward Salome, who was peering out from behind the wagon canvas. Two of the men slowly stepped toward Emilio and Archibaldus, raising their swords with smirks on their faces. Clearly, they didn't expect much of a fight.

Johann frantically tried to figure out what to do. Defend Salome and die? He had no weapons other than Tonio's knife. Peter owned a rusty short sword, and Emilio and Mustafa were tough opponents in a pub brawl, but they didn't stand a chance against half a dozen trained French mercenaries. Should he try to run away? He shot a glance at the thorny bushes by the wayside. They were just a few steps from him, but even a few steps was too far with a crossbow pointed at you. And he couldn't abandon Salome.

Meanwhile, two of the mercenaries had dragged the screaming Salome out of the wagon. She thrashed about wildly, but to no avail. The men were already tearing off her clothes, laughing as they groped her naked breasts. The rest of the troupe was herded together like a flock of chickens waiting to be slaughtered.

Salome was lying on the road with her legs spread apart, held down by two struggling soldiers. One of the mercenaries opened his fly, knelt down, and gave his comrades a triumphant look.

"C'est moi le premier," he said, rubbing his hard penis. *"Et ensuite—"*

A rumble went through the wagon as if a volcano were erupting inside. The next moment, Mustafa lunged down from the box seat, holding one of the chains he used during his performances. He roared as he swung the chain wildly above his head. It was the first sound Johann had ever heard from the dark giant. His roar sounded like that of an angry bear. The chain hissed like a snake and struck the face of the soldier kneeling in front of Salome, turning it into a bloody mess. Screaming with pain, the man fell to his side, his trousers slipping down to his knees. Mustafa swung the chain and it wrapped itself around the neck of the next man. The soldier turned red in the face, then Mustafa jerked the chain and there was a cracking sound. The man's legs gave way and he fell to the ground with a broken neck.

Everything had happened so fast that none of the remaining four soldiers had had time to react. But now they came to their senses.

"En garde!" shouted the leader, running toward Mustafa, who was standing with his back to the soldier.

When the man ran past, Johann threw his knife.

He did it with the exact same movement he'd practiced time and time again over the last few days and weeks, his face twisted into a grimace of determination and hatred. When the blade left his fingers, he felt an enormous sense of relief, as if something inside him let go. For the briefest moment, the face of the mercenary leader turned into Tonio's grinning visage.

Then the knife entered the soldier's left eye with a smacking noise. The man kept running for another yard or two, as if he hadn't noticed his own death, and then he collapsed like a puppet whose strings had been cut.

Mustafa turned around and gave Johann a nod as the giant bent down to pick up the dead man's sword. A crossbow bolt struck Mustafa's left upper arm, but he didn't even seem to react. He hurled himself at the next opponent with a dull cry. The man raised his weapon, gasping with fear, but Mustafa shoved the blade aside as if it were a twig and buried his own sword in the crook of the soldier's neck. A fountain of blood spurted from the wound and onto the dusty road.

The two remaining men didn't linger for long when they saw their comrades lying dead in the dirt. They threw down their crossbow and sword and turned to run. But Mustafa wasn't finished. He went after the men, grabbed the slower one by the collar, and yanked him back like a rag doll. Then he pummeled the mercenary's face with his fists until it was nothing but bloody pulp. When Mustafa finally let go of him, the man groaned, gave one last twitch, and died. The last mercenary got away through the bushes.

The man whose face Mustafa had demolished with the chain was still screaming. *"Mon visage, mon visage!"* he moaned over and over, rolling around on the ground. *"Je suis aveugle, je ne vois rien! O Vierge Sainte!"*

Mustafa walked over to him and slit his throat with one swift movement.

A heavy silence descended over the ravine. Blowflies found the dead bodies and landed in the gaping wounds. Among the corpses sat Salome, her dress torn, almost naked, staring straight ahead. She was trembling, but she held her head high like a proud queen of death. Eventually she stood up, leaned over the man with the slit throat, and spat in his bloodied face.

Mustafa pulled the bolt from his upper arm as if removing a splinter, and then he gently wrapped a blanket around his sister's shoulders. Johann thought about what Emilio had told him a few weeks ago. Apparently Mustafa had tried to defend Salome in faraway Alexandria, whereupon their master had cut out his tongue. No wonder Mustafa wasn't going to stand by and watch while someone tried to rape his sister again. He'd rather die—or kill.

Peter was the first to speak after a long silence. "That . . . that was damned close," he said. "Thanks, Mustafa."

Mustafa didn't deign to look at him but continued to care for Salome. Johann walked over to the body of the lead mercenary and pulled his knife from the man's eye. The blade was sticky and bloody, and the man's other eye seemed to stare at him reproachfully. It was the first time Johann had killed somebody. It had been so easy.

And if he was being honest with himself, he'd even enjoyed it.

The desire for vengeance and retribution had flowed through his veins like sweet poison, just like the time in Knittlingen when he'd met Tonio and wished for the death of Margarethe's brother. He remembered Tonio's words.

Hatred can be very healing, purging the soul like fire.

Tonio had been right. Hatred was as sweet and delicious as freshly baked honey cake. The anger that had been stewing inside Johann for so long was wiped away, and all that remained was a pleasant emptiness.

"We should get away from here," Archibaldus said warningly and brushed the dust off his frock. He was trembling, in dire need of a swig of wine. "One of them got away. We don't know if he went to fetch reinforcements."

"You're right, old pisshead," replied Peter. "Let's get going." His eyes turned to Mustafa again. Then he grinned. "I swear, that was the quickest fight I've seen in my life! You truly are—" Suddenly Peter grimaced with pain and he clutched his hands to his stomach.

"What is it?" asked Emilio. "Are you hurt?"

Peter shook his head with clenched teeth. "It's . . . nothing. Probably just an upset stomach. It's been paining me for a few days now. Perhaps the water from one of the wells I've been drinking from was foul." He gave a strained laugh and gestured at the corpses around them. "By Christ, I could be lying there getting eaten by flies, so I'm sure I can put up with a bit of stomach pain. Let's go before more of those French bastards turn up."

Peter climbed onto the box seat with much difficulty, and Johann noticed that he continued to hold his side. Johann was overcome by an uneasy feeling and wondered whether Peter had really just drunk a bit of foul water.

During the following days and weeks, they crossed the Apennines and headed south toward Florence and Siena, avoiding the smaller roads whenever possible. Most French soldiers had left the country, but the troupe didn't want to risk running into any who had stuck around. They couldn't always rely on Mustafa.

Thankfully, the crossbow bolt hadn't penetrated Mustafa's arm deeply, and the wound healed fast. Peter's stomach pains, on the other hand, persisted. Sometimes they would go away for two or three days just to return all the worse.

Peter grew visibly skinny, and his face became drawn and pale. He barely ate. But he still played fiddle during their performances; in fact, he played even more heartrendingly beautifully than before—as if his life came pouring out of him with his melodies.

"What kind of a terrible disease is it?" Johann asked Archibaldus at a tavern one evening. They had just given a show in a large, magnificent town called Pisa with an oddly tilted bell tower on its market square. The old man wiped the drops of wine from his beard before replying to Johann.

"I can't tell you for certain, but I'm afraid it's something serious. It could be a growth in his stomach that is eating him up from the inside. The Greeks call it cancer, because apparently the growth looks somewhat like a crab."

"Does that mean he's going to die?" asked Johann haltingly. He'd grown fond of Peter in the last few months, admiring the man's vivacity and leadership, but most of all his musical talent, which was unparalleled and otherworldly. But—if Johann was entirely honest—it wasn't Peter's probable death that scared him the most, but the fact that he had foreseen it in Peter's palm. He remembered what Archibaldus had said a few weeks ago about chiromancers.

I've also heard there are a few who can actually foresee a person's fate—even his death.

Johann turned pale at the thought. Could it be that Tonio had taught him such an ominous skill without his noticing?

"I think Peter knows that he won't be with us for much longer." Archibaldus sighed. "No one can say how much longer exactly. But I fear he won't be going to Venice with us."

"But . . . but Peter is our leader!" said Johann stubbornly. "What's going to happen to us?"

He had become fixated on Venice as their destination. Perhaps it had something to do with the stories his mother used to tell him about the city. Johann hoped that after so much traveling, his life would settle down a little in Venice, at least for a while. He didn't know what would come afterward.

"What's going to happen to us?" Archibaldus gave a dry laugh. "It would be worse for you if *I* drank myself to death before the autumn. Remember, it is my invitation alone that will open the gates of the Fondaco dei Tedeschi to us. With Peter, we merely lose a fiddle player—a damn good one, though." He shook his head. "It's almost as if the devil himself taught him to play! I'd love to help him, but my knowledge of healing isn't great enough. I guess I studied the wrong subject."

"Where did you study?" asked Johann.

"At one of the oldest and most venerable universities in the empire: Heidelberg."

"Heidelberg?" Johann's heart beat faster. "That's not far from where I come from. It's always been my dream to study there."

"Well, it's a beautiful city that tends to lead a young man to feast and drink more than study," Archibaldus replied with a grin. "My father, the great Karl Stovenbrannt, said I ought to at least gain my baccalaureus there. I was talented and thirsty for knowledge, and so I even gained the degree of magister. Then I went on trips to our trading posts at Bergen, Bruges, London, and also to Italy. And that's where I experienced the *dolce vita* and was forever lost to my father and the trade." He gave Johann an inquisitive look. "How come you're not at the university? You're as clever as you are learned, and you are ambitious, even though you try your best to hide it from everyone else. I've told you before: you could be a great scholar."

"The man who raised me would rather have set fire to his own house than allow me to go to the university," Johann replied bitterly. "He thought I was a good-for-nothing."

Archibaldus laughed. "I still don't know who you really are, Johann, but you're certainly no good-for-nothing. If you wish, I could teach you a few bits and pieces on our journey to Venice and throughout the winter. About the *artes liberales*, at least."

"The *artes liberales*?" Johann frowned. Evidently, he still had much to learn. "What's that?"

"The liberal arts are the prerequisite for any higher education. The three lower ones, also known as the trivium, are grammar, rhetoric, and dialectic. Then follow the four upper arts, called the quadrivium. They include arithmetic, geometry, music, and astronomy." Archibaldus looked at him sharply. "Although I think you've learned enough of the latter from your former teacher. Those arts are very old. Long taught by the Greeks and Romans, they are the foundation of all sciences."

"And you . . . you'd really instruct me in all those arts?" Johann stared at him with an open mouth. He suddenly realized how desperately he longed for knowledge; he craved it like one craves water after wandering the desert for weeks. He craved it even more than Salome's breasts and the warmth between her legs. "But how could I possibly pay you back?"

"By telling me who you really are, Johann." He raised one hand. "Don't worry—not right away. Perhaps I'll learn more about you in the course of our lessons." He took a long sip before continuing. "And perhaps I'll even find out more about your former mentor."

During the following months, they moved through the heat of upper Italy and performed in many towns and cities. For Johann, it was a time of both pain and fulfillment. Archibaldus remained true to his word and instructed him in the liberal arts. Johann's anger abated, replaced by his thirst for knowledge. Perhaps his inner rage had something to do with a frustration at the lack of mental stimuli. He felt at peace while he discussed grammar, arithmetic, and dialectic with Archibaldus. At the same time it pained him to watch Peter crumble, even though the redhead put on a brave face and continued to play his fiddle and make the announcements between their individual acts. Emilio especially tried to raise the subject of his illness with Peter every now and then, but the man cut him off every time.

"I'm going to keep playing the fiddle for as long as the dear Lord—or who-ever else—lets me play," Peter would reply gruffly. "Each one of us is only given a certain amount of time on this earth. It's pointless to grieve before my time's up. Now go practice your act, you lazybones. You dropped two balls during the last show!"

In Genoa, Archibaldus bought expensive poppy juice from a pharmacy for Peter, who took it mixed with brandy. At least it helped him to bear the pain. During the evenings, Peter would often sit by the campfire, staring into the flames and muttering to himself.

"Now he's finally come to fetch me," he said quietly. "Damn, was it really worth it? If I could only turn back time—I would gladly have paid the price for her! For her, not for this cursed fiddle."

No one knew what Peter meant by those strange words. Johann didn't have much time to ponder them, because Salome didn't give him a break. They made love so passionately under the starry skies that Johann wished the sun would never rise again. Sleeping with Salome was like a drug that helped him forget everything else—his mother, his years in Knittlingen, little Martin, Tonio, the black potion, and even Margarethe.

But as hard as they loved each other at night, Salome was no companion to him during the day. Just the opposite: she was cold and unapproachable. One day, when she and Johann followed the wagon at a little distance and Salome—as usual—said nothing and focused on picking rosemary and sage by the wayside, he grabbed her by the arm and forced her to look at him.

"Damn it, Salome, what are you playing at?" he said angrily. "Don't toy with me—I'm not a puppet. If you don't love me, just tell me to my face. But then let's stop with those games at night!"

"Games?" Salome gave a thin smile. "Is that what you really want, my little wolf? To stop doing that?"

Johann didn't answer, because he knew she was right. He needed Salome as badly as Peter needed his poppy juice. He'd never be able to leave her, no matter how poorly she treated him during the day.

"But . . . but why are you acting like this?" he asked. "I honestly have no idea what to think. You're so different at night from how you are during the day. Don't you love me, Salome?"

She looked at him for a long time before replying in a quiet voice.

"I loved for the last time when I was fifteen years old. He was a boy from Armenia, handsome like you, smart, and always had a big smile on his face. When they dragged me and Mustafa onto the ship, he tried to block their way. They cut his throat and threw him into the water like a dead rat. I watched the sharks tear his beautiful body into pieces. That was the second-to-last time I cried. The last time was when they cut out Mustafa's tongue." Her lips were thin lines, her eyes as cold as ice.

"I won't let them hurt me again. Ever! Now let go of me before I cut off your best piece. It would be a shame, no question, but I'd do it anyway."

A small knife suddenly flashed in her hand, and Johann let go. She didn't come to him for four nights. When she slipped underneath his blanket during the fifth night, they didn't utter a word. The pain when her fingernails dug into his skin was sweet and made him howl like a wolf. Johann carried red streaks on his back for many days. And Emilio studied him with a quiet smile.

"She's eating you up," he mocked. "I warned you, Johann. She devours men."

His hours with Archibaldus helped take his mind off Salome. The two men often rode in the back of the wagon on their trips between villages and towns. Archibaldus had organized a slab of slate and a piece of chalk for Johann, as well as an abacus to learn arithmetic. Of the seven liberal arts, Johann particularly enjoyed rhetoric. He and Archibaldus spent hours practicing the sequence of thesis and antithesis, whereby Archibaldus thoroughly enjoyed refuting Johann's arguments.

"Socrates likened philosophers to midwives," Archibaldus said with a smile when Johann found himself outwitted once more. "They are merely helping to deliver someone's thoughts, but the initial spark has to come from within yourself."

Johann groaned. "So much knowledge. It's a crying shame that there isn't a place where all that knowledge is stored and accessible to everyone, not just to a select few. Each monastery only hoards books for their own benefit, or you have to attend university and pay a pile of money."

Archibaldus slowly shook his head. "Times are changing. There is a public library in my hometown of Hamburg now. It's huge, and anyone can enter and browse through the books as they please."

"I want to go there one day," Johann replied. "And to Heidelberg, Prague, and Vienna—to all the great universities of the empire."

Archibaldus was now drinking much less than he used to, going to bed only moderately drunk in the evenings. The lessons with Johann seemed to have rejuvenated him. He kept trying to find out more about Johann's former teacher and master, but the young man gave almost nothing away about Tonio. On the one hand, because Johann hardly knew much about the man himself, and on the other, because he had the strange feeling that Tonio would be able to hear them if they talked about him—as if he came to life just by being spoken about. Or as if Tonio's raven and crows were circling somewhere high above them, reporting to their master.

September came, then October. There were increasingly more rainy days now, and the mild, warm weather gave way to a dull grayness that seemed to win over the sun a little bit more every day. Storms rumbled along the coast, and sea fog crept into the land from the ocean. Still, it was much warmer than the October days Johann remembered from Knittlingen. Whenever they passed slopes planted in vines heavy with grapes, he wistfully thought about the harvests back home, about the German songs and the laughter of the pretty Knittlingen girls.

When October turned to November, they decided it was time to start heading for Venice. They had been in the mighty city-state for a while now. Venice's properties stretched along the entire northeast shore of Italy and also included colonies on the shores of the Adriatic Sea and on large islands like Crete. But they hadn't come near the city itself so far.

It had been Peter's greatest wish to see the most glamorous city in the world, known as La Serenissima, or "the most serene," one last time. But he'd spent the last two weeks lying in the back of the wagon, staring at the ceiling. His daily doses of poppy juice had steadily increased. Peter's fiddle hung from a hook on the wall, gently swaying from side to side when they were on the road; he hadn't played it for a while now.

Their last performance on the mainland was in a town called Treviso, only twenty miles from Venice. That night, Johann was woken by groans coming from the wagon. Someone was calling his name.

It was Peter.

Carefully, Johann peeled himself out of the blanket, trying not to wake Salome, and climbed into the wagon. Peter had managed to light a tallow candle, and Johann could see his haggard face. The formerly proud, strong-minded fiddle player looked like death himself. When his mouth twisted into a sad smile, Johann thought he was looking at a skull. The red hair stuck to his forehead like wet straw.

"The . . . the end has come," Peter said with wheezing breath. "I can feel it."

"Shall I fetch the others?" Johann squeezed Peter's hand, which seemed to consist of nothing but skin and bones.

Peter shook his head tiredly. "I don't want them to see me like this. I . . . only wanted to speak with you."

"With me? But why—"

Peter raised a hand, cutting Johann off. "Please, Johann, tell me . . . ," said the sick man, pausing with exhaustion. "Back when we crossed the pass and you read my palm . . . something frightened you. It . . . it was because you foresaw my death, didn't you? Am I right?"

Johann hesitated briefly, but then he nodded. Why should he lie to a dying man?

Peter nodded. "I . . . I thought so. Accursed magicians and chiromancers!" He made a sound that Johann didn't immediately recognize as a laugh. "I never trusted you, lad. You've got something about you, something dark, restless. As if . . . as if the devil himself touched you."

Johann said nothing and Peter continued, his voice taking on a dreamy tone. He stared up at the ceiling as if he could see his life replay before his eyes.

"I knew a girl once. She was as beautiful as the sun, but she came from a lowly home, while my family was of noble blood, and so I wasn't permitted to marry her. We ran away together. We made a living as jugglers. It was the best time of my life." Peter smiled. "People liked it when I played the fiddle, even though I wasn't very good yet. But then . . ." He wheezed and gasped for breath. "Then she fell ill. Very ill. I had to watch her fade away before my eyes. I swore I'd do anything to save her. And . . . and someone asked me, 'Anything? Would you even give me three fingers of your right hand?' I . . . I said I would, but then I didn't give him the fingers—even though I'd promised. A fiddler needs his fingers like a fish needs gills to breathe! Do you understand, Johann? Do you understand me? And so she died, and I . . ." He paused. "I played better and better. The devil knows why." He gave another laugh. "By God, I *know* he knows! And now he's coming to take his part of the bargain."

Johann was still holding Peter's hand—the hand of the red-haired fiddler who played heavenly melodies so beautifully that they had the power to break hearts. Peter's story was confused—the last stammered words of a dying man, not making a lot of sense. But they filled Johann with a sense of dread. Suddenly Peter grasped Johann's hand so hard that Johann winced.

"Pray for me, Johann Faustus," the fiddler begged. "Pray for me, for a poor sinner who loved playing the fiddle more than he loved his girl. Pray for me! And burn . . . my . . . fiddle."

Peter's hand squeezed Johann's one last time, then life left his body with one final wheezing breath. His eyes turned glassy, and he fell back onto the bed. A nameless terror filled his gaze, as if he'd seen something horrible in the last moment of his life. Johann couldn't bear the sight and closed Peter's eyes. Then he lifted the violin from its hook and climbed outside, where the moon cast its pale light through the clouds. He walked over to the fire and threw the fiddle into the flames, which crackled hungrily as they ate their way through the wood with blue tongues. None of the others woke up.

Johann wanted to pray for Peter, but he realized that he didn't really know how. The last time he'd prayed was such a long time ago—by his mother's grave. The words fell from his mouth like dry crumbs of dirt.

"Our father in heaven, hallowed be thy name . . ."

Johann hastily made the sign of the cross before going to wake the others to tell them that Peter Nachtigall, the red-haired devil of a fiddler, leader of their small troupe of jugglers, had passed away.

And he wondered how Peter had known his nickname—the name his mother used to call him.

Faustus, the lucky one.

But it was too late to ask him.

11

THEY BURIED PETER NACHTIGALL NEXT TO THE CEMETERY of the small Treviso church. As a dishonorable juggler, he couldn't be buried within the cemetery walls, but at least the priest said a quick prayer for his soul and there was a wooden cross with his name on it. As Johann studied the crudely carved inscription on the cross, he thought about how far from Peter's home the fiddler had been put to rest, as a stranger. Johann wondered if he'd share this same fate one day.

Once the priest had left, the troupe stood around the grave in silence for a while. There was a light drizzle in the air and the hollow sound of a death knell. Eventually, Emilio spoke.

"What do we do now?" he asked the others.

"What do you think?" replied Johann. "We go to Venice. That's what Peter would have wanted."

"But we need a new leader," said Emilio.

"Indeed we do." Johann gave them a challenging look. "And that's going to be me. It was Peter's dying wish. He asked me to burn his fiddle and lead his troupe from now on."

The latter was a blatant lie, but Johann had long felt a desire to change the face of the troupe. Some of their acts were outdated, and for the last few months, Peter had treated him as a full-fledged member of the troupe and promised him a great future as a showman. Something inside Johann told him that it was time to step up.

"You?" Emilio gave a thin smile. "How old are you? Seventeen?"

"Which makes me not much younger than you," replied Johann. "You may be a good acrobat, but your speeches are dry and boring. The leader should be articulate. And you have no idea about business. I know arithmetic and how to negotiate."

"I may not be the best at delivering speeches." Emilio crossed his arms on his chest and returned Johann's defiant stare. "But you don't stand a chance in Venice, because you don't speak the language. Unlike me."

"Then you can translate for him," Archibaldus said. "I also think Johann would make a good leader. He is clever and won't let anyone pull one over on him—or us. And he certainly knows how to talk."

In the past few weeks, the sicker Peter had gotten, the more often Johann had taken over the announcements during their shows. He was good at catching people's attention with his loud voice and witty speeches, and he knew how to use just the right amount of persuasion—the mark of a good juggler. Their audience numbers had grown steadily since Johann had begun helming the shows; even Archibaldus's tattered relics had been making money again, with numerous believers paying to touch them.

"What do you think?" Emilio asked Salome, who had been watching in silence with her brother. "Do you also think our young Johann is the best for the job?" He pulled a mocking face. "You know him best of all of us."

Salome gave a little smile. "Let's give him a chance," she said. "He's pretty to look at and he's funny—the women will love him. And your speeches, Emilio, are truly as uplifting as a eulogy."

When Mustafa nodded in agreement, Emilio sighed and gave up. "All right, then. I don't feel like grappling with city officials about show permits, anyway. As long as we share fairly. I will continue to juggle, but I'll also play the wheel-fiddle like I used to—and I get a pay raise." He gave a shrug. "We need music, at least until we find someone else." He cast a dark glance at Johann. "Pity you burned the fiddle. We could've gotten good money for it."

"It was Peter's last wish, remember?" said Johann. He clapped his hands. "Now let's sell our horse and wagon. We have no use for either of them in Venice. And come springtime, I'm sure we'll find something better than that old nag."

He turned to leave, and to his secret relief, the others followed.

The city of Venice welcomed them with fog and rain.

They had boarded a barge at Mestre with all their crates and bags, and, along with numerous pilgrims, they'd set off toward the sea. The river ended in a brackish, foggy lagoon where a lonesome tower rose out of the mist.

"The Torre di Marghera," said Archibaldus, who had been to Venice as a young man. The old drunkard donned his best clothes for their arrival at the trading post, making him look almost dignified, the red nose and the matted hair aside. "The tower was the first structure the Venetians erected outside their city. And since then, they've conquered half the world."

Gradually, an entire city emerged through the dull, foggy haze. It seemed to hover above the water. Johann made out a maze of houses, palaces, churches, and bridges leading across many small canals. Fishing boats and larger ships were moored just outside the city, and a wider canal led right through town. More and more sounds came through the thick mist: the slapping of oars, the cries of the market women, the chiming of church bells. The saline smell of the water mingled with the scents of the city, and wafts of smoke, food, and filth surrounded them.

The barge was full to the last spot, and the low railing was almost level with the water. Despite the danger of falling overboard, the passengers pushed to the front to get a better view of the magnificent palaces lining the waterfront. Each building had its own dock with colorfully painted posts. Wide arches led into inner courtyards, and elaborately designed balconies adorned the upper stories.

Johann, too, was standing at the front of the boat. Black gondolas slid past him like swift fish. The gondoliers, standing at the rear, steered their boats into the smaller canals using long poles. Their passengers were ladies clad in satin and damask embroidered with gold and men wearing wide berets adorned with pearls and other trinkets. This city was so magnificent that by comparison, thought Johann, Augsburg seemed to live in an earlier era.

"Apparently, all this used to be lots of small islands," said Archibaldus, gesturing at the foggy waters in front of them, where Johann could make out several larger islands. "Over time, they grew together. The houses and even the lanes are resting on thousands of logs. But almost everything takes place on the water here."

The large canal took a bend, and then they saw a steep wooden bridge with two cranes in the middle. Both banks of the canal were bustling with people, and the lanes were full of market stalls. Just as they were heading toward the bridge, a loud horn sounded. The barge with the jugglers and pilgrims slid to one side, and Johann watched as the cranes pulled up the center piece of the bridge. A large galley with masts as tall as trees sailed past them. Waves caused the barge to sway from side to side, and some of the pilgrims cried out in fear. The galley passed through the bridge and the center piece was lowered again.

"I think it's better if we get off here," said Archibaldus, who was surprisingly sober. "God knows what other ships want to pass through the Rialto Bridge. The Fondaco dei Tedeschi isn't far from here."

Some of the pilgrims had also decided to disembark. The troupe gathered their belongings, and Mustafa carried the two heavy crates with the relics. Loaded like mules, they followed Archibaldus through a tangle of lanes and alleyways. It took Johann a few moments before he realized what was so strange about this city: there were hardly any wagons or oxcarts. Everything was transported via the canals. The lanes were so narrow that the troupe struggled to make any progress among all the pedestrians, shouting peddlers, beggars, and colorfully clad patricians. Johann noticed that the buildings' main entranceways always lay on the side of the water and included a small dock or pier, whereas the doors leading into the lanes were small and plain, more like servants' entrances. Archibaldus was right: life did take place on the water here, not on the land.

After a while they came to a building several stories high, with noise and shouting coming from inside. Johann could make out bits of German. An open gate led to a courtyard where many tables had been set up. Bales and crates were stacked up in front of the arcades surrounding the courtyard, and men wearing the bright garb of wealthy merchants walked around. Abaci and inkwells stood on the tables; pale-faced scribes sat hunched over documents bearing seals or entered numbers into lists.

Archibaldus grinned and pointed toward the courtyard. "The Fondaco dei Tedeschi. No other trading post in Venice is as busy as this one. The Germans are veritable penny-pinchers—especially the Swabians." He rubbed his hands. "Now let's go and see if the name Stovenbrannt still counts for anything in this city. Follow me."

He was about to walk into the courtyard when two broad-shouldered men wearing the typical jerkins and slit trousers of German soldiers blocked his way.

"No begging in here, old man," barked one of them in German. *"Capisci? Qui non si mendica!"*

"Dear gentlemen, I'm not here to beg but to speak with the German representative," replied Archibaldus as gracefully as possible, brushing a strand of tangled gray hair from his face. "Please tell him Archibaldus Stovenbrannt has returned after many years."

"Stovenbrannt?" The fatter of the two guards scratched his head. "Never heard of that name."

"Better not say that to the German representative," Archibaldus said sternly. "The Stovenbrannts used to sell nearly as much cloth in this town as those nouveau riche Welsers and Fuggers. Now off you go—we're expected."

The guard hesitated, clearly wondering whether he was looking at a drunk, confused old man or an influential merchant who could get him in a lot of trouble. Finally, he reached a decision.

"Wait here," he muttered.

He walked over to the arcades while the other guard continued to watch the colorful troupe in silence. After a short while, an obese man of around fifty wearing a beret and a fur-lined coat walked toward them. In his hand he carried his staff of office, which designated him as the German merchants' representative in Venice. When he saw the jugglers at the gate, his face darkened.

"You dragged me out of a business meeting for these jokers?" he snarled at the guard. "Throw them out and—"

"My dear Rieverschmitt," said Archibaldus, spreading his arms with a smile. "Don't you recognize old Archibaldus?"

The merchant frowned. "I can't say I—"

"Archibaldus Stovenbrannt. Remember?" Archibaldus pulled out his crumpled document and handed it to Rieverschmitt. "Perhaps this'll jog your memory."

The merchant skimmed through the brief letter, and his face broke into a strained smile. "Look at that, Hans Stovenbrannt's uncle. I do remember now, though it's been a long time. I was a young man then, and you were visiting your nephew in Hamburg. You . . ." He paused. "You studied for many years, they say."

Archibaldus gave a shrug. "No need to beat around the bush. I decided on a different career from the rest of my family. What you're reading there is a letter of recommendation for me and this exceptional troupe of jugglers I'm traveling with." He gestured at Johann and the others behind him. "You do need jugglers over the winter, don't you? The days are gray and boring, and if you want to close a lucrative deal, you first want to get your business partner in the right mood."

"It's true, we could do with a few jugglers, but . . ." Rieverschmitt eyed Johann and the rest of the troupe. He didn't seem particularly impressed. "Two young boys—juggling acts, I take it—and a huge Moor. And who's at the back?"

Until then, Salome had hidden her face behind a veil. Now she lowered it and took a step forward. The merchant gave a whistle and licked his lips. "By God, does this beauty have a price? I know a wealthy Venetian patrician who'd—"

Mustafa stepped forward and glowered at Rieverschmitt as if the man had just blasphemed against God and all the saints at once. The merchant sensed he'd made a mistake. "Well, I only thought—"

"Great, then we're all agreed," Johann said and positioned himself next to Archibaldus. "What about accommodation?"

"Um, well, you can't stay here at the Fondaco—not as jugglers," Rieverschmitt replied, his eyes still glued to Salome. "But many Germans stay at the Flute Inn. It's not far from here. Just tell them Rieverschmitt sent you."

"The Flute?" Salome smiled and gazed deep into Rieverschmitt's eyes. "I like to play the flute, signore. A fitting place for jugglers. I'm sure we'll get free meals and lodging there, right?"

"We . . . we can talk about that," said Rieverschmitt, squirming. "Best you move into your rooms first, and then come back and show me what you can do."

"We will," said Johann confidently. "You won't be disappointed, Master Rieverschmitt. Johann Faustus's Fabulous Troupe is the best troupe of jugglers you'll find in the entire German empire."

Johann Faustus's Fabulous Troupe . . .

Johann repeated in his mind the name he'd just come up with. It seemed to strike the right note, because Rieverschmitt grinned.

"Faustus, the lucky one? Well, we can always use a bit of luck at the counting-house. I'm expecting you back in an hour for your first show."

As promised, they performed at the Fondaco later that afternoon. Rieverschmitt seemed happy enough, but Johann got the impression that the trade representative was mainly interested in Salome. She danced her seductive veil dance to a queer melody played by Emilio on his wheel-fiddle. Mustafa tore a massive chain apart and flexed his muscles, and Johann performed magic tricks, causing the merchants watching to gasp and laugh. Archibaldus appeared to be of the opinion that he'd fulfilled his part of the day's work by talking to Rieverschmitt, and he retreated beneath the arcades with a jug of wine. The others found him passed out behind some bales of cloth later. Johann wasn't particularly upset that Archibaldus hadn't been part of this important performance.

Johann agreed to Rieverschmitt's request that over the winter they give two small performances a day—one in the morning and one in the afternoon—to keep the German traders entertained. They received free board and lodging at the Flute Inn, and Johann even managed to negotiate a small sum the Fondaco would pay them each week. It wasn't much, but enough to make their winter much more pleasurable than if they'd had to spend it north of the Alps, where it was probably snowing by now.

But even in Venice, November was cool. A thick fog covered the city, and the troupe's clothes were always damp, no matter how many times they dried them before the fire. Johann roamed through the lanes, shivering, watching the black gondolas as they appeared from the mist and vanished again. In Saint Mark's Square, the large piazza, stood the biggest, most magnificent church Johann had ever seen. It was dominated by five domes that gave the building a fairy-tale quality—like a castle from the stories his mother used to tell him. A huge tower stood in front of the structure, and right next to it was the Palazzo Ducale, where the Venetian doge ruled over the republic.

Archibaldus had explained to Johann that Venice was ruled by a powerful council of patricians led by the doge. The patricians acted like small kings. They never strutted through the city without at least a page boy by their side, if not also a Moor serving as their slave. The high and mighty kept those poor people as if they were pets.

Even more than in Augsburg, pomp and misery, wealth and poverty lived side by side here. Ladies with hair bleached with lemon juice, wearing expensive silks and high platform shoes, tottered past gaunt, hungry street urchins and condemned men who were tortured publicly beneath the arcades of the doge's palace. There was an entire street dedicated to the manufacture of extremely precious mirrors, while a few streets down people were dying in the gutter.

Exploring the city helped Johann clear his head and gave him time to think. After just a few days, the troupe had accepted him as their new leader, along with their new name. No one asked where the Latin word *faustus* came from. In Venice, they acted more as court jesters than as jugglers performing set shows;

they'd exhibit a magic trick here and do a bit of juggling over there. On good days, they even sold a few bottles of the overpriced theriac Archibaldus brewed from cheap liquor and herbs. The magister touted it as an astonishing miracle tincture and didn't mind trying it out on himself. But the relics stayed in their chests; the troupe didn't want to risk getting in trouble with the Venetian authorities. Venice boasted plenty of relics of its own in its many churches.

Everything was going as well as it could, and yet Johann felt restless. Venice had been his goal, the star he'd followed ever since leaving Tonio. But now he realized that this city was just another station in his colorful life. And he didn't know how to handle Salome. He felt jealousy creeping up in him whenever men gaped at her as she swayed her hips to Emilio's music.

"I don't think you have to dance quite so salaciously," he told Salome one evening, following their show at the Fondaco. "One day some drunk will drag you behind the cloth bales."

"Maybe I want to be dragged behind the bales," Salome replied coldly. "Always remember: you don't own me, little wolf."

To take his mind off Salome, Johann continued his lessons with Archibaldus. He worked hard, getting up before sunrise to practice arithmetic or check the grammar in his writings. When Archibaldus quizzed him at lunchtime, the old man would sometimes pause and gaze at him thoughtfully.

"You're quick, Johann," he'd say, stroking his louse-ridden beard. "Almost frightfully quick. The devil knows how you do it."

Johann grinned. "I'm only at the start. Do you happen to know Greek?"

Archibaldus groaned. "A little. But I need a fresh jug of wine for that. Be so kind and fetch one, will you?"

The Fondaco grew quiet in December. The alpine passes were blocked by snow and ice, and no more German traders arrived in Venice. Instead, Rieverschmitt frequently received Venetian guests who were interested in German linen, salt, beeswax, silver, and amber. Often they'd feast together late into the night on wine, dried fish, and roast meat. The Venetians at their food with three-pronged forks—an item that was still considered a tool of the devil north of the Alps. Johann thought it was quite practical for keeping one's hands clean.

One particularly cold afternoon, when fires were lit in iron baskets throughout the Fondaco, Rieverschmitt pulled Johann aside.

"We're expecting very important visitors this evening," he said. "Several gentlemen from the *signoria* are coming tonight. I want you to put on your best show. It is crucial the councilors are well entertained."

"The signoria?" Johann frowned. "What's that supposed to be?"

Rieverschmitt laughed. "You might as well ask who is the king of the Germans! The signoria is the elite council, the most powerful panel in Venice. The doge is elected from their ranks, and they decide the city's politics. Those councilors are more powerful than many dukes and monarchs. And they are shrewd businessmen." He grinned. "This evening could mean a lot of money for the Fondaco."

Johann nodded. "You can count on us. Johann Faustus's renowned fabulous troupe of jugglers will put on a spectacular show for the mighty gentlemen."

Shortly after dusk, Emilio and Johann juggled burning torches on the quay as the Venetians arrived in their gondolas. Afterward, Salome danced her veil dance and let Mustafa toss her high into the air. Together they balanced on thin ropes suspended above the courtyard and performed cartwheels, and Mustafa swallowed three burning torches thrown to him by Emilio—a feat they'd learned only since their arrival in Venice. Johann had left Archibaldus at the inn with a jug of wine. He didn't want to risk the old man spoiling their show in a drunken stupor.

Like so many times before, one of the highlights was Johann's trick with the egg. He'd selected one of the Venetian councilors for the purpose, a pale older gentleman in a black coat. The man wore dark eye glasses that stayed on his nose with the aid of wires that hooked around the ears, giving him the appearance of a large insect or a snake. Johann had heard of such vision aids but never seen any before, which was probably why his attention had fallen on the tall signore.

The egg appeared in an inside pocket of the old man's coat, and the audience clapped as the man extracted it with the tips of his index finger and thumb. The pale patrician seemed surprised for a moment, but then he gave a mocking smile. He pulled out a sharp dagger, pierced a hole in the egg, and sucked it empty. Johann was reminded of a hissing black snake.

After the show, while Johann sat a little off to the side, enjoying a hot cup of mulled wine, the man approached him. Johann quickly put the cup aside and bowed low. He hoped the patrician wouldn't punish Johann for making a fool of him in front of all the others. But the man was smiling. He sported a pointed beard and bushy black eyebrows, and his face looked as white as if he'd painted it with chalk.

"Not a bad trick, young man," said the Venetian. He spoke quietly; his voice was a little hoarse. His German had a soft, exotic accent that seemed strangely familiar to Johann, somehow. "How did you know I like eggs?"

Johann grinned. Evidently, the man bore him no ill will. "You forget I'm a magician," he said with a wink. "And most people like eggs, don't they? Eggs are highly symbolic and play a role in many Christian customs."

"You're right, of course." The man gave a quiet laugh. Johann had the feeling that behind the eye glasses the patrician studied him with great interest. "Eggs contain life in its purest form. When we eat them, we eat life—we practically drink it in. A lovely thought, I believe."

The patrician gave a thin smile, and Johann thought once more that he looked like an old snake. "You seem to know a lot for a simple juggler," the man said after a few moments. "Or are you perhaps a traveling scholar? A monastery student who ran away from his abbot?" He smiled again. "Or from someone else, perhaps?"

"I . . . I have studied a little," replied Johann, proud that the man thought he was a student. "And I speak a little Latin and Greek."

"Indeed?" The patrician adjusted his glasses and eyed Johann intently. *"Quemadmodum omnium rerum, sic litterarum quoque intemperantia laboramus,"* he said.

"Non vitae sed scholae discimus," replied Johann, happy because he'd understood the man's test. It was a famous quotation by Seneca, which Archibaldus had taught him not long ago. *"Si tibi libet colloqui in hoc modo: homo Deus est,"* he added.

The last phrase had come out before he knew he was saying it. Johann remembered that Archibaldus had advised him not to utter it in public. And indeed, the patrician raised an eyebrow and tilted his head to one side. Johann suddenly felt he was being scrutinized, like a mouse sitting petrified before a snake.

"How do you know this phrase?" asked the man. "Man is God. Don't you know that the church forbids such talk?"

"Oh, I . . . I didn't realize . . . ," stammered Johann. He cursed himself for failing to keep his mouth shut. At least now he knew why Archibaldus had warned him: it seemed those words were proof of heresy. There were bound to be severe inquisitors in Venice following up every account of blasphemy. "I . . . I must have heard it somewhere," he said, trying to get himself out of the situation.

The man smiled coolly. "Don't worry, I won't tell on you. I like your wit and your cleverness. You crave knowledge, don't you?"

Johann nodded, relieved the conversation was taking a different turn.

"I live in a very old house in the Sestiere San Marco," continued the patrician. "My family owns one of the biggest libraries of Italy. Would you like to see it someday? I would be glad to welcome you there."

"Thank you, but that's . . . that's too generous." Johann blushed. "I'm just a simple juggler who—"

"Nonsense." The man waved dismissively. "I can tell that there's more to you than magic tricks with eggs." The man smiled. "Although you're trying hard to hide your true self underneath that ridiculous costume. I wasn't so fortunate as to be blessed with a studious son. If it helps, consider my wish a command. I will send you an invitation."

"An invitation? Who from?"

"Expect a letter from Signore Barbarese." For a brief moment, Johann thought he could see the man's eyes light up behind the dark glasses. He licked his thin lips, like he'd done earlier when he sucked out the egg. "You will like my library, I'm sure of it. *Arrivederci.*"

He turned and disappeared into the fog beneath the arcades like a large old reptile gliding into the water.

Late that night, Johann lay in bed thinking about the strange Signore Barbarese and his invitation. What were the Venetian's intentions? Johann had heard stories of men who liked to keep pretty boys as catamites. Was that the reason for the invitation? It wasn't just since Salome that Johann had become aware of the fact that he was a handsome young man; in their travels he had noticed several older men looking at him in a certain way.

The thought of Barbarese's long, spidery fingers stroking his skin made Johann feel sick; he found the Venetian creepy with his weird glasses and black clothes, which smelled as musty as if he'd risen straight from a grave. But Johann knew he couldn't refuse. Barbarese was a member of the signoria, the most powerful council in the city. If Johann didn't follow his order, they'd probably arrest him, lock him in some dingy hole, and leave him to rot.

The entire following day, Johann was distracted. During their morning performance he botched the easiest tricks, and Emilio studied him with a frown.

"What's the matter with you today?" he asked during a break. "I would say you're hungover, but I didn't see you drinking last night."

"I slept poorly," Johann grumbled. "That's all."

He decided against telling the others about the invitation. It was just between him and Barbarese; he didn't want to drag anyone else into it and potentially get them in trouble.

So he waited the whole day and the next, but no letter arrived. When there was still no word from Barbarese on the third day, Johann decided there wouldn't be a message. Perhaps the patrician had only been messing with him, or it simply wasn't important to him and he'd forgotten all about it. Johann felt relieved and returned his focus to the shows and rehearsals. He also continued his studies with Archibaldus, but the old man was nearly at his wit's end.

"I've got nothing left to teach you, lad," said the magister. "Your Latin is better than mine now, and I only know enough Greek to teach you a few dirty poems by Sappho."

"Then tell me more about arithmetic and geometry," said Johann.

"All right." Archibaldus sighed and started drawing lines on a piece of paper. "I will teach you Euclid's theorem. Watch this . . ."

An hour later, Johann was poring over formulas and prime numbers in his chamber at the inn. Archibaldus had left him with some exercises, and Johann was so engrossed in his work that he didn't hear the knocking at first. He started with fright when the sound grew louder.

"Yes?" he called out impatiently and pushed his papers aside.

It was one of the footboys Venetian patricians liked to use as messengers. When the boy handed Johann a sealed letter, Johann knew immediately who had sent it. The coat of arms showed a roaring lion and a Latin motto, as was typical for noble families.

Aude sapere.

"Dare to know," Johann whispered. He broke the seal and read the letter. The handwriting was old fashioned and written in dark-red ink, the color of blood. Signore Barbarese asked him to wait at the quay of the Fondaco dei

Tedeschi at nine o'clock that evening. The letter didn't say what would happen after.

Johann gave the boy a small coin and sent him away. Then he gathered his study materials and left a message with the innkeeper for Salome, saying that he had some errands to run after dark.

Johann had asked the innkeeper at the Flute for a lantern to help him find his way through the lanes. It was pitch black outside and, as usual, foggy. Not a single star could be seen through the clouds. Unlike the rich citizens who were still out and about, he couldn't afford an armed bodyguard. He relied entirely on his wits and the knife he always carried. Venice at night was a dangerous place—not only because of scoundrels but also because any wrong step on the slippery stones could send a man straight into the water. Alleyways often ended abruptly by a canal, the waters cold and black. Venice was a devilish labyrinth; most of the lanes had no names, and the best way to navigate through the city was by using the churches as points of reference along with the *campi*—old meeting places, of which each of the former islands had one.

Wearing his warm hooded jerkin, Johann hurried past several taverns with lights burning behind their windows. Then the voices, music, and laughter grew fainter and eventually ceased altogether. All Johann could hear now was the gurgling of the water as it gently splashed against the slimy walls of the canals.

Luckily, it wasn't far from the inn to the Fondaco. The guards knew Johann by now and let him pass once he explained why he was there. He hurried across the deserted courtyard, past crates and bales, and onto the quay. During the day, boats came and went constantly, and the German merchants argued over the best docking spots. Now it was as quiet as a graveyard.

A solitary black gondola bobbed on the water by the quay, illuminated dimly by a golden lantern in the bow. A gondolier clad in black was standing at the stern, his face covered against the cold and partially hidden by a wide-brimmed hat. He gave Johann a wave.

"Dimmi, èquesta la gondola del Signore Barbarese?" asked Johann in broken Italian. He'd tried to learn some of the language over the last few weeks. His voice sounded strangely thin in the fog, as if the darkness was swallowing it up.

The gondolier nodded silently, and Johann climbed into the boat. There was only one bench seat in the middle, covered with red velvet. Everything else was painted a dull black, even the oar. They set off the moment Johann sat. The gondola glided through the oily water and past the many palaces whose black silhouettes blocked out the sky.

It started to drizzle; icy drops of water ran down Johann's face as the gondola silently moved through the night. The gondolier didn't say a word, and the only sound came from the occasional slapping of the oar. A few times they passed other boats going in the opposite direction that, like theirs, carried a lantern at their bow. They were small dots of light in the fog, like stars in a sea of darkness.

A few hundred paces before the doge's palace, they left the Canal Grande and turned into a small side channel that led to a stately three-story building. It was richly decorated with mosaics and frescoes in a strange style, as if from a time before Christianity. Only one window high up was illuminated. The poles in the water bore the roaring lion that Johann already knew; a stone pier and a gate formed the entrance to the first floor. The gondola docked; the gondolier remained silent.

Johann rose and climbed out. He walked up a few slippery steps and reached an inner courtyard. A deathly silence lay over the place, and Johann was confused. This was supposed to be the palace of a Venetian councilman—where were the guards and the servants? The walls were crumbling, the frescoes looked faded; the corners were covered in cobwebs and the floor with dust. Had the gondolier taken him to the wrong house? Or could this be a trap, for whatever reason?

Johann was about to turn back to the quay when he noticed a servant in golden livery standing in a small alcove. He was a tall Moor and reminded Johann of Mustafa—probably because he was just as silent. He'd been standing still as a statue, but then he lifted a candelabra with white wax candles and walked ahead of Johann. A wide set of stairs with worn marble steps led to the upper stories. Johann reluctantly walked past lugubrious portraits of men who all shared a certain resemblance with Signore Barbarese. Between the portraits hung paintings of landscapes and Bible scenes; to his growing wonder, Johann noticed that some of the paintings had been hung upside down, while others were covered with black cloth. This house was becoming stranger by the minute.

Signore Barbarese was waiting for him in the corridor of the house's top floor. He wore a black jerkin that looked as old as the furnishings. It had a high collar and was cut very low on the chest. His leggings were so tight that his legs looked like those of a giant spider. He also wore the glasses, even though the hallway was dimly lit. When Johann approached the Venetian, the man spread his arms as if Johann were a long-lost son.

"How good of you to come," said Barbarese, dismissing the servant with a lordly gesture. "Forgive me for keeping you waiting, but I was, um . . . busy. But now you're here." He gestured toward the expensive damask wall hangings and portraits in the corridor. A chandelier cast the paintings in an eerie, flickering light. "So many beautiful pictures," said Barbarese enthusiastically. "They were painted by Gentile Bellini, a good friend of mine. Have you heard of him?"

Johann shook his head.

"What a shame—he's a true master in his field. Although a while ago, an artist named Dürer visited Venice, and I like his work, too. Apparently he comes from Nuremberg." Barbarese sighed. "It's a shame hardly anyone gets to admire my paintings. My wife died young and we weren't granted any children. Yes . . . I'm afraid the long line of Barbarese ends with me." He raised a thin finger that looked oddly animallike in the twilight of the candles, like a claw or a feeler.

"Our line can be traced back all the way to the first refugees who found a new home on these islands almost a thousand years ago—on the island of Torcello, to be precise. That's where mighty Venice was born. My ancestors came from Rome, where some Barbareses even became senators. But I'm digressing." Barbarese smiled, and Johann noticed how pale he was, as if there wasn't a drop of blood flowing through the signore's veins. But the poor light in the corridor probably didn't help. "I promised you a library," said Barbarese. "Well, here it is."

He pushed open a two-winged door, and Johann saw a large room with bookshelves from floor to ceiling. There were hundreds of books, parchment scrolls, and other documents. Johann stood rooted to the spot with amazement. He had never seen so many books at once before—not even in the Maulbronn monastery!

When Barbarese saw the expression on Johann's face, he gave a quiet laugh. "I knew you'd like it. To be honest, I've only read a fraction of these books myself. My eyes are getting worse all the time, and not even the glasses can change that. Allegedly, there are documents among those scrolls that survived the great fire of Alexandria. Some books are copies of the works of Greek scholars, and there's even a handful of Arabic translations. Books have always been the passion of my family. And this newfangled book printing is just astonishing.

Written works are going to be more accessible and cheaper in the future." He made a sweeping gesture around the room. "Make yourself at home, my boy."

"Do . . . do you mean I'm allowed to read all those books?" asked Johann, stunned.

Barbarese laughed again, and it sounded a little like the hissing of an adder. "I don't think you'll quite manage to get through all of them. But you're welcome to study here and borrow some books, too. I'm looking forward to discussing the contents with you."

Still feeling like he was in a trance, Johann nodded. Then he slowly walked toward the shelves. The books were bound in old cracked leather. There were piles of parchment scrolls and tattered documents covered in Latin handwriting. Johann shyly started to pull a few books from the shelf. He leafed through a heavy tome entitled *Opus Majus*, written by someone named Roger Bacon. Then he replaced it and chose another work, *Poetics* by Aristotle, whom Father Antonius and Father Bernhard had told him about.

"Feel free to make use of the table and chair. There is ink and a quill if you want to take notes," said Barbarese. "Over there you'll find wine, cheese, and bread in case you're hungry. I'm going to leave you for a while now—and then we can discuss what you've read, if you like. My gondolier will take you back to the Fondaco at dawn. All right?"

Johann nodded, but his thoughts were with the wealth of books surrounding him. He sat down at the table and started to read.

"Enjoy," said Signore Barbarese.

Then he closed the door and left Johann on his own.

At first Johann felt like he was sitting at a table filled with so many different delicacies that he didn't know which one to sample first. He leafed through crackling pages of parchment, gently brushed his fingers over bindings, admired the colorful letters, and deciphered Latin and Greek titles just to return them to the shelf and hastily pick another volume. Some of the books were as large and heavy as cobblestones, while others were small and easy to handle, with pages made from the finest vellum. Most of them were handwritten, copied by monks who'd lived a long time ago. Johann found beautiful illustrations on some pages; the elaborately adorned first letters of chapters were true masterpieces. Johann inhaled the smell of ancient dust, glue, and lye.

After a while he started looking through the books more slowly, and he became absorbed by writings about the tides of the seas, explanations of the function of optical lenses, and illustrations of the open human body. One of the images even showed an embryo in its mother's womb. Whenever he found something particularly intriguing, he jotted down notes. Some of the books were locked with heavy padlocks, and Johann wondered what could be so bad that people weren't allowed to read it. They bore titles like *Dialectica* and *Periphyseon*. Others seemed to be about Jewish cabalism or the Cathars, a Christian sect whose treatise bore the title *Liber de Duobus Principiis*—the book of two principles. One of the locked books was by Albertus Magnus, the man whose praises Father Antonius had sung at Maulbronn so long ago. It was entitled *De Secretis Mulierum*; Johann assumed it explored the secrets of the fairer sex.

As promised, Signore Barbarese returned after a few hours. Johann hadn't touched the wine or the food; he'd been too engrossed in the books. They spoke about some of the works Johann had read, and Barbarese asked questions or made suggestions that gave Johann food for thought.

Shortly before dawn, the black gondola carried Johann back to the trading post, where he slept for an hour or two before Salome shook him awake.

"Where have you been?" she asked sulkily. "Your bed was empty and I was cold."

Johann rubbed his eyes. Despite the lack of sleep, he felt strangely refreshed and rested. "You've got your secrets and I've got mine." He placed his finger on her lips. "That was the deal, wasn't it? 'You don't own me.' Your words."

Salome studied him pensively for a while. Then she smiled. "Let's see if that hussy left anything for me," she said and grasped him between the legs.

They made love hard and fast, and Johann enjoyed the fact that Salome thought he had a lover.

Not one, but hundreds, he thought as she straddled him. *Every one of those books is like a virgin waiting to be discovered.*

~

The gondola was there for him each of the following nights. At Signore Barbarese's house, the host welcomed him politely and led him to the library. He was always dressed in his old-fashioned garb and never once took off his glasses. After a few hours of studying in solitude, they would engage in lengthy conversations, during which Johann learned more than he'd learned with Archibaldus in a month. The topic of discussion frequently was man and his position in regard to God and the church.

"The scholasticism as it is taught by the church assumes there are invariable facts—irrevocable truths—that must not be questioned," explained Barbarese. "Everything is laid down in the old scriptures. There is no room for creative thought, except perhaps in the way God's words are interpreted. But if you're not careful, you're a heretic—even though humans are perfectly capable of observing the world around us and drawing conclusions. We ourselves can dissect the world to find out what's in its innermost heart and finer veins, see all its energies and seeds. Many scholars have chosen this path by now and have turned their backs on the church. Times are changing, Johann. I own notes by a certain Leonardo da Vinci—a very clever man who works with geometry, mechanics, human anatomy, and many other subjects. His genius is like that of a creator, a god."

"But man can't be God," replied Johann. "Behind everything, even behind us, there must be something else—a higher power of some kind, God. What sort of a world would this be if it was based on coincidence, on chaos?"

Barbarese smiled. "Well, it would be a very human world, wouldn't it?"

During the day, Johann was increasingly sleep deprived, especially since Salome pushed him harder than ever. She was jealous of his imaginary new lover, and she desired him and demanded him with a passion that left Johann hollow and spent. He was frequently unfocused during their shows now, and his temper returned, especially because the troupe was beginning to make new mistakes. Their routine had become a daily grind, and the plentiful wine and good food were taking their toll. Johann, too, blundered in ways he wouldn't have a few weeks ago.

"You look more dead than alive," said Emilio one day after a show in which Johann had nearly hit Salome with a knife. "Are you ill? Do you need some rest?"

Johann shook his head grimly. "You worry about your own problems," he said gruffly. "And throw the balls to me better next time, or I'll start looking for a new juggler."

Emilio stared at him in silence, and Johann felt bad about his remark. He wasn't getting enough sleep, and that made him irritable, though his mind was awake as never before. He couldn't stop thinking about Barbarese's books—not when he was at the Fondaco or in his chamber, and not even during his time with Salome.

At least he had stopped studying with Archibaldus. The old man didn't seem to mind, believing there was nothing more he could teach Johann anyhow. But he worried about Johann.

"Something's up with you, boy. I can tell," said the old man.

"What do you mean?" Johann gave a shrug. "I'm growing up and making up my own mind about things."

"A Venetian ducat for your thoughts," murmured Archibaldus.

Johann often borrowed books from Barbarese's library now so that he could continue his studies at the inn. He was always careful to hide them under the bed so Salome and the others wouldn't see them. He didn't feel like justifying himself for being distracted. The books were his secret, his treasure, his hoard that he was protecting like a dragon.

The weeks went by, and Johann became increasingly uncommunicative and brooding. He spent Christmas alone in his chamber with his books, telling Salome that he was bed-bound with a fever. He snarled at the others during rehearsal. If something didn't work right away, he practically exploded. The only time he felt happy was during his nightly conversations with Barbarese. They still discussed God and man, but also inventions and man's latest discoveries. But they never spoke about the books with the padlocks.

It was almost February when Johann gathered his courage and asked Barbarese about those mysterious volumes. The signore smiled as if he'd been expecting the question.

"Those books contain knowledge that isn't for everybody," he said after a few moments. "Some readers might feel, well . . . overwhelmed by their contents."

"Why?" asked Johann.

"Because they question the world as we know it. No, they rattle its very foundations. Our view of the world relies on a God at its helm. But what if . . ." Barbarese paused. "What if that God doesn't exist? What if man is his own master? If he can take charge of everything? Even life and death! Man would be the architect of his own fortune."

"That would be heresy," said Johann.

The idea of there being no God was preposterous. Johann felt a black abyss opening up beneath him at the mere thought of it. Everything he knew and held dear—the whole world around him—was built on the fact that God existed. God was the beginning and the end. He made trees grow and flowers blossom; He granted good harvests and brought fertile rain and mild winters. And He alone decided when a man's time on earth was at an end. A world without God seemed impossible.

"Well, now you know why those books are locked," Barbarese replied. "Some books can kill the weak, but they can open up new worlds to the strong."

"I want to read those books," said Johann stubbornly.

Barbarese eyed him thoughtfully. "Are you sure?" Then he gave a laugh. "To hell with it! I can tell you've made up your mind. All right, then. I trust you won't hand me over to the church." He pulled a large key ring from a pocket and went over to the shelves. "I think we'll start with Leonardo da Vinci. I met him in Milan a few years ago. He had written thousands of pages of notes and drawings. When I asked him if I could have some, he didn't even look up from his work. He's a genius! A painter and inventor who represents nature as it actually is and doesn't just copy the way the church likes it." The signore smiled. "The notes are a little chaotic, but they give you a good idea of what the man is capable of. I had them bound and chose one of the artist's drawings for the cover." Barbarese picked a key and opened a book bound in black leather; on its front was an image of a naked man standing at once in a circle and a square with outstretched arms and legs. Barbarese handed the book to Johann with an almost reverent gesture. "Read it and let me know what you think. But you must promise not to take it back to your inn. The book's contents are too dangerous."

Johann promised, and Barbarese left the library. The book was like a bucketful of cold water in the face. Johann had never seen anything like it. The illustrations were the most fascinating part. With astonishing intricacy, the man had drawn war machines, boats propelled by paddle wheels, flying apparatuses, and suits that apparently enabled a person to breathe under water. Cut-open bodies displayed life so clearly that Johann thought all the sinews, bones, and organs looked like they were part of a large clock. The notes were difficult to read, especially because large sections had been written back-to-front like some kind of secret code. Still, Johann soaked up much of it like a dry sponge.

When Barbarese returned a few hours later, Johann was still spellbound.

"I'm glad you like it," said Barbarese. "I knew you were ready for it."

"He writes a lot about machines," said Johann. "But all these anatomical sketches suggest man himself is also a kind of apparatus that can be repaired. And somewhere Leonardo da Vinci writes that one day, man might be in a position to decide over life and death himself—do you think that's really possible?"

He thought about Margarethe and young Martin, and of his mother, who had died of a disease Father Antonius wanted to treat with moldy cheese. He thought about all the victims of the Black Death, which people blamed on some sort of vapors coming from the ground or on original sin—so much speculation and so many dated beliefs without any research or proof. The notes in front of him could achieve so much if they were developed in the right way!

Barbarese gave him a long, thoughtful look from behind his glasses. "To conquer death would be the crown of human achievement," he replied eventually. "If anyone can do it at all, it would take years—decades—of dedicated studying. But yes, I think it's possible."

"I want to learn it."

Barbarese laughed softly. "One thing at a time, my young adept. One thing at a time."

Over the next few weeks, Johann studied Leonardo da Vinci's notes and other books, like Roger Bacon's *Opus Majus*, in which the author turned against traditional scholasticism. Johann read that it was the people's fear of authority and their dependence on popular opinion that prevented them from thinking independently. In his *Epistola de Secretis Operibus Artis et Naturae*, Bacon prophesied that one day there would be machines that enabled humans to fly like birds. Anything was possible!

The books with the padlocks discussed science and machines, but also forbidden philosophy and magic. Increasingly Barbarese picked out volumes for Johann that weren't just about the sciences but also about magic—white as well as black. And it was no silly hocus-pocus like Johann had first practiced with Tonio del Moravia, but a secret, esoteric field of study that asked questions no one had ever asked before. There were no boundaries in that world, and nothing was forbidden.

"If we want to understand the universe as a whole, we must leave no stone unturned," said the signore. "There can't be any taboos—it's the only way for man to achieve godly wisdom. *Homo Deus est.*"

And for the first time Johann thought he truly understood what that sentence meant.

~

That night, while Johann continued to peruse da Vinci's and Bacon's works and tried his hand at a few sketches of his own, Signore Barbarese went into his secret chamber. A steep ladder led to the attic, where a well-concealed door led into Barbarese's demesne: a tiny room full of books whose contents were so frightening and revolutionary that the signore didn't dare keep them in the library.

In one corner stood a wardrobe full of wigs, fake beards, and costumes, just like in the travel chest of a juggler.

Dangling from a beam of the roof was a cage with two crows and a raven.

"I think he's ready now," said the master, sitting at a small table in front of a silver-framed Venetian mirror. He took off his glasses and wig and wiped the soot from his eyebrows. "What do you think, Baphomet, Azazel, and Belial?"

The birds screeched, cawed, and flapped their wings. The master silenced them with a wave of his hand. He carefully peeled away the beard from his lips and studied his pale reflection in the mirror. He had always been good at disguising himself.

"You can't force them," he said as he wiped away the white makeup. "Never. It's the law. They must come of their own free will. That's how it always has been. Sometimes it just takes a little longer."

Humming a tune, he took a piece of paper from a drawer in the table and started to write a long letter. When he was done, he folded and rolled it up until it was as small as the finger of a child; he sealed it with wax as red as blood. Then the master opened the cage and took out the raven. At first the animal wanted to peck at him, but then it flapped its wings with fear.

"Kraa!" cried the raven, sounding whimpering, childlike. *"Kraa, kraa!"*

"Good boy, Baphomet," said the master. "Always remember your reward. Only those who obey me will receive salvation."

The master pushed the tiny paper scroll through a ring on the raven's right claw. He double-checked that it was secured properly, then he nodded and walked over to the window with the raven.

The master pushed the shutters open wide. Pale moonlight fell into the small room and illuminated the chalky, expressionless face with its still slightly sooty eyebrows.

"Tell them that he's ready," said the master. "The arrival is near."

He threw the raven out into the night like a black snowball, and the bird spread his wings and headed north, toward the mountains.

12

JOHANN GREW INCREASINGLY WITHDRAWN, AND THE OTH-
ers hardly ever saw him. As far as they knew, he left his chamber only for the
shows. Contrary to his promise to Signore Barbarese, he had taken some of the
forbidden books with him to the inn, including some works on sorcery. It had
been easier than he'd thought—Barbarese had left them unlocked on the table in
the library. Johann simply hid them beneath the other books he was borrowing.
It was almost like Barbarese had wanted Johann to take them.

Thus passed January and February, and with March came the birds. There
was chirping all through the city, and people no longer wore long, warm coats.
Spring put a smile on everyone's face, and even the perpetual fog withdrew.
When the days started to get warmer, the jugglers began to ask how much longer they'd stay in Venice. Johann's replies were always evasive. He didn't want
to leave this city, least of all Barbarese's library, where he felt like his eyes were
being opened afresh every day. He hadn't thought of Margarethe, his mother, or
little Martin in a long time; he kept his dark memories locked up deep inside.

One afternoon in March, Johann was so engrossed in his reading that he
didn't hear the knock on the door. When he started up, it was already too late.
Archibaldus had entered his room.

"I wanted to check on you, lad," he said. "The others are worried about you
and—"

He broke off when he saw the books on the bed. "Where did you get those?"

"None of your business," snarled Johann, gathering up the books. He shoved
them under the bed, but Archibaldus had already deciphered one of the titles.

"*The Sworn Book of Honorius*?" Archibaldus turned pale. "Who gave you
that?"

"I told you it's none of your business!" shouted Johann feverishly.

"My boy, you don't know what you're doing." Archibaldus raised one hand in a placating gesture. "Whoever gave you this book dabbles in things that are too dangerous for a young student, no matter how talented."

"Perhaps they are too dangerous for an old drunkard," Johann jeered. "But not for me. Now please leave. I want to study."

Archibaldus gave him a serious look. "I always knew there was something dark inside you, Johann," he said eventually. "It went into hiding for a while, but now it seems to have returned. Please don't let it take over—I'm begging you! It would destroy you and maybe even those you love. You're clever and keen to learn, and you could become someone great—or someone very dangerous." He hesitated. "I've got a suggestion for you. You said it was your greatest dream to study at Heidelberg University. I could ensure your dream comes true."

Johann blinked with irritation. "And how are you going to do that?"

"I still have a little influence. And I know the right people. What do you say: you leave those books alone, and in return I'll get you a spot at Heidelberg." Archibaldus held out his hand. "Agreed?"

"I . . . I'll think about it," Johann said and spurned the old man's hand. "But now I'd really like you to leave."

"May God protect you," said Archibaldus. "I fear something deeply evil is trying to grab ahold of you."

Johann woke from his fixation on the books only once.

One day toward the end of March, Rieverschmitt came rushing up to him in a state of excitement.

"We need you for a bigger show tonight. The first German merchants have arrived at Venice. It was a long winter and there's still snow on the passes, so not much comes through. There is a huge demand for their wares. The Venetians want to butter them up, so please think of something special."

Johann nodded distractedly. His thoughts were on other matters. Barbarese's books robbed him of his sleep. But he knew he couldn't disappoint Rieverschmitt if he didn't want to jeopardize his stay in Venice. There were so many books left to read. It pained him to think that he wouldn't be able to visit Barbarese that night.

"You can always rely on Johann Faustus's Fabulous Troupe," he said and gave a strained smile.

A few weeks ago, Johann had taken some Venetian jugglers under contract for larger shows. One pleasant result was that it put pressure on Emilio. Johann thought the young juggler had become a little too complacent in the last few months and no longer practiced enough. And he was always badgering Johann with the question of when they'd leave Venice. But so far, Johann had managed to convince him to stay.

Even though he barely slept, Johann had his troupe under control and even managed to negotiate a higher wage with Rieverschmitt. The jugglers had become a fixture at the Fondaco. If they wanted to, they could stay for the whole year—maybe even forever, as Johann secretly hoped. He continued to spend the nights at Signore Barbarese's, although the previous night, he'd had the feeling he was being followed there. A gondola appeared to follow his at some distance, but he hadn't been able to make out any details in the evening fog.

The German merchants started to arrive at the trading post around sunset. There were more than a dozen of them, their heavily loaded vessels lying low in the water. The train of merchants included numerous footmen and even some mercenaries who had helped them to safely get their wares across the Alps. When the servants carried the crates and bales into the storehouses, Johann saw the finest Augsburg cloth, amber, furs, and chests full of silver. The risky journey had undoubtedly paid off for the merchants; they'd get an excellent price for their goods.

The troupe received the merchants with music and juggling at the quay. The tables set up in the courtyard were bending under the weight of the food. Three of the hired Venetian jugglers beat drums and played the lute while Salome danced seductively.

Their show later on was a huge success. Germans and Venetians applauded and tossed coins at them; several men lay drunkenly under the table or vomited in a quiet corner. Archibaldus snored with his head on the table, his tousled beard hanging in a puddle of wine. Johann hadn't used him for their shows in a long time. He'd avoided the old man since their argument at the inn but noticed that Archibaldus eyed him with suspicion whenever he wasn't too drunk.

Before the show and the feasting, the German merchants had closed their deals and earned a fortune. Even Rieverschmitt's face glowed red with alcohol and excitement. Visibly drunk, he waved Johann over to him late in the evening.

"Didn't you say once that you are from the Kraichgau region?" he asked with a heavy tongue. "From Knittlingen?"

Johann nodded. "Why do you ask?"

Rieverschmitt grinned and gestured at an equally drunk merchant beside him, who was struggling to sit up straight. "This gentleman here comes from a neighboring town, from Bretten. I thought perhaps you know him. His name's Klaus Reuter."

Johann was shocked. He felt a wave of homesickness at the thought of meeting someone from home here in faraway Venice. But at the same time, he was afraid the man might know him. He had made a good name for himself here at the trading post. Rieverschmitt thought Johann was much older than he actually was, and Johann had told him he was the third son of a wealthy cloth-making family. Johann nervously studied the drunk merchant, but he'd never seen the corpulent man with the saggy cheeks and the piggy eyes sunk deeply into his doughy face. Still, he knew the Reuters were a respected merchant family in Bretten and had produced many burgomasters. They also traded with the Maulbronn monastery and in Knittlingen. Did this man know his stepfather?

Johann forced himself to smile. "How nice to see someone from home. How are things in the Kraichgau?"

The man burped loudly. "Well, the Swabians are getting pushier all the time," he said with a broad Kraichgau accent. "Last year, Württemberg was made a duchy by the king and doesn't know where to put all its power. People are talking about war."

"What about Knittlingen?" asked Johann shyly, his heart beating faster. Could it be possible that Klaus Reuter knew Margarethe? Her father was the prefect, after all. "How is business going there?"

Reuter gave a shrug. "I stayed at the Lion for the first night of our trip. That was back in fall. The wine is awfully sour this year." He grinned and took a large swig from a goblet made of blue Venetian glass that sparkled in the light of the torches. "Nothing compared to this excellent grape juice."

Johann cleared his throat and made another attempt. "I knew the prefect a little. My father used to do business with him. You don't happen to know how he's doing?"

"The Knittlingen prefect?" Reuter laughed. "I can't say he's doing too well. He wanted to marry his daughter off to a Bretten merchant's son—a good match. Young Schmeltzle may not be the most handsome lad, but the family's got money. What can I say? The girl lost her mind."

"Is . . . is that right?" Johann struggled to keep the quiver from his voice. "How come?"

"No idea." Reuter wiped some drops of wine from his fleshy lips. "That was almost two years ago now. She stopped talking and just lay in bed like a cold fish." He burped again. "The wedding didn't happen, not least because she'd allegedly lain with another man—some young smart aleck. Her father gave her to another man, a vintner from Heidelberg. He was the only one who didn't ask questions and didn't mind the small dowry."

"So Margarethe lives in Heidelberg?" asked Johann quietly, more to himself.

The merchant seemed to wake from his stupor. "Margarethe, huh?" The piggy eyes scrutinized Johann closely. "How do you know her name, boy?"

"Um, didn't I mention that our fathers occasionally had dealings with each other?" replied Johann, standing up hastily. "It was nice talking with you, Master Reuter. Give my regards to the Kraichgau when you return."

Before the man could say anything else, Johann turned away. He gave Rieverschmitt one last nod and rushed out into the Venetian night. He needed to be alone now, alone with his thoughts. As the fog wet his face with dew, Johann repeated one name over and over.

"Margarethe, Margarethe, Margarethe . . ."

His greatest love, his only love, had entered his life again.

In the following days, Johann struggled to focus on his studies. Every time he bent over the books at Barbarese's library, he thought he could hear Margarethe's laughter. The signore noticed that he was distracted.

"What is it, my boy?" he asked with a frown. "I was under the impression that you were seriously interested in my collection. But now you're unfocused and keep staring out the window." Barbarese eyed him suspiciously from behind his glasses. "Has someone talked to you? Has anyone found out about our nightly meetings? Speak up!"

Johann shook his head. "I'm just tired, that's all. I think I need a little rest."

"Well, if that's the case," Barbarese said, smiling and placing an ice-cold hand on Johann's shoulder, "take a few days off. I will tell my gondolier to pick you up again next Friday. Enjoy your time off and take a good look around Venice. It's the most beautiful and most curious city in the world. But you must promise me one thing." He raised a finger and spoke slowly and intently. "You speak with no one about this library and the books inside it, understood? The consequences could be"—he hesitated—"incalculable. For you, too."

Johann nodded, glad to be dismissed. Everything had become a little too much for him in the last few days. He needed some quiet time and some distance—especially from Signore Barbarese and the books that seemed to drain him.

During the following days he only went to the Fondaco for their shows, spending the rest of the time walking the lanes of Venice. But as much as he admired all the palaces, churches, and canals, he couldn't find peace. He hadn't been able to stop thinking about Margarethe since the German merchant had told him about her. How was she doing? Was she speaking again? He was filled with a deep longing that pushed aside all other thoughts.

On the afternoon of the third day, Johann sensed that he was being followed. His pursuer didn't try very hard to hide his intentions, or perhaps he wasn't very good at it. Like a shadow, he kept ducking into gaps between houses or alcoves, always trailing twenty or thirty paces behind Johann. When the figure followed Johann into a narrow alleyway, Johann hid behind an old barrel. When he heard the quiet footsteps approach, he jumped out with his knife raised. He was about to put the blade to his pursuer's throat when he stepped back with surprise.

"Archibaldus!" exclaimed Johann. "What . . . what are you doing here? What's this about?"

Magister Archibaldus held up his palms. "Forgive me, but I saw no other way to talk to you in private."

"So you follow me halfway across Venice?" asked Johann. "You could have seen me in my room."

"It's not safe there." Archibaldus looked about himself. "And neither is it here. Come with me!"

Before Johann had time to protest, Archibaldus had dragged him into an even smaller alleyway. Washing hung on lines between the close walls of the houses; some hungry cats were fighting underneath a bridge. The air smelled of rotten fish and stagnant brackish water. They entered a small church that lay at the edge of a campus and was empty at this time of the day, apart from two elderly women in the front pew. The late-afternoon light fell through the narrow windows and onto an altar decorated with dried roses. It was as cold as winter inside the church.

"What's all this about?" asked Johann again. "Have you had too much to drink again, Archibaldus? Admit it!"

The magister gave a desperate laugh. "Oh, I wish I had! Then the truth would be easier to bear. But no, I'm stone-cold sober. Well, almost . . ." He lowered his voice. "I know now who you're visiting every night, Johann. And you ought to know the truth about him."

"So it was you who followed me the other night?"

"Salome asked me to. She . . . she thought you were with some harlot or another, and she was jealous. But I've long been suspecting something else. Your temper, the way you've become withdrawn, and then those books you had in your chamber. *The Sworn Book of Honorius* and those other books of spells—"

"What are you getting at?" snapped Johann. He wanted to get out of this cold place as fast as possible.

"I made some inquiries about your host, Johann." Archibaldus was speaking close to Johann's ear, and he reeked of alcohol. Evidently, he wasn't quite as sober as he'd said.

"Your Signore Barbarese, as he calls himself, is known to move in certain circles," whispered Archibaldus. "Oh yes, he's rich and powerful! So powerful that no one dares to touch him, no matter how much they whisper behind his back."

Johann couldn't help but smile. "And what do they whisper? That he eats snakes? Admittedly, he does look like an adder, but—"

"Signore Barbarese is a Satanist."

"A what?" Johann stared at Archibaldus with his mouth open.

"You know exactly what I'm talking about," hissed Archibaldus. "Barbarese is a devil worshipper. His family has been practicing the cult for centuries, probably since pre-Christian times. Nothing could ever be proven. But they say he's involved in horrific ceremonies, nightly rituals with human sacrifices. Sometimes he's gone for long periods of time—for years, even. But when he returns to Venice, he . . . he . . ." Archibaldus faltered.

"He what?" asked Johann.

"Well, he seems strangely rejuvenated. There are people who say he must be ancient. Not even the oldest men in Venice remember Barbarese ever being a child."

"But that's nonsense!" replied Johann. "Ghost stories spread by jealous competitors. And devil-worshipping ceremonies . . ." He gave a laugh. "If that were true, I'd know about them, wouldn't I? As you know, I've been at Signore Barbarese's house nearly every night. We talk about literature. I can't see anything satanic about that. And I've never seen him draw pentagrams on the floor of his house." He tried to sound mocking but failed. He couldn't help thinking of the meeting in the woods with Tonio and Poitou. They, too, had been followers of some kind of satanic order.

And they had sacrificed humans.

Johann thought about the squirming bodies in the trees. He'd managed to suppress that memory for so long, and now it came back with a vengeance. He shuddered, and this time it had nothing to do with the cold in the church.

"So? Have you considered my proposal?"

Archibaldus's question tore Johann from his thoughts. "What do you mean?" he asked. "What proposal?"

"You stay away from Barbarese and his books, and I get you into Heidelberg University."

Archibaldus fished a wine-stained folded document from under his coat and held it out to Johann with a trembling hand.

"This is a letter of recommendation to a friend who got somewhere with his studies—unlike me. His name is Jodocus Gallus, and he teaches as a magister of the liberal arts at Heidelberg. He's even made it to rector. The letter bears the seal of my family." Archibaldus gave a sad smile. "Lucky I haven't pawned my signet ring for a bottle of brandy yet. It came in handy for once. When we're finished in Venice, go to Heidelberg and give Jodocus my regards. You will get far with the right teacher, Johann!"

"Thank you." Feeling a little embarrassed, Johann accepted the sealed paper.

Archibaldus turned deadly serious again. "There's something else I must tell you. It's about your former mentor, Tonio del Moravia. I finally know where I've heard the name before. It sounds incredible, but—"

Archibaldus broke off when someone entered the chapel. The figure remained in the dim twilight and moved into one of the dark side aisles, where it stood in silence. The person might have been someone who'd come to pray, or the priest preparing for the next mass, or a harmless pilgrim . . .

Or someone who followed us here, thought Johann.

He shook himself. Now he was becoming as paranoid as drunken Archibaldus.

"We can't talk here," whispered Archibaldus. "I want to make a few last checks before I can be absolutely certain, anyhow. The truth would be . . ." He broke off as if afraid of his own words. "I want you to come to Torcello tomorrow morning," Archibaldus whispered. "It's a small island in the Venetian lagoon. They say the first Roman refugees settled there. Perhaps that's why they chose the place, or perhaps they've always been there."

"What do you mean, *they?*" asked Johann.

"On Torcello, follow the old canal to the Ponte del Diavolo, the devil's bridge. From there, go to the old basilica. All will be explained there. I'll be waiting for you. And now go with God."

Archibaldus squeezed Johann's hand, stood up, and hurried toward the entrance. The door opened with a squeak, and the old man disappeared into the dusk. A cool draft blew in from the door and swept the rose petals from the altar.

When Johann looked back to the dark side aisle, the figure from earlier had vanished.

13

MAGISTER ARCHIBALDUS DIDN'T COME TO THE FONDACO for the evening show, nor was he at the inn when the others returned. But no one seemed particularly worried.

"He probably just had one too many again, and now he's sleeping it off in some alleyway," said Emilio with a shrug. "Let's pray he didn't fall and drown in one of the canals."

Johann said nothing. He'd spent the last few hours contemplating what the old man had told him about Signore Barbarese and how he'd mentioned Tonio, too. Was there a connection between the two men? He thought about Barbarese's old house, about the upside-down paintings and the many books about sorcery. Tonio would have enjoyed those books.

The knowledge Johann had drunk in at Barbarese's library was enormous, as vast as the ocean, and behind every thought, every idea, lurked another flash of inspiration.

And another abyss.

Johann's thoughts returned to Margarethe. She had been afraid of Tonio the magician as a child. And, he guessed, she'd be afraid of the Johann of today, too: the grim, taciturn fellow who was consumed by books and who sought his salvation in books of spells and sorcery. Suddenly, Johann saw himself through Margarethe's eyes and realized how much he'd changed. Were the books to blame? Was Signore Barbarese actually a devil worshipper?

Johann knew he'd have to speak to Archibaldus again to find out with certainty—provided the old man wasn't dead drunk and already regretting his remarks from earlier.

"I'm going to look for Archibaldus tomorrow," he told the others. "He must be somewhere."

"Stay with me for tonight at least, and don't go running to your whore," said Salome, running her hand through his shaggy black hair.

He slept poorly that night, dreaming repeatedly of Margarethe. She staggered toward him with outstretched arms, her face covered in blood. But when he tried to approach her, she shrank back. Her face turned into that of Salome and then that of his mother.

Go away, go away, she breathed. *You . . . are . . . the . . . devil . . .*

Early in the morning, Johann awoke bathed in sweat. He turned to the sleeping Salome and kissed her gently on the cheek. Then he set off for the island of Torcello, as Archibaldus had instructed him.

He asked his way to a quiet quay in the city's east with the help of gestures and his broken Italian. Several fishing boats moored here, and apparently they also went to the smaller islands of the lagoon. For a few coins, an older fisherman with a weather-beaten face agreed to take Johann to Torcello.

While the small boat slowly sailed through the lagoon's still waters, Johann gazed at the many islands in front of them. Some were tiny, nothing more than a few rocks, while others held villages with churches and monasteries. He'd heard that the Venetians sent their sick and their lunatics to the islands, as well as seamen and travelers suspected of having contracted the plague. Other islands served as walls of defense, and others again were used to grow crops or pasture livestock. On one of the largest islands, the Venetians manufactured their world-famous glass. They guarded their secret painstakingly, and there were harsh penalties in store for any treason.

Torcello was a rather plain, swampy island whose shoreline was overgrown with impenetrable reeds. The only spot to moor was at a weathered pier, and beside it, an old canal that had almost completely filled up with silt led inland.

The fisherman had talked about Torcello during the entire crossing. From the little Johann understood, he gathered that the island was indeed the oldest settlement in the lagoon, much older than Venice. Thousands of people used to live here, but then something terrible happened. Johann wasn't sure if he'd understood correctly, but apparently Torcello had been punished by God. The people had left the island, and now only a few peasants with their sheep and cows lived there. The old fisherman had shaken his head and repeated one word several times.

Maledetta.

Johann gathered that he meant the island was cursed.

What in God's name might Archibaldus want to show him here? Maybe the old boozer had truly had too much to drink.

Johann climbed out of the wobbly boat onto the pier. The fisherman made the sign of the cross, turned his sail into the wind, and took off. Johann had asked him to return at sundown. He only hoped the superstitious old man would keep his promise—otherwise he'd be stuck there.

A towpath led along the muddy, algae-covered canal inland. Hundreds of mosquitoes buzzed around Johann and turned every step into torture. They rose in huge swarms from the salty marshes that stretched on both banks of the canal. Every now and then a solitary cow stared at Johann as he passed by, but he saw no other living soul. Ruins covered in thorny brambles showed how many people used to live on the island. Why had they all left Torcello? Had God sent a flood to punish them for their sins? And what sins could they be?

After a while he came to a low stone bridge that led across the canal. He assumed it was the Ponte del Diavolo, the devil's bridge. The old fisherman hadn't been able to tell him why it was called that—or perhaps Johann hadn't understood.

Johann could see, rising up between the trees not far from the bridge, a bell tower and the roofs of a smaller church and a taller, three-aisled basilica. Johann still hadn't seen another person. He passed by some derelict houses and finally reached the two churches that were connected by an arcade walkway. They were situated at the edge of a square that probably used to be the center of town. A few ruinous buildings surrounded the square, and the bell tower stood behind them. The square itself was overgrown with bushes, and in the middle of it stood a large chair made of stone, like a throne used in ancient heathen ceremonies. This must have been a bustling place once, with markets and court trials. Now the only sound came from the buzzing of the mosquitoes.

A sudden noise made Johann spin around. An old man was getting to his feet amid the ruins with the help of a cane. He must have been resting among the rocks.

"Buongiorno!" called Johann. But the man didn't reply. He just stood there and stared at Johann.

"Sto cercando un uomo," Johann tried again. *"Si chiama Magister Archibaldus. Lo conoscete?"*

Still the man said nothing. A flock of pigeons rose up from the ruins behind him, and then the silence returned.

Johann gave up. He entered the smaller church, whose bare stone walls inside looked naked. There was no sign of anyone. He took the walkway toward the basilica, his solitary footsteps echoing loudly.

The basilica's double doors were closed, and when Johann opened one, a heavy red curtain blocked his view. It smelled musty, as if it had been hanging there for centuries. Johann pushed it aside and gazed into the large space in front of him. Tall, narrow windows allowed some light to fall upon golden mosaics so magnificent that Johann shuddered. They showed the Virgin Mary with her child and the twelve apostles. The apse was separated from the rest of the church with columns and a splendidly decorated choir screen. High up above the screen, a sad-eyed savior looked down at Johann.

There was no sign of Magister Archibaldus.

"Archibaldus?" called Johann, his voice echoing through the huge space. "Are you here?"

The sound of dripping came from somewhere, as if it was raining and the roof had a leak.

Drip . . . drip . . . drip . . .

Johann called out once more, but there was no reply. He decided to give up. Archibaldus wasn't there. The old man had probably had too much to drink the day before and told Johann some old wives' tale. Or was he waiting somewhere else on the island? But there wasn't anything else here apart from swamp, mosquitoes, and the overgrown square. Johann feverishly tried to figure out what to do next. Clearly, his trip to the island had been for nothing. But the worst part was that the fisherman wouldn't return until sundown. He was stuck here until then.

Drip . . . drip . . . drip . . .

The steady dripping unnerved Johann. His anger at that drunken old codger grew with every second. What had Archibaldus been playing at, sending him here? Damn it, if he really had anything to tell Johann, he could have done so in Venice and not on this mosquito-infested, godforsaken island! Hopefully he'd find another fisherman to take him back to the city. Or—

Drip . . .

That goddamned dripping! It sounded like it came from somewhere behind him. What could it be? Annoyed, Johann turned around—and froze.

Since he'd set foot in the basilica, he'd looked only to the front, to the altar. The entire back wall was covered by a huge mosaic that reached right up to the high ceiling. It showed the Last Judgment. At the top, people awaited their fate before God. From a Christ medallion in the center, a glowing stream of fire fed the flames of hell below. Angels forced the unhappy souls into damnation with their lances; snakes crept out of the eye sockets of dozens of skulls, and heads of kings were roasting in the eternal fire. To the left of the door, enthroned on a seat with a dragon's head, was Hades, the lord of the underworld, and in his lap sat the Antichrist himself. He was displayed as a handsome young man wearing a toga, and his eyes seemed to stare straight at Johann, as if waiting for a reply.

And hanging beneath the Antichrist was Magister Archibaldus.

Like a mockery of the crucifixion scene, the old man had been nailed to the wall with heavy nails, his face frozen in a grimace of horror. Blood was dripping from the hole in his left hand, which hung down loosely at his side.

Drip . . . drip . . . drip . . .

For a long while Johann could do nothing but stand there and stare at the gruesomely staged scene. The culprit or culprits must have crucified Archibaldus alive, because it looked as though he'd managed to free his left hand before he died. Using his own blood, Archibaldus had written three words on the wall with his finger. They were badly smudged and barely legible, but Johann thought they spelled a French name.

Gilles . . . de . . . Rais.

"Gilles de Rais," whispered Johann, and something crept up the back of his neck as if the sound of the name alone sent waves of fear and terror through his body. "What in God's name . . ."

Speaking the name of the Lord in front of the crucified old man suddenly seemed wrong. He broke off and felt a wave of nausea wash over him; his legs almost gave way. He flashed one last look at Archibaldus's twisted face and ran out of the basilica, along the arcade walkway, through the smaller church, and finally outside.

The old man was standing directly outside the door.

Johann almost ran right into him. He screamed and jumped back. The old man grinned, baring his almost-toothless gums.

"Il diavolo," he mumbled. *"Benvenuto nella casa del diavolo."* Then he chortled softly.

Johann pushed the grinning old man aside and ran across the square toward the muddy canal. He needed to get away from here, no matter how! He ran along the canal without looking back. Almost blind from sweat and persecuted by a swarm of mosquitoes, he rushed past the devil's bridge and toward the shore, which was somewhere behind the crippled trees and the crumbling ruins. Finally he caught sight of the rotting pier. The words of the old man echoed through his head.

Benvenuto nella casa del diavolo.

Welcome to the house of the devil.

Far out in the gray waters of the lagoon he could see fishing boats, but they were too far away to hear him. There must be some way to get off this—

A solitary low bell sounded.

Johann spun around in panic. The sound had definitely come from the campanile by the two churches. Had that crazy old man rung the bell?

Another chime rang out.

In the distance, right about where the square in front of the churches lay, Johann saw a small cloud of dust rise into the air. Something was brewing there.

Something was coming closer.

A third stroke of the bell.

Without thinking about it, Johann started racing along the shore like a hunted animal. The bell was just ringing out for the fourth time when he spotted a small rowing boat covered with rotten leaves amid the reeds. A fisherman must have hidden it there, maybe one of the few people who still lived on the island. Maybe even the man from earlier. The boat was flat and looked rather rotten, with several inches of bilgewater within it. But at least there were oars. Panting, Johann pushed the boat out into the water and jumped inside. The vessel rocked dangerously, but it didn't sink and didn't take on more water. As the bells continued to toll, Johann rowed as if the devil himself was after him. His heart raced. He only slowed down a little when the shore was nothing but a thin brown stripe. He tried to catch his breath.

He scanned the distant shoreline one last time—and started with fright once more.

Someone appeared to be standing on the pier. Johann blinked several times, but he was too far away to make out any details. Still, he thought the figure wasn't the old man from before, but someone else.

It was a man, and he waved as if asking Johann to come back.

Johann knew this was impossible. What he was seeing was merely a figment of his panicked imagination. But far, far away and at the same time deep down inside him, a voice called out again and again, asking him to return to Torcello, the island of the devil.

It was the voice of Tonio del Moravia.

It took Johann a good three hours to make it back to the Flute Inn. He rowed over to the isle of Burano, from which a larger fishing boat carried him to Venice. When the fishermen gave the young man with the chalky-white face and the flickering eyes a closer look, they decided not to ask where he had come from. There was something sinister about the black-haired youth, something as ominous as the scent of pestilence, and the men were relieved when they dropped him off at the quay in Venice.

During the silent crossing, Johann had come to a decision: he would leave Venice that very day. He had no idea what had happened on Torcello or why Archibaldus had to die in such a cruel way, but evidently it had something to do with Signore Barbarese and the man's library. Archibaldus had tried to warn Johann and paid with his life—but not without leaving him one last clue. A name.

Gilles de Rais.

Johann had never heard the name before, but he sensed that he was in grave danger. Those who had crucified Archibaldus wouldn't hesitate to kill him, too. The magister had been right: Signore Barbarese really was a devil worshipper, or at least had something to do with those circles. There was no other explanation for the cynical execution at the church. Barbarese must have been afraid that Archibaldus would betray his secret. And so he'd punished the poor old man in a gruesome manner. But what was it that Archibaldus had wanted to show Johann on Torcello? What secret lay on the swampy island?

On his way back to the inn, Johann kept looking over his shoulder in the narrow lanes. His enemies could be anywhere. But try as he might, he couldn't spot any pursuers. Out of breath, he rushed up the stairs to his chamber and immediately began stuffing clothes into his travel bag. When he was about to pack his knife away, he paused with fright. For the first time in a long while he noticed the initials engraved in the handle.

G d R.

"Gilles de Rais," whispered Johann.

Could it be possible? Had this knife belonged to the man whose name Archibaldus had written on the church wall in his blood?

A sound caused him to spin around. It was Salome entering his chamber. She took only a moment to grasp what Johann was doing.

"You're leaving?" she asked, crossing her arms on her chest. "Without a word of farewell? Without telling us where you're going and why?"

Johann slipped the knife back into his pocket and continued to pack. "Trust me, Salome, it's for the best. All I'm going to bring you is misfortune—all I'm bringing anyone is misfortune!" He laughed with despair. "And I don't even know myself yet where I'm going. I've been running for so long. I think it doesn't matter where I go—they'll find me."

"They?" Salome frowned. "Who's going to find you?"

Johann didn't reply and continued to stuff things into his bag. Salome watched him in silence for a while, and then she said, "I told you once that you don't own me, Johann, and that's true. But still, I feel something with you that I've never felt with any other man."

"And what is that?"

"Jealousy. If that's the beginning of love, I'm glad it's coming to an early end." Salome gave a bitter smile. "You don't fool me, Johann. You've met another girl and you're going away with her. You haven't been with me for weeks. Even when you entered me and made me moan with lust, you were somewhere else. You were with her the whole time. And now you're leaving with her."

"Jesus Christ, I'm not going with anyone . . . ," began Johann, but then he stopped. Perhaps it was better if Salome believed it was another woman. It would help Emilio and Mustafa understand his sudden departure, too. He had never fully belonged to them, had always remained an outsider, just like in his old life.

A stranger among men.

"Did you find Archibaldus?" asked Salome abruptly.

Johann hesitated for a moment, then nodded. He didn't want his friends to find out about Archibaldus's brutal death. Whoever had done that would kill anyone who knew too much—or sacrifice them.

Twitching bodies in the trees . . .

"He . . . he told me he was tired of life with a troupe," he lied. "Apparently the German merchants offered to take him back to Hamburg with them. He still has a few living relatives there who are willing to put him up for the remainder of his days. He took a boat to the mainland first thing this morning."

"Well, his relatives better make sure they order enough wine." Salome smiled. "It's probably for the best—both for him and for you. Neither of you are jugglers. You never have been and never will be."

Johann nodded and tied up his bag.

Who am I? he wondered.

"And where are the two of you going now?" asked Salome.

"The two of us?" Johann was puzzled for a moment, then he remembered. "Oh, we'll figure something out," he replied, trying to sound lighthearted. "Just like Peter Nachtigall and his beloved back then. Remember? He loved a girl he wasn't allowed to marry. They ran away together and . . ."

He trailed off.

"What is it?" asked Salome.

Johann looked up. It was so blindingly obvious. Why hadn't he thought of it sooner?

He loved a girl . . .

Margarethe had saved him twice already. Once during the eerie ceremony in the forest near Nördlingen, and for the second time here in Venice, at Signore Barbarese's library. Both times her laughter had led him back to the right path.

He prayed she'd do it for him a third time.

Margarethe alone could show him where to go.

"We're going to Heidelberg," said Johann with a strong voice. His hand felt for the letter Archibaldus had given him the day before. He'd almost forgotten about it in all the excitement. Now it might really be of help.

"I know someone there I must go see. It's important—a matter of life and death."

"Is that so? Life and death?" Salome walked up to him and stroked his cheek. "Then go, my little wolf. I will never forget you." She winked at him. "Or one particular body part of yours, at least."

Johann leaned down to give her one last kiss, but she turned away.

"Goodbye, Salome," he whispered.

Then he shouldered his bag and walked down the stairs and out into the dusk. It took a pile of money and all his skills of persuasion to find a ferryman willing to take him to Mestre on the mainland at this time of the evening.

As the boat glided through the night like a blade, the lights of Venice sparkled behind him.

"Margarethe," said Johann softly, pushing Archibaldus's letter deep into the pocket of his jerkin, where he also kept his knife. "I'm coming, Margarethe. I'm coming to find you. Everything is going to change."

His words sounded like a magical spell more powerful than any other spell in any other book in any other library anywhere in the world.

Act IV

The Student and the Girl

14

JOHANN ARRIVED IN HEIDELBERG ON A SUNNY DAY IN JUNE in the year of the Lord 1496.

His coat was dusty and full of holes, his jerkin and shirt had been patched up half a dozen times, and his toes stuck out from gaps in his shoes. With pinched lips and grim determination in his eyes, he clutched his crudely carved staff as he walked toward the large wooden bridge spanning the Neckar River. On the other side stood the city gate, the houses and churches, and an imposing castle on a hill.

Many times during the last few months when Johann thought he couldn't go on, he had invoked two images in his mind: the moment when his eyes would first behold Heidelberg, and Margarethe's look of surprise when she recognized him and embraced him joyously. Those daydreams had carried him through the boiling heat of the Po Valley and Lombardy, across the Brenner Pass, and through the many counties, duchies, and principalities beyond. He had fallen ill on the pass, struck down by a strong fever that kept him bedridden for several weeks. Kindhearted pilgrims had found him unconscious and bathed in sweat by the wayside and carried him to a hostel. In his fever dreams Johann had seen Magister Archibaldus time and time again, nailed to a cross and always muttering the same words.

You're guilty . . .

Yes, he had loaded an enormous guilt upon himself. Archibaldus had been murdered because of something he'd wanted to tell Johann, because the old man had wanted to help him. He'd wanted to protect Johann from something unspeakably evil—and from the darkness that slumbered within Johann like a small animal and that broke out from time to time.

As Johann gradually and very slowly recovered—a gentle old monk spoon-feeding him soup three times daily, like a small child—he often thought about the name Archibaldus had written on the church wall at Torcello with his own blood.

Gilles de Rais.

Johann still didn't know what that name meant. He studied the initials on his knife repeatedly but still couldn't figure it out. Perhaps it was just coincidence that the name bore the same initials as his knife—although Johann didn't really believe in coincidence anymore.

He'd matured in the last few months like a good, earthy wine in the barrel. He was eighteen years old now, with wiry muscles tough as hemp ropes. He'd cut his curly black hair and beard with a knife the day before, making him look almost like a monk. His face had become haggard and angular, his eyes gleamed dark and mysteriously, and there had been more than a few maidservants and daughters of innkeepers who had made sheep's eyes at him along the way. He had ignored them all, as if he really were a monk. He was urged on by his love for Margarethe and the hope that everything would be different from now on. Sometimes he thought of Salome, and of Emilio, Mustafa, and poor Peter. He had enjoyed his time with the jugglers, but that journey hadn't shown him where his path was leading, what his goal was supposed to be.

Perhaps he was finally looking at his goal.

With long strides he paced across the bridge that now, around noon, was busy with peddlers carrying their willow packs and farmers steering their oxcarts toward town. Armored horsemen vociferously demanded room, and a troop of grim-looking mercenaries with slit shirtsleeves and polished cuirasses marched past Johann.

These were the days leading up to Saint John's Eve, the feast when the longest day of the year was celebrated across the Palatinate with burning wheels of straw and hill fires. Finally summer had arrived—although it wouldn't be long before fall and winter would replace the lengthy, warm days again.

Johann watched laughing children running across the bridge and holding sticks decorated with colorful ribbons, painted eggshells, or sweet yeast pretzels. Johann could hear music coming from the city and smelled delicious wafts of fried food. He realized he'd eaten nothing but a stale piece of bread that day. His savings from Venice were almost completely gone, and he'd been holding on to his last few coins for his arrival in Heidelberg.

The week before, his journey had led him very close to Knittlingen. He had been filled with a silent longing, but most of all he'd felt pain. He had no reason to return to the city of his childhood. Why would he go where everyone hated him? And those he had loved were either dead or no longer there. If he was ever going to return to Knittlingen, he wanted to do so with his head held high, as a magister or doctor, even.

Johann's hand went to the pocket where he still kept the letter Archibaldus had given him. He'd touched it so many times that the paper was thin and tearing at the edges. He prayed that this document would indeed help him get into the university. Archibaldus had gotten them into the Fondaco dei Tedeschi, after all, so perhaps the Stovenbrannt name still bore some weight.

Johann had been to Heidelberg once before, as a small child with his stepfather, and he remembered the bridge and the new castle that sat enthroned on the opposite slope beneath an older fortress. Wedged between the river and the foothills of the Odenwald Mountains lay the city, which had grown dramatically over the last decades.

On the market square, Johann bought one of those sweet pretzels he'd seen the children carrying, from a baker who had set up his stall beneath the columns of the large red sandstone Church of the Holy Spirit. He saw burghers in expensive clothing and admired the pretty gables of the houses as he walked along the paved main streets. This city didn't stink half as badly as other towns he'd passed through.

Johann stopped and cast a reverent gaze at the electoral castle. Heidelberg was no Augsburg and certainly no Venice, but it was where Philip the Upright ruled; as count palatine, he was one of the most powerful rulers in the empire. One of his ancestors had been the king, and another relative, Count Palatine Ruprecht I, had founded Heidelberg University more than a hundred years ago. It had always been Johann's dream to study here, and he could hardly believe that it might actually become reality.

The lanes around the market square were bustling, and Johann asked his way to the university buildings. They lay on both sides of a street near the Church of the Holy Spirit in the city center. A group of students clad in the typical black gowns were just emerging from a chapel, wearing their berets rakishly low on their brows. They seemed proud and aloof to Johann, who looked down at his own dirty clothes with embarrassment. All of a sudden he felt completely out of place, like a stupid peasant at the court of a king. It took all his courage to ask one of the students about the name Archibaldus had given him.

"You want to see Rector Jodocus Gallus?" The student didn't look much older than sixteen, but he eyed the taller Johann with a mix of mocking and contempt. "If you've come to beg the old man for a penny, let me tell you that the honorable doctors don't earn nearly enough to feed scroungers like you. You're better off going to the Augustinians—they'll give you a bowl of gruel."

Johann clenched his fists but forced himself to stay calm. "I haven't come to beg but to deliver a letter to Doctor Gallus," he replied coolly.

The student gave a shrug. "Try at the *schola artistarum* next to the monastery. I think old Gallus might be holding a lecture." He raised a finger. "But you better not disturb the class—or you'll be in deep trouble!"

Johann turned away without another word. After searching for a while, he finally found a smaller single-story building close to the Augustinian monastery. It looked new, like many other houses in this part of town, with whitewashed walls and expensive crown-glass windows. Johann could hear monotonous Latin recitals through the open windows. He looked inside and saw a long room filled with about two dozen students sitting on wooden benches. Some were busy taking notes, but most of them looked as though they needed to sleep off last night's feasting. Their heads kept slumping forward in regular intervals, whereupon their neighbors would giggle and elbow them. Standing by a lectern at the front of the room was an older, stern-looking man, wearing a gown and talking about arithmetic. A blackboard on the wall behind him was covered in hastily scribbled formulas and calculations. Johann knew many of the terms, and he listened intently, holding his ear as close to the window as he could. It had been a long time since he'd last exercised his mind. He drank in every word like a man dying of thirst.

To his disappointment, the lecture was soon over and the students pushed their way outside. Johann gathered from their relieved expressions and scraps of conversations that they'd meet again for their next bender in just a few hours.

Johann waited a few moments before entering the room. The man at the lectern was packing his papers into a leather satchel. He was almost completely bald and very thin; his gown hung loosely on him like clothes on a scarecrow.

He looked up with irritation, and Johann saw that he wasn't as old as he'd first thought. He was probably in his late thirties, but his serious and dignified demeanor made him appear much older.

"The lecture has just finished," the doctor said irritably. "If you overslept, ask one of your drunken pals to tell you what they learned today—although I doubt they understood anything at all." He looked Johann up and down. "And wash yourself before you show up next time. You're a disgrace to the whole university!"

"I . . . I'm not a student," replied Johann uncertainly. "Are you Doctor Jodocus Gallus?"

The skinny man nodded impatiently. "Why are you asking?"

"I've got a letter for you." Johann handed him the tattered piece of paper he'd carried next to his heart for so many weeks. Jodocus Gallus studied the seal and gasped with surprise. "A letter from old Archibaldus, after all these years! Is it true? I think I wasn't even a magister yet the last time I saw him."

He broke the seal, unfolded the paper, awkwardly put on his eye glasses, and read the letter. Finally, he looked back up at Johann. This time his expression wasn't irritable but curious. He blinked at Johann from behind his glasses.

"Well, if Archibaldus is to be believed, you're a veritable prodigy. Where did you meet my old friend from our student days?"

"On . . . on a journey to Venice. He was my teacher for a while."

"And? How is he doing?"

"Oh, he sends his regards. He's decided to stay in Venice a while longer—the climate agrees with his old bones, he says." Johann thought he better not tell the doctor about the gruesome death of his friend.

"Ah, beautiful Venice! La Serenissima!" Jodocus Gallus gave a wistful smile. "How I'd love to be there with Archibaldus now instead of here in this stinking Palatinate backwater. They call it a university town, but in reality the so-called scholars do everything to prevent learning from happening. And those lazy students aren't any better. Paris, Rome, Prague—those are modern universities, but Heidelberg? Bah! Even Leipzig has better and more advanced teachers."

Johann decided to say nothing and just give the occasional nod while the doctor grumbled and moaned. Finally, Rector Gallus concluded his litany with a dismissive gesture. "But let's quit lamenting. Archibaldus believes you're a good student. Do you have money to pay for your matriculation? Any references?"

"No," replied Johann. He still had a few coins left, but he knew that it would never be enough for the matriculation fees.

"Hang on—let me get this straight." Jodocus Gallus raised his eyebrows, looking like a bird of prey about to swoop down on a mouse. "You have no money, you don't come from a wealthy or at least honorable family, and you have no references other than this old rag?"

Johann shook his head dejectedly. Suddenly the whole plan seemed ludicrous to him. How could he have believed the university would take him in? Jodocus Gallus gave a roaring laugh.

"Typical Archibaldus!" He grinned. "Did you really think a crumpled letter from my old friend would be enough? I may be the rector, but I can't do as I please. What would the chancellor say if I simply smuggled you in?"

"I . . . I'm sorry for wasting your precious time," said Johann. He gave a shrug and gestured at the blackboard with the formulas from the lecture. "And I thank you for the introduction to Euclid's fifth postulate. I listened to your lecture from outside and thoroughly enjoyed it."

Gallus looked surprised. "You know Euclid's elements?"

"Magister Archibaldus taught me," said Johann in a low voice.

"Hmm. What do you know about the Euclidean algorithm?"

Johann thought for a moment, and then he walked to the blackboard, picked up the chalk, and started to write. "The Euclidean algorithm is a method to determine the greatest common divisor of two natural numbers," he explained. "If CD measures unequal to AB, and the smaller part is removed from the greater in turns from AB and CD, one ends up with a number that equals the previous one without leaving a remainder."

"That is correct." Gallus rubbed his beardless chin pensively. "And what about rhetoric? Do you know Plato's differentiation between sophists and philosophers?"

Johann answered this question and all that followed. The doctor quizzed him on grammar, dialectic, astronomy, and geometry. When he was finished, Gallus clapped his hands and grinned.

"I'll be damned—you know more than my students after the baccalaureate. It would seem Archibaldus was right: you are a prodigy. You've come out of nowhere and made our young dandies from wealthy families look like a bunch of slow-witted peasants." He gave a dry laugh before turning serious again, eyeing

Johann closely. "Hmm, maybe there is a solution for you after all. I'd have to speak with Partschneider . . . Yes, it might just work. If he's got space at the paupers' hostel." He turned to the door. "Wait here."

Johann sat down on a bench by the wall and stared at the formulas of the Euclidean algorithm. One moment the rector was telling him to leave, and now everything had changed again. He couldn't believe the language of mathematics might have helped to steer his life in a new direction.

After a while, Jodocus Gallus returned with two elderly men who also wore long black gowns. The doctor pointed at Johann. "That's him," Gallus told the other men, who eyed the unkempt youth with suspicion. "See for yourself."

They tested his knowledge in the trivium and then in the subjects of the quadrivium. The examination took over an hour. At the end, the three men exchanged a look of agreement.

"He shall have the spot," said the man standing on the right, who was fat and had small, deep-set eyes and saggy red cheeks. "I've rarely examined a novice who already knows so much. Truly astonishing."

"Yes, although he's no longer the youngest, it would seem," said the other man, who had gray hair and bad teeth. He scrutinized Johann closely. "How old are you, lad?"

"Eighteen," replied Johann.

"That's rather old."

"I beg your pardon, Magister Partschneider," said the fat one with a laugh. "There are even older students at your hostel. One could almost think you don't like the look of him."

"It's not his looks. It's something else," replied the magister, his eyes still fixating on Johann. "There's something about him I don't like. But I'll admit he knows a lot and seems very intelligent."

"Well, I think we'll grant him a one-year scholarship," suggested Rector Gallus. "Let's see if he proves himself worthy. Agreed?"

The others nodded, and Jodocus Gallus turned to Johann. "It is agreed. That reminds me—I haven't even asked for your name. What is it, boy?"

Johann's instincts told him it might be better not to use his real name. Heidelberg wasn't that far from Knittlingen, after all. What would happen if someone recognized him?

"My name is Faustus," he said after a brief hesitation. "Johann Faustus, from Simmern."

It was the first place that popped into his head; he'd met someone from Simmern on the road a few days before. Doctor Gallus smiled.

"Faustus, the lucky one? What an unusual name. I hope you will find your luck here in Heidelberg, young Faustus." He stood up and shook Johann's hand. "Welcome to our university," he said. "You will swear your oath to me tonight. Oh, and by the way—now you're under our instruction. And as your rector I'm telling you: go wash yourself and do something about your clothes, or else I'll have you thrown into the *Karzer*, our very own jail for students."

The first few days in Heidelberg were like an additional course of study for Johann.

He could hardly believe his luck—the famous Heidelberg University had accepted him! But this stroke of luck meant a lot of hard work. Everything was new to him, and he had to learn countless small things that were a given for all the other students. At least that way he didn't get a chance to brood over the events in Venice.

The university's campus was a maze of new buildings, former monastery buildings, churches, and squares where lectures and seminars were held according to a fixed schedule. Johann heard that the Jewish ghetto used to be situated on the university grounds, but following the expulsion of the Jews from Heidelberg more than a hundred years ago, the count palatine had all the old houses torn down and built new ones in their place. The synagogue had been turned into the university chapel, which doubled as a lecture hall.

Johann estimated there were more than a hundred students in gowns and berets strutting from lecture to lecture through the narrow lanes of the university quarter. They acted like young doctors, proudly carrying bundles of books that they'd borrowed at one of the three university libraries. Students were permitted to copy from some of the books, while others—the most precious ones—were chained to desks. Borrowing books was a bureaucratic process so difficult that Johann thought it should require its own examination.

All lectures were held in Latin, and the students mostly spoke Latin among each other, too. They wanted to distance themselves from the citizens of Heidelberg, who often considered the rebellious young lads a thorn in their side. The students would roam the streets at night, singing loudly and acting raucously, brawling or frequenting the whorehouse at Grosse Mantelgasse Lane to let off steam. Like at all universities of the empire, women weren't permitted.

Most students lived at hostels, where further classes and exercises were held under the supervision of an older magister. The hostels were noisy until late at night, in spite of the strict rules. Johann, however, was staying at the paupers' hostel, a plain building that housed six poor but gifted students and six equally poor magisters. It was considered particularly strict and was headed by Magister Partschneider, whom Johann had met during his first examination. The suspicious old man had made it clear from the first day that he was keeping an eye on Johann.

"And I still say," he grumbled, "there's something about you I don't like. Sooner or later I'll find out what it is." When Johann walked past him into his sparsely furnished chamber, he could feel Partschneider's eyes. It felt as though the man could see right through him—see who he really was.

Nothing but a juggler and a fraud.

In the first week, Johann had found a friend among the other five poor students, and now they shared a room at the hostel. The student's name was Valentin Brander, and he was a delicate boy with drooping shoulders who always looked as if he was afraid of getting a beating. But his eyes gleamed with intelligence and mischief. Valentin was the son of a plain monastery blacksmith and came from a Dominican monastery in the Palatinate. The abbot himself had recommended him to the university.

Since the wealthy students from good families avoided the inhabitants of the paupers' hostel like the plague, Johann and Valentin spent almost every evening together, playing chess—a game that Valentin had taught Johann. After the first few hours, Johann had become completely entranced by the devilish game. Its complex moves allowed him to become fully immersed and temporarily forget about everything else.

Even Margarethe.

But then a thought of her would suddenly break through again, like a lightning bolt that struck him out of nowhere. He would stare into the distance and wouldn't hear anything else around him.

"What is it now?" whispered Valentin in class one day during a lecture. "You're one of the best first-year students, you seem to know everything, and then you suddenly gawk like a stupid calf. Better watch out Partschneider doesn't catch you dreaming."

Johann shook himself and continued to focus on his studies. Originally, he had planned to start searching for Margarethe right away, but he became so busy with his new surroundings that he hadn't had a chance yet. Saint John's Eve came and went and he barely noticed it. The university was like a giant, all-devouring beast.

For the next few weeks Johann worked hard on the subjects of the trivium: grammar, dialectic, and rhetoric. He had learned much from Archibaldus and also from Tonio already, and yet it felt like he was just beginning. He wrote down everything he heard during the lectures, answered the questions of the doctors, and posed intelligent counterquestions while the other students around him slept off the previous night's excesses. Most of them had been sent by their rich fathers and would leave the university with only a bachelor's degree, which could be obtained in merely two years. Some students quit even sooner. Johann, though, was inquisitive, clever, and highly ambitious, which didn't raise his popularity among his fellow students. Sometimes he wondered why he learned so much faster than everyone else. It was uncanny: he remembered almost instantly anything he read. It was a gift he'd possessed since childhood, but it seemed to him it had grown in the last two years—since his time with Tonio.

But there was another reason why the students tended to avoid Johann. It was as if he was surrounded by something dark and mysterious, like a poisonous cloud that only few people penetrated. Magister Partschneider hadn't been the only one to notice Johann's dark aura.

Whenever Johann woke up bathed in sweat in the morning, he knew that he'd dreamed of Archibaldus again, crucified against the wall.

Of Archibaldus and of Margarethe.

He had been scouring the university's libraries for anything on a certain Gilles de Rais—the mysterious name Archibaldus had left him—but found nothing. Nor did he find anything about the phrase *homo Deus est*, and he didn't want to ask any of his teachers about it. He'd learned from Archibaldus and Signore Barbarese that there was some sort of dark secret surrounding the phrase, that it was even associated with heresy. And so he buried his blackest memories in the depths of his mind, where they sometimes surfaced to torture him in his dreams. He also postponed his search for Margarethe time and time again—partly because he was afraid of what would happen if he found her. Would she even receive him, or would she curse him and have him chased out of town? Johann always remembered the last words Margarethe had spoken to him back in Knittlingen.

You are the devil . . .

Johann barely noticed summer coming to an end. One evening, as he and Valentin once again sat together over a game of chess and Johann took particularly long to decide on his next move, Valentin addressed him with concern.

"What's the matter with you? I mean, you've never been the most talkative guy, but you've barely uttered a word in days. Something's brewing inside you, I can tell. Is it because the students from the Swabian hostel stole your lecture notes the other day?"

"Why would I care about those dimwits?" Johann shook his head and knocked over one of Valentin's knights with his rook. "The Swabians are as thick as newts. There's no point in arguing with them—even though I'd advise them against bumping into me in a dark alley at the moment," he added grimly.

"Better watch out there. Hans Altmayer, their leader, already has it in for you. If a dozen Swabians attack you at once, not even the oh-so-proud Johann Faustus stands a chance."

Valentin wagged his finger with mock severity. Johann hadn't even told his only friend among the students his real name. There had already been a few scuffles between him and other students, and Johann always left his knife at home now to avoid getting into serious trouble. Larger weapons like épées and swords were forbidden on campus. But fists were enough for Johann, and he'd even used them to help Valentin out of tricky situations. Johann was considered an unpleasant opponent who was better avoided. His fellow students respected him, and some envied his intelligence and knowledge, but no one loved him. No one wanted to go out for a beer with him, and he avoided seeking the company of anyone except Valentin.

Unlike his tall, athletic new friend, Valentin was short and scrawny. His hair was thinning even though he was only seventeen years old. Like Johann, he was smart and hungry for knowledge, but he was also highly sensitive and had been the victim of many beatings. The two of them usually sat together during lectures.

"If it isn't Altmayer bothering you, then what is it?" asked Valentin persistently.

Johann sighed and pushed the chessboard aside. Why shouldn't he tell Valentin about his fears? Maybe his friend knew how one went about finding a married girl one hadn't seen in two years and whose last name one didn't even know.

"It's about a girl," he started awkwardly. "Not just any girl, but I fear she's the love of my life. She's been part of my life for as long as I can remember."

Johann told Valentin about Margarethe, about their times together and how he'd left his hometown. He even told Valentin the real name of his birthplace. His friend frowned.

"I thought you were from Simmern."

"There were certain . . . incidents at Knittlingen that I preferred not to mention to the rector," said Johann. "I'll tell you about it another time."

"Faustus, Faustus . . . the mysterious stranger." Valentin gave him a wink. "Whatever the case," he said and placed his queen in front of his king, "now your Margarethe has married some winemaker from around here, and you're looking for her. Are you sure that's such a good idea? Maybe she's happy with her husband and you'd be bringing unwanted memories."

"If she's happy, then at least I want to know—understand?" snapped Johann. "I can't get her out of my head. Her laughter, her merry eyes—she was the sun of my life. Whenever I got too mired in brooding, she shook me awake. She . . . she rescued me more times than I can remember."

"Enough already!" Valentin shook his head and laughed. "I can tell you're incurably in love." He touched his nose. "Hmm. Do you at least know the husband's name?"

Johann shrugged. "I know nothing except that he's a vintner from Heidelberg. For all I know, she might not even live here and the merchant in Venice was talking nonsense."

"A Heidelberg vintner marries a girl from Knittlingen. That shouldn't be too hard to find out." Valentin rubbed his beardless chin. "The folks at the taverns in the Bergheim quarter might know something—that's where most winegrowers live. Could be worth a shot. Only, I don't know what the dear husband will say when his wife's old flame shows up all of a sudden. We'll have to be careful."

He grinned. "But I wouldn't mind a few mugs of Heidelberg white—as long as you're paying."

"You . . . you would help me?"

"Matter of honor among fellow students! We just need to make sure old Partschneider doesn't get wind of anything. Every night he locks this place up like a prison."

"Let that be my concern," replied Johann, smirking. "Disappearing is one of my many talents. You know, I used to be a magician in one of my former lives. And now back to the game." He leaned over the board and made his move. "Bishop beats queen. Checkmate."

Valentin smacked his forehead with one hand. "Damn, you're good for someone who's only just learned the game. I don't get you—one moment you're bemoaning your undying love, and the next you make a move as if you've been thinking about nothing else the whole time. Sometimes I'd really like to know what's going on in that head of yours, Johann Faustus."

It wasn't until the following Saturday that the two students managed to slip away in the evening. Magister Partschneider always locked the door, and the windows were barred, but in an opportune moment Johann stole the key from the hook in the hallway. Using beeswax, he cast a mold of the key and took it to the Heidelberg blacksmith the same day. With their second key, Valentin and Johann were now able to leave their quarters after dark.

The Bergheim neighborhood was in the city's western section, not far from campus. Many craftsmen lived there, but also winegrowers whose vineyards flourished along the slopes of the Neckar River. The taverns were busy on this Saturday night. Numerous students were about, drinking wine and beer from large clay mugs, bawling their filthy Latin songs, and trying to lure the Heidelberg girls into nearby barns and press houses for a quick tryst.

Valentin and Johann had decided to visit all the taverns one after another—not an easy feat in a student city like Heidelberg. To keep Johann from coming under suspicion, Valentin would lead the conversation with the locals while Johann was supposed to remain in the background. Even though they tried to go easy on the wine, Johann felt rather drunk after the fourth tavern—and they still hadn't learned a thing.

When they entered the fifth tavern late at night and with heavy steps, Johann saw immediately that it was full of students from the Swabian hostel. Among the half-drunk students was their leader, Hans Altmayer, who'd played a few dirty tricks on Johann already. Altmayer, the son of a wealthy cloth merchant from Esslingen, was an oaf who used his time at the university mainly to hone his bullying skills. When Johann walked past without acknowledging him, Altmayer doffed his beret mockingly. He was tall and of strong build but not very agile, as Johann had found out during their first run-in. Johann had easily outmaneuvered him in that scuffle.

"Look at that, the beggars from the poorhouse were allowed out tonight," jeered Altmayer, looking around at his friends. "Better keep an eye on your purses now—those paupers like to pickpocket."

His fellow students hooted with laughter, but Johann ignored them, his eyes following Valentin, who sat down at a table with some farmers. Johann leaned against a wall, where a smiling young maid soon brought him a mug of frothing beer. Hans Altmayer and the other Swabian students put their heads together and shot poisonous glances in his direction, but they didn't dare attack him openly inside the tavern.

Johann had taken only a few sips when Valentin returned to his side. His friend seemed very excited.

"I think I found something," Valentin said quietly. "Those farmers know of a winemaker who married less than two years ago. It's his second wife. The first one died of the spotted fever and didn't bear him any children—"

"And the second?"

"Comes from Knittlingen, is flaxen haired, and has freckles."

"That's Margarethe!" exclaimed Johann so loudly that the people standing nearby turned to look at them.

"Shh! Shut up and listen. Something appears to be wrong with the girl. They didn't really want to say anything else on the matter and muttered something about dark forces and witchcraft—"

"What's happened to Margarethe?"

"I don't know! You'd have to ask her husband. His name is Jakob Kohlschreiber, he's quite the boozer, and—"

"And where do I find him?" asked Johann excitedly.

"I'm trying to tell you." Valentin's mouth was close to his ear now. "He's sitting on his own in the corner over there—see him?"

Johann turned his head slowly. In a corner, a little apart from the other tables, was a man with a large jug of wine. His thinning brown hair stuck out at the sides in tufts. His face was bloated from alcohol and his lips fleshy. He might have been a strapping and muscular young man once, but now a potbelly bulged underneath his vest, and his whole body was soft like a wet sponge. His clothes were stained but also showed that he was wealthy enough.

Johann brusquely handed his mug to Valentin.

"What are you doing?" asked his friend.

"I'm going to talk to the fellow," replied Johann. "I didn't travel hundreds of miles just to chicken out now. I want to know how Margarethe is doing."

"Be careful. The man looks dangerous. And drunk."

"So am I." Johann turned away and walked toward the table in the corner.

The man stared into his mug without noticing him. But when Johann sat down opposite him, he looked up with surprise. Then his expression turned sour.

"And who said you could sit with me?" he grumbled. "Go back to your pals. Lazy student riffraff. There's nothing for you here."

"Trust me, I'm just as sick of those good-for-nothings as you are," replied Johann, trying to sound as sober as possible. "My father is a vintner and sent me to college here. But I'd rather learn a proper trade instead of all that useless nonsense. I wouldn't be much good as a merchant, either—something hands-on would suit me, like a smith or carpenter or growing wine."

"Mmh, yes, winemaking is an honest profession," said Jakob Kohlschreiber, looking a little less surly now.

Johann casually dropped a coin onto the table. It was one of the last he'd kept from Venice. It was made of pure silver, and Kohlschreiber eyed it greedily. Johann snapped his fingers at the young maid.

"Is it possible to get something better than this sour swill in here?" he asked haughtily.

When the girl saw the coin, she turned on her heel and returned shortly thereafter with a jug of wine and two fresh mugs. Johann filled them and pushed one mug over to Kohlschreiber.

"Be so kind and share a jug with a young guy who's trying to forget his misery," he said.

He didn't have to ask Kohlschreiber twice. He emptied the mug and filled it again.

"Not bad," the vintner said. "Almost as good as my own wine."

"But what use is the best wine when the wench is no good?" said Johann, taking a long sip and watching Kohlschreiber from the corner of his eye. "My girl ran away with another fellow just the other day—and I haven't stopped drinking since."

Jakob Kohlschreiber gave a bitter laugh. "My woman ran away, too, but not with another man. Her cold body would still lie in my bed, but her mind was somewhere else. Probably on Blocksberg Mountain, where the witches dance. Damned sorcery!"

Johann leaned forward. "How do you mean?"

"Well, the woman is possessed by the devil. I should have known. I met her through my brother-in-law, who sometimes goes to Knittlingen on business. Do you know Knittlingen?"

Johann nodded uncertainly. "A little."

"Well, there was a well-situated girl. The dowry wasn't very big, but she's the daughter of the Knittlingen prefect. I thought it was a good bargain. And she's easy on the eye."

Oh yes, she is, thought Johann. *As beautiful as the sun after a dark night.*

"I was deceived," Kohlschreiber went on angrily. "The devil's inside that woman—but the father never said a word! Apparently, she didn't speak for weeks following an incident in the woods with some young lad. She didn't say much with me in the beginning, either." He burped and wiped his lips. "Not the worst trait for a wife to have, really. I don't like bickering women. But when I tried to perform my marital duty, she stopped talking altogether. The only time she said a word was in her sleep—terrible words . . ." Kohlschreiber lowered his voice. "She spoke about Satan, about missing children, and about a hand reaching for her . . . 'The boogeyman, he is coming to take me, he will take us all,' she muttered in her dreams. Like I said—that woman's possessed by the devil! 'Go away, go away,' she shouted, and the next morning she couldn't remember a thing."

"So . . . so what did you do?" asked Johann.

"What do you think?" Jakob Kohlschreiber leaned back and crossed his fat arms on his chest. "At first I was going to hand her over to the authorities. I mean, who wants a witch in their house? Next thing you know, you fall under suspicion yourself. But then I changed my mind and sent her to Neuburg."

"To Neuburg?"

"The Benedictine nunnery on the Neckar. For all I care, she can spend the rest of her life kneeling before the altar. The Neuburg nuns are particularly strict. I kept the dowry, of course." He gave a malicious laugh. "I'm going to drink it away until I find a new wife. But this time I'm not going to be cheated—not for the third time. The first one couldn't have children, and the next one turned out to be a witch. Damn the useless womenfolk! Hey, where are you going?"

Johann had sprung to his feet. His drunkenness had vanished and he suddenly felt very sober. If he sat here for a moment longer, he would throw his mug at the obnoxious fellow.

"Got to get back to the hostel," he muttered. "Keep the wine."

"Well, I won't say no to that." Kohlschreiber studied Johann with his small eyes. "There's something about you I don't like, boy. You're up to something, aren't you? What is it?"

Instead of replying, Johann walked away, and the winemaker refilled his mug.

Almost blind with grief, Johann headed for the exit. He just wanted to get out of there; he didn't even take the time to look for Valentin. As he was about to go through the door, Hans Altmayer blocked his way.

"And where are you going in such a hurry?" asked Altmayer. "Did you steal something, you—"

He didn't get any further, because Johann thrust his fist into Hans Altmayer's face. All his anger discharged in one single punch. Altmayer went down with a gasp of pain, and his comrades took a step back. Johann's expression told them not to come near. Something eerie and unpredictable flickered in his eyes as if he were a wild animal.

"You will regret this," cried Altmayer, holding his nose while the blood formed a red puddle on the stone floor. "You will regret this, you arrogant bastard!"

But Johann didn't hear him. He had already rushed out into the street. A chilly breeze swept through the night, but it didn't dampen his anger and his grief. Margarethe was so close to him and yet as far as if she were in Venice or Rome—or even farther.

She was at a nunnery.

15

JOHANN STAYED IN BED FOR TWO DAYS. HE REPORTED HIM-self sick, didn't attend lectures, and spent the days staring at the ceiling of his room. Not even Valentin got through to him. His friend brought him bread, soup, and thinned wine, but Johann only drank the wine and left the rest untouched. When Valentin begged him to tell what had happened, Johann said nothing.

Johann felt as though night had descended upon him and there was no hope of daylight returning. Ever since he'd decided in Venice to seek out Margarethe, this goal had given him the strength to carry on. Now he'd found Margarethe, but she was unobtainable. He'd never even find out how she was doing. The Neuburg convent was only about an hour away from Heidelberg, but it was practically impossible for an outsider to speak with the nuns. The Benedictine sisters were very withdrawn and hardly ever left the walls of their nunnery—least of all addled young souls sent there by distraught husbands or fathers. Those were the only men who might occasionally be granted access, but no one else.

No one else.

An idea flashed through Johann's gloomy thoughts. He sat up in his bed and reached for the bowl of soup. Suddenly he felt ravenous. His usually bright mind had been boarded up for the last two days, but finally he saw a way.

A plan was ripening in his mind.

On the morning of the third day, Johann told Magister Partschneider that he was feeling better. He picked up his satchel with his quill and papers and went outside as if heading to class. He was careful not to let Valentin see him leave. His plan was only half-baked, and he was afraid his friend would talk him out of it. He turned north toward the place where small boats lay moored near the university chapel. He hired a rowboat from a fisherman and paddled up the Neckar, which was still lazy and calm in early September. To the north and the south rose Heiligenberg and Königstuhl, the two mountains that cradled Heidelberg in their middle. Vineyards stretched on both banks of the river, and sweaty winegrowers carrying packs were hard at work harvesting the first grapes. Margarethe's husband, Jakob Kohlschreiber, was probably among them, unless he was sleeping it off somewhere beneath the vines. Hatred welled up in Johann. He gritted his teeth and rowed faster.

The river went around a gentle bend, and the bridge and the city disappeared out of sight. The Neckar wound its way into the Odenwald Mountains, the wooded ranges at whose foothills Heidelberg was situated. It wasn't long before a monastery-like complex appeared on the slopes above the left bank. It lay on a plateau among meadows above a small village with a mill. A narrow path lined with linden trees led up to the imposing stone building. Johann tied the boat to a dock and walked up the hill, forcing himself not to run. Somewhere up there was Margarethe—so close and yet out of reach. He slowed down and finally arrived at the nunnery, which consisted of a church, several outbuildings, and the abbey. The entire complex was surrounded by a wall, and vineyards rose on the slopes behind it up to the edge of the forest.

Maintaining his distance, Johann circled around the complex, keeping a close eye on any window he saw. He tried to figure out which ones belonged to living quarters. On the east side, the wall ran close to a bulky building, and Johann thought he could make out moving shadows behind the second-story windows. He guessed the room beyond those windows might be the parlatory—the only place where the nuns were permitted to lead longer conversations.

Johann nodded with determination. He'd found the right place. He walked to a crumbling old wall and took the quill, inkwell, and paper from his bag and wrote down the letter he'd composed in his mind on the way. Then he pinched tiny holes with a needle in certain places. He folded the document and sealed it with the wax print of a Venetian coin that showed some kind of old crest. The sisters wouldn't be able to place the coat of arms, but that didn't matter—it was just about making an impression. He patted down his clothes, brushed his fingers through his hair, picked up his sealed letter, and approached the convent gate.

He pulled the bell three times before the small hatch in the door finally opened. The small, wrinkled face of a very old nun appeared. Like all Benedictine nuns, she wore a black bonnet.

"God bless you," she croaked in a bored tone. "What do you want?"

"I'm here to deliver a letter," replied Johann and held up the folded paper for the nun to see.

"A letter, you say? Who for?"

Johann pretended he struggled to remember the name. "Um, I think it was for a certain Margarethe . . ."

"All sisters give up their worldly names in here, you fool," snarled the nun. "Didn't you know that? There is no Sister Margarethe here."

Johann rubbed his nose. "Well, then, I don't know . . ."

"Who sent the letter?"

"Her husband, Jakob Kohlschreiber."

The old nun's face lit up. "Oh! Why didn't you say so right away? And I thought the old miser had forgotten all about his former wife. He's behind with his payments." She held out her hand. "Give it here! I'll take it to Sister Agatha in person."

"Sister Agatha?"

The nun sighed. "That's what Kohlschreiber's wife is called now. Saint Agatha defended her virginity despite being put in a whorehouse and having her breasts cut off by her enemies. And the girl who used to be called Margarethe also pledged her virginity to God, just like all of us here."

I bet it wasn't a difficult decision in your case, thought Johann.

He handed the letter to the old crone. She turned her back to him, but he could tell by the sound that she broke the seal and read the letter. He was glad he'd chosen to use the secret code he and Margarethe had used as children. The nun didn't seem to find anything suspicious. She turned back to him after a while with a look of impatience. "What else do you want?"

"Well, Master Kohlschreiber reckoned you'd give me a kreuzer for my troubles," said Johann.

"Bah, the old penny-pincher can give you a kreuzer himself. Tell him we're waiting for the money he promised. He should count himself lucky we accepted his wife as a novice at all—considering what's happened. And now go with God. Go!"

She slammed the hatch shut in his face, and Johann heard her hurried footsteps moving away. Now all he could do was hope the old woman would deliver his letter.

With quick steps he walked back to the rowboat.

In his excitement, he didn't notice he was being followed.

"You did *what?*"

Valentin gaped at his friend. Johann hadn't lasted through the evening—he was bursting with excitement and needed to share his joy with someone. And so he told Valentin that Margarethe was at the convent with the Benedictine nuns and that he was trying to get in touch with her.

"I wrote her a letter," said Johann. "At first glance, it's just a letter from a husband inquiring about his wife's well-being. But there's a hidden message, and if Margarethe still has some of her wits about her, she'll remember our secret code. I put a few things in the text that only the two of us know about—she'll realize the letter's from me."

Valentin shook his head. "You're insane! If this gets out, you'll be thrown out of the university. A student arranging a liaison with a nun!"

"It's not a liaison," retorted Johann. "And she's not a nun yet—she's a novice, so she hasn't taken her vows. I just need to know how she's doing."

"You said that before. And once you know—then what?" Valentin pointed a finger at him. "Don't fool yourself, Faustus! You won't leave her alone. Do you want to free her from the nunnery by force? Her husband will do anything to keep her there—first and foremost to protect his own reputation."

"Who knows?" Johann pressed his lips together. "Either way—two Sundays from now I'll be standing below that window like I promised in the letter. Then we'll see."

Valentin laughed. "It's madness. But I can tell you've made your decision. Love is blind. But perhaps I can offer some distraction."

"What do you mean?"

Valentin grinned and pulled out some papers full of notes. "Take a look at this. I found it in a book at the library of the college of arts. The notes are by a certain Leonardo da Vinci. Apparently, he's a court painter and scholar in Milan. Have you heard of him?"

"I . . . I might have." Johann's curiosity was immediately kindled. He leafed through the pages with trembling fingers. He saw drawings of a box with a tube coming out of one of its walls and rays of light shining out of the tube. A roaring lion was displayed on a wall—the wall of a room, it would appear. Other drawings showed a lit candle and something that seemed to be a mirror. "What in God's name is that supposed to be?" asked Johann after a while.

"Well, it's something that Leonardo da Vinci calls a *'laterna magica,'* a magic lantern. It's an apparatus that's supposed to make it possible to transfer small images from the inside of the box onto a wall."

"That does indeed sound like magic," whispered Johann.

"And yet it isn't. I read the notes. Da Vinci bases his work on the ideas of someone called Giovanni Fontana, a *medicus* and magician from Venice. Fontana's thoughts make sense to me. If we could get our hands on the materials, we might be able to build the apparatus."

"Images appearing on a wall like magic?" Johann gave a laugh. "That would be so much better than the same old lectures day in, day out. Just imagine if we made pictures appear on the wall of Saint Mary's Chapel while old Spangel drones on. Wouldn't that be a laugh?"

"So—you will help me?" asked Valentin.

Johann winked at him. "Matter of honor among fellow students."

He didn't tell Valentin that he'd already read numerous manuscripts by da Vinci—probably more than were good for him. He had never seen any of the great thinker's notes about this device before, but he knew that there was much of Leonardo da Vinci he hadn't read. Deep down inside, Johann could feel the old fever waking up: the urge to explore, to dig deeper than all the dusty scholars before him. The motto of the uncanny old Signore Barbarese came to his mind.

Aude sapere. Dare to know.

The man may have been a devil worshipper, but the motto held true for Johann, too. And what was so bad about those words? They ought to have been written above the gates of Heidelberg University. But in the few months he'd been here, Johann had realized that even at Heidelberg, only long-established truths were rehashed—nothing new was being discussed, and original thoughts and ideas were frowned upon.

For the first time in days, Johann felt like a human being again. There was the prospect of seeing Margarethe once more, and Valentin had invited him to build this magical apparatus with him. Maybe love and science could be united after all.

The laterna magica helped Johann pass the time until he could see Margarethe again. Every night following their sparse supper, he and Valentin would sit up together in their room and study da Vinci's notes. They also borrowed a book by Giovanni Fontana from the library; it was entitled *Bellicorum Instrumentorum Liber* and was about war machines just like those Leonardo da Vinci had drawn up for the duke of Milan. One image showed a fire-spitting witch with wings—evidently a puppet that moved along tracks, designed to frighten off enemies; another showed in more detail the strange laterna da Vinci had described.

"We need a box that can hold a source of light," said Valentin as he pointed at one of the sketches. "The light is intensified by the mirror and pours out through a hole. If we then place a painted glass plate in front of the hole, the picture appears enlarged on a wall."

"Hmm. We can build the box ourselves," said Johann. "But where do we get the mirror? Something like that is expensive."

"Perhaps Rector Gallus could help us," suggested Valentin. "The old fellow thinks highly of you, and he's got friends up at the castle. They have mirrors there. And I'm sure he'll know someone who can make one of those glass plates for us. It doesn't need to be big. Can you ask him?"

Johann gave a shrug and grinned. "You're right—he seems to like me. But does that mean he'll give me a mirror?"

"Ask him, at least," said Valentin.

Jodocus Gallus had become a kind of mentor to Johann. The rector was much more approachable now than during their first encounter, and several times already he had let Johann have books that other students weren't permitted to borrow. And he asked the stern Magister Partschneider about Johann regularly.

"I can try," said Johann. "But I'd have to tell him something about our doings."

"Just tell him you want to study the sun without spoiling your eyesight," suggested Valentin. "Old Gengen was talking about it in his lecture on astronomy, remember? He uses a camera obscura for his studies, and that's similar to what we're trying to build."

Johann nodded. The camera obscura had been around since the time of Aristotle. If light fell through a tiny hole in a box, an image of the world in front of the box appeared on the inside, but upside down. The camera was accepted at universities as a teaching aid. Astronomers used it so they didn't have to look directly at the sun.

"It might just work," said Johann reluctantly. "That leaves only the painted glass plates. I think getting glass won't be a problem—I've got some savings, and perhaps Gallus will lend me the rest. But who's going to paint the images? If it's an outsider, he's bound to ask questions."

"Um, I could do it," replied Valentin.

"You?" Johann looked at him with surprise. Painting was now considered a trade in its own right, like carpentry, butchery, or masonry. There were entire workshops that produced paintings for churches or wealthy citizens, just like carpenters made tables. Johann had seen many such paintings in Barbarese's house, and he knew how difficult it must be to learn this trade.

"You can paint?" he asked Valentin.

"Not particularly well, but it'll do for our purposes. Look." Valentin shyly pulled out a few tattered pieces of paper from under his bed. They were pages from old books with drawings in their margins. The images showed animals and men with bushy tails or donkey ears, a fat man with a pig's nose, and even a rumpled raven wearing a gown. Johann laughed out loud.

"Why, those are our magisters and doctors! I recognize them all. There is our Partschneider, stern old Gengen, fat Spangel, and scrawny Rentz . . . Ha, and the one with the raven wings is Gallus in his stained gown!"

Valentin grinned. "Exactly right. So you did recognize him?"

"As if he were standing right before me." Johann clapped his hands together. "Valentin, these are great. I had no idea you were so talented."

Valentin shrugged. "Just a few silly sketches. I always hide them under the bed so Partschneider won't find them—I doubt he'd be too pleased."

"Hardly." Johann grinned. "I'm afraid he wouldn't appreciate your talents as they deserve. I do, however." He gave Valentin a pat on the shoulder. "Maybe you should draw a few harmless pictures for our laterna magica to begin with."

Every evening after lectures they worked on their project, studying plans and building the box in the shed next to their hostel. They told Magister

Partschneider they were building an apparatus for their astronomy class that would allow them to watch the heavenly bodies more easily.

After two weeks elapsed, the eagerly anticipated Sunday arrived.

Johann had asked Margarethe in his letter that she show herself in one of the windows at the rear of the nunnery at noon. He hired the boat at the crack of dawn, rowed up the Neckar, and, like last time, moored near the small village by the mill. Then he roamed the nearby vineyards and woods, feeling nervous and impatient. It was the middle of September; on the mowed fields sat rows of dried hay, which the farmers hurled onto their oxcarts with pitchforks. The sky was still blue, but dark thunderclouds had started to pile up in the west. Johann guessed it would rain later that day.

When the sun stood high in the sky, Johann walked down the vineyards toward the monastery wall. The vines reached almost right up to the wall, so Johann was able to remain practically invisible in their shadows. When the bells rang the noon hour, he whistled on two fingers and waited. Nothing stirred.

Johann's heart pounded like mad. Had he come too early? Perhaps the nun hadn't even delivered the letter? Or worse: the sisters had found out about the secret code and questioned Margarethe?

Another thought was so horrible that he pushed it aside instantly: What if Margarethe had read the letter but decided not to show?

Johann whistled again, but still there was nothing. He picked up some small pebbles and threw them against the shutters.

The next few moments felt like an eternity. Then something squeaked, and the right-hand shutter of the outermost window of the second floor opened.

Johann froze. The face of a young woman appeared in the window. She held her hand to her forehead to shield her eyes against the sun, but he had no trouble recognizing her pale, freckled face. A few curly strands of flaxen hair peered out from under the black Benedictine bonnet. Her lips were full and sensual, but her cheeks were hollower than he remembered. Her eyes gleamed with a sadness, an emptiness that was new, and yet she was just as beautiful as on the day he'd left her two years ago.

Up there in the window stood Margarethe.

She looked around searchingly. She hadn't seen him yet, and Johann relished the moment, like a hunter watching a flighty deer in a clearing early in the morning. After a few moments he softly called her name.

"Margarethe, I'm here!"

Only then did she spot him among the vines. Her mouth twisted into a happy smile, but her eyes remained empty.

"Johann!" she whispered. "My God, Johann . . . It . . . it wasn't a dream, then. The letter . . ." Her voice sounded hoarse, rusty.

"I wrote the letter," said Johann, trembling with joy. To see her again after all these years was almost more than he could bear. Memories and images flooded his mind.

"Margarethe," he began. "I . . . I've been searching for you for so long. I . . ." He broke off. The sight of her was too much for him.

"Where have you been?" she asked. "So much time has passed."

Johann realized that Margarethe was talking again. The spell seemed broken, but she was changed. She was a little too far away for him to make out details, but Johann thought he could see wrinkles around her eyes. Could it be true? She was only eighteen, the same as him. He felt like an eternity had gone by since their last encounter.

"Much has happened," he said awkwardly. "I . . . I was forced to leave Knittlingen. My father no longer wanted me in the house, and Martin wasn't found. They blamed me for everything. And you . . . you didn't speak . . ."

"I know." She paused for a long moment and sighed. "Sometimes I remember, but it's just scraps, like wafts of mist. Schillingswald Forest, the boulder with the picture of the devil in the clearing, your naked shoulder in the cave. And then that man . . ."

"What man?" asked Johann.

"The man in the woods . . ." She looked around anxiously, as if someone might sneak up from behind. "Listen, Johann—what's done is done. I've got a new life here. My husband—"

"I know what your so-called husband did," said Johann gruffly.

"Johann, you don't understand. I'm grateful. I feel safe here at the convent."

"Safe from what?" asked Johann.

Margarethe said nothing. The silence tortured Johann. Some pigeons flew up from the roof. Eventually, after what felt like an eternity, Margarethe spoke so quietly that Johann struggled to understand.

"I have dreams, Johann, terrible dreams. In my dreams I see what happened that day in the woods. And I also see what's yet to come. The beast will return! It will rise from the depths and devour the earth. The man told me."

"What beast?"

"We can't see each other again, Johann." Margarethe was crying now. He saw the tears roll down her cheeks. Her words came out like hard lumps. "I'm so terribly afraid . . . Not just for me, but for you, too, and for all of mankind . . . A new age is dawning, the man said. And sometimes I think I'm the only one who knows. That he told only me."

Johann clenched his fists. What was Margarethe talking about? Had she gone crazy after all? Could her drunken husband be right?

"Margarethe, I'm begging you!" he pleaded. "I traveled through so many countries just to see you again. Don't send me away. I want to at least understand what you mean. And I want to tell you what I've been doing for the last couple of years."

Margarethe hesitated, visibly grappling with herself. "On the feast day of Saint Michael the archangel," she said eventually. "I'm scheduled to help with the grape harvest." She gave a sad smile. "Like back in Knittlingen, remember? We used to work in the vineyards together. I'll try to get away from the other sisters so we can meet again. But I beg you, Johann, you must—" She broke off and turned her head. "Someone's coming. I have to go. Go with God!"

She closed the shutters and Johann was alone. Trembling all over, he shut his eyes and saw her face once more, like he'd just seen it in the window. Saw her face and heard the laughter that had saved him twice already.

He had found Margarethe.

And he'd see her again. He would touch her and inhale her scent. And all would be well. What she'd told him of her dreams was nothing but unhappy memories that came back in her sleep—nothing but nightmares like he also suffered from time to time.

Squirming bodies in the trees . . . the forbidden books of Signore Barbarese . . . crucified Archibaldus . . . the writing on the church wall . . .

As he hurried down the fields toward his boat, the heavens suddenly opened. Thunder clapped, and late-summer rain poured down on him. Johann leaned back his head, opened his mouth, and drank the warm drops greedily.

They tasted almost like blood.

~

Below a willow tree by the river stood a figure who watched the young student climb into his boat and row away. Water dripped off the man's hood, soaked his coat, and ran down his boots. But he didn't feel it. A hatred burned inside him that evaporated any cold.

The man waited until the boat disappeared in the rain. Then he walked down to the pier and climbed into his own boat. During the long, wet journey back to Heidelberg, he wondered how he should proceed. He smiled while the rain dripped off his broken nose.

He had time.

~

Boosted by the thought of seeing Margarethe again on the feast day of Saint Michael, Johann blossomed. He worked even harder at his lessons, improved his Greek by translating Aristotle and Plato in his spare time, and badgered his teachers with questions and comments about theological discourse. He avoided Hans Altmayer as much as he could. The leader of the Swabian hostel still bore bruises from Johann's powerful punch, and his nose was crooked and swollen. Johann guessed it would never look the same again, which didn't particularly improve Altmayer's already pockmarked face.

On the few occasions that they passed each other during lectures, Altmayer hissed threats in his direction. "You're dead, Faustus. You just don't know it yet. I'm going to finish you."

"Be my guest," Johann replied coolly. "If you want to lose your teeth as well, you ugly pock-face. But I'm afraid the girls will run away screaming at the sight of you—unless they do so already."

Altmayer clenched his fists. "You'll see where your arrogance gets you," he growled. "Just you wait. You're not untouchable just because you're the rector's pet. I will strike you where you'll expect it the least. Better watch out!"

But neither Altmayer nor his friends ambushed Johann in Heidelberg's dark alleyways on any of the following nights. Evidently, word had gotten around that there was no messing with the strange black-haired student. Besides, he enjoyed the special protection of Rector Gallus.

Johann hadn't yet asked Gallus about the small mirror they needed for the laterna magica. At the end of a lecture on rhetoric, he gathered all his courage and walked up to the lectern.

"So you want to build a camera obscura with young Brander," said Gallus with a smile when Johann had finished. "An excellent tool for observing the sun. But why do you need a mirror?"

"With the mirror, we can transfer the image onto the floor of the box, making it easier for us to copy," Johann explained.

Gallus rocked his head from side to side. "Hmm. I'm not entirely sure that's permissible, but never mind—I'll try to get the mirror for you." He raised a finger. "On one condition!"

"Which is?" asked Johann. He was afraid Gallus would demand to inspect the camera obscura himself.

The rector smiled. "I want you to accompany me to a meeting tomorrow. Up at the castle."

"Up at the castle?" Johann was too puzzled to string a sentence together. "But . . . why . . . ?"

"There are some people I'd like you to meet," said Gallus. "As you've probably come to realize, the university isn't as open to the new spirit of humanism as one would like it to be. It's different at the court of the palatine elector. I belong to a group of scholars who meet there regularly to swap ideas and discuss our views. Our *sodalitas*, as we call this circle of friends, is led by no lesser man than Conrad Celtis. I'm sure you've heard of him before."

Johann nodded with surprise. Not long ago, Conrad Celtis had held a guest lecture in Saint Mary's Chapel, which had been full to the last seat. Celtis was the teacher of the two electoral princes and was considered one of the greatest scholars of the empire—although his modern views didn't always please everyone. But the students admired him all the more. Johann's jaw had dropped while he'd been listening to Celtis's lecture on rhetoric and Aristotle's poetics.

"You . . . you want me to come to the castle with you to meet . . . meet Conrad Celtis?" he stammered.

Doctor Gallus laughed. "If your Latin is as bad as your German just then, I might change my mind. Conrad Celtis himself asked me to bring a few magisters and some promising students to the meeting. The other students all have their baccalaureus, but I think you've earned this visit, as has your friend Valentin

Brander. He might not be quite as clever as you, but he's hardworking—and not as haughty." Gallus closed the book on his lectern. "Well, then, until tomorrow evening by Saint Mary's Chapel, when the bells ring seven o'clock. Be on time or we'll leave without you two." Just before he exited the room, he turned and winked at Johann. "Maybe we'll even find a mirror for your camera obscura there. Though I still don't fully understand what you intend to do with it."

Johann was far too excited that night to sleep. Not only would he see Margarethe again soon, but now he was also invited to Heidelberg Castle! It seemed like all would end well for him after all.

Partschneider gave them a grim nod as Johann and Valentin left for Saint Mary's Chapel the following evening. As they walked through the lanes at dusk, Valentin had a wide grin on his face.

"If only the Swabians could see us now! They'd choke with envy."

"Don't speak too soon," said Johann. "We don't know if Altmayer has been asked to join the group."

"Bah." Valentin waved dismissively. "The only invite he might get is to a drunken bender on Hirschgasse Lane. The Swabians know more about fighting and drinking than rhetoric and poetics."

Several magisters and students were already waiting in the light of a torch by the chapel, and everyone seemed rather excited. To Johann's relief, neither Altmayer nor any of his ruffian friends were among the group. Two night watchmen with lanterns and halberds led the small group up the hill to the castle. Johann still struggled to believe that he, the bastard of a farmer from Knittlingen, was going to visit the electoral court with all these learned men. If only his mother had lived to see it. The other students seemed to share his feelings, nudging and winking at each other while the older magisters and Rector Gallus led the way in a more dignified manner. As a sign of his office, the rector carried a gilded scepter, holding it in front of him like a monstrance.

As if the starry sky had descended upon Heidelberg, dozens of small lights illuminated the windows of the new castle. The path ran first along the castle wall and then across a drawbridge, through the outer ward, and toward a large gate, which opened from the inside with a loud creak. Beyond the gate, the castle courtyard was brightly illuminated by fire baskets. The watchmen escorted the delegation of doctors, magisters, and students into a low room with a vaulted stone ceiling. A long table full of food had been set up inside, and maidservants holding jugs of wine awaited them with smiles. The air was filled with delicious smells of roasted and smoked meats. Johann's stomach growled loudly; in his excitement, he'd hardly eaten anything all day.

Apprehensively, Johann and Valentin sat down together with the other students. No one dared to speak; an awkward silence ensued. Finally, Jodocus Gallus, sitting at the head of the table, clapped his hands.

"How does the saying go?" the rector said with a smile. "*Plenus venter, non studet libenter.* A full stomach doesn't like to study. But neither does an empty stomach—all the more true for pert young scholars who still have some growing and maturing to do. Help yourselves."

The students attacked the food hungrily. Especially those from poorer families—they hadn't eaten this well in a long time. The feast was in full swing when a side door opened and Conrad Celtis appeared. Johann quickly put down the chicken leg he was eating, and he and the students stood up and bowed respectfully.

Just like during his lecture at the chapel, Conrad Celtis radiated an almost tangible authority. Despite the still summery temperatures, the famous scholar wore a fur-collared gown and a woolen cap. His clothes were embroidered with colorful patterns, giving him the air of a magician. He seemed stern and forbidding at first, but that changed as soon as he spotted Jodocus Gallus among the guests. The two friends and colleagues hugged each other warmly and started a lively conversation in Latin. The other guests took it as a sign to continue their meal; the students also conversed in Latin now.

It wasn't long before passionate discussions started up around the long table, and Johann and Valentin eagerly participated. Johann had rarely felt so at home. His stomach was full, the wine made him talkative, and the conversation touched on subjects from a wide range of fields. They discussed the imperial diet at Worms that had brought about the everlasting public peace the year before; they debated the writings of Petrarch and the globe that a certain Martin Behaim had commissioned in Nuremberg a few years ago, which showed the world more precisely than any other model of the Earth before.

Johann was so engrossed in the conversation that he didn't notice the men approaching behind him. He felt a tap on his shoulder, spun around, and gave a start.

Facing him were Jodocus Gallus and Conrad Celtis.

"Dear colleague, I'd like you to meet an exceptional student," Gallus said to Conrad Celtis. "His name is Johann Faustus."

Celtis smiled. He looked much friendlier up close than behind the lectern of Saint Mary's Chapel. "I see: Faustus the lucky one. A happy-go-lucky, perhaps?" He grinned and gestured at Gallus beside him. "Clearly you've Latinized your name just like our dear Jodocus Gallus here, whose regular name is Rooster. And like me." He winked at Johann. "But Pick doesn't quite have the same ring as Celtis. Although the pick is a useful tool for digging—even for hidden knowledge. Where are you from, my boy?"

"From . . . from Simmern," replied Johann. The lie he'd told Rector Gallus on the day of his matriculation still didn't come easy. "My father worked in the vineyards there."

"Look at that," said Celtis. "Just like me. My father was also a vintner. That's one thing we have in common already. You see, you don't have to be the son of a king to understand the insights of this world. And don't they say *in vino veritas*?" He smiled. "Then this hall must be a true haven of wisdom."

Johann prayed that Celtis wouldn't ask him any more questions about his past, and to his relief, the scholar chose a different topic.

"What is your favorite subject among the seven liberal arts?" asked Celtis.

"Well, there is no easy answer," Johann started awkwardly, feeling his future academic career might depend on his reply. "I believe the seven liberal arts form one unit that prepares us for the higher studies. In the end, they're nothing but the tools we require for the true questions—questions that not even jurisprudence, medicine, or theology know how to answer."

"The true questions?" Celtis looked surprised. "What do you mean?"

Johann swallowed. He sensed he'd ventured out too far. In the chair beside him, Valentin shifted uneasily. Jodocus Gallus shot him a look of warning from behind Celtis. But it was too late to go back.

"I think that if we want to understand the world, we must leave the old knowledge behind and turn to new questions," he continued. "Questions to which the answers may not be found in the subjects we currently study nor in the writs of antiquity."

"Hmm . . ." Celtis considered Johann's words. "But isn't it the essence of humanism to fall back on the wisdom of antiquity?"

"The Greek and Roman scholars thought far indeed, but time hasn't stood still since then," replied Johann with a firmer voice. "We've discovered entire new worlds, so we must ask new questions."

"I think we've heard enough of this foolishness," said Jodocus Gallus, stepping forward to cut off Johann.

Celtis held him back. "Leave him, old friend. Sometimes, a wise thought is hidden at the core of a foolish one. Don't they say that children and fools often speak the truth?" He turned back to Johann. "And what are those new questions supposed to be?" asked Celtis with a smile. He appeared to like the student's nerve.

Johann hesitated. He thought about the books at Barbarese's library, about the drawings by Leonardo da Vinci, the war machines and flying apparatuses, and about the laterna magica he was constructing with Valentin. He thought about the countless questions that had crossed his mind since then, but he didn't dare bother Celtis with them. There was so much he wanted to know—far too much to break down into a few sentences, let alone answer them. That would take weeks, months, years.

Conrad Celtis was still looking at him expectantly, and suddenly Johann knew what he could ask the famous scholar. He still hadn't found in any library a clue about the mysterious name Magister Archibaldus had left for him in his own blood. Perhaps Celtis had heard of it. It was worth a shot.

"I came across a manuscript a while ago," said Johann. "And the author mentioned a certain Gilles de Rais. It sounds like a French name, but I'm not sure. I haven't been able to find anything about him anywhere—it's as if his name has been erased. Could he be a thinker or philosopher I haven't heard of before, someone the church doesn't want us to know about? Someone who might know answers to those new questions?"

"Gilles de Rais?" Celtis froze, and his face turned ashen. "Where did you come across that name?" Now Celtis's voice sounded biting and cold, and as sharp as a sword's cutting edge. "Tell me, how do you know it?"

"I . . . I don't remember exactly," stuttered Johann, feeling extremely uncomfortable all of a sudden. He felt himself blush. "I think it was in the arts library."

"Wherever it was, you need to forget that name again immediately. It brings nothing but evil."

"But—" said Johann.

"Do you believe in evil?" asked Celtis abruptly. "I don't mean the evil of everyday life, like the pickpocket cutting off a purse, the greedy murderer lurking in the dark of night, the counterfeiters, the traitors . . . I mean evil in its purest form as the antagonist to good, like Manichaeism used to teach. Do you believe in such an evil?"

Johann frowned. "I'm afraid I don't understand . . ."

"Well, I haven't fully made up my mind on the matter," continued Celtis. "But if such an evil does exist, it found its perfect vessel in Gilles de Rais. It is for the best that he is forgotten by history. And now I'd like to discuss more-pleasant matters." He gave Johann a sharp look. "Study hard, young Faustus. And before you return to your so-called new questions, find answers to the old ones."

With those words, Celtis turned away and left Johann alone with his thoughts.

16

JOHANN SPENT THE NEXT FEW HOURS IN A TRANCELIKE
state. He still took part in conversations, but everything he said and did was
mechanical, like a puppet on strings. How could he have been so presumptu-
ous? One of the greatest scholars of the empire—the teacher of the two electoral
princes—had spoken to him, and all Johann had asked about was a goddamned
name. On top of that, he had bad-mouthed everything that constituted humanism. He had made a complete fool of himself! Even Valentin shook his head
again and again.

"You shouldn't have said those things," he whispered to Johann. "Telling
Celtis that antiquity isn't the measure of all things and that the current university
courses aren't any good?" Then he snickered. "I wouldn't have had the balls."

"Shut up!" snapped Johann. "I know I messed up." He saw from the corner
of his eye how the other students stared at him and whispered. Clearly, the news
was beginning to make the rounds.

Johann angrily stabbed the slice of roast meat in front of him; it came
served on a piece of delicious-smelling white bread. He chewed without tasting
anything and kept his eyes down. He thought there was a good chance that the
university would expel him following the disastrous conversation. Why should
Rector Gallus continue to sponsor him when Johann considered everything he
learned at the university to be dated and pointless? For the remainder of dinner,
neither Celtis nor Gallus came near his end of the table, and he didn't get the
mirror for the laterna magica. It seemed Gallus had chosen to forget about his
promise. From one moment to the next, Johann had become persona non grata.

The following days, in every class he attended, Johann was also made to
feel that he had gone too far. The whole university seemed to know about his

arrogant speech at the castle. Some students smirked when he walked past, while others shoved him or jeered. Hans Altmayer used every opportunity to mock him.

"Make way for Doctor Faustus, our new deacon!" he exclaimed loudly when Johann entered a lecture hall. "I hear he's going to found his own school, where he'll teach the eighth art of snobbery and blathering."

The other students laughed, and Johann quickly sat down at his desk, keeping his head low. He soon found out that the magisters and doctors, too, were ill-disposed toward him. Old Partschneider interrupted his lecture several times to address Johann directly.

"So much for Plato's doctrine of forms," he said coldly and shut his book. "But perhaps young Faustus knows something that goes beyond Plato's idea. Or are the Greek philosophers perhaps not sophisticated enough for him? How about a brief excursus on the matter, dear colleague?"

His fellow students laughed; Johann said nothing, staring at his papers.

Life at the university became hell for him. No matter where he went and what he did, people either avoided him or mocked him. Valentin alone defended him when Altmayer and his companions riled up the other students against Johann. Johann would clench his fists in his pocket, but he never lashed out. He knew it would only make things worse. The building of the laterna magica came to a halt because they didn't have the mirror and a few other materials.

The only thing that cheered up Johann during those days was the thought of seeing Margarethe soon. He counted the days until the feast day of Archangel Michael and wrote short love poems in Greek, which he burned as soon as he finished them. When he lay awake at night, he envisioned a simple life with Margarethe at his side, making wine or farming, with a lively bunch of children around them, somewhere far away from Heidelberg and the university. He fell asleep with those images in his mind.

It was the end of September, only two days before the rendezvous with Margarethe, when Jodocus Gallus called him to the front after a lecture. Johann braced himself for the worst.

The rector looked at him with a serious expression. "I don't think I need to explain what position you got yourself into with your speech up at the castle," he said as he cleaned his glasses. "You'll understand—"

"I will pack my things today," said Johann.

Gallus paused wiping his glasses, astonished. "What are you talking about? Do you think that just because for once the wind is blowing the wrong way you have to abandon ship? Are you that weak? That's not like the Faustus I know."

"So . . . so what do you expect me to do?" asked Johann.

"I don't expect anything." Gallus smiled. "I'm merely delivering an invitation. My friend Conrad Celtis would like to see you again, tonight at the castle. Just you this time. It looks like you're getting a chance to patch things up." He put his glasses back on and studied Johann out of small, reddened eyes. "For whatever reason, Conrad has taken a liking to you. I'd advise you to hold back on the newfangled ideas this time."

"That's . . . I mean . . ." Johann was too confused for words.

"Now you've lost the power of speech for the second time." The rector laughed. "My dear Faustus, I just don't get you. One day you're as smart as three doctors, and the next you're as slow witted as a peasant." He cocked his head and wagged a finger. "Don't put me to shame! If Celtis tells me of any foolishness on your part, I won't be able to keep you here. For a student as young as you, you've made an astonishing number of enemies." Gallus waved his hand impatiently. "Now get out of here before someone sees you with me and draws the wrong conclusions. This place is worse than a bunch of gossiping fishwives."

That evening, Johann walked up to the castle by himself without any watchmen, torches, or fellow students. The guards had been expecting him and led him up a flight of stairs to the rooms of a side wing where Celtis resided during his stays at the castle. The scholar was sitting alone by a big, open fire that cast the plainly furnished room in a dancing red light. Moldy carpets covered the walls, and a rough-hewn chest stood in a corner. Apparently Celtis was no friend of luxury and comforts. When Johann lingered uncertainly in the doorway, the scholar gestured toward a stool by the fire.

"Sit," he commanded coolly.

Johann nodded humbly and took his seat. He had sworn to himself to weigh each word carefully this time.

He began, "Honorable master, I am so—" but Celtis cut him off by placing one finger against his own mouth. For a long moment Celtis just sat and scrutinized Johann while the logs in the fire crackled and crumbled into ashes.

"Do you like poems?" asked Celtis eventually.

Johann nodded, surprised. He hadn't expected this question. "I . . . I write some myself, occasionally. Nothing long, just short, silly lines."

Celtis smiled suddenly, and dimples appeared in his hitherto stony, forbidding face. "So do I, as you probably know. You remind me very much of another stupid young boy who was hell-bent on doing things his own way and exploring new worlds. That was a long time ago." He sighed. "But that's not why I invited you here tonight. It's about that one question you asked me at our last meeting."

"You mean . . . Gilles de Rais?" Johann thought he could feel a cold draft sweep through the room when he spoke the name.

"Yes, Gilles de Rais." Celtis nodded. "May his name be cursed for all eternity. I, too, was once preoccupied with Gilles de Rais, with the dark, the evil in this world. Youth is always fascinated by evil because it goes against order. It is the spirit that denies—much like small children like to say 'no' just to oppose their parents. Evil is the chaos that rails against the established truths and perpetually promises new beginnings. I admit, it's a tempting thought. And I know from personal experience: once a thought has taken root in one's mind, it gnaws and eats and doesn't go away. That is why I decided to tell you about Gilles de Rais. So it stops eating away at you." Celtis paused and stared into the fire, as if the answer to all questions lay in the flames. Then he turned back to Johann.

"Gilles de Rais was no scholar but a French military leader. In fact, he was one of the most famous and bravest knights that country full of noble warriors ever produced. He was a marshal of France and fought alongside the Maid of Orléans, whom the French venerated as a martyr and the English had burned at the stake as a sorceress and heretic. France and England were fighting a war that lasted for over a hundred years and only ended a few decades ago. De Rais was doubtlessly a brave knight, a baron from the lands near the Loire River, and a favorite of the king. He also was a friend of the arts, owned a large library, and tried his hand at acting, bookbinding, and illustrating. But as it often happens, his rapid climb was followed by a dramatic downfall—a fall right down into the depths of hell."

"What happened?" asked Johann in a whisper.

"Gilles de Rais lived the lifestyle of an emperor, holding grand tournaments and feasts. Nothing was good enough for him, and eventually he ran out of money. First he sold and mortgaged his lands. When that no longer sufficed, he turned to alchemy. He hired a throng of alchemists to find the philosopher's stone for him and turn lead to gold. He hoped to pay off his debts that way."

"And? Did he succeed?"

Celtis smiled. "Well, the alchemists, at least, became rich—from his money. De Rais himself sank deeper and deeper into poverty." He paused, and again the only sound came from the crackling logs in the fire. "It must have been around then that he first turned to the devil."

"The . . . the devil?"

Celtis nodded. "He made a pact with him. What exactly this pact entailed we don't know. The interrogation transcripts only tell us what the devil demanded of him—or at least what de Rais believed the devil wanted from him."

"His soul?" guessed Johann.

"No. That was probably too black even for the devil." Celtis shook his head. "De Rais gave him the most innocent thing that exists in the world: children."

One of the burning logs cracked loudly, and Johann shuddered despite the warmth.

Small, twitching bundles in the trees . . .

"De Rais sacrificed children to the devil," Celtis continued. "Not one, not two or three, but hundreds. He slit them open, bathed in their blood, and drank it. Sometimes he watched the children die and violated them at the same time. Others he suspended with ropes from the ceiling of his bedchamber and watched with relish as they danced and squirmed. Allegedly, he'd chant Christian hymns as they died. He also used their blood to write magic formulas to invoke the devil."

Celtis sighed; he seemed to find it hard to tell Johann all this, and yet he went on.

"Some of the children were only four or five years old, and others were older. De Rais lured them into his château by the Loire with sweets and promises, and he kept their heads as mementos. Sometimes he painted the faces and asked his servants which head they thought the prettiest. The commoners knew about it, but no one believed them. They hid their children, but de Rais sent out his henchmen and took them all, one by one. He burned the bodies on large andirons and hid the bones in his castles, where they piled up like in ossuaries. It took decades before he was found out by the authorities. The only reason it came to a trial at all was that the king dropped him."

"And . . . and what happened to him?" asked Johann with a lump in his throat.

"Threatened with torture, Gilles de Rais confessed to his crimes. He was hanged at Nantes, but he lives on in myths and tales. Till this day he is considered the personification of evil, the devil on earth, in some parts of France. But he was just an ordinary man, nothing more. Do you understand?" Conrad Celtis leaned forward. "He was wicked and evil, but he was no demon and certainly not Satan—only the people turned him into that." He breathed out audibly, as if a heavy burden fell away from him. "I told you this story because I don't want you to chase a ghost, young Faustus. No matter what you've read about Gilles de Rais, he is dead, and his bones have long rotted away. He was a person, no more and no less. We men, we don't need the devil, because we are the devil." Celtis slowly shook his head. "I'm rather alone with this opinion, I know. The church can never hear those words. I hope you won't betray me," he added.

"If there is a God, then there must also be a devil," said Johann. "Good can only exist if there is evil, too. The day only bears its name because it differs from the night."

"Yes, that's what the Manichaeans used to teach—they were a sect from the early days of Christianity that has long since perished. Who knows, maybe they were right." Celtis shrugged. "But even if the devil does exist, I'm sure it's not in the shape of a spendthrift French marshal. Still, I admit that the common people need images in order to understand the abstract concepts of good and evil. In this sense—"

"How old would Gilles de Rais be now?" asked Johann abruptly.

"I told you, he is dead. Hanged on the market square of Nantes."

"But if he hadn't been hanged—how old would he be now?" persisted Johann.

Celtis gave another shrug. "I'm guessing around ninety. The war between England and France has been over for a while now." He rose ponderously. "Now let us conclude our conversation for tonight. I'd still like to compose a few lines in Greek. Remember, I only told you all this so you can stop searching for answers that don't exist. Understand? Don't waste the intelligence and ambition you clearly possess on the unimportant. Focus on what's essential."

Johann nodded slowly. "I . . . I think I understand. Thank you."

"Very well. Oh, and . . ." Celtis stopped, turned around, and started rummaging in the chest behind him. "Jodocus asked me to keep an eye out for a mirror for you. I know a glazier here at the castle, and he had this." He held up a piece of mirror about the size of his palm, showing multiple reflections of the flames. "It's just a shard, but at least it's a mirror. Made by the hands of men, the result of intelligence and untiring aspiration—something tangible, not a flight of fancy." Celtis placed the mirror in Johann's hand. "Promise me you'll forget Gilles de Rais for this, all right?"

"I . . . I promise." Johann gratefully accepted the piece of glass. He looked at it and saw a contorted reflection of his face, as if it had been broken into pieces and put back together. He tried to smile, but the result looked strangely twisted.

Almost as if it didn't belong to him, but to Tonio the magician.

Or to a man named Gilles de Rais.

~

When Johann had left, Conrad Celtis remained sitting by the fire, staring into the flames. That accursed cold! He just couldn't get it out of his bones, not even in the middle of summer. It had lodged itself in his core and was eating him up from the inside.

In the same way as hatred and malice can eat a man up until nothing but an empty shell remains, he thought.

Shivering, Celtis rubbed his wrinkled, gouty hands together. He hadn't told the promising young student everything about Gilles de Rais. Some details were so gruesome, so horrendous, that the thought alone could make a man feel sick. It was astonishing—for example—how many different uses there were for the skins of children. Or for their eyes.

Other details sounded too far-fetched. They haunted the tales of the simple people like a poisonous mist that never quite lifted. What was reality? What was merely an old wives' tale? Certain things were so outrageous that they could never become public knowledge. It was impossible to predict how people would react if they found out.

The beast is nigh . . .

Conrad Celtis had been preoccupied with Gilles de Rais for decades. He had found the name in old chronicles and had kept digging. It had become almost an obsession over the years, and Celtis was afraid that this obsession might now be taking hold of a highly inquisitive young student who wasn't ready for such knowledge.

And so Celtis had kept certain pieces of information from Johann. They were all written down in the book where he noted anything he'd ever learned about Gilles de Rais. Celtis had traveled to Paris and Orléans; he had scouted the counties and estates along the Loire and spoken to the old folks. He had found terrible things at the châteaux Champtocé, Machecoul, and Tiffauges. Especially at Tiffauges.

Conrad Celtis closed his eyes and tried to push back the memories into the deepest corner of his consciousness. By and by, the individual pieces had come together in a horrific mosaic. He had written everything down and then locked away the book, as if he could somehow lock away the truth.

And now this young student had come along, this Faustus, and asked about Gilles de Rais. It was as if he'd reawakened the evil with his question.

How did he know the name?

Celtis decided that all his cumulative research was too dangerous to remain in the pages of one book. If it landed in the wrong hands, it could set fire to the world.

He stood up with grim determination and walked over to the chest. He opened it and took out a small, tattered book. The pages were covered with handwriting, and in some places his hand had trembled so badly that the writing was barely legible. Celtis leafed through the pages one last time and shuddered.

This goddamned cold . . .

Then he hurled the book into the flames, which immediately started to devour the pages hungrily. One by one, the pages turned to ashes, and finally the leather book covers burned away, too.

The truth about Gilles de Rais had gone up in smoke for good.

~

When Johann showed Valentin the shard of mirror the following day, his friend looked at him with surprise.

"Celtis gave this to you, on the request of Rector Gallus?" he asked. "So you aren't as deeply in disgrace as I thought. How was your conversation last night?"

"Oh, I apologized for my rash words and we talked a little about Plato and the Greek tragedies. That was all," replied Johann. "Celtis truly is a learned man."

Valentin scratched his nose. "I still don't understand what your last question was about—you know, up at the castle. About that Gilles de Rais. Who is that guy? Something about it must have angered Celtis very much."

"And now the waves are calm again," replied Johann dismissively.

Celtis's words the day before had unsettled him and stirred up old memories that he'd tried in vain to forget. He hadn't been able to sleep, tortured by those memories: the missing children at Knittlingen and later in the mountains near Innsbruck, the pentagram in the tower, and then the eerie meeting with the man named Poitou—another French name. He and Tonio had conversed in French, of that Johann was sure. But he still didn't know what had really happened in that clearing near Nördlingen.

Small, squirming bundles . . .

Just before dawn, Johann had dug out the knife that had been with him for so long now, and he studied the engraving.

G d R.

What if this knife truly had belonged to Gilles de Rais once upon a time? The blade was razor sharp. What had the knight from the Loire Valley used it for?

Johann shook himself, and Valentin gave him a quizzical look. "What is it?"

"Nothing. Let's speak of something else. What about our laterna magica? Do you think the mirror glass will be enough?"

Valentin turned the shard in his hand thoughtfully. "Hmm. We'll need a glazier to cut it first. The source of light ought to meet the mirror from as many angles as possible to achieve maximum brightness. We can't do anything else until then."

"Then we'll just have to wait a few more days. I have other obligations anyhow."

Valentin grinned. "Let me guess. Something about a girl at a nunnery?" He sighed deeply. "Afterward, don't say I didn't warn you. First the incident with Celtis and now this. If they don't throw you out of school because of arrogance, then they'll do it because you're dallying with a nun."

"Not if you keep your fresh mouth shut," retorted Johann gruffly, and he immediately regretted his words. Why had he allowed his temper to flare up again? He had hoped seeing Margarethe would finally put his mind at rest. Valentin was the only friend he had in Heidelberg—he couldn't lose him, too.

"Forgive me," he said. "Things have been getting the better of me lately. Let's take a look at our laterna magica. I need a distraction."

"There's nothing to forgive." Valentin smiled secretively and gestured toward the door. "Come to the shed. I have a little surprise for you."

Valentin had been busy indeed. The casing was finished and the oil lamp installed; they hoped it would provide a better light than a candle. Valentin shyly pulled a small wooden box from under the table. It contained several glass plates.

"I got the glass from the glazier of the Church of the Holy Spirit," he said. "It's nothing special—just a start. But I think the images might have a nice effect."

Johann picked up the glass plates and held them against the sunlight streaming through the shed's window. He laughed with surprise. Valentin had painted small animal scenes on the glass. Johann made out a wolf, a cat arching its back, and a stag with stately antlers.

"These are fantastic! The stag looks as if he's about to leap off the glass."

"I decided on animals," said Valentin. "They're easier to draw than men, and I can draw them in movement. I botched a little here and there—"

"Don't hide your light under a bushel," said Johann. "Your pictures are excellent. Provided the laterna works, the show is going to be spectacular. Just imagine how much money we could make if we charged admittance."

Valentin crossed his arms on his chest. "I didn't intend to make money out of it. This experiment serves science alone."

"Let's talk about that again another time. It would be such a shame if—"

"I said these pictures aren't for public viewing," said Valentin hotly. "There isn't going to be a spectacle on market squares or at hostels full of drunk students. That's my final word, Johann Faustus! I'm a scholar, not a dishonorable juggler."

The last words hurt Johann to the quick. Valentin had never spoken to him like this before. Clearly, Johann had offended his friend's pride, but he tried not to let anything show.

"All right," Johann said, giving a strained smile. "I heard you. And now show me the sketches one more time to remind me how to insert the glass plates."

~

For the next two days, Johann hardly went to any lectures. He avoided running into others and couldn't wait to see Margarethe again. He told Valentin he needed to prepare for his Greek exams, but the crude letters swam before his eyes, appearing to run away from him like black beetles. What if Margarethe wouldn't be able to steal away from the other nuns? Or worse—what if she regretted her decision and didn't even turn up? Did she still love him?

At the same time, his thoughts kept returning to his conversation with Conrad Celtis and what the scholar had told him about Gilles de Rais. When Archibaldus wrote the name on the church wall in his own blood—what had he been trying to say?

Johann tried to deduce logically like he'd been taught at the university. As Aristotle had done, he started with a hypothesis and supported it with arguments. The only plausible explanation for Archibaldus's death seemed to be some sort of connection to Signore Barbarese. The old magister was murdered just before he was supposed to meet Johann to tell him more about Barbarese. Evidently, the eerie Venetian was indeed a follower of some devil-worshipping sect, and Archibaldus had found out—that was why he'd had to die. But why had Archibaldus written that name on the wall? Perhaps those disciples of Satan invoked Gilles de Rais; perhaps they considered him some sort of master, even if he'd been dead for a long time. That still left the question of what Tonio del Moravia had to do with all this. Archibaldus's last words to Johann had been about Tonio, after all.

It's about your former mentor, Tonio del Moravia. I finally know where I've heard the name before . . .

What was it that Archibaldus had learned about Tonio?

Johann pushed aside his gloomy thoughts and tried to focus on the Greek text before his eyes. Conrad Celtis was right. What did he care about the long-gone Frenchman? He'd try to forget Gilles de Rais. He'd try to forget Archibaldus, the missing children, his little brother Martin, Signore Barbarese, the black potion, and Tonio the sorcerer. All that mattered was the here and now.

And Margarethe.

Finally the feast day of Saint Michael arrived. In the large Church of the Holy Spirit at the market square, the priest read a mass about the victory of the angels over Lucifer and spoke about the eternal damnation awaiting all sinners on Judgment Day. The students were obliged to attend mass, but Johann only listened with one ear. In his thoughts he was already with Margarethe.

After the service he ran down to the quay, hired one of the small boats, and rowed up the Neckar to the nunnery. The vines stretching down to the banks of the river were heavy with grapes. Johann saw the vintners with their crates between the rows; they waved at the boats and laughed as they worked. It had rained in the morning, but now the sun shone warmly and humidity rose in clouds of mist over the hills and forests. Autumn seemed far away, and yet it would be October in just a few days. Johann thought there was a faint smell of cold and wind in the air already.

He docked by the little village with the mill and ran up to the convent vineyards. He looked around nervously but couldn't see any nuns in the hills. Had he arrived early or too late? Had Margarethe changed her mind?

Then he heard giggling and whispering voices. Johann ducked behind the vines and spotted a group of four young nuns in black habits. On their backs they carried crates, which they filled rather halfheartedly. A little farther back walked an older nun, and Johann recognized her as the old hag who had taken his letter at the gate.

"*Silentium!*" she hissed, and the younger sisters flinched as if they'd been struck. Apparently they weren't allowed to speak while picking grapes.

Margarethe wasn't among them. Johann sneaked away as soundlessly as he could and continued to scour the hillside. He didn't dare call out, and so he walked about aimlessly until he finally spotted a lone figure singing softly while she carefully plucked the grapes from the vines. It was an old nursery rhyme, and Johann's heart grew as heavy as a lead weight.

Growing in our garden are parsley and thyme; our Gretchen is the bride, she's looking so fine. Red wine, white wine, tomorrow morn you shall be mine.

He and Margarethe often used to sing this song as children, and to hear it here by the Neckar so many years later almost broke his heart. He remained hidden behind the vines and watched her. Now that she thought she was alone, he could almost see her old smile. Johann drank in the moment before addressing her with a low voice.

Margarethe gave a start, then she turned to him. Her eyes looked both happy and sad at once.

"So you came," she said.

Johann nodded. "I've been longing for this day." He stepped out from between the vines and brought his hand up to her cheek. "Margarethe—"

But she pulled away. "I'm a nun now, Johann. You know what that means."

"Isn't it permitted to touch nuns?" He winked. "Has God forbidden it? Or was it just the grumpy old crone I saw back there?"

"I belong to God now. He protects me and keeps me from harm. He will also ensure that the boogeyman won't come back."

Johann rolled his eyes. "Let's talk about something else. Look what I brought you." He pulled out a deck of playing cards he'd bought off a peddler the day before. "Draw any card."

She hesitated for a while, but then she picked a card, and a smile spread across her face. "Jack of hearts . . . So you're still a magician."

"And a great one at that. After I left Knittlingen, I joined a troupe of jugglers. We crossed the Alps and stayed in Venice after we traveled Italy."

As they meandered through the vines together, Johann told Margarethe all about his adventures with the jugglers; about the gifted fiddle player, Peter Nachtigall; the old drunkard, Archibaldus; about Emilio and strong Mustafa. Only Salome he left out, and neither did he mention his time with Tonio del Moravia. Johann knew Margarethe had never liked the creepy magician, not even as a child. And he was afraid that Tonio would remind her of that fateful afternoon in the clearing in Schillingswald Forest.

"A merchant in Venice told me that you were here in Heidelberg," said Johann at the end of his report. "I left the troupe to find you. I thought . . ." He paused.

"You thought what?" She gave a sad smile. "That I'd drop everything and go with you? You knew I was married."

"But what sort of a marriage is it?" demanded Johann angrily. "Your husband sends you to a nunnery just because you told him of your nightmares!"

"Jakob did right," replied Margarethe. "I feel safe here."

"But do you love him? Have you ever loved him?"

She laughed with despair. "Where do you live, Johann? It was never about love. After the . . . incident in the forest, I was no longer an option for the merchant family from Bretten. There were . . . rumors—involving you, too. And so my father had to marry me off further afield. Jakob Kohlschreiber seemed like a good match to him. Admittedly, he's not the gentlest, and he drinks, but he's a good businessman."

"And a good businessman knows when his wife has become worthless," Johann replied bitterly. "Namely, when she has nightmares and says a few strange things."

"They are no nightmares, Johann," Margarethe said quietly. "It's the truth. The boogeyman will return. He will return and change the world. The final battle between good and evil is near. He told me so himself."

"He? What . . . what are you talking about?" Johann laughed. "If I didn't know better, I'd say you'd gone crazy." He regretted his words instantly, but it was too late. Margarethe's lips became two thin lines.

"Do you know what day it is?" she asked eventually. "It's the day of Archangel Michael. When the angel Lucifer rose against God, it was Michael who stood up to him, together with all the other good angels, the seraphim and cherubim. He threw Lucifer and his followers from the heavens and they fell deeply, right down into hell. But the bringer of light never gave up. He wants to come back—he wants to rule the earth. And very soon the day will come when he shows his evil face again!"

"Margarethe, stop! That's—"

Johann had blurted the request so unexpectedly that he didn't know what to say next. Margarethe gave him a challenging look.

"There's something inside you—I can see it. Something dark, as if the boogeyman already tried to drag you down. Has he? Tell me."

Johann thought of Tonio and the pact they sealed one rainy night in the woods.

You'll fare well with me . . . Shake on it.

He thought about the handshake in Knittlingen and the gruesome death of Margarethe's brother. He thought about the black potion in the woods near Nördlingen, the squirming bodies in the trees, and the fits of temper that had overcome him regularly ever since. But they were nothing but phantoms—ghosts of the past that could no longer touch him.

"No one tried to drag me anywhere," he replied firmly. "I'm a faithful churchgoer, Margarethe." He smiled. "Evil has no power over me."

Johann knew he was lying. He went to mass only on Sundays or when he was forced to, like today. The last time he had prayed properly was at the grave of Peter Nachtigall in Italy. And he didn't think his prayer had reached God's ears.

God was far away.

But now Margarethe was standing in front of him, his angel on earth. If he didn't want to lose her, he had to lie. What else could he do? Her time at the nunnery had left its mark, but he felt certain that he'd find the old Margarethe again if he was given enough time.

"I pray to all the saints to watch over me every day," he said imploringly.

Margarethe nodded. "Pray to Saint Anna, because she helps those who have come close to evil. Will you promise?"

"I . . . I promise," said Johann, remembering that Conrad Celtis had also asked him for a promise a few days ago. He held up a hand. "I swear it upon my mother's soul."

The words had come out before he could think too much about them, but they had a profound effect on Margarethe.

She laughed.

She laughed as merrily as back in the old days, when they'd played in the hay in Knittlingen. Johann's heart leaped with joy.

"I'm so glad, my dear Johann. We're in God's hands." She took a step toward him. "And I'm sure God won't mind you touching me now."

Slowly, he reached out and stroked her cheek. Margarethe closed her eyes and inhaled deeply, as if enjoying the scent of old memories.

"It's so good to feel you," she said softly. "It's like coming home."

He ran his hand through her hair, and Margarethe sighed. Then Johann couldn't wait any longer. He leaned down and kissed her on the mouth. Margarethe winced a little but she didn't pull away.

"God will forgive this, too," he whispered. "What can God say against love? Love is the only weapon we have to fight evil."

She trembled when she squeezed his hand. "Go with God, Johann," she breathed and turned away.

"When can I see you again?" he asked quickly.

"In three or four days, perhaps." Margarethe looked down. "That's when I'll be working in the vineyards next. And now go, before the mother superior catches you. My magician . . ."

She smiled at him one last time before turning around and disappearing between the vines.

"My magician . . . ," whispered Johann, unable to move.

But in fact it was the other way around. Margarethe had cast a spell on him.

17

FOR THE NEXT FEW MONTHS, JOHANN WAS ON A PERMANENT high. He met with Margarethe whenever possible. The nuns often worked out in the fields around Neuburg, and occasionally they even came to the convent's small outpost in Heidelberg. Johann's meetings with Margarethe were always brief and secretive—a few heartfelt words, a touch, a kiss. Johann sensed that Margarethe was opening up to him more and more. Her remarks about the boogeyman and the return of Satan became less frequent, even if she didn't drop them entirely.

Johann tried a few times to get more than a kiss, but Margarethe evaded him each time.

"I'm promised to God," she'd say as they lay together in a field, hidden behind bundles of straw and hay carts. "If the convent wants me to, I will take my vows next year. But even now as a novice, I belong to God."

"I spoke with God in my prayers," said Johann. "He only wants us to be happy."

"Aren't we happy?" asked Margarethe.

And indeed, Johann was happy. Margarethe was nearby, he was studying at the greatest university in the German empire, and his prospects of an academic career were brilliant. Most students had gradually stopped making fun of him or treating him rudely, although, Valentin aside, he still had no real friends at the university—he was too ambitious, haughty, and aloof. But Rector Gallus and several other doctors and magisters were on his side. He also met up regularly with Conrad Celtis at the castle, where they held animated discussions. Among other subjects, they discussed the latest inventions.

"I heard they are planning a clock for the bell tower at Saint Mark's Square in Venice that announces the beginning and the end of our working day," said Johann one evening as they sat in Celtis's dark study. "Until now, men followed the course of the sun—it almost seems like clocks are taking over this task."

Celtis nodded. "And I hear there are apparatuses now that not only measure the hours but the minutes and even seconds. Seconds! No longer than the blink of an eye." He rolled his eyes theatrically. "Time is racing and we race with it. Where is this going to lead?"

"Consider the advantages if everyone went by the same time," said Johann. "Merchants could arrange meetings far more easily, and labor gets a value, measured by the number of hours."

Celtis laughed. "Well, the best time will always be the one that flies along without us even noticing where it's going. I must admit, conversations with you come very close to this feeling. They are, well . . ." He smiled. "Rather refreshing. Johann Faustus certainly has a quick tongue."

They never spoke about Gilles de Rais, and most of the time, Johann managed to forget the name and everything it entailed.

The only major setback during this period involved the laterna magica. It happened during the misty month of November, when the mirror was finally installed and the casing complete. They closed the shutters of the shed and lit the oil lamp inside the box. With trembling hands, Valentin pushed one of the glass plates with the animal pictures into the designated slot. But all that showed on the wall of the shed was an obscure, flickering shadow.

"Damn it," cursed Valentin and fidgeted impatiently with the glass plate. "The light source is far too weak. All the work we put in—and now this!"

"I don't think it's just because of the source of light," Johann said with a frown. "The light is much too diffuse, shining in all directions."

"Well, you can't capture the light like a herd of wild horses," said Valentin mockingly. "As soon as it finds a way out, it goes wherever it wants to. If only I'd never seen those drawings. What a waste of time." He was about to shove the apparatus off the table when Johann held him back.

"We're not giving up yet," he said sternly. "Maybe we'll find a way to focus the light better."

"Sure, sure," jeered Valentin. "Where the great Giovanni Fontana and Leonardo da Vinci failed, the oh-so-famous Doctor Faustus will succeed."

"Who knows, perhaps they'll call me that one day," muttered Johann. A vague idea was buzzing through his mind, but every time he tried to grasp it, it slipped away.

Johann continued to be wary of Hans Altmayer. He got the impression the fellow was hatching something. Whenever they passed each other, Altmayer grinned, placed one finger at his beret, and hinted at a bow.

"Look at that—Herr Faustus, the doctors' pet," he'd say. "Just you wait. The higher you climb, the farther you fall."

"And if you never climb, you remain forever in the stinking gutter," retorted Johann as he walked away.

Johann experienced his personal eureka moment during a lecture by Rector Gallus about Archimedes's principle.

Winter had moved into Heidelberg by now. The snow piled up in the lanes and made it difficult to get around. It was so cold in the lecture halls that the students shivered in their coats and hats. Johann finally understood why the berets had padded earflaps. The small stoves weren't nearly enough to heat the large rooms. Saint Mary's Chapel was the worst, the wind howling through its drafty windows. White clouds came from the mouths of the doctors as they spoke, and thin sheets of ice spread across benches and desks.

It was a bitter cold morning in January, but at least the sun shone weakly through the windows. As usual, the rector wore his strange-looking eye glasses, but the students were accustomed to the sight by now. He took them off only occasionally, when he gazed into the distance. Gallus was talking about the buoyancy of objects when a ray of light fell through the window and directly upon his glasses, which were lying on the lectern in front of him. Johann noticed with amazement how the weak light was bundled in the glasses and appeared on the opposite wall as a bright speck. The speck was brighter than the pale sunlight streaming through the window.

Much brighter.

"Archimedes posits that the upward buoyancy . . . ," Jodocus Gallus was saying when Johann sprang to his feet and rushed out of the hall. Irritated, the rector broke off. "Let us hope it's just the call of nature urging our dear Faustus to leave us thus."

"Or the infallible Herr Faustus already knows everything about Archimedes and is off to invent his own floating object," jeered Altmayer, but no one laughed.

Johann ran over to the low, snow-covered buildings of the school of arts, where Valentin was attending one of Partschneider's classes. Out of breath, he sat down next to Valentin in the last row and leaned over to him.

"I know it now," he whispered.

Valentin turned his head in surprise. "You know what now?"

"I know how we can capture and focus the light inside the laterna magica. We use lenses made of glass! Lenses like they use for eye glasses. Rector Gallus's glasses just gave me the idea."

Johann's voice grew louder, and Magister Partschneider interrupted his lecture irritably. "If the young sirs believe they already know everything, they are welcome to leave the room."

Johann tugged at Valentin's sleeve until his friend gave in and followed him outside.

"Are you crazy?" spat Valentin. "Partschneider will never forgive us!"

"Oh, he'll get over it," replied Johann, grinning. "Much more importantly, we can now complete the laterna magica."

He quickly explained to Valentin what he'd found out. His friend seemed skeptical at first, but then he nodded. "Hmm. I think you're right—it might work with lenses. They bundle the light—I know what you mean about Gallus's glasses. And if we placed several lenses in front of each other—"

"The light would become stronger and the image clearer," added Johann.

He then suddenly remembered the strange tube he'd seen up on the tower by the Alps a long time ago, back when he was still with Tonio. He guessed the tube had also contained several lenses, one behind the other, enabling a person to see farther. He wondered where Tonio had gotten the tube. Johann had never seen anything like it again, not even here at the university.

"I admit, it's a brilliant idea, but unfortunately, we have no lenses nor the money to buy some," said Valentin, interrupting Johann's pondering. "Eye glasses are expensive—perhaps more expensive than mirrors."

"I'll get the lenses," said Johann curtly. "You just worry about fitting them."

Johann had already decided to steal Rector Gallus's glasses—in the name of science. At some distant point in the future he would tell Gallus, and Johann felt certain the man would understand. Besides, he was the rector of Heidelberg

University—surely he could purchase another pair of glasses. And in a few years' time, when Johann had become a highly esteemed doctor himself, they'd laugh about the old story.

Valentin eyed Johann suspiciously. "I don't like you much at the moment, Johann. If you go on like this—"

"Do you want the laterna to work or not?" snarled Johann, cutting him off.

Valentin gave a shrug. "All right, fine. I hope we can talk normally again once we're done with the laterna. Like friends usually talk."

The opportunity for the theft arose a few days later. During a conversation with Rector Gallus following a lecture, Johann saw that the glasses were once again lying on the lectern. It was almost too easy. Johann placed his books on top of them and picked them up together. The rector didn't notice anything.

Johann's heart beat wildly as he walked out of the chapel, but neither Gallus's cutting voice nor any hurried footsteps rang out behind him. In a shady niche between two buildings, he carefully broke the glass lenses from their frames and buried the frames in a pile of snow. A twinge of conscience overcame him; the rector had done so much for him. But then he told himself again that he was acting solely in the name of science, and that Gallus would thank him one day.

When Johann gave the lenses to Valentin, he turned them thoughtfully in his hands. "I'd be glad if they weren't what I think they are," he remarked glumly.

"I have my resources," said Johann. "Best you don't ask."

They formed a tube from a piece of tin and experimented with different distances. Conrad Celtis had also given Johann a metal concave mirror so that the light from the oil lamp was much better bundled. When they felt certain that they were on the right track, they installed the tube into their apparatus, which had grown in size.

It was an evening in February when Valentin finally lit the oil lamp of the laterna magica once more and carefully inserted one of the glass plates into the slot. It was the picture of the cat with the arched back—his favorite. Then he opened the flap at the front.

The result was so overwhelming that they cried out almost simultaneously and took a step back.

From the opposite wall of the shed, a monster stared at them that was as large as a calf and as menacing as a lion on the prowl. The cat's arched back and hissing mouth seemed as lifelike as if it had just walked into the room. The picture was slightly unfocused at the edges and it flickered a little, which added to the ghostly effect. Johann felt as though he had just entered a strange new world.

"That . . . that's incredible!" he gasped.

"It's working!" Valentin grinned from ear to ear. "Do you know what that means? The two of us—two students—have just created an apparatus that not even the great Leonardo da Vinci managed to build. When we show Rector Gallus what—"

"We can't show Rector Gallus," objected Johann.

Valentin's expression darkened. "So it's true."

"It's not just the eye glasses," explained Johann. "We told Gallus we were building a camera obscura. If we turn up with this apparatus instead, he'll know we've been lying to him the whole time."

Johann tried to sound reasonable, but he really was afraid the rector would become angry and accuse him of theft. First and foremost on his mind, however, was a different motivation: the laterna magica was *their* invention, and he didn't want to share it with other scholars. It was their treasure.

And there was another hazy idea taking shape in his head about how he could put the laterna to good use.

"They'll charge us with sorcery," he said, gesturing at the cat staring at them from the wall. "Don't you see how uncanny it looks? Partschneider and some of the other magisters aren't ready for it yet."

"So you're saying we aren't going to show the laterna to anyone at all?" asked Valentin, puzzled.

"Not yet," replied Johann. "One day, perhaps. But it should remain our secret for now."

He gazed at the cat with the arched back, and the vague idea was slowly coming together.

An idea about how he might win over Margarethe after all.

During the cold months, Johann's meetings with Margarethe had been infrequent. There was no more work in the fields, and the nuns mostly stayed indoors. Johann often had to content himself with a long, cold wait beneath one of the convent's windows until Margarethe finally appeared for a few brief moments. To arrange their meetings, they used their secret code in letters that

Johann—bowing and scraping—delivered to the mother superior. Each time, he claimed it was from Margarethe's husband, who in reality never had contacted his wife again. One time Johann even included a short love poem, hoping ardently the mother superior wouldn't notice. The fact that he sometimes felt he was being watched he put down to his fear of getting caught. He couldn't bear to imagine the consequences for him and—more so—for Margarethe if they were discovered.

One night, as he once again waited below a window in the freezing cold, Margarethe had some happy news for him.

"I'm relocating to Heidelberg," she said quietly, trying not to wake the sleeping sisters. "The mother cellarer needs an aide for our outpost there, and I have proven that I'm not only good at writing but also counting. I'll be moving in just a few months."

"But . . . but that's fantastic!" exclaimed Johann. For a brief moment he forgot to keep his voice down. "We'll be able to see much more of each other. You'll have to sell your wares at the market, after all, and—"

"We must be all the more careful, Johann," urged Margarethe. "Sometimes I feel like Mother Superior knows something. She gives me strange looks and didn't want me to go to Heidelberg at first. And then I feel eyes in my back like daggers—"

"Don't start that again," said Johann. "I prayed that the boogeyman won't appear to you again, and so he won't."

"But he will return—I know it. If not now, then later." Margarethe closed her eyes as if she could see an image in her mind's eye. "The devil may have retreated for now, but only because he is preparing for his final, great day. And we must prepare, too!"

"Listen, Margarethe!" Johann came as close to the wall covered in frozen ivy as he could. "You can't say things like that anymore! I've heard at the university that several women have been arrested as witches in the area. Apparently they were dancing on Heiligenberg Mountain, and the bishop himself wrote to the authorities, urging them to be vigilant. Two old women were burned at the stake on Dilsberg Mountain not long ago because they allegedly concocted a pestilence powder from the innards of children. It is dangerous to speak of the devil in times like these."

"And what if these women really were witches?" asked Margarethe. "What if they really murder children, grind up their innards, and celebrate the return of Satan? Have you ever considered that?" She lowered her voice. "The Odenwald Forest is ancient. They say it is named for an evil god who used to rule here."

Johann groaned inwardly. As long as Margarethe was locked up in this nunnery, she'd never get rid of her delusions. He needed to take her out of there—as soon as possible.

"Sometimes I hear voices," whispered Margarethe. "They are the voices of demons who howl and scream and wait for the day of the beast. The day of the beast is coming closer. His followers are waiting for the stars to be favorable. That's what the man said in the forest . . ."

"And what if you heard the voice of an angel?" asked Johann brusquely. "Would you believe him? Would you believe that the devil is just toying with you and that he's not coming back to earth at all? That the boogeyman only exists in your nightmares—that none of it is real?"

Margarethe smiled. "That would be nice, but I'm afraid that'll never happen." She hesitated. "Sometimes I'm not even sure anymore whether I'm not imagining it all. But what I saw back then, and what the boogeyman said to me, it . . . it seemed so real! And then those dreams—those horrible dreams . . ." She sobbed.

Johann winced. When Margarethe cried, his own fear and insecurity returned. What was real and what was imagination? What was true and what was false? He needed Margarethe's laughter like medicine.

The black potion . . .

Back in the forest near Nördlingen it had been the memory of her laughter alone that saved him.

Johann needed her the way she used to be, when her laughter was still like a bulwark against all evil and against his gloomy thoughts and musings.

What he required for Margarethe was no less than a guardian angel.

A guardian angel . . .

Johann said nothing as thoughts raced through his mind. His vague idea was taking shape and turning into a plan, still a little rough around the edges and possibly crazy, but tangible now.

"I'm going to help you," he said eventually. "And soon."

~

Spring arrived so slowly that people almost missed its arrival. Water from icicles began dripping into the lanes, forming puddles at first and then deep mud patches. The magisters lifted their long gowns with disgust and stalked across the worst of the filth. The snow melted, but the cold inside the churches and lecture halls didn't go away.

Johann focused on his studies again. In April, the month of his nineteenth birthday, he passed his baccalaureus, an exam that other students tackled only after two or more years at the university. He graduated as valedictorian, and even old Partschneider nodded approvingly.

"But don't let it go to your head," he said warningly. "Pride comes before a fall."

Johann remembered that Hans Altmayer had once said something similar to him. These days there was a kind of truce between them, but Johann still couldn't shake the feeling that Altmayer was planning something.

He saw much less of Valentin during those weeks. Johann had been very busy with his preparations for the baccalaureus, and he also avoided his friend intentionally. He didn't want Valentin to pester him with questions about Margarethe. Deep down he was hoping that Valentin assumed the liaison was finished for good. Besides, Johann was far too preoccupied with his own plans to have time for friends—plans he didn't want Valentin to know about.

While his friend was attending lectures, Johann often sneaked into the shed and worked on some secret additions to the laterna magica. The changes he made were so minute that he hoped Valentin wouldn't notice. And the additional parts he needed could be inserted and removed as required.

During their few remaining hours together, the two friends locked themselves inside the shed, sat down on stools like two little boys at a puppet show, and admired the fantastic apparitions on the wall: the leaping stag, the cat with the arched back, the wolf with its bared teeth, and all the other animals Valentin had painted onto glass plates. Dust particles danced in the beam of the oil lamp, which was strong and focused now, thanks to the concave mirror and the lenses. The air smelled of whale oil, burned paint, and hot tin. In those moments, Johann and Valentin were as close as brothers. They had created this miracle together, and they couldn't get enough of it.

"It is such a shame we can't show anyone," Valentin said with a sigh and inserted a new plate into the slot. "I mean, it's really just the common people who would consider the laterna to be witchcraft. Why can't we at least show Rector Gallus and perhaps Conrad Celtis? They'd be amazed."

"Let's wait a little longer," replied Johann. "Once I'm a magister I'll be able to present the apparatus as my own invention. That would spare us a lot of awkward questions."

"*Your* invention?" Valentin gave him a confused look. "But we built the laterna together."

"You're right, of course," said Johann. "But I think the degree of magister would elevate the laterna."

Valentin said nothing and stared straight ahead, where the wolf continued to bare his teeth.

Sometimes now, when Johann considered himself to be alone, he hummed high-pitched melodies—not just in his own chamber, but also in the long corridors of the library of arts. When Valentin caught him humming along thus, he laughed out loud.

"Are you wailing about Gretchen the bride again?" he said mockingly. "Just make sure Altmayer doesn't hear you. That would give him something new to bitch about."

Johann cleared his throat. "Spangel asked if I'd join the choir for Easter. Apparently they still need a tenor." He winked at Valentin. "Although I fear I've greased my voice too much with beer and wine."

His humming became like an obsession. Sometimes when they sat together over a game of chess, Valentin would suddenly hear the high-pitched voice from an entirely different corner of the room. He'd spin around with fright each time, but it was only Johann, sitting in front of him with a grin. On one of those occasions he pointed to the ceiling by way of explanation. "I'm merely testing the thesis of Vitruvius about the movement of sound. Conrad Celtis lent me a script by this astonishing Roman architect. Evidently, sounds travel on strange paths. That would be worth a treatise on its own."

Valentin rolled his eyes. "When do you ever *not* think of our studies?"

"Well, art is long, and life is short and fleeting," Johann replied with a shrug and continued to hum.

"Cut it out!" groused Valentin. Then he shook his head. "I'm sorry. My nerves are raw since I'm studying for that accursed baccalaureus." He sighed and pulled a face. "My Greek is a disaster, and I'm no good at dialectic. What am I going to do after the baccalaureus, when they add arithmetic, geometry, music, and astronomy? I've always wondered why you knew so much about all those things from the start. All those star signs and the calculations of the constellations."

"I had a good teacher," said Johann, lost in thought. "He used to show me the stars at night."

"Where was that?" asked Valentin.

"At . . . at a tower. A tower in the woods near the Alps."

Valentin frowned. "I thought you were from Knittlingen in the Kraichgau."

"I traveled for a while," replied Johann vaguely, inwardly cursing himself. He really needed to be more careful about what came out of his mouth. "I journeyed to the Alps once and spent a winter there."

Dark memories rose to the surface of Johann's consciousness—memories he'd been suppressing for a long time.

A blood-red circle . . . A pile of dirty, torn children's clothes . . .

"Are you all right?" asked Valentin with a concerned look. "You're very pale all of a sudden."

Johann shook himself. "It's nothing. I think I just need a little fresh air." He stood up. "Please excuse me. I need to get a few more books to prepare for the next lecture."

Valentin smirked. "Ah, there is the Faustus I know! Never at peace, always searching for something."

You have no idea how right you are, thought Johann.

He forced himself to give his friend a smile, squeezed his hand, and hurried outside, where the fresh breeze swept through his hair.

In May, Margarethe finally came to the Heidelberg house of the Neuburg convent, and now she and Johann saw much more of each other. The nunnery sold its wine, cheese, and vegetables at the market, and Margarethe paid regular visits to their stall and balanced the accounts. On those occasions Johann stood underneath the dark arcades of the Church of the Holy Spirit, waiting for a sign from Margarethe, whereupon they'd both enter the church and sit down as if in prayer, Johann taking the pew behind Margarethe's. He couldn't see her face that way, but at least they could talk.

"I've been praying again," whispered Johann. "And do you know what happened? The very same night an angel appeared in my dreams."

"That's a good sign, Johann," replied Margarethe softly. "He is holding a hand over you so that evil can't reach you."

"He also spoke to me. He said that our love alone can heal us. He holds his hand over us and gives us his blessing."

Margarethe's head was still lowered, but he could tell that she was shaking. "What . . . what do you mean?"

"I think the angel wants you to leave the nunnery. He wants you to go with me, Margarethe, for the two of us to start a new life together in another city. I'm going to be a magister in just two years, and then I'll be able to work at a university or as a teacher in a school, as a clerk, at a library, or—"

"Stop it, Johann! Stop!" Margarethe's voice rose. Several worshippers turned to look at them, and she lowered her head again immediately. "I don't want to hear such things. Nothing but silly daydreams."

"And yet those dreams could become reality, Margarethe. If you wanted them to."

She stood up and rushed out of the church.

Johann clenched his teeth. He had gone too far—too far for the first time. He'd have to proceed more slowly, take it meeting by meeting—but he was so impatient. He wanted to share his life with Margarethe, and sooner rather than later. So he decided to put his plan into action.

There was only one thing left missing.

"You want *what*?" Valentin looked at Johann with wide eyes and put down his stylus. They had met in the common area of their lodging to study up on the Greek philosophers. Valentin wanted to take his baccalaureus in half a year's time, and Johann had promised to help him. There was indeed much room for improvement in Valentin's Greek, and his translations were riddled with mistakes. On top of everything else, Johann's question completely threw him.

"I want you to paint an angel," repeated Johann. "On a glass plate, just like the animals. I'll get you one."

"What in God's name do we need an angel for?"

"Well, I think it wouldn't hurt if there were Christian motifs among our pictures," replied Johann. "If we want to present the laterna to the university scholars one day, we can hardly show them nothing but cats, stags, and wolves. An angel would bring the theologists to our side. The perfect synthesis of faith and science."

"Hmm. Perhaps you're right." Valentin put down the tome about Plutarch's comparative autobiographies of Julius Caesar and Alexander the Great. "I should have time for it after the baccalaureus."

"Why not before?"

Valentin looked surprised. "Before? But—"

"Listen," Johann interrupted. "When I said a while ago that the degree of magister would elevate the laterna—that was a stupid and vain thing to say. I can see that now, and I'm sorry. It was all your idea to begin with, so you should reap the praise for it. What do think about introducing the laterna magica during your exam? Rector Gallus would be best, I think. You could say that we started off building a camera obscura and later decided to take it further."

"And the lenses from his glasses?" asked Valentin skeptically.

"The lenses could have come from anywhere. I'm sure the old man has long forgotten about them. That was months ago, and besides, he's already wearing new ones."

Valentin shook his head. "That wouldn't be right, Johann. You put just as much work into the apparatus."

"I've got my baccalaureus already," replied Johann with a smile. "But I wouldn't mind you mentioning my name in the course of your presentation. What do you say?"

He looked at Valentin expectantly. He tried to appear casual, but inwardly he prayed that Valentin would go for it. It was too important! Important to him, but most of all to Margarethe, because he needed to get her out of that nunnery before her delusions about the devil, boogeymen, and demons consumed her completely.

"All right," said Valentin reluctantly. "Why not? I'll draw an angel. Hmm. A Virgin Mary and a cross wouldn't hurt, either." He started to draw small sketches on the edges of his papers. After just a few moments his enthusiasm seemed kindled. "The angel needs wings and a sword, of course," he said and continued his drawing. "Yes, I think I'll go for an archangel. Archangel Michael, perhaps."

Johann nodded. "I think Archangel Michael is an excellent idea. He symbolizes the fight against evil. The theologists are going to love you."

Valentin smiled and looked up from his sketches. "I never took you for someone so selfless, Johann Faustus." His expression turned more serious. "You told me so little about you and your former life. Sometimes I really don't know who you are. I've been worrying about you and me lately, but clearly for nothing." He smiled again. "You're a true friend."

Johann felt a brief stab of guilt in his chest, but the pain soon passed.

18

"So? do you like it here?"

Johann lifted the torch, and the flickering flames illuminated the many faded paintings on the cave's vaulted ceiling. Among others, there was a painting in various shades of red of the Virgin Mary with her child. The mother and baby Jesus gazed down kindly on Johann and Margarethe.

"It . . . it's so beautiful," breathed Margarethe. "How do you know this place?"

"Students have plenty of time to go for walks." Johann grinned. "I enjoy roaming Heiligenberg Mountain and being alone with my thoughts. I discovered this cave when I was seeking shelter from a thunderstorm once."

He had found the cave a few weeks earlier, at the foot of Heiligenberg Mountain—one of the last foothills of the Odenwald Mountains, wooded with oak trees and chestnuts. It lay on the other side of the Neckar River, opposite Königstuhl Mountain, and was a popular meeting place for students and young couples trying to keep their loves a secret. It always seemed a little warmer beneath the vast green canopy of the chestnut trees—unlike inside the cave, where it was as cold as winter.

Johann suspected the cave stemmed from a time when Christianity was still new to the area. The paintings were simple, as if drawn by plain peasants, but they bore a grace that many large church paintings lacked. Farther back in the cave stood a crude block of stone that might have served as an altar once.

Margarethe tightened around her shoulders the woolen scarf she wore over her nun's habit. She shivered, and small clouds of steam came from her mouth. "It's cold in here. We shouldn't stay too long. The mother cellarer is expecting me back in Heidelberg. If I stay out too long, she'll grow suspicious—if she isn't already," she said with a sigh.

"Just tell her you were delayed by a storm," said Johann. "Hear for yourself."

And indeed, there was a thunderclap outside, and they could hear the steady rushing of rain. It was the beginning of May and thunderstorms were common, especially in the hills. Since the snow had melted, Margarethe often traveled back and forth between the convent and the house in Heidelberg. The nunnery's produce needed to be transported to town, and the mothers superior and cellarer exchanged messages. The nuns used an oxcart to transport their wares and took the road that ran alongside the Neckar and past Heiligenberg Mountain. Whenever Margarethe traveled by herself, she and Johann took the opportunity for a meeting.

Margarethe's initial shyness had given way to the joy of being together with Johann. They often spoke about their childhood in Knittlingen, their games in the hay loft, playing in the fields, and Johann's little magic tricks, which he still performed for her occasionally. But they never spoke about their last few days together in their hometown. It was as if a thick fog had descended upon that period of time.

Johann's desire for Margarethe had grown continuously over the last few months. To see her without really touching her, to speak to her but not be allowed to embrace her, caused him almost physical pain. At nights he dreamed of her soft skin, the dimples in her cheeks, her deep blue eyes that seemed to absorb all his fears. The best moments were those when she laughed, because then she was back to her old self. And Johann hoped that one day she would fully be back to the way she used to be.

That's what he needed the cave for.

Finding it had been a stroke of luck. It was the one building block he'd been missing. Now everything was ready. He struggled to remain calm and tried not to tremble with excitement. Originally he'd wanted to wait a few more weeks, but when he saw the thunderclouds gathering above Heiligenberg Mountain that morning, he thought the right moment had come.

Like a sign from the heavens, he thought.

But then Johann realized that he hadn't thought of God in a very long time. He had been pretending to pray to God, the saints, and the angels for Margarethe's sake, but he'd always been his own master.

If there was a God he revered, its image was standing well hidden in a dark niche of the cave.

"I really think we ought to leave now," said Margarethe, looking about anxiously. "This place is creepy, despite the beautiful paintings. This whole area is." She lowered her voice and made the sign of the cross. "Didn't you say yourself that there were witches dancing around here? I'm sure they would have done so during Walpurgis Night last week."

"That's what folks were saying," replied Johann with a shrug. "Apparently they saw lights burning on the mountain—but that could have been fires from shepherds."

"Mother Superior says we ought to stay away from Heiligenberg Mountain, even though Saint Michael Monastery is situated on its top. The monastery is dedicated to the archangel and was built on the foundations of a heathen temple—did you know that?" Margarethe shivered as she looked around again. "Allegedly, there is a deep hole somewhere in this forest into which the heathens used to throw people as sacrifices for their gruesome rituals."

For a moment, Johann saw a large fire in his mind's eye; heavy, meaty breasts; and wrinkled hands that groped and touched him everywhere. He thought he could smell soil and something faintly fishy.

O Ostara, hear us . . . O Belial, hear us . . .

He shook himself and the memory vanished.

"Well, this is definitely not a heathen place," he said quickly. "There is an altar. And look, there are even paintings of angels." Johann led Margarethe deeper into the cave and pointed at some paintings on the ceiling. "They might be archangels. One of them is holding a sword. Perhaps the monks from Saint Michael discovered this cave a long time ago and used it as a chapel and hiding place whenever war raged in the land." He squeezed Margarethe's hand and held the torch so that he could see her face. She squinted against the light. "Margarethe, the . . . the angel spoke to me again, in my dreams. He wants us to be happy together."

"Oh, my dear Johann! Don't make it so hard for me." She returned the squeeze of his hand, and a wave of desire went through Johann. She was so close and yet so far.

"If I were a free woman, believe me, I'd do it," she said with a sad smile. "Yes, I think I'd go away with you. But I've placed my fate into God's hands."

She squeezed his hand again, and tears welled up in her eyes. "I don't know what's right and what's wrong. But I'm sure that what we're doing here is a sin."

"How can it be a sin if we love each other?" asked Johann hotly. "You're a novice, Margarethe. You haven't taken your vows yet. You are free to leave the nunnery anytime you like."

"And then? I'm afraid, Johann. Afraid of what's happening in the world out there. I'm afraid of the boogeyman."

"Do you remember the last time we were in a cave?" whispered Johann. "Back in Schillingswald Forest in Knittlingen. It was the last wonderful moment before our world collapsed. Now we're inside a cave once more—the circle is complete, and all will be well from now on."

He kissed her on the lips, and unlike with the last few attempts, she didn't turn her head away but returned his kiss. Johann shivered. She tasted just as sweet as in his memories, of summer and of juicy grapes. His hand slowly slid up to her bonnet and pushed it back until her flaxen hair came loose.

"Johann, don't," she whispered.

The torch fell to the ground and died.

There was a soft hiss and a faint, almost imperceptible smell of sulfur in the air.

It was pitch black in the cave now. He hugged her tightly and covered her cheeks with kisses.

"No one will find us here, Margarethe! We're inside the womb of Mother Earth, as safe and secure as in the womb of Mother Mary."

"Mother Mary would never condone this—she was a virgin. She—"

Margarethe broke off and stopped fighting him. But instead of returning his kisses, she stepped back and stared at the opposite wall, where the rock altar stood.

"By all the saints!" she exclaimed.

Standing inside the cave, directly behind the altar, was an angel.

He was larger than life, with outstretched wings, and he wore a helmet and cuirass as if ready for the final battle. He carried a sword in his right hand. But his eyes weren't grim like those of a soldier, no—the angel was smiling. His face showed a divine benevolence that was usually found only in depictions of Jesus Christ.

Margarethe stood as if she had turned to stone and become part of the cave—a pillar of dripstone. She didn't say anything.

But then the angel spoke.

"Don't be afraid!" he said in a whispering voice that seemed to come from all directions at once. The sound echoed repeatedly through the vaulted space.

"I've been sent from the heavens to praise your love. What God has joined together, let no church put asunder!"

The angel flickered a little, as if it was about to vanish into thin air and return to the heavens. He was almost translucent—an otherworldly creature. Now he lowered his sword in a blurred movement.

"God's love is great and it shows in the love between men!" he continued. "The devil has no power when love prevails!"

Margarethe woke from her initial shock. She fell to her knees and prayed.

"Holy Michael, our archangel," she whispered. "I thank you, I thank you . . ."

"The devil has no power when love prevails," the angel repeated and raised his sword again. His voice was quieter now, and the apparition grew weaker, twitching and jerking like a candle in the wind.

"Love . . . prevails . . . Love . . . prevails . . ." echoed through the cave.

Then the angel was gone.

Darkness spread through the cave once more, along with a faint smell of lamp oil.

Johann hoped Margarethe wouldn't notice.

"That was the angel from my dreams!" he exclaimed after a few moments. "He is real and he spoke to us!"

Margarethe nodded. She was still on her knees, tears streaming down her cheeks, and she was trembling all over.

"The devil has no power when love prevails," she repeated. "That's what he said. The devil has no power . . ."

Johann knelt down beside her and held her tightly like he used to do when they were children and she felt cold. After a while, he gently lowered her to the ground and kissed her mouth, then her neck. His fingers slid down her black habit.

"When love prevails," he whispered.

~

Archangel Michael appeared to Margarethe and Johann every week now, and sometimes even more often.

Whenever Margarethe took the oxcart from the convent to Heidelberg, Johann waited for her beneath the chestnut trees. Then they would enter the cave and pray. After a while, the angel would appear on the opposite wall and speak to them, preaching about love among men and God's victory over the devil. Sometimes Margarethe spun around in fright because she thought the voice came from right next to her, but the echo in the cave made it seem like the words came from all sides at once, reinforcing the divine effect.

And every time the angel disappeared, they made love.

It wasn't the animalistic ravishing Johann knew from Salome, but more of a tentative discovering. They'd known each other since the days of their childhood and seen each other naked before when swimming in forest lakes or playing in the hay. The last time had been in the cave at Schillingswald Forest, but Johann's memories of that afternoon were hazy. They both enjoyed seeing and feeling how the body of the other had developed, how it had grown and matured. Johann's fingers playfully caressed Margarethe's white breasts and explored between her legs. With tongue and lips he tasted her juices, and Margarethe also became more adventurous with every meeting. The only reason they stopped was because the mother cellarer was waiting—and because it was so cold inside the cave that they both had goose pimples, despite the fires burning inside their bodies.

If Margarethe sometimes cried, it was out of a mixture of shame, fear, and joy.

"Would you really go away with me?" she whispered as she pressed her shivering, naked body against his. They were lying atop an old bearskin and used their coats for blankets. "Away from Heidelberg?"

"I would go to the end of the world with you," replied Johann softly. At the same time he realized that taking Margarethe away wouldn't be as easy as he'd first thought. Her husband would search for her if she left the nunnery, and Johann had started to prepare for his magister degree, which he was determined to complete in Heidelberg. Once he had the magister, he'd be able to take Margarethe to any town he liked and find work as a scribe, teacher, or lecturer. He'd be able to get his doctorate and become a famous scholar—as famous as Conrad Celtis, perhaps. Doctor Faustus, known far and wide!

Maybe I should have waited a little longer with the angel, he sometimes thought. He didn't know how much longer he could keep up the farce. Valentin was growing suspicious, Johann could tell. And it wasn't an easy feat, smuggling the laterna out of the shed each time and reassembling it inside the cave. Sooner or later, Valentin would find out.

"What is it?" asked Margarethe, tracing his lips with her finger. "You're brooding, admit it. Even if I can't see you in this darkness, I can tell when you're brooding."

Johann laughed. "I'm Johann Faustus, remember? I always brood." He sighed theatrically and hoped Margarethe wouldn't notice the uncertainty in his voice.

She sat up, her eyes gleaming like stars in the night. "So you even brood while you're with me?"

Johann greedily kissed her, virtually drinking her in. "The brooding is fading, Margarethe. With every kiss, with every sip. You're my medicine, don't forget. Better than any quack's theriac."

She laughed. "I very much hope so!"

He kissed her again and they made love passionately.

It was the best time in Johann's life, and even though he refused to listen to it, an inkling told him that it wouldn't last forever.

It was mid-June when Conrad Celtis asked him up to the castle once again. It had been a while since they last saw each other. Celtis had been lodging at other courts—Dresden and Mainz—and Johann had focused entirely on his studies. He wanted to gain the degree of magister as fast as possible so he could finally take Margarethe away from Heidelberg.

Celtis received him in the same austere chamber as on previous occasions. The only change was that there now stood a table full of books, parchment scrolls, and documents. Johann had never seen any food or drink in Celtis's room. It was as if the scholar lived solely on literature and iron gall ink.

"So?" asked Celtis once they were both seated by the fire. "How are your studies progressing?"

Johann nodded. "I'm almost done with the works of Plutarch, and I'm well acquainted with Archimedes's mathematical formulas now. Only the Cyrenaics still give me trouble. Aristippus of Cyrene, Arete, Theodorus—"

Celtis waved dismissively. "The Cyrenaics hardly ever feature in the exams, because the doctors don't understand them, either. The sensation of lust appears to be foreign to our learned scholars, even though the Cyrenaics only mean gentle movements by that term." He laughed. "The quality of the teaching staff in Heidelberg is rather below average, as you've probably figured out for yourself by now. With the exception of my old friend Jodocus, of course."

Johann looked at Celtis expectantly. He didn't know what the purpose of this conversation was. Ever since his embarrassing faux pas at Heidelberg Castle, he'd tried not to criticize the magisters and doctors—even if he'd sometimes had to bite his tongue.

"Have you ever considered studying in another city?" asked Celtis abruptly.

Johann straightened up on his stool. He was glad about the question—it would make leaving Heidelberg so much easier. "Indeed, following my magister, I could imagine—"

"I meant sooner. This summer."

Johann's jaw dropped with surprise. He thought he must have misheard. "But . . . but . . . how? I'm in the middle of studying for my magister—"

"Which you can also complete somewhere else. A student of your scope— child's play!" Celtis grinned. "And you would have me as your sponsor."

Johann said nothing for a while. "I'm afraid you'll have to elaborate."

"I will." Celtis leaned forward and lowered his voice. "I'm going to move to Vienna this very summer. The German king, Maximilian himself, has asked me to create a chair for rhetoric and poetics. A great honor! Vienna is the center of the Holy Roman Empire and boasts one of the largest universities."

"I know," whispered Johann. "I . . . I've heard of Vienna." Suddenly he felt like the floor was swaying beneath him, and he clutched his seat tightly.

"I could do with a young assistant by my side. Someone to comb the libraries for old manuscripts for me, archive documents, and separate the wheat from the chaff. Maybe someone who will uncover long-forgotten knowledge."

"And . . . and you thought of me?"

Celtis laughed. "Who else? You may be a little arrogant, and you lack respect for us old folks, but you're smart and ambitious, just like I used to be. And you're by far the best student the university has seen in a long time. Good old Jodocus and I spoke of you just the other day. He told me you pass all your exams summa cum laude."

"You're too kind." Johann lowered his head. Inwardly, he was shaking.

What Celtis had said was true. He was one of the best, and even old Partschneider had to admit it. His intelligence, coupled with everything he'd learned from Tonio and Archibaldus, raised him above the other students. He was predestined to become a great scholar, and with Celtis's offer, there was nothing in the way of this career. Going to Vienna as Celtis's assistant was more than he'd ever hoped for. What would his mother say if she were still alive? Would he get to meet the German king?

But what about Margarethe? He'd always planned on completing his magister here at Heidelberg and then taking her with him. But as an itinerant scholar at the side of Conrad Celtis? How was that going to work?

"You hesitate?" asked Celtis and frowned. "I didn't expect that. If it's about money—"

"It's not about money," said Johann quickly. "It's . . . it's just that there are a few things I still need to see to in Heidelberg."

"Oh, I see!" Celtis winked at him. "A girl. Well, hear this advice from an old rake: love is hot and burns out fast—only art is everlasting. The desire for art—for the sciences, philosophy, literature, and painting—is the only love worth cultivating. Wouldn't you agree?"

Johann said nothing but slowly nodded.

"Your girl will understand," continued Celtis and gave him a pat on the shoulder. "Men like us are meant for greater things, Faustus. Not for child minding and church on Sunday." He stood up. "I expect your answer in two weeks at the latest. I trust you won't disappoint me."

Johann could see in Celtis's eyes that he wouldn't tolerate any objections. But he thought he also saw something else in the man's look. Celtis was studying him closely, as if trying to read his thoughts. Evidently, he wasn't inviting Johann just because he wanted a capable assistant and to support Johann's career.

He wanted to keep an eye on him.

That afternoon, Johann staggered through the lanes of Heidelberg in a daze. What should he do? An offer like this would never come again. The whole world stood open to him, and all he had to do was say yes.

He would have liked to discuss this matter with Valentin. But then he'd have to admit that he was still seeing Margarethe, and Valentin would probably draw the right conclusions. After thinking it over for a long while, Johann finally decided to do what he hadn't done in a long time: get completely and utterly drunk.

In a tavern near the university quarter, he ordered a large jug of wine. There weren't a lot of people drinking at this hour of the afternoon; most students wouldn't arrive until the evening. The sounds of laughter and music wafted in through the door. Preparations for Saint John's Eve were in full swing throughout the city, and Johann realized that he'd been studying at Heidelberg for one whole year now. He had come to find Margarethe, and he had found her. He was happier than ever before in his life, and now he was supposed to leave her again? The more he thought about it, the clearer it became to him that he couldn't do it. He couldn't possibly leave without Margarethe. But he couldn't turn down Celtis's offer, either. So what was he supposed to do?

He emptied the jug in no time. The wine was sour and cheap, but at least it was strong. He ordered another one right away. Johann's mood improved with each sip. There was a solution. He'd have to tell more lies, but he'd lied so many times in the last few years that it hardly mattered. He would take Margarethe with him to Vienna—as his maidservant. It was so easy! Celtis was bound to travel with a large household, and one girl more wouldn't even be noticed. Later, once Johann had his magister and was earning his own money, he would take Margarethe for his wife. Surely Celtis would understand. Until then, Johann would rent a room close to the university for her, and they'd be able to see each other whenever they wanted. All would be well.

Johann took another long sip while his world became simpler by the minute. His plan was genius, really, because Margarethe's husband wouldn't be able to touch them. Who would dare to bother the great Conrad Celtis just because they were looking for some runaway nun? The elector or the bishop, perhaps, but certainly no drunken Heidelberg vintner.

Johann was so thrilled about his plan and so drunk from the two jugs of wine that he didn't notice the man approaching his table.

It was Hans Altmayer.

"Look at that, the great Faustus deigns to have a drink with the common people," jeered Altmayer. His nose, which Johann had broken during their brawl, had long healed, but now it was crooked and made him look even more of a ruffian.

"Better watch out that the alcohol doesn't go to your head," he hissed, glowering at Johann from bloodshot eyes.

Altmayer had been drinking heavily in recent months and had failed his baccalaureus exams. The rector himself had cautioned him and told him that he'd be kicked out of school if he failed another test. The only thing keeping Altmayer at the university right now was the protective hand of his father, who was an influential merchant.

"Pale little students with their noses always in books can't handle anything," Altmayer went on with a smirk. "Real life looks quite different."

Johann rose to his feet. He swayed a little, and his head felt heavy and light as a feather at the same time. More than usual he felt a strong urge to pick a fight with Altmayer. A fury welled up in him like he hadn't felt in years—since his time with the jugglers. Underneath his jerkin, his fingers felt for the knife on his belt. Perhaps he needed to teach Altmayer a proper lesson so he'd finally leave him alone. Johann thought how easily the knife had glided into the eye of the French mercenary back then, as if it were butter. He'd enjoyed the feeling.

"You're right, I lack a lot of practice at drinking," he began quietly. "I'm not as lucky as a drunkard like you—drinking day in, day out, and one day ending up as a red-nosed village teacher in some godforsaken hole, unless you become a traveling student and die in the gutter like a mangy dog. Congratulations!"

Altmayer raised his fist. He, too, was drunk and ready to fight. But suddenly his lips twisted into a strange smile, and he lowered his hand again. "Why should I beat you up, Faustus? Revenge will be much more satisfying."

Then he turned around and walked away. Johann, flushed from the alcohol, staggered after him for a few steps. "Hey, stop, you useless twit, you flat-nosed newt—"

He was about to pounce on Altmayer from behind when someone held him back. He spun around angrily and saw Valentin's worried face.

"So this is where I find you," exclaimed Valentin. "And just in the nick of time, methinks." He grabbed a pitcher from a table and threw cold water into Johann's face. "Wake up before something bad happens!"

"How dare you!" Johann clenched his fist at his side. Then he felt the knife again, and it was as if it slipped into his hand all by itself. The face before him blurred and was replaced by a grinning visage.

Tonio!

Johann raised the knife, ready to strike. Only at the last moment did he realize that it wasn't Tonio standing in front of him but his sole friend. The hallucination vanished, and with it the hatred and anger. Johann dropped his arms. Suddenly he felt awfully tired and empty. What had he done? He'd almost destroyed everything he'd worked so hard for during the last year.

With a groan he collapsed into Valentin's arms.

"I . . . I'm so sorry," he mumbled. "Believe me, I didn't want to do this. Something . . . something came over me."

Johann realized what it was that had made him so angry. He had wanted to stab Tonio del Moravia! Or had it been Tonio who had nearly brought him to stab his friend to death? Would he never be rid of that evil man? The master seemed to stick to him like a curse.

Johann shook himself; his legs felt like they were made of wax. "I want to go . . . home," he slurred. "Sleep."

"No problem." Valentin grinned and caught Johann before he landed on the tavern floor. "The great Faustus, bested by a jug of wine. Finally we've found an adversary you can't outsmart."

The headache the next morning was horrendous, and when it finally subsided, all that was left behind was a feeling of emptiness. That and the realization that Johann had almost stabbed his only friend. He wasn't entirely sure what exactly had happened at the tavern and whether the wine alone was to blame. He decided to cut back on drinking wine and beer from then on. He had never handled alcohol well—it seemed to dissolve the thin wall between his reasonable self and the animal behind it. And every time he got drunk, the nightmares returned.

Small, squirming bundles . . .

Well, at least the alcohol had been good for one thing: he had come to a decision. He would travel to Vienna and take Margarethe with him. How exactly that was going to work, Johann wasn't sure yet. But he felt certain he'd find a solution—he'd always found one so far. But first he had to share the news with Margarethe.

And that meant Saint Michael would have to speak to her one more time.

Johann hadn't intended to make the angel appear anymore. He no longer needed it to, and it was just too dangerous. He wouldn't be able to keep it secret from Valentin for much longer. And he'd lately had the feeling again that he was being watched. He needed the angel just this one final time. Saint Michael would ask Margarethe to follow Johann to Vienna. The angel had to appear one last time, and then Johann would never use such hocus-pocus again. Margarethe was healed. She never spoke of the boogeyman and Satan now.

All would be well. He no longer needed the lies—at least not with Margarethe.

On the day of Saint John's Eve, children ran through the streets, holding sticks adorned with colorful paper ribbons. On the surrounding hills, the young lads were piling up pyres, which they'd set alight after sunset. Fires would also be lit on Heiligenberg Mountain. Margarethe had told Johann that all nuns had to gather at the convent on the feast day of Saint John the Baptist, but not before the late mass. Until then, the sisters enjoyed one of their few days off. And with a hushed voice Margarethe had also told him that the river liked to help itself to an offering on Saint John's night. Many times in the past, dead girls had been fished out of the Neckar the following day.

Carrying the laterna in a pack covered with cloths on his back, dressed like a plain peddler, Johann headed toward their hiding place late in the afternoon. He'd walked this way so many times now that he knew every tree and every bush. The basketlike pack on his back was bulky and heavy, holding not just the laterna but also a long fuse, the oil for the lamp, and another apparatus.

Johann had told Valentin that he was going to the library to study. But instead, he'd waited for Valentin to leave, then gone to the shed to put on his disguise and load his pack. Johann's heart was beating fast, and he kept looking back to check that he wasn't being followed. A few times, as he walked through the woods, he thought he could hear branches snapping behind him, but he guessed his nerves were playing tricks on him. He couldn't wait for all this to be over.

Once Johann arrived at the cave, he lit a torch before setting up the laterna behind the altar, like he'd done so many times before. He took the fuse out of the pack and laid it along the cave wall. The most time-consuming part of the process was setting up the water clock at the laterna. It had taken him a while to figure out how he might change the images in the laterna without having to operate the apparatus himself. Finally he'd found something in old drawings by Hero of Alexandria. The Greek mathematician had constructed machines that used the power of water to move levers. Large levers required a large quantity of water, but for Johann's mechanism, a few gallons sufficed. The water slowly dripped from one container into another, and once it reached a certain weight, the lever was pushed and the image of Saint Michael with his sword raised fell into the slot. After a while, when enough water had dripped back into the first container, the image with the lowered sword appeared. Johann had experimented until the intervals were roughly the same length. The result was a fluid movement that made the archangel appear almost real.

After about two hours, he was finished with his preparations. He covered the apparatus with a gray cloth, making it practically invisible in the dark cave. Then he went outside and waited for Margarethe.

Afternoon had turned to evening, and the first Saint John's fires had been lit on Heiligenberg Mountain. Johann thought he could hear the laughter of young folks from afar. They were probably leaping across the flames, celebrating the shortest night of the year like people had done since time immemorial. Sometimes straw puppets were burned to chase away sickness and demons. Johann had read in old books that they even used to burn real people on that night, and he thought of the alleged witches the bishop had condemned to fire only a few weeks ago—a sacrifice like the heathens used to offer to their dark deities.

A sudden noise made Johann jump, and he breathed a sigh of relief when Margarethe emerged from between the trees. As always, she wore her black nun's habit and a thin woolen scarf around her shoulders. The nights could still be chilly in June, and the cave never warmed up at all. Margarethe shivered and rushed into his arms.

"We can't go on like this for much longer," she whispered. "Living with a lie like this . . . I can't take it anymore. Would you really go away with me?"

"Yes, Margarethe, I would. That's why I traveled all the way from Venice—to be with you." He gently pulled her toward the cave entrance. "Who knows, maybe the angel will appear to us again. Maybe he knows where our path will take us."

Margarethe gave him an intent look, and for a brief moment Johann thought she'd seen right through him.

"I thought about it again last night. Why did the archangel choose us, of all people? Why does he speak to us? There are so many young couples who can't be together despite their love."

"Because you're someone very special, Margarethe. The angel wants to help you—help us—return to the path of love." Johann made a sweeping gesture at the woods around them. "And who knows? Maybe he appears to other couples in the area. This is Heiligenberg Mountain, after all. They built a monastery in the name of Michael the archangel up here. It's his realm."

They entered the cave. The temperature dropped drastically, and small clouds rose from their mouths. Margarethe tightened the scarf around her shoulders.

Johann loved the sudden darkness inside the cave. In here, the world outside, with all its noise and all that striving for glory and knowledge, seemed completely unimportant.

Only the two of them existed.

A torch that Johann had lit earlier burned from a crack in the rock. The light showed them to their bed, which they'd made over the weeks from moss and dead leaves. As they went past, Johann put out the torch, and there was a soft hissing noise that he hoped Margarethe wouldn't hear. Now it was completely dark.

They sank onto their bed and embraced like two children seeking comfort. Johann closed his eyes and inhaled the damp scent of the cave, of soil, fungi, and mossy rocks. But most of all he breathed in Margarethe's smell, which couldn't be compared to anything. He felt so close to her body, it was as if it were his own. In the same moment, he realized that he was happier than ever before.

He could have stayed like this forever.

But he knew he couldn't wait any longer. When he'd put out the torch before, he had also lit the fuse that was burning its way slowly and quietly toward the laterna. By now Johann knew exactly how long it took to get there.

"We should pray," said Johann quietly. "Perhaps the angel will return. I wish he knew the answers to all our questions."

Margarethe nodded and folded her hands in prayer.

"Oh, Saint Michael," she muttered, "I beg you, hear us sinners on earth. Deliver us from evil and show us the path to paradise."

"Deliver us from evil," repeated Johann.

As he'd expected, the fuse reached the oil lamp at that very moment. A bright speck of light appeared on the opposite wall, and inside it was the figure of Archangel Michael with his sword raised. Margarethe gave a small cry. Even though Johann knew the angel was just an image, he shivered. It was as if God was speaking to him through the apparatus.

"He has come down one more time indeed," whispered Margarethe. "Oh gracious Lord!"

"Rejoice and be merry," sounded the strange, unearthly voice of the angel. "For I bring happy tidings!"

As on the other occasions before, Johann turned his head to the side so that his voice was thrown back from the wall. He had seen jugglers use a similar technique for puppets, and for the last several weeks he'd been practicing the trick in the large halls of the library and at the Church of the Holy Spirit. The key was to avoid any sounds that required movement of the lips, or to form them using the tongue and the palate instead of the jaw. It was an ancient technique that had been used by the old Greeks.

"Don't be afraid," whispered the angel. "Loving hearts have nothing to fear. What the dear Lord put together, the world can't tear asunder."

The image changed, and Michael's sword arm pointed downward now. It was just a small movement, but the effect made the figure on the wall seem so much more real.

"Follow the call of love," the angel continued, the voice echoing through the vaulted space. "Follow the call to Vienna . . . Vienna . . . Vienna . . ." The last word echoed several times. Margarethe looked up from her prayers.

"To Vienna? But—"

"I think I know what he means," said Johann in his normal voice. "There is a university in Vienna, too. We could move there, far away from the nunnery, far away from anything preventing us from being together."

"Oh, Johann! Is that really true? Tell me I'm not dreaming!" She threw herself into his arms, and Johann once again inhaled the scent of her hair. Her bonnet slipped backward, and he covered her face with kisses. He thought he could see her cornflower-blue eyes beam in the dark.

He was so happy! There was nothing stopping them now. They would move to Vienna as part of Conrad Celtis's household, he would study, and at some point they'd marry and—

There was a jangling sound followed by the stomping of many boots.

Johann spun around with fright and saw the glow of several torches approaching from the cave entrance. Margarethe screamed. She clung to him, but Johann was paralyzed by shock. He knew right away that this was the end.

A troop of men had entered the cave.

At its front strode Hans Altmayer and Jakob Kohlschreiber, Margarethe's husband.

"Damned witch!" shouted Kohlschreiber, his bloated face glowing red in the light of the torch. "What do you think you're doing? Wallowing in the dirt like a sow with her paramour. But we saw right through you!"

"It's just like I told you," said Hans next to him. He tried to sound calm, but his voice trembled with malicious glee. "I've been watching them for a long time. They always meet in this cave. The devil knows what they're doing in here."

"Look!" cried one of the men behind them. Like the others, he was carrying a short pike and was clad in the garb of a city guard. Evidently Kohlschreiber had gathered support from the Heidelberg city watch before making his way to the cave. With a shaking hand, the guard pointed at the wall behind the altar, where the quivering image of Archangel Michael was still displayed. "By all the saints . . . an angel!"

The others also cried out in surprise. Only Hans remained calm.

"Don't worry, it's not an angel. I'm certain the apparition is somehow connected to the devilish apparatus Faustus always lugs here. He built some sort of thing with Valentin Brander. The image is a deception!"

Hans searched the cave with his torch until he discovered the hidden box beneath the blanket. "Ha! There it is, the devilish machine!"

Hans gave the laterna magica a kick, and with an ugly sound of cracking and shattering, the image of the angel disappeared forever.

Margarethe screamed again. This time the scream was high pitched and mournful, as if it came from a fallen angel.

"What were you up to with that thing, huh?" snarled Jakob Kohlschreiber, stepping toward Johann and Margarethe. "Were you trying to invoke the devil? Is it Lucifer you're praying to in this cave?"

"It . . . it's just an apparatus," replied Johann quietly. Each word came out slowly and with great difficulty, as if he'd forgotten how to speak. "Nothing but an apparatus."

"The Inquisition must learn of this," said Kohlschreiber. Trembling with fury, he pointed at Margarethe, who was covering her face with her hands. Johann wrapped his arms around her and noticed that she was as cold as the cave's rock wall. He didn't know whether she understood what he'd just said.

Nothing but an apparatus . . .

"I never trusted that woman. Cursed be the day her father gave her to me as a wife!" cried Kohlschreiber, nodding grimly. "She's possessed by the devil—he spoke from her mouth every night she lay with me. By God, I tried everything. I found her a place at a nunnery, but clearly, evil can't be driven from her. Only the fire can purge her now."

"And concerning you . . ." Jakob Kohlschreiber glared at Johann, who was still holding Margarethe tightly, as if he could protect her from all evil. "I know you! You sounded me out that time at the tavern. Tried to find out about my wife, you lecherous bastard!"

Hans grinned. "Our rector will be extremely interested to learn what kind of devilish apparatuses his favorite student has been working on—and what kind of a girl he's been dallying with. A nun!" He shook his head in mock sadness. "I believe this is the end of your time at the university, Faustus—at the very least. What did you tell me once? Many an itinerant scholar ends up in the gutter, where he dies like a mangy dog."

"Enough talk," growled Kohlschreiber. "Take them!"

The last words had been addressed to the guards, who stepped toward Johann and Margarethe with lowered pikes. Two of them grabbed Margarethe, who didn't seem to notice what was going on around her. She had started to hum a soft tune. Johann winced when he recognized the melody.

Growing in our garden are parsley and thyme; our Gretchen is the bride, she's looking so fine . . .

It was the song he and Margarethe used to sing as children.

"Take your hands off her!" he screamed. He rushed at the guards and started wrestling with them.

"Don't make it any worse!" shouted Jakob Kohlschreiber. He stepped in and grabbed Johann by the collar like a rabbit. "Or do you want to burn together with the witch? Is that what you want? Burn for this piece of trash?"

He kicked Margarethe, who whimpered and cowered on the ground. Rage swept over Johann like a dark wave. He felt angrier than ever before in his life—angrier even than the time he killed the French mercenary. Reason was blocked out, and an all-consuming hatred burned inside him. Suddenly he was holding his knife in his hand, although he had no idea how it got there. He raised his arm and stabbed wildly into the man in front of him. It felt good, and for a brief moment relief spread through his body, the sweet flavor of revenge trickling down his throat. Johann remembered Tonio's words back when he'd gifted the knife to him.

I'm giving this to you . . . It cuts skin and sinews like butter.

Gasping for breath, Kohlschreiber collapsed in front of him, blood spurting from several wounds in his stomach.

"You . . . you bloody fool," wheezed the vintner, writhing on the floor.

The guards froze with shock when they saw the seriously wounded man. They sensed that the young man with the knife wasn't entirely in control of himself, that something dark had grasped hold of him. For a few moments, the only sound was Kohlschreiber's groaning. Even Hans had taken a step back, but his eyes were flashing deviously.

"Congratulations, Faustus," he spat. "You just dug your own grave."

Johann stared at the bloodied knife in his hand with horror. He suddenly realized what he'd done. His eyes turned to Margarethe, who was holding her arms crossed in front of her chest, rocking back and forth and still humming the children's tune.

Red wine, white wine, tomorrow morn you shall be mine . . .

"Margarethe, I . . . I'm so sorry," he burst out. "I . . . I only wanted us to be happy."

Still none of the other men stirred. They stared with fright at the knife in Johann's hand. Kohlschreiber no longer made any sound, and a pool of blood grew around his plump body. Finally the guards raised their pikes again.

"Take him!" shouted Hans.

And Johann ran.

"Your grave!" rang out Hans's triumphant voice, echoing through the cave. "Your grave!"

Johann ran outside, where night had fallen in the meantime. Saint John's fires were burning on the hills all around, gleaming like eyes behind a dark mask.

"Your grave!" was the last thing Johann heard.

Then the forest swallowed him up.

Johann raced uphill for a long time, panicked like an animal in flight and unable to form a clear thought. It was just like the time he fled from Tonio del Moravia and his companions in the woods near Nördlingen. From one moment to the next he'd lost everything. But this time the shock went much deeper.

He had lost what he loved most.

Margarethe.

He noticed that he'd been running uphill only when the trees ended and he saw the sparkling lights of the Heidelberg watchtowers beneath him, with the castle above the city. He sensed he was looking back on a life he was leaving behind for good.

His life's joy had stayed behind in the cave.

Johann tore at his hair, screamed and raved, cried and whined. Eventually he cowered in a hollow of damp, foul-smelling leaves and repeated the same words over and over.

"I . . . didn't . . . want . . . this . . ."

And at the same time he knew that he alone was to blame. He had played with high stakes and lost everything. It had been his idea to win Margarethe over with the image of the archangel. He should have expected to be followed—he'd always suspected something. Every time he'd returned from the monastery or arrived at the cave, he thought he felt eyes on his back. Sobs racked his body once more.

Margarethe.

He should have stayed with her, defended her with his life. Instead he had run away and left her to the guards. Margarethe's husband had already announced that he'd hand her over to the Inquisition. She wasn't just a nun fooling around with a young student—no, she was suspected of being in league with the devil. And all that just because of the damned laterna magica! He should never have used the apparatus for his own desires. But now it was too late.

So what could he do?

Hans was right—his academic career in Heidelberg was over. And he wouldn't be going to Vienna with Conrad Celtis. Altmayer would make sure the story of Faustus, defiler of nuns and devil worshipper, would make the rounds at the taverns and university. And worse: he had stabbed Jakob Kohlschreiber—probably to death. Not that Johann regretted the man's death, but now he was a murderer and had to flee.

But then he would abandon Margarethe.

Johann swallowed hard. He'd reached a decision.

He would have to go to Heidelberg and hand himself in.

He would explain to the authorities that it was all his fault. He had led Margarethe astray and he had built the laterna magica. No devilish machine, just a simple apparatus. They'd understand, and Margarethe would be saved. At least they wouldn't condemn her as a witch. But he'd need help, and most of all he'd need a witness to confirm his story.

Johann decided to wait until the morning and then find the one person he had left.

Valentin.

He spent the night on the hilltop, gazing down at the Neckar, which wound its way through the valley like a giant black snake. The lights of Heidelberg gleamed beyond, and above them flickered the flames of the Saint John's fires. Johann occasionally thought he could hear screams, presumably from the youth dancing around the fires.

Long before dawn, he went on his way. He entered the city with the first peddlers and farmers carrying their wares to market in their packs. Johann looked like a beggar in his filthy, torn clothes, and the guards didn't recognize him. No one tried to stop him as he slipped through the gate.

He rushed to his residence as fast as he could, climbed across the low wall at the back, and knocked on the window of the room he shared with Valentin—softly at first, but then louder and louder. No one opened. Had his friend already left for the lectures? But it was much too early.

A sense of foreboding overcame Johann.

A damp mist hung in the lanes, and hardly anyone was about. Johann cautiously sneaked over to the western city fortifications. He was headed for one building in particular. The Diebsturm Tower, which served as Heidelberg's prison.

The tower was a bulky construct about ten paces high and built from massive blocks of stone. A few barred windows way up high and a narrow wrought-iron door were the only openings. In front of the tower stood a cart, enveloped in fog. On top of the cart stood a crate about as high as a man, like a mobile prison cell. Two skinny nags were hitched to the wagon.

As Johann approached the tower, the door opened with a squeak, and two guards with halberds emerged. They were followed by two other guards, who were carrying a man in torn clothes. The man's head flopped to one side like that of a ragdoll, and blood was pouring from a wound on his temple.

Johann clasped one hand to his mouth to stop himself from crying out.

The prisoner was Valentin.

Evidently, Hans had made good on his threat and reported Valentin to the authorities. Johann guessed his friend was being accused of helping to build an apparatus that was used to invoke the devil. But why hadn't the university intervened? Why hadn't Rector Gallus been called upon? He would know that the laterna was a scientific invention, not witchcraft. Johann had told the rector all about their plans, and the university had its own jurisdiction.

But then Johann realized that in this case, the city would be responsible. With the accusation of witchcraft, the authorities wasted no time. Johann guessed Valentin was about to be taken to Worms, where the bishop had his seat and where all interrogations of this type took place. Was Margarethe also on her way to Worms?

Had he come too late?

Now the guards opened the door with the barred window at the back of the large crate and shoved the prisoner inside. Johann couldn't tell whether Valentin was conscious or not—or whether he was still alive at all. Still, Johann needed to try to speak with him. Even if he risked being arrested. He waited until the cart began to move, and then he followed it quietly, using the twilight of dawn and the fog to dart from one corner to the next.

His opportunity arrived at the city gate.

The guards driving the wagon stopped to talk to the watchman. Soon the men were hooting with laughter, and it seemed as though a jug of wine was handed around. The street was still relatively empty at this hour, and the fog was thick.

Johann sneaked up to the wagon and tried to catch a glimpse through the barred window. But it was pitch black on the other side, and it smelled of rotten straw and excrement. Then Johann heard a soft groaning.

"Valentin!" he whispered. "Can you hear me? It's me, Johann!"

The groaning stopped abruptly. There was a rustling noise, and a few moments later Valentin's face appeared at the barred window. Johann saw that not only was his friend bleeding from his head, but one of his lips was split open and he was missing a few teeth. And his right eye was swollen shut. His other eye glowered angrily at Johann. There was no trace of warmth or friendship.

"What do you want?" he mumbled.

"Valentin, I . . . ," Johann began desperately. "I . . . I'm so sorry! Please forgive me, I—"

"What is it that you'd like me to forgive? The fact that you lied to me—your only friend—the entire time? That you used the apparatus we built together for your low needs? That you used me just like you use all people? That I'm going to be tried as a sorcerer because of you?" Valentin's good eye gleamed as cold and hard as a diamond. "To you, Faustus, people are nothing but scientific instruments. You use them and then you discard them. How could I be so stupid and not notice sooner? I should have listened to the others, but instead I followed you around like a dumb calf. And now the calf is being led to slaughter."

Johann tried to shake the iron bars; his face was close to Valentin's.

"Valentin . . . you . . . Don't talk like that! I didn't want any of this to happen, believe me! I'm your friend, I—"

Valentin's blood-stained saliva struck his cheek.

"Did you not hear what I said? They're taking me to the Inquisition at Worms! Not even Rector Gallus was able to do anything about it." Valentin laughed hysterically. "They are going to inflict pain on me until I confess to invoking Satan with you. And then they'll burn me alive—while you walk free!"

Johann said nothing. Then he asked the one question he needed to ask, even though he didn't think Valentin would answer it.

"What about Margarethe?"

"Your little nun?" Valentin smiled for the first time, but it was a nasty, twisted smile. "Oh, she was lucky."

Johann's heart beat wildly and he felt wide awake. "Are you saying she . . . she won't be taken to Worms?"

"No, she won't. The worst is behind her. Only God is her judge now."

Johann froze. He struggled to speak because each word was as heavy as a lead weight.

"God . . . is . . . her . . . judge? What . . . what do you mean?"

"Is it so hard to understand? She hanged herself, Faustus! Last night in her cell. I heard the guards cut her down and her dead body drop into the straw. I watched through my window as they carried her away. I guess they nailed her into a barrel and threw her in the river, like they do with all suicides."

The world stopped turning. The universe stood still. The gray morning mist covered Johann's face, but he shed no tears. He was incapable of moving, incapable of speaking.

Reality seemed like the fog wafting past him.

"She is dead, Faustus," Valentin continued. "Did you hear me? And it's your fault. Your greed, your arrogance, your lies killed her." He tilted his head to one side and studied his former friend as if for the last time. "By the way, she confessed to being a witch. I heard it myself. She said the boogeyman would come and get her now. The boogeyman . . ." Valentin's voice was just a whisper now. "Are you the boogeyman, Faustus?"

Suddenly the cart jerked forward. The gate was wide open and the cart rattled onto the bridge. Valentin's face was becoming smaller and smaller.

"Are you the boogeyman, Faustus?" shouted Valentin. "Tell me, are you?"

"Shut up!" yelled Johann. "Shut the hell up!"

Finally he managed to move again. Beside himself with anger and grief, he ran after the wagon onto the bridge. He wanted to smash Valentin's face, grind it like grain under a millstone, and punch it until the man's lips stopped moving. He noticed that he still carried Tonio's knife. He'd put it back in his pocket after he'd stabbed Jakob Kohlschreiber. Now he pulled it back out. He wanted to destroy Valentin, and himself, and the whole world.

"Are you the boogeyman, Faustus?" shouted Valentin once more.

"Shut your goddamned mouth!" Johann had reached the middle of the bridge, the river rushing down below. He was so blinded by rage that he didn't notice the two guards following him. The cart stopped, and two guards with raised halberds approached him from the front as well.

"That's him!" shouted one of them. Johann realized the man was one of the guards from the cave the night before. "The student of the devil who cast a spell on the nun and killed Kohlschreiber. I recognize him!"

The guards were closing in from two sides. Johann stood in the middle of the bridge, knife in hand, and heard Valentin laughing. It was a sad, desperate laugh—the laugh of the only true friend he'd ever had. Now Johann had lost everything. His friend and Margarethe. Everything worth living for.

Are you the boogeyman?

Johann climbed onto the bridge railing. He put the knife back in his pocket, lifted his hands toward the gray sky, and closed his eyes. The moment the guards reached out for him, he jumped.

Margarethe, I'm coming!

The waters of the Neckar swallowed him, but the Lord had no mercy. He made Johann rise to the surface and reach for a tree trunk, coughing and spluttering. Slowly Johann drifted toward the dark forests west of the Odenwald Mountains. The last sound he heard of Heidelberg was Valentin's hysterical laughter.

Though he couldn't be sure that it wasn't Tonio del Moravia's laughter. Or Signore Barbarese's. Or Gilles de Rais's, greeting him from the grave. They were all laughing at him.

Homo Deus est.

The pact was sealed.

Act V

The Awakening of the Beast

19

ON THE MARKET SQUARE, A MAN SCREAMED AS THE PYRE around him caught on fire.

He was tied to a stake with thick ropes, and the guards had stacked the logs knee high around him. The burning wood crackled and smoked while the condemned man begged for mercy—or, at the least, a quick death.

Most of the crowd watched the macabre show in silence, but there were a few who laughed, jeered, or sang dirty rhymes. Over a hundred people had gathered on the Warnheim market square, which was covered in muck and surrounded by crooked half-timbered houses and a decrepit little church. The majority of the spectators were peasants in plain tunics and drawstring shoes. The men came armed with pikes, pitchforks, and cudgels, but there were also women and children among the crowd. Awestruck, they all watched as the man on the pyre screamed. His clothes, skin, and hair were beginning to smolder, and the sweetish smell of fried meat spread across the square.

It reminded Johann of the meal he'd eaten at a tavern the night before—pork with beans and smoked ham.

Wearing his wide-brimmed hat low on his brow and a dirty coat around his shoulders, he was standing in one of the front rows, studying the flames. Blue, yellow, and red, they licked across the wood that had been doused with oil beforehand. The flames reached only to the man's thighs so far, but Johann thought he could see the first blisters forming on the man's face. He leaned forward with interest, his right hand resting on the top of the box-shaped hand-drawn cart he had lugged to the front of the crowd with much difficulty. The blisters were a fascinating phenomenon. He guessed that the heat rose up in waves against the body and increased in strength. Back at Heidelberg University, long ago, he'd read something similar in the writs of Archimedes. Or was it Pythagoras?

Meanwhile, the condemned man's hair had completely caught on fire and his screams turned to inhuman screeching. Until a few moments ago he'd been a handsome lad with soft, almost feminine eyes and long lashes. Now there wasn't much left of that. The burning figure increasingly disappeared behind the acrid black smoke that had now spread across the entire square.

The smoke . . .

With well-practiced movements, Johann removed the lid attached to the front of the box. Unfortunately it had taken too long for the smoke to become thick enough—pity, because otherwise he might have been able to save the life of the young man. But at least the dense smoke his charred body was producing served the second condemned man.

Johann's eyes turned to the second pyre, where another young man stood tied to a stake. His eyes wide with horror, the youth had watched as the first pyre was lit and the fire consumed the man in a gruesome death.

"Holy mother of God!" he pleaded loudly. "Help me!"

An elderly Hegau peasant laughed and spat into the flames, where his saliva vaporized instantly. "Do you really think the Holy Virgin is going to help a sodomite?" he jeered. "No one can help you now, you pederast—not even God himself!"

Perhaps not God, thought Johann, *but someone else can. The Antichrist . . .*

The screams of the first victim had fallen silent by now, and through the dense smoke the onlookers could make out the remains of a blackened body twisted like a doll, the mouth open as if in a final scream. One of the farmers carried a torch to the second pyre.

"Go to hell, sodomite!" he roared, holding the torch to the oil-drenched logs. "And don't forget to kiss the devil's ass!"

At that moment, the devil himself appeared.

He had horns on his head, a goat's foot, and a bushy tail, and his grin was as wide as a skull's. The larger-than-life Satan danced in the smoke of the first fire as if he'd come directly from hell onto the Warnheim market square. Deafening cracks and thunderclaps seemed to prove that the gates of hell stood wide open, and the hellish stink of sulfur spread over the onlookers.

The spectators in the front rows were the first to see the flickering devil in the smoke. They screamed and moved backward, pushing back the people behind them. There were more powerful thunderclaps, and sparks rained down on the market square.

"The devil!" shouted Johann as he hurled another pouch of gunpowder into the flames. "The devil has come upon us! Run, honest folk of Warnheim, run!"

His cries and the gunpowder had the desired effect. Wailing fearfully, the crowd moved back; only a handful of daring young men stayed put, the pikes and forks trembling in their hands.

"Now, Satan," whispered Johann.

He whistled on two fingers, and from the bottom of the cart sprang a large black mastiff. Through the haze of the smoke it looked like the hellhound Cerberus. Growling with its teeth bared, the calf-sized dog stalked toward the peasants, who turned and fled as fast as they could. Chaos broke out across the entire square; people cried, wailed, and ran; some were trampled and couldn't get back up; others threw themselves onto the ground and prayed to God and all the saints. Everyone tried to seek shelter in the lanes around the square or in one of the houses.

Only Johann stayed where he was, calmly inspecting the devil grinning down at him. He hadn't made a bad job of him, even if some strokes of the brush were a tad thick. The devil's horns looked more like those of a cow than a goat, and the cloven foot was a little smudged.

A satanic cow, he thought. *That's all you can do. What a pathetic farce for a professor and doctor, forsooth!*

He whistled Satan back before hurrying over to the second pyre, where the young man tied to the stake still trembled with horror. He was maybe eighteen or twenty years old. His smooth face was blackened by soot, and his trousers and shirt had begun to smolder in places, but other than that he seemed unharmed. Thankfully, only one side of the pile of logs had caught on fire so far.

But it wouldn't be long before the whole pyre would go up in flames.

Johann drew his knife and started to cut the ropes binding the youth to the stake. They were made from several individual strands of hemp rope and soaked in water so they wouldn't catch fire right away.

Shaking and wide eyed, the young man stared at his liberator, who was frantically sawing on the ropes.

"Are . . . are you the devil?" breathed the youth.

"No. But if we don't hurry, you'll meet him soon."

A few moments later, Johann had severed the ropes. He kicked some of the burning logs aside, then he grabbed the young man by the arm and pulled him out of the burning pile. "Quickly now, before the lamp oil in the laterna is used up!"

"The . . . lamp oil? But—"

The fellow didn't resist as Johann dragged him along. Smoke still hovered above the square, but it was growing weaker. The devil gradually dissolved into thin air.

Johann leaned over the box and pulled a few levers, and the devil disappeared as suddenly as it had arrived. A few more quick movements and the glass plate, tube, and laterna were safely stored inside the crate.

The young man gaped with amazement. "That . . . that's sorcery."

"No time for lengthy explanations. Here—put that on and help me pull the cart. Your questions will be answered later."

Johann handed a dark, stained hooded coat to the young man, who quickly put it on. Now the two of them looked like simple peddlers trying to shield their faces from the smoke with their coats. They pushed and pulled the heavy cart across the market square, which was littered with weapons, scraps of clothing, and other hastily dropped bundles. The place was still deserted for now, but already the first curious onlookers peered around the corners and out the doors again.

"The devil has gone!" called out one of them, looking at the burning pyre. "And he's taken the sodomite to hell with him!"

"That's good," he muttered through a thin smile. "Then they won't come looking for us in this world."

Together they dragged the cart through the narrow, dirty lanes away from the square; the large black dog followed them, growling at anyone coming toward them. No one gave them a second look.

Soon the two escapees reached the town gate, which stood wide open. Johann guessed that the watchmen had also rushed to the market square—unless the peasants and the rest of this accursed township had skewered them first. They pressed on without looking back. In a small wooded area not far from Warnheim, they came to a wagon like the ones used by jugglers. Strange-looking symbols, including pentagrams, were painted onto the canvas with red paint. A skinny horse tied to a tree grazed peacefully nearby. When it caught sight of the two men, it whinnied happily and pawed the ground.

The young man hadn't spoken until then, but now he could no longer remain silent.

"What . . . what's the meaning of this?" he began. "Why did you save me from those peasants? Who are you?"

"You'll learn everything in due course," said Johann. "Now help me hitch up the horse and load the laterna magica."

The youth frowned. "The laterna . . . ?"

"For Christ's sake, shut your mouth already, or else I'll feed you to Satan for breakfast!"

The black mastiff growled and bared its teeth, and the young man rushed to help Johann lift the crate off the cart and store it inside the wagon. He caught a glimpse of more crates and chests, and bunches of dried herbs hanging from the ceiling. The inside of the wagon smelled intensely of brandy and resin.

"Hop on the front with me," commanded Johann after he'd finished hitching the horse. "I'll try to answer your questions along the way."

They climbed on the box seat. "Move, old girl!" Johann cracked the reins, and the gray horse started to pull. Screeching and rattling, the wagon left the woods and the small town of Warnheim, where the people still searched for the gateway to hell.

Black columns of smoke rose up behind the walls.

"Now you can speak if you must," said Johann after a while. "But don't even think about thanking God for your life. He had nothing to do with your escape. If anyone did, then the devil."

He could see from the corner of his eye that the young man had been trying to study him furtively for a while. In his eyes lurked both fear and boundless relief. Johann smiled and hoped the boy wouldn't see it underneath the low brim of his hat.

He knew that he appeared creepy to most people. Although he was just in his early thirties, he seemed much older. His face was narrow, almost haggard, and his eyes gleamed black and mysterious. His raven-black hair reached down to his shoulders, and his hat was just as black. His pointed beard was carefully groomed and reinforced with beeswax. The cloak he wore under his old coat was made from black silk and speckled with blue spots, a pattern like stars in the night sky. With a certain amount of satisfaction Johann thought of an image he'd seen of himself not long ago. The beard and the cloak had been very faithfully reproduced. A juggler in Freiburg had sung a few mocking lines about him while holding up a series of painted canvases. Johann had considered hiring the fairground performer as a glass painter, but the man was quite old and didn't seem to be the brightest. He certainly wouldn't know how to play chess.

Johann took off the dirty overcoat and flicked the reins. "Get a move on, you old nag," he grumbled. "Or I'll turn you into a mouse and feed you to Satan. You wouldn't be the first lazy horse to land in the dog's belly."

The young man beside him finally recognized him. His eyebrows shot up and he gasped with surprise.

"You . . . you're the famous Doctor Faustus!" he called out. "The hat, the beard, the cloak—so you are real!"

"And why shouldn't I be?" replied Johann with a shrug as he continued to urge the horse forward. He could never tell how long his tricks would remain undetected. For all they knew, a mob of angry Hegau peasants might be on their way already. The Hegau region wasn't considered particularly safe for travelers—especially not those who led good, honest burghers on a merry chase using sulfur, gunpowder, and magic tricks.

"Well, there are so many rumors about you that it's hard to tell what's true and what's made up." The youth gave a chuckle. "Like the bet in Leipzig, for example."

"What is that about?"

"You straddled a barrel of wine and flew it up the cellar stairs right into the taproom. The innkeeper was forced to give you the barrel, and you emptied it, with the students' help."

"I straddled a barrel?" Johann grinned. "But why didn't I fly out the door rather than share the barrel with a bunch of red-nosed pups? What else have you heard about me?"

"In Cologne, you made a grapevine grow out of a table. And in Erfurt you turned two red roosters and one blade of straw into two oxen and a bale of hay. They say you're an infamous sorcerer and necromancer, and astrologer and alchemist. I don't even know in how many taverns I've heard tales of your adventures." The young man eyed him fearfully. "Some even say you're in league with the devil."

"So? Am I?" Johann gave his new travel companion a piercing look. When the young man gave a little start, Johann laughed. "A man is always that which people want to see in him. Out of everything they say about me, half at the most is true. But I'm not telling you which half." He winked.

It was truly astounding what sort of a reputation he had gained over the last ten years of his travels.

"Your name is Wagner, am I right?"

"Um, yes." The young man nodded, clearly surprised that Johann knew his name. "Wagner. Karl Wagner. I'm a student from Leipzig but have been traveling lately. I don't know how I can ever thank you enough for saving my life! Even if I still don't fully understand how you managed to do it." He cleared his throat and lowered his voice. "Did you use magic? Sorcery?"

Johann waved one hand. "No magic, just science. I'll show you tonight." He bared his teeth, and for a brief moment, his face took on a mocking, almost devilish expression. "And unlike you, I know how you can thank me. Nothing in this life is free, my boy."

Toward evening they came to a dense beech forest, the foliage glowing red and yellow in the fading autumn sun. To the south, the mighty rock face of Hohentwiel Mountain with its castle jutted into the sky; Lake Constance wasn't far from here and pushed fog across the woods. The two men climbed off the wagon and led the horse away from the road until they reached a small meadow lined by moss-covered rocks as tall as a man.

"We should be safe here for now," said Johann, giving the horse some barley from a bag. "Those superstitious peasants avoid this place. They believe it's haunted."

"You've been here before?" asked Karl.

"Let's say I've moved around a fair bit in the last few years. And now quit talking—go find dry wood for a fire. I'm hungry."

While Karl went looking for dry twigs and branches, Johann looked about carefully. He was glad Satan was keeping watch at the edge of the clearing. At the slightest sound, the mastiff would bark and defend its master with teeth and claws. The war in the Hegau region had finished only a few years before. The Swiss confederacy rose against the emperor and Swabia, and since then the word of the emperor didn't carry much weight in this area. The class of knights—for centuries the pillar of the empire—became increasingly impoverished, and to make a living, many knights roamed the lands, thieving and murdering. Here in the Hegau region, too. Not even the everlasting public peace Emperor Maximilian had promised had been able to change this state of affairs. The farmers also suffered, and many had chosen a life in the forests, where they banded together as groups of outlaws. Cities, on the other hand, flourished, and merchants and patricians grew wealthier by the year. The face of the world was changing.

"I think that should be enough wood."

Karl's voice tore Johann from his musings. The student was standing in front of him, his arms laden with dry wood.

"Is everything all right?" asked Karl, frowning.

"Yes, yes." Johann shook himself. "Put the wood down here."

Karl lit a small, flickering fire, and together they prepared a meal of dried meat, carrots, and wild herbs. Satan was given a bone, which it carried under the wagon. Only its glowing red eyes could be seen in the dark.

"Why did you call him Satan?" asked Karl abruptly.

"The dog?" Johann threw the mastiff a rabbit bone, which the large animal ground up noisily. "Like I said—a man is always what people want to see in him. I'm traveling by myself, without hired mercenaries or other protection. When I call Satan, people think I'm truly in league with the devil and leave me alone." He gave a shrug. "Although I must admit—the trick probably wouldn't work if Satan was a cute little poodle."

While they ate, Johann studied Karl Wagner. He was handsome; the girls most likely adored him. And the lad didn't seem stupid—a tad naive, perhaps, but he was still young.

"Can you play chess?" asked Johann brusquely.

Karl looked up from his bowl. "Chess?"

"I play according to the new rules as prescribed by Luis Ramírez Lucena in his book. It contains many interesting openings and moves, the 'smothered mate' among others. Have you heard of it?"

"Um, I'm afraid not. I've played chess a few times, but I fear I'm not very good."

"I will teach you," said Johann, trying not to let his disappointment show. He still hoped he'd chosen the right one.

"You want to know why I saved you?" he asked after a while.

Karl nodded.

"I want to show you something. Wait here." He walked to the back of the wagon and took out the laterna magica. He had installed a few improvements since the first apparatus he'd built with Valentin back in Heidelberg. The casing was now made from copper and had a tube at the front where lenses could be inserted. Another tube at the top allowed the smoke to vent. Also, a larger hollow mirror reflected the light much better.

Johann pointed the front tube toward the canvas of the wagon, opened a flap on the side of the casing, and lit the lamp inside with a burning pine chip. Instantly, a bright, perfectly round circle of light appeared on the side of the wagon.

"Now pay attention," said Johann.

He decided on the image with the white woman. Most of the time it achieved the desired effect. He opened a small container with glass plates, took one out, and inserted it into the slot on the side of the laterna.

Instead of the circle, a white, ghostly woman hovered on the wagon's canvas.

"Dear God," whispered Karl, dropping his plate of food. "What . . . what is that?"

"I don't think I did particularly well with her," said Johann with a shrug. "The white dress looks more like a sheet, and her eyes don't look real. The devil in Warnheim today was a rather sad figure, too. More cattle-beast than lord of the underworld."

"Are . . . are you saying you insert glass plates into this apparatus and then those . . . those images appear?" asked Karl breathlessly. "You deceived those Warnheim peasants?"

Johann waved dismissively. "I'll explain how exactly it works another time. The important thing right now is that you understand that it isn't black magic, just science. The laterna magica is my most important tool. I sell theriac, read palms, cast horoscopes—just like many other traveling artists. But my reputation is all down to my laterna—my wit and knowledge aside." He sighed. "But I'm not happy with the paintings. Let's say my talents lie elsewhere." Johann put out the light and the white woman disappeared. "And that's where you come in. I saw you in Leipzig—or rather, I saw your paintings."

Wagner looked at him with growing amazement. "You . . . you went to the university in Leipzig?"

"I've visited many universities in the last ten years, sometimes as a guest lecturer—if the rector believed my documents—but more frequently as a keen student. There is so much left to learn." Johann wiped his mouth with his hands. "I saw your anatomical sketches in Leipzig, the ones you prepared for the medical lectures of Doctor Joventis. I liked them very much. They . . ." He hesitated. "They reminded me of someone from years ago who also drew well. A good friend. The best and only one I ever had."

"Thank you." Karl stared into the darkness, the logs in the fire crackling quietly. "My father is a well-known surgeon in Leipzig," said the young man after a while. "He wanted me to go to college and study medicine like him. But I really want to become a painter, like Albrecht Dürer or Leonardo da Vinci. Have you heard of them?"

"It's a sin to compare oneself with Leonardo da Vinci," replied Johann gruffly. "A man like him only comes along once every thousand years. And unlike you lazy paint-slinger, he was a genius in all areas. He would easily have gained a doctor's title in medicine or law. You, however, quit your studies."

Wagner's eyes widened once more. "You know? But—"

"I was going to speak with you in Leipzig. But then you up and left. Very annoying."

"I had . . . um . . . trouble at the university that compelled me to leave."

"I think I know what sort of trouble. The same kind of trouble that got you tied to a pyre at Warnheim. It's the kind of trouble with two legs and a proud package in between."

Wagner turned red and looked down. "I . . . don't know what you're talking about."

"You're a sodomite, Karl Wagner. Personally, I couldn't care less, but the law prescribes death by fire. In Leipzig, you got away by the skin of your teeth. But in Warnheim, you found yourself another young lover—"

"It was purely platonic!"

"A term that that uneducated peasant pack doesn't understand." Johann dug a piece of meat from between his teeth. "What a stupid thing to do, letting oneself get caught in the hay with another man in the rebellious Hegau region, of all places. You can count yourself lucky that I followed you. I couldn't save your friend, though."

Wagner hung his head and tears rolled down his cheek. "We'd only known each other for a few hours. Our eyes met at a tavern, and I was overcome by fiery passion. I didn't even know his name. I . . . I know it's against nature, and I tried to fight it for so long. But the devil keeps returning to my body."

"Leave the devil out of it. He's got better things to do than possessing little sodomites. You can forget about your studies, anyhow—for good. Don't think I don't know what that means."

For the first time Johann's eyes were almost sympathetic, but the look vanished as quickly as it had arrived.

"At least I know what you can do instead. Join me on the road and paint glass plates for me. The demand is surprisingly large. Every town has its own patron saint, and in the country there are plenty of natural spirits, gnomes, and other mischievous creatures that can easily be invoked. A few animals wouldn't hurt, either—people like animals, cats in particular. Cats are always good."

Karl Wagner stared at Johann as if he were an apparition of the laterna magica. "You . . . you want me to travel with you and paint pictures on glass?"

"Well, not only that." Johann gave a shrug. "Other things also need to be done. We need to brew theriac, write flyers, announce our shows." He paused to think. "I don't suppose you play an instrument? The bagpipe, for example?"

Wagner shook his head.

"Never mind. I can't stand that instrument anyhow. I pay you one guilder per image, and free food and lodging." Johann held out his hand. "Go on—shake on it."

"I don't know," said Wagner eventually. "When I said I wanted to become a painter, I meant something a little different. I thank you for your offer, but—"

"I'm afraid you don't have a choice." Johann reached into a bag next to him and pulled out a pile of documents. "Do you know what that is?"

Wagner turned pale.

"I found this bundle among the things you had to leave behind at the inn this morning. I must say—touching love letters, even if they're a tad too flowery for me. A memento of your romance in Leipzig, I take it?" When Karl didn't reply, Johann went on. "You can choose whether I send the letters to your father first or to the Leipzig authorities."

"That . . . that's blackmail," said Karl hoarsely.

"Call it what you want." Johann gave him a wink. "In a few weeks' time you'll be glad you have accepted my offer. What could be more exciting than traveling the German lands alongside the most famous magician of the empire?"

He put the bundle of letters away and held out his hand to Wagner again. This time, the student accepted. Johann's grip was so firm that Wagner winced with pain.

"Welcome to the realm of hocus-pocus," said Johann with a grin. "And believe me, you will learn much from me."

It took a long time for Karl Wagner to fall asleep, and even then Johann heard him moan and cry out from time to time. He guessed in the student's dreams he was burning on the pyre next to his paramour. Johann was sorry he hadn't been able to save Karl's lover, but on the other hand, at least he had the young man to himself now. Who knew how Karl would have reacted to his offer otherwise.

Johann struggled to find rest. He was lying on his back, gazing up at the stars, which were the same ones as more than thirty years ago, on the day of his birth. The same stars that once foretold a great future for him.

Born a lucky child, his mother had said. *Born a Faustus.*

Johann gave a silent laugh. The stars, it would seem, played many a nasty trick.

In the thirteen years since his leap into the Neckar he had achieved much, but he hadn't found happiness. He had pulled himself ashore more dead than alive. For two weeks he was held in the firm grip of a fever, and in his dreams Margarethe and Valentin pointed at him with their fingers.

You are the devil, they called out again and again. *You are the devil!*

And they were right. The one true love of his life and his best friend—he was responsible for their deaths. Margarethe had hanged herself because of him, and Valentin had most likely been burned at the stake in Worms. On top of everything else, he had murdered Jakob Kohlschreiber, Margarethe's husband. Johann remembered how much he had enjoyed stabbing the drunken vintner. Who had he been in that moment? Himself? Or a devil in the shape of a man? Either way, he had no trouble understanding why people were afraid of him. He had laden himself with guilt, and it was a guilt that made him wake up screaming at night, a guilt that tortured him like a thousand glowing pairs of pincers, and he still didn't know how he could ever atone for it.

A kindhearted old farmer's wife had nursed him back to health back then. She had prayed for him, not knowing that any prayers for him were wasted. Once he'd recovered from the fever, all that was left of him was an empty shell, the shape of a man but without a goal, without joy, without any reason to carry on.

Then, in a ditch beside the road, he'd found a litter of puppies of which only one was still alive. The dog was as black as his soul, and Johann took it with him. Satan helped him come back to life. Johann doted on the animal so he would never have to dote on another human being again—so that he would never drag anyone down with him again. Man and dog wandered along the Neckar together, toward the Rhine and into the lands beyond. Satan grew, and with it grew Johann's will to live.

Johann.

The name seemed as distant as the stars to him now, even though only thirteen summers had passed since then.

He started with the simple diversions he'd learned from Tonio. Card tricks, juggling balls, coin tricks, the shell game, and even the egg in the blanket returned to his repertoire. Soon he'd saved enough money for a wagon, a horse, and occasionally a night under a warm roof along the imperial road, which carried him through the country like a wide, lazy river. The theriac—cheap liquor infused with herbs and alleged magic powers—caused him to become reasonably well off. He purchased the individual parts he required for the laterna magica and assembled it; he read palms, promised grand futures in his horoscopes, and called himself magister and doctor. Everyone believed him—even the universities. His wit, his gift of public speaking, and his knowledge did the rest.

And so the young Johann Faustus, a Heidelberg student wanted for sorcery and murder, became the infamous Doctor Johann Georg Faustus.

A living legend.

Out of spite and sarcasm he had kept the name he'd used to matriculate at Heidelberg University, the name his mother had lovingly called him. He sometimes went by Faust now—*fist*. No longer a lucky one, but a punch in the face to all the slow-witted, superstitious, and narrow-minded folk out there. Johann smiled. The fact that every little county, bishopric, and duchy worried only about its own affairs had its advantages. No one seemed to make the connection between the murderer from Heidelberg and the famous doctor.

Until now, at least.

Next to him, Karl moaned again, but this time the student was smiling. Johann guessed he was dreaming of happier days with his lover, just like he himself often dreamed of his one true love.

Margarethe.

No day went by that Johann didn't think of her. Of her blue eyes, her flaxen hair, and her laughter, which had saved him in the clearing near Nördlingen all those years ago.

Margarethe.

An owl hooted, and Johann started up from his bed. In the light of the moon he saw wafts of mist floating by the boulders. He suspected that once upon a time this place had been used as a sacrificial site, just like the one near Nördlingen where he had drunk the black potion and escaped from Tonio. He had never heard anything about the magician again. Nor, since leaving Heidelberg, about Gilles de Rais, the insane French marshal who had been dead for almost a hundred years now.

And Johann hoped it would stay that way.

With that thought he finally fell asleep.

The next morning, Johann was up before sunrise. He never slept much; a few hours was enough for him. Sleep was dangerous because it allowed the dreams to return, and so he tried to avoid sleeping at night as much as possible. Karl didn't seem to share this problem, as he snored and stretched under his fur blanket. A thin column of smoke still rose from their fire. Dew dripped from the leaves in the trees; fall had arrived with its damp, chilly breeze.

Johann softly whistled for Satan and fed it the remains of last night's dinner. As the mastiff slurped up the scraps, Johann watched the animal with a smile, like a father watching his child at play. He had grown fonder of Satan than of any person he'd met in the last few years. The dog had been his faithful companion on his never-ending journey through the Holy Roman Empire of the German Nation, as the empire was now called. The animal was no longer so young; the fur behind its ears and on its paws was turning gray, and it didn't run as fast as it used to. For a few weeks now it had also been limping. But Satan still provided Johann the respectability and protection he required as a lone traveler. The empire was far from safe; dangers lurked everywhere, not just in the woods. There were no laws outside the cities, and no one to keep order. Everyone had to look out for themselves.

Satan licked its jowls and gazed at its master from bloodshot eyes, evidently hoping for more. Johann stroked the mastiff behind the ears.

"Good dog," he said in a low voice. "You're a good dog." He looked over at Karl. "Let's see how we get on with our new friend. You don't like Karl very much, do you? I guess you're jealous." Satan gave a growl, and Johann laughed.

When he'd seen Karl's drawings in Leipzig, a shiver had run down his spine. The images had immediately reminded him of Valentin in Heidelberg, and so he'd continued to watch the student. The young man's slightly clumsy yet proud demeanor had awakened memories in Johann. He had seen himself as a student in Heidelberg. And then he'd almost lost Karl in the same way he had lost Margarethe and Valentin; he'd arrived just in the nick of time. On the Warnheim market square he'd sworn to himself: never again shall a student burn as a heretic. He would take Karl with him and care for him.

But if he was completely honest with himself, he wasn't doing it because of charitable, Christian feelings or because he merely needed a glass painter for his laterna. He could have hired a painter in one of the larger cities.

No, he did it because he could no longer bear the loneliness.

Despite his fame, despite all his freedom and the knowledge he had gained in recent years, Johann wasn't happy. He had forgotten how to love, because it would seem his love brought misfortune to people. He loved his dog, but the dog didn't know how to play chess. And so he wanted to give it a go with young Karl—in part also to assuage his guilt and atone for Valentin's death.

Johann hoped very much that Karl wouldn't be the next person he led into ruin.

The sound of flapping wings caused him to start from his thoughts. He looked up and saw a crow staring down at him from the branches of a nearby beech tree.

"Beat it, you damned beast!" Johann picked up a rock and threw it at the crow.

With a mocking caw, it flew away just to land on a different branch, where it continued to stare at him. Since his time with Tonio, Johann had hated crows and ravens. Perhaps that was why he always felt like they were watching him. Those birds seemed to be everywhere—in the mountains, lowlands, villages, towns, and cities. They circled above him in the sky and sat on rooftops, on the edges of wells, and on spires.

Sometimes Johann thought it was always the same three birds. Two crows and an old raven with a scuffed, jagged beak.

"Kraa!" called the crow. *"Kraa, kraa!"* Johann threw another stone and missed, and then he gave up with a sigh.

The noise woke Karl. The student rubbed his eyes and looked about. It seemed to take him a while to remember where he was and what had happened the day before. The scrapes and bruises he had suffered during his arrest would heal, but the trauma—Johann wasn't so sure. Karl had come as close to death as a man could.

Johann gave the young man a nod and threw him a piece of bread. "Here, eat," he said. "We must leave soon."

"Why so early?" asked Karl with a yawn. He was pale, and dark shadows lay beneath his eyes; a scabby scratch went right across his forehead. But even in that state, Johann noted, he was handsome.

I'm going to have to look after him, thought Johann. *Better than I looked after Martin, Margarethe, Valentin, and the others.*

"Because this area isn't safe," he replied. "The Warnheim peasants might still be out looking for us. And I won't be able to save you from the fire a second time."

"And where are you headed?" asked Karl.

"North, east, south, west—I'm at home anywhere." Johann shrugged. "But I think we'll head north. There's too much unrest in the south of the empire.

Swabia, Bavaria, the Swiss confederacy . . . war seems to love these climes." He grinned. "And I've never seen the North Sea. The cold ocean beating against the shore."

"The . . . the North Sea?" Karl was suddenly wide awake. "But that's awfully far! It's going to take us many months."

"We have all the time in the world," said Johann. "Remember? You're coming with me, no matter where! Otherwise the next post rider is taking a bundle of letters to Leipzig. Your old life is over." He walked to the wagon. "And now hurry up, you lazybones. You can eat the bread on the way. And I swear I'll teach you Lucena's chess rules before we're out of this goddamned Hegau."

When the horse pulled the wagon back onto the road, the crow was still sitting in the trees. It tilted its head to one side as if listening intently. More flapping of wings came from the low-hanging clouds, and another crow and an old raven with a scuffed beak descended from above. They greeted the first crow with a hoarse croaking that sounded almost human.

When the wagon had rolled out of sight, they spread their wings and took off together.

20

THUS JOHANN AND HIS YOUNG COMPANION HEADED NORTH from Lake Constance. The air became colder, and the autumn wind tore at the wagon's faded canvas. Most of the time, the two very different men sat side by side in silence, Karl occasionally eyeing his eerie companion furtively. Karl still couldn't believe that of all people, the famous Doctor Johann Georg Faustus had saved his life, and that he was now traveling the empire at the man's side. He was torn between admiration and fear. The doctor's black eyes were deep and mysterious, like pools in the woods; dark secrets appeared to lie at their bottom, hidden from regular mortals like him. They seemed to magically draw Karl in as well as frighten him. Even after many days on the road together, Faust remained a mystery to him—not least because the doctor wasn't particularly communicative.

"Is it true that you once found a treasure near Wittenberge by the Elbe?" asked Karl, trying to strike up conversation. They had not long left the city of Ulm.

"What? Is that what they say?" The doctor turned and met Karl's inquisitive gaze. "And? Was it gold ducats, diamonds, or the philosopher's stone? Although according to another rumor, I already found the latter in Krakow." Clearly, the never-ending questions of his new travel companion had begun to annoy Faust, and yet Karl thought he could see a vain side in the itinerant scholar.

"Well, apparently you were digging in an old cellar when you found a worm who guarded a treasure. You chased the worm away with a mirror, and the treasure—"

"Do you really think I would sit on this rickety old wagon and sell cheap swill if I'd found a treasure?"

"It makes for a good story, at least." Karl sighed. "I'm beginning to get the impression that not even half of what they say about you is true."

"You'll have plenty of time to find out what's true and what isn't. Giddyup!"

The doctor flicked the reins and the wagon rattled on, always toward the next rise, the next mountain range on the horizon. Satan stormed ahead, occasionally howling with pleasure, its jowls dripping. Satan was the hellish messenger announcing the famous Doctor Faustus, magician, chiromancer, miracle worker, and astrologer, in the townships along the imperial road. As alternative means of defense, the wagon also carried a sword and a newfangled wheel-lock pistol, but they hadn't needed the weapons so far. The sight of Satan alone made wayside robbers take to their heels.

They usually stopped in larger cities, where Faust and his assistant stayed for several days at a time. In the course of the following weeks they visited Rothenburg ob der Tauber, Würzburg, Mainz, and Frankfurt am Main, a large city of commerce, where they set up shop at the cloth market in front of the city hall and thrilled the crowds. Leipzig aside, Karl hadn't seen much of the empire.

Every city had its own smells. The pungent stench of lime kilns, the delicious smell of baked gingerbread, the numbing scent of hop mash, and the blood odor of freshly slaughtered pigs—but most of all, the stink of the gutter. Dialects changed and so did the people, who gaped at the two travelers as if they were kings from the Orient, and made the sign of the cross once they'd passed. After his initial reservations, Karl began to like this way of traveling. He enjoyed the wide world of the highway, which was so different from the drab routine at the university. His role as the announcer, assistant, and joker was growing on him, even if he'd never become an outstanding juggler.

Faust's reputation preceded him. Even from afar, people recognized the wagon with the strange-looking symbols and the mysterious man on the box seat with the blue-and-black star cloak and the floppy hat. The doctor usually rented a room in one of the better inns and set up on the market square to sell his foul and potent theriac. Faust read palms, cast quick horoscopes, and placed his hand on people's foreheads after previously rubbing his palm with his stinking miracle cure. It was one of Karl's jobs to appear as a blind young soldier who was healed by the famous Doctor Faustus.

But the biggest attraction by far was always the laterna magica.

They'd use the biggest room with shutters at the tavern. People paid two hellers' admittance and had the experience of a lifetime inside the darkened room. They'd never seen anything like it. The spectators trembled with fear as the ghastliest figures appeared on a white sheet stretched at the front of the room: devils, fiends, witches, and ghosts that Faust invoked with a loud voice and then chased away with the help of Latin spells. The cries of the audience could be heard in the streets, and people staggered outside at the end of the show and told others what they'd seen with a mix of fear and delight.

Karl usually worked on the glass paintings at night, in the flickering glow of an oil lamp. For inspiration he used whatever mythical creatures were known in the region where they had stopped: the wild man, evil Trude, the Tatzelworms, werewolves, and malevolent little elves. Occasionally the doctor would watch him at work and mutter strange words.

"Your drawings are different from his," Faust said with a nod, more to himself. "But no less good. Hmm. Not as creative, but more accurate. I think the people like them, and that's the main thing."

Karl never received an answer to the question of who the doctor was talking about.

In the course of weeks, Karl developed a sense for which sort of pictures they just got away with and which would land them at the stake. The church and the cities permitted the game with evil as long as it served their purposes. But still, it was a perpetual balancing act. More than once they had to make a hasty retreat before the town's guards threw them into jail, because some of the images seemed so real that people thought the apocalypse had begun. Karl's wolves had sharp fangs with saliva dripping from the points, and the eyes of the gnomes shone in an eerie light that couldn't stem from this world. Sometimes Karl tried his hand at flowery landscapes or handsome youths, but Faust threw them into the fire every time.

"People must be frightened—that's your job," he'd growl at Karl. "Leave the pretty and angelic to the church."

"But what we're doing here is nothing but cheap trickery!" retorted Karl indignantly. "We could put the laterna to much better use. At universities, for example, to show anatomical—"

"You paint what I tell you to paint and that's the end of it!" snapped Faust grumpily. "I'd rather work on improving your chess skills than watch you waste time on drawing muscular torsos of handsome boys. You're still a lousy player. Now go and sweep the wagon—it's like a pigsty in there."

In moments like those Karl considered leaving the doctor, even though he knew that would turn him into an outlaw. Faust possessed those accursed letters that would forever brand him as a sodomite. If they fell into the wrong hands, he would never be able to return home to Leipzig, nor set foot in any other university towns. He wasn't sure how far-reaching the doctor's influence in the empire was. He seemed to have been everywhere already, which made their travels seem strangely aimless. As far as Karl could tell, Faust's life had been one long, never-ending journey. He wasted all his knowledge, all his wisdom, on dumb peasants and thrill-seeking burghers, as if throwing pearls to the pigs.

When, in fact, the doctor was a walking library. In one of his chests, Faust was keeping books each worth several gold ducats. Karl had leafed through some of them in secret. Lucena's accursed chess book was one of them, but also Gregor Reisch's *Margarita Philosophica*, a precious encyclopedia in twelve volumes, which seemed to contain the collective knowledge of men. Karl also discovered the *Speculum Astronomiae* by Albertus Magnus, who was considered a sorcerer by scholars at Leipzig University and whose name was blacklisted. So was Faust a real magician, too?

Karl sighed deeply and packed away the juggling balls, the garishly colorful costumes, and the bottles of theriac, which reeked of cheap liquor. Then he swept out the wagon before the doctor had one of his infamous tantrums. Faust was like a haunted man, forever on the run, but Karl didn't know what from.

It would be months yet before he'd find out.

~

They took up winter quarters in Erfurt, one of the largest cities of the German empire and roughly in its center.

Johann called Satan back with a shrill whistle as they passed through the wide city gate. The guards, clad in thick woolen coats and fur hats, eyed the strange travelers skeptically at first, but when Johann gave his name and asked Wagner to hand out a few bottles of theriac, the guards allowed them through. Johann had visited the city several times before. The University of Erfurt was considered one of the best in the country, and the rector usually allowed him to hold a few lectures. The students attended in droves and relished the doctor's witty observations and theological discourse, which always bordered closely on heresy. Until a few years ago, Erfurt had been a wealthy city, but the duties the citizens had to pay the Saxon elector and the Mainz bishopric had brought the city to the brink of ruin. When they'd tried to raise the taxes again the year before, the people had rebelled and hanged one of its aldermen.

Erfurt wasn't the only place where the common people had begun to rise against the high and mighty. Johann had seen many rebellions. A few years ago, thousands of farmers had rebelled in the bishopric of Speyer, and their leader, a certain Joß Fritz, had escaped and had been busy riling up people in other regions ever since. The whole country was seething, and Johann waited for the spark that would set off the powder keg.

It couldn't be much longer.

Winter came over Erfurt with icy temperatures and snow, which piled up knee deep in the lanes. Beggars froze beneath bridges, and the poorer households struggled for firewood. The honorable and widely traveled Doctor Faustus and his assistant lodged at one of the better inns on Michaelsgasse Lane, not far from the university. In the evenings, when the musicians struck up a tune and harlots visited the tables with big smiles and low-cut dresses, Johann mostly sat in a corner by himself, while Karl—under the disapproving looks of his master—drank with the younger fellows.

Johann loved his quiet time after the shows and lectures; he despised idle gossip. He enjoyed the fact that while people respected him, they basically feared him and avoided his company—partly, of course, because of the calf-sized dog lying under his table and growling at any unwanted intruder.

Over the years, several women had tried to get close to Doctor Faustus, the mysterious man with raven-black hair and equally black eyes. He had pushed them all away. A few times, when the urge became too strong, he'd visited whores, but the moaning and sighing, the rubbing together of naked bodies, soon repulsed him. When he closed his eyes he saw Margarethe—and then he felt sick. And so he gave up on whores. He lived like a restless monk. Karl's presence didn't change that, even though the young man tried occasionally to encourage Johann to have a little fun.

In Erfurt, Johann decided to be a little nicer to his assistant. The boy was doing a decent job, and even though Karl's endless questions got on his nerves, at least he didn't feel quite as lonely.

One evening, when they sat together at a table at the back—avoided and yet watched by the locals—dining on roast meat and enjoying a jug of wine after a particularly successful show, Johann raised his goblet.

"To your latest paintings," he said to Karl with a smile. "I particularly like the hell-dragon. Three women fainted today. You're doing well!" He threw Satan a bone, which the dog caught in the air and snapped in half with one bite. Johann patted the beast's head lovingly before turning back to Karl. "But we must work on your performance as a blind soldier. People may be dumb, but they are not as stupid as sheep." He shook his head. "No one buys how easily you saunter across the stage as a blind man."

"I'm a student of medicine, not a dishonorable juggler, remember?"

"Don't mock jugglers," replied Johann with sudden coldness in his voice. "They enchant people just like we do."

He emptied his goblet in one gulp and brought it down so hard that several other guests turned their heads and whispered to one another. Karl's remark had woken memories in Johann—memories from his time in Venice, of Salome, Emilio, and Peter the fiddler, whose death he'd foreseen a long time ago. Every now and then this strange gift had befallen him again, but he had learned to handle it. He still struggled when it was young adults and children, but he never told them the truth.

He wondered if he would have foreseen Margarethe's death.

"May I ask you something?" said Karl hesitantly.

Johann forced himself to shake off the memories. When he nodded, Karl cleared his throat. It seemed something had been bothering the young man for a while.

"Why do you do it? I mean, you're a highly educated man. In the last few months, I've heard you speak about Plato and Plutarch. You know about philosophy as well as mechanics. You know Archimedes's formulas by heart as well as those of Pythagoras—even medicine isn't unknown territory to you. You could be a widely respected doctor—rector, even—at any university. Instead—" Karl hesitated.

"Instead what?" asked Johann quietly, pouring himself another glass.

"Instead you travel the lands in a rickety wagon and fool people with those . . . those images, with magic potions, and false horoscopes. They call you a necromancer and a quack. Yes, you're widely known, but you're not respected." Karl sighed. "To be honest, I think your name—and therewith mine—will soon be forgotten again. So tell me, why do you do this to yourself?"

Johann took a sip. He said nothing for a long while, staring into the goblet in front of him, the wine gleaming red as blood. He felt a strong urge to empty the goblet again and hurl it against the wall. But he restrained himself. Instead he leaned back and studied his assistant with amusement.

"Anyone else and I would have thrown the wine at your face for such insolence, but I think it is your right to receive an answer." He leaned forward. "Do you know what I hope? I hope they lock me up one day. I long for that day, even though I know it will never arrive."

"Lock you up?" Karl looked puzzled. "But why? I mean—"

Johann cut him off with a wave of his hand. "Not as a necromancer and sorcerer, silly, but as a fraudster. You know very well that everything we're doing here is fraud. And the people know it, too, but they don't want to see it." He laughed softly. "They want to be spellbound; they want to believe that the devil really exists. Because only if the devil exists does God exist. And so they play along, buy our magic potions, and let themselves be frightened by our glass images. And as long as they do, people like you and me are free to do as we please. It's our task in this world. We act the devil so God can exist."

"Don't you believe in God?" asked Karl with a frown.

Johann hesitated. "Let us imagine there was no God," he said eventually. "Then there'd be nobody to put a stop to our evildoings. After all, our laws are all based on God. There'd be no rules and everything would be allowed. All writings, all thinking . . . a tempting thought. I myself have spent much time on that idea. Too much." Johann stared into the distance for a while before going on. "Chaos would reign, because nothing would make sense any longer. We would be all alone in the universe without any solace, and without hope. That's how I imagine hell. In my darkest hours I sometimes think we're already in hell, only we haven't noticed."

"And if there is a hell, then there is a devil," replied Wagner.

"Oh yes, he exists." Johann took one last, long sip and stared into emptiness. "He exists. He just isn't quite the way we imagine him." He put down his goblet abruptly. "Enough of these gloomy, useless thoughts! It's about time you improved your chess playing. So far it's been rather sad."

Johann reached into his coat pocket and pulled out the square board with the chess pieces. He had carved them himself, during long, sleepless nights, from horn and alabaster. He placed the board on the table and started to sort the pieces like he'd done a thousand times before.

But Karl wasn't looking at the board. Instead he was gazing out the crown-glass window, where thick snowflakes had begun to tumble from the night sky.

"What is it?" asked Johann.

"Oh, nothing. Only . . ." Karl hesitated. "When we spoke of the devil before, I thought I saw someone standing outside the window. A man dressed in black. He seemed to be looking at us—watching us. And his eyes, they . . . they were burning like fire."

"A man dressed in black? And now you think it was the devil?" Johann laughed. "My dear Karl, you've got a greater imagination than I gave you credit for. Most likely it was just a student who wanted to see the great Doctor Faustus up close. Or it was a black cat." With a thin smile, Johann held up the two kings. "Which do you want to be? Black or white? These pieces right here are real, unlike some shadows outside the window."

Johann didn't let it show, but Karl's comment had rattled him more than he cared to admit. Because he, too, had glimpsed a figure in the snow outside.

A man clad in black.

And now you think it was the devil.

Johann cast a furtive glance at the window again. There was a storm brewing outside, and the wind was howling like a lonesome child.

But there was nothing else—nothing but pitch-black night.

The sensation of being watched didn't leave Johann. On the contrary, it was growing stronger by the week. When he walked over to his lectures at the university, he often spun around and looked behind himself. He started carrying his sword on him. Occasionally he thought he saw a particular pair of eyes among the students in the auditorium, and then he would falter in his lecture as he studied the rows of chairs. But all he saw were unfamiliar, guileless faces. He called himself a fool and decided it must be the dark winter's days that made him so nervous and sullen. He had known the feeling of being watched for years—it clung to him like a foul smell. Sometimes the feeling disappeared for a few months and then it returned. But it had never been as strong as here in Erfurt.

And there was something else that bothered him: with his question at the tavern, Karl had touched a sore point.

Why do you do it?

Johann had given Karl a reply, but deep down he didn't know why he was leading this life. Because he didn't know anything else? Or because he was on the run from something—because he was waiting for something to happen? Johann didn't know what that something might be. But the black figure outside the window had awakened something inside him. Something had begun to move. Which direction it would lead, he had no idea.

To improve his mood, he often took Satan on long walks along the river flats of the Gera, outside town. Karl sometimes accompanied him, and they'd discuss medicine. It turned out that the student had learned a fair amount in his time at Leipzig University. He was more intelligent than Johann had first thought, and he possessed a wit and quickness of mind that reminded Johann of Valentin.

"All they went on about in the lectures was Galen," complained Karl. "As if nothing has changed in medicine since antiquity."

"Has anything changed?" asked Johann with a smile. He was reminded of his conversations with Conrad Celtis back in Heidelberg. Back then, he'd also wanted to change the world, just like Karl did now.

"I saw the anatomical sketches of Mondino De' Luzzi," said Karl passionately. "I would love to be able to paint as accurately as he does. Not necessarily the inside of the human body, but still—his brushwork."

"You paint pictures on glass for me, and that's enough," replied Johann gruffly. "For now, at least." He gave the young man a hard look. "And stay away from the Erfurt students! I noticed the looks you were giving them last night. Death by fire is the punishment for sodomy—here in Erfurt, too."

Karl looked abashed. "I know. It's a sin. I pray every night."

"Prayers won't help you on the pyre. The only thing that'll help you there is a pouch full of gunpowder around the neck to bring you a quick death."

Johann whistled for Satan, who came running immediately. When Karl held out his hand to pat it, the animal growled at him.

"I'm afraid he doesn't like me very much. I guess he's jealous."

"She," said Johann, stroking Satan's long back. "Satan is a she."

Karl stared first at Johann and then at the dog. "A *she*? You've got to be joking!"

Johann shook his head. "Check for yourself—although I doubt she'll let you." He gave a shrug. "Unfortunately she doesn't seem able to have pups. I always hoped she'd give me a litter, but now she's too old."

"A she!" Karl shook his head and laughed. "And why not? I always had a hunch that the devil is a woman."

The weeks went by, and in March, when the snow melted on Erfurt's rooftops, Johann decided it was time to head north.

The empire's bigger roads had steadily improved in the last few years; forests had been felled, fords established, bridges built. The brothers Janetto and Francesco de Tasso—descendants of old Lombard nobility—had been instructed by the emperor to develop the German postal network. Between Schongau and Venice alone there were two dozen posthouses now, and messengers on horseback took only six days to get from the Netherlands to Innsbruck.

Post riders dashed past Johann and Wagner in rain, hail, or sunshine. Johann sometimes thought about his youth in Knittlingen and the mail station at the Lion Inn, where everything had started. He remembered how much he'd liked hanging around the Lion as a little boy. The grim-looking post riders, but especially the foreign dialects and tongues, and the strangely clad travelers with their wares from faraway countries had shown him that there was a world beyond the next hill. He had never returned to his hometown, and he didn't know what had become of his stepfather and half brothers, just like he didn't know who his real father was. But he didn't want to know. All those things lay behind him now. He felt that his old life was like Pandora's box: if he opened it, the memories would pour out like swarms of mosquitoes, including the memories of Margarethe, Valentin, Archibaldus, and young Martin . . .

Small, squirming bundles.

In his mind's eye, Johann once again saw the dark figure outside the tavern window in Erfurt. It had been like a harbinger of the past. As if someone had knocked on the window and told him to pick up the scent again. But where? Karl had been closer to the truth than he knew. Johann walked in circles, like old Satan searching for a bone that didn't exist.

Thus they passed through Jena, Halle in Saxony, and Magdeburg, from whence they followed the wide, lazy Elbe River downstream. There were towns Faust had visited before and others he was seeing for the first time, and everywhere they were received enthusiastically. But Faust barely saw his audience, as he was constantly on the lookout for a dark figure—a figure he thought he glimpsed more and more frequently now, behind the crown-glass window of an inn, in alcoves between buildings, in the fog on the fields. At nights he barred the door to his room and studied Albertus Magnus's *Speculum* and other books on astronomy until the morning. In all the years, he still couldn't see in the stars why Tonio had described him as a chosen one. His mother, too, had believed he was born under a lucky star. A traveling scholar, an astronomer from the West, had told her long ago.

Born on the day of the prophet.

What did that mean? And why had Tonio given him the black potion that night near Nördlingen? What had the master planned for him?

The world could lie at your feet—at our feet. You have the power to set the world on fire! Homo Deus est!

As the wagon rattled along the muddy towpaths by the river, Johann racked his brain. Where was this journey leading him? Was his path written in the stars—in the truest sense of the phrase? Was there something in the sky he couldn't see? He'd studied countless books, searched the libraries of every university, but he hadn't found a thing.

Then, one day in August, after so many lost years, three birds showed him the way.

Johann and Karl had passed Wittenberge, where, according to legend, Doctor Faustus had found treasure. The swampy, slightly brackish smell of the Elbe, which flowed toward the North Sea, wafted through the rooms of the plain inn with its crooked walls. As usual, Johann was lying awake in his bed. The nights were light up here in the summer, and he gazed at the few visible stars through the open window. After tossing and turning for a while longer, he got up and walked to the window. He was gazing at the sky, studying the glistening lights, when he realized that the day of his birth had come and gone for another year. The wheel of life kept turning.

At that moment he saw the raven and the two crows.

They were perched in an old oak tree directly opposite the inn and stared at him from small, mean-looking eyes. This time, Johann knew for certain that they were the same birds Tonio used to keep in the cage years ago. At least about the raven he felt certain.

His feathers were the same gray black, and a piece was missing from the bottom of his beak, as if he'd been in a fight. One of his claws was slightly twisted. Johann narrowed his eyes. Could it be possible? He'd heard that ravens could live very long—longer than men. But why should Tonio's birds be here? So much time had passed. Why now, so many years later?

The raven opened its beak and cawed. It sounded almost human.

"Sheel . . . draay . . . ," croaked the raven. "Sheel . . . draay . . ." He flapped his wings up and down and stared at Johann intently, as if trying to tell him something.

"Sheel . . . draay . . ."

With one last hoarse croak he spread his wings and flew off to the north. The crows followed.

Johann's gaze followed them for a long time. He could hardly believe it, but he thought he knew what the raven had just said to him.

Sheel . . . draay . . . Gilles de Rais . . .

Once more he stared out into the night. The birds had gone. But now he thought he could see someone standing in the field.

A man dressed in black with glowing red eyes.

Gilles de Rais . . . the devil . . . Tonio del Moravia . . .

Johann rubbed his eyes. When he opened them again, there was nothing but a scarecrow with a tattered coat. But still he knew that evil had returned to his life. He'd tried to run away for fourteen years, but nowhere was safe for him.

Not until he figured out how everything was connected.

The raven and the obscure figure had reminded Johann that there was a dark spot in his life, as black as the soul of the devil. It didn't matter whether he'd imagined everything or whether the birds had indeed been Tonio's—he had to face up to his past, or he'd never find peace. He had to find out why Tonio had called him the chosen one and why he was allegedly born beneath a special star. Everything that had happened since his first encounter with Tonio—the horror in Schillingswald Forest, the eerie events in Venice, the gruesome death of Magister Archibaldus, the stories about Gilles de Rais—they all were stones of a large mosaic that he didn't yet understand.

Johann knew deep down that the day of his birth must be the key to everything. He had to calculate his own nativity, and more accurately than any other horoscope he'd ever drawn up.

Filled with anger and a fierce determination, Johann slammed the shutters closed. Satan shot up from her sleep and looked at her master inquisitively. Johann stroked the dog and muttered some reassuring words.

And then he sat down to think.

By the time dawn broke, he knew what he had to do. Without really knowing why, he had traveled north, as if fate had led his way. And now the birds had shown him where to go next.

Hamburg.

The name of the city flashed through his mind, a tiny scrap of a memory about something Magister Archibaldus had told him many years ago. Yes—maybe he would find what he was looking for in Hamburg. There was one place he hadn't told Karl Wagner about.

A place he should have visited a long time ago.

21

THE THOUGHT OF THE RAVEN AND THE MYSTERIOUS FIGURE
in black didn't let go of Johann during the following days and weeks as they
made their way toward Hamburg. He couldn't shake the feeling he was being
watched. He often looked up at the sky or studied the trees by the wayside,
where crows sat in the branches, watching him. He kept his sword and pistol
within easy reach behind the box seat now, and sometimes he considered shooting at the crows. But there were too many.

"What's the matter with you?" asked Karl. "It's almost like you're seeing
robbers and vagabonds behind every corner."

"More like ghosts of the past," grumbled Johann.

The dark figure, at least, hadn't returned, but crows always seemed to circle
above him like birds of prey. A few times Johann thought he could see the raven
among them.

Hamburg welcomed them with a ghastly stench. Summer had made a late
comeback, and the trash and excrement in the streets reeked to the high heavens.
The Hanseatic city was situated between the wide Elbe River and a tributary
called Alster, which had been dammed to form a lake. Cadavers and garbage
floated in the many canals crisscrossing the city. Like in all other cities of the
empire, people dumped their muck directly into the gutter, where it mixed with
rotten vegetables and the blood from the butchers and got washed into the city
streams and canals. Rats scurried across dark corners and along alleyways; on
the squares, market women and peddlers proffered their wares for sale right next
to dunghills behind which people relieved themselves. Only down by the Elbe
did the air seem a little better, and that was where Johann and Karl parked their
wagon, set up a few benches, and welcomed the countless seamen to their shows.

Their spectators were mostly men with angular, weather-beaten faces. They hailed from England, Denmark, Sweden, and other countries that lay even farther away—somewhere to the north and east, beyond the horizon. Foreign-sounding scraps of conversation buzzed through the air, and much of what the eminent and wise Doctor Faustus said no one understood. But seafarers enjoyed jugglery and lighthearted magic tricks no matter where they came from. And they liked the taste of the strong theriac.

From Hamburg, the large sailboats, cogs, hulks, and caravels sailed down the Elbe to the North Sea and from there into the big world. There used to be even more ships arriving and departing from this port, but ever since a Portuguese man named Vasco da Gama had found the sea passage to India about ten years ago, many of the Augsburg and Nuremberg merchants had chosen different routes. Also, pirates occasionally frequented these shores. The heads of those captured were stuck on pikes next to the execution site on Grasbrook, an island in the Elbe.

The shows always took place in the morning, and every afternoon Johann left their camp by the river while Karl and Satan watched the wagon and prepared for the next show.

"Are you perhaps going to a bordello after all?" asked Karl, who was used to his master not telling him where he was going. "The Hamburg whores are famous. It might prove a pleasant distraction for you."

Johann shrugged. "Indeed, I am frequenting a house that brings me pleasure—even if it isn't the kind of pleasure you're imagining. Oh, and by the way, when I return, you'll have brewed two dozen bottles of theriac. Those seamen drink like fish. And remember the glass painting of the pirate. I want it done by tomorrow." With those words, he left and headed into town.

Johann followed the stinking canals until he came to the city hall by the Trostbrücke Bridge. The city hall was a redbrick building multiple stories high, and he'd visited it several times in the last few days. A small side entrance led to a flight of stairs. A little man sat behind a desk on the second floor, nodding happily at Johann.

"Ah, the famous scholar Doctor Faustus," he said and adjusted his monocle. "Yes, yes, always on the hunt for fresh knowledge. And everyone knows that studying the papers leads to a dry throat."

Like every other day, Johann handed the man a bottle of theriac. "I haven't even studied half of your books yet," he grumbled. "If you continue to drink at this pace, I'll soon be out of theriac for my shows."

The bald, scrawny old man in his fur-lined coat and dirty beret grinned with a toothless mouth. "Well, a few drunken spectators less won't hurt. What does it matter—when the door to the world of knowledge is wide open!"

He pulled a long key from his pocket and opened the door behind him. On the other side was a high-ceilinged room with bookshelves reaching from top to bottom. Ladders provided access to the books on the highest shelves. The boards were bending under the weight of the books and parchment scrolls, and the air smelled musty and leathery. To Johann the scent was like violets. The little man made a sweeping gesture. "This library is yours, venerable Doctor—at least until the bells strike six. Then my shift is over." He closed the door behind Johann.

Johann looked around reverently. He still struggled to believe he was the only person in this room, just like the days before. That night near Wittenberge by the Elbe, when he'd seen the dark figure, he'd remembered something from fifteen years ago. Magister Archibaldus came from Hamburg, and on their journey to Venice he'd told Johann about a library. The Hamburg *Ratsbibliothek* was the only public library in the entire German empire. Usually such hoards of knowledge were in private ownership of universities or monasteries whose abbots would never grant entry to the alleged sorcerer and necromancer Doctor Johann Georg Faustus. Here, however, he was free to browse for as long as he liked. The Ratsbibliothek was bigger than the library at the monastery in Maulbronn that he used to visit with Father Antonius, and bigger than that of the creepy Signore Barbarese in Venice. The Hamburg library held many ecclesiastical works but also many secular ones—philosophical treatises as well as Greek dramas and scientific books. Johann had even found some notes by Leonardo da Vinci.

But what he was really after was works on astronomy that would help him with his calculations for the day of his birth. He'd been born on a day when Jupiter and the sun had stood in the same degree of the same zodiac. While that was a little unusual, it wasn't anything extraordinary; many people were born beneath the same constellation because it occurred several times a year. So what was the secret of his birth?

So far he had found several writings by an astronomer named Heinrich von Langenstein, from Vienna, and also a book by Roger Bacon in which the well-known English Franciscan described the construction of a camera obscura for observation of the sun. But none of the books had told him why his date of birth was particularly blessed by the stars. Johann hadn't found any more on Gilles de Rais, either, nor had he found the name Tonio del Moravia in any of the documents.

Johann slowly walked along the rows of books and studied the titles. After a few moments of deliberation, he chose a book he thought sounded promising. It was written by a certain Johannes Müller and, among other topics, discussed the question whether the sun was indeed rotating around the Earth, or whether perhaps the Earth was rotating around the sun. It was a fascinating thought, which Father Bernhard back in Knittlingen had told him about and which was increasingly discussed in scholarly circles these days. Johann carried the book to a desk and started to read. It was very interesting, but it didn't help him in his quest. He was about to put it back on the shelf when he noticed another manuscript on the desk. It had been hidden under some loose pages of parchment, as if someone was in the middle of making a copy. Johann's eyes scanned the title and author.

De Occulta Philosophia by Heinrich Cornelius Agrippa of Nettesheim.

Johann frowned. He had heard of this Agrippa. A clever man who'd apparently studied at the University of Cologne and about whose sharp mind Johann had encountered a few tales. They said he completed his baccalaureus at just fourteen years old, was fluent in eight languages, and despite his young age was already more learned than most doctors in the empire. These days he was lecturing in Cologne whenever he wasn't traveling the country at the invitations of the rich and powerful. Agrippa hadn't made a lot of friends among the clergy with his witty speeches.

Much to his surprise, Johann felt a twinge of jealousy. This Agrippa might actually see eye to eye with him. An equal in a world where true knowledge still struggled in the face of old-fashioned scholasticism and bigotry.

With growing curiosity Johann studied the pages of the manuscript, which had been written in a neat, very small hand. After a few lines he was so engrossed in the work that he forgot everything around him. It was like a miracle! This writ systematically combined all known areas of magic, from chiromancy and astrology to alchemy. Everything that Johann had been taught by Tonio and everything he'd taught himself thereafter was written right here in Latin. How had this Agrippa gained his immense knowledge? A man required decades to learn all this. Johann glanced over the pages and his heart beat faster. This was the best book he'd ever read! It was brilliantly written and blessed with an insight that elevated magic to the same level as faith and science. The astrological observations, too, went further than anything Johann had known until then. He leafed through the manuscript wildly and found to his horror that he was holding only about fifty measly pages.

The book finished before it had properly begun—and the author grandly promised a work of three volumes.

Where on earth?

Johann raced along the other desks and past the rows of shelves. Eventually he picked up the manuscript, opened the door, and waved the pages under the surprised librarian's nose.

"Where is the rest?" he asked curtly.

"The rest of what?" The little man put on his monocle and studied the pages. Then his face lit up. "Oh, that! Interesting, isn't it? A merchant on his way back from England dropped it off yesterday. Apparently Agrippa was in London at the behest of the emperor, and that's where the merchant met him and bought these pages from him. I was going to copy them today. A highly—"

"Where is the rest?" repeated Johann.

The man sighed. "There is no rest. This is all the merchant brought me. He said Agrippa was still working on it."

Johann closed his eyes for a moment. For the first time in a long while he had the feeling he wasn't running in circles.

"I'm buying these pages," he said. "How much?"

"They aren't for sale. I'd have to make a copy—"

"I don't have time for that." Johann placed a gold ducat on the desk. It was the most valuable coin he owned. A fat Erfurt merchant had given it to him for a favorable nativity chart.

The librarian's eyes widened. "You could buy two dozen books for that!"

"I only want this one manuscript. And now excuse me."

Clutching the pages in his hand, Johann hurried outside and ran across the square and through the city gate toward the Elbe.

He was so lost in thought that he didn't notice the figure that entered the Ratsbibliothek the moment he had left it.

At the end of his shift, the librarian had earned three gold ducats: one from that strange Doctor Faustus everyone was talking about, and two more from a man who wanted answers to a few questions and whom the librarian tried to forget as quickly as possible.

By the end of the day all the little man could say about the strange visitor was that his coat—his whole appearance, in fact—had been as black as the night.

Only his eyes seemed to have glowed eerily.

~

Down by the port, Karl Wagner sat at a wobbly table inside the wagon and painted the beard of a pirate. Not much light came in through the curtain behind the box seat, and the tallow candles smoked terribly, so that Karl was forced to lean closely over the glass plate. He was working with very fine brushes and had to consider each stroke carefully, since the paintings on the glass plates were so small. Karl thought about the famous Nuremberg painter Albrecht Dürer, who probably let his creativity run wild on canvases as tall as a man, while he himself was painting pirate beards the size of a fingernail.

Satan was lying at his feet and growled at every little movement. Karl was increasingly under the impression that the dog wasn't guarding the wagon but him. If he tried to leave the wagon, Satan would probably tear him to pieces. Karl hated the mastiff, but he knew that his master loved her more than anything—and more than anyone. Just then Satan bared her teeth at him again, and Karl gave a strained smile.

"Lousy old mutt," he said and kept smiling. "I guess you love me about as much as I love you. We must get along, though, whether we like it or not. So you better sit like a good dog or there won't be any treats."

He tossed the tip of a sausage to Satan, appeasing the dog for the moment.

Karl tiredly rubbed his eyes and stretched his back. Outside he could hear the sounds of the river: the shouts of the seamen, the ringing of ship bells, the mocking cries of the gulls that had flown inland from the ocean shores.

Karl painted inside the wagon to avoid curious gossips, and for that purpose he'd had a little table made in Wittenberge. He'd grown tired of getting hardly any work done because of all the questions people badgered him with. The pirate he was painting today was Klaus Störtebeker, a bloodthirsty villain who was executed a long time ago. Folks were still telling ghost stories about him. According to legend, after Störtebeker was decapitated he walked past eleven of his men before the hangman tripped him.

Karl sighed and continued his work. Starting tomorrow, the doctor had rented a hall in town where they were going to show the famous Störtebeker with the laterna magica. He hoped he'd manage to capture this accursed pirate on the glass plate by then. He'd spent half the afternoon brewing that stinking theriac. Part of the job was to get up early in the morning and head to Grasbrook Island to pick mint, wormwood, and wild fennel.

Once again doubts crept into Karl's mind as to whether he had chosen the right path. Of course, Doctor Faustus had saved his life, and Karl owed him gratitude. And the man was famous—across the entire empire and beyond. But by now they'd been traveling together for almost a whole year, and the doctor was becoming more frightening by the day. Karl had found many strange books in one of the chests and begun to read them in his lonely hours, even though he didn't fully understand them. The doctor had never told him what he used to do before he took up exploring the empire, but something told Karl that Faust had a dark past, as if he'd been cursed a long time ago. Was that the price he'd had to pay for wealth and fame?

Dabbing his brush very gently, Karl gave the pirate a dashing hat. Störtebeker's gaze was both furious and mysterious at once—as mysterious as that of the doctor, who was on his way to becoming just as legendary as this buccaneer.

Doctor Faustus called himself a fraud, but Karl knew he was much more than that. Faust was the most learned man he'd ever met, blessed with a razor-sharp mind, and open to anything new. Karl worshipped the doctor—probably more than he cared to admit—but he was also afraid of him. Faust sometimes had horrendous fits of rage, and he could be arrogant and awfully sarcastic. And then there were the screams in the night.

The screams at night frightened Karl the most.

They frequently shared a room, and sometimes, when Karl stayed awake for longer than the doctor, he heard him mutter and groan in his sleep. He also cried and sighed in his dreams and repeated the same names over and over again: Margarethe, Martin, Tonio, Gilles de Rais.

The last name, especially, Faust said many times in his sleep.

On top of everything else, the doctor clearly suffered from paranoia, and it was only getting worse. During their trip north he'd often turned around to check the road behind them or stared at the birds in the sky. It was almost as if Faust feared that the birds were watching them. However, Karl had to admit that there had been a few strange occurrences lately. The black figure with the red eyes outside the Erfurt tavern window, for example. And twice more he thought he'd seen the same figure on their journey north, standing among the trees by the wayside. But he hadn't said anything to the doctor for fear of adding to his paranoia.

Karl had learned more from Faust than he ever would have learned at a university. In Leipzig he was nothing but the son of an ambitious father whom he'd never have pleased. Karl had loved his mother very dearly, but she'd passed away years before. Now, on his adventures with the doctor, he was becoming a man. Still, he had made up his mind that he wouldn't travel with the doctor forever. He felt that the heavy melancholy clinging to his master was rubbing off on him. He was going to stay with him for one more winter and then leave in the spring. He no longer cared about those stupid letters—his duty was done.

A movement by the curtain made Karl start from his thoughts. The brush jerked and the awe-inspiring sword he'd been working on turned into a long smudge. Karl swore. Now he'd have to start from the beginning. Below the table, Satan growled and pricked her ears.

"Who's there?" asked Karl harshly. "The doctor is in town. Come back tomorrow."

"Is there going to be another show tomorrow?" asked a high-pitched male voice. "I would so love to see the doctor one more time. And . . . and you, too."

"Me?" Something in the voice piqued Karl's interest. He threw Satan the bone that was supposed to go into the soup for dinner, stood up, and opened the curtain. A handsome boy of about sixteen or seventeen was standing beside the wagon. Karl had noticed him in the last few days—the chap hadn't missed a show. Their eyes had met in a way Karl knew well.

They always knew each other by their eyes.

The youth smiled uncertainly. He was pale and had fine black hair. Judging by his clothes, he was a simple dockworker, although his delicate stature didn't really fit the picture. His eyelashes were as long as a girl's. Karl carefully looked around. It was quiet by the river at the moment. About a stone's throw away, some day laborers were loading crates into a smaller boat that was probably headed for the Alster port, but none of them were looking in their direction. Karl hesitated, but not for long. The doctor wouldn't be back before six—they had enough time.

"Come in," he said and gestured behind himself, winking at the youth. "I want to show you something."

"But . . . but the dog?" the boy asked anxiously and peered through the curtain, where Satan was chewing on the bone.

"It won't hurt you. Not as long as I keep feeding it my dinner, anyhow. Come on in—you have nothing to fear."

The boy did as he was asked. He climbed inside the wagon and looked at everything with curiosity: the dried herbs dangling from the ceiling, and the many crates and chests, some of which stood open, revealing their mysterious contents. When his gaze fell upon the glass plate on the table, he giggled like a girl.

"Oh, that must be Störtebeker. Am I right? You've captured him well!"

"Thank you." Karl was also smiling now. "We're going to show him with our laterna magica."

"With your laterna what?" The youth's eyes grew wide.

"Well, it's an apparatus that allows us to make images appear against a wall," explained Karl patronizingly. "And I paint the pictures. I've even drawn the pope and the emperor. I'm a painter," he added unnecessarily. "Just like Leonardo da Vinci or Albrecht Dürer. Do you know Dürer?"

The youth shook his head.

"I copied his horsemen of the apocalypse," said Karl. "Well, to be honest, I reinterpreted the work. I don't think I've done too badly. Some even say it is better than the original."

The young lad continued to stare at the glass plate. He reverently ran his finger along the edge of the miniature painting. "These must be very valuable."

"What's your name, boy?" asked Karl, trying to change the subject.

The youth took a bow. "Sebastian, sir."

Karl laughed. "You don't need to call me sir—I'm not much older than you. Sebastian is a beautiful name." He winked at him. "And Saint Sebastian was a beautiful man. As handsome as you," he added softly.

By now he felt certain that the boy was here for a particular reason. Karl couldn't say whether it was the boy's own desire or whether he was hoping for money, but at the end of the day it didn't matter. Several times over the last few months he'd met with young men, and while Faust probably had his suspicions, Karl didn't think he noticed anything. Mostly they'd been hasty encounters beneath bridges or in the bushes. There were boys like this one in every town— one only had to find them. They were all connected by their fear of discovery. Good, upright citizens had almost less sympathy for sodomites than they had for heretics, Jews, and well poisoners.

The dainty young man turned away and started to rummage through the chests. "Those are juggling balls, right?" He pulled out one red and one golden leather ball and tried to juggle them. The balls fell to the ground and he laughed.

"Leave it," replied Karl. Suddenly he got the bad feeling that it hadn't been such a good idea to invite the handsome youth into the wagon. His demeanor seemed very experienced—calculated, even. Karl suspected this wasn't the first wagon he had sifted through.

"Leave it, I said!" he repeated more loudly. But the boy didn't listen. He continued to rummage through the chest, lifting out a black hat, red scarves, and a white wooden egg. Then he turned to the chest with the books and carelessly picked up and dropped several volumes.

"Watch out—you're damaging them!" shouted Karl.

Suddenly the youth snorted with surprise. He dropped the books he was holding, bent down, and lifted a knife from the chest. He studied it with awe in his eyes, and Karl also gazed at it with wonder. He had never seen the knife before; it must have been buried underneath all those books. The handle appeared to be carved from some kind of bone and was decorated with black patterns and lines. It looked very old and precious. The boy ran his thumb along the blade with a smile.

"It's so beautiful," he said. "Will you give it to me as a gift?"

Karl cleared his throat. This whole situation was taking a direction he didn't like at all. He gave an awkward laugh. "You're not serious, are you? That knife belongs to the doctor, and he—"

"And now it belongs to me," the boy said decisively. He eyed Karl with a cold stare and pointed the tip of the knife at him. "Or do you want to take it off me?"

Karl nervously glanced at Satan, who was happily chewing on her bone. He couldn't believe it. For once the mutt could have been useful, but she was behaving as gentle as a lamb.

The youth grinned and his eyes flashed wolfishly. "Then we have an understanding. I'm going to take this knife and—"

Suddenly, the curtain was yanked open behind him. To Karl's enormous relief, it was the doctor, arriving back much sooner than anticipated. He was out of breath, and his mouth stood open as if he'd just been about to say something when he happened upon the scene with the boy and the knife.

"What is going on here?" he snapped.

"Um, nothing," said Karl. "We were just talking."

"We?" The doctor looked the youth up and down. Faust seemed to suddenly realize what the boy was holding in his hand. His face turned ashen as if he'd seen a ghost.

"Put that down immediately," said Faust very quietly. "I'm going to count to three, and then Satan will tear you into tiny pieces. Afterward I will feed you to the gulls. One. Two."

The boy dropped the knife and ran past Faust. They could hear his footsteps for a few more moments, and then everything was silent.

"I . . . I'm so—" began Karl, but Faust cut him off with a wave.

"Pack your things. We're leaving."

"But . . . but our show with the laterna," stammered Karl. "Klaus Störtebeker . . ."

"I said we're leaving. And if I catch you with another boy like him, Satan's going to bite off the balls of both of you—understood?"

Karl lowered his eyes and nodded. "Where . . . where are we going?" he asked quietly after a while.

"To Cologne. We're going to visit someone I should have met a long time ago. Years ago. Hitch the horse to the wagon. Now!"

As Karl slunk away, he saw the doctor pick up the knife and gaze at it thoughtfully.

Then he dropped it into the chest as if it had burned his fingers.

22

THE WAGON SLOWLY RATTLED ALONG THE DUSTY ROAD
that wound endlessly through the heath. Satan jogged alongside the wagon,
panting, and stopped to relieve herself or rest up every now and then. She
no longer had the strength for long journeys and tired easily. They had left
Hamburg in the early evening and set off in the direction of Lüneburg. The
heath glowed purple in the light of the afternoon sun; they had been on the
road almost nonstop for three days now, and Johann had barely spoken.

He looked over at Karl, who was sitting next to him with a pinched expression. He probably thought Johann was still angry because of the young lad in
Hamburg. And Johann had been angry. It was encounters like those that could
cost them both their heads. He didn't care whether Karl lusted after girls, boys,
or sheep—as long as he didn't put them both in danger with his escapades.
Especially not now that Johann finally had set his sights on a goal and purpose
again. He needed to meet Heinrich Agrippa and speak with him about his masterpiece, *De Occulta Philosophia*. If anyone knew about the constellations and
prophecies, it would be Agrippa. Maybe Johann would finally learn the mystery
of his birth.

And perhaps he'd find out more about Tonio del Moravia and Gilles de Rais.

Had it been coincidence that the young thief in Hamburg found the knife?
Johann had kept it for all those years, even though he couldn't tell why. It had
brought him nothing but ill luck, but it also served to remind him of the guilt
he'd heaped upon himself. He hadn't dared to throw it away—almost as if the
act might trigger a curse. The knife had been resting at the very bottom of the
chest, and now it had reemerged. When Johann had picked it up from the floor
of the wagon, he was reminded of the engraving.

G d R.

Gilles de Rais.

Another murder of crows rose up from the wide-open space of the heath and moved across the sky like a poisonous black cloud. The birds cawed noisily, and suddenly Johann heard the name again.

Sheel draay . . . Gilles de Rais . . . sheel draay . . .

Why couldn't he get that accursed name out of his head? It had been torturing him for years now! As if the name was irrevocably connected to his fate. Like Tonio. Like everything that had happened since those days in Knittlingen.

On this trip, they didn't spend much time on shows, and so they made rapid progress. Large areas of the north of the empire were covered in moors and heath, a desolate, desertlike landscape without any hills to speak of, without valleys, and without lakes. The wind blew up small clouds of any sand the heather shrubs didn't hold down, and several times the wagon wheels got stuck in soft, sandy ruts and they'd have to push the wagon out like from a snowdrift. Once they started to travel along rivers again, the roads became better. Every time they passed through a new county or a new small barony, they had to pay road tolls. The whole empire was like a threadbare carpet sewn from countless tiny scraps and held together only by an emperor who was as far away as the moon.

The closer they came to the Rhine Valley, the lovelier the landscape became. The first vineyards appeared. Finally, twelve exhausting days of travel later, they looked upon the wide ribbon of the Rhine, and they knew it wouldn't be far to Cologne now.

So far, Johann had avoided the city of Cologne, which was one of the largest in the empire. The prior of the Dominican monastery of Cologne was also the papal inquisitor, and he had a reputation for being particularly strict with alleged heretics. Also, the city was a famous pilgrimage destination with countless relics, most notably the remains of the three wise men. Magicians and chiromancers weren't well received in such a place. But the reputation of the legendary Doctor Faustus had even reached Cologne. When Johann loudly declared his name at the city gate, the guards discussed for a while before allowing him in—not without confiscating one or two bottles of theriac. Satan was lying in the back of the wagon. It was difficult enough to gain entrance to the city without the oversized animal, and the dog had been increasingly dragging her right hind leg. Johann was worried about her.

In the northeast, the unfinished spire of the cathedral rose up. The people of Cologne had been working on this architectural masterpiece for more than two hundred and fifty years, and it still wasn't finished. The city was speckled with smaller and larger churches, and almost every single one exhibited some reliquary or other. On their way through the busy streets, they passed many pilgrims with staffs and humble clothing. After Rome and Santiago de Compostela, Cologne was the best-known pilgrimage destination in the Western world. But the city was also a place of learning and boasted one of the largest universities of the empire. The famous Albertus Magnus, whom Johann had venerated since his days at Maulbronn Monastery, had studied theology and been ordained a priest here.

"And where do you propose to find this Agrippa?" asked Karl as they drove the wagon through the narrow, unpaved lanes toward the river. By now Johann had forgiven him for the affair in Hamburg, but he hadn't told Karl what exactly he was hoping to gain from meeting Agrippa. He had merely said he was looking forward to an exchange between learned men.

"Well, Heinrich Agrippa of Nettesheim is no stranger in Cologne," replied Johann. "The bottles of theriac for the guards were a sound investment. They gave me his address. Apparently he lives near the hay market with his sister, who cooks for him. It shouldn't be far now."

They turned onto another narrow lane and neared a two-story half-timbered house that was freshly painted and appeared generally well looked-after. Johann felt himself growing nervous. What if Agrippa refused to receive him? After all, most scholars considered Johann to be nothing but a fraud. Or what if Agrippa couldn't help him? The whole idea—the hasty departure from Hamburg, the hope to learn more about his birth from the famous scholar—suddenly seemed awfully naive. What could he expect? But it was too late to turn back now.

"Wait here," said Johann to Karl. He climbed down from the box seat, walked over to the house, and pulled on the string that operated a bell inside. After a few long moments, a plump young woman wearing a bonnet and an apron opened the door. She gave Johann a friendly albeit reserved look. It seemed she was used to supplicants.

Johann cleared his throat. "My name is Doctor Johann Georg Faustus. I am looking for the eminent scholar Heinrich Cornelius Agrippa of Nettesheim. Can you tell me where to find him?"

"My brother is still at the university," the woman replied curtly. "He'll be home soon. You best wait outside."

Johann was about to make a reply, but Agrippa's sister had already closed the door. With a frown he returned to Karl, who was trying to chase away a bunch of nosy street kids. This wasn't going the way he'd hoped at all.

Soon, a crowd had gathered around the wagon. Johann was wearing his blue-and-black star cloak and the floppy hat, and the strange symbols on the wagon did the rest. Word was spreading fast that a well-known magician was waiting outside Agrippa's house.

"It's the sorcerer Doctor Faustus," whispered an elderly farmer to his wife in a broad Cologne accent. "A necromancer and devil worshipper! I've heard of him. Down at Speyer he made two calves fly to the moon! They're still up there today."

"God protect us," said the old woman, shaking her head. "When two magicians come together, terrible things will happen."

The crowd grumbled, and the first few troublemakers started to pull at the canvas, probably trying to see what sort of devilish things were hidden inside. Karl jumped down and tried to fend off the most daring fellows. But they didn't stop—on the contrary, more and more people came forward, shouting, swearing, and shaking the wagon. The lane was so full of people that they wouldn't be able to get the wagon out. Johann looked about nervously. It wouldn't be long before some city guards turned up, and that wouldn't help his cause at all. He was already considered trouble. Should he set Satan on the mob? But that would only make things worse.

"What's all this about? Off with you, there's nothing to see here!"

Johann turned around and saw a rather short man with a beret and a gown striding through the throng of people. He was probably younger than Johann, but his black university garb and lordly demeanor made him appear older and more dignified. The man had intelligent, alert eyes, a pointed nose, and a thin mouth that seemed set in a permanent sneer. Despite his youth, his hair and thin beard were already turning gray.

"Don't ask *me*—ask the people," replied Johann from the box seat.

"Well, if you are who the people think you are, you are definitely the source of all this trouble." The man smiled and suddenly looked much younger. He spoke with a Cologne accent, which made his stilted way of speaking sound like a cheap farce. "Doctor Faustus, am I right? Considering the sheer number of tales about you, I would have thought you much older."

"Considering the number of your works, Master Agrippa, I thought you, too, were older," replied Johann coolly, still annoyed about the turmoil he had caused. "Or were they written by someone else, perhaps?"

"Touché, dear colleague!" Agrippa laughed and bowed mockingly, the crowd now keeping a respectful distance. "I much prefer an open attack to the back-stabbing attempts of all those old scholars who would love nothing more than to see me convicted of heresy. Let us go inside, where we can speak undisturbed." He grinned and gestured toward an alleyway to the left of his house.

"You'll find a gate to the backyard of my humble abode down there. You must forgive my sister, Martha, for not letting you in. We simply get too many supplicants—mostly traveling students hoping for a position. But I wouldn't miss your visit, honorable Doctor. On the way home from the university alone, I heard at least a dozen stories about you."

"Only half of them are true," said Johann with a shrug.

"And he won't tell you which half," said Karl with a sigh.

Agrippa glanced at the young man. "You have an assistant?"

"A talented young man," replied Johann. "Even if his passion runs a little wild at times."

He walked through the crowd at Agrippa's side. The people readily gave way now, and some even took off their hats. But Johann also saw some men and women making the sign of the cross and other gestures to ward off evil. Meanwhile, Karl climbed back onto the box seat and steered the wagon through the crowd toward the alleyway.

The front door was followed by a plainly furnished hallway, with furs and carpets on the walls and fragrant reeds on the floor.

"Follow me into the stove room," said Agrippa as he went up the stairs. "We'll be able to converse undisturbed there. Your assistant may wait in the kitchen and let Martha spoil him. She's made fresh Cologne doughnuts—a veritable delicacy. As for you and me, we will content ourselves with the meager yet equally delicious fare of collegial dispute."

The stove room was dominated by a green tiled stove as high as a man. Such stoves were increasingly the fashion in houses of burghers. Unlike the tidy hall-way, this room was very messy. Books and loose pages were strewn across chests and small tables; a brown apple core lay rotting between an inkwell and a quill. Johann smelled parchment, dust, and sweat.

"My realm," said Agrippa with a smile and gestured for Johann to sit on a stool. They both sat down, and Agrippa eyed Johann for a long while.

"Well, well, the famous Doctor Faustus," he said eventually and leaned back. "Someone told me about your lectures at Erfurt. I was impressed by your views on the theological term of God. A little dangerous, though, because it doesn't take much to be called a heretic these days. I know what I'm talking about."

"And you are lecturing here in Cologne?" asked Johann.

"Simple theological discussions without any particular classification—on request of the rector." Agrippa gave a shrug, and Johann wasn't sure whether this show of boredom was an act or real. Agrippa was certainly clever, but he also had something pretentious and loud about him.

Just like me, thought Johann.

"I doubt I'll be staying in Cologne for much longer," continued Agrippa. "I'll probably have to travel to Italy soon. It is my duty to accompany a heavily guarded chest of war as an imperial officer. Earlier this year I helped a friend of mine in Spain to win back his castle. Oh yes, and not long ago I worked in England as an agent. The emperor sent me to develop good trade relations with the new king, Henry VIII. I speak English, you see." He paused and raised one eyebrow. "Do you know the feeling of never being satisfied, always wanting more from life, forever searching and exploring, regardless of the consequences?"

Johann nodded. "Oh yes. I know it well."

Too well.

"I guess that makes us brothers in spirit." Agrippa laughed, and his laugh was soft and melodious, almost like that of a woman. He looked around for a jug of wine, grabbed two dirty cups from a table full of books, and filled them.

"You see, I'm just as restless as you. Today I'm here, tomorrow gone—the *studium generale* includes all parts of life. But you haven't come here just to chat, have you? So why are you here?"

Johann cleared his throat. "While you were in England, you wrote a manuscript. I was fortunate enough to purchase a copy in Hamburg." He nervously pulled out the bundle of pages and smoothed them on the table in front of him. Agrippa shot a glance at them.

"The *Occulta Philosophia*," said the scholar with a nod. "I'm a long way away from finishing it." He sighed. "I should never have let that fat merchant buy a copy. But he paid well, and the emperor is once again in arrears."

"I must congratulate you. It's a masterpiece!" Johann tapped the pages. "No one has ever approached magic as systematically as you have. Astrology, invocations, spells, manticism, potions—"

"Pure theory." Agrippa waved dismissively. "I lack practical experience, and that is where you are the teacher and I am but an eager student. Why are you so interested in it?"

"Well, your work touches questions that"—Johann paused—"that concern me personally."

For the first time Agrippa seemed genuinely interested, and he leaned forward. "What do you mean?"

"Certain things have happened in my life that . . . Well, one could say I am cursed. And I've been wondering for a while now whether those incidents have anything to do with my birth chart. I was born under Jupiter. The sun and Jupiter stood in the same degree of the same zodiac on the day of my birth."

Agrippa nodded. "A strong constellation indeed. Born under the lucky star—hence your name, I guess."

"I haven't found my luck yet," Johann replied bitterly. "Have you ever heard of the expression *born on the day of the prophet*? Apparently it has something to do with my birth."

"No, I'm sorry." Agrippa shook his head. "But I think it's likely that the stars have more to say about your birth than we simple humans can see with our bare eyes." When Johann gave him a quizzical look, Agrippa continued. "I am convinced that there are many more stars out there. Some shine very weakly, as if they were far away. I've always wondered, What lies beyond?"

"Ptolemy wrote that the Earth was surrounded by eight spheres," replied Johann. "And beyond those is nothing."

"And you're content with that explanation?" Agrippa smiled. "You disappoint me, Faustus. Don't you want to find out what lies beyond the eighth sphere?"

"Beyond the eighth sphere." Johann gazed into the distance. "Someone else said those words to me once."

"That someone must have been a wise man." Agrippa emptied his cup in one gulp and refilled both their cups with wine. "But now let us speak of more worldly things. I've got a suggestion for you, Doctor Faustus. You tell me about yourself, and I tell you about the world behind the eighth sphere. If only every second story about you is true, we are going to have a few merry and stimulating weeks."

Agrippa was right. The following weeks were the most stimulating Johann had ever experienced.

Heinrich Cornelius Agrippa of Nettesheim, famous Cologne scholar, was the first person Johann had ever considered an equal. Their conversations were like duels, fought not with the sword but with wit and sharp tongues. The two men came from very different backgrounds. Agrippa was an offspring of Cologne nobility, and his father had been a diplomat in the service of the House of Hapsburg. Agrippa had grown up as a fortunate child, loved by his parents, surrounded by books, and boasting many talents. Johann, on the other hand, was a bastard who'd had to work hard for everything in his life, a juggler, and a fraud.

Even though Agrippa probably knew that most of the stories about Faust weren't true, he was happily entertained by them. A small adventure quickly turned into a scientific discourse, and the two men often sat up late into the night.

"My students told me you can make thunder and lightning," said Agrippa with a smile one evening in the stove room. "So? Can you?"

Johann shrugged. "Let's say I possess enough gunpowder to make the heavens rumble—for the simple folk, at least. The scope of this devilish mixture of sulfur, coal, and saltpeter is truly astonishing. I fear we're far from finished developing and refining this powder, however."

"And how is the real thunder in the sky created?" asked Agrippa, sipping his wine. "In his *Meteorologica*, Aristotle claims that it is the wind colliding with the clouds. What do you think?"

"Do you know Albertus Magnus's rainbow experiment?" replied Johann after some consideration. "An octagonal crystal that is partly placed into the sunlight projects the colors of the rainbow against a wall. Maybe it's a similar story with thunder. Thunder might be created by something we can't see. It is just the consequence, not the cause."

Agrippa rocked his head from side to side. "An interesting thought, dear colleague. I might use it in one of my lectures."

Agrippa mostly spent the mornings at the university, where the students flocked to his lectures to hear the scholar's thoughts, some finding them heretical while others believed they were forward thinking. Johann used the time to browse Agrippa's home library until delicious cooking smells called him to the kitchen. He took lunch with Agrippa's sister and Karl. Satan stayed in the garden by the wagon.

Thus the weeks passed, and soon it was October. The temperatures turned cooler, and rain lashed through the lanes of Cologne. Every now and then Johann still thought he was being watched, but the urge to learn more about the stars on his day of birth and about whatever lay beyond the eighth sphere was so strong that he forgot everything else around him. He and Karl slept at the Golden Crown Inn, one of the city's best taverns. Johann slept deeply and without dreams—better than he had in years. The intellectual exchange with Agrippa made him feel as satisfied as a freshly fed baby. He barely ever thought of Margarethe during that time.

They didn't give any shows with the laterna magica for fear of being accused of heresy. Johann wasn't a particularly popular man in the streets of Cologne; people gossiped about the sorcerer at the house of the controversial scholar, and a few times dung was thrown at him. But he didn't deny himself the pleasure of demonstrating the laterna in the stove room for Agrippa.

"Truly amazing," said his host once the last image—the white woman—had faded and Johann had lit the candles in the room again. "Imagine the possibilities if those images could move like real people."

"And speak," said Johann with a smile. "Who knows—perhaps that day will come, even if you or I won't be there to see it."

Johann gradually learned more about Agrippa's thoughts on the stars. The scholar thought it was possible that there were other suns in the universe—other worlds, even. The universe might be endlessly great, and planet Earth nothing but a speck of dust.

"Consider the comets," Agrippa said to Johann one day. "Where do they come from? From a distant world behind the eighth sphere? How long did it take them to travel here? Since the times of Aristotle people have believed comets are atmospheric evaporations or harbingers of bad news of future events. But I believe they come from much farther away—farther even than the wise astronomer Johannes Müller suspected, but at least he defined them as independent celestial bodies." Agrippa sighed. "It is such a pity our eyes can't see what's beyond the eighth sphere." He gestured at the laterna magica in a corner of the room. "It's a pretty toy, your apparatus. But I wonder if it could also be used differently. Those lenses you used . . ." He hesitated.

"What about them?"

Agrippa picked up the frameless eye glasses he wore occasionally and studied them pensively. "If we look through lenses, we see better. We've known that since the times of Roger Bacon. But what if we could also better see what's in the heavens? If we could see farther, we might understand what makes your birth so special. You speak of a curse—why?"

Johann hesitated.

"Have you ever heard of a Gilles de Rais?" he asked eventually.

Agrippa touched his nose, thinking. Johann thought for the briefest moment he saw a flicker in the scholar's eyes. "I'm afraid I haven't," he replied. "Should I have?"

Johann watched Agrippa closely, but the man's expression remained neutral. If he was lying, he was very good at it.

"It's not important. Please excuse the question." Johann gave a shrug. "Concerning the curse . . . it is as if someone were giving me all the wisdom, all the knowledge in the world, while at the same time placing obstacles in my way. Terrible things have happened all my life, but I was always told that I was blessed with luck. Born on the day of the prophet—how does that fit together with all the awful things that have happened to me? I finally want to know who I am. Do you understand? Only then will my searching come to an end."

"Who you are?" Agrippa couldn't hold back a smile. "Since when do people want to know who they are? An unusual question, don't you think? Somewhat . . . new." He laughed. "But then again, you are an unusual person, Doctor Faustus—almost like a new specimen of our kind."

Johann was so engrossed in his discussions with Agrippa that he sometimes forgot that he had an assistant. Karl did as he pleased in Cologne, and aside from mealtimes, they didn't see each other. Johann didn't look after Karl as he had pledged that he would after they'd first met. His thirst for knowledge was stronger than their friendship.

And so fate—or the curse Johann had spoken about—took its course once again.

~

Karl heard the sounds of music, laughter, and shattering glass as he staggered out of the tavern down by the Rhine and turned his face into the autumn rain. The Black Whale was a disreputable hole, but nevertheless it was frequented by gentlemen of the upper classes. They usually sat in the back, wearing wide-brimmed hats and plain coats to hide their expensive clothing. It wasn't long before a handsome young lad would take a seat beside one such gentleman, and a while later the pair would disappear up a narrow set of stairs.

Karl, too, had been upstairs a few times.

There were days when he cursed himself for what he was doing. Why had God punished him with this vice? He knew it was a cardinal sin punishable with death by fire, but his flesh was weak. Why couldn't he simply love girls like other young men did? It drove him crazy. If what he was doing was a sin, then why had God made him this way? Was it a test, just like the Lord had tested Job? Karl was too afraid even to confess his sins at church now—he feared the priest would disregard the seal of confession. Instead Karl launched himself from one amorous adventure to the next, drowning his guilty conscience with wine and schnapps at the Black Whale.

Suddenly Karl felt nauseated, and he staggered toward the Rhine as quickly as he could, dropped to his knees, and vomited. The lights of the taverns along the port were reflected in the water; they were low, huddled buildings near the docks, warehouses, and fish markets; they lured patrons with whores and other guilty pleasures. Karl retched. If only he could rid himself of his urge this way! Just spew it out like those possessed by the devil sometimes spewed out rusty nails and then they were cured.

For him, it seemed, there was no cure.

He was bound for hell.

What made it all the worse for him was the fact that he loved a man who was unattainable. It had started slowly and stealthily. In the beginning it was merely admiration and respect Karl had felt toward the doctor, but now it was respect coupled with true affection and—Karl quivered with embarrassment—uncouth thoughts. Doctor Faustus was a dozen years older than him, but he was still a good-looking man with soft raven-black hair and a dark, mysterious gaze. Karl thought it was mainly the eyes that attracted him so—gazing at them was like looking into two deep ponds. And he couldn't figure out the mystery that lay at their bottom, no matter how hard he tried.

Karl knew he could never reveal his feelings. The way the doctor ignored him here in Cologne pained him. Yes, they took lunch together and saw each other at the Golden Crown Inn at nights, but Faust was never really with him. His mind was always with that arrogant Agrippa, whose company the doctor found much more stimulating than a conversation with his ignorant assistant. Karl's frustration had edged him from one liaison into the next, even though he hadn't felt good about it. His latest lover in particular seemed a little creepy. He was a pretty lad with hair just as black as the doctor's. But his eyes had something calculating—nasty, even. A few times when they were lying next to each other at night, Karl had sensed the boy's eyes on him. His looks burned like glowing pieces of coal. But as soon as Karl had opened his own eyes, the boy had only smiled at him and covered him in kisses. Just now Karl had been with him again, but this time he'd felt too uncomfortable and had run outside.

Still drunk, Karl got to his feet and wiped his mouth, a bitter flavor on his tongue. He needed this to end! He would go to the doctor and ask to be released. Faust would give him back his letters, and Karl would move on and try to forget the doctor. It would be the best for everyone.

With unsteady steps, Karl walked along the Rhine while rain fell from the sky like cold tears. He had bribed the guards to leave the small gate by the Franken Tower unlocked. The guards made good money with men like him. Only a few years ago it was revealed that more than two hundred respected citizens of Cologne were engaging in sodomy. The whole affair had been swept under the carpet, and until this day honest husbands sneaked through the gate down to the houses of ill repute by the Rhine. Karl looked up at the tower that served as a jail and reminded him of what was in store for him should he be discovered.

Gently, he pushed against the gate. It opened. As soon as he was through he noticed movement in the alcove below the tower. To his relief he realized it was just one of the guards, and the man winked at him conspiratorially. Karl was about to walk past him when the soldier suddenly blocked his way. The man's expression darkened and he drew his sword.

"This is Wagner, the sodomite!" shouted the guard over his shoulder, and Karl saw more men move in the darkness. "Get him!"

Karl heard heavy footsteps, and then men with swords and pikes rushed toward him. The scene had a dreamlike quality to it; everything seemed to move slower than normally. Strangely, Karl felt no fear in that moment. All his senses were entirely focused on survival.

Before the soldiers reached him, he feinted to the right and then dashed past the astonished guard on the left. Even as a small boy Karl had always been one of the quickest. He raced like a hare and swerved left and right while a crossbow bolt whirred past his ear. Behind him the men yelled; Karl stumbled, caught himself, and stormed into a narrow alleyway. He knocked over a barrel, pressed on, and heard angry shouts behind him. He ran aimlessly through the maze of lanes, turning left here and right there until he came to the edge of the larger street that led from the port to the cathedral.

Panicked, gasping for breath, and with a wildly beating heart, Karl looked around. The men had gone. The rain was pouring down and made the moonless night even darker than it already was. It was unlikely that they'd find him now.

At first, a wave of relief washed through him. He had actually managed to shake off the soldiers. But then fear returned, doubly powerful. He was a wanted sodomite—torture and the stake awaited him. The memory of smoke and the smell of burning flesh returned. Karl started to tremble uncontrollably while he feverishly tried to figure out what to do next. Someone must have betrayed him. There was no other explanation for the fact that the fellow at the gate called him by his name.

And if they knew who he was, they'd also know whose assistant he was.

Exhausted and close to tears, Karl leaned against the wall of a house. All was lost! He couldn't return to the inn. Worse still: the doctor himself was in danger of being arrested as a sodomite. Maybe that was the real reason his bribe did no good: they were looking for a reason to arrest the sorcerer and necromancer Doctor Faustus. Karl had to warn him. That was the least he could do.

Still breathing heavily, he sneaked along the dark lane toward the cathedral. The Golden Crown Inn, a freshly whitewashed half-timbered house with crown-glass windows, stood just a stone's throw away. When Karl had a good view of the front door, he cowered in a niche between houses and piles of foul-smelling waste and waited. If he was lucky, Faust was still with Agrippa.

Rats scurried around his feet, and a night watchman walked past very closely without seeing him. After about half an hour, when Karl was soaked to the skin, a man wearing a blue-and-black cloak and a floppy hat approached the inn from the cathedral. Karl breathed a sigh of relief. It was the doctor. With Satan by his side, Faust walked with a spring in his step; Karl guessed the conversation with Agrippa had left the doctor in high spirits. Jealousy flared up in the young assistant, but only for a moment. Then he cautiously stepped out into the street and waved.

Faust took a few moments to recognize him, and even then he approached only reluctantly. When the doctor came closer to Karl, he wrinkled his nose. Satan growled and sniffed at Karl's filthy trousers.

"What happened to you?" asked Faust gruffly. "Did you wallow in the muck?"

"Something . . . something dreadful has happened, Master," burst out Karl. "By God, I . . . I'm so sorry."

Faust immediately turned serious. "What is it? Speak up!"

"May heaven forgive me. I am wanted as a sodomite and I . . . I fear so are you."

As quickly as he could, Karl told the doctor about his visit to the Black Whale, the events at the Franken Tower, and his escape. To his surprise, the doctor remained calm.

"You said they knew your name. That's bad—very bad," he muttered. "You're right. We can't go back to the inn. Nor to Agrippa if we don't want to drag him into this. But where can we go? Where . . . ?" Faust closed his eyes and rubbed his nose.

"Maybe if I hand myself in," whimpered Karl. "If I tell them that you have nothing to do with any of this—"

"Shut up!" barked Faust. "They will try to use it against me one way or another. I should never have—" He broke off and shook his head. "Whatever has happened, we must look ahead now. This running away must come to an end."

"What do you mean?" Karl looked at his master expectantly. "What are you thinking?"

"Listen closely to what I tell you," replied Faust quietly. "We'll only get out of this if we don't make any mistakes now."

"Where . . . where do you want to go?" asked Karl. "The power of the Cologne Inquisition reaches far."

The doctor nodded resolutely as if he'd just made an important decision. The rain was still beating down on them, and small waterfalls ran off Faust's hat.

"I think I know a place where we can stay awhile," said Faust eventually. "I haven't been there in a long time, but it's an ideal place to hide out for a winter—or for as long as it takes until they've forgotten about us again. I should have gone back there much sooner. There is something that might help to answer my questions." His gaze turned into the distance before he spoke again.

"It is a tower."

~

From a window on the second floor of the inn, a man watched as the doctor and his assistant walked away toward the hay market. He could only just make out their outlines through the windows. A liquid as red as blood gleamed in the expensive glass goblet he was holding. The man took a long sip, licked his lips, and smiled.

The end and the beginning were near.

When the doctor had sought out Heinrich Agrippa, the man had been a little concerned. He didn't want Faustus to learn too much—not yet. Even though it most likely wouldn't change his destiny now.

His destiny was written in the stars. Impossible to change.

Still, he'd wanted to avoid those two scholars taking their musings too far. And so he'd intervened. It had been so easy to lure young Karl Wagner in. Everyone had their weak point, their little secret, and it hadn't taken long to find out his.

The man ran his finger along the glass rim of his goblet, creating a humming, almost whining sound. His plan had been for the boy to get caught and tortured, and maybe even executed. It had annoyed him for a while now that Faustus had a companion. The doctor was weakest by himself, and most easily steered. Once his assistant had been arrested, Faust couldn't have stayed in

Cologne any longer, and his conversations with Agrippa would have come to an end.

The man took another sip of the delicious red drink. Well, now they were running away together. He'd save Karl for later. The most important thing was that he didn't lose Faust again like he'd done before. It had taken him a long time to find him once more. Now that the portentous moment had nearly arrived, he couldn't lose sight of him. He had watched Faust from a distance for years, had helped him occasionally, and had even removed obstacles from his path. But for a few weeks now he had followed him closely, like a sleuth.

The end and the beginning.

Only a few more months.

The man took one last sip, then he carried his goblet over to the cage with the birds, who greeted him with cawing and flapping.

"Here you go, my little ones," said Tonio del Moravia, pouring the rest of the red drink from the glass into the bottom of the cage. "Drink! Drink with me to the day that must come soon. We have waited long enough."

The birds greedily drank up the fresh blood. Standing in the twilight of the candles in the room, the master looked like he hadn't aged one day.

23

CREAKING AND GROANING, THE WAGON SPED ALONG THE
road by the river. It was still raining when the first glimmer of dawn appeared
above the vineyards in the east.

Johann had been whipping the horse like a madman for almost three hours.
He wanted to get as many miles between them and Cologne as possible before
the guards raised the alarm. Most likely, a delegation of soldiers was already on
its way to catch them. Johann didn't want to begin to imagine what was in store
for them if they got arrested. Two sodomites and heretics dabbling in black
magic! It was just what the Cologne Inquisition had been waiting for, and Karl
had walked straight into their trap.

After Karl had told Johann about his escape, they had rushed to Agrippa's
house. Their wagon was parked there, and Agrippa was the only one who could
help them now. With his connections and a pile of money, they had managed
to get out of the city. A brief hug goodbye had been the only farewell the two
scholars had time for. They had hastily reassured one another that they'd meet
again one day and continue their conversations.

But they'd already had the most important conversation.

Johann knew there was only one place where he might lift the secret surrounding his birth. Agrippa had sparked the idea a few days ago, but only last
night had its meaning become clear to him. They had spoken about lenses,
about eye glasses, and about the laterna magica, and then Agrippa had said
something else.

But what if we could also better see what's in the heavens? If we could see farther,
we might understand what makes your birth so special.

Johann knew of an apparatus that might enable him to do just that. But it was hidden at a very dangerous place—a place he hadn't sought out in more than fifteen years. He didn't know if Tonio still visited the place.

Back in the wagon, Satan whined. The old dog wasn't well. She struggled to walk at all now and seemed to be in grave pain, especially after eating. She slept a lot and twitched in her sleep. Johann had given her some theriac to soothe her, but he feared the worst.

I'm going to lose her. Just like I've lost everyone else I ever loved . . .

At least he'd been able to save Karl Wagner. Johann nodded grimly. It had been his fault—he hadn't looked after the boy. The meetings with Agrippa had been more important to him. Just like something had always been more important to him than those he loved. Karl was sitting beside him in silence, only occasionally casting a suffering glance at him that looked much like Satan's.

"Stop looking at me like that," snarled Johann. "What's done is done. I warned you, but I also should have looked after you more."

"I'm so sorry," pleaded Karl. "You and Agrippa—"

"Agrippa and I were reaching the end of our discussions anyhow," said Johann. "I found what I came for. It's time this journey came to an end."

"You said something similar in Cologne," replied Karl. "What do you mean? What journey?"

"The journey of my life."

Johann cracked his whip and shouted at the horse while the wind tore at the wagon's canvas.

They traveled along the Rhine toward Worms, the old imperial city. A stab went through Johann's heart when he thought about the fact that Valentin had been taken to this city to stand trial for heresy. As if the heavens were punishing him, the weather grew worse by the day. It was the coldest fall since anyone could remember, and winter was already making its presence felt at the end of October. An icy wind swept across the plains and bare fields. After about two weeks they crossed the border to Bavaria, where the Alps formed a white chain on the horizon. Johann grew more withdrawn by the day. Every time he looked at that mountain range, the memories returned—memories of Salome and Venice, but also of his time at the tower with Tonio.

The tower.

More than fifteen years ago, Tonio had introduced him to the secrets of the black guild there, but to this day Johann didn't know what the master had really been up to during those cold winter nights. Johann had avoided the area since, almost as if he feared Tonio might be waiting for him there and once again draw him into his dark rituals. But despite his unease about the place, Johann hadn't forgotten what they had buried inside a heavy crate behind the tower upon their departure.

Books and a tube.

A tube that might allow him to see the stars up close. Johann hoped it was still there.

After ten more days they reached the Alps. Meanwhile, winter had fully arrived. The snow wasn't hip deep like the first time Johann had traveled this road, but they still struggled to find the right track between the low-hanging branches. Occasionally they were forced to jump off the wagon and lead the horse through snowdrifts. In the sky above them, crows circled, and Johann tried not to think of them as Tonio's crows. In the last few days, he had frequently heard the cawing of a raven that sounded human, almost like laughter.

Sheel . . . draay . . . sheel . . . draay . . .

Finally, after more than three weeks and a long search, they arrived at the tower.

It still stood atop the hill like a broken tooth, an ancient bulwark at the edge of the Alps. The shed beside it was derelict now, but the entrance to the tower was still barred with the heavy beam, and the windows were still nailed shut the way they'd left it.

Johann breathed a sigh of relief at the sight of the solid black walls. Evidently there hadn't been any unwelcome visitors. Strange, really, because the tower stood in an elevated position and could be spotted from other hills. It was as if it was surrounded by an invisible line that only a few people dared to cross. The black pentagram on the front door probably helped—the drawing looked as clear as on the day of their hasty departure.

Johann jumped off the box seat and rushed to the tower's rear. He swept the snow aside with his feet and saw to his relief that the white stones were still in place. No one had dug around here. Then he walked back to the front and removed the beam from the entrance. He found the large key under the stone plate and turned it in the lock. The door creaked open, and a musty smell like from an ancient crypt engulfed them. It took a few moments for Johann's eyes to adjust to the dim light. At first he thought everything was as they had left it. But then he noticed the changes.

Very unsettling changes.

"This is fantastic!" exclaimed Karl from next to Johann. "I expected a filthy hole—but this looks like a knight's chamber."

Johann said nothing as he studied the furnishings. There was a newly made pinewood shelf, holding about two dozen books. Next to it stood a velvet-covered four-poster bed, a silver-studded chest, and a table with chess pieces made from ivory. Behind a folding screen by the fire stood another bed, and this one was covered in dozens of soft cushions and furs. Johann ran his fingers through the dust that had settled on the pillows.

He was here. But when?

"The complete works of Aristotle are on this shelf," said Karl. The young man had walked into the room and was pulling out books. "Ha! And if I'm not mistaken, this is Avicenna's book on healing. At Leipzig they always told us that it was burned as a work of heresy. Did you furnish this place so nicely and collect all these volumes?"

"A . . . an old friend of mine did," said Johann vaguely. His heart was beating wildly, and once more he felt he was being watched. Tonio had visited the tower in recent years and turned it into a comfortable home. Table, chest, and bed were covered in a thick layer of dust, so he guessed the last visit was a while ago—over a year, perhaps.

But who could tell when the master would return?

Strangely, Tonio hadn't unearthed the crate out back, not as far as Johann could tell, anyhow.

"You're not afraid of black magic, I take it?" said Karl, who was holding up a book with a pentagram on its leather binding.

Johann started when he read the embellished title: *The Sworn Book of Honorius*. It was one of the books he'd read at Signore Barbarese's back in Venice. How on earth had it gotten to the tower? It must have been a different edition. There was no other explanation.

"Put it back," said Johann. "Now. It's not suitable for you. Or for me," he added quietly.

He waited until Karl had placed the book back on the shelf, then he gestured upstairs. "You sleep on the second floor. There's another bed. A bit of fresh straw and some cushions should make it homely enough. The third floor is out of bounds for you, just like the rooftop—you hear me?"

Karl nodded.

"Good," said Johann. "And you'd do well to remember my words. If I ever catch you up there, I'll skin you like a rabbit. Now help me bring Satan inside and light a fire before we freeze to death."

As they got the fire going together, Johann remembered how Tonio had once used almost the exact same words with him. That was a long time ago.

But right at that moment it felt as though no time at all had passed.

They spent the following weeks almost exclusively in the bottommost chamber. Apart from brief trips outside, Satan was always sleeping by the fire. They read a lot and played chess, and Karl's skills improved with each match. Johann still beat him most of the time, but the games were no longer as boring. Sometimes Johann even had to think a little harder. Karl increasingly enjoyed the challenge.

"Ha, you're stumped. Admit it!" he said one time when Johann was taking particularly long to make his move. "I'm making you sweat."

"If anything is making me sweat, it's the damned fire," growled Johann. "You put far too many logs on. It's as hot in here as the pyre you twice narrowly avoided."

Karl's only response was a sheepish look. But there was also something else in his eyes, something Johann couldn't read. He would notice those looks more frequently over the coming weeks but never understand them. Johann was too preoccupied.

On the very first day they'd arrived, Johann had dug up the crate behind the tower and opened it nervously. The tube and books had been wrapped in waxed cloths and were undamaged. Many of the carefully hidden works were about astronomy. Johann found countless rows of tiny numbers and symbols in the margins of the books. It looked as though Tonio had made coded entries, almost like secret messages the master had left for him. Johann thought about the coded messages he and Margarethe had written to each other in Knittlingen. Surely there was a solution to this riddle, too, some kind of key to read the rows of numbers. But try as he might, he couldn't figure it out.

Johann spent many hours trying to solve the mystery, during the day as well as at night. He started with fright every time there was a noise outside—snow falling off the trees, a startled wildcat on the prowl, or the goddamned cawing of the crows. With every sound he thought Tonio had returned.

But the master didn't come. Maybe he had left this place for good?

During clear nights, Johann climbed atop the platform and watched the stars. After a few failed attempts he had finally managed to set up the tube. It wasn't so different from the laterna magica: on the inside were lenses that improved one's eyesight so much that the stars stood clear and bright before him. Everything that usually seemed so far away appeared suddenly within reach. The moon—normally a round yellowish disc with blurred edges—was suddenly covered in craters and lakes of sand, almost like a small version of the Earth. The planets, too, and even the constellations of the eighth sphere were much clearer through the tube.

But Johann still couldn't tell what lay beyond the eighth sphere; he guessed the lenses weren't quite strong enough. And so he hadn't come an inch closer to answering his pressing questions.

He had tried to inspect the lenses closely without taking them out. They appeared to be cut better and more precisely than anything he'd ever seen from glaziers in the empire. They seemed like small miracles to Johann, and not for the first time he asked himself where Tonio had gotten the apparatus. He had never seen anything like it anywhere, not at any courts or at any universities.

As if it stemmed from a foreign world.

Satan enjoyed the warmth and barely ever left the fireplace. Johann always tried to feed her the best cuts of meat, but the dog hardly ate anything. She grew skinnier and skinnier, only lapping up the theriac from time to time. Every time Johann stroked the large animal, she looked at him with loyal eyes. Those eyes nearly broke his heart.

What am I supposed to do when you're no longer with me? he wondered before calling himself a fool for posing such a question to an animal.

On their journey to the tower, they had bought enough provisions so they wouldn't have to go into the village. By now it was snowing so heavily that they couldn't have gone far even if they'd wanted to. The snow piled up outside the door and the windows, so that they had to shovel their way out every time they needed more firewood.

"I feel like we're imprisoned," moaned Karl one afternoon when they once again sat together over a game of chess.

"Don't talk nonsense," said Johann as he took Karl's queen. "I told you once before: you could be sitting in Cologne right now, waiting to be burned at the stake."

"Then why can't I at least go up to the third floor? Or up on the platform? That thing you use to watch the stars with . . . does it really bring them that much closer?"

"I said no, and that's my final word on the matter." Johann checkmated his student with his next move, turned the board around, and sorted the pieces anew. "From the beginning. You're black this time."

In fact, Johann didn't really know why he wouldn't allow Karl upstairs. There was nothing there. Only a faded brownish pentagram that wouldn't go away. Just like the bad memories.

A pile of dirty, torn children's clothes.

Johann had tried to wash away the pentagram many times—in vain. It remained a steady reminder that Tonio might return at any moment.

Satan died during one particularly cold night in December. The evening before, she had rested by the fire and lapped up a bit of theriac, and the following morning, Johann found her cold and stiff like a log—a giant skeleton held together by a bit of shaggy fur.

Johann knelt down beside her and stroked her for a long time. He remembered all the wonderful moments they'd shared. Satan had been his companion since his escape from Heidelberg, and even though she was only a dog, Johann loved her more than he'd loved most people. He curled up beside her and tried to feel the last bit of warmth. But there was nothing.

Over the last few weeks, he'd tried everything he could to help Satan. He had collected spruce sprouts and brewed a medicine from them, and he had palpated Satan's abdomen. Toward the back he had found a hardened area, and from then on he had known there was no hope. All he could do was try to ease her pain. Despite his grief, Johann was relieved that Satan had died naturally that night. If the dog had suffered for much longer, he would have had to put her down. He didn't think he would have been capable of cutting her throat.

They buried her behind the tower, in the hole where the crate with the tube and the books had been hidden. Praying seemed inappropriate to Johann, but he remained standing at the grave for a long while, in spite of the bitter cold and the icy wind that cut through his clothes like knives. Karl stayed with him for a while before sighing deeply, giving Johann one last sympathetic look, and returning to the tower's warmth.

Johann was like an empty shell for the following days. Not even chess brought him joy, and he gave up watching the stars. He had placed all his hopes on finding the secret of his life here at the tower, but he found nothing. He had been wrong. Now that Satan was dead, he had lost all remaining willpower, the force that had kept him going and pushed him on since childhood. All he ever did now was stare into the fire. He felt so tired—so many years of traveling that had been nothing but an attempt to run from himself. What had all his cleverness, all his knowledge brought him? He stayed sitting in front of the fireplace until late at night and watched the embers die.

On the third day, Karl disappeared.

He hadn't come downstairs in the morning, and when Johann checked in his chamber he found the bed empty. Karl must have sneaked past him in the early hours, when Johann had nodded off, and left him for good. Johann couldn't blame him. He knew full well that the years had turned him into a choleric, imperious, and sometimes plainly unbearable man. Now that his will to live had left him, he wasn't even a good teacher any longer. What was the young man supposed to hang around with him for? If he didn't get caught for sodomy, Karl had a promising future. He was intelligent and inquisitive, though perhaps a tad too soft for this world. When Johann thought of him, he suddenly felt real affection.

Too late.

The only thing that puzzled Johann was the fact that Karl had taken neither provisions nor blankets. And the horse was still there. How did the boy think he was going to get by in the mountains?

Johann remained sitting in front of the cold fireplace for hours while a blizzard raged outside. He considered ending his life. He would simply have to go out into the snow, lie down, and go to sleep. Although it would be more appropriate to cut his wrists with the knife Tonio had given him.

The master seemed to pursue him right until death, just like Gilles de Rais, this foreign-sounding name that had never left him in peace. The mystery about that man remained unsolved. Once again Johann asked himself whether Agrippa may have known something about Gilles de Rais after all. But now it was too late to ask him.

It was too late for everything.

A raven cawed outside. Three times, like a knock on the door.

Johann stood up abruptly, hesitated for a moment, then walked over to one of the chests.

You damned beast! You won't get me!

Never again would Tonio have any power over him! There was only one way to get away from him, and Johann was ready to choose that way. The knife with the strange initials sat at the very bottom of the chest. Johann lifted it out and ran his thumb over the razor-sharp blade. It looked like it was as old as the world, forged from the molten lava of volcanoes.

One cut and all his searching would come to an end.

Then he would finally join Margarethe, Valentin, Martin, his mother—everyone he had left and disappointed.

Only one cut.

Johann gripped the knife hard and raised it as if he were performing a ritualistic sacrifice.

You won't get me.

Just then, he heard a noise. A soft creaking of the door. Johann felt certain that it was Tonio. The master had come to get him.

But it wasn't Tonio. It was Karl. He was covered in snow from head to toe like a white monster, and his cheeks glowed red. Water dripped to the ground and formed a small puddle.

Johann lowered the blade with a trembling hand. He fought back tears. For the first time in a long while he was deeply touched. Something had burst through the cold armor of his heart, and it hadn't been a knife. The boy hadn't left him! Karl was standing in the door with a shy smile on his lips and a dirty rag in his hands that seemed to be wrapped around something woolly. The bundle whimpered and squirmed. Karl gently set it down and unwrapped it.

It was a puppy with wiry pitch-black fur. It wagged its tail and started to explore the room on unsteady paws.

"I couldn't bear your gloomy face any longer," said Karl. "So I went out to look for something that would make you happy again." He gestured at the little dog, which was awkwardly making its way toward Johann. "I found it with a shepherd not far from the village. It's a wolfhound. I know—it doesn't look like much now. But apparently it's going to grow to be an enormous beast. You could name him Satan." Karl winked. "It's a boy this time. I checked."

"Little Satan," said Johann softly, leaning down to the puppy and holding out his hand. The animal cautiously walked up to him and licked his palm. It tickled, and Johann couldn't help but smile.

"Thank you," he said to Karl. "I . . . I'll never forget this." He cleared his throat, which felt awfully dry. He realized that he hadn't uttered a word in days.

Karl shrugged, his eyes flickered, and he looked down. "To be honest, I don't like dogs very much. But I was looking for a gift for you, and the pup seemed like a sign from God."

Johann picked up the little creature and patted it. "A sign from God?"

"Don't you know, Master?" Karl said with a grin. "It's Christmas Eve. I wish you a merry Christmas!"

Outside, the snow continued to fall.

In hindsight, Johann thought that Karl's return had also been a sign from God. He had been only a second away from ending his life—on the day of Christ's birth. But the little puppy and Karl's return gave him renewed hope. Johann remembered how sad it had been to spend Christmas at the tower alone with Tonio while the church bells of the village tolled in the distance. This time, the two men were drinking sweet Rhenish wine and eating pickled eggs and ham. Even the pup got a few mouthfuls.

Johann liked the idea of calling him Little Satan, just as if the old Satan was living on inside this pup. And the young dog lived up to its name: it destroyed pillows, chewed on chair legs, and ruined the fabric of the valuable four-poster bed. It was clear he'd be a very vivacious dog. During the days following Christmas, he and Johann formed a strong bond. Little Satan would lie on his lap while Johann once more studied books for answers to his questions; the dog played around Johann's feet when he gazed at the stars from atop the tower. Johann now allowed Karl on the platform, too. Together they watched the constellations of the winter sky.

"The stars are much brighter in the winter," explained Johann on New Year's Eve. "Do you see the winter hexagon over there? Sirius, Pollux, and Procyon in

Canis Minor. If you look through the tube, you'll see more constellations behind it—constellations we would never see with our bare eyes."

Karl stared through the tube into the night sky; his jaw dropped with amazement. "There are so many," he muttered. "And there are more and more behind them. The sky is endless."

"Yes. It's enough to make you dizzy."

"Ha!" Karl cried out with surprise. "I saw a shooting star! My mother—God rest her soul—always used to say I could make a wish if I saw one."

"Well, then, make a wish," said Johann with a smile. "But don't tell me—that would bring misfortune."

Karl shot a quick look at him before shaking his head with a sigh. "What I wish for won't come true anyhow." He turned back to the tube. "The shooting star has already disappeared. I wonder where it is now?"

"I heard that some of them fall down onto the Earth. Sometimes people find remains of strange rocks. Apparently a shooting star fell to the ground somewhere in the Alsace years ago. The emperor himself owns pieces of it—so they say. As for the others . . ." He gave a shrug. "Perhaps they simply burn out."

"Couldn't it be possible that they return? Like the stars and constellations that travel across the sky?"

"The scholars say that shooting stars—like comets—are merely evaporations in the sky, like gases that sometimes come out of the ground and start to burn. Agrippa doesn't agree, but—" Suddenly Johann broke off. Karl's questions had set off something inside him; thoughts that had hitherto been as unyielding as rocks suddenly began to flow like a river.

That they return . . .

"I must check something," he said curtly. He rushed down the stairs to the bookshelf in the bottom chamber. He pulled out the books with Tonio's notes and feverishly leafed through them. Suddenly all the numbers and formulas that had posed such a riddle to him were beginning to make sense. Johann closed his eyes and pictured the starry winter sky he'd just seen from the rooftop. He tried to visualize a grid against it. When he opened his eyes again and studied the numbers, it became obvious. The numbers and letters were coordinates. They described positions, but apparently not of stars. Dates and times were written down, and even today's date was among them. The positions on the paper changed much faster than would be the case with stars. And finally Johann realized what Tonio's coded records were about. He sat down as the weight of the realization sank in.

They described the paths of comets.

Johann spent the next few hours bent over the books in deep concentration, completely unaware of anything else around him, while Little Satan played and frolicked at his feet. Karl had gone to bed.

Johann went through the numbers row by row. What Tonio had done here was incredible! Comets were considered messengers of ill omens, warnings of wars or epidemics, or signs of good fortune. But it was impossible to predict when they would come. Tonio, however, had written down countless paths of comets spanning decades. Most of them couldn't be seen with the naked eye, but it was Tonio's theory that they returned, just like the moon and stars, which also had their regular paths. But the time spans between each visit were so great that no one had ever noticed. Some comets came every seventy years, others every ten, thirty, or forty. Johann wondered whether the star of Bethlehem from the day of Jesus Christ's birth also returned in a certain rhythm.

With great excitement, Johann leafed back through the tattered pages to the beginning. The first entries were dated so far back that they couldn't be from Tonio—unless they were based on more-recent calculations. They went back centuries—back to the conquest of England by the Normans; back to the times of the Romans, when Vesuvius broke out in Italy and swallowed a whole city. And indeed, the star of Bethlehem was also recorded and even marked with red. Tonio had written the word *Messiah* above it. Johann couldn't remember ever seeing any records like the ones he was looking at. He took notes, compared entries to books on astronomy, and finally, when dawn was already breaking, he came across the one entry he'd been looking for all along. The secret of his day of birth.

There had been a comet in the heavens on the day he was born. And Tonio had given it a name.

Larua.

Johann shuddered. *Larua* was an Old Latin word for an evil spirit. A comet that brought evil. When Johann followed the rows of numbers with trembling fingers, he found that Larua returned in regular intervals, namely every sixteen years and eleven months—every seventeen years, roughly speaking.

Every seventeen years.

Johann counted. If he was born in April 1478, the comet must have next appeared in late March of 1495. A shiver ran down his spine. That was precisely when he'd been at Nördlingen and Tonio had given him the black potion. He remembered Tonio telling Poitou that they couldn't wait any longer because the stars were favorable. Johann continued to count with a thumping heart. He wrote down the date and stared at it.

End of February 1512.

That was in two months! Was that the explanation for the feeling of being watched all the time? The tense expectation that something was about to happen? But what?

Larua . . . evil spirit . . .

Johann remembered Margarethe talking about the boogeyman in Heidelberg. *He will return,* she'd said. *He will return and change the world.*

Johann had always assumed that she'd only imagined this boogeyman, or perhaps that it was some sort of scoundrel—a rogue in the woods.

But he'd never have guessed it was a comet.

He put down his quill and leaned back. His eyes hurt from all the reading. Could it be possible? And if so, what did he have to do with it all? What was the meaning of being born on Larua's day, on the day of the prophet, and why had Tonio given him the black potion on the day of the comet's return?

And most importantly, what was going to happen in two months' time?

Johann spent the following days and weeks pondering the matter and consulting the books. He found no further answers, but at least he knew now that he had to wait. Something was going to happen. His will to live had returned. During the day, he often went for walks with Little Satan and Karl and spent time atop the platform. He enjoyed the fresh air stimulating his thoughts and the easy conversations with Karl as they roamed through the woods. He still spotted crows in the branches of trees, and one time even a raven, but they no longer frightened him. They were envoys of an event that would inevitably arrive, and he would be prepared—for whatever might happen.

And then something really did happen. It was a day in early February, and Johann was standing atop the tower, wrapped in his warm coat and wearing his floppy hat, gazing at the mountains through the tube. An ice-cold wind was blowing hard into Johann's face, but there could be no doubt.

A horseman was approaching from the edge of the woods.

At first it was just a dark spot, as if a fly had landed on the front of the tube. But the spot was growing as it moved along the road. Then the figure turned off the main road and took the narrow dirt track that led to the tower.

Johann was still standing on the rooftop. Now he watched the rider's approach with his bare eyes. He was a tall man wearing a coat and a sparkling cuirass underneath. A longsword was fastened to a bag behind the saddle. The horse was black and powerful, no cheap nag but a destrier that probably cost as much as a whole tavern.

Now the man had spotted Johann. He raised his hand in greeting, galloped the last few yards up the hill, and climbed off his horse.

Then he waited.

Pensively, Johann climbed down the stairs. He didn't know who the stranger was or what had brought him to the tower. At least the man had come alone—so clearly this wasn't about arresting him and taking him to jail. Could he be a delegate from the bishop of Cologne? Johann doubted the power of the Cologne Inquisition reached this far. And the horseman looked not like a man of the church but more like a knight.

Could he be the first messenger of what was to come? A first sign of Larua's return?

"What's happened?" asked Karl, who was sitting at the chess table with a book. He looked up with confusion as Johann strode past him toward the door.

"We have a visitor. And it isn't anyone from the village."

He took one last deep breath before opening the door and stepping outside. The man awaiting him indeed seemed to be a knight. He was wearing armor, and now Johann also saw the black cross on his coat. It was the cross of the Teutonic Knights—an ancient order that had been formed in the times of the Crusades and that still wielded a lot of influence at courts throughout the empire. Johann was startled.

What in God's name could the Teutonic Knights want from him?

"Are you Doctor Johann Georg Faustus?" asked the knight, who looked like an old battle-axe with countless scars on his face. He was at least six feet tall and of impressive stature. Johann nodded and said nothing.

"I've been sent by Wolfgang von Eisenhofen," said the knight, his harness creaking in the cold. "The commander of the Nuremberg Teutonic Knights. He asks you to come to Nuremberg. An old friend is waiting for you there."

"An old friend?" Johann raised an eyebrow. "His name?"

"I'm not permitted to say. You will be told everything else at Nuremberg."

Johann watched the man closely, but his expression gave away nothing. An icy gust swept across the hilltop and rattled the shutters. Karl had come up next to Johann and was studying the knight with curiosity. Behind them, Little Satan growled almost like a grown dog sensing danger.

"And you think that just because some mysterious friend wants to see me I'm going to follow you all the way to Nuremberg?" asked Johann sharply. "You'll have to give me a little more."

The knight nodded. "Your friend anticipated you would say something along those lines. That's why I have another message for you."

"Which is?"

"He said he could tell you more about Gilles de Rais."

Johann felt as though he had been struck by lightning. He stood rooted to the spot as the name echoed through his head. The name that had been pursuing him for more than fifteen years.

Gilles de Rais.

Now he was certain that the man from Nuremberg was the first sign of Larua.

The game had begun.

It took quite a while for Johann to regain the power of speech. Finally he cleared his throat.

"Give us an hour," he told the knight. "We're coming with you."

24

THE KNIGHT'S NAME WAS EBERHART VON STREITHAGEN, BUT they wouldn't learn much more about him in the following days. With Little Satan in the wagon, they followed him to the north, having packed the laterna magica, the stargazing tube, and some of the books on astrology. At first Karl had tried to ask Johann about the reason for their hasty departure, but he'd received only vague answers. Eventually, Johann said no more on the subject at all.

Johann had no idea what to expect in Nuremberg. The only people who knew about his interest in Gilles de Rais were Agrippa and Conrad Celtis, but the latter had died a few years ago, and Johann hadn't seen him since their last conversation at the castle in Heidelberg. Who else might know about it? The mysterious person knew that Gilles de Rais preoccupied Johann—and he'd sent for Johann just when a very special comet was about to return after seventeen years.

They traveled easily with Eberhart von Streithagen by their side. No highwayman was stupid enough to challenge an armored knight with a longsword on a warhorse. And even the robber knights, who had multiplied in recent years, steered clear of them. Streithagen didn't talk much, but from the little he told them, they learned that the Nuremberg command of the Teutonic Knights was one of the emperor's last strongholds inside the city. The free imperial city of Nuremberg, which answered only to the emperor, had increasingly turned away from its former benefactor in the last few years. But the Teutonic Knights stood firmly behind the regent, and their grounds within the city were untouchable.

Johann smiled grimly. At least he'd be safe from persecution by the Cologne Inquisition there. But what might the emperor or the Teutonic Knights want from him? And who was this strange old friend?

After ten very quiet days of traveling, and with terribly sore behinds from getting bounced around on the box seat, they finally arrived in Nuremberg around noon.

From afar, they could see the mighty castle rising like a crown above the double ring of the wall, as well as churches and many neat half-timbered houses. Johann gazed at the massive city wall; it was three miles long and contained over eighty towers, and Johann was filled with awe. He had visited so many cities, and during the last year he and Karl had crisscrossed the country—from the east to the north to the west to the south—but Nuremberg was something special. Augsburg might have been the wealthiest city in the empire, and Cologne the holiest; Erfurt was the most studious and Hamburg the most adventurous, but Nuremberg was the most inventive of all, with the most intelligent, witty, and resourceful citizens. The city was both the soul and the head of the empire at once—the unofficial capital in a country that didn't have a fixed political center. Not long ago a Nuremberg man named Peter Henlein had built a spring-driven clock small enough that it could be carried in the pocket of a vest. A certain Martin Behaim had ordered the construction of a globe here that showed the world as a ball and not as a flat disc. Many other technical inventions also came from Nuremberg, and many outstanding artists called this city home, including the famous Albrecht Dürer—one more reason for Karl to be excited about Nuremberg.

"Maybe we could even visit Dürer," he said to Johann as they, along with many other rattling wagons, oxcarts, and feisty merchants, neared the city. "A handsome man, by the way, this Dürer. I saw a self-portrait of him once. He painted himself almost like our savior, with long hair and a beard. I'd love to know what the church thinks of it." Karl laughed and shook his head. "I doubt the pope would appreciate man turning himself into God."

It was February, and in all directions the fields were still covered in snow. The land was barren and the Pegnitz River impassable, but several of the major routes through the empire met at Nuremberg, making the city like a spider in the center of a web. The merchants and smaller tradesmen the group passed were dressed in heavy coats and shapeless woolen hoods.

"I mean, you're not just anybody," Karl continued, "so a visit shouldn't be—"

"I'm not just anybody but a wanted sodomite and devil worshipper, remember?" said Johann, cutting him off. "I don't really think the Cologne Inquisition has any power here, but knowing people and their love of gossip, the story might have made it to Nuremberg, beefed up into a real horror story."

"Indeed, the doctor doesn't have the best reputation in town," said Eberhart von Streithagen, riding beside them on his large destrier. "They talk about necromancy and quite a few instances of fraud. And many churchmen disliked your friendship with Agrippa. Therefore, we won't enter through the large Frauentor Gate but through Spittlertor Gate. It's close to our headquarters and not as heavily guarded."

They followed a narrower road through the icy fields until they came to the moat and one of the smaller but solid city gates, which was flanked by an equally solid tower. Displayed above the gate was the double-headed eagle, the emperor's coat of arms. When the guards saw the badge of the Teutonic Knights, they waved through Streithagen and the wagon he accompanied without questions.

It was lunchtime, and the whole city seemed to be on the move despite the cold. Peddlers with their crates rushed past them; they could hear the cries of market women from a nearby square, and the steady hammering from a smithy rang in Johann's ears. The churches of Saint Sebaldus and Saint Lorenz rose above the sea of houses and the maze of narrow lanes and alleys, and right in among this maze flowed the Pegnitz, dividing the city in roughly even halves. The air smelled of fires, braised cabbage, and horse dung. Johann thought about the horrific stench of Hamburg in the summer; by comparison, the smell of Nuremberg in the winter was almost pleasant.

From the city wall, Eberhart von Streithagen led them a short distance through the noisy crowds into the city. It wasn't long before they came to a walled-in complex holding several houses and a small church. A kind of roofed walkway bridged the lane to a second, larger church. Johann had climbed off the wagon and now led the nervous horse by the reins. His hand instinctively shot to his purse when a few pedestrians bumped into him.

"We used to be outside the city, but since the last wall extension we are like an island in a sea of disbelievers," explained Streithagen with a dark expression as they neared a gate in the wall. "The last island of the German emperor, it seems to me. Leave the wagon here. Someone will bring it in later."

He knocked on a heavy portal that had been reinforced with iron. A guard eyed them suspiciously through a hatch before letting them in. On the other side of the wall, they found themselves in a large green courtyard from which further gates led to stone houses, gardens, and even fields. In contrast to the noise outside, it was peacefully quiet within the walls, and even the air was better. Little Satan jumped out of Johann's arms and peed against one of the bushes.

"What a lush piece of land you have here," said Johann appreciatively. "The emperor was most generous."

"In return we run the largest hospital in the city, aside from the Hospital of the Holy Ghost on Pegnitz Island," replied Eberhart von Streithagen. "As I'm sure you're aware, our motto is *Help, defend, and heal*."

"Probably more defending than helping and healing," whispered Karl to Johann. "The Teutonic Knights laid waste to the east of the empire once upon a time."

Johann shot him a glance of warning. He whistled Little Satan back, and they followed Streithagen through several guarded doors until they came to a large hall. Shields with various coats of arms decorated the walls, and mighty columns held up the elaborately carved oak ceiling. A round oak table stood in the center of the hall, and bent over a few documents at the table sat a haggard old knight with a bushy beard and a monk-like, half-bald head. His expression looked serious and grim. But when he looked up and noticed the visitors, a smile spread across his careworn face.

"My dear Eberhart!" he called out happily, rising to his feet. "The guards informed me of your arrival." His eyes turned to Johann and his smile vanished. "And this must be the famous Doctor Faustus—magician, astrologer, and necromancer by trade."

"Doctor is plenty," said Johann in reply and bowed his head. "Some titles are earned, while others are bestowed without one's asking for them." He tried to keep his tone neutral; he didn't know what game was being played here. He gestured at Karl. "This is my assistant, an itinerant scholar."

The older man gave Karl a brief nod without really looking at him, and then he continued to speak to Johann. "Well, Doctor, I only know you from a few hair-raising stories that I don't particularly like. The latest come from Cologne. But it would seem there are people who think very highly of you." He motioned for his guests to take a seat at the large table, which was covered in parchment scrolls and papers. Little Satan crawled under the table and started to gnaw on one of its legs.

"My name is Wolfgang von Eisenhofen, and I am the commander here," the older man continued. "I have asked you to Nuremberg because . . . well, because we have a problem. And an old friend of yours reckoned you were the only man in the empire who might be able to solve this problem."

"We shall see," replied Johann with a shrug, trying not to let his unrest show. "It would be kind if I were allowed to meet this old friend. I traveled a long way for him, after all. Perhaps I won't even recognize him."

"You're right. It is possible he . . . changed somewhat since you last met. He told me it was a while ago that you last saw each other." With a smile, the commander turned to Knight Eberhart, who had been waiting behind them. "Very well—bring him in."

Eberhart von Streithagen walked to the double doors on the opposite end of the hall and opened them. A hunched figure had been waiting on the other side.

Johann winced and felt the blood drain from his face.

"What in God's name—" he burst out.

Behind the door stood Valentin.

Johann's former friend from Heidelberg was almost completely bald. He looked like a wrinkly old man, much older than the thirty years he must be by now. He looked as though life had sucked him dry and tossed him aside.

Only Valentin's eyes still looked as intelligent and alert as they used to. They scrutinized Johann with a mixture of disgust, curiosity, and . . .

Affection . . . Could it be true?

Johann still sat at the table, unable to move. Was he dreaming? Last time he saw Valentin, his friend was being taken to the Inquisition at Worms inside a prison cell. That had been almost fifteen years ago. Back then, Valentin was most likely going to be charged with satanism—a crime that was invariably punished with death by fire. And now here he was, approaching Johann. Changed, perhaps, but alive.

Valentin's posture was strangely bent, like a hunchback; scars disfigured his face, and his right arm hung down limply. But then he raised the hand in greeting. It was bent like a claw and missing two fingers.

"Thumbscrews are a nasty instrument," Valentin said and waved the hand as if it were a scrap of meat. His voice sounded dry and hoarse—burnt, almost. "Nearly as bad as the glowing pincers, the smoldering pokers, and the rack they use to break your back very slowly."

"You . . . you're alive . . . ," whispered Johann.

"Well, part of me." Valentin shrugged, whereby one shoulder went higher than the other. "They tortured me for three weeks, twice a day, morning and afternoon. But I stayed strong. I had no idea what hidden strengths lay inside me." He gave a lopsided grin, and Johann saw that two of his front teeth were missing. "It was probably my hatred for you that kept me alive and made me deny everything. In the end they had to let me go. That's the beauty of torture: if you make it through without confessing, you're free sooner or later." He flinched with pain as he came closer to the table with dragging steps. "But not a day goes by when my back and my hand don't remind me of that time."

"I guess it wouldn't help if I said how sorry I was," said Johann.

"No, it wouldn't." Valentin gave a dry laugh. "But do you know what, old friend? Hatred doesn't make for good company. Just like love, it can consume a man. And so I buried my hatred. And I hope it will never rise from its grave again."

"It was *you* who asked me to come here?" said Johann with a shake of his head. "How in God's name did you find me?"

Valentin hesitated briefly. "One time in Heidelberg you told me about a tower near Füssen, remember? You said you spent a winter there once. When I heard about your trouble in Cologne, I thought the tower might be a good place to hide. And so I asked the commander to search for you."

Johann ran his hand through his hair, his fingers trembling slightly. He could hardly believe that his old friend was standing in front of him—alive. Evidently, he had been mistaken at the tower when he thought the knight was the first sign of the comet.

"I kept myself above water as a traveling scribe for a while, here and there, always on the move," Valentin continued after he sat down with them. "Three years ago, the Teutonic Knights offered me a permanent position here. We were happy here."

"We?" Johann frowned. "Who?"

"I guess you're wondering how I know about your interest in Gilles de Rais," said Valentin, ignoring Johann's question. "I must admit, the thought of you never quite left me in peace, Faustus. Like a flea that bites and itches. Even years later, when you were roaming the country as the famous Doctor Johann Georg Faustus, I still wanted to know what it is that drives you. Your hunger for knowledge that was never satiated no matter how many books you read, your constant musing. In your dreams in Heidelberg you often whispered the name Gilles de Rais. Sometimes you even screamed it. You used to scream a lot." Valentin smiled sadly. "You learn a lot from sharing a room with someone. A few years after my release I had the opportunity to speak with the great Conrad Celtis once more. It was shortly before his death. The name Gilles de Rais never ceased to fascinate him, either. He told me never to say that name out loud again."

"The name is mere noise and smoke," replied Johann weakly.

"Is it?" Valentin smirked. "In any case, Celtis told me that it was the same for you. I knew the name would bring you to Nuremberg. If I'd told Eberhart von Streithagen to give my own name, your bad conscience might have stopped you from coming. Therefore I decided on Gilles de Rais—and voilà, here you are." He hesitated. "I'm afraid Celtis didn't tell me everything about that villain back then. But a scribe has plenty of time to look around old monastery libraries, and over the years I've discovered a few things."

"So you know about the children," whispered Johann. Now he noticed his own trembling fingers.

"Yes, I know." Valentin nodded. "And that is also the reason you're here."

"Excuse me," said Karl, clearing his throat. "I hate to disturb two old friends, but maybe it's about time someone explained—"

Severe looks from both Valentin and Johann cut him off.

"Gilles de Rais was a knight," said Wolfgang von Eisenhofen. "Not a Teutonic Knight, or a templar, or a knight of Saint John, but still a man who at some point lived according to the laws of chivalry and Christian virtue. He fought against a dozen knights during the liberation of Orléans and won, and he was a brave companion to the famous Joan of Arc—allegedly they were something like friends. The French king even made him a marshal of France. All the worse, what he did later." The old man bit his lip and made the sign of the cross.

"But that's hardly the reason I'm here, is it?" asked Johann with growing irritation. "Just to hear what crimes that damned Gilles de Rais committed years ago? Conrad Celtis already told me."

"No." Valentin shook his head. "You're here because it looks as if Gilles de Rais has returned."

Johann froze. The hairs on the back of his neck stood on end as if an evil beast had entered the hall.

Had he heard right?

Gilles de Rais has returned . . .

"How can you say that—" he started.

"Of course, he hasn't actually returned." Valentin gestured dismissively. "I know the monster has been dead for seventy years. But his atrocities are happening again, now, here at Nuremberg. And no one knows who might be behind them."

Wolfgang von Eisenhofen pushed a document toward Johann. About two dozen names were written on the paper. "These are the names of Nuremberg children who have gone missing in the last few months," explained the commander with a shaking voice. "Some are the children of patricians, while others are the children of common citizens and even of day laborers. None of the children was older than ten. Some of them were later found dead in the alleys, tossed aside like trash. Their throats were slit. They had been bled dry. There wasn't a single drop of blood left inside them, and a dried toad was placed in their open mouths. Gilles de Rais used to murder children in a similar manner. He slit them open, bathed in their blood, and drank it. A strange coincidence, don't you think?"

"My God, how awful!" exclaimed Karl. "How can a person do such a thing?"

"There are those who say Gilles de Rais wasn't a person," said Valentin. "Three words were written beside each body—in blood." His rough voice echoed through the vaulted room. "*Homo Deus est.* Do you know them, Johann?"

Johann felt like someone had rammed a cudgel right into his stomach.

Homo Deus est . . . Man is God . . .

"Yes, I know them," he whispered.

Valentin eyed him closely. "It would seem you know more than I thought. I was right to send for you."

"I think very highly of Master Brander. He has been working for us as a scribe for a long while now. He is clever and well read, and it was his idea to find you," said Wolfgang von Eisenhofen, squeezing Valentin's good hand. "Even though he probably has his own reasons, too," he added ominously. "He reckoned you were the only one who might be able to shed light on those horrific cases. The mood in the city is worsening by the day, and the fear is almost tangible. It feels as if we are all sitting atop a powder keg that might explode at any moment."

"I still don't understand what I can do for you," said Johann. "I'm just an itinerant doctor, a stranger in Nuremberg—"

"If what your old friend says is true, you're not just any doctor but one of the most intelligent men in the empire, and one of the shrewdest." Eisenhofen gave him a sharp look. "And you're a magician. Children who've been bled, dried toads, words written in blood . . . Clearly, we are dealing with black magic." The commander paused, choosing his next words very carefully. "So, God help us, I fear only a magician can help us now. The city—the entire empire, even—is at stake! If word gets around that the devil is on the loose in Nuremberg, the emperor's power might become seriously threatened. And he has his hands full holding both the French and the Turks at bay. Yes, we need magic!"

"Magic? You don't believe that yourself," snarled Johann, shaking his head. "I may be a scholar with unusual methods, an astrologer, healer, and chiromancer. But I'm certainly not a magician who can stand up to the devil like Archangel Michael."

"Aren't you calling yourself a magician?" asked Eisenhofen sharply.

Johann sighed. "Only to impress the simple folk. A commander and nobleman should really know better."

"Well, if you prefer, I can hand you over to my knights, who will take you and your assistant to Cologne. The reward for your capture is several hundred guilders now—did you know that?"

"That's blackmail!" Johann jumped up and slammed his fist on the table. "Has the Order of Teutonic Knights sunk this low? Blackmail?"

"Watch your tongue, Doctor!" Eisenhofen also stood up, his eyes flashing angrily. Behind the commander, Eberhart von Streithagen took a step forward, his hand on the pommel of his sword. Below the table, Little Satan growled and bared his small, sharp teeth.

"Perhaps it's better if I speak with my friend alone for a moment," Valentin said and raised his arms in a placating gesture. "A walk in the fresh air would do us both good."

Eisenhofen hesitated, but then he nodded. He turned to Valentin. "Go into the garden and tell him the rest—everything. It might change his mind. I'm expecting an answer when the bells strike one o'clock." He raised a finger and gave Johann a stern look. "And don't forget, Herr Magician: it's only a week's ride to Cologne."

A short while later, Johann and Valentin were alone in a large, tidy garden that reached from behind the knights' hall to the western wall. Paths led in a star-shaped pattern past bushes, withered roses, and pruned young fruit trees. Little Satan ran about happily, lifting his leg against a bush occasionally. The plants and trees were covered in a thin layer of frost. Their footsteps made a crunching sound as the two former friends walked along the narrow paths. They said nothing for a long while, each lost in his own memories. Eventually Johann stopped.

"Believe me, Valentin, if I could turn back time—"

"Not even God can do that." Valentin stared straight ahead. "It took me a long time to understand. But now I know that love can sometimes be destructive."

"My love for Margarethe, you mean?" asked Johann quietly.

"Do you still love her?" Valentin asked and turned toward him.

Johann hesitated. "She . . . she visits me in my dreams. But unlike years ago, they aren't happy dreams."

Valentin nodded slowly. "I understand why you can't forget her. I would have loved to paint her." With a grimace of pain, he lifted up his crippled right hand. "I took a long time to learn to draw with my left. I'm not too bad at it now."

"You still draw?"

Valentin smiled, looking at the garden, at the trees and bushes and the stone benches that would make lovely places to rest awhile in spring and summer. "I spend a lot of time here in the garden. The light is excellent." He tilted his head and studied Johann. "Perhaps I should draw you, too. You're famous now, after all."

"Why did you want to speak with me alone?" asked Johann. "The commander said you ought to tell me everything. What did he mean?"

Valentin's face darkened. "I'm sure you wonder why I asked the commander to have you of all people brought here. It is true that I believe you're the only one who might be able to help. And you owe me a favor."

Johann nodded. "Any favor in the world. I would do anything to atone for my guilt."

"Then help me to free a child."

"A child?" Johann was confused. He thought perhaps he'd misheard. "How do you mean?"

Valentin swallowed hard. "Now we come to the real reason you're here. The reason Eisenhofen hasn't told you about."

He gestured for Johann to sit on a bench in the garden's center. Blackbirds were singing all around them, and sparrows argued in the branches. It seemed like spring had already arrived here, while outside the walls winter still reigned.

"Eisenhofen said that I had my own reasons for asking you to Nuremberg," said Valentin bitterly. "And it is true. There is a girl I've grown very fond of. A child from the gutter whom I took in a few years ago. I named her Greta."

"Greta?" whispered Johann. "You named her after—"

"It seemed appropriate," said Valentin gruffly. "Maybe because I love the girl just as much as you used to love Margarethe. But not as a man. I love Gretchen—that's my nickname for her—like a father loves his child. I raised her, and she's just turned fourteen. Don't they say the love for one's children is the most powerful of all? She calls me uncle. She has no one else in this world, and . . ." He paused. "And she is in grave danger."

"What do you mean?"

"She has never enjoyed a particularly good reputation in town. Since we've moved in at the command, she's been known as a bit of a tramp, and she's even stolen the odd apple or egg at the market. When they found her near one of the dead children by the Pegnitz one night a few weeks ago, the authorities made short shrift of her. They"—Valentin's voice trembled—"they put her in Loch Prison. Not least because they found something from the devil on her—a ram's horn with some sort of strange symbols. Someone must have slipped it in her pocket."

"And now the authorities believe the child has something to do with those devilish murders?" asked Johann with disbelief.

"Don't you get it?" His old friend fought back tears. "They are trying to pin something on my Gretchen! They want her to confess that she has been with Satan and want her to tell them what she knows about the murders. But she doesn't know anything! She's still a child! They just . . . they just need a scapegoat." Valentin squeezed Johann's hand with his uninjured left. "That is the real reason I wanted you to come to Nuremberg, Johann Georg Faustus. Please help me get my Greta out of jail!"

Johann bit his lip. So that was why he was here. Not because of some comet, not to find answers to his questions, but because of a child from the gutter. Or, to be more precise, to help a friend. The only friend he'd ever had.

To atone for my guilt, he thought.

"How long?" he asked.

Valentin wiped the tears from his scarred face. "What do you mean?"

"How long until they put her on trial, damn it?"

"I . . . I don't know. She's been in jail for nearly a month. Maybe they forgot about her, or maybe they've started with the torture by now. She's only fourteen, but I heard that even with younger children . . . I know what it's like. I know the pain." Tears streamed down Valentin's cheeks now, and he trembled all over. "I told the guards that Greta is a distant niece of mine, and so—with the help of the commander—I'm allowed to visit her every few days. Until now Eisenhofen has been able to prevent the worst from happening to her. He doesn't believe she is guilty of anything. But even the power of the Teutonic Knights is limited. We can't waste any more time!"

Johann ran his hands through his hair. "And what do you imagine I can do about it? I've heard about the Loch Prison—it's heavily fortified and lies deep below the city hall. I'd gladly do anything for you, but this is impossible!"

"There must be a way!"

Johann gave a desperate laugh. "Do you want me to make a demon appear with the laterna magica to chase the guards away? That might work in a small backwater, but not here."

Valentin eyed him sharply. "So you have a laterna again? I'd heard something along those lines. My laterna . . ." He closed his eyes for a moment. "No, it probably won't work with the laterna magica. But perhaps we'll think of something else." He leaned forward. "I've got a suggestion for you, Johann. Tomorrow I'm allowed to visit Gretchen again, and I want you to come with me. If you can take a look at the prison, we might come up with an idea. I will tell them that you're a medical expert and I want you to examine her. The commander will put in a good word."

"I'll see what I can do." Johann sighed and took Valentin by the hands. For a moment they were the old friends they used to be in Heidelberg. "But I can't promise anything. Perhaps—"

He broke off when they heard footsteps on the gravel. Then the bell of the order's church tolled once, and Eberhart von Streithagen appeared.

"The commander wishes to know how you have decided, Herr Doctor," he said.

Johann exchanged a glance with Valentin.

"I will try to help you," he replied at last. "With or without magic."

~

Deep down below the city, not far from the Teutonic Knights' gardens, something rumbled.

A monotonous humming followed, echoing against the walls of the corridors until it sounded like the howling of a hundred hungry wolves. In the ancient vaults below, a man wearing a black robe stood in front of a copper basin, his hands spread far apart, his head leaning back, as if he was worshipping something lurking much deeper still below. The man's robe was covered in old symbols, and it was woven from dried sinews and tiny veins that had been cut from young bodies with sharp knives. The humming grew louder, and the man dropped something slippery into the dark waters of the basin, causing the surface to ripple.

The man smiled.

Quite a peculiar juice is blood.

He was about to continue with his invocation when a cawing disturbed his litany. The man looked up with irritation.

"Baphomet, Azazel, Belial, stop it! Or I'm going to drown you in this basin!"

The two crows and the raven stared at their master from small, nasty eyes. They shuffled back and forth excitedly on the perch in their cage, like children who can no longer hold still. The man smiled.

"You're hungry, aren't you? Not long now."

The master reached into a bag, pulled out another slippery scrap, and tossed it to the birds.

They hacked into it, tearing the scrap apart with their sharp beaks and devouring the lumps of meat.

They were surprisingly tender.

25

VALENTIN WAS ALREADY WAITING IN THE GARDEN FOR
Johann shortly after sunrise. He looked like he hadn't slept much; his scarred
face was pale and unshaven, and dark shadows lay beneath his eyes. He got up
from the bench he'd been sitting on as soon as he spotted Johann, and limped
toward him.

"Good news from the commander! Eisenhofen managed to arrange for you
to accompany me as a physician. Gretchen kind of belongs to the command
staff, after all, and Eisenhofen has a right to know how she is doing."

"I still can't believe the Nuremberg authorities want to put a fourteen-year-
old girl on trial for witchcraft. That's ludicrous!"

"She wouldn't be the first," replied Valentin with a sigh. "But thankfully it
hasn't gone that far yet. Still—the long imprisonment is getting to her. Gretchen
is such a lively, inquisitive child, you know. My heart breaks every time I think
about her sitting down there in the prison cell, all alone . . ." Valentin's voice
trembled.

"You must love her very much," said Johann sympathetically.

"There's something about her . . . something familiar." Valentin hesitated.
"You'll meet her yourself soon."

They walked out the gate and headed north toward the Pegnitz. Valentin was
carrying a small leather pouch containing a few treats for the girl, and Johann
had brought a bag with medical instruments. The lanes were still quiet; only the
hammering from the blacksmiths at the armory near the old city moat echoed
through the city. A group of nuns walked toward the Klara nunnery, their lips
moving in silent prayer. Up at the castle, last night's watch fires still burned,
bathing the sandstone in a warm light.

Johann hadn't slept much, either. The commander had given him permission to set up his stargazing tube in the tower of Saint Jakob's Church. He'd spent hours searching the night sky for any sign of the approaching comet, but without any luck. Maybe he was mistaken and there was no connection between him and Larua at all? His trip to Nuremberg seemed to be for different reasons altogether.

They walked across a stone bridge that separated the Lorenz quarter from the wealthier Sebaldus quarter, where merchants had built their houses as close to the main square as possible. This square, which was just beginning to grow busy, was flanked on one side by another large church with an elaborately adorned facade. There also was a fountain like no other Johann had seen in the empire, with a tall, thin tower of sculptures in its center.

"There is something else you should know," said Valentin slowly as they crossed the large square. "Last night another child went missing. The eight-year-old son of a bailiff from the castle. The boy was playing in a dry part of the moat. When his mother went looking for him a few moments later, he was gone. It truly hearkens to the time in France when that malicious French knight was at large." Valentin bit his lip. "I'm afraid our time is running out. The people are becoming more and more nervous—they want an explanation. It won't be long before they torture Greta."

North of the fountain stood the city hall, a gloomy, Gothic building that seemed to be from a different era. The entrance to the infamous Loch Prison lay at its rear.

Johann was glad that he had left Little Satan with Karl. The dog was eating as if he had been starved for weeks, and it was truly amazing how fast he grew. He was already as big as a full-grown poodle, and he wasn't even ten weeks old yet. Little Satan's discipline wasn't coming along quite as fast as his size, however; last night he'd defecated inside the knights' hall, much to Eisenhofen's disgust. Johann didn't want to imagine what they'd do to him and the dog should he do the same inside the city hall.

In front of a small but solid gate, two guards armed with halberds and pikes watched the two arrivals with surly, tired expressions. With his crippled hand, Valentin pulled out a folded document and handed it to one of the men. The man studied the seal of the Teutonic Knights for a long while. Clearly, he couldn't read but didn't want to admit to it.

"Valentin Brander from the command," said Valentin after a while. He gestured at Johann. "This is a physician charged with the task of examining my niece."

"The cripple and the devil's girl." The guard grinned and scratched his unkempt beard. "Best the doctor examine the wench for witches' marks, too. I bet he'll find some."

"That is just what I am here for," replied Johann with the imperious voice of a physician who still has many other patients to visit that day. "So better let us in. Promptly, if you will."

Grumbling, the guards stepped aside, and Johann and Valentin entered a paved courtyard. To the left was another guarded door, and then stairs led them down below. After a third, ironclad door, they finally stood in the antechamber to the prison. Heavily smoking torches barely managed to light up the low, vaulted room. A cold breeze swept up from a well in the center of the chamber. It smelled of smoke, watery cabbage soup, and stale air. More guards were posted here.

We'll never get in here undetected, thought Johann. *Not with all the magic in the world.*

The prison keeper, a stooped, unwashed fellow who was responsible for the welfare and feeding of the prisoners, shuffled toward them and cast a bored glance inside their bags.

"They told me you were coming," he grumbled. "Not many prisoners get visited by two gentlemen with treats at once. First the lantern and now ham and cheese. Must have cost you a fortune. My food ain't good enough for the high-class lady, is that it?"

"The girl is my niece," replied Valentin curtly. "Please direct any further questions to the Order of Teutonic Knights."

The prison keeper waved dismissively and led them down a narrow corridor past several cell doors. Johann could hear moaning from behind some of the doors. He caught a few glimpses through the windows in the cell doors and saw that the pitiful creatures on the other side were chained to bench seats or had their hands and feet locked in wooden blocks. Symbols above the doors indicated the nature of the crime the inmate was accused of: a red rooster for an arsonist, a black cat for a traitor, and so on. In regular intervals, they had to pass through more locked doors, and each time the keeper had to find the corresponding key on a large ring.

Johann looked over at Valentin, who was impatiently waiting for them to go on. He had to see the hopelessness of their endeavor—they would never get anyone out of here. Not out of a prison as heavily secured as this one. But Valentin merely gave him a tired smile, his eyes flickering with something that bordered on obsession.

Their progress was slow. Every few yards there were barred holes just below the ceiling of the narrow corridor, allowing in a few rays of morning sun and the noise from the market square. Outside, the day was starting, but inside this prison, it was forever dusk.

Finally they stopped outside a cell door almost at the end of the corridor. An upside-down pentagram had been drawn above the door—a sign for witches, Johann guessed. The prison keeper pulled out the heavy key ring one last time and unlocked the door.

"Half an hour," he said. "Not a minute longer."

The door swung open, and Johann froze.

The cell was entirely clad in timber, which was worm-eaten and covered in stains that looked like dried blood or excrement. There was a cot, as well as a small bench seat and a bucket to relieve oneself with a board on top that doubled as a table.

A sooty lantern hung from the ceiling and dispersed a little light.

A girl was sitting on the bench with her legs crossed, engrossed in a string game. She was wearing a dirty dress but no shoes, and her toes were blue with cold. Wrapped around her fingers was a thin string, which she twisted and spun into various patterns. When the two men entered, she lifted her face and looked straight at Johann.

That's impossible! he thought. *My God! How on earth . . . ?*

"Uncle Valentin!" cried the girl happily, jumping off the bench. "You're here, finally! I've been waiting for so long!"

"My little girl, let me give you a hug!" Valentin put down his pouch and wrapped his arms around Greta.

The girl closed her eyes with happiness. "Don't leave again," she whispered. "Ever."

In the dim light of the cell, the two of them merged into one single body, and for a while all that Johann heard was the moaning of the other prisoners.

Meanwhile, he studied Greta's face. It was quite dark in the cell, but still—there could be no doubt. The freckles, the soft mouth that always seemed to smile a little, the pronounced cheekbones, the flaxen hair . . . only the eyes were different. Black and mysterious like ponds in the forest.

His eyes.

Johann felt as though he were paralyzed. *Impossible,* he thought. *This must be a dream . . .*

Finally, Greta freed herself from Valentin's embrace and looked at Johann.

"Who is that?" she asked with curiosity.

"An old friend," replied Valentin with a smile. He eyed Johann closely, expectantly. "We were very close once. We were scholars in Heidelberg together."

"What are scholars?" asked Greta.

"Oh, young lads who drink too much wine and beer and think that they're immortal," replied Valentin with a wink. Then he turned to Johann. "That's right, isn't it? Immortal."

Johann didn't reply. He was still staring at Greta. She was just on the brink between girlhood and womanhood. Her stature was tall and athletic, and tiny breasts were showing beneath the dress, but her face was still childlike. Johann remembered the summer days in Knittlingen, playing in the hay, hide-and-seek in the woods. It could only be coincidence—there was no other possibility. Still, the resemblance was astonishing. Now he understood what Valentin had meant.

There's something about her . . . something familiar . . .

Greta appeared to have lost interest in Johann again.

"Did you bring me something?" she asked Valentin excitedly.

"What do you think?" Valentin held out the pouch with his crippled, pincer-like hand. "See for yourself."

Greta immediately started to rummage through the pouch. With a cry of delight she pulled out a chunk of cheese, half a loaf of bread, and a few shriveled apples. She stuffed her mouth with bread and pushed in the cheese after.

"Don't eat so fast, child," said Valentin. "You'll only make yourself sick."

The two men watched in silence as the girl ate. She was frightfully skinny, and her face and arms were dirty and covered in fleabites and scabs, but Johann couldn't see any serious injuries. Evidently the hangman hadn't started the torture yet. Johann was amazed at how well the girl looked, given the circumstances. It must be awful for her, alone in the cell at night, listening to the screams of other inmates and having not one person to talk to, apart from the hunchbacked keeper and a few surly guards. It would seem Greta possessed an inner strength that many adults lacked.

When Greta was finished eating, Valentin cleared his throat. "I brought you something else, too. I thought you could use it when you feel lonely. I know you're probably too old now, but still . . ."

From under his coat he pulled a tattered doll with matted, woolen hair and button eyes, one of which was dangling by a thin thread. Greta cried out with joy and squeezed the doll to her chest.

"My little Barbara," she whispered. "Did you miss me? I know, I didn't take good care of you in the last few years. I'm sorry." She stroked the doll, and suddenly she seemed much younger than her fourteen years.

"My friend is a physician," said Valentin. "He would like to examine you so we know how you are doing. His name is Johann."

"Hello, Greta." Johann thought his voice sounded as if it weren't his own. He tried to smile encouragingly. "May I . . . may I take a closer look at you?"

Greta pressed her lips together and gave him a frightened look. "That's what the keeper said, too," she whispered. "I don't like it."

Johann raised his hands. "I won't hurt you. I promise. I'm a physician. And I can do magic," he added mysteriously.

Greta looked at him with surprise. "Magic?"

Johann nodded. "Give me the doll. I'll show you."

Greta hesitated and looked at Valentin, who gave her a nod. Then she handed the doll to Johann. "But don't hurt her."

The idea had come spontaneously to Johann. He remembered well how much he'd loved magicians and jugglers as a little boy. Now he sat Barbara on his lap and held her little hands.

"Good day, little Barbara," he said.

"Good day, Johann," said the doll.

"I hear Greta hasn't been playing with you lately. What have you been up to, all alone?"

"Oh, I sneaked into the kitchen at the command and stole a pot of honey," the doll replied in a high-pitched voice. "And then I painted the commander's beard with it while he was sleeping. Such fun!"

The doll clapped her hands and Greta's jaw dropped with amazement. She looked up at Johann and then back at Barbara on his lap. Johann stifled a smile. He had taught himself ventriloquy all those years ago so that the archangel could speak to Margarethe—for purely selfish reasons, as he'd realized later. Now he used the trick to cheer up a girl in a prison cell.

"I would like to sing a song for Greta," said the doll. "Maybe she can join in." Johann hummed a tune in the high-pitched voice, slowly at first, then steadier and louder until the words came back to him.

"Growing in our garden are parsley and thyme." Barbara the doll clapped her small, tattered hands to the beat. *"Our Gretchen is the bride, she's looking so—"* Johann broke off. Without really thinking about it, he had chosen the song Margarethe always used to sing. The same song she'd hummed when the guards had arrested her inside the cave at Heiligenberg Mountain.

"Don't stop!" pleaded Greta. "Keep singing!"

"Do you know what, little Barbara?" said Johann to the doll, placing her on the bed beside Greta. "I think I might show you what I can do with apples."

He took the apples from the bag and started to juggle. Both Greta and Valentin watched him with amazement.

"You see five apples," said Johann, using the mysterious and seductive voice of jugglers and tricksters. "Hocus, pocus, locus—now there are just four!" One of the apples had suddenly vanished. "Hocus, pocus, three black cats—now there are just three!" Then three apples became two, and eventually Johann was only holding one last apple in his hand.

"You see," he told Greta. "You can juggle apples, you can make apples disappear, and . . . you can eat them." With the last words, he took a bite from the apple.

"Hey, that's my apple!" called out Greta and laughed.

Johann startled. Greta was laughing! The sound was as out of place inside this prison cell as the singing of angels.

And the laughter was so familiar.

"You can keep the apple if you let me examine you," replied Johann hesitantly.

Greta agreed, and Johann came closer. He examined her limbs for broken bones, cleaned the fleabites, and treated her frostbite with an ointment. Eventually he tore his overcoat to shreds and wrapped them around her feet. His hands trembled, and it wasn't because of the cold. Greta's laughter had removed any remaining doubts.

It was a laughter he hadn't heard for many years.

"Will you come back?" asked Greta with her mouth full. She was devouring her third apple since Johann had made the fruit reappear. "You must come back and do magic for me. Please!"

"I . . . I'm going to try," said Johann haltingly. He looked away when he felt his eyes well up. "And I'll bring you shoes next time."

"You can examine my little Barbara, too," said Greta. "I think one of her eyes is sick."

Johann nodded. "I will. I—"

Someone knocked on the door, and the gruff voice of the prison keeper rang out. "Half an hour is up! Come out now or you'll have to stay for good."

"I'll be back, I promise," said Johann again. He stood up, and he and Valentin walked out of the cell. He turned to catch one last glimpse of Greta waving at him, her eyes full of silent grief and hope at once.

"Come back," she said quietly.

Then the door slammed shut.

They didn't say a word as they walked the long way back out of the prison. When they stepped out into the morning sunshine in front of the city hall, Johann turned to Valentin.

"You . . . ," he said in a shaking voice. "You—"

"Let's go sit down at a tavern," said Valentin quickly. "And I'll explain."

They hurried across the square, where several grocers had set up their stalls in the meantime. There was salted meat for sale, as well as venison, eggs, poultry, and geese gaggling away in their cages. But Johann registered none of it. His whole life had been turned upside down by what had just happened in the prison cell.

They entered one of the cheaper taverns in an alley leading away from the main square and chose a quiet table in an alcove. Once a buxom serving maid had brought them two mugs of mulled wine, Valentin finally started to talk.

"Yes," he said in a low voice. "Margarethe's daughter. *Your* daughter. Did you see her eyes? They are your eyes, Johann Faustus. There can't be any doubt."

Johann sat as if he had turned to stone; all the noise around him, the loud conversations of the other people, the chinking of crockery—it all sounded like it came from behind a thick wall.

My daughter.

But how was that possible? Margarethe had hanged herself at the jail in Heidelberg—Valentin had said so himself. Even if she had been pregnant, there could have been no child, because she died.

Johann looked at Valentin, who was clutching the hot mug with his crippled hands, which were red from the cold. He kept his head low, avoiding Johann's eyes.

"Margarethe never hanged herself," whispered Johann. "You . . . you lied to me."

"Just like you lied to me for weeks and months." Valentin sighed. "I was so full of hatred for you, Johann. I wanted to hurt you where it hurt the most. And so I told you Margarethe was dead, when in reality she had been taken away shortly before me. I saw her again in Worms; she was in the cell next to mine. Twice a day when they dragged me to the torture chamber I saw her briefly, and her beauty helped me bear the pain." He blew on his mulled wine and took a sip. "During the nights, we had long whispered conversations. I learned much about you, Faustus. About little Johann in Knittlingen and his dreams and juggling tricks. I see you still know them." Valentin smiled. "You must have been a nice boy once."

"But Margarethe . . ." Johann's voice failed him. "Why . . . ?"

"Why she was spared? During her very first interrogation in Worms they found out that she was with child." Valentin gave a sad laugh. "She had known for a while, and she knew whose child it was. There could be no one else, of course—she was a nun, and you were the only man she saw." His finger traced an invisible line on the tabletop as if he was drawing her face. The sun stood above the rooftops by now and shone through the tavern windows.

"They spared her until the child was born," continued Valentin. "That's the law. Even torture has its rules, and they are recorded in the Bamberg book on the punishment of capital crimes. Shortly before I was released, Margarethe made me promise that I would care for the child when she was no more."

"And?"

"As soon as the child was born, Margarethe confessed to being in league with the devil. But the hangman took pity on her and throttled her with the garrote before the flames consumed her. She didn't suffer much."

Valentin gazed into the distance again. Men laughed, mugs clanked. The atmosphere was so peaceful that Johann felt like screaming out loud. He wanted to wail and cry, but no tears came. The last time he cried was a long time ago. It had been in Heidelberg when he'd learned of Margarethe's death.

Now she had actually died.

And been reborn at the same time.

"Margarethe seemed like she wasn't really in this world anymore during the last few weeks of her life," said Valentin. "She was convinced to the last that the devil would return to earth. She always spoke about the boogeyman she'd seen in the woods. And about Archangel Michael, who had abandoned her and all of us."

Johann closed his eyes.

The boogeyman . . . Archangel Michael.

Would this horror never end? No matter where he went, evil always got there first and waited for him.

Because you carry it within you . . .

"Greta isn't from the gutter," explained Valentin with a sigh. "I found her in an orphanage in Worms. It wasn't hard to get her out of there. No one likes to raise the child of a witch. I never told her who her mother was, and she knows nothing about her father. She thinks that her mother died while giving birth and that I'm a distant relative." He smiled, and for a moment Valentin looked like the zealous young student from their Heidelberg days. "She calls me Uncle Valentin. Isn't that beautiful? We had wonderful times together, even though she's been a little rascal at times since we took up residence at the command. She's stubborn and has an inclination for tricks and fibs. In that regard she takes after you."

Johann sat on the bench at the tavern and tried hard to remain calm. So many unexpected things had happened in the last hour. If Valentin was right, his daughter was in danger of suffering the same fate as her mother. He had to focus and find a solution. All his intelligence and all his knowledge were for nothing if he couldn't protect his daughter now.

The child he didn't even know.

26

IN THE FOLLOWING DAYS, JOHANN DESPERATELY TRIED TO figure out a way to get Greta out of Loch Prison. He felt like he was trying to square a circle—the legendary problem even the great Archimedes failed to solve.

He would often sit with Valentin and Karl at the command in the evenings. They met in the order's library, a bare room inside the church, rarely used by the knights. Valentin spent most of his time here. The only furniture was a wobbly table and a few shabby stools, but there were so many books and scrolls on the shelves along the walls that some had fallen off. More books were piled on the table. Wax from the candles of a candelabra dripped onto the tabletop, forming mounds of tallow. Little Satan lay curled up at Johann's feet.

Johann and Valentin had agreed that they wouldn't tell Karl the whole truth—not yet. As far as Karl was concerned, Valentin was Greta's uncle and an old friend in need. They didn't tell him that Greta was in fact Johann's daughter or about what had happened between the two men back in Heidelberg. Johann wanted to wait for the right moment to confess the sins from his past to his assistant. Thankfully, Karl was preoccupied with all the wonderful paintings, sculptures, and art treasures inside the churches of Nuremberg. Johann was under the impression that Karl was almost a little jealous of the effort his master put into trying to save a girl he didn't even know.

"Loch is probably the most heavily secured prison in the entire empire," said Valentin glumly. Lying on the table was a layout plan of the city hall that Valentin had secretly copied. "I visit the city hall regularly on administrative business. That building alone is heavily guarded, not to mention the jail below! All those doors . . ."

"Where do they keep the keys?" asked Johann.

"I've asked myself the same question." Valentin sighed deeply. "The prison keeper always carries one set on his belt, and there's another in the guards' chamber."

"Which is heavily guarded," said Johann. He fell silent again and thought hard, but try as he might, he couldn't work out a solution.

"What about bribes?" asked Karl.

"We might be able to bribe the keeper and one or two guards, but not all of them," said Valentin. "There are too many."

"Maybe we just have to accept that we can't save the child," said Karl with a shrug.

"If I'd said the same thing back in Warnheim, you wouldn't be here now," retorted Johann angrily. "I don't need to mention in which circle of Dante's *Inferno* you would be roasting right now."

Karl said nothing.

"There must be a solution," muttered Johann after a while as he rubbed his temples. "There simply has to be!"

By now he was convinced that it was no coincidence that Valentin had called him to Nuremberg. He had been watching the stars from the top of Saint Jakob's Church every night. The comet couldn't be far off now. It would be the third time Larua would enter Johann's life. The first time had been at his birth, the second time he'd nearly joined an occult group of devil worshippers, and now God was giving him one last chance. Because of his selfishness and arrogance, Margarethe—the love of his life—had been tortured and executed.

But now his daughter had entered his life, as unexpectedly as an angel. As if Margarethe were reaching out to him in forgiveness.

God had given him a key to turn back the wheel of time.

Now or never.

"We keep thinking," he said, staring at the map. "Worst case, we have to wait until they convict Greta. There might be a chance to free her on her way to the gallows."

But he knew that he couldn't wait that long. Every day down in that cell was one day too many for the child. It was strange that the Nuremberg authorities were holding Greta for so long without commencing torture.

Wolfgang von Eisenhofen inquired nearly every day whether Johann had found a lead regarding the devilish murders. Johann strung him along and garbled something about constellations he needed to observe more closely. He didn't really care who was behind the murders—he only wanted to free his daughter and get out of Nuremberg as fast as he could.

With the help of the commander's connections and some silver coins, Johann and Valentin managed to visit Greta most days. A few times Johann even went alone. He brought playing cards, coins, and colorful leather balls to show her all the juggling tricks he used to perform for her mother. He hoped it would distract Greta from the horror she was going through. The girl always loved it when he made her doll speak or coins appear from her ears.

But what she loved the most was Little Satan.

For a pile of hush money, the prison keeper allowed Johann to bring in the dog. Little Satan sniffed at the privy bucket, jumped onto the small bed, and licked Greta's face until she laughed. When he'd calmed down, he let her pat him while he sat quietly on her lap.

"I've always wanted a dog," she said. "But Uncle Valentin says the commander wouldn't allow it."

"He's probably afraid the dog will make a mess in the great hall." Johann smiled. "If you teach him properly, you might be allowed to keep one someday."

Suddenly Greta looked very serious. "The guards say that I'm a witch. And that I'm going to burn at the stake. I'm scared, Johann! Does it hurt to burn?"

"You . . . you're not going to burn." Johann swallowed hard. "Because you haven't done anything wrong."

"But they say that I'm a witch." Greta started to cry, and Johann's heart broke. "And I didn't even do anything! I was just by the river, by the bridge near the Hospital of the Holy Ghost, and then there was that dead little boy, and there was blood everywhere." She sobbed. "It was horrible! And I didn't even want to go to the river. But the man told me to go."

"The man?" Johann straightened up. Valentin had never mentioned this before. "What man?"

"I don't know. He wore a black coat and he . . . he was so dark, as dark as the night. And his eyes . . . his eyes looked like they were on fire, like glowing pieces of coal. He told me there were children playing down by the river and that there was music and food. When I got there, there was no one except for the dead boy under the bridge." Greta's eyes looked empty and her hands shook as she stroked the dog. "Then the guards came and found that thing in my pocket. A stinking ram's horn. They said the devil gave it to me."

"And he probably did," muttered Johann to himself. He shuddered.

His eyes . . . like glowing pieces of coal . . .

He, too, had seen such a man, first in Erfurt and then on the way to Hamburg. Evidently, someone had sent Greta to the dead boy on purpose, and the same man probably slipped the ram's horn into her pocket. But why? This case was getting stranger by the day.

Johann said nothing for a while, watching Little Satan snuggle with Greta. The dog rested his head in her lap as if he'd known her forever.

"You're not a witch," said Johann eventually. He rose to his feet when they heard the heavy steps of the prison keeper. It was time to go. "You're not a witch," he repeated. "And I promise I will get you out of here." He forced himself to smile. "Don't forget—I'm a magician. Nothing is impossible for a magician."

He hugged her so tightly that he felt Greta's pounding heart under her dress. He gave her one last smile on his way out and hoped she didn't notice the fear in his eyes.

On his way down the corridor, Johann continued to think about what Greta had just told him. A man in black with glowing red eyes had sent her to the bridge. It must have been a trick of her childish imagination, just like he once thought a scarecrow was a man on the way to Hamburg. Nature sometimes played nasty tricks on one's mind. It would be very strange indeed if someone had *wanted* Greta to find the body under the bridge. Who would want an innocent girl to be arrested as a witch?

Deep in thought, Johann didn't notice that Little Satan had run ahead. He startled when he heard wild barking and shouts in front of him. In the vaulted room at the end of the corridor, some guards were standing around the well. They were looking down the hole and laughing. Johann rushed up to the well and saw Little Satan treading water about seven paces below. It seemed he had jumped over the well's edge and was now in danger of drowning.

"Get him out right now!" ordered Johann.

"What do I care about the mutt?" jeered one of them. "Is it my dog? Maybe you shouldn't have brought it."

Little Satan whined and howled pitifully.

"If you don't, he'll keep howling like this for hours," said Johann, glaring at the guards. "Is that what you want?"

"The doctor's right, damn it," said the prison keeper from behind him. "Get the mutt out of there before the noise drives me insane."

The guards exchanged doubtful looks, and finally one of them grasped the chain holding a bucket in the center of the well and used it to climb down. He grabbed the whimpering Little Satan by the scruff of his neck while the other guards winched him up. When the dog arrived at the top, the keeper kicked Little Satan so hard that he flew across the room. He shrieked almost like a child and huddled underneath Johann's coat.

"Don't ever come here with that mutt again!" snarled the keeper. "And who are you, anyhow? I'm going to make some inquiries about your person and give notice upstairs that your visits are no longer acceptable. The brat has been spoiled for long enough!"

Johann fought back the urge to shout out loud when he left the prison. He held the trembling dog in his arms and soothed him while his thoughts raced in circles. He felt certain that the prison keeper would make sure he couldn't visit his daughter any longer. But that wasn't important right now.

What was important was the fact that he'd found a way to get Greta out of there.

"The well." Johann was pointing at the plan of the city hall spread out on the table before them. The three men had met sooner than usual, and Valentin and Karl could tell by Johann's excitement that it was urgent.

"When the guard pulled Little Satan from down there, I saw a barred door in the wall of the well," continued Johann. "I should have thought of it sooner. The well isn't a cistern, and so the water must come from somewhere!"

"The underground passages," murmured Valentin, studying the map. "You . . . you might be right."

Johann looked at him impatiently. "What are you saying?"

"Large areas of the city—on the north bank of the Pegnitz, at least—have cellars," replied Valentin slowly. "Many cellars serve to store beer, but there are also dozens of passages for the town's water supply. I once saw a map of them at the city hall. The water flows into the city from the outside—small trickles at first, which are caught in drains and directed into channels. The streams are then directed to the various wells around town, including the Schöner Brunnen fountain on the main square."

"And one of those passages leads directly beneath the city hall?" asked Karl skeptically.

Valentin sighed. "I don't know, damn it! I didn't study the map properly. They keep it closely guarded, together with the keys for the underground passages, because they don't want it to fall into the wrong hands—an entire army might be able to enter the city that way."

"When will you be at the city hall next?" asked Johann.

"Hmm." Valentin thought. "The day after tomorrow. The Hospital of the Holy Ghost is bursting at the seams, and the city wants us to take on more patients. I am supposed to report the number of beds available at the command. Why?"

"Do you remember how we took a print of a key back in Heidelberg? I want you to make prints of the keys here, too. And take another look at the map—we need to find out where those passages start!"

"Even if we find the particular passage that leads below the city hall and into the well of the prison," said Karl, "there are more guards, more doors—"

"I know that, God damn it!" shouted Johann. He thumped his fist on the table. "But it's our only chance. It's just the first part of a plan so far, but it's a start." He bit his lip. The plan was ludicrous. Karl was right. Even if they managed to get to the well, then how would they get to Greta? To his innocent daughter who had evidently been lured into a trap?

"There's something else, too," said Johann eventually. "Greta told me today that a man had persuaded her to go to the river, where she found the dead boy. Someone wanted her to be there. Why? Because the authorities needed a scapegoat? But then why a fourteen-year-old girl—why not a midwife or someone like that who normally gets accused of witchcraft?" He shook his head. "There are so many odd parts to this story. Why Greta? Why has she been sitting down there for so long without being tortured and without a trial? Something isn't right, but I just can't figure out what."

He would have liked to pat Little Satan, because he always felt calmer when the dog sat on his lap. But Little Satan had broken a paw when the prison keeper kicked him. Johann had put the leg in a splint and given the dog a little theriac, and now the animal slept peacefully inside the room the commander had assigned to Johann and Karl.

No one said anything for a while. Eventually, Valentin cleared his throat.

"I'm going to get the keys from the city hall for us," he said. "And I think I know the ideal time to break into the prison." He paused. "In four days."

"Why in four days?" asked Karl.

"It'll be the night before the Nuremberg Schembartlauf, a carnival parade where many citizens wear masks and get drunk before the start of Lent. The guards won't be as vigilant as usual, especially in the early hours of the morning."

"In four days' time." Johann nodded. "It's agreed." He looked at Valentin, who was sitting hunched over at the table. "Pray that I return with Greta."

"If you think you're going alone, you're mistaken," replied Valentin. "I may be a cripple, but I'm not going to let you free Greta on your own. I'm getting the keys, so I'm coming."

"If that is what you wish," said Johann with a sad smile. "I can hardly tie you up here." Deep down he was happy Valentin would be coming along. They'd need all the help they could get.

For a few moments the library was silent; somewhere outside, a solitary raven cawed. Then Karl gave a desperate chuckle.

"So . . . you're saying you're actually going to crawl through those dark passages? And then? Are you going to frighten off the guards with magic tricks?"

"Something like that," said Johann, standing up. "You heard it—we still have four days. Plenty of time to make plans and preparations."

The next few days were frenzied. Each night, Johann stood atop the spire of Saint Jakob's Church and watched the stars, which now almost matched their position on the day of his birth. Jupiter was nearly in the same sign as the sun, but the comet hadn't appeared yet. Could his calculations be wrong? Johann knew there could always be slight deviations, but he was all but certain that Larua would appear in the sky very soon.

Perhaps even precisely on the date of Greta's liberation.

During the days, Johann was running about town procuring things. Most of what he needed he found with merchants on the main square or at the craftsmen's quarter. When he wasn't on an errand, he roamed the lanes aimlessly, thinking and pondering until his plan took shape. Outside Frauenkirche Church on the market square at midday, he watched the *Männleinlaufen*—with the strike of the bell, a mechanical clock moved a procession of the seven prince electors around a figure of the Holy Roman emperor high above the portal—a never-ending circle. Johann felt like he, too, was coming full circle. In contrast to his usual habits, he even prayed. He visited the famous Lorenz Church with its heavily adorned western portal, sat down in one of the rear pews, and asked God for help as soft light fell through the stained-glass windows.

Lord, I have committed many sins in my life. I mocked you and I doubted you. Please help me to free my daughter. I swear I will watch over her for the rest of my life.

He imagined Greta huddled on her cot right now, afraid and confused because Johann and Valentin weren't visiting anymore. The Loch keeper had ensured that neither of them was allowed at the prison any longer. But Johann wanted to avoid the city hall in any case—he didn't want anything to happen at the last moment. Another child had vanished the previous day, down by river, near the hangman's house this time. The residents of Nuremberg were growing more upset. People whispered in the streets, and suspicions and rumors spread like a bad smell. The citizens of Nuremberg demanded a culprit—they didn't care who, just as long as the evil in town was banished.

The uncanny atmosphere affected Johann, too. During his walks through the city he sometimes thought he was being followed. But it was probably just the masks, which were becoming a common sight in the streets in the days leading up to the carnival and which reminded him of a man with glowing red eyes.

His eyes looked like they were on fire.

On the afternoon of the fourth day, Valentin asked Johann to the library, looking agitated. Johann's old friend went to one of the shelves and picked out a book. The book was cut out on the inside and contained a key ring with about a dozen keys. Valentin held it up triumphantly.

"Don't ask me what it cost to have these made. And I even managed to catch another glimpse of the map with the passageways and draw up a copy from memory."

Johann exhaled with relief. Valentin had done it! Johann hadn't really believed it would happen; his friend always used to be so nervous. The thought that Valentin had to steal a closely guarded key ring from the city hall had caused Johann many sleepless hours—hours he spent atop the church tower with his stargazing tube, but without success. The comet he anticipated so eagerly still hadn't arrived.

"Was it difficult to get your hands on the originals?" asked Johann.

"I . . . I caught an unobserved moment upstairs," said Valentin hesitantly. For a brief moment Johann thought his old friend was keeping something from him.

"All that matters now is that we have the keys," said Valentin a little too quickly. "The keys and the map. Did you get everything you needed?"

"Everything but one item. I need you to steal one more thing for me. It's not very big, and I've seen it on the commander's desk."

Johann gave Valentin the details, and his friend nodded. "That should be fine—I carry documents to his room all the time. Although the commander is starting to get impatient. He wants to know how your investigation is coming along."

"Tell him I'm preparing some very complicated magic that will help put an end to these murders once and for all," replied Johann with a tired smile. "That's not wholly false, and he is superstitious enough to buy it." He gave Valentin a thoughtful look. "You can still decide to stay here."

"I'm coming with you, and that's my final word."

"Very well," said Johann reluctantly. He was left with the strange feeling that something was awry.

"Show me the map," Johann asked Valentin to take his own mind off his worries. "Perhaps we'll find a good entry point to the passages. One that's not under constant surveillance."

Valentin pulled out the map. "I think I've already found one. It's not the nicest spot, but at least we have nothing to fear there." He indicated a particular point on the map. "No guards, at least."

Johann nodded. Valentin had chosen the spot well.

"It's decided," he said. "We're setting out tonight. And if we fail, at least we'll burn together."

"Old friends, united in the flames."

～

In the infinite vastness of the universe above them, a comet was hurtling along its path. It was nearing Earth like it did every seventeen years, though it couldn't be discerned by the naked eye. The comet was trailed by a bright fiery, bushy tail.

It was the tail of Lucifer, the light bringer, causer of chaos, he who fell from the heavens. Of the spirit that denies. The gloom that brought forth light.

There was someone who couldn't wait for this darkness to arrive.

Larua.

Not far from the command, the master closed his eyes, listening. He almost thought he could hear the rushing of the comet through the eight spheres. Then he sat down at a table and wrote messages for his crows and the raven to carry. He was gathering his followers. There were many of them, as many as the number of the beast, and their ranks were increasing.

It was the night before February 24 in the year of the Lord 1512.

A night that would change the world forever.

27

BELOW THE CLOUD-COVERED MOON, THREE FIGURES IN dark coats hurried through the lanes of Nuremberg's Lorenz quarter.

All three wore hoods that concealed their faces. One of the figures carried a cloth-covered crate on his back. The other two—one of whom was limping—carried heavy packs. They looked like itinerant peddlers or knife sharpeners. No one would have guessed that the cloths were hiding a laterna magica and that one of the figures was a famous doctor and magician. Johann was wearing his magnificent star cloak inside out, and it was blacker than a starless night.

Johann had given Karl the choice of coming or staying, and to his surprise the young man wanted to come. Johann felt deeply grateful. He wasn't sure why exactly Karl wanted to help him—perhaps he still felt indebted to Johann. In any case, he was a good fellow who didn't deserve a master who treated him as poorly as Johann had. If they came out of this business unscathed, Johann would give him back the letters and pay him handsomely.

But he struggled to believe that they would make it out unscathed.

They had left Little Satan behind at the command, hopping back and forth in Johann's chamber with his broken foot and probably relieving himself on the floor at that very moment or chewing on the furniture and rugs. The dog had sensed that something was going on. He had been restless and howled when they closed the door.

Earlier that evening, Johann had passed several men in costumes in the streets around the main square. The people of Nuremberg eagerly anticipated the Schembartlauf procession, which would lead through the entire city the following morning. The masked men all wore the same tight-fitting white-and-red garb embroidered with licking flames. They were armed with blunt pikes and wore rings of little bells around their ankles. Their faces were hidden behind smooth masks that made them look like varnished puppets.

"The timing for our plan couldn't be better," whispered Valentin to Johann and Karl as they made their way through the dark lanes. "Tomorrow, dozens of those dressed-up jesters will dance through the streets—it's an old tradition."

"Are they all hired jugglers?" asked Karl.

"Oh, no! Many of those masks are hiding the faces of wealthy patricians. They're all from respectable, influential Nuremberg families." Valentin smiled grimly. "I heard that this year, the hell is going to be an elephant—you know, one of those long-nosed monsters from beyond the sea."

"The hell?" asked Johann.

"That's what the Schembart runners call a huge wagon that, at the end of the procession, is stormed by the crowds outside city hall in a mock battle. People sometimes get hurt or even killed. Like I said—it's a raucous affair."

A door banged, and someone gave a shrill laugh. Johann looked around suspiciously and saw one of the costumed men dance across the lane and vanish in the darkness of a doorway. A second, younger man with a pike went after him, giggled girlishly, and took a mock bow in their direction. Then he, too, was swallowed up by the dark of night. Only the jangling of their little bells could be heard for a while longer, like the cackling of kobolds. Not for the first time Johann wondered whether it wasn't those masked men who had brought back his old fear of being followed these last few days. He felt for the knife that—after lengthy deliberation—he had decided to bring. The accursed knife! He was wearing it on a thin string around his neck like he used to, ready to rip it off and throw it at any moment. He didn't like it, but he knew it was the weapon he could handle the best, especially in narrow corridors and prison cells. He had given Karl the pistol and the sword, but he doubted the student was much good as a fighter.

Johann eyed the dark houses near the city wall. Once again he felt an itch between his shoulder blades as if someone was watching him. But every time he turned around, there was nothing.

Meanwhile, they had crossed the Pegnitz west of the Hospital of the Holy Ghost and were headed toward the main square. Now, in the middle of the night, the stalls of the market women and grocers had been taken down. An icy wind swept across the open space in front of the city hall. Despite the late hour, guards with pikes and halberds were on patrol outside the building.

Johann thought about his daughter, who was just a stone's throw away. How was she feeling right now? He hoped she was asleep and dreaming something pleasant. If his plan succeeded, he would be able to wrap his arms around her in just a few hours. And if he failed, they would soon see one another again in paradise. Margarethe, Greta, Valentin, Karl. But Johann didn't know whether God would have a spot for him in paradise, too.

They turned left behind the Sebaldus Church and headed toward the city wall again.

"I still don't understand why we have to leave the city to get back inside the city," grumbled Karl. "Are there no other places to access those passageways?" He groaned and tugged at the straps of the crate on his back. "The laterna is damned heavy. I don't want to carry it halfway to Fürth."

"Most access points inside the city are guarded or lie below houses of burghers who have cellars," explained Valentin. "I found an entrance that is more or less freely accessible. Probably because folks avoid it."

"And where is this entrance?" asked Karl.

"At a cemetery," replied Johann.

"At a—?"

"Shh!" Johann gestured for Karl to be quiet. "We have nothing to fear from the dead—only from the living! So be quiet."

Cautiously, they approached Neutor Gate near the castle; the gate was closed at this time of night and was guarded by a solitary watchman.

"Wait here," whispered Valentin.

He approached the guard and, after a few moments, handed him some coins. The man opened the door and let them pass through with a nod.

The highway stretched before them, desolate and empty. Some crows flew up from the icy fields. The moon emerged from behind the clouds and painted the sparsely wooded landscape with a silvery-gray light. About half a mile to the west, a few lights sparkled.

"Sankt Johannis," said Valentin, pointing at the lights. "The city's plague cemetery. Ever since the last great epidemic, Nuremberg prefers to leave its dead outside the gates."

"The entrance is at a plague cemetery?" asked Karl.

"Just yesterday they dug out a new mass grave and scattered lime over the bodies." Valentin gave a shrug. "Lucky for us. Folks avoid the place."

"And so they should," said Karl.

Johann glanced at his young assistant, wondering whether he already regretted having come along. But Karl still strode on at a fast pace with the heavy crate on his back. The laterna was part of the plan Johann had worked out in the last few days. It was a plan that required a huge dose of luck and a crucial moment of surprise.

After a while they reached the lights, which belonged to a handful of low houses. A little off to the side stood a small church surrounded by the gray silhouettes of tombstones. A low stone wall enclosed the cemetery; dry rosebushes had grown over the wall in places. Valentin stopped in front of a rusty gate and pulled out a piece of parchment that had been folded several times.

They lit a lantern, and Valentin held it close to the map, which was covered in scribbled lines and arrows.

"The entrance is in a crypt inside the plague chapel," said Valentin, pointing to the map. "It has to be somewhere in the family crypt of the Holzschuhers, who are influential patricians in Nuremberg." He looked up and gestured at the chapel among the graves nearby.

"Let's go." Johann opened the rusty gate. For a brief moment, he thought he heard the jingle of bells, but then the squeaking of the gate drowned out all other sounds. More slowly now, they walked past the old, crooked grave markers that rose out of the ground like the teeth of giants. There were several fresh mounds of dirt, including one very large one. Several black birds sat on top of it, but Johann couldn't make them out very well in the dark. Even in the chill of winter, the sweet smell of decay lay in the air.

Soon they reached the plague chapel, a small, towerlike building. Johann pushed against the door and entered the dark room on the other side. In the light of the lantern he saw wooden choir stalls and an altar farther back. The floor in front of them was covered in grave slabs with the likenesses of many long-dead Nuremberg patricians.

"The Holzschuher crypt," whispered Valentin, gesturing toward one of the slabs. "We need to get down there."

He slipped his pack off his hunched shoulders and pulled out a crowbar. Karl took it and wedged it beneath the edge of the stone slab. There was a crunching noise, and the slab lifted a tiny bit.

"Wait." Johann rushed down the apse toward a plain cross that was about as tall as a man. It took all his strength to lift it down and drag it over to the grave slab.

"Do it again," he said to Karl while sweat ran down his forehead despite the cold.

The young man groaned as he pushed up the slab, and Johann pushed the long beam of the cross into the gap. Then he walked to the other end of the cross and levered the stone slab until it crashed to the floor on the side. A cloud of fine stone dust spread through the chapel, along with a musty smell from inside the hole.

"The law of the lever, by Archimedes," Johann declared with a smile and wiped his forehead. "The mechanical advantage is proportional to the length of the lever. Yet more proof that science gets a man further than mere muscle power." He took the flickering lantern from Valentin and held it in the room below them for a few moments. Then he gathered up his cloak. "Well, then—in the beginning was the deed!"

Clutching the lantern tightly, he jumped into the crypt below.

The chamber beneath the church floor was about as high as Johann's shoulders and full of stone sarcophagi, each one bearing the emblem of the Moor with the red hat and a wooden shoe—the family crest of the Holzschuhers. The air smelled of rot, soil, and fungi.

Karl and Valentin had also climbed into the crypt by now, the younger man helping the older one. The three of them started to feel along the walls, almost completely in the dark despite the lantern.

"Over here!" called out Karl after a while. He'd found a small, narrow door that had been reinforced with pieces of iron. A rusty lock hung on the door.

"This must be the entrance," said Valentin. "Now we need this." He fished the key ring from his pack and tried one key after another. Finally, on the seventh attempt, they heard a click and the lock opened. They pushed on the little door, and on the other side lay a pitch-black corridor.

"The entrance to the Nuremberg underground passages," murmured Valentin. "We actually found it." He stared into the darkness. "From now on, we must place our trust in God. In God and in my map."

Carrying the lantern in one hand and the map in the other, he limped ahead; Karl and Johann followed.

The passageway was about as wide as two arms' lengths and just high enough for them to walk with bent knees and hunched shoulders. It had been dug into the sandstone without any bracing. Water dripped from the ceiling, and Johann tried to avoid touching the drops. The bodies of plague victims were buried above them, and their juices of putrefaction probably seeped through coffins and sand. Small puddles had formed on the ground, and Johann saw wood splinters and pieces of bone.

Their steps echoed through the tunnel. No one spoke. After what felt like an eternity, the passage ended in a small, round chamber with three doors. All three were locked. Valentin raised the lantern and studied the map.

"I believe we're near the Tiergärtner Gate now," he said. "Back inside the city and not far from the castle. I think . . ." He hesitated. "Let's take the right-hand passage."

"And if we get lost?" asked Karl.

"We won't get lost," said Johann. He had produced a black coal pencil from his pack and used it to draw a sign next to the door on the right. "Miners use such signs below ground," he explained. "If we leave a mark at every fork, we shouldn't get lost."

Valentin smiled. "I knew it was right to bring you to Nuremberg, Johann. You may have lied to me and betrayed me, but I still admire your wit and your nerve."

You have no idea, thought Johann. Inwardly, he was shaking and his fingers trembled. His whole life seemed to be coming to a head in these crucial hours.

He had to free his daughter and right an old wrong.

Valentin pulled out the key ring again, and soon they'd opened the door. The tunnel on the other side led slightly downhill. The walls and ceiling dripped and gurgled, and trickles ran down the walls like a network of veins inside a giant stone organism. A drain enclosed with bricks stretched down the center of the passageway. The water collected in the drain and rushed into the tunnel below their feet.

"Yes, it's the old Loch water supply!" said Valentin triumphantly. "The drains collect the water and direct it to the wells. Hmm . . ." He studied the map again. "The city hall should be southeast of here—"

"And this tunnel runs southeast, indeed," said Johann. "I think we're on the right track."

"How do you know that?" asked Karl.

Johann pulled his hand out from underneath his cloak and held up a small box about the size of his palm. The top of the box was covered with glass, and inside sat a quivering needle. "This is the commander's," he said. "It's a compass. It shows us our direction, even underground and without the stars. We really must return it when we're done here. It is constructed with a gimbal mounting, according to Leonardo da Vinci's design, and it's worth about as much as a destrier." He shook his head and focused on the needle. "Until very recently, the church condemned compasses as witchcraft—a terrible thought."

Using the compass and leaving pencil marks, they continued to move southeast, passing through several more chambers with doors. Each time, Valentin pulled the key ring from his pack and found the right key. Every now and then they heard rustling and scuffling noises in the dark—rats, they assumed. On one occasion Johann thought he heard the jingle of small bells again, but he guessed it was only the key ring.

They came to yet another door. Valentin unlocked it, and this time, there wasn't another corridor on the other side but a round reservoir. Johann held his breath. He lifted the lantern through the door and looked down. The black surface of the water was about three paces below them, and a bucket was floating on it. The bucket was attached to a chain that disappeared somewhere in the dark above them. Johann thought he could make out the hint of a flickering light up there, like from smoking torches.

"This is the Loch Prison well," whispered Johann as quietly as he could. "I recognize it."

"But what about voices? Or the cries of the inmates?" whispered Karl. "Shouldn't we at least be hearing a couple of guards talking to each other?"

"We have no choice but to climb up if we want to find out," said Johann.

"But then we run right into the guards' arms!"

"You forget I came prepared." Johann took the pack from his shoulders and started to rummage inside. Then he produced a small wooden keg that stank of sulfur.

"Once I light this keg, we must act fast," he whispered. "It's going to cloak everything in smoke. Karl and I climb up the chain. Valentin, you wait here." He looked at his old friend. "You said there was a set of keys in the guards' chamber?"

"I . . . I think so." Valentin nodded slowly.

"We'll take yours just in case."

"But these are just for the underground passages, not for the prison. And how are you going to get to her cell with all the guards?" asked Valentin. "The keys won't help you against those."

Johann smiled. "You brought a magician, Valentin. Remember?"

Johann lit a pine chip on the lantern and then used it to light the contents of the keg. Instantly, dense rust-colored smoke started to pour from the keg and drifted up the sides of the well in thick clouds. Johann carefully set down the keg at the edge of the reservoir and tied his damp kerchief around his nose and mouth.

"Now!" he said, and he grabbed the chain and started to climb up it.

The rusty chain links dug into his fingers, and every single muscle in his body ached. It had been years since he'd last climbed up a rope—since his time with the jugglers, in fact.

Inch by inch, Johann pulled himself up. Below him, Karl panted as he followed him with the laterna on his back. The dense smoke made Johann's eyes water, and he tried to inhale as little as possible. The mixture inside the keg included cinnabar and ocher, coloring agents he'd bought from a Nuremberg dyer. The powder produced red, almost purplish smoke, which looked particularly devilish. And the smoke was a perfect screen for projecting heinous images with the laterna magica.

Finally Johann reached the edge of the well and pulled himself up over the side. He paused cautiously and looked around. He'd expected to encounter some guards. It had been his plan to use the general chaos and the cover of the smoke to rush over to the guards' chamber and steal their keys—or to knock down the prison keeper and take his. Meanwhile, Karl was supposed to distract the other guards with images from the laterna magica. It was a terribly poor plan, but it was the only one he'd managed to come up with. Johann had calculated that it would take him five minutes to open the doors, run down the corridor, fetch Greta, and disappear back down the well with her.

But there were no guards.

The room was empty, and there were no sounds coming from the guards' chamber upstairs, either. Johann stood still and listened. No laughter, no shouts, nothing.

What on earth?

Meanwhile, Karl had also reached the smoke-filled chamber with his heavy pack. He coughed and looked about, blinking rapidly. Like Johann, he'd covered his nose and mouth with a damp cloth.

"Where are the guards?" he asked quietly.

"I don't know, damn it! And I don't have time to worry about it—let's go!"

An eerie feeling made Johann's skin crawl. What was going on here? The oil lantern in his hand, he started to run down the corridor. All the doors stood open and every cell was empty. What was happening? With rising panic, Johann raced toward Greta's cell.

He threw himself against the unlocked door, and it slammed against the wall inside.

The cell was empty.

28

THE RUST-COLORED SMOKE HAD SPREAD DOWN THE COR-ridor and flowed into the cell, but everything was still and silent as the grave.

"Damn it, what's going on here?" asked Karl, standing behind Johann in the open door. "Is it the wrong cell?"

Johann said nothing and walked inside. A few rats squeaked as they scattered. The bucket with the board had been knocked over. Greta's doll was lying on the cot. Johann picked it up and stared at it, as if little Barbara could tell him what had happened.

What in God's name was going on?

Had the guards taken Greta to the scaffold? But Valentin would have heard of it. And why were all the other cells open and empty? Where had all the prisoners gone, and the guards? Johann's thoughts raced. Something was wrong here, very wrong. Suddenly he remembered several strange incidents from the last few days—warning signs he had overlooked in the rush. He'd wanted to rescue his daughter and stormed along blindly, looking neither left nor right. He still wasn't sure exactly what was being played here, but the eerie feeling from earlier was growing stronger and stronger.

It was the feeling of having walked into a trap.

"Get back!" he shouted. "Out of here!"

He dropped the doll and they ran back up the corridor. The red smoke was so thick that they hardly saw anything. Almost blind, they reached the edge of the well, and Johann grabbed hold of the chain. He climbed down as fast as he could and entered the doorway that led into the room above the water. He'd already guessed what he was going to find there, but the reality still hit him like a blow.

Valentin was gone.

You're so stupid! he thought. *So terribly stupid! All your brains, all your knowledge didn't help. You didn't see the forest for the trees!*

Silent despair filled his body. He had failed—completely and utterly failed.

You lost everything. You lost your daughter. You fool, you—

Johann paused his silent tirade when he heard something.

It was a humming and lamenting that drifted down the depths of the tunnels. The sound rose and ebbed, and after a while, Johann thought he could make out a few strange words.

"O Mephistophiel . . . Jesum . . . Escha . . . Eloha . . . Penothot . . ."

Johann signaled to Karl behind him to be silent. He listened. Then the two of them started to walk toward the source of the sound.

"Rolamicon . . . Hipite . . . Mephistophiel . . . Koreipse . . . Loisant et Dortam . . ."

Johann walked faster, hurrying to meet his destiny. He needed certainty, even though he had a fair idea where his path was leading him.

Or, rather, to whom.

"O Mephistophiel, prasa Deus . . . O Larua . . ."

~

Fear crept up in Karl; he was almost as terrified as he'd been on the pyre in Warnheim.

While he followed the doctor down the dark passages toward the eerie chanting, Karl tried to figure out what it was that frightened him so. His heart was pounding in his throat and he struggled to breathe. His hand clutched the hilt of the sword Faust had given him, but he had a feeling that he wouldn't know what to do with the weapon, or with the wheel-lock pistol he'd stowed in the casing of the laterna magica. He still carried the laterna on his back, like a last souvenir from the old world above them.

The doctor had changed in the course of the past week. Karl was certain that this had something to do with Valentin. Something awful must have happened between the two men, something the doctor felt deeply guilty about. Ever since Faust had visited Valentin's niece at the prison, he'd acted like a man possessed. What was happening to him? The plan to free the girl had been doomed from the beginning. But still Karl had gone with the doctor, because . . . well, because he loved him. Because he couldn't allow this gifted mind, this extraordinary human being, to run straight into perdition.

Although right now it looked as though they were headed for it together.

Back in Cologne, Karl had wanted to ask Faust to release him. But then they'd had to flee the city and spent the next few months at the tower, where their bond had strengthened. Karl had almost confessed his love to the doctor there, even though he knew that he would only end up heartbroken. He was bound to Faust with an invisible tie.

The events of the last few hours had been more and more puzzling. Why in God's name was the entire prison empty, as if the plague had befallen the city? Why had Valentin run away when it was so important to him to free his niece? And what was this awful humming and chanting mixed with Latin-sounding words? He felt like his head was going to burst.

But what frightened Karl the most was the doctor.

Karl had never seen him like this. Johann Georg Faustus, the famous magician, was a sharp-witted, wise man who always kept his cool, even in the worst situations, and invariably parried every attack, every surprise with his brains alone. But now the doctor's face showed something Karl had never seen on it before.

The doctor was scared.

Sweat was running down Faust's forehead, and his face was ashen. He mumbled individual words that made about as much sense to Karl as that accursed chanting.

"The tower," whispered Faust. "He knew about the tower and told him . . . It was his raven all along . . . It must have been his raven . . . Baphomet . . . I have failed."

The last words frightened Karl the most. If the doctor had failed, then this was the end for him, too. No one could save them now—they would be buried alive.

On their way toward the mysterious voices, they passed through more chambers and cellars, and each time one of the doors stood open, almost as if someone was showing them the way. They had long left the passage they'd come from earlier. Karl thought they were heading west, but he felt quite disoriented. The humming and singing were getting very loud now. They entered a spacious cellar room with old barrels stacked up against the damp, moldy walls on both sides.

At the other end of the cellar was a large double door with strange runes carved into the wood.

And on the other side of the door, they heard the chanting of many male voices.

"*O Adonai . . . prasa Deus et praesant Deus . . . O Spiritus Mephistophiel Deuschca . . . O Larua . . .*"

Karl's fear took his breath away. He thought he was going to pass out. What was going on with him? He felt as though an invisible force was holding him back, and the feeling of being unable to breathe grew worse with every step. It was as if deep down inside, he knew that death was waiting for him beyond those doors.

Or something even worse than death.

Faust strode toward the portal.

"No!" cried Karl. "Don't open it! Don't—"

But it was too late.

The doctor had already opened the doors.

~

Johann pushed against the doors with both hands, and they swung open soundlessly.

On the other side was a large hall that was at least ten paces high and twice as long. Torches and candles bathed the room in a flickering light, and the walls were lined with glowing braziers. Johann's first impression was that he was standing in an underground church. There was a choir, a nave, a transept, massive columns holding up the painted ceiling, and a pulpit. There were an altar and a baptismal font in the apse and a cross beyond. A monk standing behind the altar had raised his arms in prayer and was preaching to his congregation in the pews before him.

"*O Mephistophiel . . . Obdesca mihy Aglam . . . O Christe meschca . . . O Larua . . .*"

On second glance, Johann saw the differences from a regular church: the paintings on the ceilings showed no tales of saints but blood, murder, torture, and wars. The cross in the apse hung upside down.

And lying on the altar was a young girl, either unconscious or dead.

"Greta!" screamed Johann. The sight of his daughter on the altar was too much for him. His knees buckled and he clung on to the doorframe to keep himself from falling.

The monk, who was wearing a black robe with a black hood, lowered his arms, and the congregation stopped singing.

"Greetings, Johann," said the monk, his voice echoing through the hall. "It's been a while since we last saw each other. Didn't I tell you back on the old post road that our pact is valid until I dismiss you?"

Johann was shaking all over, and he was unable to move, like a rabbit at the sight of the snake's open mouth. He knew that voice—he'd last heard it seventeen years ago. Since then he'd been running away from it, again and again, but it never stopped following him in his dreams.

Now it had caught up to him.

"Come, Johann," said Tonio del Moravia. "My disciples would like to take a closer look at you. They've been waiting a long time for your return. Seventeen years."

The heads of thirty men turned to face him, and Johann stared at blank masks. Beneath their shapeless black cloaks, which seemed to melt into the dark twilight, they all wore the colorful costumes of the Schembart runners. Faint jingling rang out here and there.

The bells. They followed us the whole time!

Then he noticed another figure. He had been hiding behind a column near the altar, but now he emerged, shaking.

"Valentin!" spat Johann. "You traitor!"

"Forgive me," pleaded Valentin. "They . . . they made me do it. They said it was the only way for me to save Greta. Believe me—I love your daughter just like you do."

The anger gave Johann back his strength. With a furious roar he started to storm to the front, but immediately some of the Schembart runners jumped up and stopped him. Strong muscles showed beneath the costumes of the men, and they had no trouble forcing Johann to the ground.

"Bring him to me!" commanded Tonio.

The Schembart runners dragged Johann like a sack of flour into the apse, where they forced him to his knees before his former master. Finally, Tonio took off his hood.

The sight of his face made Johann gasp.

"By all the saints," he whispered.

"Don't pray," said Tonio. "It doesn't suit you, and it won't help you."

Tonio had barely aged. His face was just as haggard and pale as seventeen years ago, his stature still tall and athletic. There might have been a few additional wrinkles, and the skin of his face seemed taut like that of a reptile. But other than that, he looked as though no more than a year had passed since they'd last met.

It's impossible!

"Pleased to see you haven't forgotten me after all these years, Johann," said Tonio. "I must admit, following your unfortunate decision to run away in Nördlingen, it took a while to find you again. At first it seemed you had vanished into thin air. But then friends from Venice told me about a handful of jugglers at the Fondaco dei Tedeschi who called themselves Johann Faustus's Fabulous Troupe. An unusual name, don't you think?" Tonio smiled his old wolfish smile. "I thought I'd pay you a visit. I always had a talent for playacting."

"You . . . you were Signore Barbarese!" gasped Johann. "They were your books!"

"Of course they were my books, you fool!" Tonio laughed. "No one else owns an original copy of *The Sworn Book of Honorius*, let alone so many manuscripts by Leonardo da Vinci. I was letting you mature like a good wine—you were supposed to find your own way back to me. I understood that you needed more time. It was beautiful to watch you grow and flourish, and entirely without the Krakow University I had intended for you." He gave a shrug. "Seventeen years is nothing if you've been waiting for as long as I have. But then the old fellow in Venice found me out."

"You murdered Magister Archibaldus!" Johann struggled against the masked men, but they held him firmly. "You . . . you . . ."

"Devil?" Tonio grinned. "Is that what you're trying to say? If it makes you feel any better—I didn't kill your drunken friend. Not personally, anyhow—followers of my order did it."

Johann said nothing. Did Tonio know that Archibaldus had left him a message in blood back then? The powerful arms of the Schembart runners still held him down. He tried to catch a glimpse of Greta on the altar from the corner of his eye. Pain shot through him worse than being stabbed with a knife.

Greta was wearing the same linen dress she had worn in her cell. Her eyes were closed, and her childlike face pale, almost translucent. Johann noticed that her chest was rising and falling ever so slightly. She was still alive. He guessed they had sedated her with some kind of herb or potion. What were these lunatics going to do to her?

Johann struggled against his captors with all his might, but in vain. Furious, he glared at Valentin by the column. The man's eyes went back and forth between Johann and Greta.

"Goddamned traitor!" snarled Johann again.

Valentin cowered as if he'd been struck. "They are powerful, Johann! What was I supposed to do?" His gaze turned to the unconscious girl again. "Just look at what they've done to my dearest treasure. *They* arranged everything. Greta was only the bait—they were after you all along!"

Johann flinched.

Only the bait.

He felt like punching himself in the face. He couldn't believe he hadn't seen this coming much sooner. He should have noticed when he first arrived at the command. Everything had been too easy. The underground passages leading straight into the prison, the key ring Valentin had stolen without a hitch, the map. It was so obvious—nothing but a cheap farce, and he, the oh-so-clever doctor, had fallen for it. He had followed the bacon like a mouse, and the trap had snapped shut.

"The tower," he whispered, looking Valentin straight in the eyes. "I told you about a tower back in Heidelberg, but never about its exact location. I only remembered later. There was just one person who could have told you where to find the tower—someone who lives there himself from time to time."

"You still don't understand how powerful this man is," said Valentin in a whisper. He trembled as he looked over to Tonio del Moravia.

"Oh yes, I do."

I've always known. I just didn't want to see.

He had never truly escaped the master; Tonio had always been one step ahead of him. That explained the prevailing sense of being watched. Tonio had never stopped watching him over all these years. But there must have been a reason for the master to bring Johann back to him now. After seventeen years.

At that moment, Johann understood.

Seventeen years.

Once again, Larua was in the sky, as on the day of his birth and as it had been in the clearing near Nördlingen. The comet was probably over Nuremberg right now. They had chosen this day for a reason. That was why Valentin hadn't stolen the key ring until now, and that was why Greta had been detained at the prison for so long. They had been waiting for this particular day.

Valentin seemed to read his thoughts. "They wanted you to figure out the plan with the tunnels yourself," he said in a shaking voice. "If you hadn't thought of it in time, I would have helped you. But it was more believable this way." He gave a sad smile. "I always knew you'd find the solution. Now you're precisely where they wanted you—where *he* wanted you."

Johann gazed at the upside-down cross in front of him. Back in the clearing near Nördlingen, he'd thought a horde of lunatics was going to kill him, sacrifice him for some satanic ritual like so many children and youths before him had been. But evidently they had different plans for him.

Something that would come to a close here in Nuremberg.

"Why didn't you just abduct me and bring me here if I'm so important to you?" asked Johann, looking at his former master. "Why this farce?"

"Well, I thought a farce was appropriate for a juggler and magician," replied Tonio nonchalantly. "Didn't you enjoy it? It allowed you to trick and perform and show off your clever mind as you always like to do. But you're right—that's not the true reason. The true reason is that you must return to me of your own free will. It is an ancient law, set down in the times before time."

Tonio studied him with black eyes, his pupils as sharp as needles.

"Back when you drank the black potion, you were almost mine. But then you got away at the last moment. Finding your daughter in Nuremberg was a stroke of luck. I'd only wanted to speak with your old friend here. I knew his name from the list at Heidelberg University." Tonio pointed his finger at Valentin, whose scarred face had lost all color. "He was very talkative. No one wants to undergo torture for a second time, do they? All we needed to do next

was lure you to Nuremberg, this resourceful city where I have the most followers in the empire. And finally we needed to get you here, into the womb of the
beast. I knew you wouldn't abandon young Greta. Not after what you did to her
mother." Tonio smiled coldly and took a step toward Johann. "You had to come
of your own free will, and now you're here. Right time, right place."

"Where are we?" asked Johann.

"Directly underneath the Sebaldus Church, one of the city's oldest churches.
The original building was dedicated to Saint Peter." Tonio smirked. "How appropriate, considering good old Peter founded the Roman Church. We've been
using this buried crypt as a gathering place for a few years now. I've had the hall
renovated, bit by bit, whenever I stopped here on my travels. Every mass needs
the right setting, don't you think?"

"And what do you want with my daughter?" asked Johann. "If you want to
take revenge on me—for whatever—then—"

Tonio waved dismissively. "Your daughter is unimportant. We want you."
He leaned down close enough so Johann could smell his sweetish breath. "*I* want
you." Tonio sniffed at him and shuddered with lust. Almost lovingly he stroked
Johann's cheeks. "You're the right one, Johann. I sensed it back in Knittlingen
when we first met—when you were just a little boy. Everything happened just
the way it was foretold."

Johann turned his face away with disgust. He realized where the smell on
Tonio's breath came from.

It was the smell of fresh blood.

"I have a suggestion for you, Johann," said Tonio. "You sit down among my
disciples and behave. And then I will tell you how you can save your daughter.
It isn't difficult—it's entirely up to you. Are you going to behave and listen,
Johann? Are you?"

Johann nodded, and the Schembart runners dragged him over to the front
row of the pews, where they sat him down in their midst. Valentin had also been
brought there, and he trembled and shook as he sat between two masked men.
Johann looked at the empty, smooth masks around him. Now he was grateful
that Greta was unconscious and didn't have to see this horror show.

Meanwhile, Tonio had walked over to the column with the pulpit and took
the narrow, winding stairs to the top. When he stood beneath the black canopy,

he paused for a moment, drinking in the ecclesial atmosphere, which was heavy with anticipation. Then he addressed his followers.

"You've been waiting for a long time," he shouted into the hall, looking like an angry, emaciated preacher. "But now the time has finally come. The reign of God ends and the age of man begins! *Homo Deus est!*"

"*Homo Deus est!*" chanted the masked men.

Johann winced at the words he'd heard again and again over the years without really understanding their full meaning. Magister Archibaldus had known who was hiding behind those words, and he'd had to die for this knowledge. It took Johann a moment to realize what Tonio's tone reminded him of. It was the same tone of voice the sorcerer had always used to seduce the crowd at the market squares.

"For hundreds of years, the church led us to believe that there was but one truth and one teaching," Tonio went on. "The church forbade you to read books and, yes, even to think! The church tried to lull you to sleep and condemned any scientific progress as heresy. They placed their obstinate, narrow-minded God at the center of the universe instead of man—but enough is enough!"

"*Homo Deus est, Deus homo est!*" chanted the masked men. Several of them had risen to their feet.

"Why has this city come so far? Why is it wealthier and more glamorous and better known than any other in the empire? Why is all the world praising Nuremberg wit and Nuremberg cleverness?" Johann could tell how much his former master and teacher enjoyed himself in the role of the zealous priest; his eyes gleamed with relish. "Because you have recognized that you can achieve greatness by yourselves! With the help of science, knowledge, inventions—you don't need a God, because you are gods yourself! Men can create paradise right here on earth. Starting from Nuremberg, our movement will conquer the world. The rebirth of man begins here!"

The masked men cheered, and Johann looked around with wonder. Who were those people? Lunatics? Followers of some dark, satanic sect? But then he remembered what Valentin had said about the participants of the Schembartlauf parade.

They're all from respectable, influential Nuremberg families.

Could that be true? Were all those masks hiding the faces of Nuremberg patricians? That would explain the lack of guards at the prison. Some powerful people had arranged for the cells to be cleared for him to walk into the trap. Who might belong to this creepy order? Patricians, merchants—perhaps even the burgomasters? And who was to say the Teutonic Knights weren't also part of this plot?

Johann wondered what Tonio was getting out of all of this. Johann had fought for science all his life, for reason and rationality instead of bigotry and dull-witted superstition, just like he had been taught by Conrad Celtis, Jodocus Gallus, and Archibaldus. He had seriously believed that a new age was dawning: independent thought instead of dogma, a society created by men instead of an angry God whose outdated rules were set down for all eternity. And now Tonio was perverting all those ideas that Johann had always championed with fervor. The rebirth of man celebrated as a satanic mass—what a mockery! Tonio was showing him a nasty caricature of man celebrating himself as God.

Homo Deus est.

Did these people truly believe that the age of God was coming to an end? Could anyone be so stupid? A horrible thought struck Johann and slowly became certainty: the lunatics surrounding him must be behind all those horrific child murders in Nuremberg.

Perhaps not only here in Nuremberg, but all over the empire?

But whether or not these madmen believed the world was coming to an end and killed innocent children—they had his daughter. He had walked into their trap like a donkey following a carrot.

Now Tonio addressed Johann from the pulpit. He was leaning down to him over the banister, smiling encouragingly with his pointed teeth. A wolf on the hunt.

"My dear Johann, the hour you've long been waiting for has finally arrived. Now you shall learn the truth—the truth that has been written in the stars since the day of your birth. I read it in your palm then. You were born on the day great prophets are born. Your mother also told you about that, remember? And she was right. You are the great prophet!"

The crowd clapped and cheered while Johann gaped at Tonio. He couldn't believe what he was hearing.

"You are the wizard Solomon's testament speaks of! You are the prophet who arrives with Larua and who we've been waiting for. *Because you're the son of a great sorcerer yourself.*" Tonio raised his voice as if reciting some ancient text.

"And when the day arrives and the great beast awakens, give it a coat. And a wizard will come when the sun and Jupiter are in the same sign, and he will be that coat. And he must give himself willingly and make the three sacrifices. Then the beast will come and no god can stop it."

Johann sat in the pew as if he'd turned to stone while Tonio gazed down at him with genuine affection. It was the loving gaze of a father upon his long-lost son. "This is your destiny, Johann. You are the wizard we have been waiting for. Many times I thought I'd found him, but every time, I was mistaken. Children who turned out to be false promises. We had almost given up hope—but then you came along! You needed more time, and I let you go. But now the moment has finally arrived—it is written in the stars! Larua, give us the strength for the three sacrifices!"

"You . . . you're insane!" gasped Johann. "I've always had an inkling. You're nothing but an insane fool!"

"Am I? A fool? Well, why not?" Tonio bared his teeth, climbed down from the pulpit, and walked to the still body on the altar. His spidery fingers brushed over her dress and slowly pushed it up over her knees.

"She is pretty, no doubt. I would love to mount her like a ram, despite her young age. It is the same as with lambs—the younger, the better tasting." Tonio licked his lips. "Perhaps I will take her with me on Walpurgis Night in a couple of years, and we can share her. We will make a child with her—your grandchild. And he will also bear the sign inside him. Who knows—maybe he would make a better coat than you? The stars will be favorable again in seventeen years' time. Seventeen years, more or less . . . We've been waiting for so long. Centuries. Millennia. Seventeen years don't matter. Even though I'd really like to choose you. I've grown very fond of you, Johann. Whether you believe it or not." Tonio's voice suddenly became icy and cutting, like hardened steel. His fingers had arrived at Greta's small breasts.

"You have the choice, Johann. Your daughter or you."

A piercing scream cut through the tense atmosphere. It came from Valentin, who had surprised his keepers and was heading for Tonio. "You monster!" screamed Valentin. "I should never have agreed to this deal. You . . . you devil!"

Tonio watched the small hunchbacked man with amusement. When Valentin reached him, Tonio made a small turn and kicked Valentin's feet out from under him. The crippled man fell to the ground with a whimper, but he started to crawl toward the altar on his elbows, trying to reach for Greta. Tonio kicked him again, this time with the heel of his boot and all his might, as if trying to squash a giant bug. There was a loud crack, and the little man lay still.

"Take him away," ordered Tonio. "I don't want his blood to soil the ceremony."

They carried off Valentin like a dirty bundle, and Tonio stepped toward Johann.

"Your daughter or you," he repeated.

Johann closed his eyes and opened them again in the hope of waking from a nightmare. But this was no nightmare—it was reality. He wanted to cry, but no tears came. What was happening here was beyond grief, beyond pain . . .

It was hell on earth.

What did these lunatics want from him? If he understood correctly, he was supposed to be sacrificed to something unfathomably evil. Something so unimaginable that men had given it a name so they might grasp it better. Just like they had done with God. But the name of this unimaginable creature wasn't God or Christ; nor was it Jahveh or Jehovah.

It was Satan. Lucifer. Light bringer.

In the old stories, Lucifer was the archangel who rose against God and was banished from heaven. Since then he'd been roasting in the depths of hell, hoping for the day he would rise again. He was the night before the day, chaos before order, the spirit that denies.

Only now did Johann fully comprehend what was going on here: these people, all of them respected citizens of Nuremberg, were awaiting Lucifer's return. They had murdered those poor children for some terrible ritual whose culmination was himself.

Johann had known for a long time that such people existed. But just as he had always taken God to be a principle of order, the devil, too, had been nothing but an abstract concept to him. His devil had no horns, no goat's foot, and he didn't stink of sulfur, even if that was what the church taught to frighten its flock. And that was why Satanists couldn't be anything other than misled fools who belonged in the madhouse or on a pyre.

That was the one side.

But if Johann was entirely honest, he had seen the devil in his dreams many, many times. Satan had seemed very real.

And now he stood in front of Johann.

"Your daughter or you," said Tonio for the third time. "You have my word that I won't touch her if you decide to join me."

Johann didn't speak. He didn't know what to believe. His entire conception of the world had been shaken. All he knew was that he had to save Greta. It was the only clear thought he could form.

The silence was broken by the cawing of a raven who was circling around the columns.

"You can have me," replied Johann quietly.

"Good choice. For you and for the world." Tonio smiled and nodded, then he snapped his fingers. "Bring me the black potion!" he commanded. His smile was certain of victory. "And believe me, Johann. This time, I'm going to make sure you drink every last drop of it."

The drink arrived in a chalice that had been cut from perfectly black obsidian and that sparkled in the light of the torches. Johann guessed it had probably been standing in the darkness between the columns the whole time. Two masked men solemnly carried the vessel to the altar and passed it to Tonio. The master held out the drink to Johann with both hands.

"You came to us of your own free will and decided to accept the black potion," he declared. "Know that it is for your best. Three painful sacrifices you must give, just like the accursed Son of God gave his sacrifice. The drink will expand your spirit and you will understand." Once again he raised up the chalice, and the congregation took up a prayer-like murmuring.

"O Satanas, O Mephistopheles, O Phosphoros!" The chanting echoed through the crypt. The master bowed to Johann, then Tonio gave him a nod.

Johann reluctantly accepted the cup, which felt cold and foreign. It was filled with a foul-smelling liquid.

"Drink," said Tonio.

Johann hesitated for another moment. He knew there would be no going back after the first sip.

For Greta, he thought. *For my daughter. May she lead a happier life than her father.*

He brought the vessel to his lips and drank. Like the last time, seventeen years ago, he retched immediately. The potion tasted like fire, burning his throat and spreading through his insides like scorching lava. Johann stood still for a while with his eyes closed, and then something seemed to explode inside him. An intense numbness spread through his body and he swayed; every sound suddenly seemed enormously amplified.

"Follow me, Johann," boomed Tonio's voice through the hall. "I am going to show you the truth. Only very few are granted this privilege."

The sorcerer led him to the baptismal font beside the altar, and Johann struggled to stay on his feet. He stumbled and caught himself by putting his hand straight into one of the braziers, but he hardly felt the pain. A very big masked man came up behind him and picked him up. Effortlessly, as if Johann were a bundle of kindling, the giant carried him toward his fate. The man conversed quietly with Tonio, and Johann thought the two were speaking French. But the words sounded strangely distorted, as if he were underwater.

The basin in front of him was a roughly hewn rock with notches and runes chiseled into the sides. Within, a dark liquid gleamed at him like a monstrous eye.

"Look into it," said Tonio.

Johann leaned over the baptismal font with great difficulty. He blinked and squinted, struggling to focus his eyes. After a while he realized that the liquid was red.

As red as blood.

Then he understood.

He was gazing into the blood of all those children who'd disappeared over the last few months.

"Quite a peculiar juice is blood," said Tonio. He dipped his finger into it and licked it off. "The tricky part is stopping it from curdling—it must remain fresh." He licked his lips with relish. "We need a lot of blood for the big day. The beast hasn't drunk in a long time. But I think we have enough now."

Tonio's lips suddenly looked a little bit fresher than before, his pale skin rosier and with less wrinkles. The red surface in the basin rippled, and Johann saw his own reflection. Then the image disappeared, and blurred forests appeared instead, partially hidden by wafts of mist. Muscular warriors wrapped in furs, their faces painted with blue streaks, stormed out of the woods, raising their swords and lances against an army on horseback. Horses neighed in panic; knights with helmets came crashing to the ground. Burning in the trees of a forest of oaks were wooden cages holding people who screamed as they hurled themselves against the bars like human torches. More warriors appeared, followed by burning pyres, blood, mouths opened in screams of agony, crying children, blood, houses on fire, ravaged fields, blood . . .

Blood everywhere.

Johann blinked. He knew it was the potion creating the illusions in his mind, but still—the images seemed as real as if everything were happening right before his eyes. He reached out with both hands and dipped his fingers into the surprisingly warm liquid. The images vanished and were replaced by a familiar face. It was Tonio and yet it wasn't—he looked younger, more handsome, almost seductive.

"Welcome, Johann Georg Faustus," said the younger Tonio with a smile. "Are you ready for the first sacrifice?"

Now Johann saw the whole figure in the basin. He was a knight in full armor on a magnificent horse, and he had the most beautiful eyes and fullest lips Faust had ever seen on a person. His mouth and cheeks looked red and healthy, as if he'd just returned from a fast ride; his body was brimming with strength and vitality. In the same instant Johann knew that this was the man he'd been looking for all these years.

Gilles de Rais.

"The little finger of the right hand," said the knight. The image shuddered, and the beautiful face was contorted into a grimace.

"*Faites vite.* The end and the beginning are close."

29

WITH A POUNDING HEART AND A METALLIC TASTE IN HIS mouth, Karl ran through the underground passages. He needed to get out of here as fast as possible! He'd left the laterna magica behind—he wouldn't have any more use for it. What he had seen and heard inside that mockery of a church was so horrific that he thought he might go insane.

After Faust had walked into the underground crypt, Karl had hidden behind the entrance. From the darkness of the cellar he had watched as the leader of the Satanists had kicked Valentin to the ground and handed Johann a chalice. He hadn't been able to understand much of what was being spoken, but the few words he'd heard made Karl's blood curdle. Then Faust had collapsed over the baptismal font.

It had taken everything Karl had to prevent himself from crying out loud during the next part of the ceremony. He had almost thrown up with fear and disgust.

With a large, curved knife, the leader had cut off Faust's little finger and tossed it into the basin.

That had been the moment Karl started to run.

He looked around in panic. The lantern in his hand barely gave off any light; the oil was almost used up. Once it went out, the darkness would swallow him up like the whale had swallowed Jonah. Which way should he turn? He wasn't sure how many forks and chambers he had crossed by now. Those damned tunnels all looked the same—it was like a labyrinth! Sometimes he thought he could hear the chanting again in the distance, and he ran even faster. He needed to get away from this hellish place of madness! At least he still had Valentin's key ring, so he could open doors if he needed to. But what good was that if he didn't know which doors led to the top?

Karl finally collapsed at the next corner. Panting heavily, he cowered down and closed his eyes. This was the end. Well, at least he wouldn't die of thirst down here—only starve to death slowly. In front of his feet flowed another one of the small streams that crisscrossed the underground like veins of the city.

When Karl looked up, he saw a sign in the flickering light of the lantern.

He cried out with surprise. It was one of the coal marks Faust had drawn on the walls to help them find their way back. Karl had completely forgotten about them in his blind panic. He jumped up and felt his strength return. If he followed the marks from here he would find the exit to the cemetery. From there he could turn west on the highway and leave this cursed place behind for good.

This cursed place and the doctor.

The doctor he loved.

Karl bit his lip. He pictured how he'd left Faust in the crypt. Like a calf at slaughter.

Like a sacrificial lamb.

He'd known the doctor for nearly two years. It hadn't always been easy with him—Faust was arrogant, cynical, and hot tempered—and yet Karl had learned much from him. The doctor had been almost like a father to him, and much more understanding than his own forbidding father, who had called him soft and never treated him with respect.

But there was more to it. Karl had had several relationships with men in his life. The first one had been at Latin School, but the other boy's parents sent him to a monastery before the affair came to light. None of his relationships had ever lasted very long—mainly because it was just too dangerous. But it was different with the doctor. The longer Karl was with him, the stronger the bond between them became. Karl thought Faust was somewhat frightening, but he was also fascinating. There seemed to be a deep, inscrutable secret in the doctor's black eyes. Karl's love for him consumed and nourished him at the same time. He knew the doctor would be his downfall, but he couldn't bring himself to leave him. And that was why Karl couldn't abandon him down here.

Karl leaned his head back and groaned. It was enough to drive a man insane! If he turned left, freedom and a fresh start awaited him. Together with Faust, the letters that threatened his safety would vanish. And the fire that was burning so hot inside him now would go out sooner or later. But if he turned right . . .

The coal marks could lead him back to the cemetery, but they also showed the way to the prison. Karl felt certain he'd be able to find the way back to the underground hall from there. It hadn't been far.

Left or right.

Swearing under his breath, Karl stood up. He cursed God, the world, and the doctor in particular, and turned right.

The marks on the walls led him back to the well below the prison. There still were no sounds coming from above. Karl turned around and tried to remember which way they'd gone earlier. The humming and chanting led him in the right direction. A few minutes later he was back in the cellar in front of the double doors. The crate with the laterna still sat where he'd left it in his panic.

Cautiously he sneaked back to the open door and peered into the crypt. The masked men were humming and murmuring strange-sounding spells, while their leader in the apse had pulled his hood back over his head.

On the altar, Greta had been replaced by the doctor.

Karl clenched his fists. Was his master already dead? Blood was dripping from Faust's right hand, which someone had bandaged after that madman had cut off his finger. His head had flopped to one side, and his eyes and forehead were also bandaged with rags. What in God's name had those men done to the doctor?

Now the leader was raising the curved dagger he had used to cut off Faust's little finger. The chanting stopped.

"The first and second sacrifice are complete!" bellowed the man in the robe. "The beast is awakening from its sleep—I can hear it! I can hear it stir deep in the innards of the earth. *Homo Deus est!*"

"*Homo Deus est, Deus homo est!*" chanted the masked men in a frenzy.

The leader held the dagger high up in the air, just like a priest lifting the cup during the Eucharist. It looked as though he was asking for the weapon to be blessed.

"O Spiritus Mephistophiel, Madeschea, Diabola, Larua . . . threefold spirit from hell . . . *Sanguis tuus, cor tuum . . .*"

Karl had given up trying to make any sense of the twisted Latin terms and names, but the last phrase he understood without a problem.

Sanguis tuus, cor tuum . . . Your blood, your heart.

He had a horrible suspicion about what would come next. The black monk would ram the dagger into Faust's body and slit him open like a fish so he could tear out his heart. Dark spells and invocations still poured from the leader's mouth, but it couldn't be long before the dagger shot down. Karl looked around with panic. Was there no way to stop the ritual or at least disrupt it for a while?

His eyes fell upon the laterna magica sitting on the ground, and from there to the small lantern in his hand. The flame was very weak, but it still burned. Karl's hands shook. He had plenty of practice setting up the apparatus quickly. Would there be enough time?

He yanked the crate closer, opened it, and pulled out one of the oil-drenched cloths they had brought along. He held it to his lantern, which had just about gone out. When the rag was alight, he used it to light the oil lamp inside the laterna magica. Then he adjusted the tube until the glowing circle of light was directly on the back wall of the apse.

The men in the underground church cried out with surprise, and their leader broke off in the middle of his litany. Annoyed, he turned around and spotted the circle, which was hovering and flickering like a supernatural being.

A not very human sound escaped the monk's throat. It sounded like the angry growl of a wolf.

Then Karl inserted the first glass plate his hands could find.

$\sim$

Johann woke up and stared into the darkness.

Where was he? What had happened? Scraps of memory returned and slowly came together to form a complete picture. Tonio . . . the underground hall . . . the black potion . . . a baptismal font with blood . . . his daughter, almost naked and lifeless on an altar . . .

Greta!

He shot up and was overwhelmed by a wave of nausea. He threw up and retched, and still everything around him was black. Had he gone blind? Was he in hell?

He tried to focus on his body. The ground below him was cold; it appeared he was lying on a stone floor. Carefully he tried to move his limbs, first his legs, then his hands. He felt damp straw. A sharp pain shot up from his right hand and made him scream out. Something had happened to his hand but he couldn't remember what. An image flashed through his mind.

A curved dagger glinting in the light.

He screamed again. It was strange to hear his own voice, as if it didn't belong to him. It echoed as if he was deep below ground. He had a terrible headache and trouble breathing, as if something was blocking his nose. Why on earth couldn't he see a thing?

With his left hand—burnt from reaching into the glowing brazier—Johann gently touched his face and found that it was almost completely wrapped up in a bandage. He started tugging at the rags and was instantly punished with excruciating pain in his head, worse than the pain in his hand. He threw up again, and his mouth burned like fire as he spat out the caustic bile.

"I would leave the bandage where it is," uttered a hoarse voice nearby. "It may be dirty, but they soaked it in oil of Saint-John's-wort to prevent inflammation. I can smell it from here."

Johann froze. He knew the voice.

"Va . . . Valentin?" he said with a raspy voice. "You . . . you're alive?"

"More dead than alive. That monster broke something inside me. I . . . I can't move. But yes, I'm alive."

"What happened?" asked Johann quietly.

"You really want to know?"

When Johann didn't reply, Valentin spoke slowly.

"After you drank the black potion, the leader cut off your little finger. He said that was the first sacrifice."

Johann winced. The wound on his hand throbbed, and he thought he could still feel his finger. But he knew it was no longer there. Another image emerged in his memory: Tonio had thrown the finger—his little finger that used to hold playing cards and make coins disappear—into the baptismal font.

But that wasn't all.

"And the second sacrifice?" he asked quietly. "What was the second sacrifice?"

Silence spread through the room, a heavy silence that was almost harder to bear than the darkness around him.

"Speak up, damn it!" gasped Johann. "What was the second sacrifice?"

"They . . . they cut out your left eye."

Johann groaned. He felt sick again but he had nothing left to throw up. He was tempted to touch the bandage with his hand, but he knew that every touch would result in agonizing pain and could lead to infection. He probably suffered from fever already.

"They went about it very professionally," said Valentin with a shaking voice. "They used proper surgical instruments—I'm guessing one of the masked men was a Nuremberg physician. I think they wanted you alive."

"For the third sacrifice," whispered Johann.

"Yes, but it never came to that. Something happened. I must have passed out for a while, but I heard shouts and swearing, and then they locked us up in here. I suspect we're in some forgotten cellar below the Sebaldus Church. I don't know what happened next."

Silence descended over their prison chamber again while Johann's eye socket throbbed. The pain was surprisingly bearable—probably an aftereffect of the black potion. Johann guessed the drink contained henbane or devil's trumpet, or both. That would also explain the hallucinations. Johann remembered seeing people in the glistening surface of the basin. First Tonio—or a younger version of Tonio—and then a knight. He'd thought the man was Gilles de Rais—a name that had been haunting his dreams for years. No wonder that it should appear in his hallucinations.

"May I ask you something, Johann?" Valentin's voice roused him from his musings. "That potion they gave you. I thought it was poison and you would never regain consciousness. And yet you're awake, you speak—"

"Ash," said Johann tiredly.

"What did you say?"

"Ash. I ate ash. When they dragged me to the basin, I held on to one of the braziers. I pretended to stumble, grabbed some cold ashes from the edge, and stuffed them into my mouth."

Johann ran his tongue along his gums and teeth. He could still feel the foul-tasting crumbs in his mouth. "The ancient Greeks knew that ash is detoxifying. I hoped it would lessen the worst effects of the potion." He added bitterly, "Even if it couldn't save my eye."

With a trembling hand he felt for the bandage again. Then he adjusted it on one side until his right eye was unobstructed. For a few moments, everything remained pitch black, and Johann was beginning to think he had gone completely blind. But then he started to make out a few outlines around him. He was lying on the floor of a dark cellar, and there was a closed door on the wall opposite him. A shivering bundle lay on the ground beside him—Valentin. His old friend looked even more miserable than Johann felt. Valentin's body was strangely twisted, like a puppet whose strings had been cut.

"I . . . I'm so sorry, Johann," stammered Valentin. "Believe me, I only wanted to save Greta. They forced me to bring you down here, and it had to be tonight. Something to do with the stars, some comet—"

"I think we're even," said Johann, cutting him off. "You—"

A noise made him jump with fright. It was a key turning in the lock.

Johann took a deep breath.

They had come to fetch him for the third sacrifice. His body stiffened and his pulse raced. He didn't want to show fear, but he knew he couldn't prevent it. Hopefully his sacrifice would at least save Greta.

"God is great and powerful," he uttered instinctively. "God, give me strength . . ." He realized he hadn't prayed for his own immortal soul in a very long time. Perhaps now was a good moment to start.

"The Lord is my shepherd," he started. It was the psalm that had comforted so many dying and frightened men before him. "I shall not want. He maketh me to lie down in green pastures—"

"Doctor, it's me!"

Johann broke off and turned his bandaged head to the door.

There were no masked men, no insane devil worshippers, no Tonio.

Just Karl Wagner.

His assistant's outline was stark against the light of a torch from behind him.

What on earth? Johann thought. For the first time he wondered whether God might be a real person made of flesh and blood, standing in front of him in the shape of Karl.

His jerkin was filthy and torn, his hair looked ruffled and wild, and in his hand he was holding Valentin's key ring.

"One of them was for this door," he said with a tired smile. "First one I tried. Lucky I took this when we climbed into the prison." He looked back down the dark corridor nervously. "I don't think we have much time. They'll return for you soon."

Johann's throat was making a rattling sound. After a few moments he realized that he was trying to laugh—a circumstance so strange given their situation that he thought he must be dreaming.

"My God, boy—heaven sent you!" he exclaimed eventually.

"I have to agree with you for once," replied Karl. "I disrupted that horrific devil's mass with an image of our savior. Jesus Christ inside a glowing circle of light—the leader of those Satanists wasn't overly thrilled. It didn't take them long to discover the laterna and destroy it, but at least they had to pause their ceremony for a while to search for me."

"And now you have come back," mumbled Johann. "You could have fled."

Karl lowered his eyes. "I still owed you something, remember? I think now I've earned the right to get back my letters."

"You certainly have." Johann struggled to his feet, and Karl stared at the bandage on Faust's face. He hadn't seen it in the dim light until then.

"What in heaven's name have they done to you?"

"That isn't important right now. The only thing that matters is where they've taken Greta."

"When I set off the turmoil with the laterna, some of those masked madmen took the girl away." Karl hesitated. "That creepy fellow at the front shouted something about taking her up to the church."

"Probably the Sebaldus Church. I guess they want to keep Greta as a pawn," said Valentin from his corner. He moaned softly. "They'll only let her go once the third sacrifice has been given—if they don't simply kill her as an undesirable witness."

"He gave me his word," said Johann pensively, more to himself. "He's bound by it." He hesitated. "We need those people to feel secure. I can't leave. If they find that I've escaped, they will kill Greta or do even worse things to her."

He thought about Tonio's words at the altar.

It is the same as with lambs—the younger, the better tasting . . . Perhaps I will take her with me on Walpurgis Night in a couple of years, and we can share her.

"Damn it!" he swore. "There must be a solution. There always is one!"

But no matter how hard he thought, he couldn't find one. Whether he stayed or whether he went—he wouldn't see his daughter again. He was doomed. Down here in this hell on earth, all his knowledge was for nothing.

"I know a solution," said Valentin all of a sudden. His voice was firm and determined.

"Which is?"

"You go and I stay."

"And how is that supposed to help?" said Karl. "They'll see right away that the doctor has fled."

"Not if I am the doctor."

"You the doctor?" With his one remaining eye Johann stared at his friend in confusion. "What are you talking about?"

"You're wearing a bandage that covers most of your face," explained Valentin. "I'm a fair bit shorter than you, but I don't think they'll notice in the dark. Not if I'm wearing your star cloak. We'll stuff my clothes with straw and put them in the corner. They won't take much notice of the dummy—most likely they assume I'm already dead. They want you, Johann!"

Johann shook his head. "You can't be serious."

"Listen, Johann. I'm dying! I can feel it. My whole body is numb, and the coldness in my limbs is spreading. I was already a cripple beforehand, but that monster broke the last few bones that weren't broken inside me. Even if I lived— I'd be a living corpse." Valentin gave Johann a pleading look. "All I have left is Greta! You must find her and save her. It is the last thing I'm asking of you. One last favor as a friend."

"I've let you down before," muttered Johann. "I might do it again."

"You won't let me down, Johann. I forgave you for lying to me and using me all those years ago. But I would never forgive you if anything happened to Greta. You would never forgive yourself, I know that."

Johann didn't reply. His head hurt, and his eye socket and his right hand burned like fire. There was a high probability that he wouldn't survive this. If those lunatics didn't kill him, fever probably would. He had made sacrifices, but now his friend was going to give his life for him.

"I'm not doing it for you, Johann," Valentin whispered. "I'm doing it for Greta."

For Greta.

Johann nodded slowly. Neither he nor Valentin mattered—all that mattered was the girl.

His daughter.

"I'm going to need a new bandage," Johann said with a heavy voice.

Then, slowly and carefully, he unwrapped the dirty rags from around his head.

30

RUSHING DOWN THE CORRIDOR A SHORT WHILE LATER,
Johann felt as though he were trudging through a swamp. His legs kept giving
way beneath him, and Karl had to hold him up. Despite the ash he'd swallowed,
the poison of the black potion was still wreaking havoc in his body. Shadows
would leap at him from the walls, and he thought he could hear the voice of the
handsome knight.

Faites vite . . . faites vite . . . faites vite . . .

The only thing keeping him going was the thought of Greta.

Before they'd gone, he and Valentin had embraced one last time, and Johann
had sensed that the strength was draining from his old friend's body. When he
looked down at Valentin with his healthy eye one last time, Johann had seen
himself on the stone floor. Bandaged head, star cloak, and the shell of a body,
nothing more.

He had learned one thing from Valentin: what really mattered wasn't what
could be seen on the outside, nor the blind pursuit of knowledge, of power.

All that mattered was love.

What use was all his cleverness if he couldn't protect those he loved? Valentin
had shown him what love was capable of by sacrificing himself for Greta. In that
moment, Johann had realized that it was love alone that gave meaning to life.
That was something Tonio would never understand.

It was this revelation that spurred him on now.

Johann staggered more than he walked. He felt as cold as ice. He wore only
a thin shirt that reached to his knees; they'd put everything else on Valentin.
Somehow he managed to climb up a steep set of stairs that led to another door.
With one of the many keys from Valentin's key ring, Karl opened the lock, and

they found themselves in a room that, unlike all the previous ones, had a window. Early morning light fell through the bluish crown-glass pane.

They were back on the surface.

Shaking with fever, Johann looked around. The door was so smoothly set into the wall that it was almost invisible from the outside. A narrow walkway lined by columns led into another room. Elegant oak chests with veneer decorations lined the walls, and gold and silver cups stood on a table in the center. Karl opened one of the chests and gasped. Reverently, he held up a gemstone-studded cross—clearly a monstrance.

"We're in the inner sanctum," he whispered. "The sacristy of the Sebaldus Church. The masked men probably took Greta the same way." Karl put down the cross and looked around. "Hmm. Somewhere in here should be . . ." He opened another chest, rummaged around for a while, and, grinning triumphantly, pulled out two musty-smelling priests' robes. "Ha, I knew it. We'll hardly find a better disguise inside a church."

With much difficulty, Johann pulled on one of the robes, the hood scarcely concealing his poorly bandaged face. He was still shaking, but at least he felt a little warmer. He could tell the fever was still spreading, however.

When Karl had also put on his robe, he gave Johann a questioning look. "And now? What is your plan?"

Johann closed his eye. He wanted to put off the moment when he'd have to admit that he had no plan. The renowned and wise doctor was nothing but a poor, half-blind fool.

"You . . . you said before that they were taking Greta to the church," he said. "Did they say anything else? Any particular place—anything at all?"

"The leader only yelled that they ought to take the girl up to the church. I guess they went into the city from here. Nuremberg is a big place."

Johann sighed and reached for the tabletop to brace himself. "Then . . . then let's go into the church, at least. Maybe we'll find a clue as to Greta's whereabouts." But even while he spoke the sentence, he knew how helpless he sounded.

They walked down another walkway, crossed another room, and came to a door whose bolt had been left open. Slowly, Karl opened the door.

The nave of the Sebaldus Church lay in front of them. The sacristy wasn't far from the altar with the silver chest containing the relics of Saint Sebaldus. The slanted light of dawn fell through the tall glass windows and bathed the many columns, arcades, and side chapels in an unearthly light.

There were no churchgoers yet, but it couldn't be long until morning mass. Farther back, an old sexton was sweeping the floor. He was hunched low over his broom and didn't notice the two strange priests.

Johann looked around desperately.

He saw nothing. No clue, nothing.

Greta had disappeared from his life as suddenly as she'd entered it.

Karl gently touched him on the shoulder. "I know you want to find this girl for your friend," he said. "But you must see that it is pointless. They took her away hours ago. She could be anywhere by now."

"We must look for her," muttered Johann. "Look . . . for her . . ." The fever and the potion made him feel so heavy, so awfully heavy.

"Listen." Karl paused. "When I told you they didn't say anything else about where they were taking the girl, I wasn't telling the whole truth. The leader shouted something else—it was rather hard to understand. But I think he said, 'Take her up to the church and then . . .'" Karl swallowed. "'And then straight to hell.'"

"To hell?" asked Johann, his voice shaking.

"To hell." Karl nodded. "Those were his words. I didn't tell you earlier because I can see that the girl means a lot to you. But I think it's safe to assume that they killed her. But we survived! We only have to go out the church door and—"

Johann slid down against a column, his consciousness fading.

To hell.

Karl crouched down beside him with concern. "You must think about yourself now, Doctor. Forget the girl, forget—"

"I can't forget her, damn it!" shouted Johann with his last strength. Then he managed a hoarse whisper. "I can't forget her. She . . . she is my daughter."

Karl gaped at him. "Your daughter? But how?"

Then Johann passed out.

~

Deep down below, a lock clicked open and Valentin Brander spoke his final prayer.

Crunching footsteps approached, and then he was picked up like a rag doll. Underneath his bandage, a smile spread across Valentin's face.

They haven't noticed.

There must have been four of them. He could feel their hands as they lifted him onto some kind of stretcher and carried him out of the chamber. Soon he heard the strange litany again as they neared the underground hall. Valentin smelled burnt oil and smoke, a lot of smoke. He couldn't cough or his voice would give him away.

The men set him down, and the chanting stopped.

"We'll catch that scoundrel soon, I swear!" hissed someone not far from Valentin. The voice reminded him of a snake. "What a pity the cripple never told me that Faust's assistant was with him. My birds need food, and he's a handsome young man. But that doesn't matter now. All that matters is the last ritual—the third sacrifice."

Valentin held perfectly still. When he'd sent word to the man named Tonio del Moravia a few hours beforehand that he was bringing Faust to the agreed place, he hadn't mentioned anything about Karl Wagner. He wasn't sure why—a whim, one last tiny attempt of resistance against the enormously powerful, inexplicable evil. Who was Tonio? A madman who had gathered followers who were just as mad as him, or was he more than that? In the few conversations Valentin had led with him at night in some foggy alleyway, he hadn't come any closer to figuring out the man's mystery. Something incredibly cold radiated from him; he seemed like an ancient reptile in a human body. Only his eyes had glowed.

Who are you?

Valentin had hoped to learn the answer before his death. But then he realized that he didn't need any more answers after death, because there would be no more questions. Nothing mattered anymore. Nothing but Greta, the girl he loved like his own daughter, the girl who had enriched his poor, pathetic life a thousandfold for the last few years. Images started to appear before his mind's eye, giving him strength.

Greta laughing on a swing, her little hands clasping the hemp ropes tight, her legs dangling . . . Greta with a bleeding knee snuggling up to him . . . Greta with her doll on her lap, her mouth smeared with honey . . . Tell me a story, Uncle Valentin! Just one more story before bedtime—please!

He wanted to leave this life with those images in his mind.

The litany rose again, and Valentin heard the snake's voice above the chanting.

"O Mephistophiel, O Satanas, O Diabolos, O Larua . . ."

Valentin no longer trembled; his body and mind felt calm. He was no longer afraid, because he knew that his life had had meaning. And that he wasn't dying for nothing. Because of him, Greta would live, and she'd even have a father. More memories rose to the surface; there were so many of them.

Greta, stark naked in a wooden tub, giggling, her little arms stretched out for him . . .

"O Samael, O Azazel, O Beelzebub . . ."

Greta and him on a horse, riding together across the fallow fields outside Nuremberg, and she laughs—oh, how she laughs!

"O Iris, O Scheitan, O Urian . . ."

Greta dancing for him, spinning around, her dress a whirling circle . . . Her laughter . . . oh, her ringing laughter . . .

"O Lucifer, accept the third sacrifice!"

Something was driven deep into Valentin's chest, but he felt no pain, only a pleasant warmth spreading all through his body.

He laughed as his soul traveled heavenward.

Far down below, in a world that was no longer his, someone screamed out loud with rage and disappointment, and Valentin knew that the devil had lost the game.

~

Johann was dreaming.

The August sun fell on him warmly from a cloudless blue sky; bees and flies buzzed around him, and the ears in the grain field were brushed by a wind as gentle as if someone were stroking his cheek. Margarethe was lying next to him, singing the old, familiar nursery rhyme.

Growing in our garden are parsley and thyme; our Gretchen is the bride, she's looking so fine . . .

Together they dozed in their favorite hiding place in the rye field, not far from the walls of Knittlingen. The grain was trampled flat in a circle around them, and in the center stood the weathered stone cross.

"Will you marry me when we're grown up, Johann?" asked Margarethe softly in his dream. "Will you look after me? Now and forever?"

Johann smiled and squeezed her hand. "I promise I will look after you. Now and forever."

"Just like you . . ." Margarethe hesitated. She brushed a strand of flaxen hair from her face; the air shimmered with heat. "Just like you . . ." Suddenly her voice took on a different tone, low and jarred as if she were speaking from inside a well, as if she were someone else.

Someone profoundly evil.

"Just like you looked after Martin, right? You bloody coward! You piece of dirt!"

Clouds moved in front of the sun and a shadow covered Margarethe's face, which ceased to be hers. It became that of Martin, then of Signore Barbarese, of Tonio, then of Gilles de Rais.

The face of Gilles de Rais, the handsome knight.

"I like to catch two children at once. Then I kill the first one and make the other one watch," said Margarethe, and her lips melted onto the ground like hot wax.

Johann wanted to scream but only managed a gargle. His tongue had been ripped out and was lying in the dirt before him.

A thunderclap announced an impending storm, and the wind whipped waves through the rye field. He could hear footsteps now, as loud as the cutting of a scythe. They plowed through the field toward him—swish, swoosh.

Closer and closer.

Swish, swoosh.

"Who's afraid of the boogeyman?" asked Margarethe in a hoarse whisper. It was the opening line of a children's game of catch. And every child knew what to answer.

"No one," replied Johann.

"And what if he comes?"

"Then we run!"

Swish, swoosh . . . swish, swoosh . . . swish . . .

He jumped up and ran across the field as the first raindrops struck his face. After a while he noticed that he hadn't thought of Margarethe. He had forgotten all about her in his fear and had simply run away.

When he turned around, she was gone.

"Margarethe!" he shouted into the rain, thunder, and howling wind. "Margarethe, where are you?"

He searched everywhere with growing desperation. There she was! She was standing among the ears, waving. But when he looked again it was only a scarecrow. The scarecrow's eyes were black, black, dead, button eyes, as piercing as needles.

"Where are you?" screamed Johann again.

"I'm in hell," said Greta, his daughter, the scarecrow with the button eyes. "Search for me in hell."

Then she stalked away on broomstick legs, a shrinking spot on the horizon until the rain washed her away. Only her words still echoed across the windswept fields.

"Search for me in hell."

The boy who used to be called Johann a long time ago—in another life— awoke with a feverish scream. His face was bathed in sweat, and his mouth as dry as a brittle Eucharist host.

"Margarethe!" gasped Johann. "Stay with me! Greta."

"You're safe, Doctor," said a voice from next to him. "All will be well."

Johann opened his one eye and the memories returned instantly. The worried face of Karl hovered above him. He was holding a wet rag, which he used to wipe Johann's forehead. From the corner of his eye, Johann saw some old wooden beams on a ceiling, a narrow window covered in cobwebs letting in some milky sunlight, a small bed, and reeds on the floor with a foul-smelling chamber pot in the middle. From afar he heard shouting and cheering, and the music of fanfares, drums, and bells.

"Where are we?" asked Johann. He was a little dizzy and his head ached, but he felt better than earlier.

"In the attic room of a tavern," replied Karl. "Not far from Sebaldus Church. You passed out and I carried you here. You slept for a few hours." He gave an exhausted smile. "The tavern keeper thought we were two drunken itinerant preachers and gave me this chamber under the roof. It's not the best room in the house, but at least I didn't have to answer any nosy questions."

Johann groaned as he felt the bandage on his face and the empty eye socket below. Carefully he touched the left side of his face; the cloths seemed fresh.

"I might not have studied medicine for very long, but I remembered a few things," said Karl, eyeing his patient with concern. "There was a pharmacy not far from here, and I used the last of my money to buy a few herbs to stanch the bleeding. Lady's mantle, shepherd's purse." He paused. "Our professor at the university said that we ought to cauterize the wound and smear it with a paste of egg and ash, but I didn't. At least your hand and face are bandaged properly now. We'll see what happens."

"Th . . . thank you." Johann slowly rose from the musty-smelling bed. He still felt nauseated from the potion Tonio had given him. "Water."

Karl handed him a jug, and he drank in long gulps.

"What's all the noise outside?" asked Johann eventually, wiping his cracked lips.

"It's the Schembartlauf parade. It started about an hour ago—the whole of Nuremberg is in the streets," Karl said. "Those masked jesters dance through town and tease the spectators, and I think at the end they storm a life-sized elephant made of wood and linen. I saw the giant contraption briefly on our way here—it was standing next to the Sebaldus Church. A truly impressive—"

Johann dropped the jug to the ground and it shattered into a hundred pieces.

"Hell," he said.

Karl put his hand on Faust's forehead. "You still have a strong fever, Doctor. You better lie down. I'll bring you a fresh—"

"Hell," said Johann again.

He stood up on shaky legs and walked to the door.

"For heaven's sake, what are you doing? You can't go outside! Where do you think you're going? You are hurt—you're hallucinating!"

"I've never been clearer in my head," said Johann as he started to climb down the stairs. "I'm going down to hell to fetch my daughter."

~

Soon they were both standing in the street. The carnival raged all around them. Throngs of people lined the sides of the lane, waiting for the costumed dancers to pass them by.

Johann squeezed through a gap and watched as half a dozen Schembart runners skipped past, with bells on their ankles and pikes in their hands. From time to time they would rush at the hooting crowd and pretend to stab them with their blunt weapons. People laughed and cheered, and the air was rich with the delicious smells of fried and boiled food.

Many musicians and jugglers who weren't Schembart runners had also joined the procession. Troupes from all over the region used this day to show off their tricks or to roam the streets playing flutes or bagpipes. Johann looked around searchingly.

Where is the hell? he thought. *Where is it?*

A hand tapped his shoulder. It was Karl, who had pushed his way through to Johann. "You have a fever," he urged. "You must go back to bed!"

Johann said nothing and continued to watch the procession. He struggled to focus. He was trembling and sometimes thought he was still dreaming. A huge, strong man wearing a costume made of dead leaves and moss was just walking past him. His face was hidden beneath a fake bushy beard, and he was swinging a tree trunk that had something tied to it that was impossible to make out in the jostle. Johann's hood covered most of his face, but still he thought the giant looked at him.

The large man slowed down.

"Any one of those masked men could be one of the lunatics from the crypt," whispered Karl, tugging at Johann's robe. "If they spot us, we're done. We must get away from here!"

Johann still wasn't reacting, staring instead at some artificial horses that came after the dancers. He could tell by the feet under the furs that inside each costume were two men. The wild man had vanished behind the next corner, and the parade was proceeding. Noise and laughter rose and fell like water on a mill.

"The elephant," uttered Johann all of a sudden, more to himself. Then he finally turned to Karl. "Where is the elephant?"

"The elephant? It was standing right next to the portal when we left the church. Why?"

"Damn, don't you get it?" Johann was almost shouting now. "The elephant is the hell! That's what the Schembart runners call their big parade wagon. Remember? Valentin told us last night. It's the hell!"

"You . . . you're saying . . ."

"By Christ, *that's* the hell Tonio was talking about. No inferno or Last Judgment, but the parade wagon!" Johann grabbed Karl by the sleeve, his one eye glaring angrily. "Take her up to the church and then straight to hell—isn't that what he said? That's where they are hiding her. Every street in town is busy because of the Schembartlauf, so they couldn't drag her away unnoticed. But it's no problem inside the parade wagon—they can smuggle her right through Nuremberg and no one will ever know." Johann's sweaty face was right up close to Karl's now. "Where is this elephant now? Where is the hell?"

"The . . . the tavern keeper said the parade would end on the main square at noon," Karl said, trying to free himself from Johann's grasp. "There'll be a huge spectacle with dancing and fireworks, and at the end they storm the elephant."

Johann looked up and saw that the cool winter sun stood high in the sky. Damn it, how long had he slept?

On the main square at noon.

"Let's go!" he shouted. "We don't have much time."

He pushed his way through the crowd, jabbing people left and right with his elbows. His right hand burned like fire, and the pain in his head nearly drove him insane, but he pressed on.

"Hey! Wait for me!"

Karl rushed after him, his robe billowing. Johann shoved aside a burly older man who cried out angrily and kicked Johann. He staggered, caught himself, and carried on, struggling to find his bearings. His field of vision was impaired by the bandage, and he fought against dizzy spells; sledgehammers seemed to thump in his temples.

Suddenly he found himself right in the middle of a group of masked Schembart runners, dancing and jumping and cartwheeling all around him. Grinning masks stared at him, bells jingled everywhere, and someone pushed Johann to the ground. Towering above him was the wild man in his costume of moss and ferns, swinging his enormous tree trunk like a club. Now Johann saw what was tied to the trunk.

It was a doll made to look like a child, about as long as his forearm and very lifelike.

The wild man was aiming his giant cudgel straight at Johann's head.

"Bienvenue en enfer!" he growled in French, and Johann thought he'd heard the voice before.

Suddenly the huge man staggered and cried out angrily as someone gave him a shove. The tree trunk missed Johann's head by an inch.

"Run!"

Karl pulled Johann up and pushed him away from the eerie giant with the club and into a throng of laughing, dancing spectators who thought Johann's stunt was part of the show.

Johann stumbled on, partly pushed by the crowd and partly dragged by his assistant. He could hardly breathe in the stench of sweat, alcohol, and horse dung; everything was so loud, so terribly loud—the drums, the bells, the shouts of the spectators, everything mixing into a monotonous mess. Behind him, Johann caught a glimpse of the wild man flanked by other masked men, the giant waving his tree trunk violently. But then Karl maneuvered the doctor around a corner, and the parade moved past them. Instantly, it was much quieter.

"They recognized us," gasped Karl, leaning against the wall of a house. "I can't really see their eyes underneath those masks, and I don't know if they are the same men as down in the crypt—but I'm certain some of them recognized us. That huge fellow just tried to kill you! We're not even safe in the crowd any longer." He shot Johann a look of warning. "Do you still want to find that elephant?"

Johann gave a curt nod. He was too exhausted for words.

"All right, then. Let's go straight to hell." He gestured to the right. "This way. The parade takes a longer loop to the main square. If we hurry, we might get there before the Schembart runners."

The narrow, filthy alleyway went around a bend, crossed a courtyard full of barrels, and finally ended on the main square. The parade was nearing from the east. There was no sight of any dancers yet, but Johann and Karl could hear the music and cheering. Something cracked and hissed, as if fireworks were going off somewhere. Johann blinked a few times; his one eye was blinded by the noon sunshine. A large crowd had already gathered, waiting for the procession to arrive. People stood tightly packed, from the city hall to the Schöner

Brunnen fountain, with its gilded towers and manifold statues, all the way over to Frauenkirche Church; even the balconies of the patricians' houses were full of people. Johann's eye scanned the crowd, his heart racing.

Where?

There! Right next to the Schöner Brunnen fountain, surrounded by a knot of people, stood the elephant. It was at least three paces high, on wheels, and crowned by a wooden tower that was surrounded by mock battlements. Four tiny cannons were fastened on the corners, and a handful of jesters stood behind the battlements, including a priest with dozens of letters of indulgence sewn onto his robe, fools with playing cards or dice patterns on their costumes, and a hunchbacked witch with a long nose and a pack on her back. The crowd cheered for the dressed-up figures when their little cannon spouted red sparks. There was cracking, smoke, thunder, and hissing.

"Hell on earth," said Johann. "We found it."

"And what do you propose we do now?" asked Karl. "Even if Greta is somewhere inside that wagon, you can't just climb up there and—hey!"

He broke off when Johann stormed toward the elephant.

The train of Schembart runners arrived from a lane next to Frauenkirche Church and was received with much fanfare. The main square was so full that Johann struggled to get through. Several of the jugglers also arrived on the square and showed their tricks and acts. The elephant swayed like a reed in the wind among all the people, and the costumed men atop the tower threw small treats into the crowd. They grabbed the treats out of the pack of the witch, who stared at the people below from nasty little eyes. Again the cannons were lit and spat out red fire.

Johann pushed through the crowd; he was close to the elephant now, but he still hadn't figured out what to do next. He was certain that Greta must be somewhere inside the structure, probably bound and gagged. He didn't think the masked men had had an opportunity to get her away yet. But what was he supposed to do? Karl was right. He couldn't climb the tower on his own, especially since it was guarded by several costumed men—and he couldn't be sure the men weren't Tonio's.

Unsure of what to do next, he paused just a few steps away from the elephant. Then, suddenly, a horde of colorfully clad soldiers in slit trousers approached from the direction where the Schembart runners had entered the square. They yelled and shouted as they carried ladders toward the elephant. Johann startled. Yelling soldiers, like in battle? Was he having another fever dream? But then he remembered what Karl had told him earlier.

At the end they storm the elephant.

Those soldiers were part of the show. They were going to storm hell.

When the men ran past them, accompanied by the cheers and hoots of the crowd, Johann joined them. He saw from the corner of his eye that Karl had caught up to him, his face a grimace of fear and determination. Johann was surprised the soldiers let them run along just like that, but then he caught another glimpse of the preacher atop the tower. The men probably thought he and Karl were also in costume.

Screaming and shouting wildly, the false mercenaries braced their ladders against the elephant and started to scale its sides. The masked men at the top bombarded them with treats and lit their cannons again and again until Johann's ears were ringing. Panting, he struggled to climb one of the ladders when he noticed that a man at the top had started to push it away from the elephant. The ladder swayed dangerously and almost toppled, but Karl managed to hold it and started to climb up himself.

Johann studied the elephant as he climbed the rungs of the ladder. It was made of wood and linen that had been painted gray, and attached to the feet were wheels on which the giant contraption could be moved through the city. He estimated there was enough room in the elephant's belly for a person, if not several. If there was an access point to the belly, then it was probably in the tower, which was about two paces taller than the top of the elephant.

Johann and Karl reached the top of the ladder and climbed over the balustrade surrounding the tower. Several soldiers had also reached the top, and they waved to the crowd, who celebrated them as conquerors. The priest with the letters of indulgence squirmed in the arms of a mercenary, squealing like a pig and rolling his eyes, and the crowd hooted with laughter. The hunchbacked witch still stood motionless, staring into the crowd.

The tower swayed under the weight of all the people; it wouldn't be long before it toppled. Johann unsteadily crept toward an artificial arch made of thin, painted wood that led inside the tower. The archway wasn't quite three feet high.

Johann peered inside but couldn't see any way into the belly of the elephant. He slammed his fist against the wall with disappointment and ripped the linen.

Damn!

Suddenly his idea seemed absurd to him, the spawn of a fever dream. How could he have thought Greta would be in here? The masked men had probably taken her away long ago—perhaps she wasn't even in the city anymore.

Perhaps she's already dead.

Johann's good hand clutched the linen, and it ripped further. He had been forcing the thought aside with all his might, fighting the unavoidable, but now it rushed back at him with a vengeance.

He had lost his daughter only a few days after meeting her.

Below him, the crowd heaved, people clapping and cheering. The first spectators were starting to tear at the gray fabric of the elephant. It wouldn't be long before the Nurembergers would shred the beast to pieces until the hell was conquered and the Schembartlauf over.

Everything would be over.

Johann looked around desperately for Karl but couldn't find him anywhere. Maybe it was just as well that his assistant didn't see him in this dark hour. Johann decided to throw himself off the elephant in the hope of putting an end to his life—just like the time he leaped off the Heidelberg bridge into the Neckar. Was the height sufficient to break his neck? As he went to look over the balustrade, his gaze was caught by the witch, who was still standing rigidly in the same spot. She wore a dress, an apron, and a headscarf like all old women, and her body was hunched over, making her seem short. For the first time Johann noticed the eyes behind the mask.

He winced as if he'd been slapped.

Eyes as black as pools in the woods.

They were his eyes.

The witch's hunchback was artificial, and Johann realized that she wasn't crippled but in fact a small person. Her hands were crossed on the balustrade and tied with thin ropes. Gray, almost invisible strings also ran up her dress and to the tower, holding her upright like a life-sized puppet; only the head beneath the mask rocked gently from side to side. Her eyes gleamed with pain and despair.

"Greta!" screamed Johann. His voice was drowned out by the noise of the crowd. "Greta!"

He tried to rush toward his daughter when someone yanked him back abruptly. A rope was thrown around his neck and pulled tight, and then someone dragged him up as if he were a rabid dog. A huge hand lifted him over the edge of the tower, and Johann treaded thin air. Panting and gasping for breath, he tried to catch a glimpse of the figure behind him.

It was the wild man.

Underneath his fake beard, the giant gave an evil grin. His black hair hung into his pockmarked face like rotting reeds. And finally Johann recognized him.

It was Poitou, Tonio's French friend he'd met in Nördlingen all those years ago.

Johann had heard his voice down in the crypt, too. Like his master, Poitou didn't seem to have aged much, although it was hard to tell with the fake beard and the wig. His strength, at least, was just as incredible as seventeen years ago.

The giant was still holding his victim over the balustrade. Johann made out a handful of masked men with their pikes below him, but unlike the ones from the parade, their lances weren't blunt. The sharp points glinted in the noontide sun, and they were aimed directly at Johann. He gagged and wheezed. If Poitou let go of him now, he'd be skewered like a rabbit. But if the giant hung on to him, he'd choke.

The crowd roared with laughter. Evidently, they thought the squirming monk was another funny stunt. Johann gasped for air and clutched the rope around his neck with his good hand, but he was far too weak to put up a fight. The voices of the spectators began to sound farther away, and his eyesight became blotchy and blurred. The world was narrowing into a tunnel, and at its end stood the loveliest apparition, glowing, surrounded by a halo . . .

Margarethe, I'm coming . . . I'm almost there . . . I . . .

Something grunted, and it took Johann a few moments to understand that it was Poitou. Then there was a crash as the hulk of a man fell backward against the tower, pulling Johann with him. The rope loosened a fraction, and Johann coughed and spluttered. From the corner of his eye he saw Karl wrestling with Poitou and guessed that his assistant must have attacked the giant from behind. One of the masked men that had followed the soldiers up the tower was just about to point one of the little cannons at Karl. And among all the chaos, Greta was still standing at the railing, stiff and quiet.

Johann tugged at the rope around his neck but it wouldn't loosen any further. It was fastened around his throat like an iron ring, and he was running out of breath. If only he had—

The knife!

Frantically he fingered for the knife under his robe—the same knife that Tonio had given him long ago. He found it, ripped it off, and cut the rope.

Fresh, life-giving air streamed down his throat.

Johann looked around, trying to grasp the situation. Karl was still grappling with Poitou, but the young man's strength seemed to fade. The giant's eyes sparkled devilishly.

"C'est la fin et le début," he snarled. *"Bienvenue en enfer!"*

At that moment, as the crowd howled and raved and the cannon next to Karl exploded into a blazing shower of red sparks, a profound calmness spread inside Johann. And even though he knew that only a few seconds passed by, he felt as though time were stretching out forever.

Greta's fearful eyes behind the mask . . . The knife cutting through her ties . . . Poitou's angry outcry . . . The blade in Johann's hand, as cold as ice . . . One last calculating look, then the throw—the one throw he had been waiting for all his life.

The knife cut through the air like an arrow.

Then the blade entered Poitou's left eye without a sound.

"An eye for an eye, and a tooth for a tooth," breathed Johann.

With a gasp of surprise, Poitou collapsed against the wall of the tower, felled by the knife of his master. His remaining eye stared lifelessly at the raven and the two crows circling in the blue sky above them. The birds cawed loudly; it sounded like laughter. Then they flew off.

The spectators hadn't yet realized what had just happened. Johann grabbed Greta under her arms and dragged her toward a ladder. The witch's mask slid to one side, and her pale face appeared beneath it. She was no longer unconscious, but she wasn't fully in her right senses, either.

"What . . . ?" she muttered. "Who . . . ?"

"Don't worry, my dear. We'll get you out of here," said Johann softly.

Meanwhile, Karl had thrown one of the masked men by the cannon over the balustrade, but part of the tower had caught on fire from the shower of sparks.

The dry timber crackled and smoked—so it would all go up in flames. Costumed men stood leaning over the dead Poitou; someone was shouting for help.

"Quick—take Greta on your back and let's get out of here!" shouted Johann.

Karl looked confused for a moment, but then he recognized the girl.

"The hell," he whispered. "You were right, Doctor."

He heaved the girl onto his back, and she clung on as he scrambled down the ladder. Johann followed. The soldiers and other masked men were too busy with the fire to notice them.

As chaos erupted all around them, they pushed their way through the crowd, away from the elephant, which by now burned like a giant torch.

The farther away they got from the main square, the quieter the streets became. It seemed as if the whole of Nuremberg was watching the grand finale, and they hardly saw a soul as they rushed through the lanes. Karl still carried Greta on his back. She sighed from time to time and cried out, barely aware of what was going on around her. Johann suspected that Tonio had also given her a potion, but unlike him, she hadn't eaten ash. What sort of nightmares were torturing the girl right now?

As Johann looked at his daughter, he felt a fire burn in his heart unlike anything he'd ever felt before. And he felt relief. It was as if he'd paid an ancient debt. But then the pain and the fever returned. His whole body started to tremble; the fight with Poitou had drained the last of his strength. His bandage and the robe were torn. He dragged himself over the cobbled streets like a walking corpse, knowing it wouldn't be long before he'd collapse. And this time he wouldn't get back up.

"We . . . we . . . must leave town," he gasped. "Tonio . . . He'll be looking for us . . . His . . . his followers will tell him what happened."

Karl didn't reply as he carried Greta through the lanes. Sweat was pouring down his face, and he was bleeding from a wound on his forehead. His strength, too, was coming to an end; he stumbled more than he walked. He stubbornly stared straight ahead to where the lane was ending in a small market square near the Hospital of the Holy Ghost. The stalls that usually sold expensive spices, loaves of bread, cheese, and salted meat stood empty. Everyone, even the market wives, had rushed over to the main square, where a column of black smoke rose to the sky. The news of the burning elephant had probably lured even the last Nuremberger out of the house.

Utterly exhausted, Karl stopped by the bridge east of the hospital. "We should go back to the command," he said. "I can't carry Greta much further. The Teutonic Knights will give us shelter and tend to her—and you."

"Out of the question." Johann shook his head and started trudging across the bridge. "Who is to say that the command isn't full of traitors? Many of Tonio's followers are patricians. Why would the command be an exception? It's too dangerous."

"But we need shelter!" said Karl urgently. "Some kind of hiding place. Just look at you!" He gave a desperate laugh. "A feverish one-eyed man who can barely walk in a straight line."

Johann looked down at himself. Karl was right. He was a shivering bundle wrapped in filthy bandages. There was nothing left of the proud, famous doctor.

"Very well," he said. "Let us . . . rest for a while. We'll find somewhere."

He knew he probably wouldn't be able to get back up once he sat down. But they couldn't keep going, either, and so he looked around for a hiding place. In the center of the bridge, stairs led down to a long, narrow island in the Pegnitz. Its sandy shores were lined with brown foam and trash washing down the river from the mills. There was a grove in the middle of the island, which probably served as a secret meeting place for lovers during the warmer months. Low trees and shrubs would offer some shelter. They walked onto the island from the west and pushed their way into the undergrowth, where they finally collapsed with exhaustion. Greta was no longer making any sound.

"I wonder if she'll recover." Karl carefully opened Greta's torn dress and leaned over her. "Her breathing is very weak."

Johann felt a stab in his chest. The thought hadn't even crossed his mind until then. Maybe the potion Tonio had given his daughter was too strong. Maybe she'd never return to him, forever caught in the twilight? But then Greta suddenly opened her eyes—his black eyes.

"Where . . . where are we?" she asked with a feeble voice.

"Somewhere safe," replied Johann and held her cold hand.

"Johann." Greta gave a tired smile. She seemed to recognize him only now, underneath his bandage. "I . . . I feel so heavy. Everything is so heavy. Can you do magic for me? I . . . I like it when you do magic."

Johann brushed her cheek with his fingers, and then he pulled a small pebble from her ear like he used to do with coins. "Your head is full of stones," he said, trying his utmost to sound calm and cheerful. "No wonder you feel heavy." He continued to pull pebble after pebble from her ear. She smiled once more.

"Are you . . . are you a real wizard?"

I am your father, my child, he thought. *I am the man who drove your mother to her death. And I am the man who loved her more than anything. Will you ever be able to forgive me?*

"Where . . . where is Uncle Valentin?"

Johann swallowed. He couldn't tell her—not yet. What should he say? But then Greta closed her eyes, and her breathing became stronger and more regular. And as Johann watched her, he felt himself grow calm, also. It was strange. He had studied so many subjects, attended so many lectures, become a master of all seven liberal arts, but there was one art no scholar in the world had taught him—not the magisters and doctors at Heidelberg, not Archibaldus, and least of all Tonio. It was a discipline that was usually hidden behind dry words in the Latin and Greek writings, as difficult to chew as stale bread. To experience it firsthand was an entirely different story. Ovid had once called it *Ars amatoria,* even if he'd meant something slightly different.

The art of loving.

The eighth liberal art.

Yes, he had loved Margarethe, and he always would. But that love rested on experiences from their childhood, from a long, common history, and also on expectations that probably would never have been fulfilled. His love for this child, however, for his daughter, had no goal. It simply existed. It filled him and gave him an inner peace he'd never experienced before. Johann wondered how his life would have evolved if he'd met Greta sooner, if he'd been her father from the start. Would it have put an end to his endless searching, his unquenchable thirst for knowledge? Probably not. But it would have steered his life down calmer roads.

Johann jutted out his chin with determination. This life—their life together—couldn't be over yet.

It had only just begun. And he would fight for it.

The noises of the spectacle on the main square blew over to them on the breeze—the crashing of a cannon, shouting, the metallic ringing of a bell.

Johann guessed the people of Nuremberg had put out the fire by now. The feast was over and folks would go home.

Johann dozed and soon nodded off, soothed by the feeling of having saved his daughter—for the moment, at least. Soft music caressed his ears, heavenly fanfares, angelic, almost . . .

So tired . . . so awfully tired . . .

"Wake up, Doctor!" Karl's voice tore him out of his dreams.

"Leave me . . . ," he said weakly. "So warm, the music . . ."

But Karl wouldn't give up. He pulled at the doctor's robe like an irritating mutt, and finally he gathered the few handfuls of snow left under the shrubs and rubbed them on Johann's chest.

"How dare you, you insolent . . ." Johann shot up, his good hand ready to strike, but as soon as he saw Karl he knew where he was. His daughter was sleeping beside him, her chest rising and falling steadily. He shook himself to dispel the fatigue.

"Those madmen are going to search for us," said Karl imploringly. "We can't stay here forever."

"Forgive me. You . . . you're right." Johann brushed the snow off his robe and felt awake again. "We need to get out of Nuremberg as fast as we can."

"Only question is, How?" Karl looked around skeptically. He shivered underneath his thin robe. The sun had moved on and stood low above the nearby city wall. The icy waters of the Pegnitz flowed past them lazily. "If it's true what you say and Tonio has men everywhere, then he's probably watching the city gates. We won't get out of town the way we look. Most likely, not even the regular city guards would let us pass. We look like outlaws."

"We must at least try. We can't stay in Nuremberg—it's much too . . ."

Johann faltered when he heard the music again. When he was half-asleep, he'd thought he was imagining it, but now he realized it was real. Flutes, drums, tambourines—soft, but clearly there. Even the quaking sound of a bagpipe was among the instruments. The music was coming not from the main square but from somewhere to the northeast, where the Laufer Gate led onto the road to Prague.

A quiet suspicion sprouted in Johann's mind.

"Quickly—follow me," he ordered.

"What's your plan?"

But instead of replying, Johann shook Greta awake. "Child, wake up! You must try to walk—just for a short while!"

"What . . . what . . . ?" she murmured. She opened her eyes and looked around with confusion.

"Pick her up and run!" said Johann to Karl. "Before it's too late!"

Without another word he hurried back to the bridge. Breathing hard, Karl lugged Greta up the narrow, steep stairs. Staggering along slowly, they headed northeast, past wells, taverns, and smaller markets that gradually filled with people again. They walked around a corner by the old Egidienkirche Church and finally reached the wide, cobblestoned street that led to the Laufer Gate. The music had steadily grown louder and sounded very close now.

And then Johann saw them.

There were about a dozen flautists, several drummers, and a short fellow playing an ancient march on the bagpipe. Never before had the quaking, mind-numbing noise sounded so sweet to Johann's ears. The musicians were followed by jesters in red-and-blue costumes doing cartwheels and juggling balls, a real camel, and a series of colorfully painted wagons hung with all sorts of household items. Striding with self-important expressions between the wagons were several itinerant preachers who probably made a living as traveling scribes and relic traders. They all headed toward the Laufer Gate like one big, glittering snake. There was no sign of any Schembart runners.

"The jugglers from the square!" cried Karl. He and Johann were holding Greta between them now, and she managed to stumble along in small steps. She was still very sluggish. "That's where the music was coming from!"

Johann nodded. "The Schembartlauf parade is over, and the jugglers move on to the next city, like they always do." He sighed. "I saw them earlier but forgot all about them."

Karl watched the bright, noisy train passing by. One of the jugglers, wearing a red fool's cap, took a mock bow and showed them his backside, making an unappetizing sound. Karl turned away in disgust.

"What are we doing here?" he asked. "I've truly had enough of jesters and masks."

"Well, I'm going to ask them if we can come along." Johann gestured at the traveling preachers in their worn-out robes. "No one is going to notice us among all those quacks and fraudsters. And I'm sure we can find a spot in one of the wagons for Greta. Wait here."

He limped toward a wagon and soon returned with a smile on his face.

"They said we can come. All the way to Prague, if we like. There's going to be a huge feast in the summer, apparently."

"Just like that?" Karl gaped at him. "How did you wrangle that so quickly? You don't have any money, so how on—?"

"I speak their language. A few words in thieves' cant, a few old tales, and the usual coin trick." Johann grinned. "We jugglers know one another."

"The great Doctor Johann Georg Faustus, a dishonorable juggler?" Karl laughed in disbelief. "Are you serious?"

Johann winked at his assistant with his one eye. "I've had many lives, my boy. You don't even know the half of it, and I'll never tell you which half is true. Now come before they move on without us."

Johann led them to one of the colorful wagons, and Greta was allowed to lie down inside. Karl joined the itinerant priests walking ahead of the wagon, while Johann sat down on the box seat with his hood pulled over his face. The driver, a young lad with red curls and a red gugel, gave him a cheeky grin.

"Got into some trouble, old man?" he jeered. "Wouldn't be the first to join the traveling folk. What do you know?"

"Oh, a few things." Johann smiled and gazed at the road that led through the Laufer Gate. The gates stood wide open, and the guards watched the lively train with dark expressions, pleased the dishonorable folks were leaving town.

When the jugglers danced through the gate, the musicians played their farewell tune and the wagons rattled across the drawbridge. Johann looked back one last time. Next to the gate stood a small boy, watching the noisy procession with his mouth open.

He looked spellbound, and Johann knew why.

Epilogue

"**BEHOLD THIS DRINK AND BE AMAZED! IT IS THE SAME** drink the Greek king Mithridates used, once upon a time, to protect himself from snakebites, and which Heracles used to capture Cerberus, the hound of hell. Thanks to this drink, Emperor Friedrich lived for more than a hundred years! The bottle is yours for just two hellers. And for three more I'll read your future in your palm. Come and learn what fate holds in store for you with the great Doctor Johann Georg Faustus!"

The people on the small market square pointed and stared. Standing in front of them on the box seat of a wagon was a man wearing a blue-and-black star-spangled cloak, watching them from beneath his floppy hat with a pair of piercing black eyes. The left eye in particular seemed to fix on the crowd ominously, gleaming like a black diamond from the depths of hell.

"The first of you to buy a bottle of the drink receives a horoscope for the whole year!" the doctor promised. He raised his hands, and the crowd saw that he wore a black leather glove on the right. "Come closer! Don't be afraid. What I foretell always comes true—the good things, at least," he added with a wink.

The people whispered and nudged one another. They knew this uncanny man from tales and from tattered, cheaply printed leaflets that made the rounds at taverns. Apparently, not long ago, the doctor flew upon a swan that he'd fed with his theriac in Basel. In Braunschweig, he made the wheels on the cart of a wealthy farmer disappear, and in the faraway Orient, he conjured deer antlers on the helmet of an imperial knight, whereupon the heathens fled in droves.

And now this widely traveled man had actually come to their small town, like a messenger from a distant world. The famous Doctor Johann Georg Faustus. He was real!

Johann stifled a smile as he gazed at the gawking crowd from atop his wagon. Here in the Breisgau region, near the Alps, the audience was especially grateful. Maybe that was because they were so far away from the big cities—from Cologne, Frankfurt, Nuremberg, and Augsburg, where the world was changing more rapidly than ever before.

"We only have a few bottles of the miracle potion left," declared Johann, making a sweeping gesture toward his wagon. "My loyal assistant, a widely traveled scholar from the University of Paris, will fetch them for you."

Ducking out of the wagon came Karl Wagner, carrying a heavy crate full of corked bottles of theriac in his arms. Karl had perfected the recipe with a mix of juniper, gentian root, a pinch of henbane, and a lot of strong brandy. People loved the brew, just like they loved Karl's painted canvases that hung down the sides of the wagon like flags. They showed fire-spitting dragons, monstrous creatures with long snouts, people with wolf heads, and a lion with the tail of a scorpion. Doctor Faustus had encountered all those creatures in the course of his travels, and there was a story to tell about each one. Karl was rightly proud of his artworks. They might not have been as perfect as those of Albrecht Dürer or the great Leonardo da Vinci, but they amazed people and transported them to another world. What more could an artist wish for?

While Karl handed out the bottles of theriac and pocketed the money, Johann invited individual spectators up onto the box seat, where he read their palms. Mostly he spoke in flowery words about happy events, like a good harvest or an impending marriage. He never foretold someone's death—even if he saw it. And he never read his own future.

All that mattered was the present.

"Good day, Herr . . . Herr Doctor. Um, may I call you 'Doctor'?" The voice of the fat farmer's wife who'd just taken a seat beside him trembled with awe. The hand she held out to him was marked by hard work, wrinkled, and covered in lines and craters like a barren field. "My dear Hans died last year," she said quietly. "All I've left is my daughter, Else. How are we going to fare in the coming years?"

"Hmm. Let me see." Johann leaned over the hand and squinted. His eyesight wasn't as good as it used to be, and the glass eye itched. It had been custom made by a Venetian craftsman and had cost him a fortune. With the false eye, his gaze appeared even more piercing and eerie. Thanks to Karl's bandaging, Johann's eye socket had healed well, as had his right hand, on which he wore a glove with an artificial finger. Following their escape from Nuremberg, Johann had remained in the grip of fever for three long weeks and only just managed to cheat death. Every now and then, a dull pressure reminded him of his little finger—the finger he'd lost in Nuremberg over a year ago.

The first sacrifice.

"I see a good summer and a rich harvest," he muttered and tapped a spot on the woman's palm. "Your Life line is as deep and wide as the Rhine."

As he continued to study the hand of the worried farmer's wife, his thoughts returned to Nuremberg. Tonio del Moravia had vanished from his life once more; Johann had never heard anything about him again. He still didn't know what exactly had happened that night in the crypt below the Sebaldus Church. His memories were sketchy—probably because of the black potion as well as the fever.

Or because he didn't *want* to remember what Tonio and his followers had tried to invoke in the underground hall and what role he had played in it.

Had Nuremberg patricians actually been involved in the madness? Had they really believed they could bring the devil to earth?

Or was the devil already among them?

"Your Head line is as straight as an arrow," said Johann in a mysterious-sounding voice. "It shows that you pitch in on your late husband's farm and that you know how to assert yourself."

"It's true!" The woman nodded. "You're incredible!"

Johann smiled inwardly. These days he knew right from the beginning what people wanted to hear. He prattled on and on while his thoughts were miles away.

The horrific child murders had stopped following their departure from Nuremberg, or so travelers had told them. He'd felt relieved, even though he still didn't know what he'd had to do with it all. Why had Tonio chosen him?

Why did the sorcerer believe that Johann was special? Just because of a comet that appeared every seventeen years? Sometimes, during the long nights on his travels through the empire, Johann woke up screaming because he'd dreamed of a beautiful knight—a knight whose French name he no longer spoke out loud.

On those nights, he thought about a phrase that Tonio the sorcerer had voiced down in the crypt and that, when he remembered it later on, struck him as deeply disturbing. He couldn't stop thinking about it.

Because you're the son of a great sorcerer yourself.

His mother had never told him who his father was. His stepfather had spoken about a traveling scholar and juggler, and that was all he knew. What did Tonio know about his father?

The son of a great sorcerer.

"Karl has finished setting up the booth stage and people are waiting for the puppet show. Are you coming, Uncle?"

Johann started up from his palm reading. It still felt strange when Greta called him by that title. He looked up and saw her cheerful face with the ever-smiling lips of her mother and the dark, mysterious eyes of her father. Greta was fifteen years old now and almost a woman. She was strong and nimble with full blonde hair to her shoulders and a constellation of freckles on her face that gave her a slightly impertinent look.

The traumatic events from a year ago didn't seem to have left a lasting effect on her—probably helped by the fact that she hardly remembered anything about them. Johann had told Greta that she'd been given a potion at the Loch Prison back then to make her docile for torture and questioning. He, Karl, and Valentin had rescued her. Whatever had happened in between was nothing but a bad dream for Greta.

And he hadn't told her about Valentin's sacrifice.

"Are you all right?" asked Greta, still smiling.

"Of course," he replied after a few moments. "I'm just focused on a particularly difficult chiromancy, that's all."

The farmer's wife nodded gravely.

In his stories by the evening campfires, Valentin was an old friend and nothing more. He had been stabbed to death while freeing Greta. The girl had cried for many nights, but now she had gotten over it. And she'd called Johann "Uncle" ever since.

One day he would tell her the truth—he just didn't know when.

"Um, you're going to get a grandson." He concluded the reading abruptly and gave the corpulent woman a pat on the back. "A healthy boy who will carry on the farm."

"When?" asked the woman, trembling with excitement.

"Oh, certainly this fall—"

"But my daughter isn't even expecting!"

"Are you absolutely sure?" Johann grinned and left the dumbfounded woman where she was.

He jumped down from the box seat and let Little Satan lick his hand. The huge wolfhound had waited patiently for his master and trotted alongside him now. Little Satan was fully grown, a giant of a dog standing more than three feet at the shoulder. Superstitious folk truly believed he was the devil.

When the commander Wolfgang von Eisenhofen had found out that Johann had left Nuremberg, he'd sent his knight Eberhart von Streithagen after him. "A gift from the commander," Streithagen had growled and, with an expression of disgust, handed him the squirming puppy as well as the box with the stargazing tube and Johann's books. "His Excellency believes that it is bad luck to keep the possessions of a wizard, most of all his dog. His only request is that you never set foot in Nuremberg again."

Johann had nodded and held Little Satan tightly. Even without the commander's request he would have given Nuremberg a wide berth in the future.

He walked around the wagon, where Karl had set up a wooden booth. There was no laterna magica—times had become too dangerous for that. People were burning at stakes far and wide as the church tried to defend itself against false preachers but also rebels with honest intentions. Johann sometimes thought the world was sitting on a powder keg that might blow up at any moment. And he wasn't planning on ending his life prematurely as a black magician and necromancer. Besides, he preferred the puppet theater to the laterna magica—there was more room for dreams.

And it didn't remind him of Margarethe.

He hadn't returned to the tower by the Alps. He feared Tonio might be there. In his dreams, the sorcerer was standing atop the platform, the strange stargazing tube that was now in Johann's possession pointed at some distant object. Tonio's eye was as big as a whale's.

I can see you, Johann . . . Always, every day . . . You can't escape me . . . Only seventeen years . . .

"Gather around!" shouted Greta to the people on the market square. She used the booming, praising tone Johann had taught her. "Be amazed at Doctor Faustus's fantastic journeys that took him to faraway lands!" cried the girl in a rhythm that seemed to entrance people. "Prepare to experience miracles you've never seen before!"

Greta called the booth her little theater, and she loved it. Karl had painted the crate with colorful exotic depictions. There was a little red curtain, along with several different backdrops and even an oil lamp that acted as the sun in the desert. With admiration Johann studied Karl's paintings of the scorching desert in the East and the distant lands they called America, named after a Florentine seafarer and explorer who believed he'd discovered a new continent. Karl had painted a green jungle and small people with spears who rode on dragons.

Johann couldn't help but grin. Karl was utterly useless as a juggler, but his talents clearly lay elsewhere. Johann was occasionally irritated by Karl's glances—looks that were more than those of an admiring assistant. One time Johann had heard Karl mutter his name in his sleep: *Faust, oh, my Faust.* But Johann hadn't said anything, because he didn't want to embarrass the young man.

They had set up wooden benches using bricks and planks of spruce in front of the small stage, and about three dozen spectators had gathered. Full of anticipation, they watched Greta as she juggled five balls at once, attracting even more people to their show. Johann nodded appreciatively. Despite her young age, it was clear that Greta was a highly talented performer—she could even play the bagpipe. What they had to offer wasn't the spectacular show Johann used to present with his laterna magica. It was smaller and less dramatic, but it made people happy.

And he was happy, too.

Karl was already crouching behind the booth, and now Greta caught her balls one by one, made them magically disappear in her dress, and joined him. Several young men in the audience made rude remarks and gestures, because Greta had developed a womanly figure. Sometimes she reminded him a little of Salome, the insatiable dancer who had bewitched him on their journey to Venice so long ago. Perhaps he would fall in love again someday, but for now his love for his daughter was enough for him.

"Watch how I, the widely traveled Doctor Faustus, once fought a lion in Africa and defeated it with the aid of white magic alone," announced Johann, who had walked up to the theater. As always, he acted as the narrator while Karl and Greta worked the puppets.

In front of a desert backdrop, a lion with a golden mane appeared, roaring so loudly that the audience gasped with fright. A second puppet materialized—clearly the doctor with his star cloak and floppy hat.

"You terrible beast," sounded Karl's voice from behind the stage. "Here—drink my theriac!" The Faust puppet threw a miniature bottle at the lion, and the animal staggered from side to side as if drunk, eventually collapsing with a grunt. The audience laughed and applauded.

"I once met the beautiful Helen herself," continued Johann. "I abducted her from Hades, where she had been sorrowfully waiting for her Paris since Troy."

The backdrop was quickly changed to a canvas showing menacing flames. The puppet of a princess with blonde hair appeared on stage and cried heartrendingly.

"Oh, poor me," wailed Greta's voice. "The devil himself has dragged me down to hell—I may never see my beloved Paris again!"

Some spectators sighed while others giggled; the Faust puppet appeared from the right, this time with a book in its hands.

"I am going to free you, beautiful Helen," announced Karl. "Not even the devil stands a chance against my book of magic spells."

"Harr, harr! We shall see about that," said Karl with a different, darker voice. At the same moment, a tinny thunderclap rang out and the devil emerged from the depths of the booth. He had goat's horns and a long tail, and there was smoke, along with the stink of sulfur. The audience screamed with horror.

"Now both of you must remain in hell!" snarled the devil and tugged at Helen. "You are mine!" The puppets fought one another, and the crowd booed the devil.

"Ha! Now you will feel the force of magic," shouted the Faust puppet at the devil. "This is my book of magic. *Vade, Satanas!*"

Doctor Faustus struck the devil on the nose with his book, and the hellish puppet disappeared with a wail. The audience hooted and clapped as the curtain fell, and Karl and Greta stepped in front of the booth and took a bow.

Johann stood next to them, smiling, pensively gazing at the devil puppet in Karl's hand. It was a cheap wooden thing with horns made of tin, a red cloak made of rags, and a scruffy tail—the butt of jokes that people laughed at, now vanquished.

But at the bottom of his heart, Johann knew that the devil would one day return.

Faust and I

A Sort of Afterword

This book exists thanks to the German silent-film director F. W. Murnau, my former German teacher Kurt Weiß, and the German Train Drivers' Union. Why? Well, I better start at the beginning . . .

I must have been about six years old when I saw Murnau's interpretation of Goethe's *Faust* on television—a masterpiece of expressionist film. I was home alone, flicking through the channels as children do. The eerie black-and-white images of a huge devil with a billowing cape, maimed plague victims, and a bearded old man wandering through foggy landscapes disturbed me more than any horror movie I watched later in life. (Take it as a warning to all parents who think they have to introduce their children to art at a young age—art can cause nightmares!)

At the start of the film, the word *Faust*—meaning "fist"—was written in old-fashioned letters, and for years I wondered what that meant. I always assumed it was about a fist punching someone's face, but eventually I learned that it was the name of the bearded old man who is later turned into a handsome youth who falls in love with a girl named Gretchen. I was less interested in the love story back then—the devil was much more fascinating, and the fog, and the terrifying grimaces of the era of silent film. Those movies still hold an almost magical fascination for me.

Years later, in high school, I happened across Faust again. This time it came from my German teacher, Kurt Weiß—one of the few teachers who truly helped to shape me. (Every one of us knows one of those—they aren't all bad, are they?)

Herr Weiß was a movie buff, and he regularly showed old Lubitsch and Chaplin movies at his home. One day, he dragged us to a matinee showing of *Faust*—the well-known 1960 adaptation by Gustaf Gründgens. Bored seventeen-year-olds never say no to getting out of the classroom, even if that means having to watch a dusty old postwar film.

Much to my surprise, the movie captivated me at once, evoking old memories from Murnau's *Faust*. I was moved by the story, but most of all I was fascinated by Goethe's verses, which have stayed with me ever since. Not long after our field trip to the cinema, I bought the drama on a dozen cassette tapes and listened to it again and again. I realized just how many of Goethe's lines had become part of everyday German language. To this day I love quoting from *Faust*, and this novel, too, is spiked with quotations. (During pub crawls, I never fail to impress by shouting "Uncertain shapes—again you haunt me" at my drinking buddies. And whenever we go hiking, I like to torture my family with excerpts from the Easter walk or the opening monologue, frowning broodingly and looking altogether Faustian.)

And I often do feel like Faust—never satisfied, forever searching for something. The beauty lies right before my eyes, but I don't see it. That's probably one of the reasons Faust is considered the most German of all mythical characters.

And this is where the German Train Drivers' Union comes into play.

In 2015, I was on a book tour near Karlsruhe when the German train drivers decided to go on strike. As a result, I got stuck in a small town called Bretten and couldn't get home. Any and all rental cars had been snatched up by wily businessmen who had smelled the rat before me. And there were no buses.

So I made the best of a bad situation, extended my hotel stay, rented a bicycle, and started to explore the beautiful Kraichgau region. That's how I came upon a small place called Knittlingen. There was an old stone church, a tiny church square that didn't really deserve to be called a "square," and next to it, a house with a sign. The sign read:

BIRTHPLACE OF DR. JOHANNES FAUST, 1480 TO 1540.

Intrigued, I climbed off my bike and looked more closely. Until then I'd always thought Faust was nothing but a myth. Had he really existed?

A small museum stood next door to the house where Faust was born, and thankfully it was open. I went inside and met a quack, astrologer, clairvoyant, alchemist, charlatan, wise doctor, and cunning conjurer who had lived around the year 1500 and made an astonishing international career following his death. Almost forty years after my first encounter with Faust, the doctor entered my life as a real person, a historical figure!

From that moment I knew that I would write a novel about him.

At this point I'd like to extend my sincere gratitude to the German Train Drivers' Union. Maybe sometimes the world needs to stand still for inspiration to sprout.

There are only a handful of sources about the historical Faust, but plenty of speculation. As a novelist I have the privilege of picking and choosing what I like from the existing literature on the subject without getting a rap on the knuckles from historians.

Knittlingen is considered the most likely birthplace for Faust. I decided on his date of birth because of a source that quotes Faust as having said to the prior of the Rebdorf Augustinian collegiate church that "when the sun and Jupiter stand in the same degree of a zodiac . . . prophets are born." I put that together with Faust's middle name, Georg—Saint George's feast day is April 23, so I got April 23, 1478. The name Jörg Gerlach (Faust's stepfather in my book) came from a farmer who lived in that very house in Knittlingen. A piece of paper with a magic spell was found in one of the thresholds, and a star-shaped alchemist's cupboard also allegedly belonged to this property.

There isn't much known about where Faust went from Knittlingen. It is possible that he studied at Heidelberg, because there is a corresponding name in the records. Then he probably roamed the empire, and the legends frequently mention a black dog and a companion by the name of Wagner. Faust cast a horoscope for the Bamberg prince-bishop Georg III; he spent time in Erfurt, at the Rebdorf monastery, in Nuremberg, and in Ingolstadt. The famous Sponheim abbot Johannes Trithemius (a type of magician himself) wrote nasty things about a charlatan and sodomite by the name of Faust in a letter. *Sodomy* was a term for homosexuality back then—a theme I pick up in my novel. A meeting between the historical Faust and polymath Heinrich Cornelius Agrippa von Nettesheim, as described in my novel, is possible but not proven.

Faust's demise is a well-known legend. Allegedly, during an alchemy experiment in the town of Staufen in the Breisgau, he blew himself up in a rather gruesome manner: "Brains stuck to the wall . . . and his eyes and teeth were strewn about." Unsurprising that people deduced the devil must have been at play, with such a theatrical exit. And thus the tale of Faust's pact with Satan was born—a topic as old as mankind.

The large number of stories and legends that started to circulate following his death show just how well known the figure of Doctor Johann Georg Faustus was in the German empire. In the year 1587, the book printer Johann Spies published the *Historia von D. Johann Fausten*, which became the first German bestseller and even sold abroad.

And now the story really gets interesting.

Toward the end of the sixteenth century, a certain Christopher Marlowe in London happened across that book. His competitor, William Shakespeare, had published one hit play after the other, and Marlowe needed a good story. Faust's suited him perfectly. The plot had everything a good play needed: action, blood, special effects, the dramatic downfall of the protagonist, and, of course, the devil. For theater owners back then, the devil was as valuable as comic-book superheroes are to the film industry today. You couldn't go wrong with the devil.

The play, *The Tragical History of Doctor Faustus*, was a great success in England. But there were too many directors and actors on the island, and so some of them immigrated to other countries, including the German empire. They brought with them Marlowe's play and performed it at fairs. But since barely any of the English actors spoke German, they introduced a comic figure who summarized the plot between acts. That was the birth of the Harlequin, also called Hanswurst or Kasper.

The play became very popular in the German empire, especially as a puppet show, and so about a hundred and fifty years later, a young boy named Johann Wolfgang—who would become famous under his last name, Goethe—was fascinated by the story. Just like me with Murnau's disturbing film, Goethe couldn't stop thinking about the material. From August 1771 until May 1772 he worked as a young lawyer in Frankfurt, where he witnessed the trial of a child murderess. In her desperation, a certain Susanna Margaretha Brandt had killed her newborn child. Goethe was deeply moved by the case, and by adding this sad story to the Faust theme, he created the Faust tragedy that is now considered the most German of all German tragedies—loved, venerated, canonized, and told and retold again and again.

An ancient story about the eternal battle between man and evil, about love and temptation, about a rise and a fall, and about a pact with the devil—the archetypal parable that was probably already known to the cavemen by their campfires.

Oh, yes, and finally my favorite joke on the matter:

The devil comes to the writer and says, "I promise you a bestseller in the millions! You will publish countless editions, enjoy fame, interviews, television appearances, and bathtubs full of money! All you have to do in return is this." The devil raises one finger and grins nastily. "You must sell me your soul."

The writer eyes the devil with suspicion for a long while. Then he says, "OK. And what's the catch?"

There is a little Faust in every one of us—and in writers, a rather large one.

This novel cost me more sweat and effort than other books, and it exists only because a whole bunch of people helped me.

First up, I'd like to thank Gerd Schweizer and Berit Bräuer, who supplied me with great amounts of literature on the topic of Faust and contributed many important details. Berit Bräuer has written an excellent nonfiction book on Faust (*Im Bann der Zeit*), which I recommend highly.

Eva-Maria Springer led me through the Faust museum in Knittlingen and Faust's birthplace; Brit Veith showed me through Knittlingen, and Barbara Gittinger was my expert for Maulbronn Monastery. Thank you also to Richard Dietz from the International Society for Faust (Internationale Faust-Gesellschaft e.V.), which manages Faust's heritage and regularly invites the public to interesting talks.

Alexander Kipphahn from the Bretten city archive supplied me with the names of wealthy Bretten merchants; Horst Kaufmann from the Schembart Society (Schembart-Gesellschaft Nürnberg e.V.) told me everything I needed to know about the Nuremberg Schembartlauf, which served as my showdown. The Nuremberg city archive was a helpful partner on the topics of Loch waterways, Loch Prison, and the Hospital of the Holy Ghost. As they have so often, the

Latin translations came from Dr. Manfred Heim; my rather poor Italian was corrected by Barbara Lambiase and Christian Platzer, and my French was checked by Alexandra Baisch. Helmut Hornung answered my questions on the subjects of comets, laterna magica, and telescopes. He pointed out to me that a telescope of the kind Tonio and later Faust own in my novel wasn't in fact invented until 1608 in Holland. Well, I think the devil was ahead of his time—in my book, at least. As always, any mistakes are on my own muddleheadedness, not on my expert helpers.

Thank you also to my father, who—being a doctor—knows how fingers and eyes are amputated. Thank you to Gerd, Martina, and Sophia from the Gerd F. Rumler Agency; they support me in every which way, from coffee to emotional support. Thank you to the entire team at Ullstein Publishing—you do a great job—and to my favorite editor, Uta Rupprecht. My son, Niklas, helped me to remove anything childish and corny from the beginning of the novel. My daughter, Lily, a keen artist, gave her blessing for the beautiful cover of the book's first edition.

A second and important editor in this project was my wife, Katrin, who was the first to notice that the final act wasn't quite working yet. I'm sorry if I was being a drama queen at first. You were right, as always!

Faust for Beginners

Are you a Faust expert? Below are quotations I borrowed from Goethe's famous tragedy *Faust* (translation by Charles T. Brooks). Did you find them in the book?

- Name is but sound and smoke. (Verse 3456)
- Quite a peculiar juice is blood. (Verse 1740)
- The mass can only be impressed by masses. (Prelude in the Theatre)
- Am called Magister, Doctor, indeed . . . (Verse 3600)
- Remember then! Of one make ten, the two let be, make even three, there's wealth for thee. (Verse 2540)
- That I may know what the world contains in its innermost heart and finer veins, see all its energies and seeds, and deal no more in words but in deeds. (Verse 382)
- Philosophy and medicine, and law, and ah! Theology, too. (Verse 354)
- The spirit that denies . . . (Verse 1338)
- Well, art is long! And life is short and fleeting. (Verse 558)
- [Part of the part am I, which once was all,] the Gloom that brought forth Light [itself from out her mighty womb.] (Verse 1350)
- In the beginning was the deed! (Verse 1237)

About the Author

Oliver Pötzsch worked for years as a journalist and scriptwriter for Bavarian television. He is the author of seven books in the international bestselling Hangman's Daughter Tales historical series, the children's novel *Knight Kyle and the Magic Silver Lance*, and the Black Musketeers series, including *Book of the Night* and *Sword of Power*. His work has been translated into more than twenty languages. Oliver lives in Munich with his family. For more information, visit www.oliver-poetzsch.de.

About the Translator

Lisa Reinhardt studied English and linguistics at University of Otago and lives with her family on the beautiful West Coast of New Zealand. Her most recent work includes *The Council of Twelve*, the seventh book in Oliver Pötzsch's Hangman's Daughter Tales series.